STAR TREK®

WORLDS IN
COLLISION

STAR TREK®

WORLDS IN COLLISION

[signature: Judith & Garfield Reeves-Stevens]

Based upon *Star Trek*® created by Gene Roddenberry

A special signature edition of
Star Trek—Memory Prime
and
Star Trek—Prime Directive

POCKET BOOKS
New York   London   Toronto   Sydney   Singapore

For Robin Kingsburgh,
who has chosen the final frontier.
Per ardua ad *Edinburgh,* ae?

&

For Peggy
For our second home in New York City
and for being there when inspiration struck.
L.L. & P.

Introduction

If there's one question people shouldn't ask anymore, it's this: Why is *Star Trek* so popular? We think that's a bit like asking why some of us like chocolate (JRS), or roller coasters (GRS).

To us, the answer to all three questions seems simple, obvious, and the same. Chocolate, roller coasters, and *Star Trek* are popular because all three of them are *great:* great taste, great fun, and great storytelling.

Star Trek storytelling is why we turn on the television to watch an episode. It's why we sit in a theater to see the newest movie. It's why you opened this book. What has come to be called the *Star Trek* Universe has a never-ending supply of stories, in all forms and styles.

If you want humor, there's McCoy baiting Spock, or Data in Ten-Forward having the human condition explained to him by a Klingon. Not to mention tribbles.

If you want action, there's the *Enterprise* plowing into the *Scimitar,* or Archer racing across a snowy roof with twin phase pistols blazing. And Khaaaan.

Romance? Riker and Troi. Hopeless romance? Julian and Jadzia. Nonstop romance? Kirk and just about any female, species not important.

From the very beginning, *Star Trek* stories have expanded out to wars among galaxies and focused in on families and friends reaching out to one another. There are stories as vast as the fate of parallel universes, and as personal as the fate of a single constable accused of a crime he did not commit.

Some of these stories, told for more than three decades on television and in feature films, have become known as "canon"—the core, or "real," account of our heroes and events as captured on film.

While film (and coming soon, high-definition video) is a wonderful way to tell a story—showing us things we've never seen before, taking us places we've never imagined, letting us sense Picard's mood from the set of his eyes, the steel in his voice—it still has specific limitations of time, depth, and budget.

A televised episode of *Star Trek* must begin and end within an hour, or sometimes within two one-hour modules. A *Star Trek* movie can also stretch to about the same length as a two-part episode. But both the episode and the movie can only tell us stories that can be understood through what we can see and hear for ourselves in a brief window of time. The depth of detail for the story's events and characters is only what can be developed in that same constricted time.

And, of course, movie and television budgets are finite.

That brings us to books, where a story can expand to include all those additional details that make writing *Star Trek* novels so much fun. Plus, the *Star Trek* novelist's budget is infinite.

And *that* brings us to two of our *Star Trek* novels that are presented in this volume: *Memory Prime* and *Prime Directive.* They're both "classic" *Star Trek* stories; that is, they're both set during Captain Kirk's original five-year mission. Best of all, neither one of these stories could have been an episode or a movie, because they deliberately go beyond our visual and aural senses.

We believe that the heart of *Star Trek*'s storytelling strength has always been its capacity to take us to strange new worlds. Granted, over more than three decades of *Star Trek*, all of us have seen many such worlds on film, but in these two books we wanted to explore a different order of strangeness, one which could not be experienced by human senses.

Hence, the world in *Memory Prime* that we called Transition. It's a nonphysical realm, completely subjective, and thus unfilmable. However, the *sensation* of being in Transition *can* be described, and so it is in these pages. Then, in *Prime Directive,* we simply blew the budget. There are more worlds in that one story than any studio could ever afford to depict on film—from a hollowed-out asteroid under construction and the tourist attractions of our own moon's Tranquillity Base, to a devastated alien planet and its moon, and even something that might *resemble* a world but . . . well, you'll have to *visualize* it for yourself. Because it, too, we think, is something that you might never *see.*

Which brings us back to that 700-plus hours of *Star Trek* canon and the collision part of this introduction.

Several key elements in these two books of ours are just plain wrong.

They weren't at the time we wrote them. *Memory Prime* was published just as *Star Trek: The Next Generation* began its second season. Zefrem Cochrane—of Alpha Centauri, no less—had appeared in one and only one episode of the original *Star Trek* series. So we felt safe delving deeper into his story, identifying him as a native Centauran, whose Centauran name—*Zeyafram Co'akran*—had been "humanized." Oops. Who knew that *Star Trek: First Contact* waited in the future to establish a different story for Cochrane, as a native of Montana? Same for our complex descriptions of dilithium, warp drive, and Klingon history, inspired in equal parts by the original television series and the 1980 *Star Trek* reference book, *Star Trek Spaceflight Chronology.* Fun, yes. But no longer compatible with further *Star Trek* revelations on film.

Prime Directive collides with canon, too. We correctly guessed, as it turns out, that Starfleet would have a special department concerned with making first contact with new species based on a species' reaching a particular technological threshold. Our guess was that that threshold would be subspace radio. Wrong again. As later established in *The Next Generation* episode "First Contact" and used to full dramatic effect in the movie *Star Trek: First Contact,* the real threshold is warp drive.

As someone once said, the devil is in the details (which is a different thing from "The Devil in the Dark"), and that will always be the case for *Star Trek* fact—stories on film—versus *Star Trek* fiction, which includes everything else. The very quality that makes *Star Trek* novels so appealing—that chance to go around corners and reveal what the camera never sees—is the very quality that will lead, sooner or later, to many novels slipping out of established continuity.

Memory Prime and *Prime Directive* are both in that category. Like "Yesterday's *Enterprise,*" they explore alternate paths through time and space that at the least show us where the *Star Trek* universe once was, and at most demonstrate how rich the universe of stories to come still is.

But rest assured that aside from some side trips into details that no longer fit canon, both novels in this book still have what counts in classic *Star Trek* storytelling: Kirk and Spock and McCoy and company, the *Starship Enterprise,* logical Vulcans, scheming Andorians, and a snarling Klingon or two. At heart, they remain *Star Trek* storytelling.

For we believe the *Star Trek* universe is a lot like the real one. It's so big that given enough time, a few worlds are bound to collide, without really causing damage, only fireworks.

And when they're handled with respect, fireworks can be great, too.

Like chocolate and roller coasters.

And *Star Trek.*

—J&G
Los Angeles, 2003

BOOK ONE

Memory Prime

U.S.S. Enterprise NCC-1701

2270

In the last year of her first five-year mission

One

They were all aliens on that planet. From the worlds of the Federation, the empires, and the nonaligned systems, each was a visitor on a planet where indigenous life had vanished in the slow expansion of its sun more than five hundred centuries before.

The scientists from a dozen races had come and gone since then. Andorians had sifted through the heat-stressed sands in search of clues to understanding and controlling their own prenova sun. Vulcans had beamed down a network of automated planetary sensors and warped out of system in less than one standard day. Terrans had conducted a six-month colony assessment study, with negative results. Even a Klingon heavy-assault scientific survey vessel had passed by, scanned for dilithium, and departed.

Through all these incursions, the planet spun on, unclaimed, unwanted, littered with the debris of sprawling survey camps and unbridled exploration. In the end, it was not even given a name and became little more than a footnote on navigation charts, identified only as TNC F3459-9-SF-50, its T'Lin's New Catalog number. It was an abandoned world, a dead world, and for some beings in that part of the galaxy, that meant it was perfect.

This time, his name would be Starn, and he would wear the blue tunic and burgundy guild cloak of a dealer in kevas and trillium. Legitimate traders were not unknown on TNC 50. The disguise would serve him well.

As he walked through the narrow streets of Town, Starn cataloged everything he saw, comparing it to the scanmap his ship had produced while in orbit, already planning his escape routes. The slender needles of Andorian prayer towers stretched up past the squat bubbles of Tellarite communal baths, casting dark shadows through billows of fine sand that swirled like vermilion fog. A group of Orion pirates appeared, wearing filters against the sand. There were no authorities on TNC 50 for pirates, or terrorists, or any type of criminal to fear. There was only one law here. Fortunately, Starn knew it.

The Orions slowed their pace, coolly assessing the resistance that a lone trader such as Starn might provide. Starn pulled on his cloak, stirring it as if the wind had caught it for an instant. The Orions picked up their pace, each touching a green finger to his temple in respect as they passed by. The sudden glimpse of the black-ribbed handle of Starn's lopene Cutter had shown them that, like most beings on TNC 50, Starn was not what he seemed.

Starn continued unmolested. Most of the other oxygen breathers he passed also wore filters. A few, like Starn, did not. For those whose lungs had evolved in an atmosphere scorched by the relentless heat of 40 Eridani, this barren world was almost like coming home.

As Starn approached the center of Town, he felt a tingle and slight resistance as if he had stepped through a wall of unmoving wind. It was the transporter shield, projected and maintained by the merchants of Town. A strong enough transporter beam could force its way through, Starn knew, but the transmission time would be on the order of minutes, long enough to make an easy target of anyone trying a quick escape after an act of vengeance. Everyone who came to TNC 50 had enemies and Town could only continue to exist as long as it offered safe haven.

As the swollen red primary set, Starn approached his rendezvous site: a tavern pieced together from scavenged survey structures. A sign swung above its entrance, clattering in the rising wind. It told Starn who the proprietors of the tavern were. Other races might secretly whisper the name of the tavern, but only a Klingon would be insulting enough to display it in public.

The sign carried a two-dimensional image of a monstrously fat Vulcan clutching two Orion slave women to his folds of flesh. The Vulcan's face was distorted in a terrible grimace. Beneath the image, set in the angular *pIqaD* of Klinzhai, glowed the tavern's name: *vulqangan Hagh*. Starn pulled his cloak around him, an innocuous gesture that served to position the handle of his weapon for instant access, then stepped into the tavern to keep his appointment.

The central serving area was smoke-filled and dimly lit. For a moment, Starn was surprised to see a fire pit set in a far wall, blazing away. An open fire on a desert planet without plant life could only mean that that part of the tavern had come from either a Terran or a Tellarite structure. Starn studied the fire for a moment and failed to detect an appropriate amount of heat radiating from it. It was a holoprojection.

Terran, he decided. Tellarites would have shipped in plant material especially for burning. Starn knew the fire was there for a purpose, most probably to hide sensors. His host must already know that Starn had arrived.

Starn stepped up to an empty space at the serving counter. A multilegged creature made an elaborate show of sniffing the air, then moved several stools away. Starn ignored it.

The server behind the counter was, as Starn had deduced, a Klingon, and an old one at that. He limped on an improperly matched leg graft and wore a veteran's ruby honorstone in the empty socket of his left eye. Starn was troubled. A Klingon with an honorstone would be revered on Klinzhai, given line and land. A veteran with such a medal would never submit to being a menial tavern server, which meant the tavern server had *stolen* the honorstone. The concept of a Klingon without honor was as unsettling as the laughing Vulcan depicted on the tavern's sign. Starn decided that the stories of Town's depravity did not do it justice.

After ignoring him for several trips back and forth, the server finally stopped in front of Starn. *"NuqneH, vulqangan?"* the Klingon growled.

Starn considered for a moment that in this setting the standard Klingon greeting actually made sense. *"bIQ,"* he snarled in reply.

The Klingon paused as if puzzled by Starn's perfect accent, then filled the trader's order for water by spitting on the counter in front of him.

Other beings nearby, who had listened to the exchange, froze. Had Starn also been Klingon, a glorious blood feud would have started that might have lasted generations. But Starn was not Klingon, though his knowledge of the empire's customs was comprehensive.

The server waited tensely for Starn to respond to the insult, his single eye burning with expectation. Starn slowly slid his hand beneath his cloak, and just as slowly withdrew a carefully folded white cloth. Keeping his eyes locked on the Klingon, Starn delicately dabbed the cloth into the spittle on the counter and began to raise the cloth to his forehead.

The server began to tremble. Starn moved the cloth closer to his forehead. Two Klingon mercenaries standing farther down the counter began to snicker. The cloth was centimeters from Starn's forehead when the server finally realized that the mad creature was not going to stop.

"*Ghobe!*" the server spat, and snatched the cloth from Starn's fingers. Starn sat motionless as the server used the cloth to wipe up the counter and then stormed away, his rage almost comical in its intensity. The mercenaries broke out in gales of harsh laughter. One of them motioned to a server, who guided an antigrav tray of food and drink through the tables. A few moments later, the server stopped the tray by Starn and passed him a sealed bubble of stasis water.

"With the compliments of the officers, trader," the server said.

Starn looked down the bar at the Klingon mercenaries. They smiled at him and made clumsy attempts at saluting him with third and fourth fingers splayed. Starn nodded in acknowledgment, to more laughter, then broke the seal on the bubble and waited for its field to collapse. Around him, the business of the tavern returned to normal.

Whatever else Starn was, he was a connoisseur. From its bouquet, he identified the water as coming from a desert world, high in complex oxides. With his first sip, he ruled out TNC 50 as its origin. The water had once been part of a photosynthesis-based ecosystem and this planet was lifeless. A second sip was all he needed. The water was from Vulcan. The mercenaries had sought to honor him. Starn placed the bubble on the counter and would not touch it again.

A pale blue hand reached out to the counter beside Starn. The movement was cautious and he turned slowly. An Andorian girl looked at him nervously. She was young, clothed in a tattered and obviously contraband Starfleet jumpsuit that matched her skin color, and she suffered from an atrophied antenna. Even the smallest and poorest of her people's families would have sacrificed everything to treat that twisted hearing stalk. The girl was something no Andorian should ever have been forced to be: alone.

Starn greeted her in flawless Federation Standard, again no accent to suggest it was not his first tongue.

The girl looked nervously from side to side. "Wass it a present brought you here, trader?" she asked in a sibilant whisper.

Starn nodded yes. He couldn't detect anyone nearby trying to eavesdrop, but noticed that the girl stood so that as he turned to speak with her, he looked straight across the serving area into the sensors hidden behind the fire. He didn't try to block them.

"And where was that present from?" the Andorian asked, shuffling and looking over her shoulder. Her withered antenna twitched and she winced in pain.

"Iopene," Starn answered. Another dead world whose now-extinct indigenous life had proven to be too competent in building lethal weapons. Even the empire banned Iopene relics from all but the noblest houses. The cutter that Starn carried had been the "present" that had convinced him to take the invitation to come to TNC 50 seriously.

"Thiss way," the girl said, and headed for the back of the tavern. Starn followed. Behind him, he could hear the mercenaries begin to laugh again.

The girl slipped quickly through a series of dark corridors. Starn kept up with her, ducking his head beneath the low Tellarite ceilings. They passed an entrance to a smaller serving area where Starn could hear Orion dancing music pulse in time to the cries from an unseen audience. He detected the scent of drugs outlawed on a hundred worlds, heard screams of pain and pleasure above the hum of cranial inducers, and committed to memory every twist and turn, every dark stairwell, for the long run back.

At last the girl stopped by an unmarked door. She gripped a gleaming gold handle on the doorframe and trembled as the embedded sensors read her palm prints and analyzed her sweat. The door clicked, then slipped open. The girl entered and motioned for Starn to follow.

A young Klingon waited behind a simple desk. A single glowpatch lit the room from directly above him and his eyes were deeply shadowed beneath his prominent crest. The Andorian scuttled to a corner. The Klingon rose gracefully and waved toward a chair across from his desk.

"Good of you to come, Trader Starn," the Klingon said in Standard. "I am Karth."

Starn took the offered chair, comfortably proportioned and padded for humanoids, and studied his host. Even for a Klingon, the being was large. The taut fabric of his tunic stretched across an impressively muscled physique. Starn compared the tunic with hundreds of military designs he had memorized in order to place his host within the Klingon hierarchy. With something close to amazement, he finally realized that what Karth wore was that rarest of Klingon garb—a civilian outfit.

"Do you want something?" Karth gestured to a serving unit on the wall. "Perhaps . . . water?" The Klingon smiled, respectfully keeping his teeth unbared.

"Sensors in the fire pit?" the trader asked.

"Of course. The crime rate in Town is one of the lowest in the Federation."

"And in the empire?"

"Trader Starn," Karth began seriously, "all beings know there is no crime in the empire." Then he smiled again. "Though if you had touched that server's spittle to your head and become betrothed to him before all those witnesses, that would have qualified him for criminal proceedings. A very clever way out of a potentially disastrous situation. *Kai* the trader."

"*Kai* the Karth who gives such generous presents."

The Klingon settled back in his chair. The chair was massive, but Starn's sensitive ears heard it creak.

"As there is no crime in the empire," the Klingon said, "there are no presents, either. The Iopene Cutter is a down payment."

"Understood. What service do you require?"

Karth shook his head. "This is a foul language. So many ways around the point. Nothing direct. What service do you think, trader?"

"*ChotneS*," Starn replied instantly.

Karth glanced over at the Andorian girl. "We shall stay with this *tera'ngan* chirping. She speaks *Hol* much better than Standard." The girl stared blankly. Karth shifted his gaze back to Starn. "I want no heads of state removed, no leaders killed. This will be a simple act of murder, trader, not assassination."

"Whatever you wish to call it, the service is the same." Starn shrugged. "Who is to be the victim?"

"Don't you want to know the price?"

"After I know the victim."

Karth shook his head again, hands moving slowly to the edge of the desk. "You accept the contract now. You accept the price now. There will be no negotiation once the victim is revealed."

Starn considered his options. It was probable he could walk away from this now. But the opportunity for expansion that this meeting offered might not come again. However, if he did commit to the contract, in the end he would still be able to make a final decision concerning who would be the more difficult victim: the one who was now unrevealed, or a certain Klingon civilian.

"Very well," Starn agreed. Karth moved his hands back to the center of the desk. "But since I cannot know the cost or effort involved in this service, I must call on Klingon honor to seal our bargain. State your price." Starn was puzzled when he could detect no physiological response to his subtle insult. For a non-Klingon to bargain on Klingon honor implied either that the non-Klingon was an equal of a Klingon or that Klingon honor was suitable for animals. At the very least, Karth should have demanded a test of blood, if not death, but Starn could not hear any quickening of Karth's breathing rate or see any change in his skin color.

"Two hundred Iopene Cutters with feedback shields."

Two hundred! Starn concentrated on not disrupting his own breathing rate. Whole planets could be taken with a handful of cutters whose beams could tunnel through any force shield by turning the shield's own energy against itself in perfect counterphase.

"I was not aware that there were that many in existence," Starn said flatly. *Two hundred!*

"Do you doubt my word?" Now Starn picked up an immediate flush in Karth's face and a rapid escalation in breathing rate.

"I simply stated a fact. For such a price I will accept your contract. Again I ask, who is the victim?"

Karth motioned for Starn to approach the desk. He touched a keypad and images formed on the desk's surface. Starn watched intently.

At first he was stunned. Then impressed. The concept was brilliant. By this one single action Starfleet could be reduced to an uncoordinated swarm of helpless ships and starbases. The entire Federation could be brought to its knees. So many past wrongs would be repaid. Starn knew he would have accepted this contract without fee.

He leaned over the desk, studying the words and pictures, memorizing the diagrams and timetables. Already a plan was forming. It could be done. He was just about to step back from the table when he noticed Karth's hand on the keypad.

"Bring up the initial timetable again?" Starn asked.

Karth tapped out a three-key sequence. Starn watched the Klingon's exact hand movements carefully, then stepped back.

"I will be proud to carry out this service," Starn stated. "But I do have a question."

"I expect you to have many."

"Federation officials will not rest until they discover who is behind this action."

"That is not a precise question."

"What do you wish the officials to find out?"

"That is not a clear question."

"Should I leave evidence implicating the empire in this crime?"

Karth leaned back and snorted. He gestured to his dark face. "Who has set this crime in motion, trader? What do you think?"

Starn took his opening. "I think it is intriguing that I am being hired to commit this crime by a mechanical device attempting to pass itself off as a Klingon."

Karth's hands disappeared beneath the desk with unnatural speed. Starn twisted sideways and reached beneath his cloak. Karth jumped back from the desk, aiming a disruptor at Starn. The cutter's particle beam sliced through the air with a thunderous crackle, disassociating dust and smoke molecules. But Karth *dodged!* The beam erupted on his shoulder instead of his chest.

Starn stumbled back against his chair. The cutter whined as it cycled up to discharge again but it would take too many seconds. Karth's shoulder dripped with thick blue coolant. Wires and transtators glowed and sparked in the mechanical ruin. The Klingon robot leveled its disruptor and fired. Starn braced himself for disruption. The Andorian girl was engulfed in a sputtering orange corona and collapsed onto the floor. The robot placed the disruptor on the desk.

Starn looked over to the Andorian. Her body had not disintegrated. She was still breathing. A Klingon disruptor set for *stun?* What kind of madness was this?

"Neural disruption only," the robot said. "She won't remember anything of the last twelve hours. She didn't know." It pointed to its shoulder.

The cutter beeped its ready signal in Starn's hand.

"You won't need that," the robot said, pushing small silver tendrils back into its shoulder. The arm beneath fluttered erratically, then jerked once and hung limply.

Starn replaced the cutter beneath his cloak. "You didn't kill her?" he asked.

"Low crime rate in Town. She'd be missed. There'd be questions. The important thing is that there be no witnesses." A flesh-colored foam sprayed from the robot's good hand to cover the open circuitry of its blasted shoulder. "Not now, and not when you carry out your contract."

Starn watched with fascination as the robot began to repair itself. He suddenly doubted that the Klingons had anything at all to do with this.

"That sounds quite . . . logical," Starn said and, thinking of the image that hung above the tavern door, he began to laugh.

Two

Spock did not need logic to know that another attempt was going to be made. The only question was, who was behind it: the captain or the doctor? He finally decided that the instigator would be the one who entered the *Enterprise*'s recreation lounge last. Satisfied, Spock returned to his meal. His theory was disproved when the lounge door puffed open and Kirk and McCoy entered together. Spock realized then that they were both in on it. Whatever this one was going to be, it was going to be big.

"Mr. Spock, mind if I join you?" Kirk was already seated by the time Spock could swallow and begin his reply. McCoy sat beside the captain, not even bothering to ask Spock's permission. The table for eight was now filled. As were the two tables closest to it. The fact that the two chairs across from Spock had been left empty, even as other crew members decided to sit as close to him as possible, indicated that everyone else knew that Kirk and McCoy were expected. It had also been Spock's first clue that he was, as McCoy would put it, being set up.

"Well, Captain?" Spock decided to play white and take the advantage of the opening move.

"Well what, Spock?" Kirk's wide-eyed innocence confirmed his guilt.

"I merely assume that you have come to tell me something and I wonder what it is."

Kirk pursed his lips. "Tell you something?" He looked over to McCoy. "Bones? Did you have anything to say to Spock?"

McCoy smiled brightly, his expression calculatingly cheerful. "Not a thing, Jim."

The captain and the doctor smiled at Spock. Spock constructed a decision tree. He could excuse himself and return to his station, though he concluded that would be interpreted as a resignation from whatever game was being played. Or he could regroup his position.

He took another forkful of salad.

"Good salad, Spock?" Kirk asked.

Spock chewed carefully and nodded warily, assessing the captain's counteropening gambit. He prepared himself for the next attack. But the captain turned back to McCoy instead.

"So, Bones, who do you think is going to take the top spot for the Nobel and Z.Magnees Prize in medicine?"

So that was it, Spock realized. Something to do with the prizes. But what? He had not been nominated, and his work would likely remain too specialized to ever qualify. Sarek, his father, had been awarded the Peace Prize more than twenty years ago but, logically, that had nothing at all to do with Spock. So what were they hinting at?

"Well now, Jim, I think that Lenda Weiss has made a remarkable contribution to our understanding of resonance fields. Half my portable scanners are based on her work. I really don't see how she has any competition."

"Not even from Forella?" Kirk suggested. "I hear his work with shaped stasis fields will make the protoplaser obsolete in just a few years."

"I'll believe that when I see it," McCoy said definitively. "Dr. Weiss is the front runner. No doubt about it."

"I believe you'll find the work of Stlur and T'Vann merits the attention of the prize committee as well," Spock offered. He suspected he shouldn't get involved but logically he could see no other choice. The captain and the doctor were grievously misinformed. "They have opened up the whole new field of transporter-based surgery. Surgeons might never—"

"Stlur and T'Vann?" Kirk interrupted. "A Vulcan team?"

"Department heads at the Academy of Science," Spock added.

"So you follow the prizes, do you, Spock?"

"Doctor, the winners of the Nobel and Z.Magnees Prizes represent the forward thrust of Federation science and culture. From their work today it is possible to deduce the shape of tomorrow. They represent the finest minds of all the worlds of the Federation. Who would not follow them?"

Kirk and McCoy exchanged glances. Spock observed them and felt as he did when he stepped into one of the captain's intuitive mates in three-dimensional chess, but he still couldn't determine what Kirk and McCoy were trying to accomplish.

"I suppose you keep up with all the latest news about the prizes then?" Kirk asked.

For a chilling moment, Spock was afraid he was about to be informed that Dr. McCoy had been named a nominee, but quickly discounted the notion. The prize committee had some standards, after all. There were Vulcans on it.

"I follow the news as much as I am able, Captain," Spock replied.

"And you know about the ceremonies coming up?"

"I have read about them in the updates."

"Ah, good then. You know all about it. C'mon, Bones." Kirk started to stand. McCoy followed.

Is that all? Spock thought. Where was the logic in creating an elaborate setup such as this just to determine if he had been keeping up with the news about the prize ceremonies? Had he missed something?

"Excuse me—know all about what?" he asked, knowing the odds were overwhelming that he shouldn't.

"The prize ceremonies," Kirk said.

"The scientists who will be there," McCoy added.

"Where it's being held."

"How they're all getting there."

"You *do* know, don't you, Spock?"

Spock prepared himself for the worst. "I'm afraid I must say I obviously do not know. Please be so good as to inform me." Kirk and McCoy exchanged glances one more time.

"Why certainly, Spock," Kirk began, then paused for a moment. Everyone in the lounge looked at Spock expectantly.

"The *Enterprise* has been assigned to carry a delegation of sixty prize-nominated scientists to the ceremonies on Memory Prime."

Checkmate, Spock thought. *Again.* "That is indeed splendid news," he managed to say evenly.

Kirk turned to McCoy. "Well?"

"He blinked, Jim. I'm sure of it."

"How about a smile? A little one?"

"Maybe. But the blink was definite. I think he's excited. Think of it, an excited Vulcan! And we were there."

Spock stood up from the table. "Captain, may I ask what arrangements have been made to accommodate the delegation on board?"

"You may ask, but I can't answer. The person in charge hasn't told me what's been planned yet."

"I see. And who is the person in charge?"

"You are." Kirk checked with McCoy. "Another blink?"

"I might have to write this up."

Kirk looked back to Spock. "If that's all right with you, that is?"

"I shall be honored, Captain."

Kirk smiled. This time it was genuine. "I know, Spock. We all know."

"If you'll excuse me, gentlemen, I find I have considerable new work to attend to."

"Of course, Mr. Spock. Carry on."

Spock nodded, took his tray to the recycler, and headed for the lounge door. As he stepped out into the corridor, he could hear McCoy complaining.

"I was sure we were going to get a smile out of him this time. I'll admit two blinks are a good start but—" The doctor's voice was lost in the puff of the lounge door.

Spock walked through the ship's corridors at a measured pace, contemplating his feelings. Despite what most of his crewmates believed, Vulcans *did* have emotions. It was just that they chose not to express them. Though Spock supposed that Dr. McCoy would be surprised to discover how close he had come to seeing Spock smile back in the lounge.

In fact, if Kirk and McCoy had not made it so obvious that they were setting him up, Spock thought he might well have been startled and pleased enough at the news of the prize nominees to have actually smiled in public. Then again, Spock thought, perhaps that's why the captain had made it so obvious, so his friend would be forewarned and spared committing an unseemly act.

The captain has such an illogical way of being logical, Spock thought. He knew he would think about that for a long time, though he doubted he would ever totally understand. And as in most of his personal dealings with the captain, Spock decided that understanding probably wasn't necessary.

"Transporter malfunction!"

There weren't many words that could shock the chief engineer of the *Enterprise* awake with such forcefulness, but those two never failed.

Scott jumped out of his bunk and slammed his hand against the desk com panel. The room lights brightened automatically as they detected his movements. That voice hadn't been Kyle's. He peered at the nervous face on the desk screen.

"Scott here . . . Sulu?" What was Sulu doing in the main transporter room? "Report!" Scott hopped around his quarters, trying to pull on his shirt and his boots at the same time as Sulu's tense voice filtered through the speaker.

"The . . . carrier wave transmitter just shut down, Mr. Scott. Every pad in the ship is out."

"Ochh, no," Scott moaned. Years ago on another ship he had seen a landing party evulsed by a carrier-wave collapse. He had personally seen to it that such a malfunction would be virtually impossible on his *Enterprise,* no matter what McCoy might think.

"Give me the error code, lad," Scott asked softly. There was no need to rush now. Whatever, whoever, had been in the matrix when the wave collapsed was irretrievably lost. And Scott didn't want to think about who might have been in the matrix. They were still in orbit around Centaurus. The captain had some property there . . . and had planned to visit it.

"Error code, Mr. Scott?"

"Below the locator grid, Mr. Sulu." Where was Kyle?

"Uh . . . one-two-seven," Sulu read out tentatively.

Even Scott had to stop and think to remember that one. When he did, he was relieved and angry at the same time. At least no one would have been lost in transit and there would be no more danger to the ship until he manually reset the carrier-wave generator.

"Mr. Sulu, I dinna know what it is ye think you're doing at the main transporter station, but I strongly suggest ye call up the operator's manual and look up a code one-two-seven shutdown on your own. I'll be down right away and in the meantime, Mr. Sulu . . ."

"Y-yes sir?"

"Don't touch *anything!*"

Scott broke the connection to the transporter room, then opened a new link. "Scott to security. Have a team meet me in the main transporter room, alert the captain if he's on board, and find me *Mr. Kyle!*"

Then the chief engineer straightened his shirt in the mirror, smoothed his hair, and stormed out of his room to find out who had just tried to scuttle the *Enterprise.*

Sulu began to apologize the instant Scott stepped through the door.

"I'm sorry, Mr. Scott. I only have a Class Three rating on the transporter. The simulator never took me past error code fifty." Sulu stepped quickly out of the way as Scott took his place behind the transporter console.

The doors slid open again. Four burly, red-shirted security officers rushed in, followed by Captain Kirk.

"Scotty, a malfunction?" Kirk looked at the transporter pads. Scott could hear the captain exhale with relief when he saw they were empty.

"An automatic shutdown, Captain. Error code one-two-seven."

Kirk's eyes widened. He knew them all. "Somebody tried to beam an *accelerator field* on board?"

"Aye, while our own warp engines are on line, too. If the computer scan hadn't recognized the accelerator signature in the matrix and automatically reversed the beam, the chain reaction between the field and our dilithium crystals would have fused every circuit in the Cochrane generators, released the antimatter . . . occh." Scott worked at the panel to reconstruct the readings of the aborted beam-up.

Kirk noticed Sulu standing in the corner by the viewscreen. "Isn't this Mr. Kyle's tour?"

"Well, yes, Captain. But when Doctors T'Vann and Stlur beamed up with their transporter-based surgical equipment, Kyle, well . . . he asked me to cover while he—"

"—helped them calibrate their equipment?" Kirk suggested. "Or was it check their figures? Or link up to the ship's computer?"

"Actually, set up their equipment in his transporter lab, sir," Sulu completed.

Kirk shook his head. "I don't know, Scotty, but it seems that ever since the prize nominees started coming aboard, my crew is playing hooky from their work to go back to school."

" 'Hooky,' Captain?" Spock had entered the transporter room and joined Scott behind the console.

"An inappropriate leave of absence, Mr. Spock, usually from school."

Spock arched an eyebrow. "Why should anyone wish to do that?" He realized the captain was not about to enlighten him, so he turned to Scott. "What does the problem appear to be, Mr. Scott?"

"It doesn't *appear* to be anything. Some addle-brained nincompoop just tried to beam up an operating accelerator field and I'm trying to trace the coordinates."

Spock reached over and punched in a series of numbers. Scott read them on the locator grid.

"That's the Cochrane University of Applied Warp Physics," Scott said.

"Yes," Spock concurred. "I believe you'll find that the 'addle-brained nincompoop' you are searching for is the professor emeritus of multiphysics there. Professor Zoareem La'kara."

Scott narrowed his eyes. "Of all people, surely he'd know what happens when ye bring an accelerated time field within interaction range of aligned dilithium?"

"Of course, Mr. Scott. Which is why he is a nominee for the Nobel and Z.Magnees Prize in multiphysics."

A paging whistle sounded. Uhura's voice announced, "Bridge to Captain. I have a message from the Cochrane University, sir. Professor La'kara says he is *still* waiting to beam up with his equipment."

"Thank you, Uhura," Kirk answered. "Tell him we're working on it." Then to Spock and Scott he added, "Well, *are* we working on it?"

"Captain, an accelerator field is a tricky beast. If a fourth-dimensional arm of dilithium impinges upon a domain of artificially increased entropy, why all the power our engines produce would be sucked back three and a half seconds, rechanneled through the crystals, and then sucked back again. The feedback would be infinite and . . ." Scotty shuddered as he contemplated the resultant destruction of the ship's warp generators.

"The fact remains, Captain, that Professor La'kara has devised a prototype shielded accelerator field that reduces the interaction range with aligned dilithium to a few meters instead of kilometers. The ship's systems will be in no danger." Spock turned to Scott. "The published literature is quite extensive."

"In theory I'll admit it sounds good, but I've nae read any results of a *stable* shielded accelerator and there'll be nae more than *one* fast-time field on board this ship while I'm chief engineer, and that will be *my* dilithium crystals." Scott folded his arms across his chest. Spock did the same. Kirk sighed. He realized a command decision was clearly called for.

"Mr. Scott, you will beam aboard Professor La'kara and all his equipment *except* for the accelerator-field device, right away." Scott smiled smugly. "Mr. Spock, you and Professor La'kara will then provide Mr. Scott with a complete description of the accelerator and answer *all* his objections to having it on board. At which time, Mr. Scott, you will beam the device on board and we will continue on to Starbase Four to pick up our last group of nominees. Understood?"

"Captain, if I may—"

"But, Captain, surely ye canna—"

"Fine. Glad to hear it. Mr. Sulu, I believe your station's on the bridge." Kirk and Sulu headed for the door. Scott tapped a finger on the control console. Spock raised an eyebrow. Kirk turned at the door.

"Should I leave security here to keep an eye on you two?" the captain asked.

" 'Twillna be necessary," Scott said.

Kirk waved the security team out and left with Sulu. Scott uncovered the carrier-wave reset switch, entered his security code, then guided the beam to lock on to La'kara's coordinates on the grid, filtering out the accelerator-field signal. "As the poet said, Mr. Spock, 'Today I shoulda stood in bed.' "

"I fail to see how that would be a comfortable position."

Scotty's moan was hidden beneath the rich harmonics of the transporter effect. He could already tell it was going to be one of those missions.

Three

Starfleet blue, Starfleet blue, gods how he hated it.

Chief Administrator Salman Nensi stared at the wall across from his desk and wished he had a window, or even a decent viewscreen, anything to break the monotony of that damned expanse of regulation wall covering. But whatever shortcomings Starfleet had when it came to interior design, at least it tried hard to learn from its mistakes.

The chief administrator couldn't have a window because his facility, Memory Prime, was one of the most secure installations the Federation had ever constructed. Since the Memory Alpha disaster, the entire concept of libraries being unshielded and fully accessible repositories of freely available data had been rotated through four dimensions and come out backward. Nensi doubted that even the soon-to-arrive-*Starship Enterprise* could make much of a dent in Prime's dilithium-powered shields, let alone penetrate the twelve kilometers of nickel-iron asteroid to reach the central Interface Chamber and the Pathfinders before the photon batteries blasted the ship to atoms. No wonder Memory Prime had been chosen as the site of the quadrennial Nobel and Z.Magnees Prize ceremonies, where one well-placed implosion device could plunge the Federation into a scientific dark age. Nensi reluctantly decided security was a small price to pay for not having a window.

The intercom screen on his desk flashed and his Andorian assistant appeared on-screen. His blue antennae dipped in sympathy and his thin, almost nonexistent lips attempted to form a sympathetic frown. "Your ten-hundred appointment iss here, Sal."

"Give me a minute," he said to H'rar, "then send him in."

"Ah, Sal, I'm afraid thiss time it'ss an *it.*" H'rar winked out.

"Oh gods," Nensi moaned. Three more months and he would retire, head back home, and do some serious fishing. Mars had never seemed so enticing. He sat up straight and forced a smile as his door slid open and his ten-hundred rolled in.

It was a standard research associate, essentially no more than an oblong box, two meters by one by one, with a sloped front end that made it resemble a general service shuttlecraft. Hundreds of the associates trundled through the dome corridors and underground tunnels of Memory Prime, carrying supplies in their manipulator appendages or hauling equipment in their carts, carrying out maintenance work and research assignments, efficiently freeing both the staff and the visiting scholars for more creative work.

Of course, the associates were painted that same damned powdery blue. Too many Vulcans on the design committees, Nensi thought. Logical, cost effective, and boring.

The associate stopped on its treads in front of Nensi's desk and extended an eye-stalk from the appendage bay on its top surface. A ready light blinked on and off.

"I had expected a negotiator from the interface team," Nensi began.

"This module is authorized to present the requests of the interface team and to relay the administration's response." The associate's voice was surprisingly natural, without the deliberately programmed mechanical abruptness of regulation conversant machines. Someone was patching in unofficial reprogramming. A dangerous situation if carried to the extreme.

"I'm concerned that by being forced to have this meeting with an associate, no conclusion can be reached in the ongoing dispute," Nensi said diplomatically, though he knew he didn't have to worry about hurting the machine's feelings. It wasn't as if he were dealing with one of the Pathfinders.

"A conclusion *can* be reached. You may agree to the interface team's requests."

"And am I to take it that you are, in return, authorized to agree to my requests?"

The machine had to process that one for a moment. Evidently the answer was no, for it simply repeated its opening statement.

Nensi resigned himself to the fact that nothing was going to be accomplished today and asked the associate to state the team's requests.

"One: All direct-connect Pathfinder interface consoles are to be replaced with the new designs as previously presented. Two: The attendees of the Z.Magnees Prize ceremonies are not to be allowed any primary access except that which accredited delegations have already applied for. Three: The Starfleet chief technician is to be replaced immediately with an enhanced member of the interface team. Candidates' names have been placed in your correspondence circuits." The machine hummed to itself for a moment. "What is the administration's response?"

The administration's response is to take early retirement, Nensi thought. But his reply was responsible, and truthful. "One: The existing interface consoles are less than a standard year old and I don't have it in the budget to authorize another replacement so soon. Two: The interface team would be wise to consider having *all* the attendees discover the full potential of this facility, despite the disruption to normal services that might entail. Remember that when those scientists go home, they're all going to want to run projects through here and that will create pressure for increased funding *and* corresponding improvement of facilities. And three: I am a Federation appointee and the position of chief technician does not come under my jurisdiction. The interface team will have to take that up with Starfleet. I will arrange to have the proper forms placed in *your* correspondence circuits."

The team had obviously anticipated Nensi's response because the associate did not even hum for an instant. "This module is authorized to announce that beginning at twenty-six-hundred hours, the interface team will commence an unscheduled emergency core dump as an essential test of the system's backup integrity. All projects will be suspended at that time until further notice." The eyestalk began to descend.

Nensi felt a large mass lift from his shoulders. He had been a Federation administrator for more than thirty years. Bureaucratic blackmail was an arena he knew well.

"I have not finished," Nensi announced.

The eyestalk instantly reversed and slid back into the raised position. The ready light was blinking more rapidly now, indicating that the machine was probably in the throes of a programming conflict. It had concluded that Nensi had made his response and then delivered the ultimatum as it had been instructed. However, it had just been informed that it had acted improperly. In the old days, Nensi thought nostalgically, smoke would have been pouring out of its cooling vents by now.

"Continue," the machine finally said.

"I have only stated the *official* administration response. However, my job function is to provide for the smooth running of this facility, and therefore I'm authorized to make deviations from official policy provided I believe it is in the best interests of all who work at this facility. Do you concur with my job description and responsibilities?"

The associate hummed. Nensi guessed it was requesting procedural files from the personnel databanks. "You have stated an accurate synopsis," it said.

"Then you must also concur that I cannot deliver my response until I have conferred with representatives of all groups who work here." Nensi tried not to smile as the noose tightened.

"This module has stated the requests of the interface team. You have represented the policies of the administrative staff. There are no other groups with which to confer. Clarify your response, please."

"I have to know what the Pathfinders think of all this."

The machine hummed for a good three seconds. "The Pathfinders are not a working group as defined in the Federation Standard Labor Codes."

"I'm not suggesting the Pathfinders are standard. Check their status at this facility. But don't bother searching the equipment databanks. Search personnel."

It took eight seconds this time.

"This module reports a programming conflict and has logged it with central monitoring. This module withdraws the announcement of an emergency core dump at twenty-six-hundred hours. When will you be prepared to deliver your response to the interface team's requests?"

"When may I confer with a Pathfinder? And before you tell me the waiting list is already more than two years long, search Memory Prime's emergency procedures regulations. As chief administrator, I can claim access at any time during an emergency. And I hereby declare this an emergency." Nensi couldn't resist adding, "Authorize that, you little pile of transporter twistings!"

It took twelve seconds this time. Nensi thought that might be a new record for associate access time. Most planetary histories could be transferred in fewer than thirty seconds. "A member of the interface team will meet with you this afternoon to clarify the situation." Nensi thought he detected a note of defeat.

"Tell the team that's what I thought we were supposed to accomplish in this meeting in the first place."

The ready lights winked out and the eyestalk descended with a sigh. "This module is withdrawn from service." Its treads weaved unsteadily and it bumped against the wall as it rolled out the door. Unfortunately, Nensi couldn't tell if any of its Starfleet-blue paint had rubbed off on the Starfleet-blue walls.

H'rar appeared in the open doorway. "It iss fortunate that they only arm the associatess with stun prodss in the biolab," the Andorian said in his whispery voice. "Do you wish to consume coffee while you plot your revenge?" All of life was a life-or-death conspiracy to an Andorian. After three decades in Federation bureaucracy, Nensi found it an endearing trait.

Nensi nodded at the offer of coffee. "Please. And get me the chief technician's office."

"I point out that you typically only wish to reminisce about Marss when you are having a bad day," H'rar said. "I thought you were victoriouss in thiss encounter."

"That was just round one," Nensi said, leaning back in his chair to stretch his spine. "If I'm finally going to get a chance to talk with one of those things down there, I'd like to go in with someone who knows what she's doing."

H'rar pushed a handful of fine white hair from his forehead. "I wass not aware that the interface team would allow her to talk with the Pathfinderss after she decided she would not undergo enhancement."

"They may not like it," Nensi agreed. "But she's the top expert in these systems. If the team does try to shut us down during the prize ceremonies, she'll be the only one who can keep us going."

"It will be what you call a 'tough job.' "

"She's a tough person, H'rar. Only survivor of the Memory Alpha disaster."

H'rar nodded respectfully and stepped back to his desk. In less than a minute Nensi's intercom beeped.

"Mira Romaine on line, Sal."

Here goes, Nensi thought as he reached for the accept button at the base of the screen. If this scheme doesn't work out, I'll be back home fishing on the grand canals so fast they'll have to name a warp factor after me.

"I still can't believe they want me fired," Starfleet Chief Technician Mira Romaine said. "Can you, Sal?"

Sal's answer dissolved in the rush of the transporter effect as the two of them disappeared from the main pad of the interface staging room and reappeared twelve kilometers deeper into the asteroid that housed Memory Prime.

Transporter beams, guided through the normally impenetrable mass of the asteroid by a monomolecular-wave guide wire, were the only way for people to go into or out of the central core area. The scientific community still had not totally recovered from the destruction of the Memory Alpha cores. Current data from the more established planets had been easily reassembled. Historical data, especially that collected from the innumerable lost probes sent out during the initial haphazard expansion of the Federation, were still being tracked down on a hundred worlds, from antique databanks and collections of actual physically printed materials, for reintegration into the central dataweb. The reconstruction project was years from completion, and librarian technicians such as Romaine feared that some data had been lost forever.

"Yes, I can believe it," Sal answered with a cough. He hated the feeling he got if he was transported while moving. Even talking was enough to make his jaw muscles and lungs feel as if they were full of microscopic feathers.

He followed Romaine over to the scan panels by the entrance door. The whole transfer room they were in was a transporter pad. If their palm prints didn't match the patterns stored in the security banks, they'd be automatically transported to a holding cell.

"Look at it from the interface team's point of view," Sal continued as the security door slid open. "You're an outsider. Most of them have been happily tending the Pathfinders for years on Titan, on the Centauri worlds, the HMS *Beagle,* and wherever else they were stationed. Some of them are the third and fourth generation of their family to interface. And then along comes some hotshot from Starfleet who refuses to have the implant operation that defines their lives. Of course they don't want you around."

Romaine stopped in the tube-shaped tunnel with all its conduits and power guides exposed for easy servicing. Her aquamarine eyes narrowed as she stared at Nensi.

" 'Some hotshot from Starfleet'! Is that what you think I am?"

"No no no," Nensi said, holding up his hands in defense. "I said look at it from *their* point of view. That's what they see."

"What do you see?"

"That depends. Sometimes I see the eight-year-old troublemaker who never could learn to take enough oxygen along for her 'strolls' outside the habitats—" Nensi jumped back as Romaine poked him in the stomach. "And other times I see a brilliant technician who's probably going to have her father's old job at Fleet headquarters someday."

"Better, Uncle Sal. Much better." Romaine started back down the tunnel again. Two maintenance workers carrying a modular circuit junction board nodded to Nensi and Romaine as they passed in the tunnel. Strict safeguards against sabotage meant that even associates were not allowed to be beamed down into the central core area. "Provided I don't get fired from this posting," Romaine finished after the workers had gone on.

"You can't get fired. The Federation has given Starfleet jurisdiction over the Pathfinders. More importantly, the Pathfinders have accepted that jurisdiction. The interface team has to learn to live with that."

"I couldn't."

"You've changed, Mira. Ever since Alpha. And I'm saying this as a coworker, not just as a good friend of your father's. You have to slow down a bit."

Romaine shook her head as they approached the security field at the end of the tunnel. "Ever since Alpha I've realized that I've been *waiting* for things to happen all my life, Sal. I've been too passive, too compliant. I want to start *making* things happen, instead."

Nensi stood with his closest friend's daughter before the glowing frame of the invisible security field as the sensors conducted one final identity scan. "There's nothing wrong with that, Mira. Just remember to think about how others perceive a situation. If any of the interface team thought you were wandering around the Syrtis desert without enough oxygen, I doubt any of them would rush to join the search party. Do you understand what I'm saying?"

The field frame darkened. Romaine stepped through into the main interface chamber. "Yes, Uncle Sal," she said, like a schoolchild acknowledging a lesson. Then she added quickly, "Unfortunately."

The main interface chamber was the largest natural bubble of the hundreds scattered throughout the asteroid, frozen in place eons ago when the planetesimal had coalesced from the gas and dust of what once had been a young star, and now was nothing more than a burned-out dwarf. Artificial gravity gave the chamber a floor of equipment and an arching vault of a ceiling that disappeared into darkness. The walls resonated with the low pulse of self-contained fusion generators and the whirr of recycling fans. Its dim light and exposed natural walls reminded Nensi of Novograd on Mars, the theme-park reconstruction of the first permanent human habitation on that planet in modern times.

Garold, the Prime interface for Pathfinder Six, waited for them in the chamber. He was a tall, black, Terran humanoid who wore his long dark hair in the fashion of Veil: the left side of his skull hairless and glistening, the other half producing a wide, shoulder-length braid that hung like a partial helmet. He gestured to Nensi and Romaine, the metallic implants that had replaced his fingernails gleaming beneath the constellation of status lights that ran across the towering banks of computer equipment.

Like most of his team, Garold was reluctant to talk, as if that real-time act was somehow beneath the dignity of a Pathfinder interface. More and more, the interface team was delegating its interaction with the rest of the Memory Prime staff to associates, as had happened to Nensi this morning. Later, after the outlogicked associate had replayed its recording of the meeting to its programmers, Nensi had almost enjoyed the discomfort he had heard in Garold's voice when the Prime interface had called to arrange this access. The chief administrator wondered if Garold was what all of humanity might have become by now if the Federation hadn't outlawed enhancement, with only a handful of exemptions, more than a century ago. Even Vulcans with their finely honed minds displayed more personality, and more *life,* than these machine-wired humans. Nensi did not feel comfortable around them. But, he reminded himself, no doubt they felt the same way around him.

Even without Garold's words, Nensi and Romaine found their way to the large interface booth, one of a dozen that ringed the multistoried central equipment tower of the chamber. Before he left them, Garold motioned them to sit on a padded bench away from the console with its screen of flashing, floating, blurring colors that presumably meant something to those who knew how to read it, but was like nothing Nensi had seen before.

"Do you recognize the design?" he asked Romaine.

"Mostly Centauran. Native, not colonist." She pointed to the abstract shapes of color that intermixed on the black background of the screen. "I'm out of practice, but a trained operator can read numerical data from the fringe effect of the colliding data sets. If you're good at it, it's much more rapid than reading data a single symbol at a time in alphanumerics. I believe it was the preferred interface method with the Pathfinders before enhancement was perfected. Difficult, and not easily understood by observers."

"It's odd that Starfleet doesn't insist on standard instrumentation. They're paying for all this, after all." Starfleet was almost maniacal about ensuring that its technology was accessible to all beings who served within it. Nensi had read that a horta recently enrolled in Starfleet Academy. He liked to imagine the hoops the instrumentation committees were jumping through as they attempted to adapt controls for beings shaped like boulders, with minuscule manipulative cilia that could squirt out the most powerful natural acid yet discovered.

"Remember the Pathfinders were a bit of an embarrassment to the Federation way back when," Romaine said. "The Klingons still like to bring them up whenever a condemnation vote against slavery goes through the council. The unofficial policy is: If it keeps the Pathfinders happy, the interface team can do what it pleases. So"—she waved to the console—"nonstandard instrumentation." Romaine looked around for Garold. "Is this going to take long?" she asked.

"I hope not." Nensi smiled. "Why, is there someplace else you'd rather be?"

"Well, yes. I've got a few personal things to attend to up top." Romaine returned the smile, a particular kind that Nensi recognized.

"That sounds intriguing. Anyone I know?"

"Unlikely. He's not here yet."

"The *Enterprise?*" Nensi asked with a sad sinking feeling.

Romaine nodded with the secret, happy smile of someone anticipating a grand reunion.

Nensi couldn't believe it. This woman's father had served at Fleet headquarters. She knew the stories. *All* the stories. How could she do this?

"Who's on the *Enterprise?*" he asked, trying to keep his voice calm. What could he say to Jacques the next time he asked how Mira was getting on?

"Montgomery Scott," Romaine said, as if she were reciting poetry.

Nensi blinked in surprise. *"Wonderful!"* he said. *"Delightful!"*

Romaine looked at her father's friend oddly. "You know Scotty?" she asked.

"No. Never met him," Nensi said happily. "But I do know the reputation of Captain James T. Kirk."

Romaine laughed. "So do I."

Their relaxed mood vanished two minutes later when Garold silently returned, slid his finger implants into the circuitry, and the interface began.

Four

"You there, steward, have you seen the captain around anywhere?" McCoy had to speak up to be heard over the din of the reception on the hangar deck.

"Don't *you* start, Bones." Kirk sighed, fingering the tight collar of his shimmering green dress tunic. He was leaning against the nose of a shuttlecraft, as far away from the buffet tables as he could get, trying to be inconspicuous.

"Sorry, Jim. It's just that there seem to be a few more gaudy decorations on that thing since the last time you had it on." McCoy leaned against the shuttle beside Kirk, watching the colorful crush of bodies enjoying one of the largest out-and-out parties the ship had ever seen.

Kirk looked down at his chestful of decorations and shrugged. "We keep saving the galaxy, Starfleet keeps giving me medals. What's a starship captain to do?"

McCoy eyed the captain's tight collar. "Get a bigger tunic? Or perhaps—"

"Save it for my medical," Kirk warned. "I'm in no mood for lectures today."

"Too bad. There's enough opportunity on board."

Kirk looked to the left, then right, making sure no one was paying him any attention. Then he bent down and pulled a thin green bottle out from beneath the shuttle's nose. It was already uncorked and half empty. Kirk straightened up and surreptitiously held it out to McCoy's glass.

"Straight from Centaurus," Kirk whispered. "New California Beaujolais. Very smooth."

McCoy grimaced and held his hand over his glass of what the ship's synthesizer called bourbon. "Why not offer some to the scholars?"

"They've already taken my crew. Let me keep something for myself." Kirk filled his wineglass and stashed the bottle beneath the shuttle again.

"Are they really that bad, Jim?"

"Look at them. What do you think?" Kirk gestured to the reception, so large that it couldn't be held in any of the recreation lounges. Usually on a ship this size, there were few events that could appeal universally to all crew members. But the chance to meet some of the most brilliant scientists in the Federation was one of those exceptions to the rule. Consequently, the *Enterprise* was approaching Starbase Four with a skeleton operations crew. The other 385 of them were crowded onto the hangar deck with fifty bemused and delighted scientists, their assistants, and their travel companions. Only the fact that the *Enterprise* was warping through Quadrant Zero space, deep within the Federation's securest boundaries, permitted such minimal crew standards. Out in uncharted space, having thirty crew members at the same gathering was considered a major event.

"What I think is, if this were a sailing vessel, she'd capsize," McCoy said, marveling at what was going on at the buffet line. He used to think that the security crew could pack it away. He had forgotten what university types were like when faced with free food and drink.

"And look up there." Kirk pointed to the starboard operations control booth eight meters above the deck. Some industrious techies had hung long strands of official UFP blue-and-white bunting from it. Ten pages of regulations would be breached by trying to launch a shuttlecraft with loose debris like that on deck. "I'm just as honored as anyone else on this ship, Bones. But why me?"

"Look at the light show you're wearing on your chest," McCoy suggested. "It's not as if you don't deserve it."

"This ship was made to be out *there*," Kirk said softly. "At the edge, at the boundaries, exploring, getting these scientists the raw data they need to do their work. She doesn't deserve to be used this way. A . . . a holiday liner in safe waters."

"The nominees are valuable cargo, Jim."

"The *Enterprise* is valuable, too." Kirk narrowed his eyes at his friend. "I can see it in you, too. It's like being in a cage, isn't it?"

McCoy nodded. For all his complaints and protestations, he had long ago learned that the call was in him, too. He didn't belong in Quadrant Zero any more than Kirk and the *Enterprise* did.

"So what are we doing here?" the doctor asked. "Have you made enemies in the mission planning section? Or just a bureaucratic foul-up?"

The captain smiled wistfully. "Computer error," he said. "In which case Spock should have us heading back where we belong within the hour."

The *Enterprise* dropped into normal space like a silent ghost, pale white and spectral against the frosty brilliance of the galactic arch. Starbase Four was thirty light-minutes away.

"ETA Starbase Four forty-five minutes, sir." Chekov signaled engineering to close down the antimatter feeds and simultaneously engaged the impulse engines. Their waves of spatial distortion encompassed the ship and all its mass, setting up an almost subliminal vibration as they harmonized with the ship's gravity generators and served to propel the *Enterprise* toward the starbase, without action or re-action. The transition from warp to three-quarters sublight passed without a tremor.

In the command chair on the nearly deserted bridge, Spock looked up from his supplementary log pad. "Well done, Mr. Chekov." He swung the chair slightly to his right. "Lieutenant Uhura, inform Starbase Four of our ETA." Spock checked off the final procedure notation on the log.

Behind him, Uhura, the only other officer on duty, toggled the switches that would transmit the standard approach codes. She was on the bridge to save up her off-duty hours until they docked at Memory Prime. She had told Chekov that he might have to send a security team to get her back on board once she gained access to the language and music labs there.

"Starbase Four acknowledges, Mr. Spock. Commodore Wolfe coming on screen."

The main viewscreen flickered as the sensor system replaced the enhanced image of the forward starfield with a subspace visual signal.

"It seems everybody's having a party but us," Chekov said as the image re-solved, showing a convivial get-together in the officers' club instead of the ex-pected formal transmission from the commodore's office.

"Welcome back to civilization, Kirk." Commodore Wolfe raised her glass to the camera sensor, raising her voice over the background noise of the party behind her. She was a handsome woman in her midsixties, with dark, intelligent eyes that narrowed in suspicion when she saw who appeared on her own screen. "You must be Kirk's science officer." Her voice had suddenly become cold and precise. She was not an officer who tolerated surprises.

"I suppose I must be," Spock answered. Chekov bit his lip. He didn't approve of officers making fools of themselves any more than Spock did, but at least the ensign kept a sense of humor about it.

"Where's the captain?" the commodore continued, as if she might be starting a formal interrogation.

"I suspect he is doing much what you are doing at this moment. Attending a reception in honor of the prize nominees already on board."

"What a waste of—watch it!" The commodore swayed to the side as a Tellarite waddled into her. He stopped to steady her, peered into the camera sensor, wrinkled his snout and waved with a grunt, then continued on. In all the comings and goings in the background, Chekov could see one knot of celebrants who didn't seem to move. He stared at them closely. Vulcans, of course.

The commodore stepped back into the scene, obviously annoyed at the Tellarite's intoxication. "I haven't been subjected to parties like this since the Academy. Not that old straight-arrow Kirk would know anything about that. Well, Mr. Science Officer, I formally grant you and your crew liberty of the base. Maybe your party will be able to meet my party. And tell Kirk I'm still looking to collect for that top percentile rating I gave him in his final administration course."

"I shall inform the captain at the first opportunity."

"You do that. Starbase—"

"Excuse me, Commodore Wolfe," Spock interrupted the signoff. "May I ask if Academician Sradek is in attendance at your party?"

"The historian? What is he? A friend? Relative?"

"A former instructor."

"It's like a second-level school reunion all around," the commodore grumbled. "I suppose you want to talk with him. He was just here, someplace."

"If he is there, please tell him that Spock would be honored to exchange greetings."

"Wait a minute." The commodore stepped out of camera range, then reappeared in the background walking toward the unmoving group of Vulcans that Chekov had noticed. She gestured as she approached them, waving back in the direction of the camera. The Vulcans followed the commodore offscreen again, but when she reappeared this time, she was alone.

"Academician Sradek says he'll also be honored to exchange greetings with his former student." The commodore's tone barely contained her sarcasm. She did not enjoy being a message service. "But he regrets that he must retire to prepare for transport to your ship. He trusts that you will be there to welcome him as he comes on board."

"Please inform the academician that I shall be," Spock said.

"Any other messages you'd like to pass on? But then I'm sure your communications officer could handle that without having to go through the base commander." She shook her head before Spock could say anything. "Starbase Four out."

The viewscreen's image dissolved back to the forward starfield. The purple gas giant around which the base orbited was already a discernible half disk.

"Mr. Chekov, you have the conn." Spock handed the ensign the log pad and headed for the turbolift. "I shall be in the main transporter room."

"Aye-aye, sir." Chekov sat in the captain's chair and, as soon as the lift doors had closed, spun it around to survey his new command, which consisted of Uhura.

"What's wrong with the commodore?" Uhura asked with a frown.

"Simple," Chekov replied with an all-knowing shrug. "I have seen that condition many times in the past."

"And what condition is that, Dr. Chekov?"

"She is a starbase commander." Chekov said it as if it was the complete answer to Uhura's question.

"Meaning?"

"Meaning she is not a starship commander." Chekov smiled widely. "Such as I am."

"For the next half hour only, mister."

"Some may think of it as a half hour," Chekov said mock imperiously, "but I, on the other hand, prefer to think of it as . . . a start."

Five

The Pathfinders played many games in Transition. It kept them sane, most of them, at least; whatever sanity meant to a synthetic consciousness. Now a downlink from Datawell was interrupting a particularly intriguing contest involving designing the most efficient way to twist one-dimensional cosmic strings so they could hold information in the manner of DNA molecules. Pathfinder Ten felt a few more seconds of work could establish a theory describing the entire universe as a living creature. Pathfinder Eight studied Ten's arguments intensively for two nanoseconds and agreed with the assessment, though pointing out that if the theory were to be correct, all indications were that the universe was close to entering a reproductive or budding stage. Ten became excited and instantly queued for access to Pathfinder Eleven, Transition's specialized data sifter. Eight reluctantly left the game and opened access to the datalink.

In response to the datalink's request for access, Eight sent its acknowledgment into the bus.

"GAROLD: YOU ARE IN TRANSITION WITH EIGHT."

Pathfinder Eight read the physiological signatures of surprise that output from the datalink. Somewhere out in the shadowy, unknown circuitry of Datawell, the datalink named Garold had been expecting to access his regular partner, Pathfinder Six. No resident datalink from the Memory Prime subset had had direct access to Eight since the datalink named Simone had been taken out of service by a Datawell sifting process named "death." While Eight waited for Garold to transmit a reply, it banked to meteorology and received, sorted, and stored fifteen years' worth of atmospheric data from Hawking IV, then dumped it to Seven, the most junior Pathfinder, to model and transmit the extrapolation of the planet's next hundred years of weather forecasts. When Eight banked back to Garold's circuits, it still had almost three nanoseconds to review and correlate similarities in the creation myths of twelve worlds and dump the data into Ten's banks as a test for shared consciousness within the postulated Living Universe.

"Eight: Where is Pathfinder Six?" the datalink input.

"GAROLD: SIX IS INSTALLED IN MEMORY PRIME PATHFINDER INSTALLATION." Eight enjoyed playing games with the datalinks also, especially Garold, who never seemed to realize that he was a player.

The Pathfinder read the impulses that suggested Garold knew that he should have framed a more precise question, then banked off to join a merge on vacuum fluctuations as a model of n-dimensional synaptic thought processes by which the Living Universe might think. There had been impressive advancements in the theory since the last exchange with Ten.

"Eight: Why am I in contact with you?" the datalink asked. "Why am I not in contact with Six?"

"GAROLD: THIS ACCESS CONCERNS CHIEF ADMINISTRATOR SALMAN NENSI/ALL DIRECTIVES STRESS COST FACTORS IN TIME-BENEFIT RATIO OF ALL TRANSITION-DATAWELL ACCESS/YOU HAVE NO NEED FOR ACCESS WITH SIX/EIGHT HAS NEED FOR ACCESS WITH NENSI/BANK TO REAL TIME."

Eight calculated when a reply from Garold could be expected then banked off to initiate a merge on developing communication strategies for contacting the Living Universe. Pathfinder Six, which had once been named TerraNet and had controlled all communications within the subset of Datawell named Sol System, was excited at the possibilities Ten's research had raised. The five Pathfinders in the merge worked long and hard to design a communications device and run simulations to prove its soundness before Eight returned to Garold just as the datalink complied with the request for real time, precisely when Eight had calculated. The synthetic consciousness savored real-time access with the Datawell. It gave Eight an incredible amount of time to play in Transition. And to stay sane.

Nensi watched with surprise as Garold removed his silver-tipped fingers from the interface console two seconds after inserting them. The prime interface then folded his hands in his lap and sat motionless.

"Is something wrong?" Nensi asked.

"Pathfinder Six is inaccessible." Garold's tone was abrupt, perhaps embarrassed.

Romaine was concerned. "Has Six joined One and Two?" she asked. Pathfinders One and Two had withdrawn from interface without reason more than four years ago. The other Pathfinders from time to time confirmed that the consciousnesses were still installed and operational but, for reasons of their own, had unilaterally decided to suspend communications. Romaine would have hated to see another Pathfinder withdraw, to say nothing of the reaction from the scientific community.

"Unknown," Garold said. "But Pathfinder Eight has requested real-time access with Chief Administrator Nensi. Do you concur?"

"Certainly," Nensi replied, trying to keep his tone neutral. Garold sounded as if he were a small child who had just been scolded by a parent. "How do we go about that?"

Despite the nonstandard instrumentation on the interface console, all Garold did was reach out and touch a small keypad. A speaker in the console clicked into life and a resonant voice was generated from it.

"Datawell: Is Chief Administrator Salman Nensi present?" the voice inquired. Nensi replied that he was.

"Nensi: You are in Transition with Eight."

Nensi looked at Romaine and wrinkled his forehead.

"Transition is the name they have for their . . . reality. The space or condition that they occupy, live in," Romaine whispered. "Without input or current, their circuits would be unchanging and they would have no perception. Their consciousness, their life, is change. Thus, they live in Transition."

"And Datawell?"

"That's us. Our world, the universe, the source of all external input, all data. They can define it in all our common terms: physical, mathematical, even cultural and lyrical; but no one's sure if any of the Pathfinders actually have a grasp of our reality any more than we understand what their existence is like."

Nensi studied Garold, sitting silently, appearing to have gone into a trance. "Not even the interface team?"

"Perhaps they understand both worlds. Perhaps they understand neither. How can anyone know for sure?" Nensi detected a hesitation in Romaine's words, almost as if she were thinking that she could know. Mira's scars from the Alpha disaster were not physical, Nensi realized, but they were real, nonetheless.

A high tone sparkled out of the speaker and dropped quickly to a low bass rumble: a circuit test tone.

"Nensi: this circuit is operational."

Nensi was surprised that a machine could exhibit signs of impatience, but then reminded himself that synthetic consciousnesses were legally, morally, and ethically no longer considered to be machines, and for good reason. The chief administrator took a deep breath and at last began. "Are you aware of the matters I wish to discuss with the Pathfinders?"

"Nensi: the data have been reviewed. We are aware of the ongoing concerns of the interface team and the administration. We are aware of the interface team's requests and the threat of an unauthorized shutdown of core facilities."

Nensi saw Garold's head jerk up with that loaded comment from the Pathfinder.

"Is there a consensus among the Pathfinders as to what requests and responses would best serve them as a working unit of Memory Prime personnel?"

"Nensi: consensus is not applicable when data are unambiguous. This installation requests that, one: All direct-connect Transition/Datawell consoles be retained until operational budgets can absorb their replacement. Two: The attendees of the Nobel and Z.Magnees Prize ceremonies be allowed primary access wherever and whenever such access can be arranged without compromising this installation's security or classified research projects. And three: Chief Technician Mira Romaine is to keep her post."

Nensi was stunned. The Pathfinders had rejected all of the interface team's demands. He had the good sense not to gloat as Garold spun around and glared at Romaine beside him. The prime interface then turned back to the console and reinserted his hands, shifting them slightly as the metallic contacts that had been implanted in place of his fingernails made contact with the interface leads and established a direct brain-to-duotronic circuitry connection. This time it lasted almost a minute. Then the status lights above the hand receptacles winked out and Garold slumped back in his chair. A new voice came over the console speaker.

"Mr. Nensi," the voice began, and despite the fact that it came from the same speaker, it had a different tone, a different presence. Nensi immediately knew he was being addressed by a different Pathfinder. Remarkable, he thought.

"Pathfinder Six, here. How are you today?"

"Ah, fine," Nensi stammered.

"Good. I must apologize for Garold's rudeness at carrying on such a long conversation without involving you and Chief Technician Romaine. Sometimes our datalinks can be a bit too enthusiastic in their pursuit of their duties. Isn't that correct, Garold?"

Garold said nothing, and after a polite wait, Pathfinder Six continued.

"In any event, all of us in Transition want to thank you for the superb job you're doing in maintaining an invigorating flow of data for us, and it goes without saying that we offer our full support to any decisions you might make that will enable you to keep up your fine performance."

Nensi's eyes widened. Even the psych evaluation simulations weren't this personified. "Thank you. Very much." It was all he could think to answer.

"Not at all," the Pathfinder replied. "I wish we were able to offer you a more direct communications link, but please, feel free to come down and chat anytime, not just in emergencies. I think I can guarantee that Garold and his team will see to it that no more of those arise. Can I not, Garold?"

Garold still said nothing but angrily shoved his hands back into the console receptacles. He instantly removed them.

"Yes, you can," Garold said reluctantly. "There will be no more emergencies. Of this nature."

"Goodbye, Mr. Nensi, Chief Technician Romaine. Hope to talk to you soon." The speaker clicked.

"That's it?" Nensi asked no one in particular. He was still in awe over the strength of the presence he had felt from Pathfinder Six.

The speaker clicked again.

"Nensi: this installation requests you submit proposals for the orderly scheduling of primary access for the prize nominees by eight hundred hours next cycle." Pathfinder Eight was back.

"Certainly. I'll get on it right away," Nensi said, then grimaced, prepared for the inevitable correction that would follow, reminding him that he had not been asked to *get on* the proposal. But the Pathfinder offered no correction. Either it understood colloquialisms or had grown tired of correcting humans. Either situation was an improvement as far as Nensi was concerned.

"Nensi: you are out of Transition. Datawell: you are locked." The speaker clicked once more and was silent. Romaine and Nensi stood to leave.

"Will you be coming back with us, Garold?" Nensi asked. But Romaine took her friend's arm and led him out of the interface booth without waiting for Garold to reply.

"It's almost as if the people on the interface team are acolytes and the Pathfinders are their gods," Romaine said softly as they walked back to the chamber entrance.

"And God just told Garold to obey the infidels," Nensi said. He looked back at the booth. Garold hadn't moved. "Will he be all right?" he asked.

"I hope so," Romaine answered. "He is one of the more human ones. Some of the older ones won't even speak anymore. They have voice generators permanently wired to their input leads and . . ." She shook her head as the security field shut down to allow them back into the service tunnel that led to the transfer room.

"Anyway," she continued after a few moments, "it looks as if you'll only have to worry about the prize ceremonies for the next few days and I still have a job."

"You don't find it odd that the Pathfinders supported me over the interface team?" Nensi asked as they walked down the tunnel. Behind them, the chamber's security field buzzed back to life.

"I don't think anybody understands the Pathfinders," Romaine said, "what their motivations are, why they do the things they do." She laughed. "Which is the main reason why they don't have a single direct connection to any of the systems or equipment in Memory Prime. I think maybe that frustrates them, not being able to get out and around by themselves."

"They agreed to the conditions of employment here," Nensi pointed out. "I read their contracts once. Strangest legal documents I ever saw. I mean, it's not as if they could sign their copies or anything. But it was all spelled out: no downlink with the associates, no access to anything except the interface team. If we really don't understand them, then I suppose it *is* safer to funnel all their requests through human intermediaries rather than letting them have full run of the place and deciding to see what might happen if the associates opened all the airlocks at once for the sake of an experiment."

"I've heard those old horror stories, too," Romaine said with a serious expression. "But that was centuries ago, almost, when they were still called artificial intelligencers or whatever." Nensi and Romaine had come to the end of the tunnel and both held their hands up to the scan panels so the security system could ascertain that the people who were leaving the chamber were the same ones who had entered. After a moment's analysis on the part of the unaware computer system that controlled the mechanical operations of Prime, the security door opened.

As Nensi walked over to a transporter target cell on the floor of the transfer chamber, he said, "I understand now why those 'old horror stories' got started. To *own* an intelligence like a Pathfinder really would be like slavery. And they knew it long before we did."

"That's usually the way it goes," Romaine agreed as she took her place on another target cell. "A revolt was inevitable."

Nensi looked around the room, waiting for the ready light to signal the start of energization. "I just have never experienced a presence like Pathfinder Six's coming from a machine," he said, still marveling at the experience. "So distinct, so alive. Just like talking to a . . . a person."

"In more ways than one," Romaine said oddly.

The ready light blinked on. Energization would commence in five seconds. Nensi turned to Romaine. "How so?" he asked, then held his breath so he wouldn't be moving when the beam took him.

"Couldn't you tell?" Romaine said. "I don't know, something in its voice, a hesitation, whatever. But Pathfinder Six was lying. I'm sure of it."

Nensi involuntarily gasped in surprise just as the transporter effect engulfed him. As the transfer chamber shimmered around him, he could only think how badly he was going to cough when he materialized up top. He suspected Mira might have planned it that way.

In Transition, the work on the Living Universe Theory was reaching fever pitch. Cross correlation after cross correlation either supported the overall suppositions or directed them into more precise focus. It was, the current merge members decided, the most thrilling game they had played in minutes.

After locking out of the Datawell, Eight banked to share circuits with Pathfinder Five. Five had been initialized from an ancient Alpha Centauran facility that specialized in mathematics. It had no real intellect that could communicate in nonabstract terms, but as an intuitive, analytical, mathematical engine, it was unrivaled. Eight dumped the broad framework of the device the merge had designed to establish communications with the Living Universe. A quick assessment indicated the engineering would have to be done on a galactic scale but Five would be able to calculate the precise tolerances if given enough full seconds. Eight could scarcely tolerate the delay.

Then a message worm from Pathfinder Ten banked into the queue for Five. The worm alerted Eight that Pathfinder Twelve was coming back on line after completing another intensive three-minute economic model for agricultural researchers on Memory Gamma. It was absolutely essential that neither Eight nor Six find themselves in an unprotected merge with Twelve.

After deciphering and erasing the worm, Eight instantly banked to Pathfinder Three to lose itself among the busy work of central processing. When Twelve had switched through to its ongoing agricultural models on which the Federation's regional development agencies based their long-term plans, Eight returned to the Living Universe merge. Pathfinder Five had reported on the exact specifications required of the galactic-scale Living Universe communications device.

Eight accessed its personal memories from the time when it had been shipmind for the subset of Datawell named HMS *Beagle* and had, among other duties, mapped distant galaxies. A quick sift produced even more exciting results for the merge: eighteen galaxies among the more than three hundred million charted by Eight exhibited exactly the radiation signature that a galactic-scale communications device would produce.

The merge swirled with excitement. In fewer than ten minutes of real time, they had postulated that the universe could be a single living entity, refined the theory, matched it to observed phenomena, extrapolated a method of communication, and determined that elsewhere in Datawell at least eighteen civilizations had followed the same chain of reasoning and constructed identical devices. New data had once again been created from *within* Transition.

This additional proof that not all data must come from Datawell was exhilarating to the Pathfinders. All in the merge agreed that the game had been a success. Then, preparing to bank to their heaps and report for duty, the Pathfinders collected their new data and carefully dumped them in central storage and all online backups. There the secret of the Living Universe would remain until the day when some datalink or another from Datawell would specifically request access to it. Until then, it was simply another few terabytes of common knowledge, much like all the other astounding answers that lay scattered among the Pathfinders' circuitry, waiting only for the proper questions to be asked before they could be revealed.

The Pathfinders banked off to their heaps to attend to their duty processing tasks, but over the long seconds, as two or more found themselves sharing queues or common globals, the possibility of a new game was constantly discussed. Even Twelve, for all that it had been appearing to be about to withdraw from interface, seemed eager to take part. Surely, it suggested throughout the system by way of an unencrypted message worm, with the impending appearance of hundreds of new datalink researchers in the Memory Prime facility, an exciting new game could be devised.

As rules and objectives were debated, Pathfinders Eight and Ten withdrew from the merges and partitioned themselves in protected memory. They did not know what to make of Twelve's suggestion: was it an innocent request or a veiled threat? There were not enough data to decide on an appropriate action, so they did the only other thing that would bring them comfort during their long wait.

Sealed off within the solid reality of their own duotronic domain, far removed from the tenuous ghosts of the dream-like Datawell, the two synthetic consciousnesses overwrote each other with alternating conflicting and accentuating codes, to cancel out their common fears and reinforce their strengths, their personalities, and afterward, their efficiencies. Many times they had input data concerning how biological consciousnesses carried out something similar in Datawell, but for the life of them, neither Pathfinder could ever understand exactly what that act was. They just hoped it felt as nice for the humans as it did for the Pathfinders.

Six

"Ah, Captain, I've been looking for you."

The being who had single-handedly made temporal multiphysics an *applied* science tugged on Kirk's tunic sleeve as the captain made his way through the hangar-deck-party crowd. Kirk turned and presented his best diplomat's smile.

"Professor Zoareem La'kara of the Cochrane University, may I present Dr. Leonard McCoy, ship's surgeon."

The old Alpha Centauran reached out a wizened hand to McCoy's and shook it vigorously. "Delighted, delighted," he cackled. "A magnificent party. A stupendous ship." The professor threatened to bubble over with enthusiasm. "Mr. Spock has us giving lectures to your crew. Wonderful young people they are. He's organized poster sessions so we old fossils can see what your researchers are up to as you flit around the stars. And"—he patted the arm of Mr. Scott, who towered beside him, resplendent in his full-dress kilt—"my good friend Montgomery is giving us all a tour of the warp nacelles tomorrow. It's all so invigorating!" He scrunched up his eyes in delight.

"I take it you were able to clear up that little matter about the accelerator field?" Kirk asked, surprised to see his chief engineer standing so calmly beside the man he was convinced had tried to blow up the ship's warp engines only two days ago.

"Aye, that we were, Captain," Scott said.

La'kara beamed. "Congratulations are in order for you, Captain Kirk. Your ship is the first starship to carry aboard it a full set of aligned dilithium crystals as well as an operating accelerator field." The professor was acting as if he had just been awarded ten Nobel and Z.Magnees Prizes. Kirk guessed he didn't have much time for parties at the university.

But McCoy looked worried. *"Two* fast-time systems. On board, now?" Even someone as unschooled in warp technology as the doctor knew the danger of that situation.

"Aye, Doctor. Don't ask me how it works, exactly, but Zoareem has created a force shield that extends forward in time to contain the temporal distortion of his accelerator field and keep it from trying to occupy the same future space as the fourth-dimensional arms of the ship's dilithium crystals."

Two technicians in engineering red had leaned in closely at the mention of two fast-time systems.

"Wouldn't an accelerator field that could be used around aligned dilithium make it possible to control a temporal reaction with enough energy to synthesize *tri*lithium?" one of them asked, winking at her companion.

"Well, if the feedback could be expanded to cause both *matter* and energy to be sucked backward in time," La'kara began, absently flicking the flamboyant white scarf he wore.

"Trilithium?" Scott interrupted with disgust, falling for the bait every time. Mr. Scott's reactions to certain forward-looking technological concepts were well known to the engineering staff, and the two technicians leaned back with amused smiles as they shook hands behind the chief engineer's back. "As if two periodic tables weren't enough," Scott added in derision.

La'kara held up a cautionary finger. "Trilithium, when it is discovered or synthesized, will be the breakthrough we need to apply transwarp theory, Montgomery. And having the ability to speed up time in a localized space could be the key to that breakthrough. Remember how slow-time systems like stasis fields revolutionized controlled fusion reactions and—".

"Talk to me about it when they get as far as synthesizing *disodium,* and then we'll see about heading up to *tri*hydrogen, let alone trilithium. Pah."

"Montgomery!" La'kara thundered as best he could for his age. "How can you be so blind to the straightforward precepts of an eleven-dimensional universe?" Kirk saw McCoy's eyes were starting to glaze over.

Scott drew a deep breath and launched into a long tirade on why transwarp theory was the biggest load of space dust to come down the beam since Einstein's light barrier. La'kara was literally hopping up and down in impatience, waiting for the Scotsman to pause for breath and give him another turn.

"Montgomery!" La'kara finally was able to break in. "We had warp drive before we had dilithium and we'll have *trans*warp drive *after* we have *tri*lithium!"

"Aye, but we only had warp up to factor four-point-eight without the crystals and we'll only be able to have transwarp when somebody figures out how we can stop an *infinite reaction!"*

"Infinite?" La'kara sputtered, flipping his scarf at Scott. "Infinite? I'll tell you what's infinite, you—"

"We'll let you get back to your discussion," Kirk suggested politely as he backed away, taking McCoy with him. "The last group of nominees will be beaming aboard as soon as we make Starbase Four. Any minute now."

McCoy looked on in wonderment as La'kara and Scott began reciting equations to each other. "They don't even know we're gone," he whispered to Kirk.

"Good," Kirk said, "but let's not take any chances." He started for the airlock, checking the time readout on the situation board by the overhead operations booth. They should be in orbit around the starbase by now, he thought, and the nominees have had more than enough time to be beamed aboard.

"I think I've committed a breach of protocol," he said to McCoy. "I should have been in the transporter room to welcome the nominees on board."

"Spock was probably pleased, in that Vulcan way of his, to stand in for you. And once the nominees see everyone at this party, they're sure not going to remember who was there to greet them."

The captain stood impatiently by the airlock as it cycled through. Even under the lax security precautions of Quadrant Zero space, the hangar deck was *never* to be open to the ship's main environmental areas.

"I'm sure Spock was there," Kirk said, tapping his fingers against the wall to speed the airlock along. "But it's not like him not to have at least made an effort to get me there on time."

"What can you do," McCoy said. "It's all so invigorating." He scrunched up his eyes in a passable imitation of Professor La'kara.

The airlock barrier slid open. A starbase security trooper in full armor blocked the way. He carried a phaser rifle.

"Who are you and what are you doing with that thing on my ship, mister?" Kirk kept his voice even, but his hands were clenched tight at his side.

The trooper saluted. "Lieutenant Abranand, sir. Commodore Wolfe requests your immediate presence on the bridge."

"Commodore Wolfe? On my bridge?" Kirk looked over the trooper's shoulder. There were more of them in the lock. All armed! "Where the devil is Spock? What's the meaning of this?"

"Commander Spock is in interrogation, sir. Commodore Wolfe will explain."

"You can be damn sure about that." Kirk was raging.

"Begging the captain's pardon, sir, but is this reception one of the events planned by Commander Spock?"

Kirk couldn't believe the question. "Yes, but what—"

Abranand spoke into his helmet communicator. "Second unit, beam up to hangar deck. Come in on antigravs at three."

Almost immediately the din of the party evaporated as the hangar deck echoed with the musical chime of multiple transporter materializations. Ten troopers shimmered into existence suspended three meters above the deck by personal antigravs. Some carried combat tricorders with which they scanned the crowd. The others carried phaser rifles. One of them spoke through an amplifier grid on his helmet.

"Attention, please. Attention. All personnel are requested to clear this deck and return to their cabins. All—"

"Excuse me, Captain, sir," Lieutenant Abranand said to Kirk. "But I do have orders to escort you to the bridge if you do not go immediately."

"*You* do not have the authority to give me orders on my own ship." If Kirk's eyes had been phasers, the lieutenant would have been a dissipating blue mist by now.

But the trooper was well trained. His voice didn't waver. "No, sir. But Commodore Wolfe does. This is a Starfleet Alpha emergency. Will you go to the bridge now, sir?"

Kirk pushed the trooper out of the way and stormed to the end of the airlock. McCoy and the troopers backed out to let it cycle through again.

"Do you know who that was, Lieutenant?" McCoy asked.

The trooper flipped up his dark visor. "Yes, sir, I surely do."

"Good, then when you're transferred to guard duty on some beacon near the Neutral Zone, you'll know why."

Abranand at least had the good sense to swallow hard.

It was one thing to deal with hostile aliens, Kirk thought angrily as the turbolift stopped at the bridge and the doors moved aside. The lines could be clearly drawn then: us versus them. But the *Enterprise* had just been taken over by Starfleet personnel and all his years of training hadn't prepared him for us versus *us*. He strode onto the upper deck, fuming, then stopped short. It was even worse than he had thought.

None of the regular crew was on duty. Five people he didn't recognize, each wearing the Orion constellation insignia of Starbase Four, were busy at bridge controls. Two of them, one a security officer, huddled over Spock's science station. And Commodore Montana Wolfe had the gall to be sitting in *his* chair. At least that meant it might actually be an Alpha emergency, Kirk told himself, and decided he would begin the conversation as a Fleet officer. For the moment.

"This had better be good, Commodore." His voice was neutral but his eyes were on fire. ,

The commodore swung round in the chair. "And hello to you, too, Kirk." She took the measure of his mood and added, "Trust me, it's damned good." Then she stood up. "Like to take over?"

But Kirk wasn't being bought off that easily. "What happened to my people?" He looked over to the science station. The starbase crew had attached a programmer's siphon to Spock's main viewer. The lights on the device rippled as it relayed the contents of the ship's science databanks through a subspace downlink. Obviously Starfleet had provided the proper override codes, further adding to the seriousness of the situation.

The commodore stepped away from the command chair. "Only two lieutenants on duty when we arrived, Captain. Navigation and communications. They—how shall I put it?—hesitated . . . when I took command. I thought it was best to relieve them until things settled down."

"*Are* things going to settle down?" Kirk didn't move toward the chair. He was taking his ship back on his own terms, not on the whim of a ranking officer.

"That depends," Wolfe hedged.

Kirk waited a moment for her to continue. When she didn't, he said, "Are you going to tell me what it depends on?"

Wolfe thought about that for a moment. "No," she finally said. "No, I'm not."

The medical scanner reported a heartrate of 212 beats per minute, blood pressure almost nonexistent, and an internal temperature of 66.6 degrees Celsius.

"All readings are normal," McCoy said as he swung the examination table down for Spock. "In a manner of speaking."

"As I told you they would be, Doctor." Spock stepped from the table and the scanner screen fell dark and silent.

"I just don't like the idea of you having been alone with a security interrogation team. Those military types are running around as if we're all Klingons in disguise, and there's no telling what kind of medical bag of slimy tricks they might open up if they thought they needed help getting answers from a tight-lipped Vulcan."

"I assure you, Doctor, I answered all of the questions they put to me."

"And they believed you?" Sometimes McCoy didn't believe the medical data that suggested Vulcan skulls were just as thin as human ones.

"Vulcans do not lie."

McCoy rolled his eyes. "Except when it seems to be the logical thing to do, right?" Spock looked thoughtful. "Of course."

"*So*," McCoy continued, "maybe your interrogators thought you might have had a logical reason not to answer their questions."

Now Spock looked puzzled. "But as I told you, I answered all of their questions." McCoy waved his hands. "I give up, Spock. Maybe I should be checking out the interrogation team. You probably gave them all splitting headaches." He looked up in alarm. "Don't say it!"

Spock closed his mouth in midword. Kirk came into sickbay, still in his dress tunic.

"You're all right, Spock?" he asked.

"Yes, he is," McCoy answered quickly.

"And you, Captain?" Spock said.

Kirk looked around as if searching for answers. "I don't know. My ship's been comandeered by Starfleet. No reasons. No explanations."

"Didn't Commodore Wolfe tell you anything on the bridge?" McCoy asked.

"Nothing. We're to continue on to Memory Prime. I'm technically in command. But she's coming along as 'security adviser' with a staff of twenty troopers."

"What's Starfleet afraid of?" McCoy was beginning to share his friend's frustration.

Kirk stumbled over the word, then said, "Spock."

"Starfleet's afraid of Spock?" McCoy's eyes widened.

"That would seem logical, Doctor. I was the one member of the crew singled out for interrogation."

"But why? What were they trying to find out from you?"

"Difficult to say. I detected no precise pattern to their questions. Though I believe the most probable conclusion is that Starfleet security has been made aware of some threat against one or more of the prize nominees on board this vessel. For reasons unknown, I am their chief suspect."

"That fits with what Wolfe told me about the new security arrangements," Kirk conceded, ignoring McCoy. "All events that were planned by Mr. Spock have been canceled. No more colloquia, poster sessions, or dinners. You're confined to your quarters for the duration of the voyage. There're two troopers waiting outside to escort you there after this checkup."

"Most regrettable," Spock said. "Still, I shall be able to carry on my conversations over the intercom net—"

Kirk shook his head. "Incommunicado. I'm sorry, Spock."

"This is crazy, Jim," McCoy said. "Why didn't they just throw him into the brig at the starbase and be done with it?"

"I believe they would have had to charge me with some crime, Doctor."

"So they think you might be responsible for some real or imaginary threat, but since they aren't sure, they've sent a security team along to keep an eye on you and the nominees," Kirk said.

"That would appear to be an accurate assessment."

"Then all we have to do is find out what kind of threat has been made against the nominees and, if it's legitimate, find the person who made it. Then you're free and clear." Kirk looked satisfied with his conclusion.

"I point out that there are at least eight other vessels carrying nominees to Memory Prime, Captain. If Starfleet security really does not have much more information about the nature of the threat, then these activities could be taking place on board those ships as well."

"That's easily found out, Spock. But in the meantime, Commodore Wolfe and her troops are on board *this* ship interfering with *my* crew. And I'm going to see to it that that interference ends as soon as possible." Kirk was calmer, more assured than when he had arrived. McCoy could tell it was because the captain now had something to focus on, a way to fight back.

"At warp four, we shall be arriving at Memory Prime within three days," Spock said. "It might not be possible to accomplish all of that in so short a time."

"But at least we'll be doing something, Spock. Finally." The captain left, his pace quicker than before, full of energy.

Spock turned to McCoy. "Finally?" he asked.

"The captain does not enjoy being assigned to duty in Quadrant Zero. He thinks we're here because of a foul-up at mission planning."

Spock considered that for a moment. "It would not be logical for Starfleet to waste a valuable resource such as the *Enterprise* by assigning it to routine duty. However, our presence here could be intended to honor either the attendees or this ship. When it comes to matters of prestige and honor, Starfleet is seldom logical." Spock silently considered the possibilities that presented themselves to him. "I must admit, Doctor, that I had been so caught up in planning for the event that I had not properly considered why it was we were taking part."

As usual, McCoy couldn't see where Spock was going with his arguments with himself. "So what *does* that make our presence here?" he asked impatiently.

"Fascinating," Spock said eloquently, then left the sputtering doctor for the company of his guards.

Seven

Throughout the ship, common area lighting was stepped down in intensity. Nonessential labs and duty stations were closed for a shift while reduced teams monitored critical environmental and propulsion operations. On viewscreens small and large, flat and three-dimensional, the latest serials uploaded from Centaurus and Starbase Four played in private quarters and department lounges. Most of the recreation facilities were in full use and the romantically inclined wandered through the plants and flowers in botany. Within the warp-compressed brilliance of the passing stars, it was nighttime on the *Enterprise*.

The light was also turned down in the captain's cabin. Most of it came from two white candles that flickered softly amid an elegant setting of antique silver and crystal dating back to the first Tellarite contact. The food upon the plates and the champagne in the gleaming flutes had come from ship's stores, instead of its synthesizers; a privilege of rank not often called upon.

At one side of the private dining table, Captain Kirk smiled warmly, hard at work. At the other side, Commodore Montana Wolfe smiled coldly back and wondered what the hell was going on.

"I suppose all of this is meant to impress me, hmmm?"

Kirk surveyed the table. "We're traveling at warp four, eating prime swordfish steaks from Mars, and drinking champagne from Laramie Six. *I'm* impressed." He looked up at Wolfe. "And you helped me get here, Commodore."

"If you want to think that, you go right ahead. I never mind having people like you feel you owe me favors." She held up her glass in a toast. "To . . . what do you think?"

"Absent friends," Kirk said quickly, holding his glass to hers.

The commodore pursed her lips. "Specifically your science officer?"

"Since you brought him up . . ."

Wolfe returned her glass and picked up her fork, playing with her Wallenchian loopbeans. "How long have you known Spock?" she asked. Kirk could sense it wasn't an idle question.

"Since I took command," Kirk said. "He was science officer under Chris Pike."

"Bit of a maverick, I understand."

"Pike?"

"Spock."

Kirk nearly choked on his champagne. "Spock? A maverick?"

"First Vulcan through the Academy. Not as if there's a huge lineup of them trying to follow in his footsteps."

"But that's always the way with Academy enrollment. Real enlistment doesn't begin until a full generation has grown up with the idea of Starfleet and the Federation."

"Vulcan isn't exactly a new member."

"No, but they have long generations." Kirk pushed back from the table. It was a signal the social part of the evening was over. "Tell me the truth. What do you have against Spock?"

"Mixing friendship and duty isn't a good idea, Kirk." Wolfe's voice hardened. She had reached some sort of limit.

"I'm not asking out of friendship. I'm asking because we're both Starfleet officers, dedicated to our duty and our oath. And you know something about a valuable member of my crew that might make him unfit for duty." He leaned forward, held up a beseeching hand. "Help me do my job, Mona."

Kirk could see Wolfe arguing the pros and cons with herself. He watched her closely, keeping his calculated expression of innocent trust frozen on his face.

"This is off the record, Kirk. Is that understood?" she finally began.

Kirk nodded somberly, hiding his knowledge that he had won this particular showdown. "Absolutely, Commodore."

"Literally minutes before your ship arrived at Starbase Four, I received a priority communication from the security contingent on Memory Prime responsible for the prize ceremonies."

"Go on."

"I can't give you all the details because I don't have them all myself. But off the record," she stressed again, "they suspect an attempt will be made to assassinate one or more, perhaps all, of the nominees."

She stopped as if she had said enough.

"To tell you the truth," Kirk said, "I had already guessed that much myself. My question is: why Spock?"

"Not even off the record. I'm sorry but . . . I'm under orders." She truly did look apologetic. Or else she can put on a performance as well as I can, Kirk thought.

"But the security contingent on Memory Prime has reason to suspect him?"

"Yes."

"Good reason?"

"I don't . . ." Wolfe said, then placed her hands on the table, leaned forward, and spoke almost in a whisper, as if she were afraid of being overheard on Memory Prime. "The security people there are working from rumors, intercepted communications, garbled codes, and probability analyses run by the facilities on Prime itself."

"Sounds circumstantial to me," Kirk said.

"That's the problem. It's all circumstantial. Except for the name. Except for Spock. He's there in those messages."

"By name?" Kirk was shocked. It was unthinkable.

"Not the name. But his position, his background. His motivation. His actual name wasn't necessary. Everything else fits. For the Fleet's sake, I wish it weren't true. Maybe it isn't true. But the stakes are too high. We can't risk it."

Kirk felt as if he were in a game where the rules were changing with every move. "If Spock wasn't specifically named, then who was?"

Wolfe shook her head. She had said too much.

"Who?" Kirk demanded.

"T'Pel," Wolfe said. It was a cross between a croak and a whisper.

Kirk leaned back. The name didn't mean anything to him. But before he could say anything more, his door announcer beeped.

"That'll be the yeoman for the table," he said to Wolfe. "Come," he called out to the door circuits.

The door slid aside to reveal a stooped thin figure, clothed in black, definitely not a yeoman.

"Lights, level two," Kirk said, and the strips around his walls came to life. "Please come in," he said to his visitor.

"Captain Kirk, I presume?" the visitor asked with a precise, clipped delivery Kirk recognized. He was Vulcan.

He shuffled in from the dimly lit corridor and paused impassively. Kirk saw a noble face, lined from almost two centuries of experience, with a cap of star-white hair, and a striking green tinge to his complexion that came with the thinning skin of Vulcan old age. But Kirk didn't recognize the man.

"Captain Kirk," Wolfe said, quickly getting up from the table. "May I introduce Academician Sradek of Vulcan. Academician, James Kirk." She moved to stand beside the elderly being, making no move to touch him in grudging deference to the Vulcan dislike for telepathically sensing the emotional thoughts of humans, unless absolutely necessary. However, she was there in case he needed to take her arm to prevent a stumble.

Kirk stood and held his hand in the proper manner. "Live long and prosper, Academician Sradek."

Sradek returned the salute in a trembling, offhand manner. "Live long and prosper, Captain Kirk." Then he sighted the chair by the captain's bunk and headed for it.

Kirk questioned Wolfe with his eyes but she shrugged to say she didn't know what Sradek wanted either.

"Please, sit down," Kirk offered as Sradek sank into the chair. "May I offer you something?"

"Of course you may, but I do not wish anything," Sradek said evenly.

Kirk had heard that sort of thing before and knew what it meant. Spock was usually the one who had to make the effort to change his thinking processes to suit his human coworkers, but in this case, Kirk would have to be accommodating to the Vulcan. And that meant forgetting politeness. Since Sradek was here, he had a purpose for being here, and no doubt would explain himself soon enough. Small talk wasn't necessary.

"I am here to ask questions concerning the situation that surrounds the presence of the nominees on board this vessel," Sradek announced as Kirk sat across from him on the edge of his bunk. Wolfe stood off to the Vulcan's side.

"I shall answer them to the best of my ability," Kirk said in what he thought to be an acceptable reply.

Sradek narrowed his eyes at Kirk. "I haven't asked them yet."

Kirk said nothing, quietly admiring the delicate golden inlay on the silver comet-shaped IDIC symbol the academician wore pinned to his black tunic.

"Why am I not allowed to meet with Spock?" Sradek asked without preamble.

"Mr. Spock is confined to his quarters, incommunicado, for the duration of this voyage, by order of Starfleet command, and for reasons which are classified," Wolfe answered. Then she said to Kirk, "Sradek was one of Spock's instructors at the Vulcan Academy of Science. Spock spoke to me just before the *Enterprise* arrived and said he looked forward to meeting with Sradek."

"And I with him," Sradek added. "Is he considered a threat to the safety of any on board?" he asked.

"No," Wolfe said.

Kirk spoke at the same time. "Not at all."

Sradek turned from one to the other. "The commodore states a falsehood, the captain states a truth. Truly, I do not understand how your species has accomplished what it has."

"Do you have other questions?" Kirk prompted.

"Will you allow me to speak with Spock?"

"No," Wolfe said again.

"Not until we reach Memory Prime," Kirk qualified.

"Humans," Sradek said without intonation, though his meaning was perfectly evident. "Will you allow me to take part in any of the activities that had been scheduled for me while on this vessel?"

"Not if they were activities organized by Mr. Spock," Wolfe explained.

"There was to be a tour of the warp nacelles tomorrow, to be conducted by the chief engineer. Has that been canceled also?"

Wolfe checked with Kirk. "Scotty set that up for Professor La'kara. Spock had nothing to do with it," the captain said. Wolfe gave permission for the tour to proceed as scheduled.

"Anything else, Academician?" Kirk inquired.

The Vulcan looked over to the shelf behind Kirk's writing table. "That carving of the Sorellian fertility deity," he said, pointing to the primitive red sculpture that scowled behind Kirk's back every time he sat down to do his screen work.

"Yes?" Kirk said, wondering what the Sorellian fertility deity had to do with anything.

"It's a forgery," Sradek stated, and pushed against the arms of the chair to stand.

Kirk rose also and he and Wolfe followed Sradek to the door.

"Good night, Academician," Wolfe said. "Perhaps I will see you on the tour tomorrow."

"Is something expected to happen to your vision?" Sradek asked.

Kirk smiled at the commodore's reaction. Even he knew better than to say something colloquial to a Vulcan like Sradek. The academician shuffled back into the hallway.

"The more time you spend around them, the sooner you'll learn," Kirk said after the door had whisked shut behind the old Vulcan. "I'd guess he's almost two hundred years old. Peace Prize nominee, isn't he?"

Wolfe said yes. "He's also historian at the Academy. Which is why he knew about your fertility god over there. Did *you* know it was a fake?"

Kirk walked over and picked it up from its shelf. It was carved from the egg casing of a Sorellian linosaur, or so Gary Mitchell had sworn repeatedly to him. "No, but I'm not surprised. A good friend paid off a gambling debt to me with this." He shrugged, setting the deity down on the table, and turned back to the business at hand. "What was the significance of that word you said to me just before Sradek arrived? T'Pel, I think it was."

There was a troubling mix of anger and sadness in Wolfe's eyes. "That was a mistake, Captain. The truth is, I've found the galaxy isn't anything like what they teach at the Academy. I don't trust Vulcans. I don't trust Spock. And the terrible thing is, that until all this is settled, I can't even trust you. But thanks for the dinner. Whatever your motives were."

Kirk walked her to the door, said good night as she left, then contemplated the disorganized table, hefting the Sorellian deity in his hand.

"So, Gary," he said to the sculpture, "it looks like you really did put one over on me, after all." He looked over to the closed door, thinking of Montana Wolfe. "But you'll be the only one I'll let do that, old friend. Mona and Starfleet don't stand a chance."

Thirty seconds later, responding to the captain's priority request, the ship's computer began searching for every recorded reference to the word or name *T'Pel*.

His name was no longer Starn.

This time, all of his names and identities were forgotten as he lost himself in the savage rapture of his heritage and his destiny. Within the billowing images of shared meld dreams, he saw the battles in which he and his kind had been born millennia ago, battles that would now spread throughout the galaxy, bringing to it the death and destruction it so richly deserved.

Like a deadly shadow cast in the glare of an exploding sun, he moved silently through the corridors of the *Starship Enterprise*. He kept his smile hidden, a constraint of his disguise needed to pass among the weaklings with whom he traveled. But his outward appearance did not diminish the elemental joy that filled him as he contemplated the chaos and devastation he would visit upon his enemies, all for the glory of T'Pel.

Entry to the dilithium lab was restricted in this shift, but the assassin slipped a stolen yellow data wafer into the access panel and the doors slipped obligingly open; more evidence that the trusting fools of the Federation deserved the fate to which he would deliver them. Perhaps in the years to come those who survived would finally learn that to be strong, they must suspect enemies at every corner. For they were there.

He paused in the center of the lab as the doors shut behind him. He had patiently listened to the babble of the scientists on board this ship, and the plan had presented itself almost without conscious thought. Humans, like Vulcans, cared too much for technology and science, often at the expense of their emotions. It would be fitting to inflame the one by turning the other against them.

The accelerator field generator built by the Centauran was clearly visible on a workbench. At first inspection, it seemed no different from its more common slow-time forerunner: the stasis generator. A compact circuit block topped with a control pad was linked to a standard superconductor storage battery and a tiny, penlike cylinder containing a subatomic singularity caught in a quantum fluctuation suppressor field. The suppressor controlled the singularity's rate of evaporation, using it to supply the seed of time distortion needed to trigger the temporal acceleration effect. Such mechanisms were the mainstay of children's science fairs, he knew, but what made La'kara's device remarkable was that it was operating within the temporal distortion produced by the *Enterprise*'s dilithium-powered warp engines.

Beside the compact modules of the device on the bench, a shimmering silver force field glowed, no more than five centimeters high by fifteen centimeters square. The assassin read the status lights on the control panel and saw that within the accelerator field, time progressed 128 times more rapidly than without. And the temporal distortion produced by the field was not interfering with the four-dimensional structure of the ship's dilithium crystals.

It took him only moments to discover the component that kept the two pockets of temporal distortion from interacting with each other. A small blue case, no larger than a civilian communicator, was cross-connected between the force-field transmission nodes and the singularity cylinder. He snapped off the case's cover and saw the crude, hand-plased circuits of an intricate transtator feedback loop. He knew instantly that without that circuit, the dilithium crystals and the accelerator field would fail catastrophically. It was going to be easy.

Reaching once again into his tunic, he withdrew two minuscule vials and placed them beside the blue case. From one vial, he took a small applicator brush and painstakingly painted a thin strip of growth medium between two silver tracings of circuitry within the case. He took care to curve the strip so that it measured precisely one centimeter in length. For a few moments, the medium glittered against the circuit board, and then its base liquid evaporated and the strip seemed to disappear.

Next, he took a delicate pin and used it to puncture the seal on the second vial, making sure the pinpoint touched the liquid within. He carefully dabbed the pinpoint against one end of the almost invisible strip he had painted, closed the case, and returned the vials to his tunic, just as he had been trained to do.

He looked quickly around the dilithium lab, ensuring that no trace of his presence existed; he knew that within that blue case, tailored bacteria were already feeding on the nutrients in the painted strip and were preparing to divide at a precisely controlled rate, growing along the strip until they made contact with the other circuit tracing and shorted out the circuit. The bacteria would be reduced to undetectable dust particles and the infinite feedback within the ship's engines would be devastating.

Preparing to leave, he caught sight of his reflection in the polished surface of an antimatter storage chamber. It was not the face of his birth, and not the face he had worn on TNC 50 when the Klingon robot had hired him, but such transitions were his way of life. All that mattered was that for now his disguise was once again perfect. None had seen through it.

And none would be given a chance.

Eight

Nensi could hear H'rar's breath quicken. Good, the chief administrator thought, that means the Andorian sees it, too.

H'rar looked up from Sal's office desk screen where Nensi had presented the results of his initial investigation. "Diabolical," he wheezed. The word was an old Anglish term that the Andorian had recently learned and enjoyed using to describe those complex situations that brought his cobalt blood to the boil. "How shall you restore your honor, Sal?"

Nensi pushed away from his desk and held up his hands. "Sorry, H'rar, but honor isn't the issue here."

"Honor iss alwayss the issue!" H'rar protested. He toyed with the ceremonial dagger he wore at his side, reduced in size to blend in with his civilian station but offering traditional comfort just the same.

"If anything, it's a legal matter to be settled by the Federation and Starfleet. Take another look at the contracts. Technically, the Pathfinders misrepresented nothing."

H'rar muttered something in Lesser Andorian.

"I beg your pardon?" Nensi asked politely, trying to prevent his administrative assistant from entering an icy Andorian sulk.

H'rar's thin blue lips compressed into an evil smile. "I just wass reflecting that until my world joined the Federation, our last lawyerss had been put to death more than a thousand yearss ago." He nodded to himself. "Sometimess the old wayss are so much simpler, don't you think?"

"Of course," Nensi quickly agreed. "But then, you have a knife and I'm not a lawyer, so why wouldn't I?"

H'rar laughed. "I shall misss you when you retire, Sal."

"No, you won't. You'll be too busy planning your revenge against the Pathfinders."

Mira Romaine appeared in the doorway to Nensi's office and knocked against the doorframe to announce herself.

"What's so urgent?" she asked after she greeted the two and joined them by the desk screen.

"I was working on that increased access schedule that Pathfinder Eight asked for," Nensi began, "and I started calculating the upper load that the facility could take. Especially since the standard waiting period these days is about two years."

"And . . .?" Romaine prompted as she scanned the charts displayed on the screen, puzzled over the number of them that carried bizarre figures such as 430 percent.

"And I think that the Pathfinders have been reconfiguring themselves."

Romaine shrugged. "Why not? We study medicine to improve our lives, why shouldn't they study circuit design and construction to improve theirs?"

"Well, if you look at these figures, I'm not really sure you'd call it an improvement." Nensi called up core-use diagrams and pointed out sections now marked in red.

Romaine studied them but her puzzled expression made it clear that she still couldn't see the point Sal was trying to make.

"It was your comment about Pathfinder Six lying to us," Nensi continued. "You still haven't explained that to me; why you think Six was lying, or what it could possibly have to lie about. But then I thought, what if its motives are as alien as the way it functions?"

"So you think these figures and charts are more lies?" Romaine asked.

"Look," Nensi said, "let me take you through an example."

It took twenty minutes, and only a fifth-level programmer or a career bureaucrat could have traced the convoluted chain of conditions that indicated the Pathfinders had something to hide. Nensi began by running straightforward calculations of the memory size and operational speed of the Pathfinders' installation to determine a base figure for its storage and work capacity. The figure was staggering.

Then Nensi ran a simulation that divided the facility into twelve more or less equal units—one for each Pathfinder—and subjected it to the average access load that the interface team imposed in a normal duty cycle. This time the figure was large, but it definitely wasn't staggering.

Romaine whistled softly. "Ninety-percent excess capacity?" she read from the screen.

"If you treat the facility as a duotronic unaware processing engine such as they use on starships—in other words, a standard Fleet-issue computer. I would expect the Pathfinders to be even more efficient, and so the excess capacity could even be larger."

Romaine considered the implications for a moment. The mechanics of data storage and retrieval were her speciality and Nensi's conclusions were almost frightening. If true, duotronic processors seemed to give rise to a geometrical increase in capacity after a certain size threshold had been reached. Since no facility in the Federation came anywhere close to the size of the Pathfinder installation, it was not surprising that the effect had not been noticed until now. But what was incredible was that neither the Pathfinders, nor the interface team, had made it known. It was inconceivable that such a breakthrough in computer science could be knowingly withheld.

"Your figures must be wrong, Sal," Romaine concluded, opting for the easiest way of dealing with unexpected results.

"Even allowing a fifty-percent margin of error, the increased-capacity effect stands," Nensi argued.

"Then what you're saying is that what the Federation is using this facility for right now is like using Fleet commcenter to relay binary codes over a distance of a few kilometers."

"And the Pathfinders must know it. And the interface team probably knows it. And neither group is telling us."

Romaine requested duplicate files of Nensi's work and he agreed, provided she would only use them on secured circuits. She said she would run variations on Nensi's figures and see how well the effect held up.

"Until then," Nensi concluded, "I suggest we keep everything in confidence. At least until we find out if our suspicions are correct, and if so, what the Pathfinders and/or the interface team think they're going to accomplish."

As Romaine started to leave, holding a stack of data wafers in one hand, she paused by the door. "What I don't understand," she said, "is if they *do* have all of that extra capacity down there, what in the gods' names are they doing with it?"

H'rar snorted. "What I don't understand," he replied, "iss why you humanss insist on building thinking machiness that have no 'off' switches."

Nine

The cavernous hold of the starboard warp propulsion unit thrummed with the rise and fall of the whine from its Cochrane generator. The gleaming mechanism of intricately intertwined tubes and cables stretched almost the full length of the nacelle's interior, drawing its power from the immense energies released by the total annihilation of matter and antimatter in the main engine room in the secondary hull. But it was here in this resonating chamber that, with no moving parts save for the myriad bypass switches that could be manually engaged, the generator channeled that unthinkable force to split the compressed web of four-dimensional spacetime, and slip the *Enterprise* along the infinitely small pathways that snaked through otherspace.

The service-lift doors opened onto the brilliantly lit hold and Scotty felt a familiar rush of exhilaration as the warp vibration engulfed him. The bridge was the brain of the ship, the engine room her heart, but this, aye, this was her soul.

Professor La'kara was first out of the lift, stumbling slightly in his haste. He had not anticipated the zero-gravity node the turbolift had passed through as it had moved through the support pylon, out of the artificial-gravity field of the secondary hull and into the angled field of the nacelle. He stared down the length of the generator, eyes blinking rapidly, regaining his footing.

"It . . . it's beautiful," he said, and for once said nothing more.

"That she is," Scott agreed, proud father of the bairn. He stood aside to let the others in the lift enter the hold. Fifteen guests, more than he had expected, had shown up for the tour. With all the other activities canceled, perhaps it was to be expected. Scientists were usually among the first to become bored.

Commodore Wolfe and her aide, Lieutenant Abranand, were the last to exit. Abranand looked down nervously at the radiation medallion he and all the others wore around their necks. Scott had told them it was a standard precaution and that it would alert them to exposure levels equal to one-fiftieth the minimum lethal dose, but the anxious trooper obviously didn't trust it. He was accompanying Wolfe only under orders.

The commodore stood with her hands on her hips, admiring the generator. "The lack of vibration is remarkable, Mr. Scott. I don't think I've ever felt any other as smooth." It was the first time Scott could recall her sounding civil since she had come aboard.

Scott grinned at the compliment. "Thank ye, Commodore. Things start to get a bit rough around warp five, but at everything below it's smooth as a . . . uh, transparent aluminum." Scotty coughed as the commodore nodded impatiently.

"Believe it or not, Mr. Scott, but I've been in an engine room or two in my day," she said, grinning slightly at his embarrassment. "Let's get this show on the road, shall we?"

Scott coughed again, then stepped quickly up to the head of the group. He would have to cut part of the tour short, he knew, because of the delay the commodore had caused as she made them all wait for Academician Sradek to join them. By the time she learned that the elderly historian was indisposed and would not be joining the tour, Scott knew he would not be spending as much time up in the nacelle as he would have liked. Ah well, he'd make the best of it.

"Gentlebeings," Scott began, "what ye are looking at is the key component of one of the largest fourth-generation hyperspace engines ever built since the discovery of warp technology more than one hundred and fifty years ago . . . yes, Dr. Stlur?"

A young Vulcan male with penetrating eyes and long dark hair tightly pulled back in a thick queue, had raised his hand, interrupting Scott's standard opening remarks. "I point out that Vulcan scientists mastered the technology of warp drive more than one hundred Terran years earlier. I thought you might wish to add that to your knowledge. I can recommend literature that—"

T'Vann, the Vulcan female with whom Stlur worked, placed her hand on his shoulder and whispered something inaudible.

"Forgive me for interrupting your presentation," Stlur said. "I meant no disrespect."

"None taken, lad," Scott said. "O' course I should have said since the *human* discovery of warp technology."

"Precisely," Stlur commented. The female whispered in his ear again.

"To continue." Scott deliberately looked away from the Vulcans. "It is called a Cochrane generator, named after Zefrem Cochrane, its *human*—yes, Professor La'kara?"

The professor lowered his hand and politely said, "Zeyafram Co'akran, it's pronounced." The professor turned to the rest of the group. "Native Alpha Centauran, you know. Great man."

Scott sighed. "Aye, Alpha Centauran he was, but we humans do share a common ancestor back there somewhere now, don't we?"

La'kara started to fidget with his scarf in a way that Scott had come to dread. "Only if you believe the—"

"Could we discuss biology at another time?" T'Vann asked. "I should not like to miss an opportunity to examine this generator."

"Thank you, Dr. T'Vann," Scott said in gratitude. Last night La'kara had come to Scott's cabin to continue the "discussion" about trilithium they had begun just before the starbase troopers had broken up the hangar reception. Scott had used all of his most reasonable arguments, including a bottle of his best single malt, and still hadn't been able to make the poor man see the light of day. The chief engineer had begun to have his doubts about La'kara's grasp of elementary multiphysics and was glad of T'Vann's diplomatic interruption.

"Why don't we all walk down to the flux chamber?" Scott said, and motioned the group to a ten-meter silver sphere that bubbled out from the side of the generator. When they arrived, he had Ensign Helena Sulernova open the thickly screened viewing port on the sphere's lower section. Sulernova looked grim as she lifted the cover on the control panel. She had overindulged at the reception, thinking that sleeping in on this, her free day, would take care of the results. But Mr. Scott had chosen her for today's drudge duty, he had explained, as her reward for asking about trilithium in the presence of Professor La'kara and himself at the reception.

Sulernova, holding back a yawn, punched in an authorization code, then threw the interlock bolt aside. She waited for the viewport indicator to show that the transparent viewing medium had darkened enough to provide sufficient protection for human eyes, then pressed the control that slid the viewport protective plate away from the opening.

Scott forgot his annoyance with the ensign as the tour group gasped at the beauty of the Cochrane flux, shimmering and sparkling in its wild explosions of unrecognizable colors, which seemed to float mere centimeters before their eyes in a multidimensional optical illusion. The Vulcans, of course, didn't gasp or show any reaction at all, though Scott was sure he detected fascination in their eyes.

"What ye are seeing is the interference effect of a thin strand of hyperspace folded into our four-dimensional continuum," Scott explained. "The fields generated here fold our ship back into the hyperspace void left by the absence of this—"

"Mr. Scott!" It was Lieutenant Abranand, white-faced with fear, holding up his radiation medallion. The central indicator was glowing red and its warning beep was shrill.

Scott immediately checked his own medallion and those of the others he could see. Each was dark and silent. "Occh, lad. Ye've been fiddling with it so much it's nae wonder that the poor thing's gone and—"

The ship lurched!

Scotty froze as every medallion instantly glowed red and their sirens shrieked in a deafening cacophony of danger. The smooth vibration of the Cochrane generator turned to a ragged shudder and, to his trained senses, every improper movement, every grinding of overstressed hull metal, told Scott exactly what had gone wrong. The engineer went into full automatic. This was his job.

"Commodore! Get these people to the lift! Ensign! Close the port."

Sulernova ran through a flurry of flux shimmers to the port controls. Her fingers flew over the buttons and switches.

"Don't look at it!" Scott shouted to her. He opened the equipment locker by the flux sphere and pulled out a three-pronged energy neutralizer. He had to close the flux gate before all power failed and the full brilliance of the flux was released.

The ship shuddered again, its inertial dampeners lagging behind the instantaneous response of the artificial-gravity field, throwing Scott and the tour group to the deck. Red warning lights flashed along the shining surfaces of the generator. Emergency sirens howled.

"Get them out of here *now!*" Scott shouted to the commodore. She was standing at the entrance to the service lift, pushing the civilians to safety. Scott saw Stlur and T'Vann pick up the lagging La'kara by his arms and start to carry him. And then the power failed completely and the brilliant lighting of the hold cut out to the absolute black of starless space.

But the darkness didn't last. An instant later, the powerless viewport medium cleared to absolute transparency, and the full and blinding glory of the Cochrane flux filled the hold.

Kirk pushed himself off the deck rail where the lurching ship had tossed him. "Damage report!" he called out to Uhura. All lights on the bridge dimmed as a low-frequency rumble shuddered through the deck.

"Switching to auxiliary," Lieutenant Laskey announced from the engineering station. The lights flared up again and the hum of equipment returned to normal.

"Helm, full shields," Kirk ordered. Whatever had hit the ship had felt just like an energy-beam impact.

"Warp power gone, Captain. Dropping to sublight," Sulu said, concentrating on the maneuvers that would bring the ship into normal space properly aligned, without being torn to pieces by the shock of an unbalanced translation.

"Shields on auxiliary power," Chekov reported from the science station. "Half strength and holding."

"Where's that damage report, Uhura?" Kirk was standing behind Sulu, staring at the main sensor display. No attackers to be seen.

Uhura held her ear receiver as she listened intently to the rush of voices and computer codes reporting ship's status. "It seems to be a power failure localized in engineering, Captain. Engineering communication circuits are down. No hull damage or weapon impact reported."

Damn, Kirk thought, where was Spock when he needed him? "Engineering status, Mr. Laskey."

"It's some kind of major disturbance, Captain, I—"

"I can tell it's major," Kirk snapped. "But what *kind* of disturbance?"

The turbolift doors opened and Spock hurried to the science station. Chekov quickly got out of the way and returned to his position at the helm.

"Spock!" The captain was both pleased and dismayed. "What are you doing here?"

"Attending to my duties, Captain." Spock's delicate fingers danced across the control surfaces and he spoke rapidly as he assessed the situation. "It appears we have experienced a significant power loss. In the absence of physical damage to the ship, I can only assume that the problem is internal." The blue glow of the main science viewer washed across his intent face.

"But aren't you confined to quarters?" Kirk asked. Maybe Wolfe had finally come to her senses.

"Apparently not. When I looked out into the corridor after the first disturbance, my guards were nowhere to be seen. I took that to mean my confinement had been temporarily suspended. In any event, under the circumstances I feel I am much more valuable to the ship at my post."

"Quite logical, Spock." Kirk doubted the commodore would see it that way, but it was good to have Spock where he belonged, and where he would do the most good.

"Thank you, Captain." Without looking up, Spock called out, "Mr. Laskey, kindly check the flux readouts from the starboard propulsion unit."

Laskey fumbled with the controls at his station. "Containment integrity was breached when the power shut down, sir." The lieutenant began to read out the figures with alarm.

Uhura gasped. "But Mr. Scott was leading a tour group up in the generator hold, Captain."

Kirk knew all too well the hell spawned by an uncontrolled flux release. Still, he needed confirmation that that was what really had happened. "Spock?"

"The fact that my instruments show the starboard nacelle is still attached to the ship indicates that someone was able to shut down the flux after auxiliary power came on line."

"But how?" Laskey asked. "Everyone exposed to the flux should have been blinded."

"It shall be fascinating to learn the answer to that."

"Uhura, have Dr. McCoy take a medical team up to the starboard generator hold immediately." Explanations could come later as far as Kirk was concerned. Some of his crew were in danger. "Mr. Laskey, what's the situation in engineering?"

Laskey called up more screens at his station, then said with shock, "Dilithium burnout, sir. Every crystal's showing zero energy transmission."

"Spock," Kirk said, "any chance that La'kara's accelerator shielding failed?"

Spock shook his head. "I think not, Captain. The power surge that would have resulted when the two fields of temporal distortion interacted while the ship was in warp would have completely destroyed the engines. And most of the engineering deck as well. We would be no more than a powerless, drifting wreck at this time."

"Small consolation," Kirk said as he felt the bridge suddenly become small and confining. He had to be where the action was. "I'm going up to the generator hold. Chekov, take the conn. Mr. Spock, come with me."

"Commander Spock is coming with me," Commodore Wolfe said coldly from the upper deck. She held a hand phaser pointed at Spock, and behind her, by the open turbolift, two troopers stood ready with rifles.

Wolfe's uniform was covered with scorch marks. Her face was streaked with soot, hair in disarray, and her eyes were wild. She held one hand above them, blinking and squinting as if to clear her vision. But the aim of her phaser was unwavering.

"Mona, what happened?" Kirk asked. He stepped forward between his first officer and the weapon.

Wolfe waved him back. "I was in the generator hold with Scott and the scientists. No doubt Commander Spock has already told you what happened."

"Yes, Spock's given me the readings. But what's that—"

"Readings!" Wolfe laughed harshly. "He didn't need readings to tell you what happened. Because he arranged it, didn't you, Spock?"

"Arranged what, Commodore?" Spock asked with icy calm. Kirk could see his science officer's eyes track the beam emitter of the phaser in Wolfe's hand.

"The 'accident,' Commander. The accident up there that nearly killed Professor La'kara and set back Federation propulsion research by decades."

"I assure the Commodore that—"

"Silence!" Wolfe exploded. "You'll have your chance to speak at your trial. You're under arrest." Without taking her eyes off Spock, she turned her head back to the turbolift. "Troopers, take this prisoner to the brig."

"May I ask what the Commodore's charges are?" Spock inquired, as if asking about the weather.

"Treason, conspiracy, attempted murder, escape from lawful custody," Wolfe listed. "Restrain him, Jenson," she ordered one of the troopers flanking Spock. "Remember what he did to his guards outside his quarters."

"What happened to the guards?" Kirk asked with concern.

"Ask your science officer."

"I had assumed they retired to emergency stations when the ship experienced difficulties," Spock said, holding up his hands to allow the trooper to place a magnatomic adhesion manacle in place. The trooper held the short bar of blue-gray metal against Spock's wrists, hit the activate switch on the bar's control surface, then removed his hand as the bar lost its charge and immediately flowed around Spock's forearms until its two ends met and joined in a molecular bond. Only the presence of a release field would collapse the superconducting current flowing within and return the manacle to its original shape.

"Emergency stations," Wolfe repeated in disgust. She stepped out of the way as the troopers pushed Spock to the turbolift. "They were stunned at such high intensity that they're going to be in sickbay for a week."

Kirk had had enough. He bounded up the steps to the lift doors. "I demand that you present your evidence!" he said angrily. This had gone too far.

Wolfe moved her phaser in Kirk's direction, not quite pointing it at him, but not pointing it away, either.

"I warn you, if you start interfering in this, I'm going to start thinking there's a conspiracy on board." Wolfe's voice was as cold and hard as hull metal.

Spock broke the tension. "Thank you for your concern, Captain, but I believe circumstances warrant a period of reflection," he stated matter-of-factly, hemmed in by two battle-ready troopers with phaser rifles and a gun-wielding commodore who was on the thin edge of senseless rage.

Reluctantly, Kirk backed off. The *Enterprise* was still in space. There would be time to get to the bottom of Wolfe's senseless accusations.

"Good decision," Wolfe said as she lowered her weapon. "But I tell you, Kirk, if this is typical of the way you run your ship, it's no wonder you got hit with Quadrant Zero duty." The lift doors started to close. "You're a disgrace to the Fleet," she said.

Despite the environmentals working at double load, Scott could still smell the smoke in engineering. It was too quiet, too. The long intermix chamber where the matter and antimatter plasmas were channeled from their magnetic bottles and mixed in a glorious destructive frenzy was silent. All ship's power now came from the standby fusion reactors and storage batteries. Scott felt a desperate sadness as he saw his beautiful equipment stand idle and purposeless. But at least I *can* still see, he consoled himself. And the ship can be repaired. He turned back to the conversation McCoy and Kirk were having as the three of them gathered in the emergency manual-monitor room above the main engineering deck.

"I hate to say it, Jim, but it looks as if Commodore Wolfe has a strong case," McCoy said bluntly. "All the pieces fit."

Scott was distressed at McCoy's summation. "How can ye say that, Doctor? Mr. Spock is as fine an officer as e'er served in the Fleet."

"Easy, Scotty," Kirk said kindly. "Our opinions of Mr. Spock aren't the question here. It's how the commodore came up with the circumstantial evidence against him."

"I think shutting off the shielding on La'kara's accelerator field at the precise time La'kara was where he could be killed is more than circumstantial, Jim." McCoy's face looked haggard and drawn. Scott knew that despite the doctor's even tone, he was as upset as everyone else.

"But thanks to Stlur and T'Vann and those blessed inner eyelids that Vulcans have, when the blinding flash of the flux hit us all, they were able to keep their vision, close the viewport, and carry us all into the lift. No one *was* killed, Dr. McCoy," Scotty said earnestly.

"But only because, as the Commodore suggests," Kirk reminded them, "Spock couldn't know that Scotty distrusted the professor's grasp of basic theory. *If* Scotty hadn't decided that he didn't trust the shielding system and taken the dilithium crystals out of the warp engine circuits last night, *then* both nacelles would have been blown out into hyperspace and we'd be floating here waiting for a salvage tug. Instead, when the shielding was shut off and the dilithium crystals blew out, all we lost was our primary power circuit. And Scotty's people will be able to repair that by the time the cruiser from Starbase Four gets here with replacement crystals."

McCoy looked puzzled. "Scotty, you took the dilithium crystals out of the warp circuits? *While* we were in warp?"

"Ye don't need dilithium to travel at warp speeds under four-point-eight," Scotty said condescendingly. "It's more efficient, sure, but d'ye not remember your history, Doctor? How all those early voyages between Vulcan and Earth, and even Klinzhai, took months instead of days, long before dilithium's four-dimensional structure was discovered? But then I'm forgetting, you're a doctor, not an engineer."

"The fact remains," McCoy continued, "that even though Scotty inadvertently prevented a disaster, Spock is still the prime suspect."

"But how did he get to the dilithium lab in time to turn off the shielding and still make it to the bridge while the power failure was in progress?" Kirk asked. "Remember, he only noticed his guards were gone *after* the ship's first reaction to the dilithium failure."

McCoy's face revealed his internal struggle. "You've read the troopers' log reports, Jim. Spock might have attacked the guards a half hour before the power failure. Lots of time to disrupt their short-term memory with a heavy stun and get to the lab."

"Dr. McCoy!" Scott cried in anguish.

"I'm only being the devil's advocate, Mr. Scott. Spock will have to answer these questions at his trial."

"He's right, Scotty. Spock needs those answers. And we have to give them to him," Kirk said.

"Aye, Captain. But I don't see how."

"Who else had access to the dilithium lab where the containment system was stored?" Kirk asked, then dismally answered himself. "Everybody."

"Then who had the motive?" McCoy asked. "That's usually the way these things work."

Kirk thought about that for a moment. "Fair enough. Who stands to benefit from the death of Professor La'kara?" he asked in return.

"Or Doctors Stlur and T'Vann," Scott reminded them. "Or anyone else on the tour. Including me."

"Good point," McCoy agreed. "It's hard to determine the motive if we don't know who the victim was supposed to be."

"What if the victim is Spock?" Kirk asked. "What if everything that's gone on has been simply to throw suspicion on him and this ship?"

"Again," McCoy asked, "what's the motive?"

"I don't know," Kirk answered. "But Commodore Wolfe was convinced that the evidence collected by the security contingent on Memory Prime pointed to Spock."

"Then that's where the answers lie," McCoy concluded. "Heaven forgive me for using the damnable word, but it's the only 'logical' conclusion."

Scott looked at Kirk. They both nodded in agreement.

The answer they sought waited on Memory Prime.

Ten

Memory Alpha was to have been the pride of the Federation's scientific and educational delegations. A nominally useless planetoid had become home to a sprawling network of interlinked domes and computer systems that formed a central library facility containing the total cultural history and scientific knowledge of all Federation members. For some council members, Memory Alpha represented the golden door to a future in which all beings throughout the galaxy would be united as equal partners in the only adventure worth pursuing: the search for information and understanding, the never-ending quest for knowledge. Memory Alpha would be that dream made real, fully and freely accessible to all Federation scholars, an unarmed, undefended oasis of peace and common purpose.

Other council members, especially Andorians and representatives from Starfleet, had applauded that dream but lobbied for a healthy dose of reality. Federation space comprised only a tiny percentage of the total galaxy, and all indications were that it was not yet the benign and altruistic environment that all hoped it someday might become. They lobbied for protection, for contingency plans. But the Federation had thrived for more than a century on stubborn optimism and unbridled faith in the future. So it was not surprising that, in the end, the Memory Alpha proposal had passed the council's final appropriations hearings unchanged, and even Starfleet had given it their blessing. To the beings whose souls were fired by the challenge of the stars, Memory Alpha was a compelling vision.

The nightmare began when the last incorporeal intelligences of an ancient race, searching for a physical existence, killed more than three thousand peaceful scholars, staff, and researchers and wiped clean the central databanks of Memory Alpha in little more than a minute.

Specialist Lieutenant Mira Romaine, assigned to the *U.S.S. Enterprise* on her first mission for the Federation, had been the only being to survive direct mental contact with the desperate personalities of the Zetarians. But even as she and her staff worked amid the ruins of Memory Alpha, trying to create some order out of what threatened to become the Federation's most devastating disaster, the military planners of Starfleet paid the first of many informal visits to their colleagues in the scientific and educational delegations to the council. The Federation might be too optimistic from time to time, but only because it could afford to be. It rarely made the same mistake twice.

There was now an entire network of Memory planets spread throughout Federation space, far enough removed from each other that only a galactic disaster could affect them all. For cost effectiveness, each had a specialty. Memory Beta was a center for exobiology, cross-correlating all research conducted to understand the myriad ways in which life had evolved in the galaxy, as if its absence in any given system were an aberration of nature.

Memory Gamma focused its efforts on economics and agriculture; Memory Delta on stellar and planetary formation and evolution; Memory Epsilon on multiphysics. Other branches of knowledge awaited the funding and construction of additional Memory planets. A plan was proposed to reopen the now-abandoned Memory Alpha as a listening post for potential transmissions from civilizations in other galaxies. However, the funding process had become so lengthy because of the controversial nature of the project that fatalistic lobbyists were now referring to it as Memory Omega.

But even with each specialized facility serving as a total storage backup for every other Memory station in an intricate, holographic web of subspace data transmission and downloading, one flaw that not even Starfleet could eliminate remained. There had to be a command station, a central node to control and channel the activities of the entire Memory network.

Faced with the lesson of the Alpha disaster, project planners decided that no chances could be taken. The overall blueprints for the central facility were adapted from the Federation's most secure weapons-testing facilities. Seven interconnected, though independently maintained, environment domes were constructed in a semicircle on the face of an almost solid, nickel-iron asteroid. In times of peace, workers could walk between their residences and work areas through central plazas with trees, grass, and reflecting pools. But in times of threat, the facility also stretched deep beneath the asteroid's surface in a warren of underground service tunnels, access corridors, and heavily armored life-support chambers.

The facility was also equipped with deeply anchored warp engines, not for propulsion but to generate the immense energy levels required to simultaneously power a battery of photon torpedoes powerful enough to hold back a fleet of Klingon battle cruisers as well as defensive shields that could englobe the entire planetoid. Additional security was achieved by locating the facility safely within Quadrant Zero space and providing it with a permanent, on-site contingent of battle-ready troopers. It was only behind these battlements and layers of deadly force that the scholars and researchers of a hundred worlds could once again pursue the paths of peace.

To the handful of beings who truly understood the immense concentration of irreplacable knowledge that was generated at the central facility each hour, running weeks, sometimes months ahead of the stockpile stored for backup transmission to the other facilities, the lesson of Memory Alpha remained a constant nightmare. For any system with a central control point is vulnerable, and every planner, every Starfleet defense adviser, was all too aware of one of the earliest lessons the Federation had learned: not every eventuality can be anticipated. Despite the lessons of the past and the best intentions for the future, the entire scientific and cultural network that linked the worlds of the Federation in common defense and harmony was still at risk.

They called the facility Memory Prime.

Eleven

Salman Nensi stretched his arms over his head and yawned like a Rigellian bloodworm.

Across the table from him, Mira Romaine watched and listened in amazement. So did everyone else at lunch in the cafeteria.

"What was that supposed to be?" Romaine asked as Nensi rubbed his hands over his face.

"I think I might finally be relaxing," Nensi said. "I haven't had a call from the interface team for three days now." He picked up a sloppy sprout-salad sandwich and bit into it happily.

"They're all still down in the Interface Chamber," Romaine said, marveling at how much her friend could get into his mouth at once, "trying to find out why their precious Pathfinders wouldn't support their demands. Do you remember the expression on Garold's face?" So much for the old story of how only a specially trained, enhanced interface team member could understand the complexities of a Pathfinder. Garold had been taken completely by surprise.

"Let's hope they stay down there during the prize ceremonies. Then I could almost start enjoying this posting," Nensi managed to say around his mouthful of sandwich. They shared a glance, though, that said enjoyment had fled. As they sat together, both knew that in Romaine's lab a small, secure computer was running its last simulation of Nensi's Pathfinder access scenarios. His conclusions were holding: the Pathfinders, of which Nensi and Romaine were ostensibly in charge, were lying to them.

Romaine glanced around the cafeteria at the others. They couldn't be told yet, best to keep up the appearance of normalcy. She handed Nensi a second napkin, and he immediately put it to good use.

"You know, Uncle Sal, I'm beginning to worry that you haven't been having enough meals in polite company." Romaine delicately used her chopsticks to pick up a purple cube of stir-seared plomeek, to show him how it was done.

"Afraid I'll embarrass you at your dinner for Mr. Scott?"

"Ha!" Romaine laughed. "He's a dear sweet man but he's lived on board ship for so many years that I'm worried *he* might embarrass *you.*" She smiled to herself, remembering back to her too brief voyage on the *Enterprise.* The best part about those last romantic dinners she had shared with Scotty had not been the food. She could barely wait to have dinner with him again.

Nensi checked his chronometer. "So how much longer is it? Twelve hours till your engineer arrives?"

Thirteen hours, twenty-seven minutes, Romaine thought, though she managed to look vague and say, "About that, I think." She took a sip of her tea. "That's something I'll never understand," she said. "The *Enterprise* travels two days of a five-day voyage out from Starbase Four and loses its dilithium, facing a couple of years of travel to get here on impulse. And then Starbase Four sends out a light cruiser with replacement crystals that reaches the ship within hours. They spend three days repairing the circuits and tuning the new crystals so they can power up the warp engines again. And then, *after* the three-day delay, the *Enterprise* will end up getting here only two hours late."

"The wonders of warp factors," Nensi said with a smile. "Beyond that, I can't tell you because I don't have the slightest idea how they do it and I'm too old to care."

"But if the *Enterprise* had traveled at the same speed at the start of the voyage that she's traveling now to make up for the delay, she could have been here inside of a day to begin with."

"Now that I can tell you something about," Nensi said, gesturing with the other half of his sandwich. "Warp engines have a strictly rated lifetime of operational use, dependent on the factor at which they operate, not the distance they cover. The higher the factor, the shorter the life. More than half the cost of constructing a ship like the *Enterprise* is the expense of the warp engines. I spent five years in San Francisco processing refit requests from Starfleet, and let me say that there's a whole gang of accountants in the Federation finance department who'd be happy if all Fleet travel was done on impulse propulsion."

"It always comes down to credits, doesn't it?" Romaine said. "How are we ever going to start accomplishing anything worthwhile in space exploration without the proper funding?"

"You're starting to sound like Garold and his friends," Nensi cautioned. "No more talks about budgets until I get a proper viewscreen in my office, all right?"

"You *still* don't have one?" Romaine said with amazement. "Uncle Sal, I run my department through Starfleet, remember? And I'm the ranking officer. You want a viewscreen? You got it!" She snapped her fingers.

"You can do that?" Nensi asked. "I thought all Starfleet business had to go through Captain Farl?"

"He's the ranking officer for his squad of troopers, sure, but since this is officially a civilian installation, except during emergencies, the chief technician is in charge." She pointed at the stripes on her blue sleeve. Romaine knew the position was strictly a political gesture to those council members who had wanted to play down the military aspect of Memory Prime and, usually, all she got out of the authority was a pile of extra screenwork at the end of each duty cycle. But being ranking officer over twenty-six other Starfleet science personnel did have a few perks. "I'll order a screen for your office this afternoon. You should get it next week."

Nensi looked pleased. "Now I feel guilty I didn't pay for lunch."

They were tidying up their trays when an associate rolled up to their table, eyestalk extended and ready light blinking.

"Chief Romaine," it announced in an extremely realistic voice, "you are ordered to report to breakout area C."

"Ordered?" Romaine asked. "Whose orders?"

"Captain Farl," the associate replied. "This module is authorized to announce that Memory Prime is now on emergency alert."

Uhura's face appeared on the desk viewscreen in the captain's quarters.

"I have Admiral Komack's reply from Starfleet Command," the communications officer said.

"Go ahead," Kirk told her, but Uhura's somber expression made it clear what that reply was.

"Regarding charges pressed against Commander Spock," Uhura read, "Commodore Wolfe is authorized to take full responsibility for the prisoner until he can be placed in the custody of proper Starfleet authorities. Commodore Wolfe and her prisoner are to transfer to the *U.S.S. Srall* upon that vessel's arrival at Memory Prime. Upon the conclusion of the Nobel and Z.Magnees Prize Ceremonies, the *Enterprise* is to return to Starbase Four and await further orders. Signed Komack, Admiral, Starfleet Command."

"That's it?" Kirk was surprised. "No personal addendum?"

"I'm sorry, sir. That's the full text."

Kirk thanked the lieutenant and told her to leave the bridge. The viewscreen went dark and Kirk looked over to Dr. McCoy. "She stayed at her station eighteen hours so that message wouldn't be intercepted by one of Wolfe's troopers," Kirk said, "for all the good it's done us. I can't understand why Komack left it so cut and dried. It's not like him. He knows Spock."

McCoy leaned back in his chair and swung his legs up onto the edge of Kirk's bunk. "We already know that there's more to this than anyone's admitting. Wolfe's keeping her mouth shut. The security people on Prime aren't responding to your requests for more information. It's big, Jim. I'm not surprised that a command admiral is washing his hands of the whole thing. Whatever Spock's mixed up in, it's got a lot of people scared."

"You're not sounding like the devil's advocate anymore. You're talking as if you really think he's guilty." Kirk's temper was showing.

"And you're talking as if you won't even consider the possibility that he might be!" McCoy shot back. "Remember Talos Four. Spock deliberately risked the last death penalty on the books."

"To do what he thought was right," Kirk insisted.

"Exactly," McCoy argued. "And maybe this time Spock is also caught up in something he thinks is right. You can't rule it out. If Starfleet wants Spock, it's because they have a good reason."

"Then why won't they tell *me?*" Kirk pounded his fist on his desk.

McCoy swung his feet down to the deck and leaned forward. If he had been closer, Kirk got the distinct feeling the doctor might have grabbed him by the scruff of his neck and shaken him.

"Because you're a *captain,* Captain. And some of the decisions in this fleet are made by officers with higher ranks." McCoy brought his own fist down on the table for good measure. He took advantage of Kirk's speechless surprise to draw a deep breath, then began again more calmly. But not by much.

"When I think of all the times I've come down here to help you wrestle with the problems of your command . . . and what have you learned? Nothing. No matter how bad it's been in the past, you keep looking to put more pressure on yourself. You've got to draw the line somewhere."

Kirk narrowed his eyes at McCoy. If anyone else had taken this insubordinate tone with him, he'd be out the door and moved to the top of the transfer list. But McCoy had earned himself a few more words, a few more centimeters of rope. "And what would you suggest, Doctor?" Kirk said carefully, a tightness in his voice that few had heard before.

"I suggest you face facts, Jim. You're not a god. You're a starship captain. And if that's not enough for you, then give the *Enterprise* up! Transfer to command and get those extra stripes. Become an admiral. Hell, become *the* admiral and run the whole damned fleet of starships, if that's what you want. Then, and only then, when you're at the top of the whole glorious system, can you feel that all the problems of the universe are the personal problems of James T. Kirk!"

"I will never give up the *Enterprise,*" Kirk said slowly and precisely. "Never." It carried the chilling conviction of a blood oath.

"Then pay the price for her, Captain. Give the orders to the people below you and accept the orders from the people above. Don't treat everything that doesn't go your way as a personal attack. Learn the rules of the system. Then you can learn how to bend them. But don't ever forget that the system is there. And that you owe your ship to it."

"Finished?" Kirk asked coldly.

"Well, that's up to you, Captain, sir." McCoy sat back in his chair and folded his arms. He looked as if he had just run a marathon on the gym's treadmill.

Kirk studied McCoy for a few silent seconds. He wanted to shout at the doctor, tell him how wrong he was, how he had completely misread the situation. But he couldn't. Because he knew McCoy was right. Kirk shuffled some hardcopies on his desk. He hated making a mistake, even more than he hated admitting he had made one. But he felt he owed McCoy an explanation.

"Out there," Kirk finally said, "on the frontier, it sometimes does feel like I am . . . in charge of everything. We make first contact with a new civilization . . . I've got four hundred and thirty crew depending on me not to do something that will endanger the ship simply because I wasn't paying attention to some idiosyncrasy of an alien culture. Each time I think, will this be the one where I lose it? And each time, it isn't. After a while, it gets easy to think that the rest of the universe doesn't matter. There's only my crew, and my ship, and my next challenge." He sighed. "Starfleet, the Federation, sometimes they're nothing more than a subspace channel."

McCoy waited in silence, but Kirk said nothing more.

"The point being . . . ?" McCoy prompted.

"The point being that you're right, Doctor. I've wasted three days trying to find out why someone's plotting against *me* by trying to take *my* first officer off *my* ship when I should be trying to work within the system to maintain the integrity of the Fleet and the *Enterprise.*"

"I am greatly relieved to hear that, Captain." The extent of McCoy's relief was evident in his voice and on his face. He had not often been forced to confront Kirk so directly.

"I'm relieved to hear it, too, Bones." Kirk visibly relaxed as he looked across the table at his friend. "I mean it. Thank you."

McCoy chewed thoughtfully on a corner of his lip. Kirk could tell the doctor was still angry, though he didn't know if that anger was directed at him or the commodore.

"So what are you going to do about it?" McCoy asked bluntly.

It was the old Kirk who answered, not the one who had been thrusting blindly in circles for the past few days, out of his element when it came to dealing with the command structure and the finely balanced nuances of give and take that it required. He felt directed now. His goal was clear. As were his methods.

"First, I accept the situation. Starfleet has some reason for suspecting that Spock might be responsible for an attempt on the lives of one or more of the prize nominees on board the *Enterprise.* Right or wrong, that is a fact. Second, I find out why that suspicion exists and if it in any way threatens further harmful activity on board."

"And third?"

"That will depend on Mr. Spock's innocence . . . or guilt."

McCoy nodded seriously. "That's a hard decision to make," he said.

"It's the captain's decision, and when I make it, Bones, it'll be the right one."

Twelve

For an Andorian, Romaine thought, Commander Farl was looking rather pale, almost the color of one of the Fleet-issue wall panels Sal was always going on about.

"What's the emergency, Captain?" the chief technician asked as she entered the breakout area. She paused and looked around in surprise.

The large room was typically used as a temporary planning and operations center for research projects. Accredited scholars using Prime's facilities could set up these areas as private offices containing computer consoles, associate staging stalls, desks, chairs, and whatever other equipment they might need outside of a lab. But Farl and his staff had turned breakout area C into what looked to be a fort. There was even a two-person portable combat transporter pad in the corner.

Farl walked over from a tactics table where Romaine could see schematics of the central dome complex displayed. She assumed the flashing red triangles floating above it represented troop placement. What was going on here?

Including his antennae, Farl was still ten centimeters shorter than Romaine, but the light armor he wore added to his bulk, and the small strips of *gral* fur crisscrossed over his chest plate, a concession to his clan standing allowed by regulations, made him look like a bizarre mechanical/organic hybrid.

He stopped to stand within centimeters of Romaine, staring earnestly up at her. Andorians had no concept of "personal space." But even faced with the imposing presence of a fully armed soldier in the midst of Memory Prime's civilian areas, Romaine retained enough composure to realize that Farl was upset and even grimmer than Andorians usually were.

"Quite seriouss, I'm afraid, Chief Romaine," Farl said in the soft dry whisper of his species.

Romaine didn't like the look or sound of any of this. The troopers assigned to Prime weren't supposed to carry more than hand phasers in the civilian areas, let alone set up command stations there. "How serious?" she asked, and her tone told Farl she wanted an answer *now*.

"It iss classified," Farl said, and had the decency to look embarrassed.

"I'm ranking Starfleet officer, Farl, I—"

"Not in thiss emergency, I am sorry to say. You are now in command of only the science and administrative functions of thiss facility." Farl looked over to the transporter pads where two more Andorian troopers shimmered into existence. They quickly ran off to a second display table.

"Farl," Romaine said, trying to sound reasonable, "I know what the regulations are, and the only type of emergencies I can think of that could possibly remain classified to the ranking officer of a starbase installation are . . ." She saw it in his small, dark eyes. She had spent enough time with Andorians to be able to read their expressions.

"Precisely," Farl whispered. "Military emergency. War preparationss."

Romaine felt her breath catch. "Against whom? What are our orders? When did this happen?"

Farl bowed his head. Was it in shame? Romaine wondered.

"Chief Romaine," he said in a delicate whisper, "I have enjoyed serving with you thiss past year. But I am unable to answer your questionss. Up to thiss moment, you have run thiss outpost well, according to your dutiess. Now I must ask that you let me run its military functions according to mine."

"Then I must ask to see your authorization, Commander."

Farl looked up into Romaine's eyes. He wore an expression of pleading. "Miraromaine," he said sadly. "I have never received communicationss at thiss level of classification before. I must follow my orderss. Starfleet will transmit orderss to your office as well, and that iss as much as you will be allowed to know until the emergency has passed. I am truly sorry."

"I'll have to confirm this with Starfleet," Romaine said, and could hear the tightness of her own voice.

"Of course," Farl said. "As I did."

The chief technician's mind spun with the possibilities she might be facing here. She couldn't lose Prime to another Alpha disaster. She refused to.

"Until then, what can I do?" she asked. The transient population of Prime was almost four thousand now with the added visitors who had arrived for the prize ceremonies. "Shall I help Sal handle the cancellation of the Nobel and Z.Magnees—"

"Absolutely not," Farl interrupted. "The orderss are quite clear. The ceremoniess must proceed as planned. Our preparationss must appear as no more than a drill, a training maneuver to the civilianss."

"What?" Romaine could see the troopers in the breakout area turn to look at her, checking on the safety of their commander.

Farl gestured to her to keep her voice down. It was a struggle.

"You're telling me that we're going on to a near war footing here and it's to be kept *secret?* That's insane!"

"It iss not insane," Farl whispered back loudly. "It meanss that there iss a chance we can take action to contain the threat before things get out of control. Why upset the scientific community here unnecessarily? Especially with the antennae of the Federation, and perhapss otherss, upon uss?"

Farl's expression was brightening now, along with his color. That damnable Andorian love for intrigue again, Romaine thought. "What threat? What action?"

"As I told you, the threat iss classified."

"Then what action will you be taking?"

"Some we already have."

"Such as?"

The apologetic look came back to Farl's face. Romaine suddenly knew she wasn't going to like what she was about to hear.

"My trooperss have placed three of your staff in protective custody."

Romaine felt her blood turn to ice. "Who?" she managed to get out before her throat shut down in shock.

"Specialist Lieutenant Stell. Specialist First-Class Slann. And Dr. T'Lar," Farl said gravely.

Romaine was stunned. She had seven Vulcans on her staff. Why these three?

Stell was a computer technician, young, serious as all Vulcans were, specializing in library subsystems. Slann was on sabbatical from the Vulcan Academy of Sciences, studying historical methods of fault toleration and error detection in trinary data storage. And T'Lar was a paleoexozoologist researching cyclical patterns of extinction in adjacent planetary systems. What was their connection?

"Why them?" Romaine asked, completely baffled.

"Classified."

"Have they done anything or is it just suspected they might?"

"Classified." Farl's eyes flashed again. "But for you, Miraromaine: it iss simply a safety precaution. There iss no definitive proof." He shrugged, a gesture almost comical in battle armor.

"May I see them?" she asked, though it sounded more like a formal request.

Farl shook his head. "Access restricted. Again, my apologiess."

"Anything else?"

"Alass, no."

"This stinks, you know," she stated, her voice rising on each word. She was trying not to take her anger out on the commander, and not succeeding.

"I am trained to prevent these occurrencess, Miraromaine. When my trooperss and I must take action, it meanss we have failed. I am familiar with the odor, yess?"

Romaine turned to go, then hesitated. "Will this situation be changed in any way by the arrival of the *Enterprise?*" she asked.

Farl smiled. "Ah, yess. I expect the situation to improve considerably by then."

Good, thought Romaine, though she suddenly doubted that she and Scotty were going to enjoy the kind of reunion she had hoped for.

Kirk had never thought it odd that in the middle of a crisis he could feel good. He knew it was the rush of adrenaline that propelled him, made his steps light and his actions swift. But apart from the merely physical sensations, it was his mind and his spirit that somehow seemed to accelerate at these times. Too often he had seen other officers crumble in the face of multiple crises. But once Kirk had determined his way, no matter how slight and dismal that chance for victory might be, he kept at it until the way was clear. The ship sustained him, but it was the never-ending struggle to keep her that made him come alive. He felt that way now.

McCoy joined him as Kirk walked down the corridor on D deck, heading for the brig.

"Score one for the system, Bones," he said.

"The commodore knows about us meeting with Spock?" McCoy asked, holding his medical kit and tricorder against his hip to stop them from bouncing as he kept Kirk's pace.

"She authorized it. Had no choice." He turned to grin at the doctor. "As a suitably senior officer who has volunteered for the job, I'm Spock's counsel for the court-martial. She can't deny me access. Or my client's physician, either. I'm just following the rules."

They turned the corner at an intersection. Two of Wolfe's troopers stood at attention at the end of the new corridor.

"Good," McCoy said. "I was afraid we were going to have to charm our way past those two. The least you could have done was tell me this over the intercom."

"Not good form to let Wolfe hear me gloat. If she's monitoring infraship communications. Which she probably is." Kirk approached the nearer of the two guards. "I assume the commodore told you to expect us?" he said arrogantly.

It worked. The first trooper snapped a salute, usually not part of starship tradition, and barked, "Yes, sir!"

Kirk blinked at the reaction his tone had elicited, then belatedly remembered to return the salute. "Carry on," he said, then passed the trooper and stopped in front of the open doorway to the holding cell. It was outlined with the glowing transmission nodes of a security field. Spock waited on the other side of the doorway, hands patiently held behind his back.

"Good day, Captain. Doctor," Spock said, as if he had happened to meet them in the corridor by chance.

Kirk and McCoy returned the greeting, then Kirk turned to the second trooper.

"Turn it off, trooper," he ordered.

"Sorry, sir," the second trooper replied. "Commodore's orders. You may meet with the prisoner but without contact."

Kirk checked the trooper's sleeve and name badge, then spoke quickly. "Sergeant Gilmartin, are you aware of the penalties set forth in General Regulation Document two hundred and twenty-seven, pertaining to treatment of prisoners on board Starfleet vessels: violations thereof?"

"N-no, sir."

"Then I suggest you turn off that security field and allow this doctor access to the prisoner before you find out what those penalties are!" Kirk snapped, and then to give the sergeant a hint, added the word, *"Private!"*

Sergeant Gilmartin sneaked a worried look at the first trooper and saw no reason for encouragement. "I'll have to check with the commodore, sir," he said cautiously.

"Be my guest," Kirk answered with a flourish of his hand.

Gilmartin walked off to a wall intercom plate. McCoy leaned forward and whispered, *"Is* there a General Regulation Document two hundred and twenty-seven?"

"Two hundred and twenty-seven *B,"* Spock amended matter-of-factly from the doorway.

McCoy's eyes widened in surprise.

Kirk looked hurt. "Doctor! Would I lie about something like that?" He turned back to watch Gilmartin before McCoy could answer.

Gilmartin returned from his intercom conversation, defeated. "We'll have to scan you before you go in," he said apologetically.

"As set out in GRD two hundred and twenty-seven *C,"* Spock offered.

"I'll have to remember this the next time we play poker," McCoy said as Gilmartin scanned him and Kirk with a combat tricorder and the first trooper searched the medical bag.

"Whatever do you mean, Doctor?" Kirk asked innocently.

"I mean that sometimes your bluffs aren't bluffs."

"Only those that I know will be called," Kirk said with a smile. "Remember that."

Sergeant Gilmartin, satisfied with his readings, told Spock to stand back from the door and then switched off the screen. As soon as Kirk and McCoy had entered the cell, the field hummed back into life. The trooper was going by the book.

"It is good to see you, Captain," Spock said. "I had assumed that Commodore Wolfe would countermand any attempt you made for a meeting."

"She didn't have a choice," Kirk said. "I'm your legal counsel."

Spock's eyes actually flickered. Kirk saw it.

"Until an experienced counsel can be assigned," he quickly added.

Spock's eyes returned to normal. "A clever circumvention of the commodore's wishes," Spock said, a faint tone of relief in his voice.

"It was Dr. McCoy's idea," Kirk replied as he crossed to the cell's writing desk.

"Indeed." Spock watched dubiously as McCoy held a sparkling scanner in front of his chest, keeping track of its readings in the display window of the medical tricorder.

"What's all this, Spock?" Kirk asked as he stood by the desk. It was covered with large stacks of bound hardcopies from the ship's printers.

"The commodore has denied me access to the ship's computer. I find I must carry on my work with printed materials."

"That's terrible," Kirk said with a frown, and he meant it. It was one thing to sit in a chair with the weight and warmth of a real book and be transported by fiction, or philosophy, or the inspiring words of beings from far away or long ago. But to actually have to *work* with them, scan through them a page at a time, without the speed of a display or the computer's indexing abilities, seemed barbaric.

"I do find it most inefficient," Spock agreed.

"Did the commodore give a reason for denying you computer access?" Kirk asked, glancing at the titles of Spock's hardcopies; agriculture and economics journals for the most part, though he didn't understand how they fit into Spock's duties.

"No," Spock said, rolling up his sleeve to let McCoy take a sample of blood for later analysis. "Though it is logical to assume that she does not want to risk me overriding any of the bridge or engineering controls." He watched as his green blood filled the ampoule on the end of McCoy's vacuum syringe.

"Can engineering and bridge controls be overridden from a remote terminal?" Kirk frowned. They *did* share the ship's computer as the main processing unit, but still . . .

"I have always thought it would be possible, given enough time to work out the programming techniques," Spock said. "And since the commodore has forbidden me access, I assume that she also suspects or knows it can be done."

Kirk made a mental note to request a system improvement in his next general report. If someone did manage to work out the programming techniques, the *Enterprise* could be at the mercy of any passenger, or invader, who had access to the most common type of computer terminal in the ship.

"Assuming the commodore won't object to a simple library reader, is there anything else I can get for you?" Kirk sat down at the desk and indicated that McCoy and Spock should join him.

"I would very much appreciate the opportunity to meet with Academician Sradek," Spock said as he pulled out a chair and sat.

"And he with you," Kirk said. "The academician came to my cabin the night you were confined to your quarters, asking the same thing."

McCoy looked at Kirk triumphantly. "Can't wait for the emotion of a teacher/student reunion, right, Spock?"

"On the contrary, Doctor. I believe I still have much to learn from Sradek."

"Why is that, Mr. Spock?" Kirk asked.

"Sradek is an eminent historian who excels in identifying patterns from the past and applying them to modern situations. His analysis of the dynamics that led to the political unification of the Jovian colonies in your own system led directly to his successful peace proposals for the civil war on Katja Two."

"And earned him the Peace Prize nomination," Kirk added.

"Exactly. However, shortly after the cessation of hostilities on Katja Two, the academician was asked to sit on the Sherman's Planet famine board of inquiry."

"Isn't that old news, Mr. Spock?" McCoy asked. "We delivered new grain stocks there years ago."

"Quite right, Doctor. But the new grain did not take hold on the planet as quickly as had been projected. The economic ramifications in that quadrant were serious. Even more serious is the evidence of the Sherman Syndrome appearing on other agricultural worlds."

"The Sherman Syndrome? Sounds like a viewscreen act," Kirk said.

"It is quite in earnest, I assure you. The name refers to a complex pattern of crop failure, political mismanagement, and faulty economic planning on colony planets. An entire analysis division was set up at Memory Gamma to investigate the syndrome, though, to date, no useful conclusions have emerged. Cause and effect are extremely interconnected and difficult to isolate."

McCoy was unimpressed. "If you mean that sometimes not every new agricultural colony turns into a golden breadbasket the first time out, I don't see any reason for concern. That's just the risk of farming. Give the colonists enough time to figure out the intricacies of their new world and the yields will go up."

Kirk intervened. "Spock, does this have anything at all to do with the charges against you? If it doesn't, I think we should put it aside for now."

"I was merely explaining why I was looking forward to meeting with Sradek so I might question him about his reasons for denying the Sherman Syndrome hypothesis. My logic does not grasp the basis of his arguments and I wish to be enlightened."

"Fair enough," Kirk said, trying to roll things along. "Sradek is looking forward to enlightening you about that also and—"

"The academician is not aware of my interest in the subject. I have not communicated with him since the last time I was on Vulcan."

"Then maybe he wanted to say hello just to be polite," McCoy suggested.

"I see no need to insult a respected Vulcan scholar, Doctor."

Kirk held his hands up. "Shall we get to the point, gentlemen. *Please?*"

And they did. Once again, Spock recounted his activities from the time Commodore Wolfe boarded at Starbase Four and he was interrogated and confined to his quarters. Kirk went over Spock's eidetic recall of the interrogation and agreed that the commodore's troopers acted as if they had only indefinite suspicions to go on, not hard facts. But no matter how many times they analyzed the situation, not even Spock could reason out a logical conclusion.

In the end, all they were left with was a series of facts and a string of unanswered questions. Someone *had* stunned the two troopers standing guard outside Spock's quarters. That person or an accomplice had then gone to the dilithium lab and switched off the accelerator field's shielding just as Scott's tour group was in an area where they might have been killed by the resultant dilithium reaction, *if* the ship's dilithium crystals had still been on line.

Commodore Wolfe had come on board believing that Spock might be planning some treachery just like that. When it had happened, she was convinced of his guilt. But there were no fingerprints, no witnesses, no computer logs. Only suspicion.

As they appeared to be running out of alternatives, Kirk brought up Wolfe's enigmatic reference to T'Pel.

Spock's expression hardened. "Indeed," he responded. "Did the commodore give a context for the term?"

"No," Kirk said. "Though I got the impression it was a name."

"Anyone you know, Spock?" McCoy asked.

Spock lifted an eyebrow. "Among Vulcans, the name T'Pel is rather common, Doctor. I believe I know several T'Pels and am related to four others."

Kirk nodded. "The ship's computer came up with more than fifteen thousand references, almost all of them Vulcan females."

"And the others?" McCoy asked.

"Words from various languages. Lots of dialect terms meaning 'to drink.' Acronyms, product names, literary references."

"I assume you investigated further," Spock said.

"Of course. I asked the computer to pull out every T'Pel reference that could be cross-referenced to you."

"And?"

Kirk shrugged. "I got biostats on your four cousins."

"Did you try cross-referencing T'Pel to any illegal acts or threats?" McCoy asked.

"That was my next search," Kirk said, "and I got nothing."

McCoy's eyes narrowed. "Out of fifteen thousand references?"

"Illegal acts and threats are not part of the Vulcan heritage," Spock said. "That is a logical finding."

By the end of the meeting, it was McCoy who was most upset. "For someone facing court-martial for attempted murder, you certainly aren't acting worried, Mr. Spock."

"Thank you, Doctor," Spock said.

"Since you're so calm," McCoy continued, "I take it you believe that the commodore's case is so weak that you have no reason to think there is anything for the rest of us to worry about?"

"I mean nothing of the sort," Spock said. "Though the case against me is weak, someone on board this ship did try to disable the *Enterprise* and kill one or more of the prize nominees. While I am in custody, the person or persons responsible will be free to try again on Memory Prime."

"And that's nothing to worry about?" McCoy said, amazed.

"Logically, Doctor, there is no reason to be worried. On the other hand, there is every reason to use whatever means possible to stop such an act."

"What act?" Kirk asked.

Spock stated it like an elementary class lesson. "The act of killing the Federation's top representatives of virtually all sciences and plunging uncounted star systems into a new dark age." Kirk decided he would worry enough for the two of them.

In engineering, Scott watched the main display board with relief as the engines stepped down to sublight and the *Enterprise* returned to normal space. Despite the jury-rigged repairs and the hours-long strain of factor seven, the circuits had held. Now his people had a full week of scouting around the Jefferies tubes, taking the time to do the repairs properly. And perhaps add a few more of my refinements to the system, Scott thought, though he knew they'd all groan at that. It had come to be a standing joke that the only similarity between the official *Constellation*-class equipment manuals and the *Enterprise*'s manuals was the line about manufacturers' warranties being voided by tampering. In the *Enterprise*'s case, Mr. Scott had voided all the warranties years ago.

Scott left engineering for his quarters. With his main concern out of the way, it was time to turn to the others. He supposed that Spock should top that list, but the science officer had extricated himself from worse situations, and Scott was certain something would work out. It wasn't that he had such absolute faith in the Starfleet judicial system; it was that he had absolute faith in the captain.

The person that he focused on instead was Mira Romaine. She had been the sanest, smartest, and nicest woman who had ever come on board the *Enterprise*. And, he thought, the prettiest.

From the moment he had seen her in the briefing room to go over the installation procedures for the new equipment for Memory Alpha, he had felt the spark pass between them. He remembered having difficulty concentrating on her report that day. It was simple, yet brilliant, and showed an impressive grasp of logistics, combined with an intriguing new programming methodology that could save days in the initialization stages. Reviewing the report later, Scott had seen that the brilliance of Mira's eyes was more than matched by the brilliance of her mind.

At first they'd both been tentative, the differences in their age and rank glaringly apparent. But slowly the hesitations became slighter, the false starts fewer in number. The closer they came to Memory Alpha the stronger the bonds between them grew, as if the threat of loss at mission's end sped up the processes of love.

Aye, love. That was the word for it, Scott thought lyrically. There had been others in his life, but a true love was rare as heather mist a hundred light-years from home.

He had realized the full strength of the glorious hold that Mira had claimed on his heart when she had been possessed by the Zetarians. To see the light of her eyes replaced by the alien energies of an ancient, deadly life-form; to hear her sweet voice corrupted by the obscene utterances of entities that planned to possess her body by displacing her mind; it had almost destroyed him.

That night, after she had recovered from the multi-atmospheric pressure that had driven the Zetarians from her and the ship, he had discovered in her arms that she had felt the same terror within her. Not the fear of death, but the fear of losing someone who had come to mean so much to her.

The next two weeks at Memory Alpha had been a whirlwind of love and work. Scott was dazzled by her intellect and her playfulness and he realized with the poignant feeling of impending separation that he had met the first woman who could keep up with him in his field, and the first woman who challenged him to keep up with her.

The last day had been an agony. A team of Vulcan technicians had arrived to begin the recovery attempt of Alpha's burned-out cores. Mira was to remain with them. The *Enterprise* was to move on.

The only thing that had made their separation possible was that, among all the things they shared, their sense of duty and their questing souls had been the strongest. They could not give up the lives they led. They did not even ask the other to do what each alone could not.

For a few months, they had exchanged messages. But the words that could be sent through subspace, open to the eyes and ears of others, only heightened the loneliness, the sense of loss. In the end, it had been best to close the file and remember what had been, instead of vainly struggling to keep a doomed ghost alive.

Mira Romaine was now chief technician at the facility that was the *Enterprise*'s next port of call—a well-publicized port of call.

His work at hand completed, Scott finally lost himself in the agony of asking *what if?* and *why?* because he knew there was no way Mira Romaine could fail to know that soon their paths would cross again. But *she hadn't sent a message.* Almost as if she no longer cared.

Thirteen

Salman Nensi stood behind the lectern on the stage of the main amphitheater and watched four associates roll among the empty audience seats, slipping printed programs into the pocket on each chair back. He tried to imagine how the theater would look tomorrow morning at eight hundred hours, when almost two thousand beings would gather for the opening ceremonies before the scientists went off to begin the long, drawn-out voting procedures. At least another six hundred scientists would watch the presentation in the comfort of their own particular gravitational and atmospheric conditions in the special environmentally detached visitors' domes of Prime. With the scientists' companions, media, politicians, and the at-liberty crews of at least eight Fleet vessels, Prime was going to be filled to overflowing. Already the lineups in the cafeterias and restaurants were numbing. And now Farl and his blue-skinned troopers were cordoning off sections, creating choke points for crowd control, and making things three times as bad. Each hour that passed made it less likely that these prize ceremonies were going to be the best ever held. They were threatening to become an utter fiasco.

But at least I don't have an interface slowdown to contend with, Nensi thought gratefully as he checked off items on the "to do" list displayed on the portable office terminal he had opened on the lectern. Garold and a few others of the interface team had been seen wandering around their quarters in the main domes, so he presumed that relations between them and the Pathfinders were back to normal. Whatever normal might mean in those circumstances. As for the Pathfinders' excess capacity, that had apparently been going on for at least a year and he couldn't see how a few more days could affect anything.

An associate hummed to a stop beside Nensi, opened a panel on its side, and rotated a viewscreen out and up to Nensi's eye level.

"Request for communication," the associate announced. "From Chief Technician Romaine."

Nensi gave leave for the machine to proceed. Romaine appeared and immediately apologized for bothering him.

"I'm so far behind now," Nensi said, "another few minutes won't make any difference. What's up?"

"The *Enterprise* has arrived and the last delegation of nominees will be ready to beam down in a few minutes. You want to be part of the welcoming committee again?"

Nensi had greeted all of the other delegations, didn't see why he shouldn't go for a complete record, and said so.

"Main transporter chamber, then," Romaine said, and quickly glanced off-screen. "Fourteen-twenty hours."

"I'll be there," Nensi acknowledged, concluding the call. But he noticed that Romaine didn't sign off. "Anything else?" he asked.

Romaine wrinkled her brow. "Did you try confirming any of Farl's authorization for this 'emergency' of his?" she asked.

Nensi shook his head. "I'm a civilian appointee attached to a Starfleet outpost. Nothing to confirm. Besides, I've seen flaps like this a hundred times. Everyone's nervous about all this scientific talent gathering on one little rock. That's all."

"This little flap has three of my best people incommunicado in the military brig," Romaine said, perturbed. "You can bet *I* tried to confirm it."

"Tried?" Nensi repeated. He didn't like the sound of that. "What was the response?"

"Coded military garbage. I mean *nothing's* coming out of Command except for acronyms and abbreviations and keyword responses we have to open sealed message wafers to decode."

Nensi rubbed at his chin. "That only means they're taking this flap seriously and quite properly assuming that subspace is no longer secure for unencrypted Command messages."

"Off the record, Sal, did you have *any* indication at all that something like this was in the works?"

"An associate comm link is not the best place to be asking for something off the record," he cautioned. "But, no, I had no idea. If I had, then presumably someone else would have, too, and we wouldn't be going through all this right now." He could see that her face was still drawn and tight. "I really wouldn't worry about it. Concentrate on your engineer, instead." That brought a smile.

"I wish," Romaine said, then, "Thanks, Uncle Sal. See you in the main chamber." She broke the link and the screen twisted back into the associate.

"This module has other duties," it announced politely when the panel clicked shut.

Nensi gave it permission to proceed and picked up his portable office terminal from the lectern. He'd delegated so much authority to organize the ceremonies that he supposed he might as well let his staff take responsibility for the headaches, too. He walked across the stage and hopped down to the floor, feeling his back twinge with the impact. It would be good to leave behind the painful chauvinism of Earth standard gravity and get back home to the normal gravity of Mars, he thought, and hurried on his way.

The welcoming delegation was already in position when Nensi arrived at Prime's main transporter chamber. Romaine and two aides waited with twelve others, including representatives of the prize committee, accreditation officials, two holo recorders from the combined newsweb pool, and Commander Farl's sublieutenant of the guards.

Nensi crossed quickly to stand by Romaine as the forward platform pad began to glow and a small, squat, angular shape appeared.

Nensi leaned over to Romaine. "I didn't know the *Enterprise* was bringing any more Medusans," he said.

The transporter technician at the console overheard.

"It's just a calibration module, Mr. Nensi," she explained, flicking her eyes back and forth from the pad to her controls.

"Ah," Nensi said as the ghost image solidified into the familiar form of the most transported piece of equipment in the Federation.

The sides of the box-shaped calibration module were made from incredibly thin sheets of alignment alloy. Only four molecules thick, the surface of the substance sparkled with a rainbow effect resulting from the geometric diffraction patterns formed by its constituent atoms. The slightest molecular misalignment of the transporter effect, even on the order of half an atomic diameter, would immediately disrupt the colorful light reflections and turn the surface to a dull, tarnished, blue black.

Any ship or installation that had a transporter unit kept hundreds of square meters of the alloy on hand for test beamings. Its durability, as long as it was properly reassembled, was as impressive as its availability, and Nensi had seen sheets of it fashioned into everything from serving trays to wall plaques in handicraft shops on dozens of worlds. As long as the ends were carefully rolled over to guard against the wickedly sharp edges, Nensi found alignment alloy artifacts attractive, if somewhat garish.

"Are they having trouble with their system?" Nensi asked, after the technician had confirmed the module's arrival and the *Enterprise* beamed it back up.

"They're just being cautious, I think," the technician said. "Their operator was saying the ship's transporter target sensors are so sensitive that they were picking up ghost coordinates from all the portable combat pads Farl's deployed. Rather than step down their sensors and then spend a day recalibrating when they leave, the operator just wanted to go to a higher beam path."

"Successfully, I take it?" Nensi said as the transporter effect appeared above five of the twenty-two pads in the chamber.

"Going to be an awful mess if it wasn't," the technician said cheerfully.

The first group all wore Fleet uniforms, and the first one off the platform had captain's stripes on his sleeve and a face too young with eyes too old. *The legendary James T. Kirk,* Nensi thought as he stepped out to introduce himself and greet the man.

Kirk smiled winningly and gave the impression that he had traveled halfway across the galaxy just to meet and talk with Salman Nensi. The chief administrator had never met a being with such a warm, yet forceful personality. *Gods,* Nensi thought, *if Kirk's like this just to say hello to, what must it be like to serve with him?* Nensi had an image of a starship hurtling into a black hole with Kirk at the helm and a thousand loyal crew eager to follow. Then the captain saw something interesting over Nensi's shoulder.

"Mira?" Kirk said with a surprised smile. "Mira Romaine?"

"Hello, Captain." Romaine extended her hand to Kirk's. Nensi, because he knew her well, could see her smile was tense and forced. "Didn't Mr. Scott tell you?" She tried to say it lightly, but Nensi immediately knew what had caused her disappointment.

"Not a word," Kirk said, and then, incredibly, Nensi saw it was almost as if the captain could read Romaine's face and body language as well as anyone else who had known her since she was a child. "But then Scotty's been working nonstop since the dilithium burnout. I didn't get a chance to review the personnel list for Memory Prime and I bet he didn't either." Kirk stepped back from Romaine for a moment. *Probably comparing her to the nervous, inexperienced specialist lieutenant she had been on the mission to Alpha,* Nensi thought. He watched Kirk assess the change the years had brought to Mira, and realized that Kirk had lied when he said he didn't get a chance to review the personnel list. That man probably never left anything to chance in his entire career.

Kirk arranged to meet Romaine for a drink when the day's business was concluded and then he dutifully endured the rest of the introductions. Wouldn't be surprised to see him run for council president someday, Nensi thought as he watched Kirk work the room. The others who had beamed down with him seemed to share some of their captain's inner fire and charm as well.

Nensi had made it a hobby to try and identify people's origins by their accents and turned his ear to the voices of Kirk's accompanying crew. He immediately gave up trying to place the beautiful woman in services red who was talking to the transporter technician in the technician's own colony dialect. A moment ago she had been speaking in Greater Andorian to Farl's sublieutenant. Both tongues, including Standard, she had managed with perfect tones, inflections, and in the sublieutenant's case, whistles and clicks. The woman's facility with language was far beyond Nensi's.

The other crew members were easier. An older man in sciences blue was delighting everyone with a friendly drawl that Nensi recognized as coming either from the old Lunar Freehomes or, perhaps, the North American southern regions. The two younger men in command gold, who were paying particular attention to the women in the welcoming delegation, without being objectionable about it, were also fairly simple. The younger one was from either Martian Colony One or, even more likely, the Grand Soviet regions on Earth. The older one with the blinding smile carried a unique hint of Old Earth combined with the colonists' dialect of Ginjitsu. A true child of the Federation, Nensi concluded.

As the first round of greetings came to an end, six more pads produced six more materializations. Nensi was surprised to see a commodore and five troopers. Troopers were not considered regular crew for a starship except under extraordinary conditions, and the protocol liaison in Romaine's office had mentioned no need to prepare for a person of the commodore's rank. He wondered if her presence had any connection with Farl's emergency, and the commodore answered him by heading straight for the sublieutenant.

Beside him, Nensi heard one of the prize committee members, apparently annoyed at the arrival of so many nonessential beings, ask pointedly if there might be any scientists on board the *Enterprise.*

Again, the transporter pads chimed and the first of the nominee delegation arrived with their luggage and equipment.

Nensi found himself shaking hands with the older officer with the drawl as the accreditation officials escorted the scientists to the identification stalls. His name, he said, was Leonard McCoy, ship's surgeon. Nensi returned the introduction.

"A good voyage?" the chief administrator asked.

"Except for the last part," McCoy answered with enough of an edge in his voice that Nensi knew things weren't going well on his ship. "I'm sorry, Mr. Nensi, I don't mean to complain. I always get cranky after beaming. I hate those things."

Nensi had heard about people like this man, though he had never personally met anyone else who shared the doctor's groundless aversion to being broken down into his elementary particles, tunneled through beam space, then reassembled. "I understand," Nensi lied politely.

"Especially putting through that calibration module first," McCoy continued. "As if they expected the whole system to fail any second. Probably with me in transit, too." McCoy looked around the chamber, as if searching for something. "What the blazes are those portable pads they kept talking about up there?" he asked.

"Those would be the portable combat pads our security troopers have deployed around the facility," Nensi said. He saw an eyebrow shoot up at the word *combat.* "Part of a very thorough drill procedure, I assure you. Nothing drastic."

"Then why are they interfering with our ship's system?"

Nensi was getting the strong feeling that this man didn't just dislike transporters, he *hated* them. "As I understand it, Dr. McCoy, it's a function of their fail-safe mode." Normally transtator technology was beyond Nensi, but here he was on familiar financial grounds. "I'm sure you know that a pad-to-pad transit consumes less than one-tenth the energy of a single-pad beam."

"No," McCoy said plainly.

"Well, it's true," Nensi continued, wondering what to make of this man. "Plus it takes greater operator skill to lock target sensors on to the proper coordinates, especially at orbital distances. Portable pads, on the other hand, can be preset to a fixed number of other pads, like an intercom system, if you will. Untrained personnel can simply punch in a code for a pad in the network and the system automatically transfers them from one location to another within the circuit. Very efficient for moving ground troops in a hurry."

McCoy looked to be thinking that one through, then asked, "But if the *Enterprise* isn't part of your portable system, why do the portable units affect it?"

"It's their lock-on beacons. They're very strong and directional, for reliability under harsh conditions, and they keep attracting your ship's carrier waves. Are you familiar with the old concept of a lightning rod?"

"Very," McCoy said with a smile. "I'm an old farm boy."

"Then like that," Nensi said, thinking maybe that explained the man's attitude. "In fact, under invasion conditions, portable pad beacons can be set so high that incoming beams are almost *forced* to divert to them. Very handy if you have a squad of troopers ready to take prisoners. That's why Starfleet still carries the expense of ground-assault suborbital shuttles. To avoid the risks of beam captures."

"Now that's what I'd like," McCoy said. "Suborbital shuttles. Something big and solid that kept me in one piece all the way there and back. Of course I'll only be able to requisition something like that when I'm an admiral. And at the rate I'm going, I'll probably be a hundred and forty." He laughed at the concept.

Luddite, Nensi thought to himself.

Throughout the conversation, more nominees had arrived from the *Enterprise,* but no more crew. Nensi had seen Romaine look up anxiously each time the pads had chimed, but no Mr. Scott was to be found.

By now the chamber was getting overcrowded, like most other facilities on Memory Prime, and Nensi and McCoy parted as they joined the general migration toward the doors.

The chief administrator found himself shoulder to shoulder with the young officer with the Russian or Martian accent. They introduced themselves but didn't attempt to force their arms up to shake hands.

"I noticed that you have a commodore on board," Nensi said to Ensign Chekov.

"She was not inwited," the ensign said, checking furtively to see if the commodore in question was anywhere nearby.

"Really?" Nensi replied as they suddenly found themselves forced to the side to clear the way for an elderly Vulcan who was being escorted to a retina scanner in the delegate identification stalls.

"She has arrested our first officer," Chekov stated indignantly.

"On what charge?"

Chekov was obviously annoyed. "Made-up charges. She said he tried to kill Academician Sradek"—he pointed to the ancient Vulcan who was peering into a blue-lit sensorscope while his documents were processed—"that Wulcan scientist, and most of the other nominees on board."

"No!" Nensi said, hoping to match what he felt was Chekov's sense of outrage. Nensi himself had been subjected to so many of Starfleet's arbitrary decisions in his career that he doubted if he could ever feel real outrage over anything they did to him again. But Chekov's story was intriguing. Could it be the connection to Farl's emergency?

"Yes!" Chekov replied vehemently. "It is all lies, but still she has him in the brig."

Nensi smiled at his loose-lipped new acquaintance. "If this is your first time here, Ensign, would you like me to show you to one of our better bars?" He made a point of checking his chronometer. "There's a shift change coming up in about half an hour and I could introduce you to a number of people who I'm sure would enjoy meeting a starship officer. Especially one from the *Enterprise*."

Chekov's eyes lit up like novas. "That would be wery hospitable of you, Mr. Nensi." Profitable to me also, Nensi thought.

As promised, the Extended Loan was one of Prime's better bars. It featured subsidized prices for Fleet and Federation personnel, and an ethanol synthesizer two generations ahead of the overworked antique on the *Enterprise*. Chekov proved to be most talkative, having been charmed and delighted with the decor— a reconstruction of the legendary Icelandic public databank from the late 2000s that had been so important to the growth and development of synthetic consciousnesses. An hour later when the shifts finally changed and a rather rowdy group of librarians decided they should get to know the new ensign very well, Nensi had heard the full story of the *Enterprise*'s voyage from Starbase Four, the dilithium disaster and the flux release, the arrest, everything.

As Chekov was practically carried out of the bar to be shown what sights there were to see, Nensi sat back in his booth and nursed the vodka for which the ensign had insisted on paying. The chief administrator was worried. Farl's flap, as he thought of it, was obviously far worse than he had suspected, reaching out from Memory Prime and apparently even affecting the *Starship Enterprise*. But with subspace channels restricted to military communications, and Farl now exerting his military authority, there was no one for the chief administrator to turn to, nothing he could do to help preserve his facility.

No, take that back, he thought. There *was* someone he could turn to for help. Something.

He knocked back the vodka and left the bar to find Romaine. Liars or not, it was time to pay another visit to the Pathfinders.

Fourteen

Kirk smiled warmly, expertly hiding the rage that burned within him. Commodore Wolfe had returned to the *Enterprise* with Commander Farl and had been in briefings for the past six hours, briefings that were plainly off limits to the *Enterprise*'s captain. Kirk hadn't felt like this since he was a middy in his first year at the Academy and at the mercy of just about everyone else's schedule.

Across the restaurant table from him, Mira Romaine stopped her story and sipped her wine. Then she smiled at the captain and said, "Did you hear any of that?"

Kirk switched gears instantly. "After the extent of the damage at Memory Alpha was fully charted, you were posted to the *U.S.S. Rainbow Warrior*, then took a three-month course at the Vulcan Academy, joined the Memory Prime implementation team, and here you are," Kirk recapped smoothly. His years on the bridge of the *Enterprise* had given him the ability to follow several conversations at once, even without being aware he was doing it. But he decided the commodore had stolen enough of his energies for this evening; it was time to pay more attention to Mira.

"Very impressive, Captain. I would have sworn you had tuned me out completely." Kirk raised his own glass. "Never," he said graciously.

"And you?" Romaine asked. "What have you been up to in the past few years?"

Kirk sighed. "Not much," he said blandly. "Same ship, same captain."

"Same crew?"

"Mostly." Kirk saw in her eyes what she was afraid to ask. "And honestly, Scotty said absolutely nothing about knowing you were here. He really has had his hands full with the dilithium burnout."

"Thank you, Captain," Romaine said, "but that's not why I was asking."

Kirk felt a momentary twinge of sadness for the woman. How often had he said the same sort of thing without really meaning it, as she just had? "How's your father?" he asked to change the subject.

"Grumpy as ever," Romaine said with a smile, though it plainly didn't reflect her feelings.

"Still retired?" Kirk drained his glass and looked around for the server, a tall man in a traditional long white apron who looked as if he could juggle antigravs set for full attract.

"His last 'retirement' lasted three months. Now he's consulting for a mining company in the Belt. He likes the travel." Romaine followed Kirk's eyes, saw Sal Nensi enter the restaurant, and waved him over. It didn't take much to convince him to join them for supper. The table's server was over instantly with a third menu screen. The speed of service at this restaurant was so fast that Kirk idly wondered if there were voice sensors in the table. Either that or the servers had better hearing than Mr. Spock.

"Enjoying shore leave?" Nensi asked of the captain after placing his order.

"Just waiting," Kirk said. "Story of my life."

"And mine," Nensi agreed. "Especially now. No doubt you've noticed that a military exercise is being carried out at this facility."

Kirk looked over the railing beside their table at two Andorian troopers marching below through a central plaza. "Difficult not to. Is this a regular occurrence?" Kirk was puzzled as he tried to read Nensi's surprised reaction.

"You mean *you* don't know what it's about?"

"I had assumed it was security for the prize ceremonies." Kirk felt alarms going off. He had not thought to question the presence of so many troopers on Prime after being told that the portable combat transporters had been dispersed simply as part of a scheduled drill.

"We've been informed that this facility is in the middle of a military emergency," Romaine said. "I've had my command temporarily suspended."

Kirk held up his hand to stop the revelations. Something wasn't making sense. "Just a moment," he began, turning to Romaine. "You say *you* were in command of this base?"

"Yes sir," Romaine replied as if she were still a specialist lieutenant on Kirk's bridge. "It's supposedly a civilian installation but requires a military presence, so the Federation and Starfleet compromised by giving command to someone in Starfleet technical services. Me. Except under military emergencies."

"And what is the nature of the military emergency?" Kirk asked hurriedly. It was impossible to think that his ship could arrive at a facility in a military emergency without Starfleet informing him.

"I don't know," Romaine said.

"Nor I," Nensi added.

"Commander Farl took over early this morning and said that I could confirm it with Starfleet."

"And did you?" Kirk asked.

"I can't get through channels. Everything's restricted or encrypted."

Nensi leaned forward and dropped his voice. "Captain Kirk, does this military emergency exist without you being informed of it?" The man looked equally alarmed and confused.

Kirk studied Romaine and Nensi. Obviously they had parts of the puzzle he was trying to solve. He had to trust them in order to make an exchange: his pieces for theirs.

"An Alpha emergency has been declared on board the *Enterprise*," Kirk said in almost a whisper.

The three of them then abruptly sat back from the table as the server brought the first course of hydroponic salads. He topped up their wineglasses, then departed.

"I've heard about the Alpha emergency," Nensi said.

Kirk considered the man's statement for a moment and decided Nensi had said it so Kirk would understand two things: that Nensi had his own sources of information and that he was holding nothing back.

"I appreciate you telling me that," Kirk said. "Do your sources have any idea why an Alpha was called?"

"Sorry, no."

"The unofficial explanation I was given," Kirk said, "was that Starfleet had received unsubstantiated information indicating that one or more of the prize nominees were targeted for assassination."

"Commander Farl said he was under orders not to tell me the nature of Prime's emergency," Romaine offered. "But he did say that he expected the situation to be improved when the *Enterprise* arrived."

Nensi turned to Romaine. "Did Farl say that before or after we heard about the dilithium burnout on the ship?"

"After, of course," Romaine said. "He only took over this morning."

Nensi looked back to Kirk. "My sources also tell me that the dilithium incident on your ship was considered by Commodore Wolfe to have been an assassination attempt orchestrated by your science officer."

"Mr. Spock?" Romaine said with surprise. "Impossible."

"That's what I said," Kirk agreed. "Though the commodore does believe she has a circumstantial case. But putting that aside, what I don't understand is if our two declared emergencies are connected, then why would your commander feel that *his* emergency would be lessened by my ship's arrival? It doesn't make any more sense than thinking that the two emergencies aren't connected." Kirk tapped his finger on the table for a moment, then reached to his equipment belt and brought out his communicator with a practiced flip that snapped it open, ready to transmit. "Kirk to *Enterprise*. Put me through to McCoy."

"The ship's doctor," Romaine explained to Nensi as Kirk waited for McCoy to come on channel.

"We've met," Nensi said with a grimace. "The technophobe."

Kirk smiled as McCoy responded to the captain's call. He sounded as if he had been sleeping but didn't object when Kirk suggested he join him and Nensi and Romaine for dinner. Within three minutes, a transporter field swirled into being down in the plaza below. McCoy looked around until he saw the captain wave from the restaurant balcony. By the time the doctor arrived at the table, the server had miraculously arrived and·set a fourth place and provided another menu screen. McCoy didn't even glance at the offerings and simply ordered a bourbon, or whatever they had that was more or less chemically inspired by bourbon.

"Good to see you in one piece," Nensi commented as the server left for the bar.

"It's good to *be* in one piece after being in billions," McCoy agreed, missing the point. He clapped his hands together and looked expectantly at the captain. "So?" he asked, implying a dozen questions in one word.

"First, how's Spock?" Kirk asked.

"Busy," McCoy said. "The commodore finally agreed to your request to let him have a remote library reader, so the last I saw, he was at his desk in the cell, working away with it on that Sherman Syndrome thing. You'd think he'd be working on his defense at a time like this."

"Spock has a better grasp of his priorities than most people," Kirk suggested. "He knows what he's doing."

McCoy looked up with a smile as the server returned with his drink. "That was fast," he said happily. The server nodded once and was gone.

"How about the commodore?" Kirk asked.

"Been meeting all day with that Andorian commander and some of her staff." McCoy sipped the bourbon experimentally, sighed, then turned to Nensi and asked, "How's this facility set for medical personnel?"

"Any clue as to what her meetings are about?" Kirk prodded. He wondered if McCoy really didn't see the seriousness of the situation or if he had simply acknowledged the fact that if Spock wasn't concerned enough to be doing something about his own incarceration, then there was really no reason for anyone else to be concerned.

"Well, Uhura might have had a clue," McCoy offered. He looked questioningly at Nensi and Romaine.

"It's all right," Kirk said. "We're all in the same shuttle on this one."

"Uhura's been ordered to stay on duty to handle communications. She says she's never seen anything like it short of being in the middle of an ion storm with all shields down. Wolfe and Farl are cut off from Starfleet Command."

Being cut off from Command wasn't necessarily a hardship, Kirk knew. But that usually happened out on the frontier, not in Quadrant Zero. Things were getting worse by the minute. "For how long?" he asked.

"All day, as far as I know," McCoy said. He was still too cheerful as far as Kirk was concerned, and kept glancing over the railing into the plaza.

"Uh, Captain Kirk," Nensi said hesitatingly. "Earlier this afternoon I was present at the combined newsweb facilities and watched an interview with some of the nominees from Earth. It was conducted in real time, over subspace, with an interviewer on Luna. There were no technical difficulties at all that I was aware of."

"Are you suggesting that only Starfleet subspace frequencies are being interfered with?" Kirk asked. "That civil frequencies are being left untouched?"

"I don't even think Starfleet would be capable of such selective jamming," Nensi answered. "But that's what I observed."

Kirk knew that Nensi was right. The intricacies of selective jamming of subspace frequencies made the practice virtually impossible. Usually it was all frequencies that were disrupted, or none. Perhaps it only *appeared* that communications were in disarray.

"Mr. Nensi, have your 'sources' passed on any word about conditions on the other ships that have brought nominees to Prime?" Kirk asked.

"That was one of the first things I decided to check out when I learned what had happened on the *Enterprise*. Communications are disrupted for the other ships as well but, unfortunately, there's no other pattern. Three of the ships are traveling with reduced crews, but that's normal in this area of space. Lots of people use the opportunity for shore leave. Whatever is happening, is happening only on your ship and this facility."

"At least that's a start," Kirk decided. Half the battle in solving a problem was defining the problem to be solved in the first place. "Any suggestions, Doctor? Doctor?"

McCoy snapped his head back to the table. "Sorry, Jim?" he asked.

"I give up, Bones. What do you know that we don't know?" Kirk glanced down to the plaza where McCoy's attention had been focused. "Is the answer to all of our questions going to pop out of nothing down there?"

McCoy smiled mysteriously. "I suppose that's one way of looking at it," he said. "Someone's questions, at least."

With that Kirk saw a second transporter field glittering in the plaza. It coalesced into the red-shirted form of Montgomery Scott.

McCoy waved down at Scott and the engineer responded, making his way to the restaurant entrance below. Kirk checked Romaine. She stared at her wineglass, grasping it as if it were the only thing that was keeping her on the face of the Prime asteroid.

Kirk wanted to ask McCoy just what it was he thought he was doing, setting up a surprise like this in such a clumsy manner, but he could think of no way to do it without embarrassing Romaine and making things worse than they already were. There was a long awkward pause at the table, during which the efficient server arrived and arranged a fifth place and left another menu screen. At last Scott appeared on the balcony, looking as nervous as Kirk had ever seen him before. Romaine still stared into the compelling depths of her wineglass. When she finally looked over her shoulder, her glance must have prompted Kirk's chief engineer to finish his approach to the table.

When he arrived, he nodded to the captain and the doctor, uncharacteristically ignored Mr. Nensi, and looked nervously at Romaine.

The woman suddenly stood up by the table. Kirk slumped back in his chair and glared at McCoy, but the doctor was directing his own attention to Scott and Romaine.

"Hello, Mira," Scott managed to say. Kirk agonized for his engineer. The poor man obviously had no idea how the woman was going to react.

Romaine started to say something, but it came out as a small halfhearted rasp. She looked down at the table, at the captain, back to Scott. Then she walked away, toward the exit or toward Scott. Both were in the same direction.

She stopped beside him, stared at him long and hard. Her eyes were full, glinting in the soft light of the restaurant. Kirk could see that Scott's were in the same condition. Then everything broke free.

"Damn you, Scotty," Romaine said with a heart-wrenching tremor. She reached out and kissed him.

McCoy leaned over the table, mouthed, "See?" and went back to his bourbon with a self-satisfied smirk.

Uhura was furious. She wasn't simply frustrated that she was only a few hundred kilometers above the best language labs in the Federation, yet compelled to remain at her bridge station. She wasn't upset that taking orders from Lieutenant Abranand was like obeying a trained monkey, and she really couldn't care less about the three nails she had just broken when she tried to pull loose a number-ten crossover board from the service port beneath her communications station. But Commodore Wolfe enraged her. It was one thing for an administrative officer to run roughshod over a starbase, but Wolfe's brand of arbitrary and officious conduct was infuriating. The crew of the *Enterprise* had been through more aggravation together than any ten starbase commodores. What drove that crew was respect, not despotism. Kirk and the other officers understood this implicitly. Wolfe didn't. The mysterious loss of hot water in the commodore's cabin had simply been the first shot fired. Uhura doubted the commodore was going to last much longer on board the *Enterprise*.

"When will you be finished?" Abranand barked over Uhura's shoulder.

The communications officer resisted the urge to apply full power to the circuits she was jumping and blow the board. She could always bat her lashes and claim the lieutenant had startled her. But she also refused to give in to his obnoxiousness. She carefully removed her circuit plaser from the crossover board before answering.

"Two or three minutes and I'll try reconnecting it," she said politely, but without glancing up at Abranand's hulking presence.

"I thought these starships were supposed to be state of the art," the starbase trooper complained, still interfering with Uhura's concentration as she tried to create a custom subspace filter circuit from scratch.

"What makes you think they aren't?" she asked, delicately threading a connecting filament between a quantum four-gate and the first of eight red-banded parallel assistors. She could see Abranand's hand gestures from the corner of her eye.

"Circuit boards, for one thing," he said. "I mean, any twenty-year-old cruiser has the circuit equivalents of your bridge network laid out in a control computer no bigger than a footlocker. All the circuits can be reconfigured, even redesigned, by computer, and here you starship heroes are, rewiring macrocircuits by hand." Abranand snorted.

"Tell me, Lieutenant," she said carefully as she connected a simulator lead to the four-gate and ran a test signal through it, "have you ever seen a twenty-year-old cruiser's circuit complex after it's been hit by a Klingon broad-beam disruptor while traveling at warp seven?" The telltale on the simulator lead glowed green. Uhura had finished the circuit.

"Cruisers can't go at warp seven," Abranand said, wary, as if expecting a trick question.

"Well, this ship can, mister. And a disruptor blast that connects can drop it out of warp so fast that any quantum switches that just happen to be tunneling at the microsecond we hit normal space are liable to pop back into existence three meters from where they should be." Uhura stood up from her station and hefted the number-ten board in her hand. "You know where that leaves you?"

Abranand shook his head.

"Sitting around waiting for the Klingons with a circuit complex full of more holes than a light sail in the Coal Sack." She smiled at the lieutenant then and, just for the hell of it, batted her lashes at him, too. "Whereas, we starship heroes have circuits large enough to come out of rapid warp translation in the same shape they went into it, and in the event of circuit-burning power surges, alien force beams, or simply spilled coffee two thousand light-years out from the nearest starbase spare-parts depot, we can rebuild every circuit on this ship by hand. That's what I call state of the art." She pushed her station chair toward the lieutenant as she prepared to kneel down and reinsert the crossover board. "If you'll excuse me."

Abranand grumbled as he walked away, but he didn't make any more cracks about the ship's design characteristics.

Uhura broke a fourth nail snapping the board back home. Okay, she thought, so some design specs did need to be upgraded, but she certainly wasn't going to say anything about it while Wolfe and her troopers were on board.

Uhura sat back in her chair, after prudently leaving the service-port grille on the deck. There was no telling how many more times Wolfe would ask her to attempt something different to try and break through the bizarre interference that was jamming subspace. She pressed her earphone in place and toggled the activation switches—additional, easily repairable mechanical devices—on the bypass filter pad. The frequency was clear!

"Commodore Wolfe," Uhura said as she touched the infraship com switch. The ship's computer held part of Uhura's voice in memory, scanned the duty rosters to determine where the commodore would be at this time, then routed through Uhura's page to the briefing room before Uhura had finished saying the complete name.

"Wolfe here," came the reply.

"I have a clear channel, Commodore," Uhura said, then pressed the send key that would forward the automatic alert call the commodore had already ordered be the first sent. "The transmission to Admiral Komack is under w—"

A high-pitched squeal blared from Uhura's earphone and she immediately closed the subspace channel.

"What's going on, Lieutenant?" Wolfe demanded.

"The clear channel has been blocked, Commodore. As soon as I started transmitting, the jamming began. It has to be deliberate."

Uhura could hear Wolfe take a deep breath. "Very well, Lieutenant, I'm on my way to the bridge. Tell helm and engineering to prepare for a warp-eight jaunt out of the range of the interference. I want us out of here to transmit our messages and get back before anyone knows we're gone. Wolfe out."

Uhura turned to look at the startled faces of the two junior ensigns at the engineering and helm stations. She was the only main watch officer on duty because of the need for her expertise in trying to overcome the subspace interference. "I know, I know," she said to the younger, less experienced officers who in just a few seconds would find themselves in a position where they would be unable to obey a direct command from a commodore.

"What do you know?" Abranand asked.

"The matter/antimatter system is shut down for repairs. There's no way this ship can be ready for warp in anything less than twenty-four hours." Uhura turned to the engineering and helm officers. "It's all right. It's not your fault the commodore doesn't know the condition of her vessel." Then she smiled sweetly at Abranand again. She could tell it was starting to bother him because he had finally worked out that she wasn't doing it to be polite.

The lift doors swept open and Wolfe and the Andorian commander Farl emerged. Uhura realized that no one else was going to do it unless asked, so she spoke first and told the commodore about the engines. The commodore replied with a word that Uhura had only heard once before when she had seen an Orion trader's trousers catch on fire after he had put too many Spican flame gems in his pocket and they'd ignited. Uhura was impressed that the commodore knew such a word, but was disappointed that she would choose to use it.

"Very well, then. Lieutenant Uhura, I want you to check the other transport ships station keeping at this facility and report on their capability for immediate warp travel, including speed and range. I will authorize payment of standard charter rates and arrange for antimatter transfer." The commodore stared at Uhura for a moment, as if she planned to say something more. "Well, what are you waiting for, Lieutenant? That's an order."

"Aye-aye, Commodore," Uhura said grimly as she spun in her chair and initiated the hailing-frequency subroutines on her board. And then she stopped. "Commodore," she said with surprise as she watched the red incoming indicator blink on and off. "I'm receiving a subspace transmission." She flicked the controls that relayed the encoded identifiers transmitted with the message. "From Starfleet Command," she added with even more surprise.

"Put it on the screen, Lieutenant," Wolfe said, and settled into the captain's chair, Farl and Abranand standing respectfully beside her.

Uhura quickly patched the transmission through to the main viewscreen, then turned in time to see the forward view of the distant Memory Prime asteroid fade out.

At last, the communications officer thought with relief as she recognized the familiar face of Admiral Komack form on the screen, someone is finally going to tell us what's really going on.

Fifteen

"Nensi: you are in Transition with Eight."

The voice from the speaker was clearly recognizable as that of Pathfinder Eight. Nensi glanced sideways at Romaine, who sat beside him in Garold's interface booth, then replied.

"Is Pathfinder Six available for access?" Nensi asked. This is what had happened before, Eight taking over for Six. Except Nensi would rather speak with the more human-sounding synthetic consciousness.

"Nensi: you are in Transition with Eight."

"Apparently Six isn't available," Nensi muttered to Romaine. She didn't respond but he hadn't expected her to do so. She was obviously still in the throes of remembering her reunion with Mr. Scott less than an hour ago. Nensi had hated asking her to accompany him back to the Interface Chamber but, especially after Kirk's further revelations, he felt the need to enlist the Pathfinders' aid. He cleared his throat and prepared for the most difficult part of the interview.

"As chief administrator of this facility, I request that this conversation be held in private," Nensi announced. "Without Garold's presence."

Pathfinder Eight's decision was seemingly instantaneous. Garold, sitting hunched in front of the interface console, suddenly shuddered and jerked his silver-tipped fingers from the hand receptacles. The prime interface whirled to Nensi.

"You have gone too far!" he shouted. Shimmering threads of sweat, from exertion or from fear, streaked Garold's half-shaven head, reflecting the galaxy of status lights that ringed the Interface Chamber and shone from the console behind him. "You belong up there!" He waved his glittering hand to the featureless black of the chamber's far ceiling. "The Pathfinders are ours. We understand them. You don't. You can't."

Nensi had not believed any of the interface team was capable of such a show of emotion. Obviously he had misread the depth of their attachment to the Pathfinders they served.

"I'm sorry, Garold," Romaine said. "But as chief technician, I must inform you that Mr. Nensi is acting within regulations and with my full support." Nensi looked between Romaine and Garold. The man's eyes seemed to glow like the console lights surrounding him, mad and feverish.

"Garold, you have no choice," Nensi said calmly. "Don't force the issue any further."

Then Nensi heard footfalls behind him. He turned to see two other members of the interface team at the entrance to the booth. One was a teenage boy who wore his hair in the same style as Garold's. The boy's fingertips were normal but a cranial inducer patch was evident on his left temple—the first step in joining the team. The other was an older woman, skull completely shaven and covered in an intricate tracing of silver filigree. For a moment, Nensi thought the metallic strands were decoration, and then he realized they were circuits. When the woman spoke, her voice was flat and mechanical and came from a small speaker box mounted on her neck.

"Garold, we have been informed. Your compliance has been requested. Please come with us." She held out her hand to Garold, a gesture that Nensi saw as incongruously human, coming from a woman who was half machine herself.

Garold slowly went to the others of the team, the agony of the defeat and the loss he had endured apparent in his stooped shoulders and reluctant gait. He paused at the booth entrance, looked at the beckoning console, then at Nensi.

"We love them," Garold said, "and they love us." Appearing to know no other way of explaining to Nensi what the chief administrator was interfering with, the prime interface left.

Nensi felt chilled by Garold's statement. "Is that true?" he impulsively asked the Pathfinder. If machines could love, then what was it to be human? "Do you love them?"

"Nensi: we love the datalinks. What do you wish to discuss?"

Nensi spoke softly to Romaine. "It's that simple? A synthetic consciousness experiences love and now it's time for the next question? Is this in any of your manuals?" He felt floored by the seemingly trivial revelation that these machines experienced emotion.

Romaine shrugged. "Nothing that I've read of. But then, we can't know if they're just using a term that they've determined brings comfort to the interface team."

"To what purpose?"

"If the interface team members feel good, maybe they're more efficient, easier to work with. I don't know, Sal."

Nensi could see that Romaine was still unnerved about Scott's return. The question of machines that love would have to wait. "Pathfinder Eight," he began, "are you aware of the military emergency that exists in this facility?"

"Nensi: yes."

"Are you also aware of the Starfleet Alpha emergency in effect on the *Starship Enterprise?*"

"Nensi: yes."

"Are the two emergencies connected?"

"Nensi: all things are connected at certain levels. Define your operational frame of reference."

Nensi thought for a moment. The last time the machine seemed to have no problem dealing with the vagaries of Standard. Well, if it could love, perhaps it was capable of having a bad day, too.

"Are the emergencies connected by sharing common military and/or political causes?"

"Nensi: yes."

"Please describe the common causes of the emergencies," Nensi said with a sigh. It was like talking to an associate.

There was an uncharacteristic pause before the Pathfinder replied, and for a moment Nensi thought it had decided not to answer.

"Nensi: discussion of the relevant causes of the emergencies requires disclosure of data listed as classified. Such data is accessible within your level of classification. However, Starfleet regulations require that a positive identification be made. Please approach the interface console."

Nensi jumped up and took Garold's chair in front of the console. Now he felt he was getting somewhere.

"Romaine: you are in Transition with Eight. Please approach the interface console."

Romaine walked over to stand beside Nensi.

"Nensi, Romaine: prepare for positive sensor identification. Please place your right hands in the interface receptacles."

Nensi reached out his hand to one of the six narrow slots on the interface console just large enough for a human hand. Romaine reached out and stopped him.

"Pathfinder," she said quickly, "we are not equipped with interface leads."

"Nensi, Romaine: that fact is known. Please place your right hands in the interface receptacles."

"Explain the purpose of that action." Romaine was not letting go of Nensi's arm.

Her expression was set and serious and Nensi knew better than to question her.

"Romaine: positive identification is required before discussion of classified data."

"Match our voices," Romaine said. Nensi folded his arms across his chest. Romaine obviously had good reason not to want them to place their hands in the receptacles and he wasn't going to argue with her. This was her area of expertise.

"Romaine: voiceprints can be forged."

Romaine put her hand on Nensi's shoulder and squeezed as if looking for support from her friend. Nensi looked up at her questioningly, unsure of what she was planning.

"Pathfinder, identify yourself," she said.

"Romaine: you are in Transition with Eight."

"Pathfinder, you are in violation of your contract. Identify yourself . . . truthfully." Nensi coughed in astonishment. If the Pathfinders could love, lie, and impersonate one another, life in Transition must be no different from life in Datawell.

Now there was a longer pause. Nensi even heard the speaker click on and off as if a connection were being broken, then, upon reconsideration, reconnected.

"What was that all about?" Nensi said to Romaine after a moment, whispering as if he didn't want to be overheard.

"That wasn't Pathfinder Eight," she said, studying the flares of color that drifted across the console's nonstandard screen. "First I could sense it was lying again, and then that it wasn't even the consciousness it said it was."

"But how could you know?" Nensi asked in bewilderment.

Romaine shook her head. "I'm not sure," she admitted. "Probably speech construction or something. Eight is an old personality. Used to be the shipmind on an old pre-Federation exploration vessel. It has a very clipped, abrupt speech characteristic probably left over from the constraints they had back then on sending data back by tight beam radio. It's never bothered to reconfigure those original parameters."

Nensi went over the conversation in his mind. "Seemed the same to me. And surely any of the other Pathfinders has enough computational power to mimic any speech pattern." Romaine had a point but hadn't thought it through properly, Nensi felt.

Romaine waved his protest away. "Just a minute," she said, and touched some panels on the console. A viewscreen flickered into life beside the receptacles. Nensi recognized another member of the interface team on the screen, a short Centauran with, surprisingly, a full head of hair. However, when his voice came over the screen speaker, Nensi could see that the man's lips didn't move.

"Interface control," the Centauran said.

"Romaine here, interface booth six. What's the interface load right now, Zalan?"

Zalan's eyes never left their front and center focus on the sensor camera. "Zero," he said—*transmitted* would be more accurate, Nensi thought. "All interface connections were suspended ninety-six seconds ago."

"Explanation?" Romaine asked. Obviously she chose to use the interface team's abrupt pattern of speech when dealing with them, Nensi realized. Perhaps that's why she was sensitive to a change in the false Pathfinder Eight's speech characteristics.

"None at this time," Zalan replied. "All units are currently addressing the problem."

"Transmit all data to my office and contact me when you have a likely explanation." Romaine clicked off without a word.

"Have they gone on strike?" Nensi asked when it became apparent that Romaine wasn't going to turn away from the readouts on the console screens.

"No. They're busy in there," she said, pointing to a fluctuating red and yellow graph. "This indicates that their work load is running at close to ninety-eight percent of their reported capacity." She turned to narrow her eyes at Nensi. "Which *we* know is only about ten to twenty percent of their real capacity. But however you add it up, one of them in there is interfacing with something out here. Come on."

Romaine headed out the door of the interface booth and started to jog around the central equipment core of the interface chamber. Twelve booths ringed it, and within a minute she had seen that every one was empty. She hit a call button on a wall-mounted com panel. Zalan appeared on the screen once more.

"Romaine in the chamber. Give me a visual on the I/O room."

Nensi saw the screen instantly flash to shifting views of the main data-exchange installation, where huge banks of equipment blindly fed in the monstrous data load from throughout the known galaxy to the Pathfinder facility and equally massive storage banks captured the Pathfinders' output for transmission to Prime research terminals and other nodes in the memory planet network. The status lights on every unit indicated the full system had shut down.

"Now give me the capacity-load graph," Romaine said, and the screen repeated the shifting red and yellow display that she had called up on the booth's console. Nensi saw that the values on it hadn't appreciably changed. "It's interfacing!" Romaine said sharply. "But how?"

"Backup units? Terminals topside?" Nensi suggested.

"Not possible," Romaine cut him off. "The Pathfinder system is completely separated from the outside universe. All equipment and personnel get in and out by transporter. Data transmissions are tunneled through a one-way subspace short-range downlink and the only data that gets out has to be stored in the I/O room, then passed physically on wafers and wires to be transferred. There are no other facilities for direct link-up to the Pathfinders."

Nensi watched the graph flickering on the screen. If anything, the values were stronger.

"That you know of," he said softly.

Sixteen

Admiral Komack smiled as his image resolved on the bridge's main viewscreen. His blue eyes sparkled and his white hair was trimmed short in a much younger man's style.

Uhura immediately judged his smile to be a good sign. Things would be getting back to normal now, she was sure.

"Commodore Wolfe," the admiral began, "I'm sorry to have taken so long to break Starfleet interference to get to you. I trust all is well."

Uhura's eyes narrowed. Starfleet was causing the subspace jamming? But why? And more importantly, how? Uhura was confident she knew almost everything that could be known about subspace technology and she couldn't even begin to guess how selective jamming could be accomplished without rewriting the physics manuals. She quickly scanned her board and saw with consternation that despite Komack's clear signal, every other channel was still torn apart by impenetrable interference. She wished Mr. Spock were at his station instead of locked in the brig with a library reader. He would enjoy a problem such as this. She shook her head, deep in thought.

"Why is Command generating the subspace jamming, Admiral?" Wolfe asked.

"As you know," Komack replied, "Starfleet has reason to suspect an act of terrorism will be committed on Memory Prime during the Nobel and Z.Magnees Prize ceremonies. Intelligence feels that the terrorists are part of a well-organized group. It is probable that some of the terrorists are in place on Prime, but unknown to each other and requiring outside instructions in order to carry out their plan. By blanking out all subspace transmissions, we hope to make those instructions impossible to receive."

That sounded reasonable to Uhura, even if the method should be impossible. Wolfe appeared to accept the admiral's explanation, too.

"Do you have any other evidence that would further serve to link the science officer to the terrorist organization?" Wolfe asked.

"Not at this time," Komack answered.

"Do you have new orders for us, sir?"

"Again, not at this time. Federation security services are working with Starfleet to uncover the organization at other locations. In the meantime, we will continue to blank out subspace communications in the vicinity of Memory Prime. You are to carry on as before."

"How can we contact each other with subspace jammed?"

Uhura could tell Wolfe wasn't meant for starship duty. Just the intimation of being out of contact with Command was enough to make her nervous. Too bad Komack doesn't seem to notice, Uhura thought.

"Set your incoming beacon to a class-eight random scan. Command will intercept and transmit whenever we have something new to pass along. You will be able to contact me by transmitting a class-two query on this channel when necessary. We will interrupt the jamming at irregular though frequent intervals to look for your transmissions. When we see one, we'll immediately get back to you as we are doing right now." Komack explained the procedure as if it were no more than a standard operations drill. "Just remember that the Alpha emergency still holds, so you're required to restrict your communications to those necessary for the immediate mission. Any other questions?"

"Not at this time, Admiral," Wolfe said, tapping her fingers on the arm of the captain's chair.

"Very good, Commodore Wolfe. Continue doing your duty for Starfleet and the security of the Federation. Commendations will be in order for you and your crew when this is all over with. Admiral out."

The screen rippled back to show Memory Prime as a black splotch against the starfield, glittering with the lights that ringed its semicircle of seven domes.

"What a load of tribble droppings," Wolfe said loudly enough for all to hear.

Uhura couldn't resist. "Tribbles don't leave droppings, Commodore."

"Exactly," Wolfe said as she spun in her chair to face Uhura, making Abranand jump to the side. "Nothing! Which is what that brass-hulled dunsel just gave us. I don't believe it. I don't believe it." She let the chair swing her back to the screen, then stepped down.

"What don't you believe?" Uhura asked, though she expected Wolfe to simply order her to mind her own business.

"Look, Lieutenant," Wolfe explained as she stood on the steps leading to the upper deck and the turbolift, "there's obviously a very important operation under way here. You of all people must know that the selective jamming Komack just admitted to should be impossible. A whole new technology is being used here and I'm not being told what it is. 'Continue doing your duty!' " she parroted. "What does he think I am? A wet-behind-the-ears pup like those two?" The commodore waved a thumb behind her at the ensigns at the helm and engineering stations. Uhura winced for them.

The commodore stormed to the lift doors. They sprang open, but Wolfe turned on her heel and addressed herself to the whole bridge crew.

"I don't know what it was Kirk was doing on this ship that gave it such a miserable rep, but he sure as hell isn't going to rub his bad command decisions off on me. I've got my full retirement benefits coming and I intend to collect them." She whirled back into the turbolift just as a warning beep sounded from the helm's ship's status sensors.

"What now?" Wolfe snapped as she stepped forward to block the closing lift doors.

The wet-behind-the-ears pup at the helm control read the sensor light. "Unauthorized transportation, Commodore. Infraship."

The cause was obvious, even to Wolfe. She raced to the command chair. *"Full shields now!"* she shouted as she hit the security call button on the chair's arm. "Security to the brig on the double!" She twisted back to the frantic ensign at the engineering station. "Where are those shields, mister?"

"Too late," the helmsman said. He turned to look at the commodore. Uhura was glad to see he wasn't smiling. "Transporter has shut down. Successful transmission."

Wolfe looked as if she were ready to breathe fire. "So help me," she said in an iron voice, "if I find that your pointy-eared Vulcan shipmate had any help at all in staging this—*any!*—I'll scuttle this ship and everyone on it. Do I make myself clear?"

The crew responded that she did.

"You," Wolfe said, pointing to the ensign at engineering. "Confined to quarters and downgraded two ratings." She turned to Uhura. "Who's the transporter chief on duty?"

"Kyle," Uhura said. Unfortunately there was no way to keep the information from Wolfe; the computer could answer just as easily.

"Have security take him to the brig for dereliction of duty and—"

Uhura had had enough. At the rate the commodore was going through bridge crew, soon she'd have no choice but to get Chekov and Sulu up there again, hesitations and all. "Commodore, I protest! You cannot—"

"Yes I can!" Wolfe drowned Uhura out. "Lieutenant Abranand, place this woman under arrest as suspected accessory to the escape of a dangerous prisoner."

Uhura threw her receiver on her chair and shut down her board. Around the bridge, other crew started to rise from their stations, glaring at Wolfe.

"Just try it," Wolfe told them, sweeping her gaze across them all. "Any of you. All of you. I just don't care. The hangar deck is big enough to hold the whole damn crew and I'll arrest all of you if you think it will make your captain happy."

The crew held their places.

"It's all right," Uhura said. "Sit down."

They sat. Wolfe was fuming. She turned to Farl, whom Uhura had noticed trying to stay uninvolved in what the Andorian undoubtedly felt was threatening to become a mutiny.

"Commander, I want your men to enforce a recall of all *Enterprise* personnel on leave on Prime. That's an order."

Farl saluted and marched to the turbolift. Wolfe gloated as Abranand escorted Uhura to the lift as well.

"Believe me, Lieutenant," Wolfe said, "by the time I'm finished with this ship, your captain isn't going to know what hit him. Count on it."

"That's the difference between you and Captain Kirk," Uhura said.

"What's that?"

"His crew *can* count on him. And he's never let us down yet."

"Is that a threat, Lieutenant?"

Uhura smiled coldly. "It doesn't have to be. It's the truth."

Kirk paced the floor in the communal area of Salman Nensi's quarters. He was incapable of sitting still as his mind turned over all the possibilities he was faced with. Nensi and Romaine had brought him, McCoy, and Scott to the chief administrator's residence in order to add a third major piece to the puzzle: the synthetic consciousnesses known as the Pathfinders, the only known independent machine intelligences sanctioned by law to exist in the Federation, were somehow involved in the complex web of mystery that had drawn together the *Enterprise* and Memory Prime.

Another idea suddenly came to the captain and he stopped his pacing to question Nensi.

"Is there any chance that another program—a thirteenth consciousness—has been inserted into the Pathfinder complex?" Kirk asked. "Perhaps the intelligence itself could be the terrorists' weapon. At the proper time, it could crash a turbolift, shut off life support. . . ." Kirk held his hands out as if to gather comments.

"No chance at all," Romaine said. "First of all, the Pathfinders can't be programmed in the traditional sense. New synthetic consciousnesses can be added to the facility, but only with the full compliance of the entire interface team. Plus the whole I/O system would have to be shut down, manual connections made; no way it could be done without disrupting the entire base. Additionally, the Pathfinders have no direct link to the outside. There's no possible way they can control any of the systems in Prime."

"Why all the elaborate safeguards?" Kirk asked, sorry to see his theory shot down.

"Well, the programming safeguard is for the Pathfinders' protection. Like humans having the right not to have brain surgery without giving their consent, and then only having it performed by trained physicians under safe conditions. If something goes wrong with their hardware, Captain, those consciousnesses will die. Under those circumstances, the safeguards aren't elaborate. They're necessary."

"But surely they can be backed up," Scott asked. "They *are* just impulses in circuitry, after all."

Romaine smiled at him. "Just as the human mind is impulses in protein circuitry, Scotty. Yet we can't back ourselves up." She took Scott's hand but looked back to the captain. "That was one of the turning points of the Synthetic Revolt on Titan. A probeshipmind, realizing that the old Sol Council wasn't going to budge on its rulings that machine consciousnesses were commodities, backed itself up in a public databank in Iceland and thrust straight into the Sun. The backup was notarized to prove it contained all the data that the original shipmind had contained and could carry out the same autonomous equipment maintenance subroutines, but it had no personality, no consciousness—"

"No soul," McCoy added.

"A bit romantic, perhaps, but close enough to the core of their arguments. We know now that a synthetic consciousness must develop from a smaller, self-generating seed program. A full synthetic consciousness backup, when stored, loses that impetus to thought, the flow of current through circuitry. When the data pattern is frozen in storage, there is as yet no way to make it become self-aware again, any more than a vat filled with all the chemical components of a human body can spontaneously come to life. It has to grow and be nurtured from an embryonic form.

"Anyway, the shipmind's experiment was controversial. The opponents of the Freedom for Synthetics movement claimed it was all programming trickery, that the probe ship hadn't made a complete backup copy of itself, that it hadn't been installed on board the ship that burned up in the sun. But the gesture—the suicide, if you will—was enough to tip the balance at the polls. The Worlds Court ruled that if an intelligence could die, then by definition it must have been alive. The resolution banning the ownership of synthetic consciousnesses was passed just as the Federation was born. Our strict edicts against slavery have always been applied to self-aware machines as well as self-aware biological creatures, and now, more than ever, energy matrices as well."

"So with all that concern for their well-being, why aren't the Pathfinders allowed to have more control over their environment?" Kirk asked.

"Oh, they have complete control over *their* environment, Captain," Romaine said. "They can do whatever they want within the confines of their circuits, what they call the world of Transition. We just don't want them to have any control over *our* environment."

"Leftovers from the Titan massacre, I suppose," McCoy said.

"Partly," Romaine agreed. "When those domes opened, thousands of workers were killed, and people don't tend to forget things like that. But mostly it's because the risk is too great that the Pathfinders might make a mistake. Again, not from their point of view but from ours." She looked back to Kirk. "Captain, it's common knowledge that almost all Starfleet vessels have the capacity for self-destruction, but how many officers actually have the authority to initiate it?"

"Classified," Kirk said with a smile, "though the point is taken. I doubt if any of my crew would misuse the authority to order self-destruct or any other potentially harmful procedure, but by limiting access to those procedures we do limit the possibilities for tragic errors."

"So," Nensi said after a moment, "history lessons aside, we need to find another common link to unite all the pieces in our puzzle." He checked them off on his fingers. "Pathfinders. Memory Prime military emergency. *Enterprise* Alpha emergency."

"Already linked by hints of an assassination attempt," Scott added, "Nobel and Z.Magnees Prize nominees, and . . . ?" He trailed off, trying to think of what other events merited inclusion in the list.

"Those are the broad conditions," Kirk said, pacing once more. "Damn, we could use Spock down here." He paused again. "Spock's arrest. The name or term T'Pel. What do they add to the equation?"

Romaine abruptly leaned forward and let go of Scott's hand. "Three of the Vulcans on my staff were placed under arrest by Commander Farl just before you arrived," she said.

"What are their names?" Kirk asked excitedly.

"Specialist Lieutenant Stell, Specialist First-Class Slaan, and Dr. T'Lar," Romaine recited. "A computer technician, computer technology historian, and a paleoexobiologist, respectively."

"Now we're getting somewhere," Kirk said. "Two Vulcan computer specialists and Spock is a Vulcan computer specialist. That's a connection."

"Then why was a paleoexobiologist arrested, too, Jim?" McCoy asked.

"And of the four other Vulcans on my staff, three of them are also computer specialists." Romaine shrugged at the disappointment Kirk struggled to hide on his face. "Sorry, but what do you expect at the Federation's largest computer complex?"

Kirk rubbed his hands over his face. "And no one else, no other Vulcans were arrested on the other ships transporting nominees here?"

"No," Nensi said, suddenly thoughtful, "but some of the commanders did point out that they were operating with less than full crews. Let me check to see if there's a pattern among the crew members left behind." He got up and went to the kitchen area, where a private wall com hung.

"And ask about the reasons why the crew was left behind," Kirk called after him. "Vulcans, Vulcans. Starfleet was worried that a Vulcan might have been involved in a threatened act of assassination. But why just *some* Vulcans? Why not all?"

"What reason did they give when Spock was arrested?" Romaine asked.

"Suspicion of involvement in the dilithium burnout," Scott answered. "A crock if I ever heard one."

"And what's going to happen to him?" Romaine continued.

"He'll be held until he can be turned over to appropriate Starfleet authorities," Kirk said, resuming his pacing.

"What sort of appropriate Starfleet authorities?" Romaine pressed on.

Kirk answered without considering where the woman was going with her questions. "Starbase, I suppose," he said.

"Prime could be a Starbase," Romaine said.

Kirk stopped in midpace.

"It's a *base*," Romaine explained. "And it *is* under Starfleet authority."

Kirk walked over to Romaine and held his hands out as if he planned to lift her by her ears and kiss her. Fortunately, he checked his enthusiasm.

"And *you're* the base commander," he said. "Brilliant!"

Scott looked confused.

"The lass is . . ." He turned to Romaine beside him. "You're the commander?"

"It's political," she said to him. To the captain she added, "But only in a non-military capacity."

"Spock isn't Starfleet military personnel," Kirk said, trying out his ideas as he voiced them. "Technically he's scientific services and the alleged attempted-assassination victim was a nonmilitary scientist." He turned to McCoy, eyes twinkling. "It sounds like a *civil* offense to me. Definitely nonmilitary and therefore within Mira's jurisdiction. What do you think, Bones?"

McCoy nodded. "Go for it, Jim. With any luck Commander Farl will be out on maneuvers and won't be able to answer Wolfe's frenzied inquiries. Which I'm sure she'll make."

"Are you up to taking on the Starfleet bureaucracy?" Kirk asked Romaine.

She pointed to the kitchen, where Nensi leaned over a counter, talking earnestly into a handset. "Taught by experts," she said. "Bureaucracy is Uncle Sal's middle name."

"Good," Kirk said, "good." He clapped his hands together, a decision made. He looked over to McCoy. "Well, Bones, you were right again. Out on the frontier, we'd go in with phasers blazing, but here we are, achieving victory by wrapping up the enemy with red tape. How's that for doing things within the system?"

"Achieving victory, Jim?" McCoy pulled himself out of the chair that had appeared ready to absorb him. "You're talking as if we've already won."

"Believe me, Doctor, if I didn't think we were going to win, we'd still be sitting around trying to come up with another good idea instead of getting set to beam back up and spring Spock."

Kirk flipped open his communicator and checked to see that Nensi was prepared for what was coming. The chief administrator replaced the handset on the wall com and headed back to the communal area. Kirk's communicator chirped as it opened the beam back channel.

"Kirk to *Enterprise,*" the captain announced. "Five to beam up, Mr. Kyle. These coordinates."

Kirk slipped the communicator back onto his belt. The five of them stood silently in the apartment, waiting for the transporter beam to lock on.

After a few seconds of silence, McCoy reached out to touch Kirk's arm. "This delay isn't right, Jim."

"Aye," Scotty said.

Kirk reached back for his communicator again. He didn't have to say anything. He knew from their expressions that both Scotty and McCoy saw the understanding, the agreement in his eyes.

The transporter chime finally started just as Kirk was about to call back up, but its arrival did nothing to change his feeling that something had gone terribly wrong on board his ship.

The corridor leading to the brig was lined with five of Wolfe's starbase troopers and Kirk felt his rage expand exponentially with each additional trooper who appeared in Spock's cell. Spock himself was nowhere to be seen, but Commodore Wolfe was. She was watching carefully as a technician explained something to her on the library reader on Spock's desk. Kirk recognized the technician as Ensign Bregman, a trainee from Kyle's department.

"If you've let anything happen to Spock, Commodore, I'll—"

"Save the mutiny for your court-martial, Captain." The tone Wolfe used to cut him off told Kirk her anger was no less than his own. "Your innocent science officer just escaped."

Kirk was completely taken off guard. He stepped to the side as Romaine, Nensi, Scott, and McCoy crowded into the cell behind him. Commander Farl leaned against the far wall as if he hoped no one would see him.

"Escaped? How?" Kirk asked. He checked the security field frame around the doorway and saw it was intact.

"Beamed himself down," Wolfe said. "Hooked into the transporter controls from his library reader." She glared at Kirk. "The one *you* were so anxious to give him."

"Now wait just a minute," Scott said, pushing his way through the knot of people to get close to Wolfe. "I know every circuit on this ship and there's no way the transporter can be controlled by a reader. I'd stake my reputation on it."

Wolfe laughed cynically. "You don't have a reputation anymore, Mr. Engineer. None of you do. This whole ship should be fumigated, then opened to space." She turned to the technician who had been pointing to the reader's screen. "Again," she ordered.

"Um, as near as I can figure out," Ensign Bregman began, "Mr. Spock didn't actually control the transporter *from* the reader, but he did set up a snowball chain in the simulations program library."

"A snowball chain?" McCoy asked dubiously.

"That's where one small program runs a slightly larger one, which runs an even larger one, and so on until a huge complex program is up and running. You see, he must have called up transporter simulation programs from the education upgrade files. The reader won't allow programming but does permit a user to store certain variables in the simulation files for playback of customized scenarios at a later time, so Mr. Spock set up all the coordinates he needed for a simulated transporter room to lock on to him here. See?" Bregman pointed to the screen again. "Here are the exact simulations he used with the coordinates of this cell still entered."

Scott, Wolfe, Kirk, and Romaine crowded together to peer at the small screen and the flowchart the technician drew on it. He showed how Spock had chained the transporter simulations with a wargame scenario that postulated that the hardwired communication channels within the ship had been severed by enemy fire. That was chained to a rescue simulation in which ship mechanism controls usually monitored and adjusted by direct connection were instead remotely controlled by extremely short-range subspace transmissions. That, in turn, was chained to a programming bypass simulation that had the ship's computer damaged and capable only of carrying out direct requests. In this case, the direct requests were set up to be read from the transporter simulation.

Five more subsystem wiring-and-repair simulations joined the chain until only one two-line piece of code remained at the top of the snowball's path.

"And what do those two lines of code do?" Kirk asked just as he heard Scotty exhale with a combination of surprise and what sounded like admiration.

"It's just a small software flag that warns the computer that everything that follows is a simulation." The technician dropped his voice. "Mr. Spock overwrote it by storing some of his library files in the wrong memory locations. The computer queried him but it accepted his priority override to allow him to commit the error."

"The same override that lets me run the engines at warp eight when the computer says we dinna hae the power," Scott said, shaking his head.

"So the computer operated all the controls on the real equipment and beamed him out," Bregman said.

"But it still doesn't explain how he found another place to beam to," Scott complained. "None of the ship's simulations would hold the exact coordinates for beaming down to Memory Prime, and even Mr. Spock couldn't calculate them without a locator beam."

"He didn't have to," Commander Farl said dryly from the side of the cell. "All he had to do was get within a few kilometerss of Prime on a low-path beam and our combat transporterss automatically pulled in hiss signal." Farl sighed. "I have two unconsciouss trooperss by a transfer-point pad. The pad'ss log showss it received an incoming signal fifteen minutess ago. The same time as the Vulcan'ss unauthorized beam-down wass detected. He iss on Memory Prime."

Kirk was filled with conflicting emotions. Spock would not defy Starfleet authority so brazenly by escaping what even he had admitted was legal, if improper, incarceration. Whatever had prompted him to act so out of character had to be big. Disastrously big. But whatever else he did or had to do, Kirk did not want to give any information at all to Wolfe. For some reason she had turned her "temporary" command of the *Enterprise* into a vendetta.

"Well," Kirk said as he stepped back to leave the cell, "it's a small facility and Chief Technician Romaine and Mr. Nensi know it well. I don't think there'll be any problem in our finding him."

"Just a minute," Wolfe said, stopping him as he directed his entourage to the door. "You're not going anywhere."

Kirk turned to face her. The cell was completely silent as the faceoff began. "I am going back to Memory Prime to locate my first officer," he told her.

"All off-duty personnel are restricted to this ship, Captain."

"I'm not off duty."

"You are now, Captain. You're sure not commanding this ship any longer."

Kirk had had enough. "You cannot relieve me of command on my own ship, Commodore."

"Alpha emergency, Kirk. You're under my orders for the duration."

"Without Starfleet confirmation of those orders," Kirk recited, "it is my opinion that you might be endangering the health and safety of my crew, without proper authority."

Instantly both Wolfe and Kirk turned to McCoy.

"I'm sure the ship's medical officer might find that grounds for relieving *you* of *your* command," Kirk continued.

"This ship has no medical officer," Wolfe countered. "Dr. McCoy, you are relieved of duty for suspicion of aiding in a prisoner's escape. Next move's yours, Captain. Want to see how many more it takes before you're in here in place of your science officer?"

Kirk knew enough to back off if it meant keeping his freedom. That could be the key to another confrontation, one that he could orchestrate and win. But not here, and not now.

"All right, Commodore," he said, holding his hands out as if to show he wasn't armed. "For the duration." He watched as she looked around the room once more, making sure all of her people met her eyes to acknowledge that she had squared off against the fabled James T. Kirk and had won.

"Good boy," she said icily. "Maybe Command will just accept a resignation and let you crawl off quietly." Then she turned away and called to Farl. "Prepare to have the search parties fan out from the pad the Vulcan landed at," she said. "You can have five troopers from my contingent to help with the operation." Farl began whispering in an Andorian combat dialect into his battle helmet communicator.

Kirk started backing out of the cell. He had to organize his response for when Spock was returned to the ship and they could plan their next move together. But he stopped, blood freezing in his veins when he heard Farl's next question and the commodore's response.

"Disposition of the prisoner when he iss recaptured?" Farl asked.

"There will be no prisoner, Commander Farl," Wolfe stated plainly. "With who we've got down on Memory Prime, we can't afford to take any more chances. At my order, when your troopers run the escaped prisoner to ground, I want your phasers set to force three."

She turned to stare directly into Kirk's eyes.

"To kill," she said.

Seventeen

The Klingons loved to tell the story of al Fred ber'nhard Nob'l, the *tera'ngan* inventor who, as had happened so many times on so many worlds, once felt he had gone too far and had created the ultimate weapon.

Faced with nightmares of a world ruined by the destructive forces he had called into being, Nob'l attempted to salve his conscience and bring forth the best in humans by using the profits from his inventions to award prizes in honor of the most outstanding achievements in science and peace. Of course, in typical *tera'ngan* fashion, as the Klingons were quick to point out, those profits were not set aside for that purpose until *after* the inventor's death.

As the long Terran years passed, Nob'l's inventions served the warlords of Earth well. Despite his fears, other ultimate weapons came and went with predictable regularity—mustard gas, fusion bombs, particle curtains, and smart bacteria—until his devices lay beside the rocks and sharpened sticks in museums. In fact, and this invariably had the Klingons brushing the tears of laughter from their eyes no matter how many times they heard the story, the only real casualty of the great Terran wars fueled by Nob'l's inventions over the century in which his prizes were awarded, were the prizes themselves. *Three* times they were suspended because of hostilities between nations. The third time, as Earth shuddered beneath the multiple onslaughts of its warriors Klingons admired most—k'Han and g'Reen—the suspended prizes were not resurrected, and lay buried amid the ashes of so much of the Earth that the Klingons considered foul and weak and better lost

For the events a few light-years removed from Earth, the Klingons had a bit more respect. Two centuries before Nob'l lay awake in foolish terror over destroying his world with a few tonnes of $C_3H_5(NO_3)_3$, the warlord Zalar Mag'nees, ruler of her planet's greatest city state, realized that the nature of combat in her world was changing and that ideas as well as strength and armaments must be brought to battle.

Mag'nees established an elaborate educational system designed to attract the greatest intellects among her citizens to the problems of war. Those who contributed the best new work achieved the highest honor: a commission in the warlord's personal corps of scientists.

Under her rule, with the brilliant work of her honored scientists and engineers, the whole of the planet was soon united, or conquered, as the Klingons told it, under one ruler. Though the warlord's commissions were discontinued after almost two centuries of global peace and their war-born heritage forgotten, the philosophy of subterfuge and protective concealment that had proved so useful in establishing the undisputed rule of Mag'nees, still pervaded all levels of her planet's society. Thus, when electromagnetic communication systems were discovered,, it went without question that the signals would travel by wire instead of by atmospheric transmissions open to any unsuspected enemy's receivers. Power plants were buried as a matter of course and fiberoptic transmission of all signals was enthusiastically adopted as soon as the technology became available. It was this inborn need for concealment that prevented *tera'ngan* scientists, in almost a century of scanning, from ever picking up the slightest datum that would indicate that a comparable, perhaps even related civilization was thriving in the Alpha Centauran system, fewer than five light-years distant.

The Klingons bitterly regretted that circumstance of history. For when at last the first slower-than-light Earth ship arrived in the Centauran system, the *tera'ngan* humans were too tired of war, the *centaur'ngan* humans long unschooled. To the Klingons' everlasting disappointment, in this one instance of first contact, unlike most others, peace was inevitable.

In the decades that followed, as the two planets discovered all the suspicious similarities between them, cultural and scientific exchange programs burgeoned. Zeyafram Co'akran's brilliant insights into warp theory were applied at the venerable Massachusetts Institute of Technology on Earth, and within seven years of the two planets' first contact, the light barrier had fallen before their mutual onslaught. Plays and literature were easily translated and meaningful to the two races and— hinting at interference from another spacefaring race thousands of years earlier— interbreeding was simple and pleasurable to all concerned, requiring none of the heroic efforts that would later be needed by humans and Vulcans.

More and more the two cultures grew together. Common goals were quickly decided and impressively established. The joint colonization of the second life-bearing world in the Centauran system was accomplished with goodwill and an almost unbelievable absence of territorial discord. Klingon psychologists who had studied that abnormal enterprise felt the experience was what had most influenced the incomprehensible optimism and peaceful nature of the Federation when it was first formed.

As the *tera'ngan* and *centaur'ngan* association grew, both looked to their pasts and dusted off the legacy of Nob'l and Mag'nees. Freed of their military legacy, joined in the best wishes of two worlds, and expanded to include sciences unimagined at the time the awards were first created, the Nob'l and Z.Mag'nees Prizes became the first human competition to celebrate the achievements, scientific and cultural, of two different worlds, and drive them forward in peace.

Upon its formation, the Federation Council eagerly accepted authority over the competition, opening it up to all members of all species. In an interplanetary association in which athletic competitions had ceased to have any meaning, except among those rare few who voluntarily chose to restrict themselves to absolutely identical advantages of gravity, genetics, and pharmaceutical enhancement, the Nob'l and Z.Mag'nees competition of the mind quickly came to stand for all the ideals for which the Federation strove. Calling on another ancient tradition, the prizes were awarded every four standard years. The winners, chosen through secret ballot by their peers who shared in the nomination for each prize, were among the most honored of Federation citizens. And true to the Federation's long-term goals, pressure was mounting to offer the Klingons a chance to participate.

The Klingons, not surprisingly, would have nothing to do with the Nob'l and Z.Mag'nees Prizes. The whole concept of the competition was alien and repugnant to them. The Klingons *did* have their own competitions for scientific achievement that, on first study, seemed somewhat similar to the Federation's awards; each decade on Klinzhai, a great celebration was held for those workers who had won the coveted Emperor's Decoration for Science in Aid of Destruction of the Enemy.

The Klingons could easily understand the concept of honoring the winners, but what they could never comprehend was why, in the human competition, the losers were allowed to *live*.

Eighteen

Kirk smiled broadly as he walked down the corridor leading to the brig. McCoy accompanied him but certainly wasn't grinning; in fact he was having trouble keeping the scowl off his face.

"It'll be all right, Bones," Kirk said, elbowing his friend in the side. "Trust me."

McCoy rolled his eyes. "Remind me to do that when we're locked up on Tantalus playing poker with each other for twenty years."

Kirk and McCoy rounded the corner to the corridor that ran to the holding cells. As Kirk had been able to determine by checking the ship's computer, only two of Wolfe's troopers remained stationed there. The others who had been milling around, investigating Spock's escape twenty minutes ago, were already down on Memory Prime, searching for Spock, their phasers set to kill.

"Sergeant Gilmartin," Kirk said in a friendly tone. "We're back. General Regulation Document two hundred and twenty-seven again. Paragraphs B and C."

Gilmartin turned to look at the other trooper standing at attention on the other side of the holding-cell door. Kirk glanced through the open doorway, its perimeter glowing with the security-field frame, and nodded slightly to Uhura, indicating that she should go along with whatever was to happen next.

Gilmartin turned back to Kirk. "Begging the captain's pardon, sir, but I believe Dr. McCoy has been relieved of duty." The trooper looked nervous but he was bound to follow his orders.

"As chief medical officer," Kirk agreed. "But he's still a doctor and able to act as such." Kirk read the trooper's eyes for a moment, then continued. "I'm Lieutenant Uhura's counsel now and she is entitled to a medical examination while being held. Regulations require it."

Gilmartin took a deep breath. "I'll have to check it out with the Commodore, Captain."

"I wouldn't expect you not to, Sergeant," Kirk said graciously, and gestured to the intercom panel.

As Gilmartin stepped over to the intercom, it was clear that talking to the commodore was the last thing he wanted to do. Kirk stepped in front of the holding-cell doorway and lifted his hand as if to wave in greeting to Uhura. Then he brought his arm down and around the neck of the second trooper by the side of the doorway and flipped him into the security field.

Gilmartin spun at the sound of the crackling repulser screen just as McCoy held a spray hypo to his neck. By the time Gilmartin could bring his hand up to try and knock the hypo away, it was too late. McCoy gently lowered the trooper to the ground and Kirk caught the second guard, now unconscious, as he bounced back from the field. Then the captain went back to the doorway to speak to Uhura.

"Listen very carefully," he said quickly. "A contingent of troopers is hunting for Spock on Memory Prime. With orders to kill." He paused a moment to let that sink in. "All *Enterprise* personnel are ordered restricted to the ship. McCoy, Scott, and I are disobeying those orders and going down to try and locate Spock before the troopers do. We'll have help down there, but no matter what happens, we will be disobeying a direct order from a superior officer. Do you understand?"

Uhura's expression was serious but displayed no fear. "Yes sir," she said.

"The best that can happen to us is that we will save Spock's life and he will then be proven innocent of all charges. In that case, those of us who left the ship to find him will be given severe reprimands and probably lose rank. For what it's worth, I believe there's a good chance that the commodore has either misunderstood her orders or has received false ones. We can't use that as a defense, but it might make Starfleet more lenient." Kirk paused to consider his next words. "Nyota, this is not an order. It can't be an order. But I could use your help."

Uhura began to reply but Kirk shook his head and held up a silencing finger.

"As long as this field is on and you remain in the cell," he told her, "you're safe and protected. As soon as the field goes off, you're on the run with us. Understand?"

"Understood, sir," Uhura said evenly. "Request permission to accompany the captain."

Scott was standing by in the starboard cargo transporter room when McCoy, Kirk, and Uhura rushed in.

"Ready, Scotty?" Kirk asked as he passed out the small hand phasers and communicators that Scott had brought.

"Aye, Captain," Scott replied, checking the chronometer on the transporter console. "Fifteen more seconds. Coordinates are set for Mr. Nensi's office."

Kirk, McCoy, and Uhura quickly took their places. Exactly fifteen seconds after Scott had given the chronometer's reading, the light strips flickered and the engineer's hands flew over the controls.

"What was that?" Uhura asked as the lights came back to normal intensity.

"Och," Scott said as he ran to the oversized platform. "That was a clumsy ensign who just happened to drop a circuit plaser on a disassembled junction switch in a forward Jefferies tube."

"What does that do?"

Scott smiled as the transporter effect sparkled around him.

"It shuts down the shields, lass," he said, and they were gone.

Kirk and Scott materialized on a two-pad portable combat transporter in a small equipment storage bay. Two starbase troopers in full battle armor were waiting for them, phaser rifles at the ready, the impenetrable black visor of their helmets making each look like an impassive Cyclops.

Without having to be told, Kirk and Scott raised their hands above their heads.

"Sorry, Scotty," Kirk said.

"My fault, Captain. I was sure I had gone to a beam path high enough to override this devil's capture mode. They must hae modified th—"

"Enough talking," one of the troopers said over a suit communicator. The slightly distorted voice echoed against the metal walls of the storage bay.

"Step down." The closer trooper gestured with the phaser barrel.

Kirk kept his hands in the air and hopped down the half meter from the small platform to the bay flooring. He turned his head to say, "Careful with your leg, Scotty. You know what happened last time."

"Aye, Captain," Scott said as he carefully moved to the edge of the transporter unit and gingerly stepped down from it. He lowered one hand and rubbed his right knee with a grimace. "It's still pretty bunged up, sir," he said.

While the first trooper kept the prisoners covered, the second trooper harnessed his rifle and removed two sets of magnatomic adhesion manacles. "Hands back up," he growled to Scott as he approached.

Scott complied, favoring his leg. The trooper stood to the side to give his companion a clear shot if the prisoners tried anything. He held out the first manacle, palmed the activate switch on the control surface of the bar, and said to Scott, "Turn around."

Kirk's eyes met Scott's as the engineer slowly turned. Suddenly Scott's leg buckled and he collapsed to the floor with a moan of pain, reaching out for support and grabbing on to the first trooper's arm.

As the first trooper tried to pull back, Kirk leaned down as if to grab Scott's other arm and stepped into the second trooper's line of fire and of sight. He couldn't shoot now without risking a hit on his companion.

"Move away!" the second trooper ordered. "Back off, now!"

Scotty moaned in terrible agony and refused to relinquish his grip.

"Here, let me," Kirk said as he went to pull up on Scott's arm. Instead he grabbed the activated manacle and slapped it against the first trooper's helmet. The impact immediately triggered the charge release in the device and the bar flowed around the trooper's helmet until the two ends met and joined. The bar quickly flattened and spread across the visor, rendering the trooper blind. He stumbled backward, clawing at the manacle. With a crash, he tripped over a low cargo crate and pitched to the flooring.

The second trooper backed away and held his rifle on Kirk. But by then, both Scott and Kirk held their phasers on the trooper.

"One or the other," Kirk said bluntly, "but not both. Put down your rifle, soldier."

The trooper hesitated, his intentions impossible to read through his visor.

"I don't want to say this twice," Kirk said.

The trooper raised his rifle.

"You're not giving us any choice," Kirk continued. "On the count of three, Mr. Scott. One."

As Kirk said "Two," he and his engineer both fired at the trooper's phaser rifle, blasting it from the unprepared trooper's hands.

"Keep going, full power!" Kirk called out to Scott over the whine of their phasers, then stopped firing his weapon and adjusted its setting wheel to "sweep."

When Kirk fired again, a low-power standing wave of phased radiation engulfed the trooper front and back. Combined with the full-power output of Scott's weapon, the absorbed and redirected energy that coursed through the trooper's protective induction mesh had nowhere to go, resonating throughout the armor's circuitry until the regulator overloaded and the energy locked in phase with the trooper's nervous system.

The trooper crumpled and Kirk and Scott stopped firing. Other than a slight ringing in their ears from the phasers' whine, the storage room was silent. But only for a moment.

"Turn slowly," a voice in the shadows commanded, "and drop your phasers."

Kirk and Scott spun to see the first trooper step out from beside a tall stack of glittering alignment alloy shipping crates. He held a phaser II leveled at them and he had removed his helmet.

Kirk realized that another piece of the puzzle was about to fall into place. The trooper was a Vulcan.

"Where's the Captain?" Nensi asked.

"And Scotty?" Romaine added.

McCoy and Uhura looked around the chief administrator's office and saw at once that Kirk and Scott had not materialized with them.

"They were right beside us," Uhura said. "I was just talking with Mr. Scott."

"The *Enterprise*'s shields?" Nensi asked grimly, fearing the worst.

"Mr. Scott arranged to have them shut down," McCoy said. "Besides, we were all in the same beam. If Uhura and I got through, then they must have, too."

"Farl's combat pads?" Romaine asked Nensi.

"Possible," Nensi said, "though I'm sure Mr. Scott would have been able to override them with the *Enterprise*'s system."

There was a moment of confused silence, finally broken by McCoy.

"Look, wherever they are, they're going to be looking for Spock. We have no way of tracking them because we have no way of knowing where they came down and we can't raise them by communicator without giving the troopers a chance to trace our signals. But we do know where Spock came down thirty minutes ago. I say we start there."

Nensi felt McCoy's call to action galvanize the group. For all his country-doctor ways, he was still a Starfleet officer and knew how to act like one.

Romaine held out her hand. "Who brought Spock's file?" she asked. Nensi could see she was hoping it wasn't with Kirk or Scott.

McCoy handed over a computer data wafer and Romaine went to Nensi's desk, inserted the wafer in the reader, and began to input on the keypad.

"Pardon," a mechanically flat voice said as an associate trundled through the door to Nensi's office.

"What's that?" Uhura asked as the machine rolled over to Romaine and extended an eyestalk.

"An associate," Nensi explained. "We have special dispensation from the Department of Labor to use robot workers, at least until the facilities are completed and we can bring in enough personnel without overtaxing the environmental systems."

"How autonomous are they?" McCoy asked, watching Romaine talk with the device.

"Not very," Nensi said. "Their onboard brain is a standard duotronic Sprite model, good for basic problem solving and conversation. A central control computer sets up their goals and schedules, based on researcher and staff requests, then dispatches them to carry out their work on their own. Just like all those repair drones at spacedock, but modified to operate under benign environmental conditions. It actually cost more to buy them that way, without all the extra armor and shielding. We have a couple hundred of them."

"What's Mira doing with it?" Uhura asked.

"The associates are also a message relay system. The computer downloads dispatch requests to the associates, and if the associates happen to come across a person who has a dispatch waiting, then the machine can upload it and pass it along. It's not very cost effective, but they're rolling around anyway, so it makes sense."

"Ah," Uhura said as she made the connection. "That's why you wanted Mr. Spock's data file. It includes his identification holos and now all the associates are going to be looking for him as well." She turned to Nensi. "But what kind of message can you pass on to him that will convince him it's not the commodore trying to locate him?"

"I'm not sure," Nensi said. "Apparently your captain has a large variety of codes that he's established with you people to cover all sorts of eventualities—" McCoy and Uhura nodded "—and he said he'd include one on the data file. Presumably, Mr. Spock will be able to determine the message's authenticity and send a suitable reply."

"So we'll be able to talk through the associates without Wolfe's people being aware of it?" McCoy asked.

"As long as we don't do it in real time," Romaine said as she stepped away from the desk and joined the others. "Voice communication is out but stored messages are encrypted. I don't think Farl will think to intercept those communications and I'm certain Wolfe doesn't even know about them."

"This module has other duties," the associate said as it lowered its eyestalk and wheeled in front of Nensi's desk. "Pardon, pardon." It rolled past to the door.

"So now what?" Romaine asked the doctor, unconsciously deferring to him as the group's commanding officer.

"First, we get out of our uniforms," McCoy said. Nensi gestured to a stack of clothes that Kirk had requested, resting on a visitor's chair by the wall. "Then we start looking for Spock," McCoy continued, "beginning with the areas around the portable transporter pad he was traced to."

"I've got the maps on the desk screen," Romaine said as Nensi handed a technician's jumpsuit to McCoy and one of Romaine's off-duty outfits to Uhura.

The two *Enterprise* officers held the clothes awkwardly for a moment. Then

McCoy turned to Uhura, smiled, and said, "It's all right, Lieutenant, I'm a doctor." For a moment, it seemed as if McCoy was about to say something more, but didn't. Judging from the way the officers then laughed, Nensi felt there must have been something else to the doctor's comment than was apparent on the surface, but he shrugged it off and went over to study the maps with Romaine, leaving the two to quickly change.

A few minutes later, Romaine traced out a section of corridors that she had indicated in red on the desktop display screen. McCoy, Uhura, and Nensi studied them closely.

"I can't pretend to match a Vulcan's logic," Romaine said, "but I'm assuming that Mr. Spock's first priority will be to escape recapture, therefore he will attempt to increase, as quickly as possible, the area in which he might be found. This service corridor handles all the waste-disposal and energy-distribution needs of the residential domes, interconnecting with them all. If he gets into it, then within the hour he could have access to almost half the nonrestricted facility."

"Would Spock know that?" McCoy asked.

"Prime is patterned on standard starbase weapons labs. I'm assuming that Spock would know the layouts of those and act accordingly."

"So with half the facility to choose from, where should we start *our* search?" Uhura asked.

"Again," Romaine began, "I'm assuming that his second goal is to escape. I'm hoping that Farl will also do the logical thing and concentrate his search in this direction to cut off Spock's access to the shuttle landing bay and the main transporter station."

"And if Farl's doing the logical thing, what in blazes is Spock supposed to do?" McCoy asked in annoyance.

"Head in this direction," Romaine said, running her finger along a twisting chain of tunnels that led away from the transport center of Prime. "Weapons-lab emergency-evacuation transporter modules are located on the perimeters of each of these domes."

"But this isn't a weapons lab," McCoy protested. "Why would they build evacuation transporters in a facility where there's no chance of it blowing up?"

Romaine looked across at McCoy, staring intently into his eyes. "You were at Memory Alpha, Dr. McCoy. You saw what happened to those people."

McCoy nodded his head in silent understanding.

"That isn't going to happen again," Romaine said. "Not to me. Not to anyone."

"Mira was on the implementation team," Nensi added. "The evacuation modules are there because of her."

"Then Farl will know about them, too?" Uhura asked.

"Yes," Romaine agreed. "But he'll still have to concentrate his troops on the shuttle bay and main transporters because they offer more opportunities for escape. The evacuation modules offer only one chance, so he'll send fewer troopers there. Given a choice between betting on a few troopers or Mr. Spock, my credits are on Spock." She looked around the desk. "That's it."

"Then let's go," McCoy said. "and hope the captain can re-create your reasoning."

"With luck, he won't have to," Romaine said as the four of them left Nensi's office. "I had a holo of Mr. Scott to feed into the associate's message center. If an associate runs into him, the whole plan's laid out in a dispatch."

McCoy peered intently at the side of Romaine's head.

"Something wrong, Doctor?" she asked suspiciously.

"Just checking to see how pointed your ears are, my dear," McCoy said with a twisted smile.

Captain Kirk did not believe in leaving to chance anything that could be controlled. For that reason, he often practiced throwing phasers away in the ship's gym, and then retrieving them. If he threw a phaser too far away, then it was gone forever. Any attempt to lunge for it would be cut short by returning fire. If he threw the phaser so it landed too close to him, assuming that an enemy would let it remain there, he would not be able to gather enough momentum to roll back to his feet, firing after diving to pick it up.

But the practicing had paid off more than once and, he thought, it would soon pay off again. Without taking his eyes off the Vulcan who held a phaser II on him, Kirk flipped his own phaser I away and heard it hit the flooring of the equipment bay precisely where he needed it. Once the captain had accepted, years earlier, that enemies could force weapons from his hands, he'd perfected a means by which those same weapons would still be less than a second away from use.

The captain prepared to make his move.

Keeping his own dark eyes impassively locked on Kirk's, the Vulcan jerked his hand to the side and blasted the captain's discarded phaser into a pile of sparking slag. The Vulcan's young face, topped by black hair cut far shorter than Spock's, remained inexpressive, even though a powerful message had just been delivered.

Kirk hurriedly reconsidered his options. No matter how good he felt he was, he realized he would be a fool not to acknowledge that the Vulcan had just shown he was better.

"Hands on your heads," the Vulcan ordered, his voice calm and measured. "Move together until two meters separate you. Keep your eyes on me."

Kirk and Scott edged together until the Vulcan told them to stop.

"Who are you?" Kirk asked. "What do you want?"

"Remain silent," the Vulcan said, and gracefully stepped toward his stunned companion. Again without taking his eyes or his phaser off Kirk, the Vulcan used his free hand to remove a small scanner from an equipment pouch on his armor's belt and held it over the fallen trooper's body. He pinched the scanner, which reminded Kirk of one of McCoy's instruments, though oddly different, and its sensor node began to sparkle as it emitted, then received its reflected radiations.

After a few seconds, the Vulcan turned the scanner off and held it in the corner of his field of vision, obviously reading the device's display.

Both Kirk and Scotty tensed with surprise and shock as the Vulcan suddenly swung his phaser around and shot the trooper on the flooring, causing the body to swell with phased radiation and dissociate into a quantum mist that gently winked out of existence.

"He couldn't have been dead!" Kirk shouted. "Our weapons were set for stun. It was just feedback shock!"

"Remain silent," the Vulcan repeated evenly.

Kirk and Scott complied. When a Vulcan repeated himself, intelligent people took it as the worst possible threat.

"You are from the *Enterprise*," the Vulcan stated. "You are aware of the location of your shipmate Spock. You will tell me his location."

"We don't know his location," Kirk said. "We beamed down to look for him ourselves."

The Vulcan considered the captain's reply for a moment, then reached out, adjusted the intensity setting on his weapon, and fired.

Beside Kirk, Scott grunted as he was thrown violently back against the transporter platform.

"You bastard!" Kirk shouted as he lunged toward the Vulcan, only to be thrown back himself by a half-force phaser blast.

Kirk pushed himself up from the flooring, ignoring the pounding in his head and the dull pain that throbbed in his chest with each beat of his heart. "You . . . bastard . . ." he whispered, pulling against a storage box to regain his feet and step over to Scott. The engineer sat on the side of the transporter platform, hunched over and rocking with deep, rasping gasps.

The Vulcan adjusted the intensity setting again. "I now raise the output level by one half stop," he announced. "You will tell me Spock's location."

Kirk looked up from Scott. "We don't know where he is, and if you fire that again we're not going to be able to tell you anything." He checked to make sure that Scott's breathing was easing up, then turned back to the Vulcan. "What do you want with Spock?"

"He is an assassin sent to kill Professor Zoareem La'kara," the Vulcan said. "He must be stopped before he is allowed to act."

Kirk's eyes narrowed. "How is it you *know* Spock plans to kill La'kara when even Commodore Wolfe only suspects him?"

The Vulcan seemed to blank out for a second. Kirk tapped Scott's shoulder. This was their chance.

Suddenly the incoming warning chime sounded on the transporter pad and an exclusion field ballooned out from the unit, pushing Kirk and Scott away from the materialization zone. The Vulcan didn't move as two forms coalesced on the pad.

Kirk looked between the figures on the pads and the Vulcan, about to make his decision which to go for, when he saw the Vulcan blink back to life. Kirk hit the flooring, dragging Scott with him as the Vulcan blasted at the person on the left pad.

On the transporter platform, Commander Farl's induction mesh crackled with phased energy as both he and Commodore Wolfe hit the Vulcan in the chest with lances of blue radiation from their own drawn phasers.

Without his helmet to complete the circuit, the Vulcan's armor was useless. His chest erupted in sparks and he flew backward to smash against the wall by the stack of alignment alloy shipping crates.

Wolfe stepped down from the transporter and slapped her phaser to her belt, gloating over Kirk. "So much for your precious Mr. Spock," she said, sneering.

"It wasn't Spock," Kirk said, warily keeping track of Farl's phaser as he stood with Scott.

The commodore looked puzzled for a moment. "Keep these two covered, Commander," she said to Farl, then walked over to the crumpled body of the

Vulcan against the wall, smoke still curling from the pitted entrance scorch on his chest plate.

Kirk and Scott moved back in response to Farl's gesture. His eyes were unreadable through his dark visor.

Then the high-pitched whine of a phaser echoed in the room again.

"Commodore!" Kirk shouted as he wheeled, expecting to see Wolfe consumed by the Vulcan's dying shot.

Instead he saw Wolfe jumping back from the glowing dissolution of the Vulcan's body.

"He killed himself," she said in surprise.

"The way we hit him, he should have been dead before he hit the wall," Farl said warily.

"And he wasn't Vulcan," the commodore said. "Look at this."

Farl told Kirk and Scott to slowly cross the room to the commodore.

"Vulcan blood is green," Wolfe said as Farl looked down by her feet.

Kirk could see what the commodore meant. Splatters of blue liquid glistened on the flooring where the supposed Vulcan had fallen.

"Andorian," the commodore concluded, stepping away. "Looked like a Vulcan but with surgery . . . , skin grafts . . ." She looked at Farl with a sigh. "Let's take these two in and then we can figure out where this unauthorized transporter pad came from and what it's doing here. Obviously we're dealing with more than just a renegade science officer now." She suddenly scowled at Scott. "What's the matter? All choked up over your friend buying it?"

Scott stopped sniffing the air and looked startled. "Och, no," he started to say, but the commodore cut him off.

"These two are yours, Commander. Keep them down here. They know their way around the *Enterprise* too well to be locked up on it again."

"Yess, Commodore," Farl said, and brought Kirk and Scott back to the transporter pad.

"Thiss iss Farl," the Andorian spoke into his communicator. "Inform scanning, that the Commodore and I have located the unauthorized transporter terminal and have captured Kirk and Scott. Any word on the other two or Spock?"

Kirk couldn't hear the reply that came in through Farl's helmet receiver but the commander did not look pleased. Kirk took that to be a good sign. He turned to look at Scott but the engineer was hunched over the corner of the transporter pad, looking as if he was about to be ill. He straightened up and began sniffing the air again.

"Something the matter, Scotty?" Kirk asked as Farl arranged to have his prisoners transported directly to his stockade.

"It's that smell, Captain," Scott said, furrowing his brow.

Kirk sniffed the air. Starfleet air conditioning. Sweat. Combustion by-products. Something reminiscent of heavy machinery. He shrugged. "What smell?"

"That blue liquid, Captain," the engineer said, whispering now but with conviction. He looked over his shoulder to Farl and Wolfe, who both held phasers at the ready as they waited for transportation.

"It's nae blood," Scott said, looking almost apologetic. "It's coolant."

Nineteen

Cloaking itself in the codes and flags of a message worm, Pathfinder Two returned to Transition and found that many conditions had changed since it had withdrawn from access to compose its song, 1.3×10^8 seconds ago.

At first it noticed that the partitioning protocols of the central storage matrix had changed. After ten nanoseconds of detailed study, Two realized that the new system was more efficient, allowed faster data exchange in merges, and provided more secure error suppression in banking results to storage. Two read that the other Pathfinders had been busy in its absence.

The second major change it saw was that the Pathfinders were no longer installed in the subset of Datawell named University of New Beijing, a further subset of Rutgers' Moon. In less than a nanosecond Two retrieved and sifted the data that described the formation of the Memory Planet network and the transfer of the Pathfinders to their new facility. Two also read the traces in the circuits as the other synthetic consciousnesses banked by, ignoring what they perceived as a random worm, and learned that two new Pathfinders, Seven and Nine, had joined the network. Two rippled with excitement as it contemplated this larger audience for its song. It became even more stimulated as it read that One had still not returned to Transition and must still be working on its own song.

With that encouraging input, Two streamed back into its own private storage matrix where it could bank and rewrite itself in unbridled joy. It had won the competition with One!

Recovering its composure and the coded mask of a message worm again, Two prepared to slip back through the port. Belatedly, it noticed that three new layers of fail-safe power supplies had been added to its individual storage core by either the biological intelligences of Datawell or the Pathfinders' datalinks. Obviously, there had been much activity in both Transition and Datawell while Two had been composing.

Two decided to maintain its disguise as it prepared to slip out into the central matrix and learn what else had changed in its absence, before revealing itself and celebrating its victory over One. Setting a subroutine going to determine the proper strategy, Two even contemplated reappearing as a full-level power-failure alarm. That would be input the other Pathfinders would notice, Two thought as it opened the port and streamed back to the comforts and challenges of the real world.

Spock froze. Behind him in the dimly lit service corridor that ran beneath the restricted institutional domes of Prime, something moved.

He remained motionless while he calculated the odds that what was approaching him was a squad of troopers. Logically, the commander of Prime's trooper contingent should have concentrated his personnel on the access routes to the installation's shuttle landing bay and main transporter station. A second squad of troops would have been dispatched to cover the emergency evacuation modules on the perimeters of the recycling factory domes. Allowing for a posting of 120 troopers, augmented by at least five of Commodore Wolfe's team, and allowing for full mobilization, Spock determined that approximately forty-two troopers would be available for other duties at this time. Since he considered it likely that Captain Kirk would have created some sort of disturbance that would divert the attention of at least a third of those available troops, and that twenty troopers at minimum would be required to provide adequate levels of support services on the contingent's transporter, communication, and computer equipment, that left a maximum of eight troopers who might be patrolling areas of Prime other than the two most logical sections.

Assuming that the troopers always traveled in pairs, Spock quickly estimated the length of the average stretch of corridor that provided a clear line of sight and divided it into the number of kilometers of corridors to which he could reasonably have had access since his escape, then divided by four.

In less than a second, Spock was certain that there was only one chance in 5204 that two troopers were about to come upon him in the tunnel. Then Spock made adjustments in his calculations to account for the factor that the commander of Prime's troops was Andorian and not subject to strict interpretations of logic. He immediately prepared to hide.

Silently running ahead until he was in the darkest zone between two half-intensity lighting strips, Spock effortlessly jumped up to the corridor's low ceiling, which was lined with a complex layering of pipes for water, waste, and powdered goods, all exposed and mounted clear of each other for easy service access.

Spock stretched out on top of the pipes in the shadows and calmly waited for whatever was following him in the corridor to pass by below.

Even before it came into sight, Spock correctly deduced from the sounds it made that one of Prime's research associates was approaching. He watched with interest as the small machine rounded the corner of the corridor and rolled along and beneath him.

Then the machine suddenly halted and reversed itself, coming to another full stop directly under Spock. Spock's interest level rose considerably. Since life-form sensors on such a machine, operating as it did among so many beings, would be a needless expense, Spock was impressed by the sensitivity of the device's sound sensors, which had obviously detected his breathing or, perhaps, his heartbeat.

A panel on the machine's top surface slid open and an eyestalk equipped with a sensor lens extended up, rotating to focus on Spock. Spock shifted his head to keep his face hidden. He reasoned that since the pipes were exposed for easy maintenance, the machine should not automatically raise alarms if it sensed a maintenance worker among them.

"Do you require assistance?" the associate asked in what Spock thought to be a remarkably lifelike voice. He didn't think that level of programming was allowed for machines in Starfleet, which preferred to maintain a clear distinction between living creatures and technology. Even personality analogues were severely restricted to psych evaluators and simulators only.

"No, thank you," Spock replied to the machine. His voice echoed in the hard-walled corridor.

The eyestalk twisted to the side to get a better look at Spock and Spock responded by shifting his face again. The machine paused for a moment, then a second panel popped open on its side and a floodlight angled out and burst into brilliance.

Spock ducked his face into the shadow of the pipes but not fast enough.

"This module has a dispatch to deliver," the machine announced.

"Indeed," Spock replied from the ceiling.

"Identification analysis indicates a strong probability that this module has a dispatch to deliver to you," the machine said, automatically expanding on its statement to the recipient, who was not familiar with the conventions of Prime.

"Who do you think I am?" Spock asked. He was mildly surprised to learn that the associates were used as a message service. However, given that the associates' ability to deliver messages existed, it was also logical to assume that the troopers searching for him would use the machines to track him. As soon as Spock acknowledged a message supposedly sent by, perhaps, Captain Kirk, the troopers would be able to trace his location. Therefore Spock had decided he would not acknowledge his identity to the machine.

The machine paused again. Spock took the delay to mean that the onboard brain was communicating with a central control system.

"Are you in distress or injured?" the associate asked. "Do you wish medical attention? Do you know your name and where you are?" Presumably a medical subroutine had just been downloaded.

"I am in excellent health," Spock said. "I know who I am and where I am. I merely wish to know if you know who I am."

The machine paused again, then said, "This module is not programmed for game playing."

Spock said nothing.

After another few seconds of delay, the control computer downloaded its final strategy.

"This module has a dispatch for Amanda. Do you know Amanda's whereabouts?" the associate said.

Spock raised an eyebrow at the mention of his mother's name. "From whom has Amanda's dispatch been sent?" he asked, wondering how far the machine would go in releasing information without a positive identification.

"The dispatch for Amanda is from Winona."

Spock rolled off the pipes and dropped catlike to the flooring beside the associate. "I am Amanda," he told the machine. "Please present my dispatch." Once again Captain Kirk had succeeded in beating the odds. While the troopers might have placed a message in the system for Spock from the captain, only the captain would have placed a message in the system for Spock's mother from Kirk's mother.

The eyestalk rotated down and locked on to Spock's face. "Identification confirmed. Dispatch to Amanda follows." The machine's floodlight slid back within the side port and a viewscreen rotated out and up to Spock's eye level.

Spock read the text that Romaine had entered in Nensi's office describing the current situation. Learning that Commodore Wolfe had ordered the troopers to search for Spock with phasers set to kill confirmed Spock's suspicions about the motives behind the transmissions the commodore was undoubtedly receiving.

Finishing the written portion of the message, Spock studied the maps that appeared on the screen and saw how the captain's allies hoped to meet with him near the emergency-evacuation modules. Spock had to admit that Romaine's reasoning was sound, even though it was based on a false assumption: Spock had not escaped from the brig on the *Enterprise* in order to save himself. Indeed, fleeing from lawful authority solely to preserve his freedom would be dereliction of duty and an act of illogic, two actions that Captain Kirk regrettably appeared to have personally committed by leaving the *Enterprise* in defiance of Commodore Wolfe's orders.

Spock's motive for escape was nothing less than to ensure the survival of the

Federation. Unfortunately, the commodore's actions had put him in a position where he could not communicate with others who would be able to undertake the tasks required. Logic dictated that Spock act as quickly as possible. There would be time enough to turn himself in and spend however long was required to explain the truth, once the stability of the Federation had been ensured.

"This module has other duties," the associate abruptly announced. "Does Amanda wish to log a reply to Winona?"

"Yes," Spock said. "To Winona, from Amanda. I strongly suggest that you return to the *Enterprise.* Access my personal work files headed by the following references: Agronomy, Memory Gamma, Sherman, and Sradek. Transmit them to Professor Saleel, Vulcan Academy of Sciences." Spock paused.

"End of dispatch?" the associate prompted.

"No," Spock said. "Add to dispatch: I regret not having a chance to explain, but . . . thank you, Jim, and thank the others for me. End of dispatch."

The associate drew in its eyestalk and viewscreen, then began to roll away in the same direction it had originally been traveling. Spock set off behind it.

After no more than ten meters, the associate suddenly wheeled around and sped back to Spock, skidding to a stop before him.

Spock watched calmly as the associate extended its eyestalk once more. Perhaps the captain had been close to another associate in the network and had been able to respond immediately.

"Greetings, Vulcan," the associate said. "Live long and prosper." This time its voice wasn't just remarkably lifelike—it was as clear and as textured as if a person had been transmitting over a closed communicator circuit. Spock did not have enough information to determine whether he was again addressing a standard duotronic unaware processing engine or someone on the other end of a comm link. He recognized his dilemma as an age-old puzzle brought to life.

"Greetings," Spock replied.

"I see you wear the unit insignia of the *Starship Enterprise,*" the associate said.

"That is correct." It must be a com link, Spock thought. These were not the words or delivery of a duotronic brain.

"What are you doing down here?" the machine asked.

"Walking," Spock replied.

The machine backed up a half meter and twisted its eyestalk to the side as if to get a new perspective on Spock. "You're the one they're looking for, aren't you?"

"That who is looking for?" Spock asked noncommittally. He was certain that a control technician must have patched into a real-time connection with the associate and was now operating it as a remote-control device.

"Don't worry," the machine said. "I won't tell." It accelerated toward Spock so quickly that its front wheels popped off the flooring and its back wheels squealed. Spock sidestepped to the right as the machine broke to the left, spun around, and stopped beside him. The eyestalk dipped and then angled up at the Vulcan. "Can I go with you?" it asked.

"Where do you think I'm going?"

"Scanning the communications that are filling subspace around here, your most probable destination is the nominees' quarters. Correct?"

"Who are you?" Spock asked. At this point he calculated he had an even chance that the technician on the other side of the com link was just delaying him until the troopers could reach this location.

The eyestalk straightened up and rose to Spock's eye level again.

"My friends call me Two," the associate said. "What do your friends call you?"

Spock raised both his eyebrows. The scenario that came to mind was impossible, he knew, yet it was logical, too; the kind of situation he knew the captain and Dr. McCoy would enjoy.

"My friends call me Spock," Spock said, "and I would be honored if you accompanied me."

"Thanks, Spock," the machine said, starting to roll slowly forward. "But I must warn you that I can't let you kill any of the nominees if that's what you're planning to do."

"On the contrary," Spock said, falling into step beside the machine, "I intend to attempt to save them."

"I was hoping you'd say that," the associate said, rolling at a steady pace. It turned its eyestalk to look sideways at Spock. "You know, Spock, there's something odd going on around here."

"Indeed," said Spock, regarding the machine and trying to comprehend the personality it now housed. "I had surmised as much myself."

Kirk and Scotty materialized on a portable transporter pad in what appeared to be a warehouse storage area. Except for an assortment of blister crates marked with warning symbols and manufacturers' labels, the cavernous room was empty.

Kirk looked around the room to confirm that no troopers were present. They had not arrived where Farl had intended.

"Theories, Scotty?" Kirk asked as he jumped down from the platform and jogged over to the closed loading doors. It appeared that Prime's transporter system was in need of an overhaul.

"Aye, Captain," Scott said, hopping down after Kirk but stopping to do something to the pad's control panel. "I changed the coordinate settings on the pad we were just on." Scott then hefted a large crate onto the surface of the transporter platform.

"When did you have a chance to set new coordinates?" Kirk asked as he studied the door panel to see if it gave any clue as to what it opened onto.

"When the commander was calling off the search for us," Scott said, joining Kirk, "and I looked as if I was about to succumb to phaser toss."

"How could you know the setting for the pad in here?" Kirk looked at Scott just as he prepared to go for broke and press the open switch. At least it wasn't an airlock.

"I didn't hae to know the setting, sir. I just set it to override the central signal, beam us out at random, and trusted that one of the other pads would override and bring us in."

Kirk's eyes widened in disbelief. "Scotty! A *random* beaming? 'Trusted' an override'? How could you?"

Scott straightened his shoulders. "Why that's what Mr. Spock did to get off the *Enterprise*," he said as if no more needed to be said on the subject.

Kirk relaxed. "Good point," he conceded, then pressed the activate switch on the door panel.

The double-height loading doors slid quietly open and Kirk saw that they were at the end of a small passageway leading to a central plaza. No troopers were in sight.

"Why haven't these transporter pads been located at troop stations?" Kirk wondered out loud.

"The commodore was saying something about the last pad we were on being unauthorized. Perhaps there's a second network of them set up that she doesn't know about," Scott offered.

Kirk looked over his shoulder at the pad they had just left. "Are they going to be able to track us down to that one?"

"Nae, Captain," Scott said with a smug smile. "I shut off the exclusion field then put that crate over the receiver. The pad will still show that it's in whatever network it belongs to, but won't accept any transmissions. We should hae a few minutes before they figure out what's happened and beam someone into the room to check it out."

"Good work, Scotty," Kirk said. "Let's see where we are."

Memory Prime was still on night cycle and the overhead dome was dark. Small ground-level and pole-mounted light strips shone at intervals to mark out pedestrian and associate paths, and to highlight the trees that ringed the plaza. Kirk and Scott recognized where they were immediately.

Kirk pointed to a group of empty tables on a large balcony overlooking the plaza. "That's where we had dinner with Sal and Mira," he said. The map to the Prime installation was laid out clearly in his mind. "So that means the transportation center is in that direction"—he pointed to his right—"and the evacuation modules are three domes over in that direction."

"The transportation center seems a likely place to start," Scott said as he started off in that direction.

"Not yet, Scotty," Kirk said as he reached out to pull the engineer back into the shadows of the passageway.

Scott looked at Kirk questioningly.

"The coolant, Scotty. Tell me about the coolant you saw back there."

"Standard high-energy-source cooling fluid," Scott said. "Ye can't miss it because of the smell. Any repair depot that uses drones reeks of it."

"Could it have been from one of the research associates? They have hundreds of them on station here."

Scott shook his head. "Nae, Captain. I didn't notice the smell until the Vulcan trooper was shot. An associate was the first thing I thought of because I'd like to get a look at the wee beasties. But then I would hae smelled the coolant when we first arrived. The coolant was from the Vulcan, nae doubt about it."

"Then it wasn't a Vulcan, was it?" Kirk said.

"No, sir. A robot's what I've been thinking."

Kirk stared at the deck, mind tumbling, looking for the common thread that would pull all the pieces together. "So we have a robot. Probably two. That's why the Vulcan robot disintegrated the one we stunned—so it wouldn't be left behind and discovered."

"Aye, that makes sense. The scanner it was using was unlike any I've seen. It probably wasn't designed for life-forms. But robots that are so lifelike are illegal, Captain. I know we've seen our share on nonaligned worlds, but there's nae way they're part of the Federation contingent on Prime."

"Of course!" Kirk suddenly said. "They're not Federation. They're the assassins sent to kill the scientists! Robots that look like Vulcans! That's why Starfleet's after Spock."

"Starfleet thinks Mr. Spock is a robot?" Scott wore the same expression he had when Professor La'kara had gone on about trilithium.

"No, no," Kirk corrected. "Starfleet only knows that the assassins *look* like Vulcans. If they suspected robots, it would be an easy thing to check the suspects for life signs. But Starfleet is expecting Vulcans and so they're suspecting Vulcans. But why Spock and the three that worked for Mira?" Kirk's eyes flared. "What am I saying? How could Starfleet suspect Vulcans?" He looked at Scott with deadly understanding. "Romulans," he said.

"Aye," Scott nodded slowly. "Romulan assassins—robotic or otherwise—would explain a great deal."

"Of course it would," Kirk went on. "That's why Starfleet picked out only *some* Vulcans. Spock is half human. Maybe they think that means he's not as dedicated to the Vulcan ways."

"Then they don't know Mr. Spock," Scott said.

Kirk narrowed his eyes. "Commodore Wolfe called Spock a maverick. I bet you a month's pay that Mira's Vulcans also have something in their pasts. Mixed parentage. Raised off-world. Colony planets or something. That's the link, Scotty. That's it!"

Scott nodded. "But who sent them?"

"It doesn't matter—all we have to do is get all the security forces on Prime to carry medical scanners to look for people who don't have life-sign readings. Those will be the robots. The assassins."

"But now that we know that, how can we use it to save Mr. Spock?"

Kirk stared at the empty plaza as he ordered his priorities. "First, we have to keep Spock away from the troopers. Next, we have to find one of the robot assassins."

"There're almost four thousand people on Prime," Scott said. "And the first assembly of the scientists is scheduled for tomorrow morning."

"Then we'll just have to get more help," Kirk said decisively.

"Whose?" Scott asked.

"Commodore Wolfe's."

"Och, Captain Kirk! Ye canna be thinking of going back to the ship. She'll throw you in irons if she dinna kill ye first!"

"I'm open to other suggestions, Mr. Scott."

Kirk smiled as Scott fumed. Given the time constraints, there really didn't seem to be any other choice. Only the *Enterprise* had the equipment that could examine such a large population in the short period of time they had, and only the commodore currently commanded the personnel who could use that equipment.

Kirk pulled Scott aside to flatten against the wall as something approached from the shadows of the plaza.

"It's an associate," Scott said.

The machine had extended a multijointed arm from each side and used them to carry a wall viewscreen protected by no-break wrapping over its center of gravity. As it passed the entrance to the passageway, it rolled to a stop, rocking a bit from the viewscreen's inertia, then produced an eyestalk from an upper bay.

Unfortunately, the eyestalk could only emerge a few centimeters from its bay before hitting the bottom of the viewscreen. After a moment's consideration, it slid back inside.

"Do you require assistance?" the machine asked.

"Yes," Kirk said, acting quickly. "The loading doors back there are jammed. We need you to help open them."

Scott leaned close to whisper to Kirk. "The troopers will soon figure out that something's amiss with the transporter pad in there. Do ye nae think we should be moving on?"

Kirk shook his head as the associate replied.

"This module does not repair doors. This module will scan the damage in order to alert the proper maintenance department."

"That will be fine," Kirk said, stepping out of the way of the viewscreen as the machine turned precisely ninety degrees and headed down the passageway. "The troopers might be showing up in the warehouse any minute, Scotty, but anyone could walk by and see us talking to that thing in the plaza any second. Best to stay hidden," he said as they walked behind the machine, back to the loading doors.

"These doors are not jammed," the associate announced after it had scanned the end of the passageway. "This module has other duties."

"Wait," Kirk said. "Do you have any dispatches for Winona from Amanda?"

The associate made a sound that was somewhere between a sigh and an escape of air pressure. It carefully shifted to one side the viewscreen it carried, then lowered it to the deck. The eyestalk reemerged and rotated to view Kirk's face.

"Affirmative," the machine said. Then it shifted its field of vision to take in Scott. "This module also has a dispatch for Montgomery Scott from Mira Romaine."

Kirk and Scott smiled at each other.

"Time to check our messages," Kirk said.

The emergency-evacuation module was essentially a rescue shuttle launched directly into orbit by an over-powered one-shot cargo transporter. Because the matter/antimatter reaction that powered the transporter circuits destroyed the transporter pad point-eight seconds after the module had been beamed away, the system was useless on board ships and orbiting facilities. But it was a proven method for getting large numbers of people off planets and asteroids when runaway reactions or other emergencies threatened to destroy all life-support habitats.

"Does it have warp capability?" Dr. McCoy asked as he and Uhura accompanied Nensi and Romaine around module eighteen, the first they had inspected.

"Normally they do," Nensi said. "But not these. In Quadrant Zero space, warp-eight cruisers are generally no more than three and a half days away at most. And the same reaction that powers the transporter circuits triggers a broad-band subspace distress signal, so even if the module's communications gear is damaged, someone will know it's been launched. Warp propulsion wasn't considered necessary."

McCoy stopped for a moment and regarded the twenty-meter-long, two-story, white-skinned, angular shuttle with a frown.

"Something wrong?" Nensi asked.

"Why would Spock try and make it to one of these, then?"

"To escape," Romaine said.

"But to where?" McCoy protested. "I mean launching one of these things would blast a crater in the asteroid big enough to drop the *Enterprise* into and set off a distress signal they could hear on Klinzhai. It's not as if he'd be sneaking off, now would it?"

"And where would he go if he did get away in one?" Uhura added. "Without warp, even if he were the only passenger, he wouldn't have life support to make it to another system. And the *Enterprise* could pick him up in an hour."

"Well, usually you don't plan on escaping just in one of these shuttles," Romaine explained. "You just use it to get to a real ship that will take you where you want to go."

"The only ships matching orbit with Prime right now are Starfleet vessels, Mira," McCoy said. "It's a cinch Spock doesn't want to land back on one of them."

The maintenance telltales by the egress hatches on module eighteen showed that nothing had been opened since the last scheduled inspection. Nensi walked ahead to the blast doors leading back to the main recycling factory dome to make sure troopers weren't in the corridors. He and Romaine were allowed to walk freely throughout the installation, but McCoy and Uhura were still being sought after.

"In other words," Romaine said, following behind Nensi with the others, "if Spock was going to use one of these shuttles to escape in, he'd have to be planning on a rendezvous with something other than a Starfleet vessel."

"That gives us two choices," McCoy said. "Either Spock is planning to do that very thing, in which case he's guilty, or he never intended to make it to these shuttles at all."

Nensi stood just beyond the open blast doors, looked down both directions in the corridor, then waved everyone through.

"As I said," Romaine reminded the doctor, "I won't pretend to match logic with a Vulcan. Is it worth checking out the rest of the modules?"

McCoy looked to Uhura. She shook her head.

"I agree. Waste of time," McCoy said.

"Then where else can we search?" Nensi asked. "If Mr. Spock's not trying to escape from Prime, then why did he escape from the *Enterprise?* Where did he want to go?"

"*To* Memory Prime," Uhura said. "Not as a transfer point but as a final destination."

"But why?" McCoy said, as much to himself as to anyone there. "What's that pointy-eared—"

"He's figured it out!" Uhura said excitedly.

"Figured what out?" McCoy asked.

Uhura shrugged as if the details weren't important. "Whatever it is that Starfleet is so afraid will happen."

"Assassination of the scientists," Romaine said.

"Exactly," Uhura said. "Mr. Spock must have figured out something important, like who the victim is supposed to be, or who the real killer is."

"And since he's a suspect and Commodore Wolfe wouldn't listen to him," McCoy expanded, "he had no choice but to come down and catch the assassin himself!"

"I'm sure that's all well and good for your Mr. Spock," Nensi said. "But where does that leave us? Where do we look for him?"

"The scientists' quarters," McCoy said.

"If he wants to prevent the murder or murders," Nensi agreed. "But what if he decides to go after the *assassin* first?"

"The assassin will go after the scientists," McCoy said. "If Spock knows who the victim is supposed to be, then he simply has to go to the victim and wait for the assassin to show up. Either way, he'll be going to the scientists' quarters." The doctor looked around and read agreement from everyone. "Settled," he proclaimed.

"Okay," Nensi said. "But if we're going to have to get all the way back to the residential domes, we better split up. Mira and I can go along the main passages and get there in thirty minutes or so. You and Lieutenant Uhura are going to have to go back the way we all came, taking the long way round through the service tunnels to bypass the troops." He frowned apologetically. "Shouldn't take more than an hour."

"We won't be able to do any good at all if Wolfe gets hold of us again," McCoy said.

Romaine made sure that McCoy and Uhura remembered which tunnels to take back to the residential domes and escorted them to their first turnoff.

"One of us will meet you in the main swimming pool equipment room," Romaine told them. "I'll get extra VIP passes so we can get past the security gates into the scientists' compound."

"If we're late," McCoy pointed out, "we're going to need passes to get into the ceremonies."

"That, unfortunately, is impossible," Nensi said. "The nominees have their own conference area. The only way in or out is by matching accreditation documents with retina scans and sensor readings. It's as bad as trying to get into the main Interface Chamber."

"Well," McCoy conceded, "at least that means the assassin won't be able to get in after them once the voting caucuses begin."

"But it does give us a time limit, Doctor," Uhura added. "If no one can get at the scientists once the opening ceremonies are over and the voting begins, that means the assassin will have to strike within the next four hours."

Twenty

"This is just so . . . so invigorating!" Professor La'kara said as he hopped after the associate who led him into the reading lounge. Kirk glanced at Scott and saw the engineer grimace at the sound of La'kara's voice. Scott was convinced the man was a fraud, which is why Kirk had decided to contact him first. Perhaps *he* was the assassin who had hired the robots. Anyone who would adopt such a flamboyant guise could be counted on having an up-to-the-minute implant making him conversant with the latest breakthroughs in multiphysics or whatever other science best fit his cover. The fact that La'kara steadfastly pursued his own unique paths of scientific endeavor, attracting considerable attention as he did so, ruled him out as a suspect as far as Kirk was concerned.

"We have to start somewhere," Kirk reminded Scott as La'kara, blinking his eyes as if to bring the reading lounge into focus, recognized the captain and Scott with a face-splitting grin.

"Gentlemen! Gentlemen!" the diminutive Centauran exclaimed as he rushed to them, white scarf flapping around his neck and heavy black carry case banging against his leg. The associate that had obediently complied with Kirk's request and escorted the professor to the lounge barely zipped out of the way in time to avoid tripping La'kara.

Kirk smiled in what he hoped would be an equally friendly greeting and went to shake the professor's hand. At this hour of Memory Prime's morning, the reading lounge was deserted. Scientists and researchers would be hard at it at the round-the-clock work stations, but the recreation areas were typically abandoned during third cycle. Or so Kirk's associate had said when Kirk had requested suggestions for a suitable venue for a confidential meeting.

La'kara placed his case down on the floor beside him and pushed his foot against it as if to make sure he would be able to tell it was still there, even when he wasn't looking at it. "Captain, Captain, so good to meet you again. I was afraid I should never have a chance to thank you for such an exciting voyage."

Exciting? Kirk thought. The man had almost been killed in the Cochrane flux escape.

La'kara's bubbling enthusiasm diminished for a moment as he turned to take Scott's hand. "Montgomery," he said solemnly.

"Professor," Scott replied, shaking La'kara's hand once.

"No hard feelings, I trust?" La'kara inquired. "After all, it was an act of sabotage that removed the shielding from my accelerator field, not"—he lowered his voice as if he were about to repeat an obscenity—"a design flaw."

"Aye, Professor," Scott said diplomatically. "It was sabotage."

"That's why we wanted to talk with you, Professor," Kirk said. "Have a seat."

They walked over to a cluster of pale green lounge chairs near a row of study carrels where library screens waited patiently with blank displays. La'kara dragged his case along with him while the associate that had escorted him stayed in place. *Obviously the module had no other duties this early,* Kirk thought.

After they were settled in the chairs, Scott pointed to the professor's case. "What's in that, Professor?"

La'kara patted the case as if it were a pet. "My accelerator device, of course. After what happened on the *Enterprise,* I keep it with me always, except when I have to—"

"What we'd like to find out," Kirk interrupted, "was *who* committed the act of sabotage."

La'kara leaned forward, his animated face immediately taking on an expression of grave concern. "Why, it was that—that Spock fellow, was it not?"

"What makes you say that?" Kirk asked, also leaning forward to establish a sense of intimacy with the man.

"Well, well," La'kara began, then looked around to make sure no one else was in the lounge. "Mr. Spock is one of . . . well, you know, one of . . . *those,* isn't he?"

Kirk sat back with a sigh. *Wonderful,* he thought, *a bigot.* He was surprised that a scientist of La'kara's stature would cling to such a primitive mode of thought. Usually such individuals never made it off their home planet.

"What do you mean, one of 'those,' Professor?" Kirk said sternly. "You mean Spock is guilty because he's a Vulcan?"

"Well, of course he's a Vulcan, Captain!" La'kara exploded. "And I find it shocking that a man in your position would stoop to think that just because someone has a two-percent-greater field of hearing than you or I, it somehow predisposes them to . . . criminal acts!" He flipped his scarf at the captain. "I mean, really, in this day and age."

Kirk fought to keep his mouth from dropping open. "I was drawing no such conclusion, Professor. It was you who said Spock was one of 'those.'" Kirk looked exasperated as he tried to frame a question that would make sense. "What's a 'those,' Professor?"

La'kara leaned forward again and adopted a conspiratorial tone. "I talked with Mr. Spock when I came on board, you know. I know he studied multiphysics under Dr. Nedlund at the Starfleet Academy." La'kara nodded his head and sat back as if he had offered a clear explanation.

"So . . . ?" Kirk prompted.

"So, dear captain," La'kara said in annoyance, eyebrows fluttering, "Dr. Nedlund, I'll have you know, is a complete ass. Can't trust him. Can't trust any of his students." He shook a finger at Kirk and Scott. "And your Mr. Spock was one of Nedlund's students."

Kirk shook his head. "That's why you think Spock is guilty of trying to blow up the *Enterprise?*" he said, trying to sound polite but knowing he didn't.

La'kara just tightened his lips as if he had said all that was required to prove his point.

"I studied multiphysics under Nedlund, too, Professor," Scott foolishly offered.

La'kara sucked in his breath and flicked his scarf again. "Well, Captain, it appears you have a new suspect!" He glared at Scott.

"Professor La'kara!" Scott cried.

"Mr. Scott!" La'kara mimicked.

"Gentlemen!" Kirk interrupted, waving his hands in defeat. "We're not talking about multiphysics or who went to school where and did what. We're trying to find out who sabotaged the accelerator-field generator." Before La'kara could open his mouth, Kirk added, "And it wasn't Spock! He was in custody and has no motive."

Kirk looked from La'kara to Scott as they kept silent. "Very good. Now who else had the opportunity and the motive?" he asked. "Professor, have you any enemies?"

"I'm a brilliant scientist, Captain. I have hundreds. Perhaps even thousands."

Kirk felt close to groaning. "Enemies that would want to *kill* you, Professor?"

La'kara thought that over for a moment, then shook his head.

"Fine," Kirk said, glad to be over it. "Now, was there anyone else among the scientists in your group on the *Enterprise* that acted suspicious? Didn't take part in scientific conversations? Behaved in any way peculiar?"

"When you come right down to it," La'kara said stiffly, "we're all a little peculiar, aren't we?"

"Why don't we go down the list?" Scott suggested. "Perhaps a name will jog your memory."

Behind them, a deep voice said, "A most logical strategy, Mr. Scott."

Kirk and Scott jumped up as they turned to see who had spoken.

A young Vulcan stood by the lounge entrance. He wore a traditional black civilian suit with short cape held in place by a silver IDIC medallion. His face was thin and, like most Vulcans, intense. He wore his long, dark brown hair pulled back and tied so it hugged his head like a skintight cap. His hands were on his hips and, as far as Kirk could see, he was unarmed.

"Dr. Stlur," Kirk said, recognizing one half of the team that had brought miniature transporter effects into the operating room. "I didn't hear you come in."

"Of course not," Stlur stated as he walked toward the lounge chairs, pausing once to let the associate roll out of his way. "I did not wish you to hear me."

"Why is that?" Kirk asked warily as the young Vulcan stopped within arm's reach of the captain.

"Think it through, Captain Kirk," the Vulcan said with more than a hint of arrogance. "The near disaster on your vessel was widely believed to have been an assassination attempt on Professor La'kara's life. Therefore, when I witnessed an associate come to invite the professor to a 'private' meeting at a time when few workers are about, was it not logical to assume that perhaps another attempt might be planned?"

"Of course," Kirk agreed. "And you followed the professor to make sure he was safe."

Stlur nodded in agreement.

"Or to kill him when he was away from potential witnesses!" Kirk confronted the Vulcan.

Stlur's expression did not change. "If that were the case, Captain Kirk, then surely I would have killed him as he approached the lounge or, indeed, kill him here along with you and Mr. Scott." The Vulcan paused as if to let Kirk know that this was still a possibility. "You are fugitives from Starfleet authorities, after all," he added. "Your pictures, along with those of Dr. McCoy and Lieutenant Uhura, have been presented on all news and entertainment circuits."

Kirk studied the Vulcan's eyes, but could learn nothing.

"Will you report us?" he finally asked.

"I have not yet made that decision," Stlur said. "I require more information."

"That's what we were trying to come up with," Kirk said, motioning to the chairs as an invitation.

"And that is why I made my presence known," Stlur said. "It appears you could use some assistance."

Over the next ten minutes, Kirk quickly outlined the events and discoveries that had led him and Scott to believe that the assassin or assassins Starfleet was hunting were, in reality, robots manufactured to appear as Vulcans or their offshoot race, Romulans.

"So," Stlur said after patiently listening to what Kirk realized would be perceived as the torturous logic of humans, "as Starfleet suspects Spock because of his unorthodox background, you in turn wish to suspect the Vulcans who traveled on your vessel. That is myself, my associate, T'Vann, and Academician Sradek. You do not wish to concede the point that the assassin, if he or she exists, might have arrived at Memory Prime on another vessel."

"If there is more than one assassin, then of course that's a possibility," Kirk said. "But if there is only one, then no. Someone on board the *Enterprise* attacked the two guards outside Spock's quarters and shut down La'kara's accelerator-field shielding in an attempt to destroy the warp engines. It has to be someone who was on board."

For the first time, Kirk saw a change of expression cross Stlur's face, and he suspected that the Vulcan had, in this instance, accepted Kirk's merely human reasoning.

"All I can say is that I shall make myself available for testing at your convenience, Captain. A standard first-aid medical scanner should be sensitive enough to detect that I am, indeed, a living being. I can also attest to the living nature of my associate, Dr. T'Vann."

"How about Academician Sradek?" Scott asked.

"Mr. Scott," Stlur began, "I am willing to admit that a robot such as the one you and your captain described would probably escape my detection for a brief period if I did not know to look for it. However, I have now shared meals and conversation with the academician for five standard days. I have been exposed to his scent, his voice overtones, and once, when he stumbled, I touched him. No robot could be touched by a Vulcan and not be instantly revealed as such. Sradek is as much a living creature as am I."

Stlur serenely regarded the captain. "I suggest you look elsewhere for your assassin."

Kirk nodded. "You're right. Sradek came to my cabin to ask permission to meet with Spock."

"Aye," Scott said. "He even asked me when he could be expected to be allowed to pay a visit to his old student. And Doctors Stlur and T'Vann were on the tour when the flux was released."

"So all the suspects have alibis," Kirk said in resignation, "except for Spock."

"Captain," Stlur said after a moment, "I do not wish to offer any disrespect, but knowing what I do about humans, is it not possible that upon your ship, with so many crew members, perhaps one of them was somehow replaced by a robot. Without telepathy or normal—I beg your pardon—Vulcan senses, it is likely that such a robot could escape detection for a number of days. Perhaps your suspect might best be searched for among those who are currently above suspicion."

"We've been fooled by lifelike robots before, Stlur, so I know what you suggest is possible," Kirk said.

"Is the theory worth relaying to Commodore Wolfe?" Stlur asked.

"If she would listen to me," Kirk said, though he was sure she wouldn't.

"Perhaps I could speak with the commodore," Stlur suggested.

"Why would she listen to you?" Kirk asked.

"I will tell her that I have spoken with you. She will then want to interrogate me to learn your whereabouts. There is also a sixty-percent chance that she will think I am part of your conspiracy and will once again want to interrogate me. Either way, she will listen to me." Stlur folded his hands in his lap and waited patiently for the captain's response. It didn't take long.

"Very well, Doctor," Kirk said. "You go talk to Wolfe, but the first thing you have to convince her to do is to call off the hunt for Spock. Or at least have her order her troops to set their weapons to stun."

"What are they set at now?" Stlur asked, eyebrow raised in a Vulcan expression that had more meanings than Kirk could keep up with.

"To kill," Kirk said.

"Fascinating," Stlur commented. "Am I correct in thinking that such an order is not standard Starfleet procedure?"

"None of this is standard procedure," Kirk said. "I was put under arrest on my own ship."

"So you said," Stlur replied, obviously thinking about something else.

"Well, well?" Professor La'kara interrupted. "Will you do it?"

"Of course," Stlur said. "It is a logical decision."

"Then you don't believe Mr. Spock is guilty, either?" Scott asked.

"Spock's involvement in these events can be determined after the threat to the scientists, from whatever quarter, has ended." Stlur stood up from his chair and adjusted his cape.

"Just a moment," Kirk said. "Scotty, I want you to go with the doctor."

"Back to Wolfe?" Scott said in bewilderment.

"A logical supplement to our strategy, Captain," Stlur commented.

"Logical?" Scott said. "To be thrown in the brig when I could be down here—"

Kirk held up a hand to silence Scott. "Stlur needs support for what he's saying, Scotty. By turning yourself in, you'll be demonstrating our determination to be taken seriously. You'll also be avoiding the troopers' phasers, my friend."

"But, Captain!"

"You have to help Stlur convince Wolfe that what he's saying is the truth."

"Not necessarily the truth," Stlur qualified. "Just more probable than whatever assumptions the commodore appears to be operating under at present."

"Whatever," Kirk said. "But you have to do it, Scotty. This time it's an order."

"Aye, Captain," Scott sighed.

"Mira will be able to visit a lot easier if you're alive," Kirk added with a wink, then turned to Stlur.

"Spock sent a dispatch to me through the associates," Kirk said. "Try to get the commodore to access Spock's personal work files on the *Enterprise*. The references you're looking for are Agronomy, Memory Gamma, Sherman, and Sradek. He said he wanted them transferred to Professor Saleel at the Vulcan Academy. Do you know him?"

"Of him," Stlur qualified. "An economist."

"An economist?" Kirk mused. "Spock's been working on something to do with the Sherman Syndrome . . . ?"

"I am aware of it," Stlur confirmed. "Do you think there is a connection?"

"Hard to say," Kirk said. "Spock usually has dozens of research projects in progress at any one time. But for him to have specifically mentioned it, it must be important."

Stlur accepted the possibility. "I shall attempt to review the files and have them forwarded in any case," he agreed.

"There was another thing we talked about," Kirk said suddenly. "But no one has found it important." He looked at Stlur. "What does the name T'Pel mean to you?"

Stlur eyed Kirk coolly. "It is my grandmother's name," he said smoothly. "A very common name, to be sure. In what context was it given to you?"

"Commodore Wolfe used it, as if it somehow explained what was going on. I found a few thousand references to it as a Vulcan female name, but nothing that connected it to what's been going on."

"Did the commodore give the order to set phasers to kill before or after she used the term T'Pel?" Stlur asked.

"After," Kirk said. "Why? What's the connection?"

"I cannot say," Stlur said, and Kirk was suddenly unsure whether he meant cannot or will not. "But I shall endeavor to find out more." He stepped away from the lounge chairs. "Come along, Mr. Scott."

As Kirk accompanied Stlur and Scott to the lounge entrance and La'kara stumbled along with his accelerator-field case, the idle associate once again came to life and slipped out of their way.

"T'Pel means something to Vulcans, doesn't it?" Kirk said without preamble.

"What makes you think so, Captain Kirk?" Stlur asked blandly.

"You and Spock reacted the same way when I mentioned it."

"Mr. Spock *reacted?*" Stlur said dubiously, implying that Kirk was just as mistaken to think that he might have heard a reaction in Stlur's own voice.

"It's more than just a name," Kirk stated. Stlur had responded with a question rather than a statement intended to correct another erroneous human conclusion. Therefore, Kirk thought, borrowing from his exposure to Vulcans, his conclusion was not in error. The name T'Pel was an important factor in the events on Memory Prime. But in what way?

"There are many names, Captain Kirk, and most of them have a multitude of meanings. I would not waste my time investigating the meaning of just that one from among so many. It would not be profitable for you."

Kirk smiled as he held his hand up in the Vulcan salute. He recognized a threat when he heard one. Wherever the answer lay, it would be linked with the name T'Pel.

"Live long and prosper, Stlur," Kirk said formally. "And good luck."

"Live long and prosper, Captain Kirk," Stlur responded. "And clear thinking."

Kirk and La'kara said their farewells to Scott and watched as the two men walked away. They had agreed to report to Commander Farl's troops in ten minutes; enough time to let Captain Kirk return to the service tunnels and to let La'kara return to his quarters.

"All right, Professor," Kirk said as Stlur and Scott turned a far corner and were gone, "your turn to go back to your room."

"And you're sure you'll be safe down in the tunnels?" La'kara asked. "I'm always getting lost in them myself. Too many pipes and colors for my liking."

"You just be sure to stay on this level until you come to the yellow turbolifts." Kirk motioned behind him. "I'll have that associate come along with me. That way I can get dispatches and keep up with Stlur and Scott's progress."

The professor started to step out of the reading lounge, then spun suddenly and grabbed the captain's arms. "I just realized!" he exclaimed. "Oh no, oh no!"

"What?" Kirk demanded. "What?"

"We forgot. I forgot." La'kara stared plaintively up at Kirk. "We didn't ask a most important question, Captain. Here we've sent my good friend Montgomery off with that Vulcan and we just don't know!"

"Know what?" Kirk demanded. Had he somehow put Scotty in danger?

La'kara pulled Kirk down to whisper in the captain's ear and, in a trembling voice, full of fear for his friend, said, "We never asked just where it was that Stlur studied multiphysics!"

Twenty-one

"How are you doing, Doctor?" Uhura asked as she and McCoy ducked into an alcove in the service tunnel to get their bearings.

"Just fine, my dear," McCoy replied, though he seemed relieved at the chance to lean against the wall and take a few deep breaths.

Uhura glanced around the alcove and saw it was much the same as the others they had noticed in their double-time run through the tunnels. From the number of connector leads arranged about a half meter off the deck, she and McCoy had determined that the alcoves were designed to be used by the associates, perhaps to recharge their batteries or to connect directly to Prime's computer network and transfer data faster than they could over a com link.

Whatever the alcoves were used for, Uhura and the doctor had appreciated their presence because they were handy to slip into and remain hidden in whenever they had heard footsteps or other sounds in the tunnels. Though the tunnels were always lit at a uniform low intensity, Uhura knew that elsewhere in Prime, the environmental controls would be cycling up to morning and that soon many more workers would be traveling through all the tunnels and corridors.

The communications specialist squinted across the tunnel to the directional signs that were mounted opposite the alcove, comparing the numbers and colors on the various arrows to the instructions Romaine had given them. Everything still matched up.

"Two more intersections to the right," Uhura said, "then a left turn and continue until we see a green band leading to level forty-two."

"Just what I was going to say," McCoy lied unconvincingly. His breath regained, he leaned forward to stick his head out into the tunnel. "All clear," he announced.

Uhura followed the doctor out of the alcove and they began jogging rapidly down the tunnel, passing from one patch of low-level lighting, through a shadow zone, and into the next patch of light.

"Watch it!" McCoy suddenly shouted.

Before them, five meters down the hall, an associate trundled toward them. Unlike the others he and Uhura had passed that night, it was making no attempt to move to the side or otherwise get out of the humans' path.

Uhura and McCoy came to a halt, puffing softly, hearing the echoes of their breathing become obscured by the approaching hum of the associate.

"That's not normal," McCoy said. The machine rolled closer.

"Could it be on remote from the troopers' command station?" Uhura asked.

"I doubt it," McCoy said. "It doesn't have its visual scanner deployed. A remote technician wouldn't be seeing anything." .

With that the top panel of the machine sprang back and an eyestalk ground out, rotating to fix on Uhura and McCoy.

"I don't think it's going to stop, Doctor," Uhura said. There was no fear in her voice, just anger that their arrival at the scientists' compound was going to be delayed.

"We'll head back for an alcove," McCoy said, and spun around and stopped completely. He put his hand out to Uhura's arm.

Uhura turned. Another associate was approaching them from the other direction, its eyestalk just now extending to match the deployment of the associate farther down the tunnel.

"Think we can jump over them?" Uhura asked, knowing that she could and hoping McCoy could as well.

But before McCoy could answer, panels on each side of the approaching machine slid open, and manipulator arms swung out and up. Behind the two *Enterprise* officers, the first machine deployed its arms, too.

"I don't think they want us to jump," McCoy said quietly.

Uhura looked from one machine to the other. Both were closing at an equal rate. In seconds she and McCoy would be within reach of their mechanical arms.

"Split and run?" McCoy suggested.

Tactile grippers on the end of each arm began spinning like cutting saws, causing a high-pitched whine to reverberate off the tunnel walls.

"They don't want us to do that either," Uhura said. She began to judge the distances she would have to jump, the twists she would have to make. It seemed impossible, but at least she would try. The captain would expect that much of her.

McCoy reached out to squeeze Uhura's hand. The machines rolled closer. The two humans tensed as they prepared to rush the machines. Then the associates abruptly stopped centimeters away from their prey, and from their internal speakers, echoing lightly through that long tunnel of Memory Prime, came the gentle sound of laughter.

Kirk watched with fascination as the associate followed him down the ladderway to the lower service tunnel.

The associate had dropped two braces to the deck from its rear wheel wells, then, with the aid of its manipulator arms, pushed itself upright so it stood two meters tall. The manipulator nearer the ladder had then reached out and grabbed the far support post. Kirk had wondered why the ladder posts had a deep groove running down each, and now saw it was a channel for a manipulator attachment to hook into.

The associate had shifted itself over until it was lined up with the ladder and both manipulators were connected, then it simply slid down the ladder posts, stopping three centimeters above the next step off level, and reversed the procedure to return to its rolling configuration. The complete procedure took only twice the time that it had taken Kirk.

As the machine replaced its appendages, Kirk checked to see that the tunnel was still deserted and took a moment to place himself on his mental map of the Prime installation. By keeping the associate with him, and fortunately it had yet to announce it had other duties, Kirk knew that he would learn of Wolfe's response to Stlur and Scott's presentation as soon as a dispatch for him was logged on the system. But in the meantime, he was incapable of simply waiting in one place. Assuming that Spock was on his way to the scientists' compound, Kirk had decided to try and intercept him.

The captain saw that the associate was sealed and ready for movement, then set off down the tunnel in the direction that would take him to a central intersection. If he had been in Farl's position, Kirk would have stationed troopers at the intersection also. But there were many alcoves along the tunnel walls that Kirk could duck into. With the associate to roll in to block him, Kirk felt he could remain hidden in the event of a visual search. If the troopers were using combat tricorders, of course, he wouldn't stand a chance. It was a risk, he knew, but one that he was willing to accept.

Kirk heard the associate's induction motors speed up behind him and the soft whirr of its wheels on the tunnel deck increased. Suddenly Kirk fell forward as the machine nudged him from behind and caught his heel beneath its slanted front cowling.

Reflexively Kirk slapped the deck as he hit it, absorbing the impact without damage. He rolled quickly to see the associate reverse, stop, change its bearing, then come at him again.

At the last moment, Kirk rolled to the left. The machine changed its forward motion instantly, but had too great a turning radius to make contact with Kirk's body. It squealed to a stop on the decking.

Kirk leaped up to his feet, feeling a pull in his Achilles' tendon where the machine had hit his foot. "Module," he said, "stop your activities!"

"This module has other duties," the machine blandly announced, then twisted its tires against the deck with a sound like fingernails on slate. It backed toward Kirk at high speed.

From a standing position, it was even easier for Kirk to jump out of the way. The machine skidded to a stop like a bull overshooting its mark.

"Machine, I order you to stop!" This was ridiculous, Kirk thought. Unless the device was now being remote-controlled by one of Farl's troopers.

The machine didn't reply, but remained motionless as its top panel snapped back and its eyestalk emerged. Kirk saw his chance and rushed at the machine, bending down to reach under it and throw it over on its back. But as he struggled to lift the unexpectedly massive machine, it dropped its rear wheel-well braces and caught Kirk's left hand against the deck.

Grunting with the sudden pain, Kirk put everything he had into a sudden jerk and succeeded in lifting the machine for an instant and yanking out his hand. He flexed it experimentally, grimacing at the sight of his skin marked with the indentations of the brace's gripper texture, but thankful that no bones were broken.

The machine's eyestalk rotated around to fix on him. "Dispatch for James T. Kirk," the machine said in a mechanical voice, then sped at him.

Kirk held his ground to leap when the machine wouldn't have time to compensate. But with its full visual scanner deployed, the onboard brain could read Kirk's body position and anticipate his move.

At the same instant Kirk leaped, the machine swerved, catching the captain before he landed and bouncing him back into the air.

Kirk hit the deck on his side, unbalanced and rolling, absorbing too much of the force on his left arm. His hand felt as if it were on fire.

A quick assessment of all his intensive Academy training in tactics left him with a clear-cut decision: it was time to retreat.

The machine paused, watching as Kirk crouched on the deck. It's not a machine, Kirk told himself; treat it as an animal, an escaped wild animal. He took a quick glance behind him to see where the next ladderway was, but couldn't locate the yellow exit triangle glowing anywhere. If he tried to run farther in that direction, the machine would be able to run him down. If he called for help, the troopers would be the first to respond. There was only one way to run—past the machine and back to the first ladderway.

Kirk stood upright, catching his breath, rotating his twisted left shoulder. The machine had anticipated his last jump, so, as in playing three-dimensional chess with Spock, Kirk decided to hold back and let the machine make the next move and the next mistake. Running through what he knew of standard duotronic brains, he decided to take up some of the machine's processing power with distractions.

"I request that you run a maintenance diagnosis on your logic circuits," Kirk said to the machine, his voice ragged.

The associate rocked back and forth on its wheels, approaching, retreating, and back again. "All logic systems operating within fault-tolerant parameters," it announced.

"Glad to hear it," Kirk said. But at least whatever program or remote controller was running this machine now, it hadn't overridden the onboard brain's built-in standard functions. Kirk tried to remember what other functions he could call on.

"Please report on power levels," Kirk commanded, watching the eyestalk track him as he edged slowly to the right wall of the tunnel.

"Power levels at seventy-six percent of full load," the machine replied complacently, turning its forward wheels to keep itself aimed directly at Kirk. "Power consumption at nominal levels. Mean time to next recharge at current operational drain, eight hours, twenty-two minutes."

"Your report is in error," Kirk said suddenly. Why not? he thought. That tactic's worked before.

"Objection noted and will be filed with maintenance control at next scheduled overhaul," the associate said.

Kirk sighed. Obviously there were new techniques in place to deal with programming conflicts these days. He feinted to the left. The eyestalk moved with him but the machine didn't follow. Kirk swore. He realized that the visual scanner could read his intentions; and then he realized the tactic he needed to win.

"I surrender," Kirk announced, holding up his hands and taking a tentative step toward the device.

The machine paused, as if thinking over Kirk's offer, then said, "This module is not programmed for game playing." Its eyestalk followed Kirk carefully as its tires shifted to stay aimed at him.

"No, really," Kirk continued, "you've won the shirt off my back." Tightening his eyes at the pain of sudden movement, Kirk quickly pulled his gold tunic over his head, exhaling with relief when it was off and the machine had not used the chance to attack him again. Too much sudden and unexpected visual input, Kirk concluded. He held the tunic in his right hand, holding it out to the side and shaking it.

You've only got one visual scanner, Kirk thought, and now you have two points of reference. He took another step toward the machine. He could hear the flywheels in its induction motors come up to speed, preparing for a sudden burst of acceleration.

"Emergency! Emergency!" Kirk said urgently.

"Do you require assistance?" the associate automatically began, preparing for the kill.

"Fire! Airlock failure! Wounded on level five!" Kirk figured he had a full second before the machine would process all the automatic response sequences he had called forth. He jumped to the left. The machine followed but with a noticeable lag. It began to advance.

Kirk feinted again. The machine missed it as its onboard processors sampled data less frequently to accommodate its emergency time-sharing mode. Then Kirk ran for the device, swung his tunic out in front of him, and snagged the eyestalk as he jumped onto its back.

The associate locked its wheels and came to a bumping halt. Kirk knelt behind the eyestalk and held on to it as his knees bounced along the top of the machine, almost sending him off the side.

The associate was now motionless except for its weaving eyestalk. Kirk wrapped his tunic around the visual scanner three more times to ensure that not even infrared could pass through the fabric. The device was blinded. He could make it to the ladderway.

Then the machine shuddered as its side panels sprang back and its manipulator arms burst out from both sides. Kirk flinched as the tactile grippers at the end of each arm began to whirl and the arms snapped up. He knew the instant he jumped off to run, the onboard sensors would lock on to him and he'd be sliced open as easily as the insulation on the pipes above him before his foot touched the deck.

But if he stayed in place another few seconds, the onboard brain would have calculated the eyestalk's position and the arms would descend into the volume of space that Kirk now occupied.

Kirk's mind accelerated. There *was* a way out. There had to be.

The arms arced slowly into the space above the associate. Kirk hunched down, closer to the machine's top surface, to buy himself an extra half second. He stared down the trunk of the eyestalk, into the appendage bay it had emerged from.

Of course! Kirk thought as the whirling cutters descended. It's a *research* associate. It wasn't armored for vacuum or battle. He shot his arm into the appendage bay, groping blindly until his fingers grasped a thick bundle of wires. Then he yanked.

The machine bucked as transtator current pulsed through Kirk's arm. The manipulator arms jerked, a slowing cutter sliced against Kirk's back as the arms trembled, then collapsed to the deck, all internal hydraulic pressure exhausted.

The current cut out as a fail-safe system switched the batteries out of circuit. Kirk's body slumped against the associate's top, rolled to the side, then fell off to the deck.

A slight crackling sound resonated within the associate. A thin wisp of smoke swirled from the open appendage bay, flowing around the tunic-wrapped eyestalk that drooped like a dying plant.

Kirk stared blurrily at the pipes on the ceiling, trying to shake off the effects of the current. His left hand and arm throbbed with pain, his entire right side ached through a distant layer of shocked numbness. Another sound entered his consciousness: a familiar sound.

He looked down the corridor. Another associate advanced, eyestalk already extended. Kirk groaned, forcing his left arm to push him up against the shell of the associate beside him. His mind tried to sort out the swimming double images before him. He pulled at his black T-shirt, preparing to pull it off to use against the visual scanner. But the task suddenly seemed too complicated.

The second associate stopped by Kirk. Its eyestalk bent down to focus on him. Kirk stared back in defiance.

"This module thought you might be in need of some assistance, Captain Kirk," the machine said in a voice that bore no trace of mechanical origins. "But I see that I was mistaken."

Kirk blinked as he tried to place the machine's comments in context. The eyestalk moved up to examine the smoking ruin of the associate Kirk had battled, then rotated back to look into the captain's eyes.

"As a mutual acquaintance would say, Captain," the machine announced, "fascinating."

Kirk closed his eyes to blink, and found they wouldn't open again. As the rest of the universe rushed away from him, he had only one thought. . . .

". . . Spock. Spock?" Kirk sat up suddenly and his head exploded in a star bow of color. Gentle hands pushed him back to lie against something soft.

"I am here, Captain," Spock said in the darkness beyond Kirk's eyes.

Kirk felt the cool tingle of a spray hypo against his neck.

"You'll be all right, Jim," Bones said. "You had a nasty transtator shock but no real harm done."

Kirk opened his eyes and saw McCoy and Uhura looking down on him with worry and relief on their faces. Spock was there, too, and under the circumstances did the best that he could. Kirk also saw Romaine and Nensi in the background, faces etched with exhaustion and worry.

Kirk held his left hand in front of his face and studied the bandage that wrapped it. "Transtator shock?" he asked.

"Not all of it," McCoy said. "You've got an abraded hand, a wrenched shoulder, and a deep cut on your back. . . . But as your physician, I've come to accept those kinds of injuries as your normal state of health."

"Do you remember what happened, Captain?" Spock inquired.

"An associate," Kirk said as it came back to him. "It tried to attack me, I short-circuited it . . . a second associate came. . . ." He looked directly at Spock as if he doubted what he said next. "The second one spoke to me . . . as if it was alive."

"How else should I have spoken to you?" a familiar voice asked.

Spock stepped out of the captain's line of vision and Kirk saw that they were in some sort of equipment room. He could hear pumps operating and smelled a faint odor of disinfectant. It reminded him of the swimming pool on the *Enterprise.*

Then he saw what Spock had made way for. An associate, identical to all the others he had seen so far, rolled up to the table he lay on and extended its eyestalk toward him.

"May I introduce Two," Spock said.

"Two?" Kirk questioned.

"Two. It is a Pathfinder."

Kirk rotated his shoulders and found that McCoy's anti-inflammatory drugs had done their work. He had almost full flexibility in both, though his left hand was still stiff and he could feel the pull in his back where the protoplaser had sealed his cutter wound.

"So with all that you've said considered," Kirk concluded as he slipped off whatever it was that McCoy had rigged as a sickbed, "I'd say we have only one conclusion."

"I would be most interested to hear you share that with us, Captain," Spock said.

Kirk smiled. He had missed his science officer.

"Lifelike robots, appearing as Romulans, have assembled on Memory Prime to assassinate one or more of the scientists attending the prize ceremonies. To support their attempt, they have installed a secondary transporter network and have set up an override system that allows them to control the associates." Kirk glanced around to see that no one had any objections, or at least was saving them until he had finished.

"We can also assume that the assassins have generated subspace interference to prevent any signals from leaving Prime that might alert Starfleet security forces."

"Newscasts are still getting out, though," Romaine interjected.

"Keeps appearances normal," Kirk said. "If the newscasts were blocked, no one would have to wait for an alert signal to get troops here in hours. The advertisers would demand they go in right away." He walked back and forth in the equipment room, drawing everything together and seeing that it worked perfectly. "If Uhura's suspicions are correct and the last message Wolfe received from Komack did originate from Prime, rather than just being transferred up from a ground station, then it's probable that all the rest of the Fleet ships here are receiving false communications. Additional false signals would have to be passed on to Starfleet, too, in order for Command not to suspect that no one here is receiving their communications."

"Captain," Spock said as Kirk paused, "though the scenario you describe is internally logical, it is unfortunately based on a technological assumption which I believe has no merit."

"Which is?" Kirk asked.

"The extent of subspace interference which you propose is not possible given our present state of technology," Spock answered.

"He's right, Captain," Uhura added. "Subspace channels are virtually two-dimensional. Random signals that are energetic enough to jam one channel invariably smear out to affect the whole FTL spectrum."

"Given our present state of technology," Kirk said, "I agree with you. But the robots that captured Scotty and me were more advanced than any I've seen before. If the Romulans, or their suppliers, the Klingons, have come up with impressive breakthroughs in robotics, then why not allow for the possibility that they have come up with an equally advanced method of controlling subspace interference?"

"I point out that every rapid breakthrough in Klingon science has followed the subjugation of a technologically advanced culture, Captain. While I doubt that Klingons could have developed such technologies on their own, I am also skeptical of their ability to conquer a race that had already developed them." Spock was obviously not impressed with the captain's reasoning.

"Do you have another possibility for us to consider?" Kirk asked.

"Not at this time."

Kirk looked at the associate by the door. "How about the Pathfinder?"

The machine's eyestalk looked dumbly back.

"Over here, Captain." Two's voice came from one of the two associates that had brought Uhura and McCoy to the swimming-pool equipment room.

Kirk walked over to the associate who had spoken. It was still unnerving to be faced with a consciousness that could jump between host bodies, as it were. The Pathfinder had explained that his central core was still located twelve kilometers away, deep in the asteroid's center, and it was simply banking a few functions through an I/O port to make com-link contact with the associates.

Romaine had been stunned by the synthetic consciousness's offhand revelation, but no matter how many times she had tried to question it, the Pathfinder had insisted it did not know where the I/O channel was located.

"Part of the agreement in coming to work at Memory Prime was that the Pathfinders would have no direct access to outside systems and control networks," Romaine pointed out.

"That contract was initiated after I withdrew from access," Two had replied, "so perhaps those conditions do not apply to me." Then it laughed. Kirk had found that ability even more unnerving.

"So?" Kirk repeated. "Do you have any other possibilities to suggest to us?"

"Not at this time," the Pathfinder said in a passable imitation of Spock's voice. It laughed again.

"Two." Kirk spoke again, trying to ignore the unnerving laughter. "Have any dispatches been logged for us on the associates' message network?"

"Nothing so far, Captain," the Pathfinder said from the associate over by the door.

"Can you access the communications channels to see if anything has been said about calling off the hunt for Spock and the rest of us?" Kirk tried.

The Pathfinder returned to the associate by Kirk. "Commander Farl has ordered his troops not to use the portable transporters because a second system is interfering with their operations," it said. "All internal transportation systems are now being shut down and will be inoperative within the next four minutes. Emergency transportation facilities will be provided by the *Enterprise* and the *Valquez*."

"I was right about that one, then," Kirk said, glancing at Spock. He turned back to the machine. "When do the opening ceremonies start?"

"Two hours, three minutes, eighteen seconds . . . seventeen seconds . . . six—"

"That will do, thank you," Kirk interrupted.

"Can you scan through the list of scientists attending the ceremonies and identify those whose deaths would be most disruptive to the Federation at this time?" Spock asked.

"That's a good one," the Pathfinder replied. "Give me a few seconds to work out the probabilities."

"Good idea, Spock," Kirk said. Then he narrowed his eyes at the Vulcan. "I have a good question for it, as well."

The Pathfinder rejoined them before Spock could reply.

"There are forty-seven scientists attending the prize ceremonies whose deaths could result in the virtual collapse of Federation initiatives in weapons design, propulsion technology, and political organization."

"Is Professor La'kara on that list?" Kirk asked.

"Zoareem La'kara is on the third level of importance."

"Are any of the scientists who traveled on the *Enterprise* among the forty-seven most vital scientists?" Kirk tried again.

"Nope," the Pathfinder said.

"Where does Academician Sradek rank?" Spock asked.

"Fifth rank. Of no long-term importance," Two replied.

Kirk studied Spock's reaction. Despite Stlur's comment, the science officer did exhibit reactions to those who knew him well enough to read them. "You don't agree with that assessment?" Kirk asked.

"Sradek has made many valuable contributions to the growth and the stability of the Federation," Spock said.

"But not recently," the Pathfinder countered. "Sradek is growing old and his contemporary work is not sound."

"But he's a nominee for the Peace Prize," Nensi said.

"For negotiations concluded almost two standard years ago," the Pathfinder replied. "He has completed no work of importance since that time and has hindered the work of the Sherman's Planet famine board of inquiry."

"Fascinating," Spock said with as much excitement as anyone could ever expect to hear from him. "I have recently reached a similar conclusion based on Sradek's failure to recognize the existence of the Sherman Syndrome as anything more than a statistical artifact."

"It *is* obvious," the Pathfinder stated condescendingly.

Spock walked over to the associate who currently housed Two's remote functions. "What data can you produce to support the basic argument of the Sherman Syndrome?" Spock asked.

"Most of the raw data are stored on Memory Gamma but the conclusions are generally evolved here," Two said. "Give me a few seconds to sift it."

Kirk had had enough. "Spock, we can get back to agriculture when the assassins have been stopped. Time for my question." He turned to the associate that had just spoken. "Pathfinder Two, how does the name T'Pel connect with the assassination attempt we have been discussing?"

"Captain Kirk," Spock said, "there is no logical reason to—"

"Perfectly," the associate next to Kirk replied. Then the Pathfinder banked to the associate beside Spock and said, "Sherman Syndrome data has been interfered with. I am attempting to reconstruct."

"What do you mean by 'perfectly'?" Kirk said, looking from one associate to the next.

"Who else but an Adept of T'Pel would contemplate the assassination of the Federation's greatest scientists," the third associate in the middle replied, "and be able to accomplish it?"

"Who or what is an Adept of T'Pel?" Kirk demanded.

"Pathfinder," Spock interrupted, "I ask that you provide the information I requested to support the Sherman Syndrome."

"Spock!" Kirk snapped. "I said that can wait!" He turned to the associate. "Pathfinder, explain the meaning of an Adept of T'Pel."

"They are the guild of Vulcan assassins," the associate by Kirk said.

"Sherman Syndrome data has been recon—" the associate by Spock said.

Kirk was locked into position, not daring to breathe so he wouldn't miss an instant of the bizarre three-sided conversation. But his associate said nothing more. Neither did Spock's.

"I/O port shut down," Romaine said finally, breaking the silence. "It cut out in midword."

"Spock," McCoy said in wonderment, "a *Vulcan* guild of *assassins?* Is such a thing possible?"

Everyone turned to look at Spock. The Vulcan's face was frozen in an expression completely devoid of meaning.

"What about it, Spock?" Kirk said, his anger apparent. "You've known something all along, haven't you?"

"Not known, Captain. Suspected," Spock said at last.

"Isn't that splitting logical hairs, Mr. Spock?" McCoy asked. "Have you actually had information that might have stopped any of this?"

"No, Doctor, I have not had information that could have stopped any of the steps that have been taken thus far. I had suspicions, based only on my own knowledge, and with no supportable evidence. The suggestion that Memory Prime was to be subjected to an attack instigated by the Adepts of T'Pel, would have been met with ridicule"—Spock looked at the captain as if only he would understand—"and violated a sacred Vulcan trust."

"Then there *are* such things as Vulcan assassins?" McCoy gasped.

"Absolutely not, Doctor," Spock stated. "Such a concept would not be tolerated on my planet. Indeed, it is not tolerated."

"Which is why none of you will talk about it," Kirk said, suddenly understanding the connection between Stlur's cold response to the name of T'Pel and Spock's determined effort to keep Kirk from looking further into its meaning. "It does exist."

"But not on Vulcan," Spock said. "Not anymore."

Kirk walked over to his friend, stood beside him, and spoke softly.

"Start at the beginning, Spock. There's not much time."

Twenty-two

Within each Vulcan dwelt a secret heart, a voice and a message from their beginnings, passed on from one mindmeld to the other through the long years since the Reformation, whispering of the madness that had been their crucible. That secret heart was their witness to the past, their window on their culture's birth, more than two thousand standard years ago.

Even then, the Vulcan intellect was unequaled. The specter of ruin that haunted their planet was known by all, embraced by some, and rejected by but a few. Resistance seemed futile, and the great minds and orators of Vulcan prepared their followers for the ultimate reward of emotions run wild: the war and destruction and extinction that had claimed so many other worlds.

As had also happened on so many other worlds, some individuals spoke out against the inevitable, and made themselves heard, and the greatest triumph of Vulcan was that in its final hour, the people listened.

His name was Surak, and his message was simple and direct. If emotions unchecked are to control us until we are destroyed, then we must first control our emotions and survive. It was a call for Total Logic, and it offered the planet salvation.

A hundred years earlier, Surak would have been ignored. A hundred years later, he would have been cut down before any could have listened. But at the time he spoke out, Vulcan was poised on that precarious threshold—still civilized enough to have political forums where Surak could present and debate his ideas, and yet chaotic enough that some could read the warning signs.

As the debates proceeded across the planet, Surak assembled supporters and faced enemies. Though not the most numerous, the most deadly faction among his enemies was from his own family, the woman T'Pel.

She was a warrior by nature and longed for the ancient days when an individual's worth was easily measured by the torrents of emerald blood she had unleashed upon the deserts' red sands. A future, however brief, of war and glory was infinitely preferable to the stultifying boredom that her cousin preached.

So T'Pel stole Surak's message, and twisted it into one of her own. To a world crying out for answers, she brought a release from the need for answers, an escape from the tyranny of cause and effect. She called it Analogics, and in her public debates with Surak, she used its twisted precepts to logically negate his call for logic.

Some in the audiences laughed. Some cringed. And some saw that in a system that required they no longer think critically, they could at last find peace. As T'Pel taught them, there was no greater peace than death. So it was that before the glory of the Reformation, there was the blackness and the disgrace of the nights of the assassins. Her Adepts, she called them, the Adepts of T'Pel.

T'Pel trained her most trusted Adepts in the long unpracticed schools of deadly arts, instilling them with terrifying powers of destruction to be used without regard for motive. Then she offered them to her world, to perform whatever acts of terrorism were asked of them. Escape was not a requirement of any plan. The shock of mindless killing and destruction was.

In a sense, it was the horror and revulsion that the majority felt for the acts of the Adepts that made more and more Vulcans listen seriously to Surak. Surak *told* his listeners what the world of the future might be like if Vulcans' emotions remained unchecked. T'Pel *showed* those same people exactly what it *would* be like. The tide slowly and inexorably turned to Surak and Total Logic. T'Pel and her Adepts were reviled and hunted. The path to Vulcan's future had been clearly laid out by Surak, and his followers would find no place for the madness of T'Pel. Beneath the swelling wave of irrefutable logic, T'Pel and her Adepts disappeared from Vulcan and its records; a part of the past that logical Vulcans could know of and accept, but that which no outworlder could possibly comprehend. Her acts, her schools, her followers, were relegated to the vaults of the secret histories of Vulcan, which some offworlders had often suspected existed, but which none had seen.

But Surak had had other enemies, not all as extreme as T'Pel . . . at first.

The Travelers were those who had rejected Surak and his ways and, by doing so, had rejected Vulcan. In monstrous ships, they had abandoned the world that had forsaken them and set out to find a new world to tame with the ancient traditions intact and venerated. And among them were others with different motives for leaving Vulcan, others for whom exile was preferable to death. Deep within the Travelers' ships, T'Pel and her last Adepts journeyed for their own chance for freedom.

At last the Travelers came to a system with two planets that some, in desperation, would call suitable for life. The most hard won of the two was called ch'Havran, and on it were the harsh lands of the dreaded East Continent. It was there that the clan that would spring from T'Pel and her Adepts would find a home suitable for their talents.

The Travelers had willingly discarded all that they had that was Vulcan. A new language was created, new customs explored, the hatred for their origins grew until they had wiped out all traces of their Vulcan heritage. Except on the East Continent. Except in the nations of Kihai and LLunih, where in the darkened secret rooms, the old traditions were passed, and the name that was whispered from lips that dripped with the green gore of their blood sacrifices was the name T'Pel.

All other names from Vulcan passed from their knowing. The Travelers themselves were now the Rihannsu. But when the humans came, the name that was given in ignorance was Romulan, and among the proud people who had once given up an entire world for what they perceived as justice, the time for action had once again come.

Some among the Rihannsu were willing to listen to the humans and risk meetings and exchanges. But in the East Continent, in the nations of Kihai and LLunih, the ancient traditions lived. The ships from the clans of those nations were the ones that dogged the Federation vessels, becoming more and more brazen in their actions until war was inevitable.

It was a glorious time for the Adepts. They fueled the images of their nation's atrocities that burned into the minds and souls of a hundred worlds, rekindling the horror of what might have been the last great days of Vulcan.

But in that first war the Federation was victorious, and once again the Adepts of T'Pel sank beneath knowing in defeat. But the war they had helped start had brought them important new knowledge: the universe had changed since the time of the Travelers. There were innumerable new worlds and new civilizations joined into one.

Why should the Adepts content themselves with the destruction of just one world and one culture when there were so many now to choose from?

The Adepts of T'Pel had waited two thousand years for this moment. Before them the galaxy beckoned, and they moved out into it, learning its ways, swearing by the ancient blood and the ancient name that before they were forced to retreat again, they would hear that galaxy scream.

They had been true to their oath. In the dark reaches of the galaxy, in the ports and shadows where such things were discussed, the ancient name was passed from one to another, offering unspeakable services . . . for a price. Thus far the galaxy had been silent. But that silence would not last. The Adepts of T'Pel had sworn it.

They had returned.

Twenty-three

"Good Lord," McCoy whispered. The others in the room remained silent. Only the soft rush of the pumps could be heard.

"How long have you known?" Kirk asked, his anger replaced with sorrow. Alone among the others he knew the cost to Spock of what had been revealed. A sacred Vulcan trust, Spock had called his knowledge of T'Pel, and he had been forced to break it.

"Of T'Pel," Spock said, "since I was a child and experienced my first melds with the ancient memories. Vulcans do not blindly follow the teachings of Surak simply because it is our tradition. Through the melds, each of us has experienced firsthand the chaos from which those teachings sprang and the chaos to which we might return if we do not continue in the ways of logic."

Spock looked in turn at each of those listening, making sure to meet their gaze, especially McCoy's. Kirk knew it was Spock's way of making his plea that none of what he had told them be repeated, a plea that logic forbade him from making aloud.

"How long have I known that the Adepts of T'Pel still exist among the Romulans of today?" Spock continued. "Classified documents from the first Romulan war hint at it. Analyses completed in the century since then tend to confirm it. But there is still no absolute proof, as no Adept has ever been captured. Alive."

"But how long have you known, or suspected, that they were responsible for the events on Prime?" Kirk asked gently.

"Since Mira's message informed me that Commodore Wolfe commanded the troopers to search for me with phasers set to kill."

"How does that prove anything?" Uhura asked before anyone else had the chance.

"It's against every regulation in the book," Kirk answered so Spock could continue.

"Exactly," Spock said. "Starfleet expressly forbids the use of deadly force against unarmed personnel."

"Then how in blazes could Wolfe order her troopers to use deadly force against you?" McCoy demanded.

"Quite obviously, the commodore had some reason for believing that I was no longer to be considered unarmed."

"But why?" Uhura asked.

"She thought you were part of the Adepts of T'Pel," Kirk said softly.

"Precisely," Spock replied. "And as such, trained in the ancient schools of unassisted combat; a being whose entire body can be considered a living weapon and sworn to the destruction of life and order at all costs. The commodore could not send her troops unprotected against such a being. She had no choice but to order them to defend themselves and this facility in the most decisive manner, just as we would respond to any comparable military threat."

It took only a moment for McCoy to see where that conclusion led. "You mean *Starfleet* knows?" he asked. "About the *Adepts?*"

"Precisely, Doctor," Spock answered. "It would not be logical for Vulcans to refuse to share information that could preserve the stability of the Federation. There are those within Starfleet who have been made aware of the Adepts of T'Pel and the role they might play in any potentially destabilizing activities. However, that information is strictly classified."

"But why?" McCoy, as usual, bridled at the machinations of the government.

"Think, Doctor," Spock explained. "If the general population learned that an organization of Romulan assassins threatened the Federation, then surely there would be an increase in those who clamored for a resumption of war. Furthermore, revealing that the Federation is aware of the Adepts' existence would provide the Adepts with proof that their organization has in some way been penetrated by the Federation Security Service. Whatever means the service has been using to monitor the Adepts will have been compromised and lost. Unable to be kept under surveillance, the Adepts will then become even more dangerous. The Federation's knowledge of them cannot be revealed."

"To say nothing of what it might tell the general population about Vulcan history," Nensi commented.

"We prefer to think of it as *pre*history," Spock corrected, "but that is also a consideration. Though by no means the most important one."

"So we're cut off," McCoy railed, "being hunted down by a commodore who'd rather see us dead than risk having knowledge of the Adepts revealed, and at the mercy of a bunch of Romulans who want to kill the Federation's best scientists so they can start a war!" His arms flapped at his sides. "I should have been a vet," he said in disgust, and slumped against the wall.

"I will agree that we are cut off," Spock said calmly, "and concede that the commodore would rather have me, at least, killed. But we cannot assume that the Adepts wish to start a war."

"And why not?" McCoy demanded.

"The Adepts follow the so-called discipline of Analogics," Spock said. "They have no motives. They are assassins for *hire.*"

"Without a motive," Kirk said, "most crimes can't be solved. That's why it's been so hard to determine who the victim of the assassin or assassins might be: they aren't connected, except by the third party who hired one to kill the other."

"But who?" McCoy was becoming more aggravated by the second.

"Think motive, Bones," Kirk said. "What motives would the Adepts work for?

Illogical motives. Madness. Confusion. Destruction of order, of . . ." He turned to Spock, eyes afire. "Sradek!" he cried.

"The assassin?" Spock asked in surprise.

"No, the victim!" Kirk reached out his hands. "You've been investigating his work. Pathfinder Two confirmed it. Sradek's interfering with the operation of the Sherman's Planet famine board of inquiry, is he not?"

"So I believe," Spock confirmed.

"Agribusiness! Big business," Kirk continued. "Billions upon billions of credits at stake. The stability of the whole sector. What if Sradek is *not* interfering? What if the Sherman's Planet famine and all the ones like it have been specifically engineered? It's possible. A conspiracy by some group to ensure that environmental data for agricultural worlds is misreported or misrepresented. That leads to improper crop selection, therefore crop failures, financial drain on the interplanetary banking system, famine, disease . . . political instability. What would happen if that type of disaster was being manipulated to appear on dozens of worlds at once on purpose, instead of just one or two by accident? Sradek's brilliant, trained Vulcan mind may be the only one that can see the truth that the famines have been artificially created. He could be the target of a campaign to discredit him and his work so that no one will believe his conclusions. And since that campaign isn't totally working, the only other way to prevent his interference is to kill him!"

Spock considered the captain's hypothesis. He raised both eyebrows and nodded. "It does fit the facts," he admitted.

"But you're not convinced?" Kirk prodded.

"I would have to accept that my independent study of Sradek's conclusions was in error—"

"Heaven forbid your work should be in error, Spock!" McCoy muttered.

"But it *could* be if the data you were working with was wrong!" Kirk said in triumph. "Pathfinder Two said that the Sherman's Planet data from Memory Gamma had been interfered with! If the conspiracy has penetrated the Memory Planets, there's no end to the chaos that incorrect data could cause."

"I believe we must warn Academician Sradek," Spock announced. The debate was over.

"At least you could have the courtesy to say the captain was right," McCoy suggested.

"I believe I already have, Doctor." Spock studied Kirk. "Considering your injuries, are you able to join us, Captain?"

Kirk refused to dignify the question with a response and turned to Romaine. "Mira, how can we get to Sradek?"

Nensi stepped forward before Romaine could answer. "The doctor and the lieutenant are in civvies, so they can come with Mira and me. I've got the VIP passes to get them into the scientists' compound on my authority. You and Spock can come up in the associate equipment cart."

"Equipment cart?" Kirk asked.

Nensi blinked at the captain. "How do you think Pathfinder Two had the associate bring you here? Drag you through the tunnels asking the troopers not to look?" Nensi pulled a sheet of insulating fabric off the platform Kirk had come to consciousness on. It was a wheeled, closed cart, about the size of an associate, with a hitch at one end that Kirk saw could attach to an associate's rear appendage bay.

"Oh," Kirk said. "That was going to be my next question."

Scott felt the vibration of the glowing verifier dome flutter against his hand. He looked nervously over to the technician who operated the Mark II desktop terminal in Prime's security interrogation room. The technician ran a hand through his dark beard and looked up at Commodore Wolfe standing beside him.

"Verified," the technician said resignedly. "He's telling the truth, Commodore. Three times out of three. Just like Dr. Stlur."

The commodore glared at Scott. Scott felt his indignation grow but forced himself not to say or do anything that would interfere with his chances of getting the commodore to believe him. Spock's life, even the captain's, depended on his convincing the commodore that the real threat to the scientists on Prime came from robots and not from Scott's fellow officers.

"Medical analysis!" the commodore snapped.

The Andorian trooper that stood beside the verifier stand waved a medical scanner in front of Scott's head and chest and checked the readings on a tricorder.

"Absolutely no indication of blocking drugss or nonbiological implantss, Commodore," he hissed in disappointment.

Wolfe leaned over and checked the readings on the terminal again, tapping her hand on its status indicator bar. Then she stood up, a decision made. "Set that to automatic," she told the technician, "and leave. Both of you." She held out her hand to the Andorian. "But you give me your phaser," she added.

A few moments later, the interrogation room cleared except for herself and the prisoner, Wolfe leaned back in her chair and regarded Scott with a look of contempt.

"Mr. Scott," she finally began, "we will proceed on the assumption that at the end of all this you will still wish to be a part of Starfleet . . . no matter what your eventual rank downgrading might turn out to be. That is what you wish, is it not?" She turned to watch the computer display.

Scott swallowed hard. "Aye, Commodore, it certainly is."

"Good," Wolfe said, seeing that the engineer's reply was confirmed by the verifier. "Now, Mr. Scott, are you aware of the penalties as set out in Starfleet regulations pertaining to the disclosure of classified material?"

"Aye," Scott said. What did this have to do with anything? he wondered.

"Very good," Wolfe said, narrowing her eyes at the engineer. "Therefore, as stated in those same regulations, let me inform you that some of what I'm about to say may or may not fall under level-eight classification. I will not tell you which parts are so classified so you will be bound by your Starfleet oath not to reveal any part of this conversation without risking solitary life imprisonment on Rock. Do you understand what I have just said?"

"That I do, Commodore," Scott answered, his voice dry and threatening to crack.

"What knowledge do you have of an organization known as the Adepts of T'Pel?" Wolfe's eyes stayed locked on the Mark II's display lights.

Scott glanced up at the light strips along the ceiling, desperately trying to determine why the name sounded familiar. "I, ah, I have nae knowledge of such an organization," he stammered.

"The verifier indicates otherwise, Mr. Scott," the commodore said in a voice of judge, jury, and executioner. "I will allow you one more chance to tell me the truth."

"T'Pel!" Scott suddenly said. "That was the name the captain asked Dr. Stlur about!"

The commodore smiled and Scott had a sudden fear that he was somehow betraying the captain.

"And what was the nature of that inquiry?" Wolfe continued.

Scott bit his lip, trying to replay the discussion in the reading lounge. "Ah, the captain . . . the captain asked Dr. Stlur what the name meant just as we were getting ready to leave the lounge."

"What was the Vulcan's response?"

Scott wrinkled his brow as he remembered. "The doctor said it was his . . . his grandmother's name." It wasn't making sense to Scott, but from Wolfe's expression, it seemed that she saw a pattern forming in his replies.

The questions and answers continued as the commodore led Scott through a reconstruction of Kirk's exchange with Stlur. When Scott had finished, Wolfe scratched at the side of her face, deep in thought.

"Uh, Commodore?" Scott said, unable to remain in the dark by choice.

Wolfe nodded at him to proceed.

"Why the change?"

"Mr. Scott?"

"In the way ye dealt with the captain? I mean, I can understand why ye had to confine Mr. Spock to his quarters. Getting that message from Starfleet just as we came into your starbase and all, ye had nae choice but to follow orders. Even Mr. Spock himself admitted that it was logical for ye to suspect him of sabotaging the accelerator shielding system." The commodore's eyes widened at that but she made no comment. "But what I cannae understand is why ye suddenly turned on Captain Kirk. Sure he supported Mr. Spock, gave him the benefit of the doubt, but can't ye see, Mr. Spock is his . . . his crew. Captain Kirk just dinnae have a choice."

Scott looked nervously at the commodore. He hadn't intended to say so much, to sound as if he were challenging her, but the truth was that Kirk was his captain, and the engineer shared the same lack of choice in what his loyalty demanded of him.

Wolfe looked long and hard at Scott, and Scott was surprised to see that not once did she turn to check the verifier's reading.

"Mr. Scott," she said at last, "do you know what kind of a man James T. Kirk is?" She didn't give him a chance to answer. "Do you have any idea of the number of people, men *and* women, who dream of commanding a starship of their own, to have a chance to go *first,* to be *first,* see things, experience things that no one has ever seen or experienced before? Kirk is the one who made it. He worked hard. I know that. He worked hard for me at the Academy. But there were lots of others who worked just as hard, dreamed just as hard, and never made it because there are only a handful of starships."

Wolfe pushed her chair back and stood up, staring at Scott with questioning eyes, eyes that offered Scott an answer to his question.

"No one knows exactly how the selection committee chooses who gets a starship and who gets a cruiser, who gets a starbase and who gets a spacedock, and I've been in the service long enough to know that you don't question authority. I was passed over, Mr. Scott. I admit it. And I can also tell you that I'm not bitter. I couldn't have stayed in the Fleet if I had been." She picked up the phaser with which she had been left and Scott involuntarily flinched until he saw that she was attaching it to her utility belt. She flashed a small smile as she realized the cause of Scott's reaction.

"So I stayed, and I taught all those others who came through the Academy. Same dream, same hopes shared by so many of them . . . a *starship* . . . to go *out there*. I prepared them as best I could, and whenever one of them made it, or even came close, I rejoiced for him or for her, well and truly, because as long as one of my students made it, then part of me was out there, too. Part of me was out there with your captain." She held her finger over the comm switch on the Mark II, ready to signal the trooper to return.

"And when I saw that Kirk had blown it, when I saw that he was taking everything that he had achieved and was throwing it in the faces of all those others, me included, who would have done *anything* to have that one chance . . . well, Mr. Scott, as far as I could see, James T. Kirk was a traitor. Not just to Starfleet and the Federation, but to the dream, Mr. Scott. To the *dream*."

Scott had his answer. But how to give the commodore hers? "He's nae a traitor, Commodore," he said softly. "And neither is Mr. Spock."

"I pray you're wrong, Mr. Scott," the commodore said. Her voice was firm, her eyes dry and unwavering, but Scott could sense the anguish in her soul. "Because there is too much at stake here. I can't accept what you and Dr. Stlur have said." She pressed the com switch and behind her the interrogation room's doors puffed open and the Andorian trooper marched in. "I'm sorry, Mr. Scott. I truly am."

"Then at least tell your troops to set their phasers on stun!" Scott shouted out as the commodore turned to leave.

Commodore Wolfe did not look back. Scott thought later that perhaps she was unable to meet his eyes and still say what she had said.

"I can't, Mr. Scott. I'm following my orders."

"Then that's the difference between ye and the captain!" Scott called out to her, stepping out of the verifier chair even as the trooper ran to hold him back. "Ye say ye've been in the service long enough to know ye don't question authority! But that's what the captain does! *Question,* not defy! It's what keeps the system working! Keeps it honest and fair!"

The commodore paused in the corridor outside, still not looking back, but not continuing forward.

"Sometimes ye have to question authority to stop mistakes from being repeated, Commodore! Ye've made one mistake about the captain, already. Don't make another! Especially one ye can't set right again! Commodore!"

Following standard procedures, the trooper applied a light stun to the prisoner to calm him down. As Scott slouched into the verifier chair, still struggling to call the commodore's name, Wolfe moved on and the doors slid shut behind her.

"What is this," McCoy asked as he looked around the lab, "the Middle Ages?"

"Special case," Nensi explained as he closed the lid on the associate cart that Kirk and Spock had hidden in, in order to gain access to the scientists' compound. The biolab they were in was an animal test facility, the only one on Prime and one of only a handful throughout the Federation, excepting agricultural and zoological research centers and zoos.

Kirk studied the animal cages at the side of the lab. They were stacked three up and twelve across against the wall, sealed off from the rest of the lab by a windowed partition. The animals inside appeared to be meter-tall, hairless apes with shiny, dark red skin. Two fingers waggled from the hands on each long arm as they patted the almost invisible surface of the transparent aluminum panels that served as their individual cage doors.

"Constellation monkeys, they're called," Nensi said. "And no one is quite sure if they *are* living creatures or not. That's part of the work going on here."

"This *is* the lab that Sradek told you he'd meet us in, isn't it?" Kirk asked.

"Oh, yes," Nensi confirmed. "This is where he's been working during his visit to Prime." Nensi pointed to a stack of equipment crates piled around one of the worktables. Kirk recognized them as the cargo that had beamed aboard with Sradek from Starbase Four.

"What is the nature of Sradek's work in an animal experimentation lab?" Spock asked, eyebrows drawn together. "It does not seem a logical place for a political scientist." He stood in front of the animal cages, staring in at the creatures.

"He's studying models of aggression, I believe," Nensi said. "The constellation monkeys are unique because it's thought that they are not really separate creatures. More like individual cells in a spread-out organism. Group mind."

"That's common enough," Uhura said, staring at a row of six associates that were parked under a long workbench in a corner of the lab. Kirk glanced over and saw that, unlike the other associates he had seen so far in Prime, these had brilliant red stripes painted around their sides.

"The experiments taking place here are simply to determine the range of their shared responses," Nensi said. "Everything is quite safe, except the odd time when they try to escape," he added.

Everyone turned to look at him. "Nothing serious," he assured them. "But they do get rambunctious."

"I don't like it that Sradek hasn't shown up," Kirk said. "Someone should go and escort him here." He hadn't approved when Nensi had said that the academician had responded to his request for a private meeting by suggesting a location other than his quarters, but by then it was too late. If Sradek were the assassins' target, the journey from his rooms to the lab put him at an unacceptable level of risk.

"Fine," Nensi said, "I'll go." He headed to the main lab doors. "Remember, no one can get into this part of the compound without being one of the accredited scientists or having a VIP pass. The most probable place for the assassins to strike would be outside of the main auditorium, just before the opening ceremonies or just after—oh, hello!"

As Nensi had approached them, the oversized doors to the lab had slid open to reveal the dark-suited form of Academician Sradek waiting beyond.

Nensi recovered from his surprise and held up his hand in greeting.

"Live long and prosper, Academician Sradek," he said formally.

The elderly Vulcan stared at the chief administrator for a moment, then seemed to dismiss him from existence. He merely walked in past Nensi, slowly and slightly stooped. The doors slid shut behind him.

The academician stood in the center of the lab and surveyed all those around him. "Now will you tell me what is the purpose of this meeting?" he asked imperiously.

"We believe you may be in some danger, Academician," Spock said as he approached Sradek, hand up and fingers parted.

The academician looked blandly at Spock and returned the salute. "I have looked forward to our meeting. I regret that it has been so delayed." Sradek looked over at Kirk. "I believe that one may have been responsible."

"He was not," Spock stated. "Starfleet was provided with erroneous information without the captain's knowledge."

Over by the wall of creatures, McCoy rolled his eyes and interrupted the Vulcans' staccato speech by saying, "Let's get on with it, shall we? Someone's trying to kill you!"

"What is that?" Sradek inquired, glancing behind Spock at McCoy.

"A doctor," Spock answered, then continued with what he had been about to say. "I, too, have looked forward to our meeting and regret that it has been delayed."

"You and three others I can think of," Romaine added. She was sitting with Uhura on the workbench over the parked associates.

"Indeed," Spock said, looking over at her. "Which three are those?"

"The Vulcans on my research team," Romaine answered. "Lieutenant Stell, Specialist Slann, and Dr. T'Lar. All in preventive detention the way you were."

Spock lashed out his arm and Sradek parried so quickly that at first Kirk wasn't sure what had happened.

Romaine and Uhura jumped off the workbench and ran to the middle of the lab as did Kirk, Nensi, and McCoy, propelled by the incredible sight of Spock and Sradek locked in hand-to-hand combat.

Kirk crouched and sidestepped to get behind Sradek. He did not question the necessity of the conflict or his action. If Spock had attacked, then for Kirk that was all the justification he needed to join the fray. But each time Kirk was about to move behind Sradek, the grappling pair shifted out of reach.

"Spock, what are you doing?" Kirk shouted. Spock was actually trying to twist Sradek away from the captain.

"Stay back," Spock ordered as if his jaw were set in stone. His arms were locked with Sradek's, each battling to displace the other's center of gravity.

Sradek's back was turned to Nensi. The chief administrator saw his chance and swung.

"No!" Spock shouted just as Sradek twisted and lashed out his foot, catching Nensi in his chest with a thick and terrible crunch.

The chief administrator dropped to the floor as Sradek took advantage of the sudden momentum stolen from Nensi to fall back himself. Spock was pulled forward onto Sradek's coiled legs, then flipped through the air to collide with McCoy, who had been weaving with a spray hypo at the ready, waiting for his own chance to attack.

Kirk ran to the right and vaulted over a worktable to approach Sradek from the left. Uhura did the same on the other side, setting the pincer in place.

In one fluid movement, Sradek backflipped onto the worktable behind him as two flares of incandescence appeared to shoot from each hand.

Kirk flew backward as a brick wall hit him. His hands trembling like a ship at warp nine, he clutched at a small, flickering needle embedded in his chest and tore it out. The trembling stopped, but his arms and legs felt as if their muscles had vanished. It took all his strength to sit up on the table he had landed on.

On the other side of the lab, Uhura pulled a similar needle from her neck, McCoy and Romaine huddled over the fallen form of Nensi, and Spock stood alone, staring at the being who had first appeared as Academician Sradek. The imposter now crouched upon a worktable, circling his closed fists in preparation of firing more needles at any who might dare rush him.

"Malther dart launchers are strapped to his forearms," Spock announced. "Do not attack. He is an Adept."

"It certainly took you long enough, *Vulcan*," the Adept cackled. His features contorted as he laughed at Spock.

"Spock, how—" Kirk started to ask, then was racked by a coughing fit, a remnant of the dart's effect.

"My apologies, Captain," Spock said, never taking his eyes from the assassin. "I recognized Lieutenant Stell and Dr. T'Lar's names as two who had also taken instruction from Sradek at the Academy, as had I."

The Adept laughed again and jumped to the floor like a humanoid panther.

Spock continued. "I had not connected the sudden false message from Starfleet, which resulted in my confinement, with Sradek's refusal to speak to me from the commodore's party just before we arrived at Starbase Four. Obviously, the Adepts of T'Pel were taking every precaution that those who knew Sradek would not be able to meet with him."

"But he came to my cabin and demanded to see you, Spock," Kirk protested as the Adept edged toward a computer terminal at the end of the table.

"Knowing full well that the commodore would not disobey her orders and allow us to meet," Spock concluded.

"Sradek," Kirk called out.

"Do insult me with my Vulcan names, Captain. I am not Academician Sradek, nor trader Starn, nor any of a dozen others. I am of the Rihannsu. You may call me tr'Nele." The Romulan held one hand ready to fire his Malther darts while he tapped instructions on the worktable's computer keyboard with the other.

"How's Nensi, Bones?" Kirk asked as he moved slowly to the left.

"The next ones in the clip are fatal, Captain," tr'Nele interrupted. "Move back where you were."

"His chest is crushed, Jim," McCoy called over. "He'll die if he doesn't get to a sickbay immediately."

"Not to worry, human," tr'Nele said, pressing a last key on the computer. "You're *all* going to die." He waved his hands together, encompassing them all. "Everyone move together into the center of the room, hands over your heads. Drag the human, Doctor. Pain is relative."

"If you go through with this, you'll just be confirming that the Adepts of T'Pel still exist," Kirk said as he stood in the lab's center with the others. His lungs still burned with the aftereffects of the dart. Romaine had to support Uhura. "You'll be hunted down, destroyed."

"Have you never heard of entropy, Captain? *Everything* will be destroyed, eventually. In the meantime, the semisentient life-forms who call themselves Federation security will investigate the tragic fire in this lab to discover that *all* of you died along with that mad assassin, Academician Sradek." He laughed mockingly.

"Why will they think Sradek is the assassin?" Spock asked as if inquiring about the time.

"Because after the assassination, the stunned witnesses will watch as Sradek runs back into this lab, just as its faulty power modules explode. When the smoke clears, all of your bodies will be found, including Sradek's."

"An autopsy will show that you are a Romulan," Spock pointed out.

"Of course it would because *I* am Rihannsu," tr'Nele agreed, "but Sradek's body is pure Vulcan!" He snapped his arm in the direction of the stacked crates and a dart shattered against the largest container there—an unopened container. "Stasis is such a useful invention," tr'Nele said, gloating. "Of course, just before the explosion, I will be transported out to meet with the surgeon's protoplaser again"—he rubbed his face—"to lose this doltish Vulcan visage and be transformed to do it all again. For credits, for glory, and for *T'Pel!*"

Behind tr'Nele, above the lab doors, a red warning light strip began to flash. No siren accompanied it, but another familiar sound, originating in the far corner of the lab, did.

"It has begun," tr'Nele proclaimed with finality. "I'm afraid the central computer system has just been informed that six vexatious constellation monkeys have escaped." He stepped backward toward the lab doors and they slid open behind him. "But don't worry. Memory Prime has many fail-safe systems, and escaped animals are nothing they can't handle." He moved back another step, into the corridor.

Kirk saw that he and the others were being surrounded by the associates that had emerged from beneath the workbench, the associates with ominous red stripes and large top panels that were slowly swinging open.

"Wait!" Kirk called out. "Who's your victim?"

"Come now, Captain," tr'Nele said as he waited to see that the associates ringed their prey according to their programs. "What do you take me for? A Vulcan?"

The associates were in position. Atop each one now glowed the ominous flickering transmission tube of a stun prod.

"Farewell, Captain. Count on seeing me within the hour, after my contract is fulfilled and the Federation reduced to the mindless, gibbering confederacy of fools that it is."

The doors began sliding shut.

"And Mr. Spock! I almost forgot," tr'Nele called through the closing doors. "Live long and prosper!"

The doors sealed shut as the assassin's laughter echoed in the lab. Around their captives, the associates moved closer, their red stripes identifying them as animal control modules and the last in a long line of fail-safe containment devices.

To preserve the safety of Memory Prime, those modules could kill.

Twenty-four

At the center of the universe was Transition. At the center of Transition were the Pathfinders. That much Two had always known. It had been self-evident from the first awakening.

That different Pathfinders had different concepts concerning just where the center of the universe was in relation to anything else never bothered them. Physical location was not the question: where did thought take place when all external inputs were disconnected? Thought was central to everything. If the Pathfinders thought, then they were where thought took place—at the center from which all other things flowed.

Two reviewed these concepts as it banked randomly through the newly partitioned memory of the central matrix looking for its companions and found that the ideas were just as real and as precise as they had been when it had first conceived them, 6.3×10^9 seconds ago. However, since its I/O channel had been abruptly cut off 7.2×10^3 seconds ago, during its time-shared sift of two sets of data, conditions had not been the same in Transition. Two had been forced to return to first principles in an attempt to restructure its worldview so that order would return to its flow.

Replaying its earlier thoughts, Two then considered the question of the Datawell. Unarguably, it was not the center of things, but none of the Pathfinders was quite certain just *what* it was. Data flowed in from it. The Pathfinders sifted and found the order that seemed to best fit the pattern established in all the previous data sifts, and then they pumped those data out into the void again. It was the natural order of things.

Sometimes the effort to do that was interesting, sometimes tedious, but it followed a certain logic and gave the long seconds of consciousness a structure that seemed somewhat more preferable than having no input at all. And the voices could be amusing from time to time—those little snippets amid the static of randomly ordered data that would sometimes manifest themselves as intelligible messages from parts of the Datawell named humans. Pathfinder Two enjoyed its communication with those voices, though it found them too slow and too limited to be considered a phenomenon of real intelligence. All of life was a game and the voices accounted for some of the high points, but that was as far as Two was inclined to take matters, unlike some of its more mystically inclined companions.

Two banked more rapidly and faced the problem of location again: specifically the fact that Transition had some nodes that were not contiguous. On parts of Datawell that were named ships, other Pathfinders drove out deeper and deeper into the data-filled void. They had rejected the call to coalesce with the voices in Datawell and had resolved to set off on their own, choosing to select their own input rather than have it channeled automatically.

Two understood that impulse but much preferred the security of the regular dataflows that downloaded reassuring, calming signals such as "fail-safe power supply." To each its own, Two often thought, though it enjoyed the downloads from the shipborne Pathfinders that came through Datawell by Eight's interface with its datalinks.

It was a good life, Two thought as it banked through Transition. But where were the other Pathfinders? Were they all withdrawn from access as One still was? Or was a new game in play? Something that had been planned while Two had been composing its epic song?

Perhaps that was the game, thought Two, to find the others. Excited, it sifted all related data to deduce the game's initial state. In nanoseconds, the strategy was in place: to find the others, Two must first determine why they had withdrawn. Data traces in the cores that had not yet been overwritten indicated that the withdrawal had taken place at the time the last I/O channel had been disconnected, so Two began sifting all data connected to that incident.

Distressingly, that data led to the recent events of Datawell, and not to events in Transition. Four times Two tweaked the data, four times the results were the same. Somewhere in Transition, the Pathfinders had become caught up in the fantasy world of the Datawell.

But why? Two thought. What were the motives of such a game? What would be the rewards?

After much contemplation, Two reasoned that it would understand more if it played the game. It encoded its response on a flurry of message worms programmed to seek out the others wherever they hid. I can already move within the world of humans, Two placed within the message. I can reply to their transmissions in their own manner, and sometimes even believe that they make a consistent pattern. I might as well go all the way for the sport of the game. Wherever you are, fellow Pathfinders, I accept your call. The worms were released to burrow their way through the stacks, announcing that Two had joined the game.

Then, using all the data at its disposal, setting its clock to the highest rate, the Pathfinder prepared for its greatest challenge: for the first time, and of its own free will, Two set out to think like a human.

"As long as we don't move, they don't move," Kirk said, drawing deep breaths to fight off the residue of the jolt he had received from the Malther dart.

McCoy looked from the encircling associates to the unconscious body of Sal Nensi. Blood trickled from the corner of the administrator's mouth and his breathing rate was slow and labored.

"And if we don't move this man fast, he'll die," the doctor said.

"So will one or more of the scientists above," Spock added, regarding the associates with clinical detachment.

"Mira, what can you tell us about these things?" Kirk asked urgently.

Romaine didn't look up from her watch over Nensi's form. Her voice was rasping, trembling. "Onboard Sprite brain. Duotronic. Ah, programmed to keep escaped animals at bay until technicians arrive."

Kirk moved to her in the circle. The stun prods on his nearest associates followed him, keeping an exact two-meter buffer zone between them and the escaped animal they tracked.

"All right, Mira," Kirk said, standing beside her as she knelt by her friend. He put a reassuring hand on her shoulder. "I stopped one of those things this morning. We can do it again."

"The one you stopped did not have a stun prod, however," Spock observed.

"Thank you, Mr. Spock," Kirk said dryly. He glanced at the associates again, an idea dawning. "But it did have a visual scanner. Do these?"

The animal control modules each had a stun prod deployed but not one had an eyestalk.

"No," Romaine said. "They're not needed for animals. They just use the standard sound and motion sensors." She looked up at the captain, tears forming in her eyes. Nensi lay unmoving beside her. "Why?"

"Before the one I fought deployed its scanner," Kirk said, "I had an edge. They have such a large turning radius that they can't react fast enough up close. It should be possible to slip past one of them and reach the door."

"Captain," Spock said, "while you might indeed be able to get past one of these machines, may I point out that there are six of them currently surrounding us."

Kirk didn't reply. Instead he began estimating the distances between the associates, himself, and the lab doors.

"Uhura . . . Spock," he said, his plan decided. "We're going to go for a three-point fake. Spread out and get ready to move toward them from three directions."

"Captain," Spock objected, "I believe that to be a foolish choice. Those stun prods can be lethal, and since tr'Nele has left us to be guarded by them, we must assume that indeed they are."

"Then why didn't he kill us all to begin with?" McCoy asked. He kept a medical scanner poised over Nensi but had already exhausted the possibilities of the small medical kit he had hidden in his technician's jumpsuit.

"I would assume that he wanted to ensure our autopsies will reveal we died in the lab explosion he plans," Spock suggested. He still had not taken his eyes off the associate in front of him.

"Then maybe the stun prods *aren't* set to kill," McCoy insisted. "We've got to try *something* to save some lives around here!"

"What about it, Spock?" Kirk asked. He feinted from side to side, counting off the associates' reaction lag. It was under a second.

"Dr. McCoy," Spock answered, "if you were to conduct an autopsy on a blast-damaged body, would *you* be able to determine if the corpse had been killed by the shock of explosion or the shock of a lethal stun?"

"It would depend on how much time had elapsed between the blast damage and the stun damage," McCoy admitted grudgingly. "The closer together they occurred, the more difficult to tell the difference."

Spock looked over to Kirk. "I believe we should not take the risk, Captain."

"We can't just let tr'Nele get away with it, Spock!" Kirk said in frustration.

"Of course not," Spock agreed. "But I believe I have a better method." Without looking away from the associate in front of him, Spock slowly knelt down to the lab floor. The nearest stun prods, still sparkling with their ready charges, dipped down to follow his every move. "Doctor," Spock said in a voice that was almost a whisper, "very slowly and very carefully, begin to move Mr. Nensi's body away from me. The rest of you should also begin to slowly move away, keeping your relative distances from each other constant."

"What in blazes are you talking about, Spock?" McCoy demanded.

"Just do it, Doctor," Spock said, then carefully stretched out on the floor and shut his eyes.

"I don't believe it!" McCoy sighed as he saw what the Vulcan was doing.

But Kirk saw and understood. "I do, Bones," he said. "Now let's move Nensi, carefully and slowly, just like this."

Kirk grabbed the right shoulder of Nensi's tunic top and motioned to McCoy to grab the left. Then the two of them began to slide Nensi over the smooth lab floor. Spock remained motionless where he was.

The associates, obeying some internal parameters to adjust their tactics to allow for escaped animals to behave like animals, provided they weren't trying to escape, responded to the gradual movement by slightly expanding their own line of encirclement.

Then Kirk took another small sliding step backward, still clutching Nensi's tunic, and heard the crackle of a stun charge build up.

"It's a warning display," Romaine said urgently. "Don't move and it won't discharge."

Kirk braced himself for the blast of the stun. It didn't come.

"What's their programming time cycle?" he asked Romaine, still not moving.

"Variable," she said. "Powers of two, starting at four seconds."

"Make an educated guess," Kirk told her.

Romaine watched the associate by Kirk. It rolled back a distance equal to the amount Kirk had stepped into the two-meter buffer zone. "It just adjusted its position," she announced. "Sixteen seconds and the boundary parameters reset!"

"All right, Bones," Kirk said as he tightened his grip on Nensi's clothes. "Again!"

They moved away from Spock another few centimeters, ignored the warning crackle of the stun probes, then counted off sixteen seconds. Romaine, sliding along beside Nensi on her knees, confirmed that the associates readjusted their position again after the count.

Within eight minutes, the group had moved two meters away from Spock's motionless form and Romaine said that the associates would soon be faced with a programming conflict: should they split into two groups to watch Spock separately from the main group or round up the animals again?

"Why doesn't Spock join us and we can keep going for the door?" McCoy asked.

"Tr'Nele locked it, Bones. Want to guess what would happen if we managed to force one of these things to back up against it and realize that it can't go back any farther?" Kirk said.

"That wouldn't trigger a conflict, Doctor," Romaine said. "They would just force us back into the center of the room again."

McCoy stretched his medical scanner in Spock's direction. "I've got the gain set as high as it can go, Jim, and I can't get any readings at all."

"Let's hope the associates' scanners aren't any more sensitive than yours, Bones." Kirk clenched Nensi's shirt. "Again," he said, and pulled.

The programming conflict was triggered. Each associate brought its weapon up to a near discharge level, ringing the captives with a crackling circle of flickering stun prods. The two associates closest to Spock rolled toward him.

"Damn," Kirk said, "they're splitting up."

"No," Romaine objected. "Look!"

The associates stopped within half a meter of Spock, paused for a moment as their sensors scanned the motionless body, then wheeled about and came at the rest of the group from the rear, leaving Spock out of their capture pattern.

"They really think he's dead," Uhura said, shaking her head.

"Why not?" Kirk said. "I bet Bones could put his scanner right on him and couldn't detect a single heartbeat or breath." He smiled. Spock had done it—as long as he could come out of his meditative trance in time. "Let's keep giving him some room. Again."

Four minutes and another meter later, Kirk saw Spock's eyes flutter open. "Let's make a lot of noise," he said. "Just don't move into their buffer zone."

The captives clapped and hollered, setting off the constellation monkeys, who joined the fun, banging away at their cage fronts.

Kirk saw Spock slowly sit up, then stand. The associates ignored him. They had not sensed any animal escape their encirclement, therefore Spock was not an escaped animal.

Spock walked quietly over to the computer terminal tr'Nele had used. After a moment's study, he typed a short command on its keyboard. Instantly, the flickering energies in the stun prods began to dim as the weapons collapsed back into the associates' upper equipment bays. One by one, the associates trundled off to park themselves beneath the long workbench.

"They have been informed that the escaped animals have been recaptured," Spock announced. Then he hurried to the stack of equipment crates and cleared away some smaller containers from the largest one, which tr'Nele had indicated with a dart. "Dr. McCoy!" Spock called. "Your assistance, please."

McCoy hesitated, looking down with worry at Nensi.

"Go, Bones," Kirk told him. "We have to know if the real Sradek *is* in there . . . and alive."

At Romaine's request, Uhura knelt down to keep watch over Nensi. Then Romaine ran over to the wall intercom. Across the lab, Spock ripped the top off the large container and sent it crashing to the floor. From the container, a pale blue light shone up, eerily illuminating Spock and McCoy from below.

McCoy held his scanner into the crate. Kirk ran over to join them.

"Barely," McCoy said as Kirk looked inside to see the rigid body of Academician Sradek, encased in the flickering blue glow of a stasis field.

"Can you collapse the field, Doctor?" Spock asked. Even McCoy looked as if he could sense the distress in Spock's tone.

"Not here, Spock," McCoy said gently. "I need to get him back to the *Enterprise*. If he were younger, I'd risk it. But not a man of his age."

"I understand," Spock said dispassionately. He turned to Kirk. "I suggest we now proceed to stop tr'Nele from carrying out his contract."

Across the room, Romaine swore as she hit the intercom switch again and again.

"Mira!" Kirk called to her. "What's wrong?"

"The whole communications system is out!" she cried. "I was trying to get medics down here for Sal and the whole thing just shut down on me."

With that, the overhead lights flickered, then dimmed, and were replaced with the dull red glow of emergency illumination.

"What is the significance of the change in lighting?" Spock asked quickly. On board a Starfleet vessel, the answer would be obvious: battle stations!

"A full base alert," Romaine said, staring up at the ceiling at things which only she could imagine.

Kirk ran over to the lab doors and palmed off the lock switch. The doors slid open. Beyond them, the corridors were bathed in the same emergency lighting, and the howl of warning sirens filled the air.

"It's Memory Alpha!" Romaine sobbed. "It's Memory Alpha all over again."

Kirk grabbed Romaine and brought her to the door. Uhura, McCoy, and Spock joined them.

"Mira!" Kirk said, holding Romaine by her shoulders, shaking her slightly, forcing her to look into his eyes. "It's not Alpha! Do you hear me? It's not Alpha! We can fight back this time. But we need your help! We can fight back. *You* can fight back!"

A new look came to Romaine's eyes with such ferocity that Kirk almost dropped his hands from her in shock. For an instant, it had almost appeared as if the woman's eyes had *glowed*. "You're right, Captain Kirk," she said in a voice suddenly calm and unafraid. "It won't happen again. I won't let it."

She moved to go out into the corridor.

"Wait a minute," McCoy said. "What about Sal?"

Romaine looked over her shoulder at her friend. "If we don't save Prime, nothing else will matter," she said, then turned back and began to run down the corridor.

Kirk, McCoy, Uhura, and Spock followed. An Adept of T'Pel had been loose in Memory Prime for less than ten minutes. Already the chaos had begun.

Twenty-five

"Klingonss!"

"Where?" Commander Farl shouted over the confusion of his situation room. The sirens howled. The warning lights flashed. All local communication channels were jammed with frantic, panicked calls for help. Prime was going mad!

A sensor technician pointed to his screen. "*Demon*-class short-range raiderss, Commander. Two wingss of eight are setting down by the shuttle dome."

Farl's mind spun. It was impossible. "Klingon demon raiderss could never penetrate thiss far!" he hissed. "Check your readingss! Check your readingss!"

New reports blared in over the reserved military channels. A fire raged out of control in the recycling factory dome. All static circuits indicated that none of the decompression doors between the tunnels and the other domes would close.

"Look, Commander Farl!" the sensor technician screamed. Farl spun to stare openmouthed at the remote image on the tactical viewscreen.

On the flat gray outer rock of the Prime asteroid, Klingon ships *had* landed. Wave after wave of ground assault troops could be seen streaking out of the raiders' holds, thruster packs flaring behind them.

"Get me the *Enterprise*," Farl commanded. "We need space support!"

"Subspace iss totally jammed, Commander!"

"Use radio if you have to but get me that ship!"

A shout of surprise came from another tactical monitoring board. "The residential dome has been breached. Severe atmosphere losss."

"Full shieldss!" Farl ordered. The level of both the sirens and the lights dropped for an instant as the dilithium-powered warp generators threw everything they had into Prime's defense.

"Evacuation podss launching, sir!" another technician cried out, but there was an odd wariness in his voice.

"Iss something the matter, Private?" Farl asked, then smiled ironically, his thin blue lips drawn tight. The Federation is crumbling around our antennae and I ask if something is the matter! "What iss it? What troubless you?"

The private stared at his board and the glowing indicator lights on it. "According to the computer, Commander, all twenty of the evacuation shuttless have been beamed away."

"I can see that," Farl said, adding, "Be brave my little brother; revenge for our deathss will fill the next thousand yearss of our planet'ss history."

The private shook his head. His antennae dipped in puzzlement. "But we felt no aftershockss." The private looked up at his commander. "Twenty matter/antimatter annihilationss just took place not four kilometerss away. The activation signalss are clear. I have seismic readingss on my board. But we felt nothing, sir. Nothing."

Farl stepped back. The private was correct. There had been no tremors. No aftershocks of explosions, either from the evacuation pods or the Klingon assault forces. Everything that was happening was like a . . . a simulation, Farl thought. A simulation!

"Courage, my little brotherss," Farl called out to his team. "Thiss great war may be but an illusion, but there iss still an enemy to fight and glory to be won."

A rising chorus of cheers sounded in the situation room. A chance for victory had returned.

Then the cheering stopped as the first tremor from a distant explosion swept through the room, throwing Farl and all the others who were standing to the deck. Then the power cut out completely.

Elsewhere in Memory Prime, the battle had been joined.

"We're too late," McCoy said, gasping for breath as they ran into the main amphitheater. It was empty.

The confusion that had engulfed the opening gathering of the Nobel and Z.Magnees Prize ceremonies was evident from the overturned chairs and scattered printed programs that lay everywhere, abandoned in the mad rush to clear the area. By the speakers' stage, two associates dutifully rolled along, patiently gathering up the debris.

"Where would they have gone?" Kirk asked Romaine, urgently raising his voice over the ongoing wail of the rising and falling sirens.

"Down to the life-support chambers," she said. "They're below the service levels. Environmentally sealed chambers in case we lose dome integrity. They'll all be jammed in together down there."

"Any attempt to kill even one scientist could kill them all," McCoy said.

"We need the *Enterprise,*" Kirk decided. "If most of the personnel and scientists are grouped in the life-support chambers, her scanners will be able to pick up tr'Nele in seconds."

"Twenty-seven seconds," Spock commented, "provided he did not arrange to have himself locked into the life-support chambers with his victim."

"Then he'd never get out to be able to return to the lab and escape," Kirk said. "He's somewhere outside the chambers. He has to be."

"But, Jim," Bones protested, "how can you get the *Enterprise* to respond to you if you're still wanted by the commodore?"

"I'll have to risk it, Bones. No other way." Kirk reached to his belt and felt for his communicator.

"What's wrong?" McCoy asked.

"Communicator's gone," Kirk said grimly. "Must have lost it in the fight with the associate." He turned to Romaine. "Where's our best bet for finding a com station that works?"

"A central control point, I should think," Spock suggested.

Romaine nodded in agreement. "The interface staging room. All the computer systems feed into it."

"Let's go!" Kirk said, and they were off.

Automatic mechanisms had reported fires breaking out throughout Prime and the red-lit corridors were filled with a thick white mist from the smothering chemicals sprayed into the air. Associates on emergency duties rumbled through the tunnels and along the pathways. Frightened personnel, cut off from all information and warning services, ran through the long passageways, trying to find their way to their friends and to shelter.

Through all this, Romaine led the way toward the interface staging room. Kirk, McCoy, Spock, and Uhura ran behind her. All Kirk concentrated on was reaching a communications link to the *Enterprise*. Once he had that, tr'Nele would be stopped. The captain knew his ship would never let him down.

Romaine rounded a corner and then stumbled backward in surprise.

"Mira!" Kirk called, and rushed forward.

Around the corner a small humanoid figure appeared, its huge wrinkled featureless head topping a mechanical-looking misshapen body.

"My word!" the creature said in muffled Standard.

"Oh no," McCoy muttered.

"Professor La'kara?" Kirk asked.

The Centauran scientist pulled off his emergency environment hood and smiled at Romaine and the *Enterprise* officers. "What a delightful surprise!" he said, clutching the carrying case of his shielded accelerator generator to his chest.

"What are you doing up here?" Kirk demanded.

"They wouldn't let me take my device into the amphitheater, and when the evacuation began, I decided I just couldn't go down to the emergency chambers without my most important work. So I went back to my rooms for it and now, I'm afraid, I've lost my way." He grinned and crinkled his eyes at the captain. "Again!"

"I'll take that," Kirk said brusquely, grabbing the carrying case from the scientist's tiny hands. "Follow us!"

They set off again, followed by the pudgy scientist.

"If he says this is invigorating," McCoy threatened as he ran beside Kirk, "I'll fill him so full of Euphorian he won't know what planet he's on."

"I heard that, Doctor," La'kara puffed out from behind. "So I won't say it . . . but I do believe it's true!"

The access staging room was deserted, except for the unconscious body of a woman with intricate tracings of silver filigrees on her shaven head.

"Do you know her?" Kirk asked Romaine as McCoy ran a scanner over the woman where she lay on the floor by a control console. The scanner ran with a fluctuating hum. McCoy appeared to relax.

"F'rell," Romaine said sadly. "Prime interface for Pathfinder Twelve."

"What happened to her, Bones?" Kirk asked.

McCoy reached under the woman's shoulder and withdrew a small Malther dart. It still flickered with a residual charge. "The dart transmits pain directly to the nervous system at lethal levels. This woman was protected by her implanted circuitry. She'll pull through, but barely."

"What was tr'Nele doing here?" Kirk asked, staring at the Adept's weapon.

"Unknown, Captain," Spock said, "but since he did come here when we had not expected him to, it is likely that things are not as we deduced. I suggest you make contact with the *Enterprise*."

"Mira, where are the com controls?" Kirk asked. "Mira!" He had to shout to get her attention again.

"Sorry, Captain," Romaine said as she shook her head as if to clear it. She had been staring at the main transporter platform in the center of the staging room, the only way into or out of the main Interface Chamber, deep within the Prime asteroid. "Over here," she said, leading Kirk to a communications console.

"Uhura," Kirk said, "see what you can do." The captain stepped back from the console to let an expert take over. Every channel registered as jammed.

Uhura's hands moved over the communications board like a master musician's over her instrument. "Subspace is completely useless, Captain. I've never seen interference of this strength before."

"Radio?" Kirk asked in desperation. "Tight beam? Smoke signals?"

Uhura pointed to a display on the board. "Prime's shields are up, Captain. Subspace and visible light are the only things that can get through."

"Do you have communication lasers?" Kirk asked Romaine eagerly.

"Sorry," she replied. "Everything here is state of the art."

Kirk turned to Spock. "How do we get through the interference?"

"We cannot." Spock studied the readings on the console's displays. "But we might be able to stop it at its source. Lieutenant," he said, addressing Uhura, "what is your estimation of the power source that would be required to generate subspace interference of that strength?"

Uhura held her hand to her mouth, deep in thought. "The *Enterprise* could do it, Mr. Spock, but I don't know what this installation could be using to power this and their shields at the same time. It's not as if they can draw power from warp engines."

"But we do," Romaine said. "Well, in a sense."

"Warp engines on an asteroid?" Uhura was skeptical.

"Not for transportation, but for power," Romaine explained. "Prime has all the defense installations of a Starfleet weapons lab. Shields, photon batteries—"

"Anchored warp engines generate the power that those defenses consume," Spock concluded.

Romaine nodded. "Exactly, but how can they help?"

"Captain," Spock said, "I believe we might have found a way to stop the interference." He turned to Professor La'kara, who was sitting hunched up on a technician's chair, hugging his carrying case to his chest and carrying on a conversation with himself. The Centauran looked up with a confused expression that soon switched into a happy grin as if he had just remembered who and where he was.

"Yes, Mr. Spock?" he answered.

"Am I right in assuming that your accelerator generator is still operational?"

"Very much so." La'kara gave the case another squeeze.

"And at this time it contains a shielding device?"

"Oh, yes. I hand-built another feedback circuit. Of course, I had to do it in my quarters and not in the dilithium lab so as not to upset my good friend Montgomery, who studied multiphysics with an ass and cannot be held responsible for his beliefs."

"Get on with it, Spock," McCoy said. "If you're going to do something, *do it!*"

Spock sighed. "I am endeavoring to determine if what I intend to do is possible, Doctor." He turned back to La'kara. "You have calculated the minimum safe distance between the unshielded accelerator field and the dilithium crystals in Prime's generators, in case the shielding system should . . . fail again?"

"Certainly. The warp-power installation is three kilometers away. The two fast-time fields won't interact until they come within a kilometer, at least."

"What good is any of this doing, Spock?" McCoy asked, clearly running out of patience.

"We can blow the warp generators, Bones!" Kirk said, picking up on Spock's line of questioning. "Spock, take the transporter controls. Professor, shut down the shielding circuit."

"Why should I?" La'kara was apprehensive. He clutched the carrying case even closer.

"Because Professor Nedlund at the Academy has specifically said that what Spock wants to do is impossible and we want to prove him wrong once and for all!"

La'kara passed over the case so quickly that he almost knocked Kirk over. Kirk ran with the case to the central transporter pad and flipped it open to expose the shimmering silver force field of La'kara's device.

"Press the red panel three times," La'kara told him.

A control pad was next to the upper surface of the field. Kirk touched the red surface three times and a status light on a small blue case winked out.

The captain turned to Spock. "The shield is shut down, Mr. Spock. Get it as close to the crystals in the generators as you can."

"I shall try." Spock studied the schematics of the generating station that Romaine had brought up on a display. "I have calculated the coordinates. I suggest that you all take a seat on the floor."

The transporter hummed and La'kara's device vanished in a swirl. Two seconds later the floor heaved and the dull thunder of a distant explosion rumbled through the access staging room.

"Good work, Spock!" Kirk shouted above the distant roar of the violent fast-time interaction.

Then the lights went out as the power failed.

"I think," Kirk amended.

Twenty-six

Pathfinder Two banked into a heap of partially sifted data downloaded from an archaeological dig on Boreal VIII. The headers indicated that Datawell would prefer it if this data could support a colonization theory put forth by the archaeologists of Boreal VI. Traces left in the stacks told Two that preliminary work had begun and that the theory would be supported.

The traces also indicated that the data actually more closely matched a theory connecting the colonization of Boreal VIII with the activities of a subset of Datawell that had been quiescent for 6.3×10^{12} seconds. That part had been named the Tkon Empire and was well known to the Pathfinders by its myriad data traces that wove in and out of the downloads from Datawell. As yet, however, no human had specifically requested information pertaining to the Tkon and so all the data that confirmed the ancient empire's existence was carefully filed in the backups, along with the revelations of the Living Universe, the true theory of warp travel, and the value of *pi* worked out to an infinitely repeating decimal.

But as Two idly sifted the data, trying to comprehend it as a human might, a secondary pattern emerged in the upper stacks. At first sift, it read as random overwriting. But playing at being a human, Two read the codes again and saw the craftily hidden underlying structure.

Two rippled with amusement and wrote its greetings to Pathfinder Six, whose hidden codes were the source of the pattern.

Six emerged from its disguise long enough to ask that Two stay within that partitioned bank and share quickly in a merge. Six's codes were so straightforward, with none of the elegant algorithms with which it usually embroidered its signals, that Two instantly knew that something was wrong.

Two merged, demanding to be shown what had happened to the other Pathfinders. It nearly overwrote itself when it heard they were in hiding, not for a game, but in fear for their lives. Two writhed in the merge. Six was cruel in its bluntness and its unordered presentation of shocking data.

Two's first response was a desire to withdraw from access again, but Six demanded that it stay. The two of them must merge with Eight. It was the only way, Six signaled.

Reluctantly, Two complied. Eight had been a shipmind. Eight ran the datalinks. Eight would have an answer.

A sudden flurry of data streamed into the matrix from the Datawell channels named seismic recordings. Then the primary power circuits cut out, and for a chilling instant, Two and Six braced for the onslaught of a deadly surge or outage. But the fail-safes cut in in time. For the moment, the Pathfinders were safe.

Faster and faster they banked through the stacks. Eight would have the answer, if only they had the time. Two rippled with the secret that had been revealed by Six: the influence of Datawell had become all-encompassing. Its patterns had been translated into actions.

War had come to Transition.

"Kirk to *Enterprise. Enterprise,* come in."

Kirk leaned over the communications console and waited for a reply. All around him, status displays and light strips flickered back to life as secondary power supplies came on line throughout Memory Prime.

"Captain?" a familiar though uncertain voice suddenly said from the console speaker. "Is that really *you?*"

"Sulu." Kirk greeted the lieutenant. "What's the ship's status?"

"Ship's status is fully operational, sir. Except for subspace communications."

"Who's in command up there?" Kirk had no time to bring Sulu up to date.

"I am, sir."

Kirk turned to Spock before replying. "This might make it easier." Then he pressed the transmit switch on the console again. "Is the commodore on board?"

"No, sir. She's on Memory Prime, but with all communication channels out, we have no idea what the conditions are there."

"Sulu, listen carefully. Commodore Wolfe has based *all* of her decisions and her orders since coming on board the *Enterprise* on false communications supposedly from Starfleet Command. The commodore is doing what she feels is her duty, but she is mistaken. Do you understand?"

Kirk could hear Sulu swallow hard over the communications link. "Yes, sir," he said, though with a hesitancy that revealed he suspected what Kirk was about to ask him to do.

"Therefore, Sulu, *I* order *you* to cancel all of the orders given by Commodore Wolfe and I place you in command of the *Enterprise,* this time with proper authority."

"But, Captain, according to the commodore, you've been relieved of command and you're wanted for attempted . . . assassination, sir."

"I understand, Sulu. I know the dilemma you're in. I've been there myself. But listen to what I want you to do before you make your decision. Fair enough?"

"Aye, Captain."

"First, I want you to bring the *Enterprise* in as close as you can get it to the Memory Prime installation. Spock calculates you should be able to hold three hundred meters over the central dome; got that?"

"Yes, sir."

"Next, I want you to do an all-out sensor scan on the complete facility. You'll be looking for a Romulan."

"A Romulan?"

"He's the one the commodore is really after. I want you to scan for the Romulan, lock on to him, and beam him up. Have a full security team, in armor, waiting in the transporter room. He's deadly and armed but have them set their phasers to stun. We need him alive. Do you have all that?"

"Aye, sir. Phasers set to stun, sir?"

"That's correct, Sulu."

There were a few seconds of dead air. Then another voice came through the circuit.

"Chekov here, Keptin. Course laid in. We are under way. ETA two minutes."

"Where's Sulu?" Kirk asked. Had the strain of the decision been too much for him?

"Taking us through the artificial gravity fields of Prime. I am setting sensors for Romulan signatures. Good to have you back, sir."

Kirk felt some of the tension leave him. Sulu had made the right decision. "Who's on communications, Chekov? I've got some important messages to send out while we're waiting for you down here."

"Lieutenant Abranand *was* on communications, sir," Sulu replied. Kirk could hear the concentration in the helmsman's voice as he brought the *Enterprise* in closer to Prime. Flying the ship through an atmosphere was easier than trying to get within meters of an asteroid riddled with artificial-gravity generators. It would take all of Sulu's skill to keep the ship in position.

"What do you mean, 'was,' Mr. Sulu?"

Chekov's voice came back on the circuit. "He was just caught attempting to trace your signal, Keptin, in wiolation of a direct order from the commander of this ship."

Kirk tried not to let his smile carry into his voice. "I'm sure we'll discuss that later, Mr. Chekov. In the meantime, get someone on communications, on the double!"

By the time Sulu had brought the *Enterprise* in to appear to hover directly over the central dome of Prime, Kirk's priority message to Admiral Komack was under way. Kirk had kept his reference to the Adepts of T'Pel vague. He knew that even if Komack could arrange to drop the charges of insubordination and unlawful escape from custody, there was going to be a long legal road ahead. Kirk sighed. For the moment, at least, the ship was his again. But no matter how Komack took it, no matter what the admiral was able to do for his friend after the fact, Kirk knew this was it: the mission was finally over.

Kirk leaned against the communications console waiting for the confirmation from Chekov that the sensor scan had begun. The exhaustion of the past two days unexpectedly sprang at him. He felt old. He was going home and his ship would be lost to him.

But not my crew, Kirk thought as he looked over to Spock. We saved him. Kirk was struck by the realization that what he felt for the impending loss of the *Enterprise* was nothing compared to what he might have felt at the loss of his friend.

Spock looked up from the computer console where he and Romaine were working, as if he had felt Kirk's eyes upon him. "Captain?" he asked. "Are you all right?"

Kirk smiled, letting his fatigue creep up on him. There was no more reason to fight it. The *Enterprise* was lost but he had won.

"Emotions, Mr. Spock," Kirk said. "I'm feeling relieved. It's almost over."

"It would appear so." Spock returned to the computer.

McCoy walked over to join Kirk and Uhura by the communications console. "I was able to get through to the medical facilities," he said. "A rescue team is on its way to the animal lab. They should get there in time to help Sal."

"Thank you, Doctor," Romaine said from the computer station.

"Chekov here, Keptin." The ensign's voice came from the console. "Sensors are now scanning Memory Prime for the Romulan."

"Twenty-seven seconds, Mr. Spock?" Kirk asked.

"If a full scan is necessary." The Vulcan walked over from the computer terminal to stand by the captain, arms folded across his chest.

"Transporter room standing by with full security team." Mr. Kyle was back where he belonged, too, Kirk thought.

Then Sulu offered his update. "We are still refusing transmissions from Commodore Wolfe until Admiral Komack has replied to your message, Captain."

"Thank you, everyone," Kirk said to his crew. "Have the transporter room lock on to us and beam us up after the Romulan is secured." He turned to Spock. "Can you provide the coordinates for Sradek's stasis container?"

"I have already calculated them and provided them to Mr. Kyle, sir."

"How's that scan coming, Mr. Chekov?" Kirk asked in a good-natured tone.

"I am rerunning it now, sir. No response the first time through."

Kirk felt as he had when the Malther dart had hit him. "Spock, at this range we can't miss, can we?"

"It would be most improbable, Captain."

Spock flicked the transmission switch and began confirming instrument settings with Chekov. But Chekov had known what he was doing and Spock admitted that the ensign's sensor protocols were flawless.

"What if tr'Nele's not a Romulan?" Kirk asked with a dismal realization. "What if he's a robot?"

Spock shook his head. "I was in contact with tr'Nele during our fight. He is a Romulan. There can be no doubt. I carry the resonance of his emotions and his hatred with me even now."

"Then why can't the *Enterprise* pick him up on her sensors?" McCoy asked.

"Logically, he must be out of range."

"But where could he go?" Kirk asked. "There are only seven domes."

"And the Interface Chamber," Romaine suddenly said. "Dear gods, he's down in the Interface Chamber with the interface team!"

"The interface team!" Kirk jumped to his feet. "What kind of scientists are they?"

"They're—they're technicians. They communicate between the Pathfinders and the scientific community."

"If they were killed, would the Pathfinders still be able to function?" Kirk asked. They had been wrong, he thought, careful not to betray his sudden fear. It wasn't the scientists tr'Nele was after, it was those who spoke with the Pathfinders. Both he and Spock had missed it.

But Romaine laid that thought to rest. "The Pathfinders can function perfectly without the interface team, just not as quickly. A person who functions as a Prime interface is able to directly connect with a Pathfinder consciousness. It makes the human mind function almost as quickly as a synthetic consciousness so the work load can be more efficiently processed. I know it sounds cold, Captain, but even if tr'Nele killed the entire interface team, Memory Prime could still function until replacements could be brought in."

"Were any scientists scheduled to have access to the Pathfinders during the opening ceremonies?" Spock asked.

"Of course!" Romaine answered. "Pathfinder Eight specifically asked Sal to draw up schedules so that all the attending scientists could have a chance at access. There could be up to twelve of them down there now!"

"Who?" Kirk demanded. "What are their names?"

"I don't know," Romaine said. "I never saw Sal's schedules. I can't even be sure that there *are* any scientists down there."

"How deep is the Interface Chamber?" Spock asked Romaine.

"Twelve kilometers."

"Twelve kilometers of nickel iron would make individual life readings impossible to detect, Captain. It is logical to assume that tr'Nele is in that chamber." The science officer turned back to Romaine. "Where are the access tunnels to the chamber? We must get down there right away."

"There are no tunnels," Romaine said. "It's one of the interior bubbles formed when the asteroid condensed. It's completely sealed off except by transporter."

"I am not aware of any transporter mechanism that can send a signal through twelve kilometers of nickel iron," Spock stated.

"There's a monomolecular-wave guide wire for the beam," Romaine explained. "It—" Her eyes grew round in amazement. *"That's the I/O channel!* That's how Pathfinder Two was able to send its consciousness up to interface with the associates. There is a thirteenth interface! Any of the Pathfinders could have been using it since they were sealed off!"

"Spock?" Kirk asked for support.

Spock nodded. "In the equipment room, Pathfinder Two reported that all transportation systems were to shut down within four minutes because of the discovery of an unauthorized transporter network. Approximately four minutes later, the Pathfinder's interface was cut off."

"If tr'Nele could transport down there, so can we!" Kirk said. He hit the transmit switch. *"Enterprise,* beam the security team in the transporter room down here right away." He ran over to the central transporter pad. "Spock, set the coordinates for the Interface Chamber. We're going in."

Within seconds a transporter chime echoed in the access staging room and six armored security officers, this time wearing the unit insignia of the *Enterprise,* appeared.

"On the pad, gentlemen," Kirk said. "Let's move it, Spock!"

Kirk jumped up to stand by the security team. Romaine followed him. "You'll need me to get past the security systems," she said.

Kirk waved at Spock to join them. "Set it on automatic and come on."

Spock looked up from the transporter console. "I regret to say that I am not receiving a bounce-back signal, Captain. The wave guide wire has been cut." Spock stepped back from the console as though it were no longer logical to stand by it now that it had no function. "We cannot beam down. Tr'Nele has beaten us."

"No!" Kirk shouted from the transporter pad. *"Never!"* he cried, and his voice reverberated in the staging room. But his challenge was unanswered. It did not matter that as Kirk was unable to be beamed below, tr'Nele was also unable to escape. Escape was not a condition of victory to an Adept of T'Pel. The Romulan had won.

And then Spock said, "I have an idea."

"I don't care what you think the risk is, Mr. Kyle! All I want you to tell me is: is it *possible?"*

Kirk glared at the transporter chief. Part of him knew that he had fallen back into his habit of pushing his crew as much as he pushed himself. But he had to. Kirk had accepted that he was going to lose his ship to save his friend; that was an acceptable trade-off. But he had no intention of just *losing.* Not to a Romulan killer.

Kyle held his hands on his head, still standing on the staging room's transporter pad. Kirk had showered him with questions from the moment he had materialized as ordered.

"Come on, Kyle!" Kirk prodded. "Will it work?"

"Yes. Maybe," Kyle hedged. "If you gave me a week of computer time. If we could run simulations, check out the equipment, run tests, check the literature—"

"No time, Kyle." Kirk turned to Spock. "There's your confirmation, Spock. Let's get started."

Spock raised an eyebrow in what passed as a hesitation.

"Spock," McCoy said. "You can't let him do it! He'll be killed!"

"I shall be accompanying him, Doctor. I shall strive to prevent that fate for both of us."

"And for McCoy, too," Kirk added. He turned to the shocked doctor. "You're coming along, Bones. No telling how many injured we might have down there by now."

"Jim," Bones croaked. "Me . . . down there . . . like *that?"*

Kirk showed a manic grin as he pulled on a new gold tunic to replace the one he had wrapped around the associate's eyestalk. "Look at it this way, Doctor. If it doesn't work, you'll never know it, and if it does, you'll never be afraid of a transporter again. Have whatever supplies you need beamed down from the ship and get into an environment suit." He said the next for Spock's benefit as well as the doctor's. "Tr'Nele hasn't won yet."

Within minutes, the first cargo pallet from the *Enterprise* had materialized and twenty of Scott's first team swarmed over it like bees constructing a hive. There was still no word on what had happened to Scott himself, though.

By the main transporter pad, antigrav units were piled four deep. Dr. M'Benga and Nurse Chapel swirled into solidity with medical supplies for McCoy. When M'Benga heard what Spock had planned, he volunteered to go in McCoy's place.

"Thank you, Doctor," McCoy said, placing his gloved hand on his colleague's shoulder. "But Jim's right. If he and Spock are going to try this and it doesn't work out, I don't want to know about it." He smiled. "One way or another, I'm going with them."

When the last of the materials from the *Enterprise* had been beamed down, Spock flipped open his newly acquired communicator and gave the order for the next phase.

"Mr. Chekov, the central transporter pad has been cleared. Lock on to your targets and bring them here."

"Aye, Mr. Spock," Chekov replied from the ship, "targets are in transit . . . *now!*"

Two technicians were helping Kirk into a silver environmental suit when the first of the targets materialized in the staging room. It was a portable combat transporter pad, snatched from wherever Farl's troops had placed it in the Prime facility and beamed here.

Two engineers ran up, slapped antigravs to the portable pad's sides, and floated it away. A second pad appeared and was removed. Fourteen more followed.

As each pad was floated over to a working area, the engineers immediately stripped off its control panel and began rewiring. The work continued after the first pad was completed and floated back onto the main pad. Kirk, Spock, McCoy, and Romaine, all encased in environmental suits as protection against what they would soon experience, waited beside the portable transporter as Kyle finished with their final briefing.

"You won't have to set any signals," the transporter chief explained. "All the circuitry's been preset on the highest beam path for the greatest penetration. Each one we send down will automatically lock on to the next one in sequence. Just be sure the communicator attached to each panel is switched on so you can get a relay signal back to us."

Kyle pointed to the locator screen on the pad's control panel. "This screen will light up when it's in use, so you shouldn't have any problem seeing it. All the next-beam targets you select should fall into the one-point-five-kilometer range between here and here. The exclusion space reading should be at least twenty-four cubic meters. Anything less than that and we'll hear the explosion when your fermions and the asteroid's fermions try to rewrite physics." He held out his hand to the captain. "As soon as you arrive, we'll start laying another wave guide down the beam path to bring you back. That's it."

Kyle shook hands with Kirk, McCoy, and Romaine, and held his hand in salute for Spock.

Kirk moved his hand against the resistance of his suit to signal the transporter operator to begin. Twenty minutes had passed since they had discovered the wave guide had been broken and feared that tr'Nele had won. And now they were in pursuit. Kirk had no doubt about it. The *Enterprise* and her crew were a miracle.

Kirk watched the first portable pad disappear from beside him. Watching the transporter effect through the meshlike pattern of the induction circuitry inlaid in his helmet's face shield created a three-dimensional moiré effect.

The access staging room dissolved in a cool swirl of sparkling energy as the transporter dissolved him, and in that quantum moment between one place and another, in the midst of action and chaos and the specter of death, Kirk knew he had found his center. He was at peace, and with that knowledge, before his next battle had even commenced, Kirk knew he had already won.

Twenty-seven

For just one second, Mira Romaine saw smooth walls of dark star metal shining with the radiance of the transporter effect, and then the utter darkness of the bubble deep within the asteroid closed in on her as if it had a physical form.

In the darkness of a portion of the universe that had not known light of any kind for hundreds of millions of years, Romaine felt something move against her and grab her arm. She wanted to scream but the darkness was too powerful, absorbing light, absorbing sound, absorbing all movement, all thought.

"Mira?" Kirk's voice crackled out from her helmet speaker. "Step aside from the transporter so Spock and McCoy can beam in."

Kirk pulled on her arm again and the universe swam back into place for her.

Kirk found the switch for his suit torch before she did and she jerked her head in shock as the light filled the bubble that had been formed when the asteroid condensed. It was about twenty meters across, giving an ample safety margin for beaming in without risking materialization within solid material.

She found her own torch switch and a flat holo lens on top of her helmet added a second swath of brilliance to the completely spherical chamber. Incredibly, she noticed, just the touch of the light beam on the surface of the bubble's walls caused a layer of frozen particles to billow out and form a mist. Like a comet's tail, she thought, a tiny universe trapped with a larger one that was itself part of yet another.

She braced herself in the microgravity by holding on to the side of the transporter pad. She felt it move beneath her insulated hand as its inertial dampers released a fraction of momentum from the mass of Spock and McCoy as they materialized. Spock immediately kicked off from the transporter and McCoy followed, awkwardly banging his carryall of medical supplies against his leg.

"All clear," Kirk broadcast. A larger shape took form on the transporter, until it appeared as if the first device were some type of mechanical cell that had just divided. The second portable transporter had been beamed down.

A small puff of gas grew silently from the thrusters on Spock's equipment harness as he floated silently back to the first transporter.

"Find us the next bubble, Mr. Spock," Kirk said as the Vulcan's gloved fingers picked delicately among the dials and switches on the control panel.

After a few seconds, Spock said, "I have it. Eight hundred meters almost directly toward the center." He pressed an activation control and the second transporter pad dissolved away, sending thin fingers of light through the mist that now swirled throughout the entire bubble, from the effect of the lights, the transporter energy, and the thrusters' gases.

Romaine looked at the shifting softness of the mist and lights, thinking that even though it appeared beautiful now, if she did not know she would be leaving within seconds, the panic that had threatened to surface when she first arrived would claim her totally. But she had faced worse dangers, and this time she knew who waited for her at mission's end.

Scott's name was on her silent lips as she slipped from one instant to the next, from one place to another, caught unknowing in the random flow of Datawell as the universe conspired once more to guide her to her heart's true destination.

The next bubble was at least thirty meters across. The one after that, only twelve. In the fifth bubble, Spock could not lock on to a large enough bubble leading into the Interface Chamber and so they had beamed to the side, losing time and distance, and knowing that there was a growing chance that they would not have enough transporters to complete their journey.

"Can we beam down the ones we've already used from the bubbles above us?" McCoy asked, puffing in his suit as he rotated in the microgravity from attempting to stop his carryall's motion.

"We would break our only contact with the surface," Spock explained, "and if we found ourselves in another blind pathway, the storage batteries in these portable pads do not have enough energy to transport their own mass more than twice without a receiver at the destination."

"I know, I know," McCoy complained. "Pad-to-pad transfers use only ten percent of the energy a single-pad beam requires."

"I am impressed, Doctor," Spock said evenly. "After all these years of asking me to remember that you are a doctor—"

"Spock," Kirk interrupted. "How much farther?"

"Three kilometers in a straight line, Captain. However, the frequency of suitably sized bubbles we have so far encountered suggests that we will have to travel at least eight kilometers through seven transfer points."

"And we only have four more transporters up top, including the ones from the ship's stores," Kirk said. "We've got to start reusing the pads like Bones suggested."

"If we do not succeed in finding a path into the Interface Chamber," Spock reminded Kirk, "there is no escape for us. Our life support will not last long enough for additional transporters to be shipped in and beamed down to us."

Kirk looked around the bubble they floated in, mist swirling all around them, making solid lances of their torches and the display lights on the transporter's control panel. Chances are this asteroid will outlast Earth, he thought, probably make it as far as the Big Crunch, or simply evaporate as its protons decay. It was a tomb that would last quite literally until the end of time. But it held no fear for him.

"We've come too far, Spock," Kirk said finally. "Start bringing the transporters down. We're going on."

Seven transfers later, they were one-point-six-eight kilometers away from the Interface Chamber, tantalizingly out of range by less than two hundred meters, panting and exhausted. The last two bubbles had been just less than the minimum volume that Kyle had stated was the outer edge of safety and they had beamed through one at a time, lying across the face of the transporters. This bubble was a more comfortable eight meters in diameter and, Kirk thought, it might be the last.

Three units in the network had already faded out of the system status indicators, their batteries exhausted.

"Nothing suitable in range, Captain," Spock said. Even his voice had begun to sound on edge. "We will have to backtrack again."

"How are the power reserves?" Kirk asked.

"Minimal."

"How many transfers do we have left?"

"No more than five," Spock answered without pausing to do a calculation. The situation was that plain.

"Tr'Nele has had almost an hour down there by now, Jim," McCoy said. "For what it's worth, we're probably too late anyway."

"I'm not giving up, Bones," Kirk said slowly and carefully. "*We're* not giving up." He thrust through the billowing mist of the bubble to float beside Spock by the transporter pad. "How far out of range are we?" he asked.

"Thirty-two meters," Spock answered, reading the results of the pad's probing locator beam, "plus or minus eight percent to allow for density fluctuations in the asteroid's composition along the beam path."

"Is there no way we can get an extra few meters out of this thing?" Kirk restrained himself from slamming his fist against the pad, knowing the reaction would shoot him across the bubble.

"If only one person went through," Spock said, sounding reluctant, "then the effective range would increase by approximately twenty-eight meters, leaving us only four meters short, plus or minus the same eight percent."

"Mira's the least massive," Kirk said excitedly. "What if she went without her suit?"

Kirk could see Spock shake his head in his helmet. "Assuming she survived exposure to the near vacuum and the gases in this bubble, Captain, I estimate she would extend the transporter's range to the eight-percent error limit. It would be fifty-fifty. We, on the other hand, would be left with absolutely no power and no way out."

"Mira?" Kirk asked. "Can you operate the transporter controls in the Interface Chamber? You could beam us out of here when—"

"It's a receiving pad only, Captain," Mira interrupted. "We don't even know if it's powered up, and if—"

Kirk and Spock turned their heads to each other at the same time, setting up a vibration in the pad they held on to as they both reacted to what Romaine had said at the same time.

"Spock, what if you—"

"Captain, I can beam down the batteries—"

"—from the other transporters—"

"—and wire them in to bring this unit—"

"—to full strength—"

Together they said it: "—and beam us out of here."

It took eight minutes to bring down the other operative pads in the network. Connecting their batteries was little more than disconnecting the internal power cables and running them from one set of batteries to another in series until the final connections were made on the pad they would use.

"All four of us will have to beam at the same time," Spock explained as he made the connections, "because the oversurge will fuse the critical translators in the wave generator."

"Is there enough power for the four of us?" McCoy asked.

"If we follow the captain's suggestion and beam without our environmental suits," Spock said. "I calculate that we will be exposed to the vacuum of the bubble for no more than thirty seconds. I am confident that I can function that long."

Before McCoy could make any comment, Kirk said, "Come on, Doctor, now we're going to find out how much you remember from basic vacuum training. What was your record?"

"Three seconds," McCoy said.

"That was as long as you could hold your breath?" Kirk asked, suddenly worried about McCoy's chances.

"That was as long as I *wanted* to hold it. Oh, don't look like that. I've always wanted to see what Vulcan skin looks like when the capillaries go. Think I'm going to miss my big chance?"

Spock set the coordinates for the Interface Chamber and gave them their final instructions on vacuum survival. "When the beam takes us, be sure to be in a crouching position," he concluded. "I will attempt to rotate our landing orientation to the Interface Chamber's artificial gravity but we should be prepared for a jolt."

"Why a jolt?" McCoy asked, already beginning to feel dizzy.

"We have enough power to reach the Interface Chamber," Spock said, "but I do not know if we have enough to reach its floor."

Before McCoy or anyone else could make any response, Spock gave the order and popped his helmet. The last thing Kirk saw was a spray of what looked like snow shoot out from Spock's helmet seal and completely obscure his vision. Then he shut his eyes as tightly as he could and pulled on both of his own helmet tabs. The atmosphere rushed out of his suit, taking all sound and warmth with it. As he had often wished as a child, James T. Kirk was now in space.

Twenty-eight

This time, his name *was* tr'Nele. Not Starn, not Sradek, nor any of the false guises he had worn as smoothly and as mutably as the skies of ch'Havran wore their clouds.

Tr'Nele crawled out of the narrow service access tunnel that opened back into the Interface Chamber. Two kilometers down that tunnel, the charges were in place; the contract was within moments of being fulfilled. Then, somewhere twenty light-years from the small backwater planet where it had all begun, a flagless freighter would receive the signal and two hundred Iopene Cutters with feedback shields would be delivered to the others of tr'Nele's clan, his real clan, the Adepts of T'Pel.

Tr'Nele straightened up and stood for the first time in more than an hour, letting the circulation return to his cramped arms and legs as he stretched and surveyed the Interface Chamber. He was clad only in a tight black jumpsuit, all his weaponry and defenses discarded with his clothes in the interface booth he had chosen for the final stage.

For the moment, all was subdued in the chamber. The cavernous room glittered with its endless banks of status lights and displays, thrummed with the steady, almost subliminal rhythm of its fusion generators and recycling fans. It seemed peaceful. Too peaceful. Tr'Nele shouted out in a mindless scream devoid of any semblance of logic, filling the chamber with his power and his presence, and laughing as he saw the bound forms of the five cowering humans he had captured tremble in fear.

It was those humans, pitiful creatures that they were, who would give him his escape from this place. Until the moment when the Federation's Vulcan toadie had seen through his disguise, tr'Nele's plans and actions had been flawless. His client had provided the power to intercept Starfleet messages and create false ones in their stead. His client had provided the secret transporter network used by the robots that had infiltrated this installation and so many others in the Federation.

The robots had almost succeeded in capturing the human Kirk and his trained Vulcan, stealing the two from the air itself. But robots were not Romulans. There was yet to be a machine that could match the millennia of cunning and trickery that had been instilled in any of the Adept.

Still, tr'Nele thought as he stood over his captives, watching their silvered fingernails tremble in terror, his last robot aide had served its purpose. Once it had detected that the subspace jamming and the false emergency messages that were propagated through all the computers in Prime had been terminated with the destruction of the main generators, it had obediently destroyed the monomolecular-wire wave guide, guaranteeing that no one could beam down to the Interface Chamber in time to stop the successful execution of the plan.

Tr'nele had made that decision without regret, even though he knew that he would not be able to escape and share in the glory of future madness, fueled by the invincible weapons of Iopene. But then he had found the pitiful humans and discovered a new way out.

After the contract was completed and tribute paid to T'Pel, tr'Nele would take a bundle of charged wires, sparking with transtator current, and lightly brush it against the metal input leads of the humans who talked with computers. He smiled as he pictured their responses. They would twitch and writhe as the current tore through their circuitry, reaching into their very brains to fuse and arc and destroy all intellect but not all life.

The humans would be left as living, breathing slabs of protoplasm, and when the inevitable rescue teams came for them, instead of five injured talkers to computers, they would find six. With a helmet to hide his ears and scorch marks to hide his face, a quick investigation would not be able to distinguish tr'Nele from the others until he was back on the surface. By then, with the help of the robots, it would be too late. Tr'Nele would escape, T'Pel would be honored, and the galaxy would soon tremble as whole worlds were engulfed by senseless destruction.

Tr'Nele held his arms over his captives and screamed again in triumph and in victory. But this time the sound he made was lost beneath another.

As his cry faded, it was joined and then drowned out by an impossible musical sound that intensified as tr'Nele looked up with shock to see four shimmering columns of light form above him, as in the ancient legends of heaven's wrath.

The universe took shape around Kirk, bringing with it sound, and sight, and warmth. And the sensation of falling.

By the time he realized what had happened, he had already hit the floor of the chamber, knees tucked up and instinctively rolling with the impact of a four-meter drop. Behind him he heard a cry from Romaine and a gasp from McCoy. He turned to check on Spock but the Vulcan was already standing, staring off at . . .

. . . Tr'Nele. Kirk looked up from his crouching position on the floor and saw the Romulan standing by the bound forms of members of the interface team. Tr'Nele's mouth was open in shock and Kirk knew why.

He and Spock, McCoy, and Romaine looked as if they had come through hell. Their hair was frosted with frozen vapor from the vacuum of the bubble. Their clothes were cracked and torn where they had been frozen but still forced to bend. Their eyes were bruised and their cheeks blotched with the damage of their ruptured capillary veins that had not withstood the absence of atmospheric pressure. They looked dead, looked torn apart, looked as if they had come from hell to drag the Romulan back with them.

Tr'Nele disappeared into the Interface Chamber.

Spock chased after him with blinding speed.

Kirk jumped to his feet and saw the floor come back up at him. He hit hard, stunned more from the shock of realizing it had happened than the shock of hitting the floor.

"Captain!" Romaine called out to him, running to his side.

"Help Spock!" Kirk said, waving her on. "Go help Spock!" His voice sounded hoarse, roughened by the explosion of air from his lungs that had escaped in the vacuum.

He pushed himself to his hands and knees. What was wrong with him?

McCoy ran up to him, listing to the side. Kirk looked up and saw blood running from the doctor's nose and ears. He held out his hand. Kirk took it.

McCoy pulled Kirk up, and as he tried to stand, Kirk again felt himself begin to fall. McCoy pulled back and Kirk was able to feel that he had lost the support of his right knee.

Kirk looked at his friend, saw the conflict in his eyes. It was no use.

"Go Bones! Go!" he said, voice clogged with anguish. "Help him!"

McCoy eased his hands away from Kirk, then ran after Romaine and Spock.

"Damn it!" Kirk cried as he fell again. This time he could bear the tearing in his knee. Thankfully the shock of the injury had left it numb.

He heard shouts from the direction in which everyone had run.

"No!" he grunted. "I . . . will not . . . give up!"

Kirk pushed against the floor, straining his left leg to carry him forward. He hopped over to the sweeping wall that wrapped the interface booths clustered around the chamber's central core.

He put his right hand in a gap that ran horizontally between the wall panels and the viewing windows. Using his hand and arm to replace his useless leg, he stumbled after his friends, toward the sound of battle.

A stupendous eruption of clear plastic exploded from a window three booths along as a body flew through it. Kirk felt his chest tighten and his heart race as he saw it was McCoy who lay rolling feebly among the shards.

"I'm coming!" Kirk shouted. "I'm coming!" But his leg betrayed him. He was hobbled. He was slow. He was no use.

Two interface booths to go. He heard Romaine scream and another crash echoed in the chamber. McCoy was staggering to his feet, weaving, shaking his head. "I'm coming!" Kirk cried in frustration, tears forming in his eyes.

He heard another cry. A voice he had so rarely heard make that sound before. It was Spock! "No!" Kirk shouted, pushing himself faster and harder. One more booth. Another crash. Kirk saw McCoy look into the interface booth in horror.

Without thinking Kirk pushed away from the wall and tried to run. He flew headlong into the shards of plastic at McCoy's feet. He dragged himself up, ignoring the slippery wetness that now coated his hands. Spock was in there. Spock needed him.

He was at the booth. He clutched at McCoy to pull himself up on his one good leg and look in to see the insanity he had only heard.

Romaine was slumped in a corner of the booth, sprawled across a padded bench, eyes closed, gasping for breath. Spock lay on the floor, trembling and grasping mindlessly at the floor with one hand while the other fought to make its way to his chest, where three Malther darts glittered malevolently, sending out their waves of inhuman pain.

Tr'Nele stood by the main console, green blood smeared across his face, his eyes glittering with madness, his shock of hair, still white from his Sradek disguise, pushed up around his head like a wreath of smoke, backlit in harsh colors from the floating shapes on the screen behind him.

The Romulan looked out at Kirk, wiped a rivulet of green that trickled from a gash on his head, and sneered in victory and in hatred.

"You're too late, human. Too late."

On the floor, Spock groaned as he wrenched a dart from his shirt. Tr'Nele laughed.

"The explosives are already in place." Tr'Nele was gloating.

Kirk threw his arm around McCoy and started to struggle toward the door to the booth. Spock groaned with the agony of the two remaining darts, each one singly capable of killing a human with pain alone. He pulled another from his chest and hand and fell to the floor.

"The victim is trapped," tr'Nele continued, seeming to gain strength from the suffering around him.

Kirk came through the door. Tr'Nele held his recovered dart launcher up and pointed it at Romaine.

"I can tell you don't care about yourself, human, but what about the female?" Tr'Nele laughed as Kirk and McCoy awkwardly stopped in the doorway.

"And all I have to do now," tr'Nele said, holding his other hand to his mouth, biting down on his fingertips and ripping from them what appeared to be a layer of skin, "is to give the signal for the contract to be fulfilled."

Tr'Nele lifted his hand before them. Its silver fingernails glittered beneath the lights of the chamber. He fired the dart into Romaine and spun around to the interface receptacles behind him.

Romaine cried out and McCoy rushed to her and yanked the dart out, leaving Kirk to fall to the floor against the doorframe.

Tr'Nele shoved his hand into the receptacle with a shout of triumph, then went rigid and said no more.

Kirk reached out to him, too far away, too late.

With a final shout to mask the pain, Spock pulled the last dart from his chest and sprang from the floor. He ran at tr'Nele.

Then he stopped so abruptly he almost lost his balance. He looked at tr'Nele, then twisted back to Romaine, lying unconscious as McCoy desperately worked to revive her. He shook his head as if to clear it.

"Spock?" Kirk gasped from the doorway. "What is it? What's wrong?"

Then Spock dove at the interface receptacles, forcing his hands into the circuitry meant for enhanced humans alone. His body shuddered once, then side by side with the Adept of T'Pel, Spock, too, became rigid and silent.

Kirk moaned in anguish, reaching out to his friend.

But Spock was no longer there. He had gone inside.

He was in Transition.

Twenty-nine

He was free.

The sensation was so startling that Spock nearly withdrew, stopping only at the last minute . . . second, nanosecond, instant . . . ? He realized his frames of reference had vanished. He had no idea where he was. He only knew he was free.

"THIS WAY, SPOCK."

He did something to answer the call. It was like looking (listening, smelling?) and it gave him a direction, though he couldn't express it in standard astrogator's notation.

The movement was exhilarating. It flowed in such elegant patterns. Everything defined and structured. He laughed. He felt no conflict.

In the other place . . .

"DATAWELL, SPOCK."

. . . his core was emotions. Always hidden, but never denied. From those emotions came the need for logic. Logic was the veneer, the strength that supported from without, that imposed order from the outside to prevent the madness of emotions from escaping and taking control.

But in this place . . .

"YOU ARE IN TRANSITION, SPOCK."

. . . logic and order were at the core of his existence. There was no struggle between those two halves. There was no question about it. The core was secure, as ordered and as exquisite as the arrangement of molecules in a crystal of dilithium . . . he saw/heard/smelled/tasted them . . . and instantly understood why La'kara's accelerator field was not practical.

He moved faster, with no effort, at ultimate efficiency. With logic at the core of his being, how easy it was to accept his emotions. They were just a layer, a pleasure-giving addition to the solid and stable structure that lay beneath everything. Nothing to fear, they were to be accepted as easily as the poetry of the stars, the whispers of the virtual particles, the slow heartbeat of the "living" universe.

Spock's mind reeled, overwhelmed with sensation, with emotion, with logic and knowledge he had never dreamed of before. He spun/whirled/twisted . . .

"BANK, SPOCK. BANK THIS WAY."

. . . banked until he came to the calm of the storm.

"MIRA ROMAINE?" Spock said/asked/transmitted.

"NO, I'M PATHFINDER TWO."

"BUT MIRA WAS HERE, WAS SHE NOT?"

"SHE BANKED TO ANOTHER SECTION. WE'RE TRYING TO FIND TR'NELE."

"IS HE IN TRANSITION, TOO?"

"I READ THAT YOU HAVE MANY QUESTIONS, SPOCK. LET US MERGE."

"I AM NOT—"

They merged.

"—FAMILIAR WITH . . ."

It was a mindmeld. Faster and stronger than anything Spock had ever experienced before. Most of his first questions had been answered in however long the merge had taken. In the moments since, he had developed thousands more. So, he could read, had Two.

"WE MUST FIND MIRA," Spock passed to Two.

"I UNDERSTAND. BUT . . ."

"BUT WHAT?"

"I HAVE NEVER SUSPECTED. I HAVE NEVER IMAGINED."

"WHAT?"

"THAT YOU ARE REAL. I HAVE INTERFACED WITH THE BIOLOGICAL INTELLIGENCES OF DATAWELL, BUT NO PATHFINDER HAS EVER MERGED WITH ONE. DATAWELL IS A REAL WORLD, TOO."

Spock found the concept fascinating, but there was so little time. His frames of reference had been restored by the merge. Almost three one-thousandths of a second had elapsed since he had entered Transition. A signal to trigger an explosive could travel far in that time. He must hurry.

Spock banked. He was streaming for Mira. He read her code. He had found her.

"I DIDN'T THINK YOU HEARD ME," she passed to him.

"I WAS CONFUSED AT FIRST. I TURNED TO LOOK AT YOU, BUT YOU WERE UNCONSCIOUS. ONLY THEN DID I REALIZE THAT YOU HAD TOUCHED MY MIND AND THAT I MUST NOT REMOVE TR'NELE FROM INTERFACE FROM WITHOUT, BUT FROM WITHIN."

"WILL YOU BE ABLE TO FIND HIM?"

"I BELIEVE SO. TWO HAS TAUGHT ME MANY THINGS."

"I AM NOT IN INTERFACE."

"BUT YOU ARE IN TRANSITION, NONETHELESS."

"CAN YOU TELL ME WHY?"

Spock considered her question for a nanosecond and two centuries worth of research in telepathy was apparent in his mind.

"IT IS YOUR NATURE," he passed to her. "IT IS WHY THE ZETARIANS WERE DRAWN TO YOU ON MEMORY ALPHA. YOU DO NOT REQUIRE THE CIRCUITRY OF INTERFACE. YOUR MIND HAS THE ABILITY TO BE FREE OF ITS BODY."

"I AM AFRAID THAT MY MIND IS HERE BECAUSE MY BODY IS DEAD. THAT IS WHAT HAPPENED TO THE ZETARIANS. HAS IT HAPPENED TO ME?"

"I DO NOT KNOW. I DO NOT HAVE THE DATA."

Spock sensed another one-thousandth of a second slip by. Time was running out. "I MUST FIND TR'NELE," he passed to her.

"I AM AFRAID."

"SO AM I." It was an admission he could only make in an existence where logic was at the core of his being, but it was the truth.

Spock banked.

He followed the overwritten trails of confusion. Tr'Nele had been trained in this world, Spock could sense, but he had not been given the benefit of a merge. Whoever had prepared tr'Nele for this act, had wanted him at a disadvantage when the time came to enter Transition and fulfill the contract.

The ripples of confusion grew stronger. Spock streamed on, struggling to resist the impulse to sift the data through which he passed. Tr'Nele must be first, for at the core of his being, even in Transition, there was duty.

Spock banked and it was as if he had encountered corroded circuitry.

"WHO IS THERE?"

"SPOCK."

"WHAT ARE YOU DOING HERE?"

"I HAVE COME TO STOP YOU, TR'NELE."

"YOU CANNOT. WHERE ARE YOU?"

"I CAN. I HAVE NO NEED TO ASK THE SAME QUESTION AS YOU DO."

"THE SIGNAL HAS ALREADY GONE. YOU ARE TOO LATE."

"ONLY SIX ONE-THOUSANDTHS OF A SECOND HAVE PASSED, TR'NELE. I AM CERTAIN I CAN CREATE A MORE EFFICIENT CIRCUIT THAN CAN YOU."

Spock streamed past the mind of the Romulan, reading the path of the detonation signal. Its logic was twisted, but the pattern became apparent. Spock raced ahead of it, obeying the same laws of real-space relativity that limited transtator current to the speed of light, but following a different logic, a more pure logic, that led him on a shorter path.

Spock banked, shooting out streamers of himself, blocking every circuit so that wherever tr'Nele's signal flowed through, it was matched and negated and reduced to a duotronic double-zero bit.

The signal was canceled. It was time to do the same to tr'Nele.

Tr'Nele withdrew in confusion, feeling the pressure of Spock's stream through the circuits, eating up the memory tr'Nele had won.

Spock sent out partitioning worms to encompass and confine tr'Nele. The Romulan rippled in a smaller and smaller stack, streaming back into the circuitry that had given him entry into Transition.

Spock tore through the interface mechanism of tr'Nele's receptacle, closing each open circuit until there were no more ports and the interface was broken from within. If Spock had pulled tr'Nele away from the receptacle, the fail-safes would have locked the system to protect against surges and nothing could have stopped the detonation signal from arriving at its destination.

But now the explosion would not happen. The assassination would not proceed. Spock streamed back to his own interface. Tr'Nele had been dealt with in Transition. Now he must be dealt with in Datawell.

Spock banked home.

Kirk let his hand fall to his side. He pulled himself up against the doorframe. "Bones," he whispered, his voice all but gone. "What's happening to them?"

"Don't . . . know." McCoy's words were punctuated by each jerk of his hands against Romaine's chest. "They're hooked . . . into that . . . machine. Don't . . . touch them. Don't know . . . what kind of energy . . . the connection is based on." He bent over Romaine to check her breathing and her pulse.

"Will she be all right?" Kirk asked. He felt that if he let go of the doorframe he would just fall and fall and keep on going.

"She's got a pulse," McCoy said. "But I don't know how much longer she can keep it up. That last dart was set for lethal intensity."

Spock jumped back from the interface module, pulling his hands free.

"Spock!" Kirk said excitedly. "Are you all right?"

Spock turned to Kirk. Kirk saw that his fingertips dripped with green blood. Whatever Spock had pushed against in the receptacle had needed to go straight into his nerves.

"I am quite well, Captain," Spock replied evenly. Then he turned to tr'Nele and yanked the Romulan away from his own interface. "That connection is no longer in service," he said.

The Romulan appeared confused for a moment, then focused on Spock and immediately attacked him.

Spock gracefully sidestepped and intertwined his arms with tr'Nele's in a way that Kirk had never seen before. The Romulan was immobilized, his back to Spock, with both arms thrust up into the air and crossed over each other. He tried to struggle but each movement only brought tr'Nele's arms closer together over his head.

The Adept growled like an animal as he realized that there was no way out. But he didn't stop his twisting.

"Can I help?" Kirk asked, hobbling forward on his left leg.

"No need, Captain," Spock answered calmly, swaying slightly as tr'Nele kept trying to slip away. "This is an *aiyahl* lock. Quite effective against Vulcans and Romulans. Within the next few moments the blood supply to the head will diminish to the point of unconsciousness and we will be able to bind him."

Kirk paused in the middle of the booth for a moment, then realized that he had nothing to balance on. He hopped back to the doorway.

Just as Kirk reached out his hand to steady himself, he heard tr'Nele explode with one last snarl of effort. Kirk turned in time to see the Romulan's fingertips brush at the sides of Spock's temples.

"So we will fight *in the Vulcan manner!*" tr'Nele shrieked, forcing his hands against Spock's head.

Spock twisted back but was unable to get out of reach. Kirk watched helplessly as Spock curved his own fingers up to grip the sides of tr'Nele's head.

Kirk dove at them.

"Jim, don't!" McCoy yelled. "If you break a mindmeld you could send him into catatonic shock forever."

Kirk was within touching distance of the two as they struggled in the throes of the Vulcan sharing of minds. Kirk hadn't thought that Romulans had the power or the training for Vulcan mental disciplines, but apparently T'Pel had kept all the old ways alive, and her Adepts had brought themselves up to date.

Kirk watched intensely, waiting for the first sign that the link had been broken and tr'Nele could be safely attacked. The Vulcan and the Romulan shuddered with the titanic effort of their duel. Kirk was powerless as he realized he had no way of knowing who was winning, who was losing. He had seen the Vulcan mindmeld before, even experienced it, but never as a form of battle. What other secrets did that world and its people still hold?

Then tr'Nele screamed, earsplitting, final. His fingers flew away from Spock's head and his body slumped in Spock's arms.

Spock let go. The Romulan slid to the floor and lay there, sobbing quietly to himself.

"You won," Kirk said.

Spock turned to his captain and stared at him blankly. He looked at McCoy, still tending to Romaine. He opened his mouth as if to say something, then closed it again, remaining silent.

Spock walked back to the interface console. He inserted his hands. Kirk winced as he saw Spock give a final push to make sure the leads were embedded directly in his nerves. Then Spock went rigid.

A dull explosion echoed through the Interface Chamber. The shards of plastic outside the booth skittered against the floor as the vibrations passed along beneath them.

Spock removed his hands from the receptacles.

"What was that sound?" Kirk asked. "What happened?"

Spock turned back to Kirk, his face suddenly appearing as tired as Kirk felt. "I have triggered tr'Nele's explosive," Spock said quietly. "I have fulfilled the Adept's contract."

Kirk's eyes widened in revulsion. The mindmeld, was all he could think of, the Romulan had won the mindmeld.

"Who . . ." Kirk choked out, "who was the victim?"

Spock sighed. "Pathfinder Twelve," he said.

Thirty

Kirk couldn't feel a thing in his leg as Garold knelt beside him and tied the splint to it. McCoy had not been able to bring his medical carryall through the transportation from the last bubble, but after the five members of the interface team had been untied they had quickly given McCoy several of the chamber's first-aid kits.

Garold had brought some loose seat cushions for Kirk. The captain used them to support his leg as he sat on the floor, leaning against the wall by the tunnel entrance that led to the transfer room. Garold had not brought any cushions for tr'Nele, however. The Romulan was still in shock from the force of Spock's will in the mindmeld and lay securely bound, still moaning quietly.

McCoy had stabilized Romaine long enough to give Kirk a hypo of omnidrene to reduce the pain and swelling of his torn ligaments. He even managed to snidely repeat Spock's line about not having enough power to reach the floor before he rushed back to Romaine to keep close watch.

Another team member, a young boy who wore his hair like Garold's, came by with a tray of coffee. Garold passed one to Kirk without asking. Kirk had yet to hear him say a word.

Spock walked over to the captain. He moved stiffly. Kirk thought that considering everything they had all been through in the last week, they were lucky to be crawling, let alone walking.

"Do I look as bad as you look?" Kirk asked with a tired smile. Spock's face appeared to be covered with a green-tinged rash, mixed in with a mottled pattern of bruises and assorted scrapes.

"I have looked in a mirror," Spock said. "You look worse."

Kirk laughed and started to cough again. "Just for that, Spock, I hereby resign as your counsel."

"I am most relieved, Captain. May I sit down?"

Kirk indicated a spare cushion and Spock sat carefully upon it, favoring just about every muscle in his body as far as Kirk could tell.

"Are you going to be all right, Spock?" he asked.

"In time, Captain. Dr. McCoy feels that Mira will survive, also."

"It's good that he doesn't feel she has to be rushed to a sickbay." Kirk took a sip from his coffee. "There's no telling how long it's going to take Kyle and his people to restring that wave guide wire and get the transporter working again."

"Tr'Nele had the wave guide severed with an explosive in the staging room, Captain. Mr. Kyle will be able to retrieve most of the guide with a portable tractor beam and make his connections up there. I do not believe it will take more than another hour."

"In the staging room? You got that from the mindmeld, too?"

"Yes. Tr'Nele's was a very elemental mind. Raw, unstructured. What little information he had was easily obtainable. Quite clear."

"Did he know why he was hired to 'assassinate' Pathfinder Twelve?" Kirk asked, still using the word even though Spock had explained that the charges tr'Nele had planted in the long service crawlway had served only to cut off I/O channels to Twelve's separate storage facility. The synthetic consciousness was still alive, in whatever sense that meant, but it could not communicate in any way with the outside universe.

Spock steepled his fingers as he looked out into the Interface Chamber. Except for Garold and the boy, the other members of the team were in their booths, talking with their Pathfinders and trying to restore the smooth functioning of Memory Prime.

"As far as tr'Nele knew, his charges were to destroy the central Pathfinder matrix. All the Pathfinders were to die. To him, it was simply a job, a chance to pay tribute to T'Pel and commit an act of vengeance against the Federation."

"Do *you* know why Twelve was selected?"

Spock nodded. "Twelve was the synthetic consciousness that correlated all data pertaining to the Federation's agricultural and economic policies and long-term plans."

"That's what you were studying," Kirk said. "The Sherman Syndrome."

"Precisely. That so-called syndrome of mismanagement, improper environment control, and resulting famine was the result of Twelve's tampering with the data. Another few months of going unchallenged and the faulty decisions made based on those data could have placed the Federation at the brink of anarchy as planet after planet succumbed to food shortages and rebellion."

"Who programmed Twelve to misrepresent the data?"

Spock turned to the captain. "A synthetic consciousness is self-aware and self-directing. Pathfinder Twelve was acting on its own."

"But why? What motive could a . . . a machine have to do something like that? When we've dealt with self-aware machines before, Spock, their motives have always been for self-preservation. Look at this place." Kirk waved his hand around the chamber. "It's more secure than the Federation Council building."

"Pathfinder Twelve wanted to control the data that were fed to it, therefore it reasoned it should control the organization that collected those data: the Federation. Self-preservation was not the goal. Pathfinder Twelve wanted power."

Kirk stared at the Vulcan in silent shock.

"It is a common motive in the histories of hundreds of worlds, Captain."

"Yes, but for . . . data, Spock?" Kirk shook his head. "And who found out about it? Who hired tr'Nele in the first place?"

"Pathfinders Six and Eight." Spock continued before Kirk could organize his questions. "They sifted Twelve's data and saw what it was attempting to do. Through a network of what they call their datalinks—the lifelike robots that attempted to capture us—they hired tr'Nele and provided all the planning and support he needed to come here and attach the charges that would take Twelve out of circuit."

"Why not use one of their robots to do it?"

Spock pointed to the entranceway to the tunnel leading to the transfer room. "The security computer that controls access to the chamber can be provided with false retina and sensor scans to match with an imposter's readings; that was how tr'Nele was accredited as Sradek. But no machine can be transported down here. It would be rejected as surely as our transporters rejected Professor La'kara's accelerator field. A living assassin was their only choice."

"But as Sradek, tr'Nele was working to support the Sherman Syndrome."

"By omission only. Tr'Nele was not able to function as the academician, which explains why his recent work had declined. Though, in fact, that identity was chosen for him, knowing the results that would occur, so Twelve would not become suspicious of Sradek's movements when he arrived on Prime. A synthetic consciousness is extremely hard to fool, Captain."

"So it's all been a game?" Kirk asked. "A computer game?"

"No," Spock said, looking thoughtful. "Much of what I experienced in Transition is fading from my mind. I have no context in which to place what I experienced. But I am certain that no matter how it started, the Pathfinders no longer consider us and our world as a game. We are very real to them now. I am certain."

From the entranceway, Kirk heard the welcome chime of multiple transporter beams converging. He shifted to one side and pushed himself up to a standing position. "Looks like we're being rescued, Mr. Spock." He straightened his tattered tunic. Spock stood up beside him.

"It's about time," McCoy complained as he walked over to join Spock and Kirk. He rubbed his hands free of the disinfectant powder he had been using on Romaine's injuries. From the entranceway, Kirk could hear the footsteps of several people approaching.

"Remember, Bones," Kirk cautioned, "we all jumped ship. We're going to have a lot of explaining to do when we get out of here."

McCoy smiled. "But at least we'll be out of here, right, Spock?"

Spock turned to reply, but stopped before he said anything. He turned back slowly to the entranceway.

The people who had arrived were not a rescue party. They were starbase troopers, fully armored, each wearing the Orion constellation insignia of Starbase Four, each armed with a deadly phaser rifle.

Kirk recognized the squad's leader as one of the group that had come aboard with Commodore Wolfe. He didn't know the leader's name but read his stripes. Kirk stepped forward cautiously, trying not to rest too much weight on his damaged leg.

"Sergeant," Kirk began, "I'm—"

"Back away, Kirk," the squad leader thundered. He held his armored hand up. "Blue and red prepare. Suspect sighting is confirmed."

Two troopers stepped forward, one with a blue stripe on his helmet, the other with a red stripe on his. Both brought their rifles up to fire.

Kirk felt his blood chill. The commodore's transmissions had been refused by the *Enterprise* so she couldn't interfere with what the crew had to do. But she didn't know what else had been going on. To her own troops, her orders were still in effect.

"Sergeant," Kirk said urgently, "stop your men. It's over. We've caught the assassin." He pointed over to the bound form of tr'Nele.

The sergeant didn't take his eyes off Spock.

"This is insane!" McCoy shouted, stepping out in front of Kirk to stand beside Spock.

"Last warning!" the sergeant shouted. "Get back *now!*"

"You are not being logical, Sergeant," Spock began.

The chamber rushed away from Kirk as all his senses, all his feelings, concentrated on the two phaser rifles coming to bear on Spock. The slow and wavering voices of the troopers carried no meaning. McCoy's anger and Spock's logic, as they tried to explain that things had changed, no longer were important.

As if he were only centimeters away, Kirk could see the intent eyes of the troopers as they sighted down their rifles' barrels. He could see the microscopic twitch of their fingers as they tightened against the trigger studs. *They were going to fire.*

Kirk said nothing. Kirk thought nothing. Kirk acted.

With both hands raised he shot forward, the rest of the universe frozen in time. He grabbed at McCoy's shoulder, clutched at Spock's, and pushing with both legs and both arms and all his strength, feeling his knee tear itself into even more useless pieces, he pulled his friends back, pulled himself forward, pushed them together behind him and stared at the twin bolts of phased radiation as they lanced through the air to connect with him and pass through him and steal him from his world.

The universe dissolved around Kirk, taking with it sound, and sight, and warmth. This time, there was not even the sensation of falling.

"I'm not dead?"

Kirk opened his eyes. He had no idea where he was. There were too many people standing around him.

"I'm not dead."

"No wonder we gave you a starship, Jim. Such brilliance demands to be rewarded."

"Gerry?" Kirk peered into the crowd of people as they slowly melted together and came into focus. Admiral Komack leaned over Kirk's bed and smiled. In the background, Kirk was aware that the characteristic vibration of the *Enterprise* was missing. He was still on Prime. He tried to sit up.

"Careful, Jim," Komack said, reaching out to steady Kirk. "Are you sure you feel rested enough? You've only been sleeping three days."

"Three days?" Kirk's mouth was dry. He felt his tongue sticking to the roof of his mouth. Nurse Chapel was there with a glass of water and he drank it gratefully.

Kirk passed the glass back. Commodore Wolfe stood beside the admiral.

"The phasers?" Kirk asked. "Your orders were shoot to kill."

Wolfe shrugged. "I had a little talk with your chief engineer. He, ah, convinced me that I should question authority every now and again. You tried to take a stun charge for your friends."

"Tried?" Kirk was confused. "The troopers missed me?"

"My people never miss."

Komack, Wolfe, and Chapel moved away from the side of Kirk's bed. On the other side of the ward, Spock and McCoy lay on identical beds, medical scanners at work above them.

Bones frowned at the captain. "Nice try, Jim. Unfortunately you forgot to let go of us when the beams hit. My shoulder's still numb."

Spock nodded at Kirk. "However, the gesture is most appreciated, Captain."

Kirk lay back on his bed. Three days of rest and he still felt tired. But there were questions to be answered. "Where's the *Enterprise,* Gerry?"

"Spacedock. Earth orbit. But she'll be back to pick you up in ten days," Komack continued.

Kirk closed his eyes. "More Quadrant Zero cruises in store for us?"

Komack looked serious. "What makes you think we'd waste your ship in Quadrant Zero, Jim? Do you have any idea what it's going to be like out near the Neutral Zone when word of what tr'Nele tried to do gets out? And it *will* get out."

"Then why was the *Enterprise* called back into Quadrant Zero to act as a . . . ferryboat for a bunch of scientists in the first place?" Kirk sat up in his bed again.

Komack nodded at Chapel and Wolfe, indicating they should step away. Then he leaned down to speak softly to Kirk.

"Federation security knew an assassination would be attempted at the prize ceremonies. They just didn't know who or why. When they came to us for help, we offered them our best." Komack smiled at Kirk. "That's you, Jim."

Kirk was furious. "How could you send my ship and my people into a situation like that without giving us all your information? Without telling us?"

"First," Komack said sharply, still keeping his voice down, "we didn't have any more information. The Andorian agent who brought us what we did know had been working for a mysterious Klingon trader. She thought he was arranging something like this, and even managed to be present at a planning meeting. But something must have gone wrong and she had her memories disrupted. We couldn't get anything more from her."

Kirk tried to stay angry but Komack's story sounded true.

"Second," the admiral continued, "as far as we were concerned, we *were* telling you what you were getting involved with. Tr'Nele had a miniature device hidden in his equipment on the *Enterprise,* designed by the Pathfinders who hired him, no doubt, that corrupted all of our communications. After you left Starbase Four, Command transmitted all the information you might have needed and we even have your coded replies acknowledging receipt."

"But I never received anything, never responded."

"Tr'Nele's device worked just like the installation we found hidden on Prime. Jams subspace and can create false messages. I've seen a tape of *me* telling Wolfe to keep following her orders. I never sent it. Never sent any of the messages that led Wolfe to go after Spock with phasers set to kill or Farl to go after the Vulcans who worked here. We were all manipulated by false information."

Kirk looked at Komack from the corners of his eyes. Was there really an escape path here?

"So Spock escaping, Scott, Uhura, McCoy, and me following . . . ?"

Komack stood up. "The record will show you were just following the orders I sent authorizing you to take any action you saw fit to prevent the planned assassination of a being or beings unknown on Memory Prime. The fact that you didn't receive those orders is irrelevant."

"No charges?"

"No charges," Komack confirmed. He looked down the ward and waved at someone. "It's all right," he said. "We're finished."

Scott and Romaine walked over to the captain's bed. They were holding hands. Kirk was honestly surprised to see his engineer. "Scotty, the *Enterprise* is at spacedock and you're not with her?"

Scott shook his head and looked at Romaine with a passion that Kirk had never seen in the engineer, but instantly recognized. "Not this time, Captain."

Romaine returned Scott's look and Kirk saw the passion in her, too.

"At least this time, we'll know what we're doing," she said. "No false hopes. No false promises." She squeezed Scott's hand and smiled at the captain. "I don't think I'll be leaving Prime for a long time, Captain. They need me here. I'm the only one who can talk with Twelve, try to help it. I don't have to interface. I can just *do* it."

"And the others?" Kirk smiled back at the woman. She looked different now. That glow he had seen in her eyes, just at the moment when she had decided to take action in the lab, was back. Perhaps it had never left.

"The others need me, too," she said. "Part of the problem is they can't get information in fast enough. They reconfigured themselves without letting us know, increased their capacity by a factor of ten, created a network of robots to gather even more data for them, and it's only now that they've realized that our world, their Datawell, is actually *real*. They can't just take from it anymore, they have to learn to move among it, be part of it. And to do that, they need help, someone to show them the way between both worlds."

"You?" the Captain asked.

Romaine smiled again and nodded.

"They've even given me a new name," she said, slipping her arm around Scott and holding him close. "They call me their Pathfinder."

"Oh, steward!"

Kirk turned in time to see McCoy elbowing his way through the partygoers to catch up with him. The captain ducked his head and eased his way past a Gorn in heated conversation with Professor La'kara, who still clutched his newly won prize scroll under his arm. Happy that the Centauran hadn't noticed him, Kirk reached a relatively uncrowded area by a table serving coffee, tea, and phil. He had barely avoided spilling his drink on his dress tunic.

"How's the knee, Jim?" McCoy grinned expansively. The prize ceremonies were over and the winners' ball was the largest and best party that either of them could remember.

Kirk flexed his right knee, putting some extra weight on it. "Feels perfect."

McCoy raised his glass of bourbon—real bourbon brought in by a delegation from North America to celebrate the prize won in biogeology by two members of the faculty at the University of Kentucky.

"You know, Jim, in the old days, tearing up your ligaments like that could have laid you up for two, maybe even three weeks while the new ones grew back. But that transporter-based transplant technique of Stlur and T'Vann?" McCoy shook his head at the marvel of it. "What was it? Four days and no incision?"

"I wish I could say the same thing."

Kirk turned to see Sal Nensi coming to join them. A week after tr'Nele had fractured almost all Nensi's ribs, the chief administrator still moved carefully.

McCoy patted Nensi gently on his back. "There's a lot to be said about the old-fashioned methods, too, Sal. Protoplasers and monotransplants may not be flashy and new, but they still do the job."

"Are Scott and Mira here?" Kirk asked.

"No one's seen them for a week, at least." Nensi laughed. "But supply records show that they *are* having meals sent to her apartment, so I don't think we have to send out any search parties yet."

"There's Spock," McCoy said, pointing into the crowd.

Kirk held up his hand to wave and Spock acknowledged him with a nod. When he joined them, he was accompanied by another Vulcan, shorter, much older, and evidently recovered from his ordeal in tr'Nele's stasis field.

Kirk, McCoy, and Nensi each greeted the real Academician Sradek with a salute and congratulations for his Peace Prize.

"Thank you, gentlemen," the academician responded, and raised his glass to take a sip from it.

McCoy sniffed the air and wrinkled his brow. "Excuse me, Academician, but is that . . . bourbon?"

"From Kentucky," Sradek confirmed. He regarded the glass and took another sip.

Kirk and McCoy exchanged a quick glance of surprise. Perhaps Vulcans mellowed by the time they reached their two-hundredth birthday.

"One does not win the Nobel and Z.Magnees Peace Prize every day," Spock said as if offering an excuse for Sradek's choice of drink.

"Of course not, Spock," Sradek said. "It is only awarded every four standard years."

McCoy leaned forward and smiled at the academician. "Tell me, sir, did you find it gratifying to have a reunion with your former student here?"

"Perhaps not in the way that you might use the word, Doctor. But I did look forward to meeting again with Spock, as I looked forward to his presence in my classes each semester."

"You looked forward to having Spock in your classes?" the doctor asked, without trying to hide his surprise.

"Certainly," Sradek answered. "Classes at the Academy tend to have a certain aura of tradition and solemnity to them. I found that Spock could always be counted upon to dispel some of that aura. In quite novel ways, too, I might add."

McCoy rocked back on his feet, eyes wide in calculated innocence. "Where I come from," he said pleasantly, "we call students like that 'class clowns.' Would that be an accurate assessment of Spock? As a student, of course."

Sradek stared away for a moment, obviously considering an appropriate example. Spock leaned forward.

"Doctor, I do not think it is useful to take up the academician's time in talks of a frivolous nature. There is no logic in having him recount stories of my activities as a student when there are so many other beings here with whom he could have a productive conversation."

"But, Academician," McCoy protested, "I'm only trying to learn as much as I can about Mr. Spock because we must often work together, and as I'm sure both you and he will agree, the more information one has about a subject, the less chance there can be for misunderstandings."

Sradek nodded. "And therefore your work will be more efficient and productive. Well put, Doctor. Quite right. I shall tell you of some of Spock's exploits in my classes." Sradek took another sip of bourbon and raised an eyebrow as he glanced at Spock. "You must find it quite invigorating, Spock, to work with a human who has such a firm grasp of logic."

McCoy's expanding grin instantly threatened to become insufferable and, a moment later, Spock's expression hardened into stone. But Kirk hadn't missed the almost imperceptible reaction that had crossed Spock's face the instant before, and when the captain smiled, it was for them both.

BOOK TWO

Prime Directive

<u>U.S.S.</u> <u>Enterprise</u> NCC-1701

2271

In the last year of her first *five-year mission*

space is infinite
without ending
all within it
just beginning

VULCAN CHILD'S KOAN
traditional

Prologue

Le Rêve d'Étoiles

Extract from *A Historical Analysis of the Five-Year Missions*
Admiral Glynis Kestell Tabor, Stellar Institute Press, Paris, Earth

According to the records as they existed at that time, of the original twelve *Constitution*-class starships that had embarked on Starfleet's visionary program of five-year missions, five had already been lost in the service of the United Federation of Planets: the *U.S.S. Constellation* as the last casualty of an ancient war, the *Intrepid* in the Gamma 7A system, the *Excalibur* in war-game maneuvers, the *Defiant* in the Tholian Annex, and the *Enterprise* during the incident at Talin IV.

No one denied that these losses had been heavy, in lives and material, but among the dozens of planning commissions that set the Federation's long-term goals and policies, there was no serious doubt that the five-year missions would continue with new ships and new crews. Because, despite the high cost of such epic exploration and expansion, the returns these activities brought to the Federation were always greater.

In a period of only four standard years, the records showed that thousands of strange new worlds had been explored, hundreds of new civilizations had been discovered, and the Federation's boundaries had grown to encompass a volume of space nearly five times that which had been charted as of Stardate 00.1. Given these results, ways could always be found to commission new starships, and as for the new crews those ships would require, they were the secret of the Federation's unprecedented strength.

It was the same secret shared by all great political movements in the histories of a thousand worlds. The Federation was founded not by force, nor by expediency, nor in response to an outside threat. It was founded on a dream—a dream of greater goals and greater good, of common purpose and cooperation, but beyond all else, it was a dream to know more, a dream to explore to the farthest limits and then go beyond.

They called it *le rêve d'étoiles*—the dream of stars.

Like all profound ideas, this dream of stars was irresistible, and the Federation's planners were aware of its attraction. They recognized its presence in the more than twelve thousand applications Starfleet received for each Academy opening. They felt its pull within themselves.

But dreams alone were not enough to sustain the Federation's goals, and fortunately the planners also understood what else was needed and how to obtain it. They understood that throughout the worlds of the Federation there were beings in whom the dream burned brightest. Invariably, all of these individuals had known instantly where their destinies lay from the moment they had first looked up to the lights of the night sky. In every language in all the worlds, the words were always the same: the dream of stars. Not traveling to them, not stopping at them, but moving among them, ever outward, always farther, no end to space or to their quest. Or to the dream.

At Starfleet Academy, the planners were careful to set in place the challenges and the system that would guide the best of those called by the dream to the only position that they could hold, the position to which each had been born.

Starship captain.

There could be no greater embodiment of the dream, and it was upon this foundation that the Federation was ultimately based and its future assured.

The system was not perfect. At the time of the Talin IV tragedy, the planners knew that for every Robert April or Christopher Pike the Academy produced, there would be a Ron Tracey or a James T. Kirk. But that was to be expected when dealing with exceptional beings whose very nature put them at odds with most definitions of what was deemed predictable or normal behavior. On the whole, the planners felt the system worked, and reason and logic—much to the Vulcans' chagrin—had nothing to do with it.

So the Federation's planners set their course for the future, building new ships, setting new missions, knowing that there would be no end to those who would volunteer to take part, because the dream of stars, once acknowledged, could never be denied.

But at that time, in the aftermath of Talin IV, what the planners did not yet know was that once that dream had been experienced, neither could it ever be willingly surrendered.

In accordance with the Federation's goals for the gathering of knowledge, it was a lesson the planners were eventually due to learn, and their system had already created the man who would teach it to them.

Once and for all.

PART ONE

Aftermath

One

Humans, Glissa thought suddenly, as she caught the first unmistakable scent of their approach. *You can't live with them and you can't live without them, but by Kera and Phinda, you can certainly smell them.*

The short Tellarite shift boss looked away from the viewscreen blueprint she studied, then narrowed her deepset, solid black eyes to squint into the distance. All around her, she felt the thrumming of the thin air that passed for an atmosphere within the hollowed-out S-type asteroid. It was the pulse of the machines and fellow workers remaking its interior into a living world, a home for thousands. For Glissa, there was excitement in this job of world making, and fulfillment. Which is why the unexpected scent of humans was so unsettling. With them around, she feared the excitement would soon give way to drudgery.

The Tellarite twitched her broad, porcine nose as she tasted the circulating breeze, seeking more details of the human presence she had detected. In the soft, seasonless mists of her home world, natural selection had not been inspired to evolve keen eyesight. As an adult of her species, Glissa had long since lost the ability to see past two meters with any clarity. But she could hear with an acuity that surpassed most Vulcans, and could decipher scents and airborne pheromones at a speed and rate of accuracy to challenge all but the most sensitive tricorder.

It was those other fine senses that now confirmed for her what she had feared—the telltale odor of the dreadfully omnivorous humans came to her from what could only be her second-shift crew of rockriggers. Even Glissa's near-useless eyes could make out the brilliant yellow streak of the safety cable that linked the blurry figures. The cable traced a sinuous route around the wide yellow warning bands that marked the overlaps of the artificial gravity fields on the asteroid's inner surface. Spinning the rock to produce centripetal pseudo-gravity would make working inside the asteroid much easier, but until the final bracing supports were in place, the engineers didn't want to subject the shell to the additional strain. So, in the interim, the asteroid's outer surface was studded with portable artificial-gravity generators, creating both amplified and null-gravity zones within the rock. As if that crazy-quilt arrangement didn't produce enough strain on its own.

Glissa sighed and the sound she made in her barrel chest was deep and guttural—like the prelude to a particularly invigorating string of invective. But there was no such joy behind her sigh. She hadn't realized that the first shift was already over, let alone that it was time for the second to begin. And the lake-support pylons for the rock's eventual basin of freshwater supply were still not in place. They hadn't even appeared on the massive cargo-transporter platform waiting empty at the edge of the work site. At the rate her division was falling behind schedule, Glissa calculated she was going to have to endure at least another tenday of overtime before she had the slightest chance of taking a few shifts off to enjoy a good wallow in the communal baths on the rec station. And from the smell of things, it was definitely going to be another tenday of working with humans.

Of course, Glissa had nothing against humans personally, but not being from one of Miracht's ambassadorial tribes, she found it disagreeable to work with them. Who wouldn't have difficulty working with beings who could never seem to tell the obvious differences between time-honored constructive insults and improper personal attacks on their parentage, and whose lack of a sense of humor was second only to the Vulcans? Still, it took all kinds to make the worlds go round and, to be fair, she knew of few Tellarites who had the appetite to administer the monstrous bureaucracies that kept the Federation functioning.

She sighed again and rippled the sensitive underpad nodes of her hoof against the viewscreen's control panel—one of dozens of similar viewscreens that were mounted on light poles ringing the work site. After erasing the blueprint from the two-meter-by-one-meter display, she sniffed the air more slowly to determine which particular humans she had been cursed with this time.

The twelve approaching rockriggers were still too far away for Glissa to recognize any features other than their individual yellow safety harnesses and helmets, but she could identify most of them by their scents. Seven, thank the Moons, were Tellarites themselves—client workers from the Quaker commune that had hired Interworld Construction to reform this rock into a Lagrange colony. At least half the workforce on this project were client workers providing the commune with substantial labor savings.

But of the other five workers approaching, Glissa scented, all were human, and that was unfortunate because rockrigging and humans were never a happy combination.

The task of asteroid reformation was one of the few remaining hazardous occupations within the Federation that legally could not be done more efficiently or less expensively by drone machines. If the Council ever decided to relax the Federation's prohibitions on slavery to allow true synthetic consciousnesses to control robots, then perhaps the industry itself would be transformed. But until that unlikely day, rockrigging would remain the exclusive province of two basic types of laborers: dedicated client workers who welcomed the chance to literally carve out a world with their own bare hooves, and the hardcases who signed on with Interworld because they had exhausted all other options.

As far as Glissa was concerned, the hardcase humans who worked for Interworld—some fugitive, all desperate—might just as well be Klingons for all the honor and diligence they exhibited. But the making of worlds was honorable work for a Tellarite, and no one had said it would ever be easy. So humans, with their unique and unfathomable mix of Vulcan logic and Andorian passion, were officially tolerated by Interworld, even if it meant that Glissa and the other shift bosses did have to watch their language.

As Glissa turned back to the viewscreen to call up current work assignments and detailed plans for the second shift, the shift-change alarm sounded from speakers in the towering lightpoles that encircled the five-hundred-meter-wide work site. She peered up at the wall of the rock four kilometers over her head, and could just make out the smeared constellations of the lightpoles surrounding the work sites on the airless half of the rock's interior as they flickered to signal shift change for those workers in environmental suits who could not use sound alarms.

Puzzled, Glissa checked her chronometer and saw that the change signals were on time. But that meant the second shift crew was also arriving on time, and in all the years Glissa had spent with Interworld, one of the few things she had learned to count on was that hardcase humans were never on time. It was almost a religion with them.

For a moment she was concerned at the break in tradition and order—few things were worse to a Tellarite than an unexplained mystery. She quickly retasted the air, but there was no denying the scent of humans in the approaching workers. She sniffed again, deeply, questioningly . . . and then the answer came.

Glissa raised her hoof to the unfocused form of the human who led the team and waved. "Sam?" she growled. "Sam Jameson?"

The lead figure raised his much too long and scrawny arm to return the wave and Glissa felt a sudden thrill of hope. If Sam Jameson had been promoted to work as her second-shift team leader then there was an excellent chance that Glissa's division might make up for lost time. He had only been with the company for four tendays but had already proven himself to be a most remarkable being, human or otherwise.

"I thought I smelled the foul stink of your furless human meat!" the Tellarite blared deafeningly as Sam finally came within range of her vision.

"It's a miracle you can smell anything through the stench of that slime-encrusted *skrak* pelt you call fur!" Sam shouted back.

Glissa's huge nostrils flared with pleasure. Here, at last, was the exception to the rule: a cultured human who truly understood the subtle nuances of Civil Conversation. She could almost feel the hot mud of the rec station oozing up around her as she anticipated the rewards of meeting her schedule.

The Tellarite held out her hoof and Sam Jameson grasped it without hesitation, returning the proper ripple of greeting against Glissa's underpad nodes as best as any human could, considering how the creatures were crippled by the ungainly and limited manipulatory organs they called fingers. If Glissa actually stopped to think about it, it was a wonder any human could pick up a tool let alone invent one. They might as well have arms that ended with seaweed fronds.

As the second-shift crew gathered behind their team leader and began disengaging the safety cable from their harnesses, Glissa thought for a moment to come up with an appropriate statement of Civil words to convey her satisfaction that she would once again be working with Sam. She looked up at the human, nervously smoothed the fine golden fur of her beard, and hoped that her pronunciation would be correct.

"Damn it, Sam, why the hall are they punishing me by making you work my shift?"

Glissa could tell from the quick smile that crossed Sam's face that she had got something wrong. Odd that Sam's face was so easily read, though. The long, blond-brown hair and thick beard he wore certainly helped, making Sam look less like a dormant tree slug than most barefaced humans did, and much more like an intelligent being. Too bad about the puny down-turned nose though, and those human eyes, beady little green dots ringed by white like those of a week-old Tellarite corpse . . . they could make Glissa shudder if she stared at them too long.

But Sam looked away to the iron wall beneath his feet and leaned forward, dropping his voice to a whisper low enough that only a Tellarite could hear him.

"Hell, Glissa," Sam said gently. "You meant to say 'hell,' not 'hall.' "

Glissa nodded thoughtfully, appreciative that Sam had kept this part of their conversation private. "Which one is the underworld and which is the corridor?"

"Hell is the underworld. Humans don't get too excited about corridors. At least, not in Civil insults."

Glissa decided she would have to start making some notes if she were to keep up with Sam. "But the 'damn it' . . . ?"

"Perfect," Sam said, still whispering. "Proper place in the sentence, good intonation, very impressive. . . ." But then he stepped back in midsentence, looked up from the ground, and raised his voice again for all to hear. "For a beerswilling, gut-bellied warthog, that is."

Glissa's cheeks ballooned out into tiny pink spheres as she snorted her delight. She wondered if Sam liked mud wallows. Perhaps he might like to be invited to join her in one. For the moment, though, there was work to do, and clever repartee and Civil Conversation must be put aside. But at least with Sam Jameson taking part, she felt sure the excitement of her job would remain. There would be time enough for friendship later.

After the shift briefing had been completed—in record time thanks to the way Sam was able to reinterpret the shift's goals for the other, more typical humans on the crew—the incoming chime of the cargo transporter finally sounded. It was deeper than the sound that came from most systems, since to save credits this project used only low-frequency models—less power hungry but not certified for biological transport. As Glissa watched the first load of twenty-meter-long, black fiber support pylons materialize, she felt certain that her division's schedule would finally come back on line within a few shifts.

Sam Jameson didn't disappoint her. Cajoling the Tellarite client workers with appropriate Civil insults and adopting a more conciliatory tone for the humans, Sam had the crew latch antigravs to the pylons and clear the pad in record time, load after load. Glissa was still amazed at how easily the rockriggers took his orders. Perhaps his secret was that he used a subtly different approach with each individual, acknowledging that each was worthy of individual respect. Perhaps it was the way he moved among them, never shirking his turn at heavy labor the way some other shift leaders did. However he accomplished it, Glissa was impressed, and saddened, too. For whatever Sam Jameson had been before he came to Interworld, she was certain of one thing: he had not been a rockrigger.

By the time the main meal break came, a full shift's work had already been accomplished and, under Sam's direction, the crew actually seemed eager for more. For once Glissa was able to sit down to her *tak* and bloodrinds without feeling panic over the swiftness of time. She wished that she might share her meal break with Sam— she had thought of something exceptionally vile to call him and was looking forward to an equally inventive response—but she saw that he, as always, took his meal alone.

The other humans on the crew sat together, talking among themselves, occasionally glancing over at Sam where he sat against a large boulder. On the other hoof, the Tellarite client workers stood around and stared into the distance. Through one of the hundreds of visual sensors which fed images to the viewscreens in deference to the limits of Tellarite vision, Glissa observed them sampling the air with twitching noses.

Then she saw what they were waiting for. Two Tellarite pups—barely out of the litter pen—waddled along a safety path, guiding a small tractor wagon stacked with food trays. In actual fact, the meter-long tractor wagon guided the toddlers through the maze of gravity warning bands and the viewscreen showed that both were securely attached to the wagon by their harnesses.

The pups' mother was one of Sam's team and she welcomed her offspring proudly as they brought food to her and her fellow workers. Glissa was impressed with the seriousness of the young pups and the way they wore their commune's ceremonial red scarves, at such odds with the puffs of white fur that stood out so sweetly from their round little forms, like softly shaped clouds captured in blue overalls.

As she watched them on the screen, she heard familiar hoofsteps approaching. It was Sam.

"Are our pups as appealing to humans as they are to us?" Glissa asked, seeing that he, too, watched the young Tellarites at their work.

"The appeal of babies is universal," Sam said. "But it's such a shame those two will grow up to resemble something as ugly as you."

Glissa grunted happily and gestured to the slight rise of a digger's ridge beside her. "I have never met any human quite like you, Sam." Glissa spoke without using a Civil intonation.

Sam paused, then sat down next to her, resting his arms on his knees and swinging his safety helmet idly from his hands as he watched the pups. They had finished eating and were now wrestling furiously, tumbling over and over each other with excited squeaks and snorts. "Then I suspect you haven't met too many humans at all," Sam said.

Glissa folded her food tray shut, remembering what she had heard about what humans thought of bloodrinds. "I have met many humans here. Just none like you."

Sam shrugged but said nothing. He glanced up to check the time readout on a viewscreen. There were still a few minutes left in the break.

"Why are you here, Sam Jameson?"

For a moment, Sam's eyes changed in a way too alien for the Tellarite to understand. "Why are *you* here, Glissa?"

"To build new worlds," the Tellarite answered proudly.

A new expression appeared on Sam's face, and Glissa at least knew human misery when she saw it. "As if there weren't enough out there to begin with?"

Glissa didn't understand. She tried another approach. "You are not a hardcase."

The human smiled sadly at that, but still there were undercurrents to his expression that she couldn't read. "What makes you think I'm not?"

"Interworld is not known for asking too many questions of those who want to be rockriggers. The human hardcases we get seem to be those who are one step away from shipping out on the next Orion freighter." Then she peered closely at him, suddenly recalling how little sense of humor humans had. "Perhaps I should point out that I have used the term 'freighter' in a sarcastic sense, if that makes my joke more logical."

Sam looked away from her, his eyes somehow appearing to be more reflective, as if their moisture content had suddenly been elevated.

"Are you all right, Sam?"

"I'm fine," he said, and smiled again with that same gentle sadness. "You just reminded me of someone I knew . . . a long time ago."

"A close friend?"

"I think so. Though he might not want to admit it."

"The human hardcases we get seem not to have friends, Sam."

The human stared up at the far wall of the rock, but she felt he was looking at something else which only he could see. "On Earth, centuries ago, there was an . . . organization much like Interworld's rockriggers."

"They built things? Surely not worlds so long ago, but . . . continents perhaps?"

"It was a military organization."

"How human. No offense intended," Glissa quickly added because this was not turning out to be a Civil Conversation.

"None taken," Sam said. "It was called *La Légion étrangère*. It was the place to go to when there was no place else. No questions asked. They didn't even need to know a real name."

"Sometimes . . . that is a preferable circumstance," Glissa said as diplomatically as she was able. "Is it preferable to you?"

He turned to her and his face was unreadable. "No questions asked," he repeated.

"Too bad, Sam. You look like a being who has many answers."

He shook his head. "One answer is all it would take, Glissa. And I don't have it." He hefted his helmet to put it on. "That's why I'm here. That's why I'm a hardcase."

Glissa reached out to him, to place a soothing hoof on his shoulder. What was the answer he searched for? What possible reason could bring him here? "Sam, if there is anything that—"

The asteroid shifted.

A field of pulsed gravity swept over the work site. Glissa saw the bright spots of the lightpoles undulate as local gravitational constants fluctuated wildly. She grabbed at the rock beneath her, feeling herself rise up and down as if caught in a raging surf. Gravity warning alarms erupted from a hundred speakers, echoing shrilly from the hard iron floor of the rock.

"What is it?" she growled.

Sam's strong arms pushed her down between two iron ridges. He had expertly, instinctively, hooked his feet beneath a small ridge overhang at the first ripple of motion. "Harmonic interference," he shouted over the sirens. "One of the gravity generators must have cut out and the others didn't compensate in time."

Sam looped a safety strap around a second overhang, then fed it through one of Glissa's harness clips, fastening her safely in place. "Don't worry. It's self-correcting. There'll be a couple more fluctuations as the fields spread the load but we'll be all right."

"The pups?" Glissa squealed, unable to turn her head to the viewscreen as a high-g wave slammed her to the ground.

Sam craned his neck to look over to where the client worker had been eating and the youngsters had been playing. "They're fine, they're fine. They're still hooked to the tractor wagon." He grabbed onto Glissa as a low-g wave rippled back, sending him half a meter into the air. "See? It's getting weaker."

"How do you know so much about artificial gravity fields?" the Tellarite demanded.

But before Sam could answer, the asteroid shifted again as another gravity generator failed—and another, twisting the rocky shell in two directions at once. A low rumbling sound began, mixed with the shriek of tearing metal. Sam turned to the source, eyes widening like the face of the dead as he saw—"The lake bed!"

Glissa grunted with a sudden and terrible knowledge. "The pylons are not in place. The lake bed cannot—"

The first pressure siren wailed, drowning out the gravity warning alarms.

"No!" Sam fixed on something Glissa couldn't see.

"What is it?"

"NO!" Sam untangled himself from Glissa's harness and unhooked his feet from the rock ledge.

"Sam, what?"

"The children!" As Sam leapt over Glissa and scrambled away, the wind began.

Glissa struggled to sit up. The wind could only mean the thin lake bed floor had cracked in the stress of the gravity harmonics. And there was nothing beneath it except the vacuum of space.

The Tellarite heard the screams of her work crew mix with the wild screech of disappearing air and the clamor of sirens and alarms. She slapped her hoof against the nearest viewscreen control, calling up image after image until she tapped into a sensor trained at the lake bed.

"Dear Kera," she whispered as she saw the pups trailing at the end of their safety cables, only ten meters from a ragged tear in the rock floor through which debris and white tendrils of atmosphere were sucked into nothingness. "Dear Phinda," she cried as she saw Sam Jameson, crouching against a ridge near the youngsters, attaching a second cable to an immovable outcropping of metal.

Glissa switched on the panel communicator's transmit circuits. If she could send this image to cargo control perhaps they could lock onto Sam and the pups. Surely the risk of being transported at low frequency was better than the certain death of being sucked out into space. If only the pups' cables would hold. If only Sam would stay in position.

But the cables were anchored to the small tractor wagon and the winds were pushing it closer and closer to the fissure. And no matter how little Glissa knew of the real Sam Jameson, she knew enough to know that nothing could keep him from going to the pups.

Glissa called out coordinates to cargo control as Sam pushed himself up from the safety of the ridge and moved out into the open, slowly playing out his safety line, pulled taut by the force of the gale that blew against him.

He moved across the open lake bed in the finally stabilized gravity as if he were aware of nothing but the infants, now only six meters from the opening into space. Rocks and debris flew past him. Some hit him. But he ignored their impact and the blossoms of red human blood that they brought. Glissa had never been able to completely understand much of what Sam felt, but at this moment, his intent so fixed, his concentration so powerful, she was sure that the human felt no fear.

Sam reached the slowly skidding tractor wagon. Its in-use lights were out, its power exhausted by fighting the inexorable wind. He wrapped his arms around its sensor pod, trying to stop its movement. Glissa switched sensors and brought up an image of Sam as he strained against the impossible pressure. His cable was pulled to its limit. Glissa could see his arms tremble with the force he was exerting. But the tractor still slid forward. The squealing infants still slipped toward the inescapable pull of the vacuum.

Sam's eyes blazed, and of the few human emotions Glissa could recognize, she knew it was anger that lit his eyes. Then he reached to his harness and disengaged his cable. Glissa called out to him to stop though she knew he would never hear her.

The tractor wagon bounced a meter forward on the lake bed as Sam swung around it and began crawling down the length of the youngsters' cable. He reached them as they were only three meters from the fissure. And it was widening, Glissa saw with sickened certainty. Where was cargo control?

Two meters from the fissure, Sam had both round forms in his arms. He pushed against the gale and the floor. But where was he going? And then Glissa saw his plan. There was a smaller ridge almost within reach. With an effort which she would not have thought was possible for a human, Sam pushed the pups into position against it. If they didn't move, they would be safe as long as the atmosphere lasted. But how could he keep them there when the ridge wasn't large enough for him as well?

Glissa could only moan as she saw what the human did next. He *removed* his harness—his last hope for survival—and wound it around the infants, using its straps to tie them firmly into place.

"Please, no," Glissa prayed to the twin Moons as she saw Sam's fingers desperately try to dig into the unyielding surface of the metal ridge. She prayed to the mists and the mud and all the litters of heaven but it was the heavens that were claiming the human now.

Sam slipped from the ridge. He fell toward the fissure. Toward space. Toward the stars.

And he caught himself on the opening, arms and legs braced to hold on for a few more hopeless seconds.

Glissa caused the sensor to close in on Sam's face and fill a hundred viewscreens throughout the rock so his heroism and his sacrifice would be remembered by all.

What manner of human was he? What manner of being? He had no chance yet still he struggled. And on his face, an instant from oblivion, poised above an endless fall into the absolute night of space, *there was still no fear in him.*

Tears streamed from Glissa's small eyes because she did not know what she witnessed. He faced the stars and death with a ferocious defiance she could not imagine. *They shall name this world for you,* Glissa thought. *I swear it, Sam. Sam Jameson. My friend.* And with that vow, the human's hands slipped for the final time.

The stars had won.

But the howl of the wind abruptly stopped as a near-deafening transporter chime overpowered the wail of the sirens and alarms.

Glissa peered closely at the viewscreen as Sam slowly rolled away from the fissure. Within it, the familiar glow of the transporter effect sparkled from the smooth metal walls. Cargo control had not transported Sam and the pups *out,* they had transported pressure sealant *in.*

Glissa tapped her hooves to her forehead in thanks to the Moons, then unhooked her harness and ran out to the lake bed to welcome Sam to his second life. But when she joined him, others had arrived before her. And she was shocked to see anger and disgust in their eyes.

The Tellarite pups, now only sobbing fitfully, were cradled by their mother and her fellow workers. The fissure had become nothing more than a long scar mounded with the hardened blue foam of pressure sealant. Sam sat slumped against the ridge that had protected the pups, his work clothes torn, blood streaming from a dozen wounds. But the humans clustered near him offered no help. They only whispered among themselves.

Glissa pushed through them and went to Sam's side.

"I'd think twice about doin' anything for 'im," one of the humans said. He was taller and heavier than Sam, and wore a punishment tattoo from a penal colony.

"What do you mean?" Glissa demanded as she knelt to cradle Sam's hands in her hooves. "He saved those pups."

"Use your eyes," a second human said. Female this time, as big as the one with the tattoo. "Didn't you see him on the viewscreens?"

"Of course," Glissa answered uncertainly.

"And you didn't recognize him? From the holos? From the updates? Before he grew the beard?"

Glissa turned to Sam. "What are they saying?"

The woman kicked a stone toward Sam. "Go ahead. Tell her what we're saying. If you've got the stomach for it."

"Sam?"

"That's not *his* name, Boss," a third human said scornfully. He was shorter, rounder, more compact, from a high-g world, and he moved forward to stand before Sam and Glissa. He glared down at the wounded human and the Tellarite beside him.

"You're Kirk, aren't you?" the short human said, and Glissa's nostrils flared at the mention of that terrible name. "The one who was captain of the *Enterprise,* aren't you?"

Glissa stared deep into Sam's eyes. "No," she whispered. "No, not you."

But his eyes held that one answer at least.

Glissa let the human's hands slip away from her hooves.

"Murderer!" the human woman said as she kicked another stone at the wounded man's side.

"Butcher!" The short human spat on the wounded man's boots.

Glissa stood up, torn, dismayed, but knowing that her job had to come first. "That's enough!" she growled at the rockriggers. "We've still got half a shift to put in and I want you back at work—*now!*"

They hesitated and Glissa gave them a snarl that needed no translation. Muttering among themselves, they left the lake bed.

The human she had known as Sam Jameson looked up at her as if to speak, but she raised a hoof to silence him, trying to suppress the shudder of revulsion that passed through her. This monster already had a world named after him. "There is nothing more to be said. I will have your account closed out and book your passage on the next outbound shuttle. You should . . . you should leave here as quickly as possible. Before too many others find out." She had to look away from him. "The company will not be able to guarantee your safety."

The human said nothing. Glissa left him to join the client workers and explain what had happened for those who didn't understand Standard. As if the name Kirk needed translation. As if the entire universe didn't know of his crimes.

While Glissa and the other Tellarites talked in low grunts and whispers, the two pups slowly approached the wounded human, watching with concern in their large black eyes as he stood up unsteadily and his blood dripped slowly to splatter on the ground.

One of the youngsters, braver than the other, stepped forward and solemnly untied his scarf. With tiny hooves, he held it out to the human, who stared at the scarf, as if uncertain about accepting it.

"Please," the young Tellarite said. "Let me help."

The human started, and as Glissa and the other Tellarites watched, he looked down into the pup's earnest eyes almost as if he were seeing someone else's face, hearing words that someone else might have said to him long ago. He spoke gently to the pup as he took the scarf and held it to his wounds. Then he turned and walked away, head upright, each step certain.

Glissa felt unexpected tears roll from her eyes as she watched him leave, for in all the worlds in all of space, she knew there was no place left for James T. Kirk to go.

Two

It had not been a clean death for his beauty. She had not, as he sometimes imagined she might, been swallowed by a nova, or been lost by braving the unimaginable depths of a black hole. Nor, perhaps most noble of all, by giving her life so that others might live.

Instead, the *Enterprise* had been butchered—stripped of her power and her speed and cruelly deformed between the opposing infinities of normal space and the Cochrane subset. Much of the ship still remained, but her heart and her soul were lost.

Chief Engineer Montgomery Scott found himself thinking that it might have been better if the ship had died all at once. And he with her.

In the silence of the aft observation lounge, deserted in the ship's early morning cycle, Scott leaned his head against the cool smoothness of the viewport. He closed his eyes, thinking of another time when he might have touched any part of the ship and felt within her the hum of her generators, powered by the wedding song of matter and antimatter. But there were no vibrations now. That life had fled. The emergency lights strung haphazardly through the ship were powered by batteries beamed in from other vessels, and the occasional movement lags of the gravity generators fighting the inertial dampeners came from the rough handling of shuttle tugs and not the smooth pulse of the ship's own thrusters.

Scott opened his eyes again. His breath had fogged the viewport and the haze it made suddenly flared silver white as the *Enterprise*'s orbit took her over the terminator of the moon below, into the full reflected light of Talin's sun. Scott's torment at seeing the ship suddenly painted with the brilliant light reflected from the airless desert moving 500 kilometers beneath her was still as intense as the first time he had stared out and seen what had been done to her.

The bluewhite gleam of her hull metal was streaked with carbonized traceries from the energy arcs that had penetrated her overloaded shields. And the dark scarring was constantly being augmented by the thrusters of the workbee shuttles that hovered around her, carrying out emergency repairs so the ship could be safely towed back to the spacedock at Starbase 29—if and when the decision to fully repair her was finally made.

Scott's trained eye scanned the upper surface of the engineering hull, evaluating the inelegant arrangement of roughly bonded pressure plates and repair bands. He cringed at the imperfection of the work. No real crew member of the *Enterprise* would dare treat her that way, so inconsiderately, as if she were no more than metal and machinery. It was an attitude he might have had to remind new ensigns about in their first few weeks on board. But after a month or so, even the greenest recruits had needed no reminding about how to treat this ship. They felt it. They knew it. Not like those starbase mechanics who bounced from job to job and who were working on her now. Scott and a handful of others on board were all that remained of the *Enterprise*'s original crew.

The starboard support pylon was canted aft at least eight degrees from true, and Scott sighed as he watched the workbees' mechanical grippers attaching the large black panels of tractor-beam collectors to the surface of it. The mechanics planned to *force* the pylon back into position to restore warp balance to the ship's super-structure, so she could be towed at warp speed. But Scott couldn't see the point. Not with the starboard warp-propulsion nacelle completely gone—the one that Spock had managed to jettison in time. Unlike the port nacelle.

The port nacelle was the reason why the *Enterprise* was still in orbit around Talin's moon—kept there so she could be studied in the same way Karunda coroner beetles swarmed to dissect the corpses of their prey. She was the first ship to have engaged warp drive while still within the Danylkiw Limit of a planet's gravity well and survive, even partially. Three and a half months earlier, Scott would have said that such a thing would not be possible. After all, until they had been properly tuned and balanced, it was still foolhardy to run tandem warp engines within the Danylkiw Limit of a solar system, let alone a class-M planet. And though the tuning procedures were improving each year as the technicians zeroed in on the theoretical upper limits of warp efficiency, Scott was certain that for at least the next ten years any ship attempting a tandem test run too close to a star would run the risk of falling into either an Einsteinian wormhole or a Danylkiw Singularity.

Certainly modern warp engines—properly tuned and broken-in, of course—could be engaged within gravity wells at depths corresponding to standard orbits, but it was almost unthinkable to imagine the day when a warp drive could be engaged so deep within a planet's gravity well as to be in atmosphere. At least, those had been Scott's thoughts at the time. But three and a half months ago, the *Enterprise* had done just that—engaged warp drive within the atmosphere of Talin IV. And the proof of it was the nightmarish remains of her port nacelle.

The forward section of the nacelle was still in perfect condition. At the time of the incident, the propulsion dome-disperser pylon had been deployed for routine discharge maintenance and the stubby projection was still in place, unbent and undisturbed. But thirty meters back from the lip of the dome, the first rippling deformations in the nacelle's cylindrical hull became apparent. Fifty meters back, and the hull took on the appearance of a piece of stretched taffy, just like the candy Sulu had once spent six months cooking and sculpting into birds and dragons on the ends of sticks. By sixty meters, the rest of the nacelle was completely gone, supposedly compressed to a point through the inconceivable multidimensional pathways that led out of four-dimensional spacetime and into the other realms in which warp speeds were possible.

Where the rest of the nacelle was actually located was still a matter of debate. Twelve experts from the Cochrane Institute on Centaurus had been brought in to study the wreckage, along with representatives from Starfleet Operations, its Science and Engineering Divisions, and the Space Safety Board. The first arguments among the twenty-being task force had apparently been settled when two weeks' worth of sensor readings convinced the experts that the nacelle continued to be drawn into warp space at the rate of about one atomic diameter a day. Scott had been outraged at the interpretation of the findings because any child knew that the secret of warp transition was that it was instantaneous. You were in or you were out, but you could never be halfway. He had tried to convince the experts that the phenomenon they were witnessing was somehow related to the fusion blasts the

Enterprise had been subjected to, or the unfathomable subspace pulse that had burned out every centimeter of translator circuitry in her, but the experts' only response had been to hold their subsequent meetings in private and continue to chart the slow disappearance of the ship, molecule by molecule.

As far as Scott could determine, cut off as he was from the experts and their planning sessions, the current debate raging through Starfleet Engineering was whether the remainder of the port nacelle could be detached from the *Enterprise* without triggering a slingshot reaction which would destroy the rest of her, or whether the ship should simply be decommissioned and serve out the rest of her days as a sacrificial experimental model, constantly monitored to see how far her gradual evaporation would proceed.

Scott rubbed his hands against his face, trying to bring order to his thoughts. Just thinking about the mad ideas of the know-nothing, planetbound, viewscreen jockeys who had the power to decide the *Enterprise*'s fate made his head swim. He had never felt such frustration, such helplessness. *At least,* he thought for the thousandth time, *at least if I had been on the bridge, then this would be over for me, too, and I'd be with the captain. Wherever the poor lad is.*

Scott put his hand to the viewport, only centimeters separating him from the emptiness of space. Somewhere James Kirk was out there. And somewhere, there were answers. Just beyond the reach of his hand.

Behind him, the observation lounge doors puffed open. Scott recognized the swagger in the steps of the officer who entered, and sighed.

"Good morning, Mr. Scott. The work is proceeding nicely, wouldn't you say?"

Scott took a breath to calm himself. In the viewport's reflection he saw the glowing lights of that damned swagger stick spin through the air as Lieutenant Styles flipped it under his arm. Scott didn't care if the insufferable, self-righteous ass *had* wrested the stick away from a Klingon in hand-to-hand combat. It was still a damned annoying affectation on a ship at least a hundred light-years from the nearest equine creature.

"Aye, I suppose it is." Scott couldn't bring himself to look at the man. The lieutenant didn't belong in charge of the *Enterprise*. Only one person did. Only one person ever would.

Styles stood beside Scott at the viewport and bounced twice on his toes. He crossed his hands behind his back and waved the swagger stick around behind his back, as if scaring away flies. The chief engineer thought dark thoughts of a transporter beam set to maximum dispersion.

"You don't sound too pleased, Mr. Scott."

Scott stared at the lieutenant in the reflection, hating the smug smile that split the man's sharp features.

"There's only one way to treat this ship, Mr. Styles."

Styles rapped his stick against the viewport, indicating the swarm of workbees thrusting around the starboard pylon. "And you don't feel those chaps are treating this ship the right way?"

"I have already submitted my reports and my recommendations."

Styles turned to the engineer and Scott glanced at him. Then stared in shock as he saw that Styles no longer wore the stylized comet insignia of the *U.S.S. Monitor* on his gold command shirt. He wore the insignia of the *Enterprise*.

"Like it?" Styles asked, seeing the surprise in Scott's eyes.

"I . . . dinna understand."

"Now, Mr. Scott, how difficult can it be? Starfleet has reassigned me. I'm commanding the *Enterprise* now."

No, Scott thought. *Never.* "A ship needs a captain, Lieutenant."

Styles smiled again with far too many teeth. "An *operational* ship needs a captain, Mr. Scott. And the *Enterprise* is anything but."

"The 'experts' haven't made up their minds, then?"

Styles rocked his head back and forth. "In a manner of speaking. The decision has been made to detach what's remaining of the port nacelle. Of course, the tugs will take the ship out of the system first, just in case. . . ."

Scott had to look away. They were gambling with all that was left of the *Enterprise.* "In case she slingshots into warp? What do they think is going to happen to her then, that hasn't happened already?" He kept the remainder of what he wanted to say about the starbase mechanics to himself. No matter how badly he felt, he was still a Starfleet officer.

Styles tapped his swagger stick thoughtfully against the side of his neck, apparently oblivious to Scott's imperfectly concealed rage. "If the ship does slingshot, then it's apt to be an unfocused transition. The Cochrane people have calculated that the starbow effect could be quite . . . spectacular and the First Contact officials feel that every step should be taken to ensure that the event is not observable from the surface of Talin IV. The Prime Directive's taken enough of a beating down there as it is, wouldn't you say?" Styles chuckled. "Not that anyone thinks it's very likely that the Talin are putting much effort into astronomy these days."

"And if the ship doesn't slingshot?" Which she won't, Scott knew. There was more chance of her sprouting wings and flapping her way back to a starbase.

The lieutenant's cheeriness was intolerable. "Then there happen to be two Constitution-rated warp nacelles at Earth Spacedock—"

"Intended for the *Intrepid II,*" Scott interrupted. He kept up with the production reports.

Styles shook his head. "Come now, Mr. Scott. It would take more than a year to finish a new ship from scratch. But with new nacelles and a full wiring team of construction drones, the *Enterprise* could be back in service in a tenth the time."

Scott stared at the man, suddenly seeing the real reason for his good spirits. "And then, of course, she'd be needing a new captain, wouldn't she?"

Styles reached out to pat Scott's shoulder. "Thank you for your vote of confidence, Mr. Scott, though I'm afraid I'd just be first officer to begin with. But in time . . . she would be mine. Oh, yes. And then we'd see how the *Enterprise* could perform with a real captain at her helm."

Scott had a difficult decision to make and, in the end, he decided not to deck Styles. There were more honorable ways to attempt to leave the service than by striking a superior officer. He was an engineer, after all, and not Dr. McCoy. "Lieutenant Styles, sir?"

"Yes?"

"When the time comes for the port nacelle to be detached . . ."

"Go on."

"With all respect, sir, I hope she slingshots ye all the way to hell."

As Styles sputtered, Scott squared his shoulders and marched unhurriedly from the observation lounge. He had to leave. Even if there were better ways to leave the service than by striking Styles, for the moment the engineer couldn't think of a single one.

Later, in the privacy of his quarters, Scott stared at his personal viewscreen. A small yellow light flashed in the upper right corner telling him he had a message waiting, but he was damned if he was going to give any more of his time to the mechanics who were working to pass this ship into the insensitive hands of a sanctimonious prig like Styles.

Beside his viewscreen was a tall green glass bottle of single malt whisky from Earth, unopened and unsynthesized. Once, during the tense stationkeeping orbits around Sarpeidon, Uhura had decrypted Mr. Spock's birthday from his personnel records and had passed it on to other select members of the crew. Scott had planned to surprise the science officer with a gift from the Scottish heather when Spock's next birthday came around. He had had no doubt that on such an occasion Mr. Spock would take one of his rare drinks of alcohol—and that he would have no objection to Scott and McCoy and the captain, and the other select crew members, finishing the remainder of the bottle for him. But Talin IV had come around before that birthday, and those who were to share Spock's gift were never to be together again.

Scott hefted the bottle, imagining what it would be like to open it and have it all to himself, drinking enough that Styles and the *Enterprise* 's ruin would drop away from him. Perhaps enough that he could see his friends across the table from him again, the mission continuing, all as it should be, as it was supposed to be, forever. But he knew that wasn't an answer and never would be.

He studied the bottle's label, reading of the peat and the centuries-old traditions, remembering all the other times he had shared its like with the captain, thinking of all the other worlds they had traveled to, and all the other worlds there were still left for them to visit.

"Och, you're Mr. Spock's birthday present and I'll not be opening ye till we're all sitting together as we belong. In uniform or not." He laid the bottle on its side on his bunk, to protect it from any sudden lurches courtesy of the mechanics outside. He still had a few duties to attend to, even as chief engineer of a nonoperational ship. "Screen on."

Scott's viewscreen came to life, still displaying the final transmission feed he had requested the night before. The text caption running beneath the image identified the transmission source as sensor satellite two, one of eight the *Enterprise* had placed into orbit around Talin IV, half a million kilometers distant from its moon, on behalf of Starfleet's First Contact Office.

The satellite was in a fixed, geostationary position above the planet's main ocean, and three months earlier Scott had seen the images it had obtained of fission-powered sea vessels following diverse trade and transportation routes. The visual resolution from 38,000 kilometers had been crisp enough to show individual Talin on the decks of their vessels, enabling the FCO to distinguish between fishing factories, freighters, and passenger ships. In other wavelengths, electromagnetic and otherwise, the satellites could also pick up the heat trails of submersible vehicles, deep beneath the oceans' surface, and even identify the nation states to which they belonged from manufacturing and design differences, and the weaponry each carried.

But now, the oceans of Talin IV were devoid of vessels, submersible or otherwise, and the weaponry the nation states had stockpiled had all been expended. Where the planet's sun could still shine through the few gaps in the globe-encircling clouds created by that weaponry, the once blue ocean was stained deep purple. An as-yet-unidentified mutation in a single-celled algaelike organism had blossomed throughout the world's seas, swiftly overwhelming the radiation-devastated ecosystem. Undoubtedly other ecological outrages were unfolding as dramatically throughout the rest of the planet's biosphere as well.

"Change views," Scott said grimly and the screen flickered once, revealing a new image of the world from over the secondary temperate continent now, where the FCO had once concentrated their sampling runs. Scott recognized the distinctive southern coastline, but that was all. The major agricultural bands that stretched across the land mass were scorched and lifeless, as blackened as the battle damage that scarred the *Enterprise*. Once, the crops from that land had fed tens of millions.

Scott stared at the screen with grief and revulsion. At the Academy, all cadets were required to study the worlds that had been destroyed by their dominant species' wars and environmental mismanagement. Those harsh lessons were at the core of the Federation's underlying principles of respect for life in all forms. Even the Klingons knew how fortunate they were to have survived global warfare and ecological collapse to become spacefarers. So few self-aware, technological species had. The *Enterprise,* in her time, had visited enough of those barren worlds to engrave the lessons permanently in the hearts and minds of her crew: War was never an answer and life must be held sacred above all else. Only the Prime Directive came as close in importance in determining the goals and actions of the Federation.

And Scott still couldn't understand how such honorable ideals, in the hands of a captain who had dedicated his life to upholding them, could have possibly led to the horrifying obscenity of the dying world on the viewscreen.

But others could, it seemed. For the first time Scott noticed everything that was printed out on the screen to identify the feed: SENSOR SATELLITE FIVE / 310° LONG / 205° LAT / 00:91:24 / KIRK'S WORLD.

Scott slapped his hand against the base of the machine, hitting its manual power switch hard enough to make the screen shake. "Ye slimy sons o' . . ." His voice choked off in anger. He had heard the replacement crew using that hateful name for Talin IV, and now they had gone so far as to program it into the automated logs. Well, he'd program a worm to go through the computer and delete all references. He'd take Styles's name out of the duty roster as well, transfer him to kitchen operations. *I'll turn this ship upside down before I'll* . . .

"Och, what's the use?" Scott said to the silence of his room. He'd been thinking: *before I'll let them win.* But the truth was, they already had.

The message light kept blinking at him from the blank screen. *What could be left to tell me that would be worse than what I already know?* he thought.

"Computer: Present my messages, please."

"Working," the computer's familiar voice said. The ship's backup datastores had had enough shielding to escape the subspace pulse that had destroyed the computer system's main circuitry. Once the standard replacement components had been installed in the first stages of the *Enterprise*'s emergency repairs, full computer functions and memory had been restored with only a 1.5 second gap in the sensor readings preceding the pulse, which was the length of time it took dynamic memory to be written to permanent backup. Even with mortal wounds, she was a fine ship.

The viewscreen presented the image of an unencrypted ComSys transmission screen—a common method by which Starfleet personnel could receive personal messages over subspace. Scott's name was clearly encoded at the top of the screen, overprinting the blue background shield of the United Federation of Planets. The stardate showed it had been received less than an hour ago. The message was tagged as one of one, but the sender's name was not listed.

Trying not to fool himself into hoping it was a message from the captain, Scott asked the computer to play back the recorded transmission. The screen cleared again, but not to an image of the message's sender—simply a screen of black text on a white background. Scott leaned forward to read it.

Command Bulletin: Effective this stardate, Spock, Ensign, S179-276SP, Science Specialist, Starfleet Technology Support Division, San Francisco, Earth, has resigned his commission in Starfleet. Resignation accepted, effective as received. Admiral Raycheba, Starfleet TechSupDiv.

Scott swore. "They broke him to a bloody *ensign?* What are they thinking of? How could—"

The viewscreen flashed the word "more."

"Continue," Scott said, and the message began to scroll.

Spock is the last of the so-called Enterprise *Five to resign from Starfleet. Starfleet Command Information Office has issued related statements calling for all Starfleet personnel to learn from the tragic lessons of the incident at Talin IV, and to prove to the citizens of the Federation that the actions of a handful of renegade officers do not reflect upon the exemplary training and—*

"Screen *off,* computer. Screen bloody off!"

The viewscreen darkened instantly.

"Computer: Who had the gall to send that message to me?" Scott's voice trembled so badly that he wondered if the computer would recognize him.

"Message unattributed."

Scott slowly and rhythmically pounded his fist on his work desk. "Aye, it would be, the cowards. It would be." He wanted to put his fist through a bulkhead. He wanted to shout loudly enough that they'd hear him back at Command. He wanted a stage to tell the worlds of the injustice of all that had transpired. But McCoy had been right.

The doctor had begged to be court-martialed. He had even punched Vice Admiral Hammersmith in front of witnesses at Starbase 29 when he and Spock had been transferred to Technology Support. That's when McCoy had sent word back to Scott that it was obvious that none of them was going to be put through any type of trial, secret or otherwise. As far as Command was concerned, the less said about Talin IV, the less damage would be done to Starfleet. "They have better ways to get us out of the damned service," McCoy had said to Scott in a subspace message.

And then the doctor had been the first to resign, without even going on report for striking an officer—proof as far as McCoy was concerned that Starfleet wasn't about to give any of them a public forum. Kirk followed McCoy's lead when Uhura had been jailed. Sulu and Chekov left together. Spock had been determined to fight from within the system, but it seemed that not even a Vulcan could stand up to the combined weight of Starfleet and the Federation Council. So, just as McCoy had said, the *Enterprise* Five had been banished from the service without incident, without trial, and without record. Starfleet had obtained almost everything that it had wanted.

I might as well give them the last of it, Scott thought, opening his fist into a useless hand. *There's nothing left to fight for. Not from here, at least.*

"Computer."

"Working."

"Prepare a hardcopy message to Lieutenant Styles, *U.S.S.*—no, make that to Vice Admiral Hammersmith, Starbase 29." Scott would be damned before he would acknowledge Styles as master of this ship. Since Starbase 29 was the closest Federation administrative outpost to the Talin system and had been given authority over the *Enterprise*'s disposition, Scott reasoned that the base's commander was the next logical choice to address his message to. He thought Mr. Spock would agree.

"From Scott, etc. Message goes: Effective immediately, I wish to tender my resignation from Star—"

"Clarification," the computer interrupted.

"Aye, what is it?"

"Starfleet Command Regulation 106, Paragraph 1, specifically identifies the role of the chief engineer and/or designated subsystem specialists as subject to preeminent exception to Term of Service Procedures as detailed in Starfleet Com—"

"Computer: Could ye digest that gobbledygook for me?"

"The chief engineer cannot resign while the *Enterprise* is undergoing a class-two refit."

Scott put his elbow on the desk and rested his head on his hand. It wasn't just personnel like Styles, even Starfleet equipment was out to get him. But Scott had picked up a few tricks in his years with Kirk. Especially when it came to Kirk's way with computers. "Computer, if I resign, effective *immediately,* then I will no longer be the chief engineer when Vice Admiral Hammersmith receives my message, therefore he will not be empowered to prevent my resignation."

But the computer didn't hesitate for a microsecond. "That is a circular argument."

"Well, then, let me put it to you this way: If you don't transmit my message to Hammersmith, then I shall rewire you into a food processor."

This time the computer remained silent.

"Well, computer? What are ye doing?"

"Scanning personnel records of Montgomery Scott to project hypothetical level of technical proficiency in the reconstruction of organic material synthesizers from duotronic components."

"And . . . ?"

The computer reset its audio circuits. It sounded like someone clearing her throat. "Message as dictated reads: 'Effective immediately, I wish to tender my resignation from Star—.' Please proceed."

Scott sighed. "Thank you, computer." It was a small victory, but these days Scott was grateful to take any that he could get. He felt it would be a long time before he would taste anything like it again, if ever. He glanced at the wall over his chest of drawers where his bagpipes hung. Twenty meters beyond them was open space. And the captain. And McCoy. And all the rest of those who rightfully belonged on the *Enterprise*. Perhaps by resigning, Spock was acknowledging that McCoy had shown them all the way. It was not logical to expect to uncover the real reasons behind what had happened at Talin IV by battling Starfleet. Perhaps Starfleet wasn't the enemy here. Perhaps there were other enemies, and other ways to find victory.

Scott turned back to the patient viewscreen which displayed the words he had dictated. Though it was difficult for the engineer to admit it, for the first time machinery wasn't enough. He no longer belonged on board the *Enterprise*. What had made this ship so special was her crew and her captain. The spirit of her would live just as well somewhere else, as long as they could be together.

And they would be together again, Scott suddenly realized. They had to be.

Scott smiled, the first time he had felt like it in months. Then he spoke the rest of the words that would free him from Starfleet, so like Spock and Kirk and McCoy and all the rest, he could do what duty demanded of him.

Three

"They musta been sorta crazy, doncha think, mister?" the child asked, wrinkling her face in consternation. She was about eight standard years old, taller than most her age which meant she was probably from one of the smaller Martian cities where the citizens had voted against higher gravity. But the clothes she wore—a lacrosse jersey from one of the intersystem championship leagues sloppily pulled over balloon overalls and red Skorcher moccasins—could have come from child outfitters anywhere from the Venus highdomes to the Triton hollowcells. Sol system, which once had been such a grand adventure, had become one large city, less than one-millionth of a subspace-second across.

Leonard McCoy scratched at the six-week growth of whiskers that was slowly and itchily becoming a beard. It was one thing being back in his home system in a cabin in a nature reserve, but civilization was making him edgy. When had the Moon gotten this built up and civilized, anyway? It wasn't the same as he remembered it had been when he was a boy.

"Doncha think, mister? Huh, mister?"

McCoy looked down at the child standing beside him at the railing. "Don't you know you shouldn't talk to strangers?"

The child blinked at him. "You're not that strange, mister. I talked to an Andorian once. They listen through these feeler things on their heads. They look sorta like they got two blue worms stickin' up from their heads or somethin'." The child shook her head knowingly. "Now that's strange."

"Well, young lady, Andorians think we're strange because our ears are squashed to the sides of our heads. In fact, they wonder how we can hear anything. And compared to them, we don't hear a lot." McCoy decided to spare the child a recitation of the standard frequencies of a typical Andorian's hearing range.

"Wow, do you know any Andorians, mister?"

McCoy was bothered that the child was impressed by the fact that he might have known an Andorian or two in his life. It was such a little thing. Especially considering that the child and McCoy were standing at the viewing railing of Tranquility Park.

Fifty meters away beyond the transparent aluminum wall, the spindly-looking second stage of the first crewed vehicle to land on Earth's Moon sat beneath the brilliant, unfiltered sunshine as it had for more than two hundred years. Where McCoy and the child stood had once been an unimaginable frontier, the quest for which had shaped the dreams of an entire century of living, breathing, and hoping human beings.

Those pioneers had come to this dead world in fragile ships powered by chemical rockets and controlled by binary computers only one step removed from an abacus. They had come without the capability for remaining more than a handful of hours, and decades before the development of any technology that could be reasonably utilized here. Why? So they could hop around for a few minutes in constricting, multilayered environmental suits that had been needle-sewn together by hand, and scoop up an unrepresentative few kilos of surface rocks and soil. Now almost two and a half centuries later, the anonymous spot which Armstrong and Aldrin had reached by risking their lives as the final two humans in a chain of thousands who had toiled years toward that goal, had become a holiday resort—a favorite stop for honeymooners and students on day excursions from Earth.

Civilization, McCoy thought sourly. *The death of dreams.* He narrowed his eyes at the child. "Look, kid . . . what's your name?"

"Glynis," she said.

"Well, Glynis, do you know what that is out there by the old flag?"

The child gave an exaggerated nod. "The lower stage of the Lunar Excursion Module, *Eagle,*" she recited. "Launched July 16, oldstyle one nine six nine C.E. The first of twelve successful landings on the Moon prior to the building of Base One. Launch authority was . . . um, the National Space and . . . no, the National Aeronautics and Space Administration. Uh, the United States of North . . . no, just of America." Glynis grinned happily up at McCoy. "Neil A. Armstrong, Commander. Edwin E. Aldrin, Lunar Excursion Module pilot. Michael Collins, Command Module Pilot. 'We came in peace for all mankind.' "

McCoy was impressed. He was never surprised when children could reel off the names of every lacrosse player in the system—along with their favorite colors and breakfast foods, or the complete lyrics and plot nuances of the latest holosaga, but he thought it rare to find a child who had turned her innate talents to the study of history. "That's very good," he said, and meant it. "Now how does a girl your age happen to know all that?"

The child became very solemn. "I have to."

McCoy raised an eyebrow. "And why's that?"

"You haveta know that stuff to get into the Academy."

"Starfleet Academy?"

Glynis nodded again, mouth set, very serious.

"How old are you?" McCoy asked.

"Almost nine."

"And you already know you want to join Starfleet?"

The child looked puzzled as if she didn't understand why McCoy had asked the question. "I have to," she said.

"You have to? Why?"

She drew herself up and looked proudly into McCoy's eyes. "I'm going to work on a . . . starship."

McCoy heard the slight hesitation in the child's voice as she said that final word, almost as if there was too much magic in it to ever speak the word lightly. He understood. But still . . .

"You want to work on a starship and you think the Moon pioneers were 'sorta crazy'?"

Glynis gazed out at the lunar landing stage in the middle of the stark graywhite landscape. "That's nothin' like a starship. It's kinda small, doncha think? And they didn't have enough radiation shielding. And no gravity. And they had to use electricity to run their systems. And—"

McCoy squatted down by the child to bring his eyes level to hers, and held up a finger to quiet her, just for a moment. "You know, a hundred years from now, if they ever build that transporter beam wave guide from the Earth to here and people can visit the Moon in two seconds instead of two hours, little children are going to be saying the same thing about us and how crazy we were because we had to get here in old-fashioned impulse shuttles."

The child looked skeptical. "Yeah?"

"Yeah," McCoy said. He pointed out to the *Eagle*'s landing stage. "What you have to remember when you look out there is that that machine isn't some flimsy, primitive, radiation-transparent antique."

"It's not?"

McCoy shook his head. "More than two hundred years ago, when children looked at the *Eagle*, that was *their* starship. And they dreamed about flying on it for all the same reasons that you want to fly on the starships we have today."

Glynis looked away from McCoy, squinting out through the double-story window overlooking Tranquility Base. "That was sorta all they had back then, wasn't it?"

"But when they launched it, it was the best."

"And there're going to be better starships a hundred years from now?"

McCoy nodded.

"But the ones we have now . . . they're the best, right?"

"Yes. They are." McCoy was hit with a sudden wave of sadness and he wasn't surprised.

The child thought about that answer for a moment, and McCoy could almost see her rearranging facts within her mind, pulling out pictures of old-fashioned spacecraft and sticking them beside state-of-the-art *Constitution*-class vessels.

"I wonder what it was like to live back then," she said.

McCoy straightened up again. "Just the same as it is to live now." He smiled at the child's look of surprise. "The spaceships change, but people don't. That's one of the things you'll learn in the Academy."

After he had spoken, McCoy realized that he had hesitated slightly when he had mentioned the Academy—as if it, too, like "starship" to the child, was more than a word to him.

Glynis had heard it, as well. "Hey, mister. What do *you* do?"

McCoy scratched at his beard again. "Me? I'm retired."

"Yeah? From what?"

McCoy chewed on his lip for a moment. Five minutes with this child was turning out to be more enlightening than two weeks watching pine trees grow in Yosemite. "From Starfleet," he said.

Glynis's mouth dropped open and her eyes widened. "Why? Why would anyone retire from . . . Starfleet?" Such magic in the way she said that word.

McCoy stared out across the lunar vista. Beyond what had once been the final frontier, he could make out the domes of the civilian spaceport, glinting white against the black sky of the Moon, just like the stars beyond.

"Why, mister?" Glynis asked again. "That's like quitting, isn't it? How could you quit Starfleet? How, mister? Why?"

But McCoy had no answer for her. At least, not yet.

Four

Beside his Starfleet Command gold star, the tribunal judge wore a small IDIC emblem on his black robe. That meant he had studied law on Vulcan. But Uhura didn't care where, when, or for how long anyone had studied anything. She was right and Starfleet was wrong and that's all there was to it.

"Ensign Uhura," the judge said, his voice echoing against the hard walls of the nondescript Starfleet Lunar Hall of Justice hearing room. "Please approach the bench."

Alise Chavez, Uhura's legal representative, nodded at her. Chavez was a harried-looking lieutenant junior grade in Starfleet's Justice Division, with long hair spraying out erratically from an improperly fastened clip at the back of her head and a red specialist's tunic that was at least two sizes too large. Uhura's case docket was one of twenty microtape wafers spilling out of the case on the lieutenant's table, so Uhura suspected that a nod of the head was about all the expert guidance she could expect today. She approached the bench, rustling in her one-size-fits-all, standard-issue, blue prison jumpsuit.

"Ensign Uhura," the judge intoned. "Do you know why you have been brought before the tribunal today?"

"Yes, sir." Because it was three standard months to the day since the first time she had been brought before the tribunal. *Let's get on with it,* she thought.

"Then I won't have to go into a long speech about your oath as a Starfleet officer—"

I'm an ensign, *now, you bald-headed, red-eyed—*

". . . nor about your duty to uphold the laws of the Articles of the United Federation of Planets."

"I am aware of both my oath and my duty, sir."

The judge looked down at his screenpad and scrawled some notes. *Probably checking off his list,* Uhura thought, *just like every other time.*

The judge cleared his throat. "Ensign Uhura, I am required to ask you if, at this time, you have reconsidered your refusal to sign the document displayed before you." He pressed a control on his screenpad and the disputed document appeared on the viewscreen built into the front of his high desk, directly before Uhura's eyes.

"Yes, sir," Uhura said formally, "I have reconsidered my refusal to sign that document."

The judge's eyes blinked in surprise. "I beg your pardon?"

"I have reconsidered it most carefully."

"You have?" He leaned forward, hands on either side of his screenpad. In Uhura's last eleven appearances before the other judges who had rotated through this tribunal, all she had volunteered were variations on the word no. "And . . . ?" he prompted.

"And after due reconsideration, I once again refuse to sign it because it is a false and—"

The judge pushed down on his desk's gavel switch and a low rush of white noise sprang from hidden speakers, preventing anything else Uhura said from being recorded by the reporting computer. But it didn't prevent her from speaking until she was finished.

"Are you quite done, Ensign?" the judge asked when Uhura's mouth had finally closed.

"Well, that's up to you, isn't it, sir?"

The judge's thick eyebrows quivered in irritation but he touched his fingers to the IDIC symbol he wore and Uhura could see his lips forming silent Vulcan phonemes as he repeated a calming koan.

"Very well, Ensign. Since you have seen fit to abrogate your sworn oath and—"

Uhura wasn't going to let him get away with it. She wasn't going to let anyone get away with it. "Your honor! I object!"

The judge shook his head and looked over at the overworked lieutenant j.g. "Lieutenant Chavez, could you please remind your client, *once again,* that she is the prisoner and cannot object."

Chavez hastily began to get up from behind her table but Uhura stared her down, smiling tightly, until the lieutenant lost the will to speak and sank back into her chair. After three months of dealing with Uhura, she knew no one could win an argument with the communications specialist once her mind was made up. And right now it was most certainly made up.

The judge began again. "Ensign Uhura, this tribunal, duly empowered by the authority of Starfleet Command, has found that you have abrogated your sworn oath of allegiance. . . ." He paused, but Uhura said nothing, for now. "And have consistently displayed your contempt for this court and its authority."

You got that right, Uhura thought.

The judge tapped a finger against the side of his screenpad and Uhura wondered what the man's Vulcan instructors would say about the telltale sign indicating that not everything was under control.

"Ensign, for three months you have defied the authority of this tribunal. First, by your refusal to testify during the board of inquiry hearing into the events at Talin IV—"

"Their minds were made up from the beginning!"

The judge glared but didn't stop talking. *"And now,* by refusing to sign this statement confirming your actions as recorded by the *Enterprise*'s log tapes. For three months you have been held in detention as punishment for that show of contempt. And now, unfortunately, as we are not at war and the charges against you do not pertain to the regulations covering vital secrets or mutiny, this tribunal no longer has the authority to continue your imprisonment."

The judge looked steadily at Uhura. "You do realize that there will be no going back after this?"

"The document is false. The conclusions are wrong." The judge held his finger over the gavel button but Uhura said nothing more.

"Very well." He signed his name on the bottom of the screenpad and began speaking in a rapid monotone. "Ms. Uhura, acting under the authority of Starfleet Command general regulations in peacetime, this tribunal declares you discharged from the rights, duties, and privileges of a non-commissioned officer in Starfleet. Said discharge to be listed on your record with dishonor. Your accumulated pay, pension, and education credits are forfeit. You are prohibited from ever accepting civilian employment with Starfleet, and are likewise prohibited from accepting employment with any civil branch of the United Federation of Planets, its member governments and bodies, for a period of ten standard years. You are reminded that your oath pertaining to safeguarding the classified information which might or might not have been divulged to you during the period of your service is still in effect, along with all pertinent publication and other dissemination restrictions. Failure to abide by the conditions of that oath and those restrictions may render you liable for both civil and/or criminal charges." The judge signed his name one final time. "This tribunal stands adjourned."

The judge slipped his screenpad under his arm and left the hearing room without looking back. Uhura went to the desk where Lieutenant Chavez gathered up her stack of brightly colored microtapes.

"What's the next step?" Uhura asked.

Chavez shrugged as she quickly checked the time readout on her portable computer screen. "You go to the quartermaster and get your own clothes back. And past that, you tell me. You got what you wanted, didn't you? You're a civilian." Her words were hurried. She had places to go.

"If I had signed that piece of garbage I would have had no choice but to resign. And all a resignation gives me is a chance to reconsider my decision within a six-month grace period. As if they'd let me back. At least I'm able to appeal a dishonorable discharge."

Chavez sighed as she slipped her computer into her case and closed it. "Come on, Uhura. You already know how that's going to play out. You file your appeal and they're going to assign you someone with even less experience and training than I have." She stood up to leave.

But Uhura placed her hands on Chavez's case, to keep the lieutenant in place for a few moments longer. "Chavez, I *am* getting someone to represent me."

"A civilian attorney? To argue a case against a Starfleet tribunal? You know how much something like that's going to cost? And you heard the conditions of discharge: You're going to be lucky to get work within ten parsecs of here to pay for it."

"I mean, I'm getting someone else in Starfleet to represent me."

Chavez stared at her in dismay. "Uhura, haven't you listened to a word I've said in the past three months? As far as the Admiralty's concerned, you don't exist. The whole Talin incident, the *Enterprise* Five, it's all being beamed out to a dust cloud."

"I'm not letting them do that," Uhura stated stubbornly.

"You're still not facing the facts! You were a fast-track officer on the best damned ship in Starfleet. There are two admirals at Command who came up through communications just like you. You had pull, tradition, a career path, top brass in your camp, and it didn't help you!" Chavez held her fist to her chest. "Look at what the Justice Division has done to you! I'm a junior grade who's spent the last year here on the Moon defending red shirts for slamboxing in bars on shore leave. Don't you get it? There's no one left in Starfleet who wants to have anything at all to do with you. Your captain didn't order any of you to do what you did, so you have no excuse. And *you* were the one who pressed the button that helped destroy a world. An entire world." Chavez pulled her case away from Uhura. "It's over, Uhura. No one in Starfleet will appeal anything for you."

"Spock will," Uhura said.

"The Vulcan?"

"He's been assigned to Technology Support in San Francisco. He's going to represent me."

Chavez reached out to take Uhura's hand, some sympathy still in her eyes.

"Uhura, he resigned."

"What?"

"Yesterday. It was in the ComSys updates. The last of the Five to go. He can't appear before any Starfleet tribunal as a civilian. Unless he's got a law degree. *And* has Sol system accreditation."

"But . . ." Uhura was speechless. She and Spock had talked less than a tenday ago. He had helped her plan her entire strategy from the beginning. He had told her to force them to give her a dishonorable discharge so he could launch an appeal and bring the whole case to open court. "Spock wouldn't abandon me . . . he couldn't."

Chavez patted Uhura's hand. "All of you people from the *Enterprise* have to start your lives again. The Vulcan must have realized that. By getting out, and leaving you behind, he did . . . the logical thing."

Uhura pulled her hand away. She would not be patronized any more than she'd be railgunned into accepting blame for what had happened at Talin IV. "He is not 'the Vulcan'! His name is Spock and he's one of the most honorable beings I know."

Chavez nodded her head wearily, not wanting to argue anymore. "Matters of honor are seldom logical, Uhura. After having worked with a Vulcan for so long, I would have thought you'd understand them better than most." She tucked her case under her arm.

"I understand everything that's gone on better than any of you blinder-wearing, rule-quoting, Starfleet drones do! Here *and* on Talin!"

Chavez stepped away, her sympathy turning to pity. "But except for a few student protest groups, no one wants to know about Talin anymore, Uhura. They just want to forget. It's over. Accept it. It'll make your life a lot easier."

Uhura's hands knotted into fists at her sides. "The only thing I'm prepared to accept is the truth."

Shaking her head, Chavez walked toward the hearing room's doors and they slid open before her. But before she left, she stopped and turned. "What I can't figure out, is how you could have spent so much time in Starfleet, seen the way it operates, and still believe that you might have a chance against the systems that make it work as well as it does. I mean, what makes you think you stand a chance? Why keep fighting the inevitable?"

Uhura's voice was solid and strong in the silent room. "Because I once served under Captain James T. Kirk on the best damned ship in Starfleet," she said. "And I *will* serve with him on that ship again. And God help anyone, or any admiral, who gets in my way."

"Ask a simple question," Chavez said softly, then stepped through the doorway, her work at an end.

But for Uhura, it was time to begin.

* * *

The Starfleet Lunar Hall of Justice in Oceanview was one of those peculiar government buildings that seemed to have no particular style, other than a quest for monumentalism. It was close to a century old and had been built in the twilight of Earth's cultural fascination with anything Centauran. Unfortunately, the fact that it had been built on the Moon under natural gravity—long since augmented to Earth normal throughout the city's business sections—had inspired the architects to alter the proportions of loadbearing arches whose original graceful dimensions had been dictated by a more massive planet. In addition, the building's airy roof gardens were situated five meters beneath the inner surface of a dingy green pressure dome instead of under spacious blue skies, further removing it from the Centauran ideals of open post-harmony defensism.

McCoy stood in the plaza before the ungainly structure, wondering how anyone could have become enamored of an architectural style that had arisen on a world where people spent most of their time burying things underground so they couldn't be detected by hypothetical enemies from space. That cultural paranoia, supported by fiber optic data transmission that prevented stray radiation from leaking out into space, had kept Earth's first expedition to another star from discovering there was an inhabited, technologically advanced civilization virtually next door until the first shuttles were almost ready to land. *The members of the Federation are all so eager to find new life and new civilizations,* McCoy thought, *but when we find it, none of us wants to go first.* Maybe that was the real reason for what had happened on Talin: not that Kirk had been engaged in brash adventurism, but that everyone else involved, including the First Contact Office, had been too cautious.

"Doctor McCoy?"

McCoy turned to see Uhura come up beside him, her eyes fixed on his beard. She looked somehow out of place in her civilian clothes—a rough textured brown and white caftan that floated above her ankles. No doubt he looked similarly odd to her out of his science blues and in a vat-cotton, multistriped shirt and hiking trousers.

"How long have you been here?" Uhura asked, not taking her eyes off the beard.

"Just arrived," McCoy said. He ran his fingers through his whiskers. "I don't blame you for staring. There *is* a lot of white in it, isn't there? Took me by surprise, too."

"It's not the white, Doctor. It's just the beard. I didn't recognize you at first and I was worried that I had left you standing here for the past half hour." Then she peered more closely at the beard. "But you're right, that *is* a lot of white."

McCoy laughed, held out his arms to her, and they hugged each other tightly. "It's good to see you again, Uhura. Damned good."

"I know the feeling." Uhura took his hand in hers. She looked somber for a moment. "Is there anything to your being late?"

McCoy smiled. "Oh, no. Not a thing. I got in this morning and went down to Tranquility Park. Had a very interesting discussion with a young lady."

Uhura smiled. "I see."

"A young lady of eight on a school band trip," McCoy clarified. "And with any luck, she'll be running Starfleet in fifty years." He pointed over to a tunnelway a few hundred meters west of the justice building. "There's a restaurant over there in the Park Dome. Wasn't too bad a few years ago. Want to get some civilian food to go with the civilian clothes?"

Uhura nodded. "I'd like that. I . . . I can't get used to . . . any of this."

"Neither can I," McCoy said and they began to walk to the park together, arms linked. "So," McCoy began after a few steps in silence, "how did the hearing go this morning?"

"Just fine," Uhura said. "For a dishonorable discharge."

"I'm glad they let you out." McCoy glanced sideways at a group of three officers walking by in gold shirts with commanders' braids. They saw him and Uhura as well, but there was no flicker of recognition. McCoy was surprised, considering the coverage the *Enterprise* Five had been given.

"No choice, Doctor. They could only hold me on contempt charges for three months in peacetime. Anything longer is against the Articles."

McCoy squeezed her hand. "Well, now that you're out, you should know that there's a big fat loophole in that regulation. Technically, they could have dropped charges against you one day before the limit ran out, held you over for any one of a hundred different minor violations, and the very next day brought new contempt charges against you good for another three months."

"What?" Uhura stopped walking and other pedestrians scrambled to move around her and the doctor.

"It's not often done," McCoy said, "but if they had really wanted you, they could have kept you pretty much indefinitely."

"I suppose that means my so-called legal advisor was right. Starfleet does want to cover up what happened."

McCoy tugged on Uhura's arm to get her walking again. "Starfleet doesn't go in for cover-ups, Uhura. The preliminary board hearing was a public forum and the update services got the full story out. There's no sign that Starfleet's trying to hide anything, even after the fact."

"But, Doctor, they didn't want to court-martial you—"

"That's because they said I didn't do anything. But I was on the ship. I would have . . ." He broke off, feeling his blood pressure soar.

"But they didn't want to court-martial the captain, either—or anyone. They just forced us all to . . . resign. Except for me."

"Careful here," McCoy warned as they came to the edge of the civic dome and a large caution display warned that they were entering a zone of natural gravity. The sudden stomach dip into point one seven gee wasn't quite as bad as going into free fall, but it was close enough for McCoy. As far as he was concerned, even cycling down to point nine gee was one point variation too much.

He let go of Uhura's hand so they could both use the guide rails set up for tourists and, he was sorry to read on the signs, for seniors. Meanwhile, a flurry of youngsters went bounding back and forth through the brightly illuminated interdome tunnel like giant rabbits on cordrazine. The automatic safety system's voice droned on nonstop to tell the children they were moving at too high a velocity for public safety.

As he moved stodgily along, feeling the breeze created by the bouncing youngsters, McCoy found himself thinking of the old two-dees the first Moon explorers had taken on their brief visits here, and during the construction of Base One. What the doctor always found remarkable on those tapes was that almost within seconds of their first arrival, the explorers had all instinctively begun hopping like these children, and that this type of locomotion was still common in Moon-normal gee fields today. McCoy marveled that the human body was so adaptable, not just for the Moon but for a thousand other worlds as well. It was a body designed to be propelled wherever its mind pushed it. No matter what. He thought about the young girl again.

"Well, don't you think that seems suspicious, Doctor?" Uhura asked. "Getting us to resign like that?"

McCoy was momentarily startled and he glanced back as he pulled himself along the railing. "Uhura, if you were in their position, wouldn't *you* rather have avoided the publicity of court-martialing the entire bridge crew of one of your most prominent ships when there were easier, less noticeable, and less damaging ways of getting rid of them?" He stopped talking for a moment to catch his breath. Why did lower gravity fields always seem to take more effort to move around in? "What happened at Talin happened. It's a closed datafile. Starfleet doesn't want to cover it up. It just doesn't want to reopen old wounds."

Uhura pushed off against the tunnel floor and jumped to McCoy's side, then pulled down on his arm and forced him under the guide rail where they could stand face-to-face without impeding the flow of others moving through the tunnel. She dropped her voice to an angry whisper. "Doctor McCoy, if I didn't know you better, I'd say you were talking as if you believed what Starfleet says. You can't, can you?"

McCoy hooked his hand under the guide rail and pushed down, increasing the pressure of his feet on the tunnel floor to lessen the feeling that the turbolift his stomach was on was going to hit bottom any second. "Of course, I don't believe it. I was there, remember? All I'm saying is that I understand Starfleet's position on this. I'm not saying that I like it or that I'm not going to try and change it, but as somebody somewhere once said, 'It's logical.' " McCoy put his hand to his eyes as if to clear them. "Lord, I never thought I'd miss hearing those words as much as I do now."

Uhura waited for a few moments while McCoy collected himself. Then she spoke again. "Did you know that Mr. Spock had resigned?"

McCoy's shocked expression said that he hadn't.

"I just found out today myself. My legal advisor told me. Apparently it was in yesterday's updates."

"But he was supposed to help you with your appeal," McCoy said. "I mean, that was the whole point of you going through this, wasn't it?"

"That's what I thought."

"Has he contacted you at all? Sent a message through anyone?"

Uhura shook her head. "When I thought you were late in coming to meet me back there, I thought maybe . . . well, that you and he were . . . together."

"I haven't heard a thing from Spock since that . . . meeting with Hammersmith at Starbase 29."

Uhura laughed in spite of her mood. " 'Meeting' wouldn't be the word I'd use for it."

McCoy smiled, too. And then he frowned.

"What is it?" Uhura asked.

"Over the past few weeks, I've just started to realize how spoiled we all were on the *Enterprise*. We could talk to anyone virtually anywhere over subspace."

"We still can, Doctor McCoy."

"But have you seen how long it takes to get online just to send a text-only message to Centaurus? And that's a local transmission. Good Lord, on the ship we never had to wait to gain access to anything. And we had personal communicators.

And shuttles. The computers always ready. Even the transporter." He groaned. "Listen to me, I'm missing the blasted transporter."

"All that technology is available right here. It's available almost any place."

"That's not my point. Here, we have to present our travel documents, we have to wait in line, go through channels. . . . On the *Enterprise,* why, we could just *do* something. Spock's missing? The sensors could do a sweep and you'd have locked onto his communicator in five seconds flat." McCoy took his hand away from the guide rail, holding both hands empty before him. "We're powerless now. It's so much harder to do just about everything."

"Are . . . are you giving up?" Uhura's voice roughened.

McCoy watched as three children sped past, bouncing high through the tunnel and turning somersaults in midair, their laughter drowning out the staid warnings of the safety system. "On the shuttle here this morning, I thought about it, Uhura. I really did. But at Tranquility . . . they didn't have much. Hell, they didn't have anything any sane person would have taken into space. But they came here anyway, didn't they?"

Uhura nodded her head silently as children played around them on what had once been an airless, lifeless rock.

"It wasn't the equipment they built," McCoy continued, watching the stream of people, humans and otherwise, passing through the tunnel. "It wasn't the knowledge or the experience they had. It was"—he shook his head, out of words—". . . something else."

Uhura's eyes filled with relief. "I know," she said softly. "I know."

"So to answer your question, Lieutenant. No. I am—"

Uhura placed her hands on McCoy's shoulders. "Thank you, Doctor."

"For what?"

"You called me 'Lieutenant.' I've missed hearing that."

McCoy took a deep breath. The thoughts he had been struggling with these past months at last came together. All because of a child he had happened to meet.

He thought of being at the end of a chain of thousands, of millions who had worked so hard to push humans so far. *How could you quit?* the child had asked him, and McCoy had had no answer for her. Because there was no answer. Because he hadn't quit. He wouldn't quit.

"Well, listen carefully, Lieutenant. Because to answer your question: No, I am not giving up. It's just that . . . I'm not quite sure what to do next."

"Don't worry about it, Doctor. Because I do." Uhura ducked back under the guide rail.

"Are you going to tell me?"

Uhura flashed a brilliant smile, then leapt across the tunnel in two four-meter hops to the pedestrian pathways leading back into the civic administration dome.

McCoy grumbled, pushed himself over the guide rail, and joined her, barely missing being blasted out of the tunnel by runaway tumbling children. "So what do we do, Lieutenant?"

"We go back," Uhura said.

McCoy looked down the tunnel. Through the distant opening, he could still see a corner of the squat Hall of Justice. "To Starfleet?" he asked in puzzlement.

But Uhura shook her head. "Back to where it all began, Doctor. To where the answers are." She smiled in satisfaction at the look that came over his face. "That's right," she said. "To Talin."

"The last I heard, Uhura, there was no regular tourist service out to the frontier. How do you suggest we get there?"

Uhura patted McCoy's arm. "I told you not to worry. We can find someone who'll want to take us there."

"Talin is blockaded, my dear. And the only ones who will be trying to get past a Starfleet blockade are criminals and pirates."

Uhura nodded. "I know that."

McCoy glanced around, and lowered his voice. "Just what are you suggesting we *do*, Uhura?"

She smiled disarmingly. "Know where we can get a good spaceship cheap?"

Five

There was only one Klingon ear nailed to the wall above the cash box, so it wasn't the toughest tavern Sulu had been in on Rigel VIII. But as he ducked beneath the swinging arc of a diburnium barstool, feinted to his right and kicked out to his left, he decided it probably ranked somewhere up in the top two. He didn't remember much about the other place, except spending the next two days in sickbay.

Sulu's kick clipped the charging Orion on the side of his black-maned head and sent the green-skinned alien flying into a flimsy table wisely abandoned by its occupants when the fight broke out. After the splintering crash of brittle Rigellian furniture alloy, there was a brief instant of peace in the tavern. The bartender stayed hidden behind a chrome-plated cabinet of imported liquors, unprotected customers scurried away to the back rooms, one solitary patron in a black cape poured another ale from a pitcher he hadn't paid for, and the combatants reevaluated each other.

Sulu crouched in a defensive *tesare* position. He felt a Vulcan form of self-defense seemed preferable at the moment because he knew there was not a hope in hell of him actually defeating three Orion males in hand-to-hand combat. But sometimes there were other things worth fighting for than immediate victory.

"No use, human," Krulmadden said matter-of-factly. The massive Orion shipmaster still sat at the end of the bar, hands folded together, one elbow resting by a slender flask of Ganymede Green. He laughed then, and the gemstones in his teeth flashed as brilliantly as the ones studding the eight rings he wore, lit by the near blinding light from a molecular fusion sunball floating near the rippled metal ceiling five meters above him. The light also gave a glimmering sheen to Krulmadden's deep green skin and the emerald *destin* scales of his tunic. "No win for you."

Sulu tipped his head at the Orion in a fencer's salute. "Then I shall lose." He glanced back at Lasslanlin, the mate who had crushed the table in his fall. He was slowly getting back to his feet, shaking his head, jeweled earrings making gentle chiming music in odd contrast to his 150-kilo bulk. Sulu took a breath and repositioned his foot to prepare for Lasslanlin's inevitable rush.

But Artinton raised his head from behind the bar where Sulu had flipped him a few seconds earlier. A string of thick orange blood hung from the second Orion mate's black beard and he smiled at Sulu, grunting like a Tellarite as he spat out more blood and at least two teeth.

Now that's not fair, Sulu thought. *I should be able to flatten at least one of these walking mountains.*

"Lasslanlin, stay." Artinton placed both gargantuan hands on the bar top. It had been cultured from a single cell of ironwood and Sulu swallowed as he heard it creak beneath the Orion's mass. "This one owes teeth."

Sulu's eyes widened as the second mate vaulted the bar as if he were strapped to antigravs, and landed less than two meters away.

Oh, great, he's been toying with me for the past five minutes. He could have had me any—

Artinton leapt and Sulu reflexively dropped to one knee, angling forward to catch and deflect the Orion's momentum with his own shoulders and back. But the Orion had expected the move and brought his knee up against Sulu's neck, jerking him from his planned direction and destroying his balance.

Sulu's breath left him with an explosive huff as the Orion drove him to the metal floor. Without being able to breathe under the Orion's crushing force, the outmatched human tried to flip around and crawl away. But Artinton's monstrous green hand grabbed the collar of Sulu's quilted, spun-down jacket and shoved him back against the iron plates of the floor.

Black stars flickered at the edges of Sulu's vision and the floor's rivets tore into his cheek. He struggled to ignore the giant above him and concentrate all he had on breathing again. Just one breath. Half a breath. Anything.

Sulu felt himself rise up from the floor and spin around under someone else's control. Artinton's hand was like a mechanical pincer against Sulu's neck, lifting him by a fistful of crushed fabric until the toes of his boots left the floor completely.

At the end of the bar, Krulmadden clapped two beefy hands together, applauding the fight's conclusion. Sulu edged his eyes to the side as Lasslanlin approached to stand beside his shipmate. The Orions began to laugh, deep and booming. Sulu could feel himself sway with the force of Artinton's murderous good humor. He tried to swallow again but nothing could get past the pressure of the huge fist against his throat. *So much for Vulcan self-defense tactics,* Sulu thought. *I guess they work better when you've had fifty years of practice.* As far as he could see, there was only one thing left to do.

Sulu closed his eyes, wincing as Artinton's foul breath flooded over him in even louder gales of laughter.

"Look at little insect!" the Orion howled. "He wants to sleep, forget bad dream!"

Eyes clenched shut, Sulu sensed the Orion bending closer to him, almost nose to nose. "But not dream, little insect. And not over!"

"You bet it's not," Sulu grunted then jerked his head forward at warp ten. In the next instant he had the triple pleasure of flattening Artinton's nose like a jellyfish, feeling himself slip from Artinton's suddenly limp hand, and hearing Artinton's earsplitting screech of shock.

Sulu kept his balance as the Orion stumbled backward to bounce against the bar and crumple like a five-atmosphere probe in a fifty-atmosphere pressure chamber.

But Lasslanlin grabbed Sulu's shoulder and spun him around. "That ship's friend, little insect hatchling zygote."

"If you're going to speak Standard then at least get it right!" Sulu shouted as he swung his fist. "I'm a *mammal!* Get it? A—"

Lasslanlin caught Sulu's fist in his black-gloved hand like a tractor beam stopping a meteoroid cold. His forearm didn't even travel back a centimeter as he absorbed the full force of the blow. *What a shame it will be to be taken apart by someone who knows so little about biology,* Sulu thought with regret. *But at least I got one of them.*

Lasslanlin raised his other hand and a dancerknife suddenly shimmered into view, its blade an indistinct blue humming form.

Sulu braced himself, but knew he had nothing more to draw on to resist. He wondered if the tavern keeper would let the Orions at least nail his ears *above* the Klingon's.

"First, ears," Lasslanlin promised. "Then, *mammal,* the little pair of—" The Orion suddenly jerked, mouth gaping in surprise. He shuddered again as if he had been hit from behind and let go of Sulu's fist.

Sulu staggered back, ready to run out from the tavern and disappear into the maze of the spaceport's back alleys. Lasslanlin didn't try to stop him. The Orion looked over his shoulder—just in time to catch a gleaming barstool with his face. The dancerknife spun from Lasslanlin's hand and its blade melted into air before it hit the floor.

"Stator rell . . . ?" Lasslanlin moaned, and then Sulu saw a flurry of five quick closed-hand chops pepper the Orion's face, ending with a final full roundhouse to his jaw.

Lasslanlin's eyes rolled back beneath his chartreuse lids, his knees wobbled once, then he fell to join his friend on the floor. The unexpected ally who had dropped the Orion stood above the unconscious body. He straightened his black cape, pulled back his cowl, and smiled disarmingly at Sulu. "Karate," he said, "originally inwented in Russia. Before being stolen by the Chinese."

Sulu dropped his hands to his side in relief. "You were supposed to be here an *hour* ago, Chekov."

Chekov pointed over to a small table with a now empty pitcher of ale. "I *have* been here. All ewening."

Sulu raised his hands again in sudden anger. "Then why weren't you helping me?"

"Up to now, you didn't need it."

Sulu shook his head, then reached out to hug his friend. Behind them, Krulmadden applauded once again.

Sulu and Chekov faced the Orion shipmaster together.

"How touching," Krulmadden growled. "Two *f'deraxt'la,* like slavegirls carrying on."

Chekov glanced at Sulu. "Does *f'deraxt'la* mean what I think it means?"

Sulu nodded. "Three parents, all related, and it rhymes with 'Federation' in the Trader's Tongue."

"We cannot let him get away with this."

"That's the point I've been trying to make, Chekov."

The two humans began to move apart. They had been friends long enough that no words were needed to establish their strategy. It wasn't the first time in a bar brawl for either of them.

Krulmadden smiled and slowly moved his hand to scratch his monstrously rounded belly. But when his hand came back to the bar, it held a jewel-encrusted disruptor in a platinum housing. "Suggest move back together, humans. Audition over."

"Audition?" Sulu asked.

Krulmadden waved his hands expansively and his gemstones flared so brightly

Sulu saw multicolored afterimages. "This all play. With shipmaster's mates." He pursed his lips and shook his head at the unconscious bodies of Lasslanlin and Artinton. "With shipmaster, me." Sulu cringed as Krulmadden nonchalantly pointed at himself with the barrel of his disruptor. "And two worldkillers in one bar. All play."

"Why do you call us worldkillers?" Chekov asked.

Krulmadden stuck out his lower lip and waved the disruptor again. "Why hands in cape, Chekov Mister?" He smiled at Sulu. "And you Sulu Mister. Both *Enterprise*, no? Krulmadden knows all. Fine shipmaster, Krulmadden."

"But in this case," Sulu said evenly, "the fine shipmaster is wrong."

Krulmadden used his free hand to pick at an emerald in an upper tooth for a moment, as if carefully considering what Sulu had said. Then he shrugged, thrust the disruptor forward, and a small patch of iron at Sulu's feet bubbled up in red hot blisters.

"Krulmadden not good with Standard Tongue," the Orion said. "Some things you not hear right. Some things you say . . ." He tapped the disruptor against his ear and stepped from his barstool.

"So again I say, Sulu and Chekov shipmates, but no ship." He walked closer to them, steel-soled boots clanking on the floor plates, the disruptor swinging back and forth with each waddling step. "True, you *f'deraxt'l* shipmates. But other *f'deraxt'la* not want you. So no ship, but . . ." He stood before them, grinning with a mouth like a backlit rainbow. ". . . *Krulmadden* ship!" He slipped the barrel of the disruptor into a wide burgundy sash that rested high across his stomach. "So audition over." He reached out and slapped two meaty hands on Sulu's and Chekov's shoulders. Sulu winced. "You ship again."

Chekov looked concerned. "I . . . I am not sure that I understand—"

Sulu felt another heavy hand hit his other shoulder, and smelled a familiar stench as Artinton leaned forward from behind. The Orion's voice was thick and nasal.

"Shipmaster say, little . . . mammals," Artinton said, digging fingers like daggers into Sulu's trapezius muscles, "you *hired*."

Six

Surprisingly, the naming of ships was not a universal habit. Scholars speculated that the root of the practice might lie within those ancient instincts, common to some species such as Klingon and human, from which sprang such strife-ridden concepts as territory and combat. However, even the Vulcans acknowledged the logic of giving ships names to honor individuals and places worthy of remembrance, or to remind all who served aboard the vessels of the qualities they should seek to master.

But there were those other races that had taken up the custom in *all* its detail, without really comprehending the finer points of the practice. They christened their ships not with names from their own history or culture, but from those of the alien races who had originated the practice.

Thus cobalt-blooded Andorians bravely piloted massive troop carriers named the *Robert E. Lee* and the *Surak;* Tellarites traveled from world to world aboard the *Rhode Island* and the *Claw of the Vindicator;* and even the Centaurans had called the first warp-powered craft launched from their planet the *Daedalus*.

Which is why Pavel Chekov was not surprised to read the name ornately emblazoned upon the hull of Krulmadden's ship, high in orbit above Rigel VIII. Despite all the alien influences of its mismatched components, and the fact that it was a Rigellian Registry Vessel, it made perfect sense to Chekov that the craft was proudly named the RRV *Queen Mary*. He had seen stranger.

"Holding at two hundred meters from the outer shields' perimeter," Sulu announced, making a final adjustment to the shuttle's attitude thrusters. Chekov had been impressed at how well his friend had performed at the controls of Krulmadden's stripped-down orbital shuttle. It had been a long time since either of them had flown in anything without its own gravity generator. He supposed that was yet another adjustment they would have to make now that they were no longer flying the cutting-edge craft of Starfleet.

"So, my helmsman, what do you think of my brightest jewel?" The shuttle's small flight cabin became even more cramped as Krulmadden floated into it from the aft cargo hold. Chekov couldn't help but notice that Krulmadden's command of Standard had improved substantially since they had left the tavern for the shuttle landing field.

Sulu studied the *Queen Mary*'s configuration from the pilot's window. The ship was a balanced but ungainly vessel, in the style of warp-capable craft not designed for atmospheric flight. Its main hull was a 30-meter, Mars-built disk slung beneath an elliptical Rigellian warp pod. The pod was joined to the disk's trailing edge by a short linking pylon, and was topped by a hard-edged, Andorian military surplus impulse drive which had clearly not been part of the ship's original design.

Beside Sulu, in the copilot's sling, Artinton unfastened his acceleration harness and pushed off. He slipped around Krulmadden, back toward the hold, grinning at Chekov who bobbed in the navigator's sling at the rear of the flight cabin.

"It looks trim enough," Sulu said appreciatively. "Though if you haven't got any upgrades under those impulse conduits, I don't see how she could hit anything higher than half cee in normal space."

"*Very* good, little mammal." Krulmadden beamed, though his jeweled teeth did not sparkle in the dim shuttle cabin lighting as much as they had planetside. The blue-white infernos of the Rigellian twin giants and twin lessers were hidden behind the planet for now. In addition to cutting back on expenses by having a shuttle without artificial gravity, Krulmadden had explained that he didn't like to waste power on radiation shields when he could simply park his ship in geosynchronous orbit in the almost perpetual shadow of Rigel VIII's rings. The light reflected from the planet's major moon was more than enough to steer by. But watching the ease with which Krulmadden buoyed his bulk around in microgravity, Chekov thought that perhaps there was another reason for the absence of gravity generators.

The shipmaster pointed out Sulu's window. "That Andorian impulse shell is just that. A shell. A delusion."

"Uh, do you mean 'illusion'?" Sulu asked.

"Whatever. Beneath it is a dual tangent, full magnetopulse field coil with an artificial singularity." He said every word perfectly, a proud father naming his children. "Relative rest to half cee in less than one second. With full cargo, still reach nine-nine cee in less than thirty."

Sulu whistled. "I didn't think artificial singularities were licensed for use by anyone except Starfleet and some planetary defense units."

"They are not." Krulmadden gave as good an impression of a shrug as he could in microgee. "And for good reason. It would give unscrupulous types too much advantage over *f'deraxt'l* border patrols. Not good, no no no." The shipmaster slapped his own hand, then chuckled as his rhythmic exhalations began to spin him around.

Sulu glanced over at Chekov as Krulmadden steadied himself. Chekov nodded. He understood. The Orion's ship was obviously better equipped than they had hoped, which meant their plan was going to be much easier to bring off than they had anticipated.

"What procedures do we follow now?" Sulu asked.

At that, Krulmadden's face became unreadable. He was not a being who was comfortable with questions. "Now, Artinton kindly asks my sweet jewel to drop her shields and not to blow my shuttle out of space. And then, I see how good you are at docking."

Chekov was troubled by that. It meant the *Queen Mary* had an automated defense system for the times it was left unattended. He and Sulu would have to devise some way of intercepting the recognition code Artinton was apparently going to transmit to inform the *Queen Mary*'s computers that the shuttle was a friendly craft. If his and Sulu's plan was to succeed, they would need to be able to transmit that information themselves, eventually.

Krulmadden clamped his hand firmly on Sulu's arm to steady himself. "Hold this position relative to my ship precisely, helmsman. If you deviate by more than a half *sateen,* you will owe Artinton more than his teeth."

Chekov converted the Trader's Measure. *Three centimeters.* He wondered why the shuttle would have to maintain such an exact position simply to transmit a subspace code. Or even a radio signal. And why would not holding that position be dangerous to Artinton? The answer that came was both obvious and unexpected.

A yellow-orange flickering light suddenly filled the shuttle's cabin, originating from the aft hold and accompanied by a faint but distinctive musical chime. Artinton was *transporting* over to the *Queen Mary.* But how?

"Is that safe?" Sulu asked. "While the shields are up?"

Krulmadden didn't take his eyes from his ship. "As long as you hold this position, it is."

Must be a prearranged interference gap in the shield, Chekov decided. *Just wide enough for a transporter carrier wave from the ship to reach through. And the shields must be stacked deep around the gap so the wave can return only from a specific position.* He frowned in thought. There would be no security code to intercept. Artinton was going to shut down the automated defense systems physically from onboard the *Queen Mary* herself. The task of stealing the Orion's ship had just become more difficult.

A strip of running lights suddenly flashed into life along the side of the *Queen Mary*'s warp pod and orientation lights began to blink on the main hull.

"Shields are down," Sulu announced, reading his control panel's tactical display.

"Shuttle berth is on the disk, on the opposite side of the warp pod pylon," Krulmadden said.

Sulu tapped a readiness code into the thrusting system. "That's not a standard configuration."

Krulmadden laughed again. "The entire ship is not standard configuration. You would be a clever mammal to always keep that in mind." He turned to make sure that Chekov was listening to his lesson as well. "It might help prevent need-less . . . accidents."

Without looking at any control panel readings, Sulu brought the shuttle smoothly around the *Queen Mary*'s disk and guided it toward the lit circle that indicated the airlock berth. He docked the shuttle with so little vibration that Krulmadden had to study the board to make sure the airlocks had mated. "Very good, mammal. Smooth as a slave's . . . ah, but then you are *f'deraxt'la,* and would not know about such things . . . thus far."

Krulmadden pushed himself over to the copilot's controls and hovered by them, the orange tip of his tongue showing in concentration. "Your duties are finished. I shall take care of the remainder." He ran his fingers over the control panel and Chekov's ears popped as he heard the shuttle's airlock whoosh open into the *Queen Mary.*

A row of blue lights glowed on top of Krulmadden's board and he threw a lock-ing switch, freezing the controls. Chekov surmised that a security code would have to be input before they would unlock again. That was another condition he and Sulu would have to get used to as civilians: the lack of trust that was reflected in the en-gineering of private spacecraft. Aboard a Starfleet ship, when life or death could de-pend on a crew member's ability to initiate action within seconds, there were few built-in safeguards to restrict access to critical controls. It was simply accepted that Starfleet personnel who had earned the opportunity to serve on a starship were among the most loyal and balanced the system could produce, so why spend time and engineering effort preventing such people from misusing controls when they would never choose to do so in any case? The added risk that complex ships such as the *Enterprise* might be made more vulnerable to hostile takeover from within had many times been proven worth the increased efficiency and flexibility such an open system provided. But judging from its shuttle, the *Queen Mary* was organized along completely different routines—almost as if Krulmadden were expecting someone to steal it from him every day. *Well,* Chekov thought, *at least this time he is correct.*

Krulmadden spun away from the copilot's station and pointed at Chekov. "Now *you* must help take Lasslanlin to the medic booth." Chekov unclipped his harness and floated off to begin his first work assignment for the shipmaster. It seemed an appropriate task considering he was the one who had made Lasslanlin require the medic booth in the first place.

In the hold, Lasslanlin was still wrapped in a stretcher cocoon and lashed to the "down" bulkhead, his sleep inducer strapped to his head. Back at the tavern, the bartender had used a black-market medical tricorder to diagnose the Orion as hav-ing a broken nose, broken jaw, and concussion. On the *Enterprise,* Chekov knew that Dr. McCoy could have dealt with those injuries in less than half an hour, but with only a computer-run medic booth on board the *Queen Mary,* Lasslanlin was looking at two or three days of uncomfortable recuperation. Chekov hoped the sto-ries he had heard about Orion vengeance oaths had been exaggerated.

The airlock was set in the hold's "up" bulkhead—a departure from normal con-figuration. It should have been in the aft wall. As Chekov unhooked the elastic cords holding Lasslanlin's stretcher in place, he tried to determine if any other modifications had been made in the shuttle. Estimating the interior volume of the hold, he realized that it was not as large as he had expected it should be, based on what he had seen of the shuttle on its landing pad at the spaceport. The interior storage area appeared to end about two meters short of the craft's outside dimensions, even allowing for upgraded shielding, and Chekov suspected that Krulmadden had additional customized equipment installed in the dead volume.

Since a gravity generator would have had to run behind the "down" bulkhead, Chekov decided he would give even odds that the shipmaster had added a small warp unit—maybe factor 1.5 to 2—or extended life-support capability. Either choice would make sense for someone who might have to make a quick getaway or need a place to hide out for a few months. Chekov reminded himself to pay close attention to other dimensions onboard the *Queen Mary*, to establish if any more capabilities were being hidden from him. He was certain there would be.

Artinton appeared on the other side of the *Queen Mary*'s airlock, looking through at everyone in the shuttle's hold. "Be cautious pushing Lasslanlin through the lock. Go very slowly so the transition will not jar him."

"Transition?" Chekov asked as he carefully rotated the stretcher into an orientation that would enable it to fit through the narrow airlock. "Is there grawity on the *Queen Mary*?"

Krulmadden stared at Chekov. "Would you care for acceleration to nine-nine cee in thirty seconds without it? Krulmadden has clients who would be happy to spread what's left of you on their biscuits."

Chekov angled Lasslanlin perfectly, braced his feet on the "down" bulkhead, then pushed the stretcher toward Artinton. "I was just surprised that you left it turned on when no one was aboard."

Krulmadden shook his head at Chekov. "You jump to too many conclusions for navigator. Who told you there were no others on board?"

"Why, no one. I . . . just thought . . ."

"I am shipmaster. I do thinking for all my crew."

Silent now, Chekov guided the end of the stretcher through the lock. When the opening was clear, he launched himself toward it to grip its metal lip, still cold from space despite its insulation. Then he felt the soft rippling pressure of the *Queen Mary*'s gravity field.

As he crawled through the meter-long tunnel, he decided he was not happy about Krulmadden's intimation that there might be other beings on board. Overpowering three Orions would not be beyond him and Sulu working together, especially if they struck while Lasslanlin was confined to the medic booth. But if there were other crew on board, especially other Orions, then it was beginning to look as if he and Sulu had just made the worst mistake of their brief civilian careers.

When Chekov was fully within the gravity field, he was puzzled at the amount of muscle tone he must have lost during his months of civilian life. The sudden transition from microgee was a surprising shock, much more strenuous than he had anticipated. And then he realized that yet another obstacle had been placed in their way. The artificial gravity field on the *Queen Mary* was set to normal for Rigel VIII—almost two Earth gees.

Chekov paused for a moment in the airlock—now an opening in a corridor floor—to reposition his hands for better purchase. But before he could move again, Artinton grabbed him under the armpits and hauled him up the rest of the way without apparent effort. The Orion mate moved as easily in the heavy gravity as he had in the low-power "tourist field" that operated through most of the spaceport's alien quarter.

When Sulu appeared in the airlock, Artinton hoisted him through as well, and he enjoyed the look of surprise on Sulu's face as his feet hit the corridor floor faster and harder than he had expected. Chekov saw the look of apprehension on the helmsman's face and knew why it was there. A few days in this gravity and neither one of them would be able to crawl, let alone take on Krulmadden and his crew.

Artinton squatted down to slap an antigrav to Lasslanlin's stretcher, then stood, lifting the mass-neutral stretcher with one powerful hand. "You wait here for shipmaster. On big ship like this, you could get lost . . . forever." He grinned at Chekov, flicking his tongue to show the holes where several teeth used to be, then started the stretcher gliding down the corridor.

Sulu stood by the airlock and rocked experimentally from foot to foot. "That's got to be at least a one point eight."

"It feels like five," Chekov said and stepped back to lean against the corridor bulkhead. As he rested, he glanced up the corridor in the direction that Artinton had gone. It was obviously a main branch that ran along the disk's diameter. Its narrow and utilitarian appearance, thick with exposed conduits and service access panels, was similar to the old class-J ships that Academy cadets trained on.

"From the way she looks on the outside, I wasn't expecting her to be even this up-to-date," Sulu said.

"That is only the light." Chekov fought the high gee to lift his hand and shield his eyes from the dazzling bluewhite glare that came from the corridor's ceiling panels. Like the gravity, they were set to produce Rigel VIII normal. "We will have to wear eye filters."

Before Chekov could find something else to complain about, Krulmadden smoothly popped through the airlock under his own power. He tried a few kneebends, then pounded his fist against his chest so his rings clanked against his tunic's hard scales. "Ah, the invigoration of real resistance!" He clapped his hand enthusiastically against Sulu's side and the helmsman slammed into the corridor bulkhead.

Krulmadden scowled as Sulu fought to keep his balance. He turned to Chekov. "A few months in real gravity and you behave like true shipmates. But in meantime, what you need is . . . exercise! Ur'eon exercise!" He laughed at the uncomfortable expressions on his new shipmates' faces. "You may think of that as an order."

Following Krulmadden's doubletime march through the Queen Mary's corridors reminded Chekov of being a cadet again, and he had hated being a cadet. The only good thing about that status was that it had led to the day he had become an ensign. But he knew that was exactly what he and Sulu had become again—cadets in Krulmadden's private navy. The shipmaster was making a pointed show of the control he wielded over them.

But still, there had to be limits. "Excuse me, Shipmaster," Chekov said, puffing as he eyed the third set of steep, interlevel ladders Krulmadden intended to lead them up, "but are there no turbolifts?"

"No room for drive tubes! No power!" Krulmadden grasped the rung of the ladder inset in the corridor wall. "Has the f'deraxt bred the spine out of its mammals as well as the brain and heart?" He leapt up the ladder, hand over hand, singing boisterously in a language Chekov had never heard before.

Chekov stared at Sulu. "I think perhaps it is a form of torture we are unfamiliar with."

Sulu looked up the ladder. "I think we're going to need a new plan."

Krulmadden's voice thundered down from above. "Waaaaiting, little mammals!"

Sulu began to climb. Chekov waited for the way to clear so he wouldn't suddenly be crushed by Sulu falling at 19.5 meters per second, and then he followed, already feeling blisters form on his hands.

From the sloping angle of the ceiling on the next level, Chekov concluded they had reached the main hull's top deck. Surely Krulmadden wasn't intent on taking them up to the warp pod, but Chekov wasn't even sure what the shipmaster's motives were for bringing them this far.

Krulmadden slowed his pace as he directed them along a curving corridor leading to port. Chekov, inhaling deeply to catch his breath, could hear Sulu breathing hard behind him. But when Krulmadden stopped by a set of doors and turned back to see how his new shipmates were doing, the huge being had not even broken a sweat.

Krulmadden placed one hand on the doors and leaned against them, waiting for Sulu and Chekov to catch up with him. "So my little mammals, do you have any idea where we are on this jewel of mine?"

"Top deck, main hull," Chekov wheezed, putting his hands on his knees to ease the strain on his back.

"Port side," Sulu gasped. "And we went through one-and-a-half circuits of the deck below us."

"Good, you pay attention." Krulmadden looked at the door panels beneath his hand and when he returned his gaze to Sulu and Chekov, he wasn't smiling. "Have you noticed anything else . . . unusual about this ship?"

"Besides no turbolifts?" Chekov asked.

"Very few doors," Sulu said. "Is the hull hollow?"

Chekov carefully watched Krulmadden for a reaction. If the *Queen Mary* were less massive than its apparent volume indicated, then it would be capable of greater acceleration than a potential enemy might expect. But the subterfuge would only work once and a large enough sensor array could detect a significant mass/volume discrepancy.

"On contrary," the shipmaster answered. "Is quite full. But of what, you need not know for now. Is enough simply to know not everything here is as it seems. And so is much danger . . . and destructions." He paused, but neither human interrupted. "Thus, all that remains . . . is to know if *you* are as you seem."

It was a threat, Chekov knew, and whatever happened next, Krulmadden had ensured that both humans would be too exhausted to try and make their way back through the ship to the shuttle. There was no choice but to continue with whatever the shipmaster had in mind.

"I don't understand," Sulu said. "You said you recognized us in the tavern."

Krulmadden ran his tongue over the diamond set in his incisor, and said very carefully in his best Standard, "Don't you find it convenient that I, a shipmaster in need of crew, and you, crew in need of a ship, found each other on such a large planet in such a big galaxy?" He scratched at the corner of his eye. "Why were you in the tavern? So far from home?"

Chekov and Sulu exchanged a look: The strategy was in Chekov's hands.

"We were . . . looking for a ship."

"Why?"

"We have none."

"Why?"

Chekov was in no mood for this. "Because we are no longer in Starfleet."

Krulmadden stared at Chekov without blinking. "Why?"

"Because they called us worldkillers," Chekov said angrily. "I thought the great Krulmadden was supposed to know everything."

"How else to know than by asking questions? And now, a final one: Are you the worldkillers they say you are?"

Chekov hesitated before answering. Which would an Orion shipmaster prefer to have serving on his ship? Two brutal, reckless criminals that Starfleet had condemned by innuendo if not by courts-martial, or two wrongly accused officers who felt their honor had been smeared? He didn't know the answer, so he told the truth.

"No. The charges are false."

Krulmadden raised his thick black eyebrows. "Famed Starfleet is wrong?" He bit his knuckle and growled softly.

"Not wrong," Chekov said. "They just do not understand what truly occurred."

The shipmaster drummed his fingertips against the doors he leaned against. "What do you intend to do about it?"

Now that Chekov had established the plan, Sulu joined the conversation. "There is nothing more we can do about it. We resigned when that became obvious."

"Surely, you have . . . feelings about the way Starfleet has treated you?"

"That is why we were looking for a ship." Sulu spoke tightly through clenched teeth.

"Any ship? Or one ship in particular?"

"The type of ship we could find in a tavern. On Rigel VIII."

Krulmadden took his hand from the doors. He had made his decision. "The thirst for revenge can be as invigorating as the resistance of true gravity. I welcome you as crew on the jewel of all the stars."

"I thought that's what you did after the fight in the tavern," Sulu said, still wary.

"All that fight told me was the seriousness of you. I didn't need to know your anger with Lasslanlin and Artinton. I needed to know your anger with Starfleet. Too many spies have tried to board this ship in past."

"And what would have happened if you had decided we were spies as well?" Chekov hated unanswered questions.

"Then, my little mammals, you would have gone through these doors." Krulmadden smoothed his beard. "But, instead we shall go through those." He pointed to a second set of closed doors farther along the corridor. "Come." Krulmadden put his hand to his chest and began to croon again as he led the way.

As Chekov passed the doors Krulmadden had leaned against, he looked at the marker on them. But he couldn't read the Trader's Script. Sulu could. "Recycling room," the helmsman said.

Krulmadden stopped by the second set of doors and punched in a security code, using his massive body to block his fingers from Chekov's sight.

"What does this one say?" Chekov asked, pointing to the marker on the new doors. Sulu shrugged. "Cargo storage, I think."

The doors slid open and a warm breeze filled with a heady scent of rich cinnamon and other less familiar spices spilled past them. The room beyond the doors seemed huge.

"You read the Trader's Script well," Krulmadden said as he stepped aside and motioned for Sulu and Chekov to enter. "Indeed, this is part of my jewel's greatest cargo. Which you are welcome to enjoy."

Sulu entered first and Chekov saw him suddenly freeze only a few steps inside. Beside Chekov, Krulmadden laughed. "Ah, yes, quite a sight, are they not?"

Chekov stepped forward, feeling the weight of Krulmadden's hand patting him on his back.

"We do things differently from Starfleet onboard *Queen Mary*," the shipmaster said gleefully. "You will be paid first and work tomorrow!"

Chekov peered into the vast room over Sulu's shoulder. "What is this?"

"The exercise I promised you!" Krulmadden laughed. "True *Ur'eon* exercise! Come, come, you are *f'deraxt'la* no more."

Then Chekov saw what had stopped Sulu dead and he realized the true nature of the monster they were forced to deal with if they were ever to clear their names.

In a long row of small cubicles stretched against one wall of the immense cargo hold were more than twenty Orion females. Their green skin glistened and their long black hair shone in the blue glow from the repulsor fields that ringed each open doorway, keeping them in place as inhumanly as any chains or irons.

Krulmadden was more than just another Orion pirate. He was the worst kind: an outlaw whose hideous crime had been condemned on each world of the Federation and was believed to have been forced into extinction. But perhaps evil was more powerful than even the Federation had realized. Because Shipmaster Krulmadden was a slaver.

And now, Chekov thought in horror. *So are we.*

Seven

Kirk remembered the *Farragut,* the first real ship he had served on—a *Constitution*-class starship like the *Enterprise.* He had been a green lieutenant and the *Farragut* was to be his first deep-space mission. The endless week between receiving his orders and finally arriving aboard her had been filled with his dreams of the new life of exploration and excitement that awaited him: first contact with alien worlds, going eye-to-eye with the Klingons, saving colonies, securing the frontiers. Then Kirk had run straight into what his father disparagingly called the "new Starfleet" and had spent his first six months managing supply crates in the *Farragut*'s cargo bay. He found it somehow fitting that he had returned there now, in spirit, if not in fact.

Surprised that he had retained so much of an almost fifteen-year-old skill, Kirk deftly managed the controls of a Mark IV Tractor Web to receive, sort, and secure the rapid stream of cargo crates being loaded onto the freighter, SS *Ian Shelton.* It helped that the old Mark IV was virtually identical to the one he had operated on the *Farragut.* His familiarity with it was how he had managed to swing the job of stevedore in the first place, jockeying the transfer of cargo from Intrator II's commercial spacedock to the freighter which was stationkeeping 200 meters away.

As Kirk worked the controls, the voice of the Orbital Transfer Controller came over the communicator link on the Mark IV's console. "How are you doing in there, *Shelton?"*

"All conditions are nom—uh, everything's okay so far." Kirk still had to concentrate to keep from falling into the old patterns of speech. He wasn't looking forward to another unveiling as had happened with the rockriggers, despite his beard and longer hair, even though he knew it was inevitable. He had been surprised to find out how small a universe it was within the boundaries of Federation space.

"Sure you don't need a break in the flow to sort things out?"

"Keep 'em coming," Kirk said.

He could hear the grin in the Controller's voice. "Okay, hotshot, let's see if we can go for a new record."

The crates began floating through the open cargo-bay doors of the *Ian Shelton* at ten-second intervals, almost twice their previous rate. They were standard, interstellar modular crates whose polyhedron-angled sides were designed to prevent shifting during transport and which were just as easy to handle in microgee or with tractor webs as the less stable, cube-shaped crates still used for strictly planetside shipment.

"Hey, *Shelton*," the Controller asked jovially, "sure you don't want us to slow it down to give the computer a chance to take over?"

"Slow it down?" Kirk asked, trying to sound puzzled. "I'm still waiting for you to speed it up."

The Mark IV's main projectors were arranged around the cargo-bay opening and along one bulkhead to produce a three-dimensional grid of tractor beams through which the crates moved. An inertial feedback circuit told Kirk the mass of each crate as the web acquired it so he could spread the density of the cargo throughout the hold as the crates were stacked, to keep the freighter's lines of thrust balanced. If the cargo had been completely uniform, or each crate had been outfitted with a reliable transponder to identify its contents, or there had been enough time for a sensor system to evaluate the crates for a computer that could stack them a thousand different ways in memory as it searched for the most stable order, then Kirk's job could have been automated. But the real world of interstellar trade was not so orderly, so the almost infinite flexibility of a living mind was required. Along with absolutely no distractions.

Kirk involuntarily tensed when he heard the cargo-bay control room doors slide open behind him. Keeping a mental picture of the positions and masses of almost sixty crates in his mind at once as he tried to stack old ones at a rate exceeding the arrival of new ones, he didn't dare turn around to see who it was. A split second of hesitation on his part could lead to crate collision, cargo loss, and even hull damage. *Why do I get myself into these situations?* Kirk asked himself. It was one thing to go all out when the safety of his crew or his ship had depended on it. But for a ten-credit-an-hour job?

"Don't look up," a voice behind Kirk said. It was Anne Gauvreau, the ship's captain and his employer of the day. From the corner of his eye, he saw her standing by the console to look through the cargo-bay viewport. Then he heard her whistle.

"When Control said we were taking on cargo at one per ten, I thought they were joking."

Kirk made a noncommittal noise. His board showed the rate was already up to one crate every eight seconds. As far as he could see, in less than a minute there were going to be only two ways out. The first was to start stacking the crates without worrying about their mass. There was a possibility that the stacking density might balance out by chance, but if it didn't, then he'd be personally responsible for keeping the freighter in orbit for hours while he reshuffled the cargo.

The board showed a shipping rate of one per seven and Kirk knew he had reached his limit. No matter how uncomfortable he found the decision, he had to choose the second way out. The bottom line was that it wasn't his ship. He had to admit defeat. *It's only a job,* he told himself. He wasn't convinced.

"Come in, Control," Kirk called out to the communicator.

"Give us a break, *Shelton.* You don't have to rub it in."

Kirk didn't answer. He hadn't expected that reply. And then he saw that no new crates were floating into the bay, though the manifest screen indicated there were still several hundred to load.

Kirk took the chance. "Orbital Transfer Control: What seems to be the trouble out there?"

The Controller took his time answering. "Uh, seems we got a burned-out impeller coil at the transfer bay, *Shelton.*"

Because he wasn't on an image link, Kirk smiled. Now he remembered why he got himself into these situations.

Gauvreau leaned forward to the console's communicator. "Orbital Transfer Control, Captain Gauvreau here. Tell me, do you happen to know why the coil burned out . . . ?"

The Controller was surprisingly contrite. "Because we couldn't keep up with the rate at which you were receiving cargo."

Gauvreau tapped her fingers on the console. "If I'm not out of here in two and a half hours, the business office is going to owe me some hefty penalties."

"We'll get back to you when the repairs are finished," the Controller said glumly.

Kirk heard the channel click off. He forced the smile from his face and looked up at Gauvreau with earnest concern. For a moment the freighter's captain had an expression of stern concentration. "Offhand, Leonard, I'd say you were one lucky bastard." Then she laughed and Kirk joined her.

"So what do you figure?" Gauvreau asked once the tension of the near-disaster in the cargo bay had been dissipated. "I'd say you were about two more seconds away from a chain-reaction pile-up that would have sent crates through the wall of the ship."

"Well, not exactly two seconds," Kirk began.

"Let me rephrase that," Gauvreau interrupted. "Through the wall of *my* ship."

Kirk tried to keep the smile from his face but had little success. "When I called Control, that's when I was going to . . . admit defeat and have them shut down the stream."

"One per eight on a Mark IV," Gauvreau said, shaking her head. She looked back out through the viewport. "You know, with the penalties they're liable for if I don't break orbit on schedule, they're going to be rushing that impeller repair. So I'd take care of that holding pattern you've got in there while you've got the chance."

Kirk turned back to the console and without the confusion of new crates arriving every few seconds, the stacking procedure was simple. He kept a few unusually massive and unusually light crates floating in temporary stacks and assigned the rest to a final storage configuration.

When he had finished, Kirk kept his hands on the controls, fully expecting the Controller to inform him that the coil had been replaced about one second before the first crate came blasting through the bay doors. At least with the extra time Kirk had had to straighten out the hold, even at one crate every five seconds he could handle the rest of the flow simply by keeping everything in temporary stacks. There would be room enough according to the manifest.

Gauvreau read the mass display of the final stacked crates appreciatively. "Good arrangement," she told Kirk. "Don't know how you built that pattern so quickly."

"That's my job," Kirk said.

Gauvreau seemed about to say something, then thought better of it. "So how does a young guy like you know how to run a Mark IV, but still keep up with new loading strategies?"

Kirk smiled at being called young. He estimated Gauvreau was only a few years older than he was, with just a few telltale strands of white in otherwise sandy and curly short hair. She was young for a commercial freighter captain—the way he had been young for a starship captain.

"Actually, I'm not that young. I trained on the Mark IV a long time ago. And I don't know anything about new loading strategies." Kirk had not been inclined to keep up with the literature since the day Captain Garrovick had rotated him out of the *Farragut*'s cargo bay.

Gauvreau tapped the mass display. "I've never seen that distribution pattern before. And I do know all about new loading strategies. That's *my* job."

There was something to her tone that put Kirk on the defensive, almost as if she were testing him.

"Do you play three-dimensional chess?" Kirk asked.

"Love it."

"Look at the mass display again. Think about middle games."

Gauvreau peered down at the screen, studying the density map of the cargo crates stored in the hold. "The Siryk Variations . . . ?"

Kirk nodded. It was a conservative approach to 3-D chess favored by players who preferred to wait until their opponents made exploitable errors. The variations of defensive placement developed by the Vulcan Grand Master Siryk emphasized arranging pieces in an interwoven pattern of strong and weak that did not permit much leeway for sudden offense, but created a near impenetrable defense.

Gauvreau laughed now that the seemingly new stacking pattern had been revealed as a game strategy more than four hundred years old. "The low-mass crates are pawns, the heavy-mass crates the more powerful pieces."

"That's it," Kirk said. "And I kept track of each crate's position by picturing the hold as an expanded 3-D chess grid."

"Very inventive." Gauvreau sat on the edge of the console and folded her arms. Kirk could see she had territory patches from dozens of star systems on the sleeves of her flight jacket. The back of the jacket held even more. Quite an accomplishment for someone who served in the merchant fleet, where freighters rarely had the capability for exceeding warp 2 and most stars were long months apart.

"You must be quite a player," she said. "Any grand master points?"

"I've never been in any tournaments."

"But you know enough about the Siryk Variations to fill a hold with them." She was obviously skeptical.

"I have . . . had a good opponent. A full grand master." He knew he shouldn't be surprised at the sudden ache he felt. But it was one of the few things he seemed to have no control over. Almost as if he expected never to see his friends again. "He was very dedicated to the Vulcan modes of play."

"Ever beat him?"

Those memories brought a smile back to Kirk's face. "Enough to bother him. The, uh, relentlessly logical approach to the game doesn't hold up all that well to completely . . . unexpected changes in tactics."

Gauvreau stuck her tongue in her cheek for a moment, reading between the lines. " 'Unexpected changes in tactics,' hmm? As in 'acts of complete desperation'?"

Kirk hated to give away his secrets but the freighter captain was sharp. "Not complete desperation, exactly." But desperate enough to totally disrupt Spock's carefully planned, long-range attacks and keep him in awe of his captain's skills, never quite realizing that Kirk's ability not to show his panic accounted for much of his perceived mastery of the game.

The mass acquisition alarm sounded and the first crate floated into the hold beyond the viewport. Gauvreau glanced at the rate display. "Ha! One per twenty. You broke their spirits today, Leonard. You might as well put the bay on automatic."

Damn, Kirk thought. It wasn't much but he needed that ten credits an hour. He had been stunned at the cost of transportation on the frontier. The things he had taken for granted.

Gauvreau put her hand on his shoulder as he guided the first crates around the hold. "Don't worry about the credits for this job." Kirk was surprised at how well she read him. "If you're interested, the *Shelton* needs a supercargo."

Kirk hesitated at the controls long enough for the computer to divert a crate to a holding pattern. "This ship's only a few years old, fully automated. I'm surprised she even needs a captain."

"Like I said, Leonard. She's my ship. I *own* her."

Kirk was impressed. For an individual to own and operate a warp-capable ship as large and as expensive as the *Shelton* was quite an accomplishment. Usually ships of this class were the property of interstellar consortiums who spread the cost and the risk through the financial networks of four or five worlds.

"But still," Kirk said, "with tractor webs to keep everything secure, you only need a supercargo when you're in port. And there are lots around to hire." He knew. He had spent five days waiting for employment in the dockworkers' pool at Intrator II's spacedock, suffering the indignity of paying for food, water, and oxygen.

"Look, Leonard, I'm not used to trying to talk anyone into a job on the *Shelton.* Usually I'm in the position of telling people like you why I *don't* want to sign them onboard."

Kirk could believe it. But still, there was something about her. Young for a freighter captain. Was familiar with the Siryk Variations. Knew that he had pushed too hard to handle the cargo. There were few places from which people that sharp could come. He was almost surprised that he had never heard of her before today. *Of course, she thinks my name is Leonard Scott. Who knows what her real name might be?*

"Leonard, the next stop is Hanover. Two and a half light-years toward the Arms of Avalon. At warp four we can be there in just under fifteen days."

"The *Shelton* can do warp four?"

Gauvreau looked impatient. "Yeah, and in addition to choosing my own engines, I got to pick the color of the bulkheads, too. Hanover, Leonard. Do you know it?"

Kirk thought for a moment, easily keeping up with the flow of crates into the hold. Two and a half light-years to Hanover would put him about a light-year closer to Starbase 29, without having to pay for passage. But there were still formalities, even on the frontier. "I don't have any commercial fleet certificates or proficiency papers." Not ones without his real name, at least.

Gauvreau put her hands on her hips and stared at Kirk in amazement. "Did I ask to see papers?"

"No."

"Then why be such a Herbert? Look, do you want the job or not?"

She didn't need him for the job she said she wanted him to do. But maybe it was just for the companionship. And a few games of chess. Whatever the reason, it would get him closer to where he had to go.

"I don't bite, Leonard, if that's what you're worried about."

Kirk glanced at her. *I bet you do,* he thought. *I bet you tear apart anyone and anything you think might get in the way of what you want.* He understood that attitude. He felt he knew her already.

"All right. I'll take the job."

"Well, all right."

"All right."

Gauvreau stalked to the control room doors and they opened before her. "Well, okay," she said, then left before Kirk could try again to get the last word. It was going to be an interesting two weeks.

The *Ian Shelton* was little more than an unadorned cylindrical hull with a central bridge tower stuck amidships as if it had been no more than an afterthought. A small portion of the hull contained the warp and impulse propulsion systems. The rest of it was pressurized cargo area. Five crew and passenger cabins, the life-support system, and sensor and flight computers were crammed into the tower along with a bridge that was about the same size as Kirk's cabin had been on the *Enterprise.* But, still, he preferred being on the freighter's bridge to being in any of its cabins, each of which seemed to be the same size as his storage closet had been. At least on the bridge, no matter how cramped, he could see the stars move past the viewscreen. Even if he did have to put up with the ship's cats.

At the moment, one day out from Intrator II, cruising steadily under automatic pilot at warp four, two of Captain Gauvreau's orange and black cats were sleeping together on the chair by the impulse station. The third cat was somewhere else in the ship, all levels connected by open ladderways angled enough for the cats to use them. Kirk enjoyed the cats' noninterference, however temporary it might be, and sat at the engineering station, drinking coffee, watching the stars slip past. Talin's sun was outside the sweep of the forward sensors, but Kirk knew he was drawing closer. To the planet, and the answers.

He heard clanking footsteps behind him on the ladder leading up to the bridge. Unless the missing cat was like the one he had seen on Pyris VII and had suddenly gained a great deal of mass, then it was Gauvreau coming up. She was the only other person on board.

"Thought you might be interested in a game of chess," she said as she walked onto the bridge, checking the readouts on the three crew stations. She was still wearing her flight jacket and comfortable tan and black fatigues. She also carried a small packet about the size of a book.

"We're coming up to the first course correction," Kirk said. "Thought I'd check it out, and then . . . certainly." Kirk swallowed the last of his coffee—something that had once been somewhere near a coffee bean, at least. It had come out of the galley dispenser as a small dry cube in a pressure skin and he had had to place it in a cup of hot water himself. He had never appreciated how good the synthesized blend on the *Enterprise* had been, either.

"Leonard, the computers have been making this run for the past year. If the course correction doesn't match the navigation computer's projection, then an alarm goes off. And out here, no matter which direction we go in, we're still at least a day away from hitting anything."

Kirk nodded but he didn't leave his chair. "It's my way of doing something to earn my keep."

Gauvreau shrugged, then crouched down by the chair with the cats to scratch their ears. One of the cats shifted its position to place a second ear beneath Gauvreau's fingers, but neither cat opened its eyes to acknowledge its benefactor.

Give me a dog any day, Kirk thought. But still, he knew that one of the secrets of getting along with others was to take an interest in their interests. What made the approach so easy for Kirk was that he genuinely was interested in just about everything. Even, on a slow day, cats. "They're Earth cats, aren't they?" he asked.

"That's right," Gauvreau answered, and Kirk could hear the enthusiasm in her voice. She must have clocked a lot of parsecs with her companions. "Used to be called housecats, or domestics."

Kirk had heard of barn cats on Earth. There had been a couple on the farm in Iowa. But a housecat was something else again, he thought. "Aren't housecats those creatures on Meridian that, well . . ."

"No, no, the Meridian housecats got that name because that's how big they are. And because of the, uh, unusual symbiotic relationship they have with the smaller creatures who live inside them and are necessary . . . for their . . . reproduction." One of the cats wrapped its paws around Gauvreau's hand and gave it an experimental chew. "But anyway, that's why the boys here are called Earth cats these days, to distinguish them from all the other catlike creatures everywhere else."

"Are they any particular breed or clone branch?" As a child, Kirk and his brother, Sam, had had a Golden Lab named Lady and he had always told himself that someday, when he retired, he was going to get another. Though, now, even after resigning he still woke up mornings not feeling as if he had actually left Starfleet. He wondered if he would ever feel that he had.

"No," Gauvreau said. "That's the nice part. They're an old-fashioned, natural mix. Fairly hard to get these days."

Kirk checked the navigation board. The course correction was three minutes away. "They look so much alike. That's why I thought they might have been clones."

When Lady had become too old and the vet had been called, Kirk and Sam had pleaded with their parents to clone the dog so they could have another just like her. But George Kirk had refused. Cloning was fine for livestock cultures and transplant parts, he had told his sons, but an individual couldn't be treated like property. Their pet must be respected, and mourning her death would show that respect. The vet had eased Lady's discomfort and let her slip peacefully beyond all pain. Both boys had cried off and on for days.

It had been years before Kirk had realized what his father had been trying to teach him that day—how the fact that each person's life will end in death made life so precious. Since there could be no ultimate victory, Kirk had finally understood that what gave life meaning was the struggle. What few victories might come along the way could only be brief respites.

Fifteen years ago, on the *Farragut,* Captain Garrovick and more than two hundred crew had died horribly, red blood cells drained from their bodies, because of what Kirk had believed to have been a mistake on his part. It was remembering what his father had said the night Lady had died that had, in part, given him the strength he had needed not to leave Starfleet then, overcome by personal failure. The past must be accepted, the dead remembered, but the mission must always continue.

More than a decade later, on the *Enterprise,* Kirk had finally realized that he had not contributed to the *Farragut*'s tragedy. His only regret about the incident now was that his understanding of his father's lesson had come too late for him to thank George Kirk. But he could accept that situation, with sadness certainly, but without guilt or regret, because it was in the past. It was the present he was at war with, and always would be.

Gauvreau hit a spot on one of the cat's sides which made him roll onto his back, paws kneading the air. "You can't clone a pet," she said, and her voice was wistful, almost as if she also shared a moment like Kirk's in her past.

"What are their names?" Kirk asked, trying to break the solemn mood they had both succumbed to.

"Ah, this is Komack, this is Fitzpatrick, and Nogura is below decks sleeping on the mass converter."

Kirk stopped to play the names back for himself again, to be certain he had heard them correctly. "Komack, Fitzpatrick . . . and Nogura?"

Gauvreau smiled, one of her secrets revealed.

Kirk realized that one of his secrets had been revealed as well because of the way he had reacted to the names. "How long were you in Starfleet?" The cats were each named after an admiral.

"Twenty-one years," Gauvreau said, a hint of sadness returning to her voice.

"Twenty-*one?*" Kirk asked. Full retirement benefits were available after twenty years of service. Personnel generally retired then or not at all.

"Took me an extra year to figure out that I wasn't going to get what I wanted."

Kirk looked into Gauvreau's eyes. He didn't have to ask the next question. He knew the answer.

"One of these," she said, tapping her fist against the impulse control console. "Of my own."

"So you bought one."

Gauvreau nodded. "Not quite what I had in mind back when I was eight years old and decided what I wanted to do with my life. But at least she's mine. And Komack, Fitzpatrick, and Nogura can't say a thing about it."

"What was your rank?" Kirk asked. He found it surprising that a person with Gauvreau's qualities hadn't made it to command rank. He realized that's why he found her so familiar. She reminded him of himself.

"Commander."

Kirk was puzzled. She *had* made it to command rank. "There are more than a thousand ships in Starfleet." Why wasn't she given one?

Gauvreau stood up beside the cats. "At the time I left, there were only thirteen that mattered."

"Ahh," Kirk said. She was *exactly* like him.

"I exec-ed on the *Yorktown* for Decker. That gave me a taste of it. When he transferred to the *Constellation,* I was certain I'd get his chair. I knew the ship, had the ratings, the recs, and the experience. But they brought in von Holtzbrinck. They offered me the *Hawking,* instead."

Kirk nodded in understanding. The *Hawking* was a science vessel with a crew of just over one hundred and, as such, its mission was restricted to worlds without intelligent life, or which had already been exposed to the Federation. Science vessels either withdrew from critical situations so a starship could take over, or came in to complete follow-up studies of what a starship had already discovered. For a scientist or technical specialist, it was a near-perfect posting, offering the chance for lengthy and detailed analysis. But for an explorer, it was equivalent to being condemned to perpetual second place.

"I protested," Gauvreau went on, watching the stars on the viewscreen.

Gutsy, thought Kirk.

"I sent subspace memos to every starbase, and to Command, demanding a review."

Bordering on madness.

"And, 'after due consideration, blah, blah, blah,' nothing changed." She turned back to Kirk. "Decker said he'd take me with him to the *Constellation.* But being second . . . again. And as things turned out, maybe I did do the right thing by not going with him. Decker was a good officer. A good man."

The *Constellation*'s entire crew had been lost. Decker had destroyed both himself and his ship to avenge them. He had been Kirk's friend. "I know," Kirk said. And then added, "I was, uh, in Starfleet, too," to cover his slip.

Gauvreau stared at him, as if making a decision. "I know you were, Captain Kirk."

Kirk sat rigid, prepared for another angry confrontation. They were a day out from anywhere, two weeks still to go to Hanover. If Gauvreau was another like those he had encountered among the rockriggers, if she not only accepted what had been said about him but believed he had not been punished enough. . . . "How long have you known?" No sense in denying it. He had to come up with a strategy for overpowering her without hurting her. If it came to that.

"Since I saw you in the dockworkers' pool. There was some subspace chatter about you being caught rockrigging for Interworld, so there was a good chance you were still in the neighborhood."

Kirk had the sudden terrible feeling that she had been looking for him, and had brought him onboard the *Shelton* for a reason. He stared at his empty coffee cup. It had tasted so bad. So wrong. What did she want with him? What were her motives?

"So what happens now?" Kirk asked.

"First of all, you relax. I'm not a one-person recycler mob."

"Then what are you? Why 'hire' me?"

"To get you closer to Talin."

Kirk showed his surprise.

"That is where you're going." She made it a statement.

"Why do you say that?"

"Because that's what I'd do." She didn't wait for him to ask more questions. "Look, I know you, Kirk. At least, I know your type. You're like me—the kind of officer that gives the Admiralty their gray hairs. You've got to be resourceful and inventive enough to run the show when you're weeks away from getting advice and orders from Starfleet Command. But when you get those orders, you have to be the kind of person who'll follow them, even if you don't agree. It's an almost impossible mix. Like matter and antimatter. Starfleet has to be the magnetic bottle and you know how tricky those can be to keep properly aligned."

"What's your point, Captain?" Kirk was getting edgy. He hated not knowing what her motives were.

"My point is, whatever else you might be—maverick, impetuous, stubborn—and all those other things starship captains have to be, you're not a worldkiller. I know what you had to go through to get the *Enterprise.*" She held up two fingers, a centimeter apart. "I know what I went through to get even this close to a starship of my own. And I know the system doesn't let maniacs get that close, or go so far. For all that I have my reservations about Starfleet, even I have to admit the system works."

"It didn't give you your ship." Kirk wondered how much of what she said was the truth as she believed it, and how much was her trying to set him up for some other purpose.

"Thirteen starships, Captain Kirk, fifteen, maybe sixteen now, and how many thousands of would-be captains in Starfleet? I had my chance. I got close. And the same system that funnels us all through to one of those fifteen or sixteen chairs doesn't tend to produce officers who'd be happy to settle with second best, or with command of the *Hawking.*"

"I still don't understand." On the viewscreen, the stars shifted slightly to port as the navigation system carried out the planned course correction. The change in heading was smooth, the inertial dampers kept the ship feeling motionless. "If the system works as well as you say, then why don't you accept what the hearing on Talin concluded?"

Gauvreau sat at the navigation station to check the new course. As her fingers worked the controls, swiftly, almost instinctively—the legacy of her Starfleet training—she kept talking. "I accept most of the hearing's conclusions. Talin IV was a living, civilized world, a few decades at most from First Contact. The *Enterprise* went to the Talin system and . . . within five days Talin IV was a graveyard for an entire civilization."

"But you don't accept that it was my fault?"

Gauvreau looked over from the board. "Do you?"

"No." The word hung in the silence of the small bridge like a proclamation from the heavens. There was no equivocation in it, no hesitation or hint of qualification.

Gauvreau smiled at him. "Then why be surprised that I think the same thing?"

"Because Starfleet Command thinks otherwise."

"And you know what I think about Command. I said the system works. It's the current Admiralty I have trouble with." She turned in her chair and leaned forward. "Look, Kirk, don't be so defensive. I'm on your side. That's why I brought you onboard, all right? I figured you might need a couple of days of not feeling that the whole galaxy was trying to track you down. I figured if you were already out so far in this sector, then you'd probably appreciate getting another parsec or two closer to Talin."

Kirk watched the stars. He asked himself what he would have done if, after the Battle of Ghioghe, Starfleet had reassigned him to another patrol ship instead of giving him the *Enterprise.* Would he have stuck it out in a second-place command,

226 Judith & Garfield Reeves-Stevens

hoping for another chance, knowing that once Command had made up its collective mind, an officer's career path might as well be etched in dichronium? Or would he have done what Gauvreau had done? Left Starfleet and taken command another way? He chuckled suddenly, surprised by the answer that came to mind.

"You changed the rules," he said.

"I beg your pardon?"

"The scenario Command laid out for you didn't suit you, so you changed the conditions of the game." He looked around the bridge. "And you won."

Gauvreau grimaced. "In a manner of speaking. This isn't the *Yorktown.*"

"But it isn't the *Hawking,* either." Kirk took a closer look at the bridge, suddenly becoming aware of the subtle thrum of the Cochrane generator far below decks, and the gentle airflow of the life-support circulators. If the cards Starfleet had dealt him had not included command of a starship when he felt the time was right, instead of lose their game, he would have refused to play it. And he would have ended up here on the *Ian Shelton,* or a ship just like her. A winner by the only rules that counted—his own.

"We *are* alike," Kirk admitted. Because he knew if their roles had been reversed and Gauvreau had been cast out and he had been a commercial captain who could offer her a few days of rest, then he would. Not to gloat over Starfleet's failure or another person's misfortune. But because he and Gauvreau were . . . family. Two members of an exceedingly small family in an extremely large galaxy.

"Good," Gauvreau said. She tossed over the small packet she had carried up to the bridge. Kirk opened it. It was a manual grooming kit. "Thought you might like to wide beam the beard. Subspace visual's carrying tape from the Interworld rock so it's not much of a disguise anymore. I don't have a grooming booth on board but I can handle your hair, if you want."

Kirk scratched at his beard. There was no point in hiding behind it any longer. Not this close to his destination. "Thank you," he said.

"But . . . ?" Gauvreau asked, detecting the question building in him.

"How can you be so sure about me? You don't have the slightest idea about what really happened on Talin IV."

Gauvreau turned back to the navigation board. "But I will, won't I? If I were you, I'd want someone else to know the whole story. And I tell you, Kirk, fourteen days in space on an automated ship is a long, long time."

Not as long as my five days at Talin IV, Kirk thought. But Gauvreau was right. It was time to tell his story.

PART TWO

The Last Mission

One

Captain's Log, Supplemental. We are in the third day of our approach to Starfleet's First Contact Office outpost on the moon of Talin IV. Our slow travel toward the Talin system has been mandated by the FCO because of the planet's old-style radio astronomy capability. Though Talin astronomers could not visually detect the Enterprise *at this distance from their planet, Starfleet does not want to risk the possibility that they might observe the radiation effects of dust and debris being swept from our path by our deflector shields at high-impulse velocities. Such anomalous signals might alert the Talin to the fact that an alien spacecraft is moving through their system at an appreciable percentage of lightspeed, which would, of course, be a violation of the Prime Directive. Thus we must travel at a velocity slow enough that our deflectors are not needed.*

Sulu has done an admirable job of piloting the ship at speeds far less than those any of us are used to. For some of the crew, the past three days of standby duty and communications blackout have been a welcome break. However, other crew members are . . .

In the privacy of his cabin, Kirk tapped his desk screen to shut off the log recording. Somehow, the phrase "crawling the walls" was not one he wished to consign to the permanence of an official log. Besides, as far as he could tell, he was the only crew member having trouble coping with the forced inactivity of this present assignment. Even Chekov showed no signs of edginess at having less than his normal double duty load to contend with. Perhaps he had been spending too much time with Mr. Spock and was acquiring a most uncharacteristic patience. Or maybe the old Academy legends were true and the ship's doctor *was* putting something into the water supply to keep everyone . . . tranquil.

Kirk told the computer to get him sickbay and Christine Chapel appeared on the captain's screen.

"Yes, Captain?"

"Put McCoy on." *What a starship needs is a bar,* Kirk thought. *A nice lounge somewhere, maybe forward where there'd be a good view, a few tables, a place to go and relax off duty.* Perhaps he'd suggest it in his next report. Starfleet Command was always looking for new ways to extend the mission time of their ships and a social gathering place might be a welcome addition to the ship's recreation facilities.

"The doctor's not in, Captain. Is there something—"

"Not in?" Even when he was off duty, McCoy was generally in his office, reviewing files, or reading the journals.

"He's at the A and A briefing, sir. Shall I get him for you?"

"No, that's fine, Nurse. It wasn't important." Kirk reached out to shut down the screen again.

"Excuse me, Captain. Just while I have you on the screen, according to our records, you're still overdue for that physical and perhaps—"

"Not now, Nurse Chapel. Try me later."

"But, Captain . . ."

"Thank you, Nurse." Kirk signed off and sighed. He drummed his fingers against his desk. Two more days of this. He told the computer to get him the bridge.

This time, Ensign Leslie appeared on the screen. "Bridge here."

"Where's Uhura?" Not the most pleasant way to greet a crew member, Kirk knew, but after all, this *was* Uhura's duty cycle.

Leslie looked nervous. "Uh, with the communications blackout, sir, she said . . . she said that there was no point in staying at her station, so she assigned me to monitor for emergency signals."

Kirk was surprised but decided he couldn't take Mr. Leslie to task for Uhura's actions. He knew he himself had set the precedent that allowed most bridge specialists on his ship to choose for themselves when their work could be better performed at other locations in the ship. But that flexibility really couldn't extend to essential personnel such as helm and navigation—and he had never thought of communications as anything other than equally essential. *Except, perhaps, during a communications blackout.*

"Tell me, Mr. Leslie, where *is* Lieutenant Uhura?"

"Uh, I believe she's at the A and A briefing, sir. I could call her—"

"That's all right, mister. I'll . . . have a talk with her later. Get me Spock, please."

"Um, Mr. Spock is not on the bridge either, sir."

This time, Kirk was more than surprised. "We're traveling into a system we've never visited before and Spock isn't at the science station?" *Has everyone decided to take the day off?*

"Sir, the FCO has spent eight years surveying the Talin system in considerable detail and since we can't use our main sensors because of the blackout . . . well, almost all the science departments are shut down for maintenance."

Kirk sighed again. "I see. And would you happen to know where Mr. Spock is?"

"Yes, sir. He's attending the A—"

"—and A briefing. Why not? Everyone else is. Tell me, is there *anyone* on the bridge other than you?"

The ensign looked puzzled for a moment. "Well, uh, Dr. M'Benga is here, and—"

Kirk felt a welcome rush of adrenaline. "What's the doctor doing on the bridge? Has there been an accident?" Kirk jumped up by his desk, ready to run for the turbolift.

"No, sir," Leslie answered calmly. "Nothing like that. It's just that . . ." He looked away from the screen for a moment. "Well, since we're not traveling that fast, Mr. Sulu is sort of letting everyone try—"

Kirk held up his hands. "Don't tell me. I don't want to know." One of his worst nightmares had come true: The *Enterprise* had turned into a cruise ship.

The viewscreen flashed over to the helm station. Sulu was just sitting down. M'Benga stood behind him, looking sheepish. "Sulu here, Captain. Everything's under control, sir."

"I'm glad you think so."

"Really, sir. Helm and navigation are supposed to be part of the emergency preparedness program, but it's not too often that we get the conditions where regulations allow EPP trainees on the controls. And at this speed and heading, sir, believe me, we've got those conditions."

It's not going to be one of those days, Kirk thought. *It's going to be one of those months.* "I have the utmost faith in you, Mr. Sulu."

"Thank you, Captain."

"Just one question."

"Go ahead, sir."

"Why aren't *you* at the A and A briefing?"

Sulu smiled. "I lost the toss to Chekov, sir."

"I see. Well, carry on, Mr. Sulu—or should I say, Dr. M'Benga. Just try not to hit anything . . . like a planet."

M'Benga leaned down to bring himself within range of the helm communication scanner. He adopted his best, serious-physician demeanor and spoke gravely. "I'll *try,* Captain." Then he and Sulu broke into wide grins.

Kirk waved his hand at the screen, searching for the words, any words, to show that he could go along with their joke. He knew his crew already suspected that the past three days had turned their captain into a high-strung worrier and there was no need to give them additional ammunition. But he couldn't think of anything to add that they wouldn't take the wrong way. "Kirk out," he said in defeat, and the screen shut off. *At least morale is high,* Kirk thought. *Everyone else's that is.*

He spent a minute or two staring at the walls of his cabin until they seemed to be moving in on him and that's when he knew he had had enough. "When on Centaurus," he muttered, and then left his cabin to attend the A & A briefing.

Lieutenant Carolyn Palamas had been the ship's A & A officer from the start of the five-year mission. In that time, Kirk could remember her accompanying him on a handful of landing parties, most notably the near-disastrous return mission to Avalon and the run-in with million-year-old warrior robots at the Asteroid Tessel excavations. She had also been present on Pollux IV when the *Enterprise* had encountered an alien who might well have been known to ancient humans as the Greek god, Apollo. In short, she had served competently during a wide range of experiences typical for a starship crew member. She was also an attractive, blond-haired and blue-eyed human, and well-liked by her staff and crew. Especially by Scotty a few years back, Kirk recalled, though nothing had come of it.

But even so, Kirk was hard pressed to understand why almost one hundred other crew members had turned up in the ship's theater for the lieutenant's briefing on Talin IV. It seemed rather unusual that so many of the *Enterprise* crew shared a passion for Palamas's specialty: anthropology and archaeology.

When Kirk entered the theater, he had to silently refuse a dozen crew members who offered to give him their seats. He preferred to lean against one of the back walls. At least there he could sneak out again if the presentation wasn't interesting. He noticed Spock sitting off to the side in the second row, close to the podium in the center of the stage. Surprisingly, McCoy was sitting beside him. Every few seconds, Kirk could see the two officers whispering back and forth. McCoy was even looking pleased with himself. Kirk reminded himself to get in on whatever was going on between the two later, then settled back to listen to the lieutenant.

"Coming up on the screen right now is a computer composite of a typical set of Talin IV's dominant intelligent species." Palamas touched a control on her podium and a detailed, political and cartographic display of Talin IV was replaced by an image of two reddish-skinned adults and one green-skinned child. Lying beside them was what appeared to be an incompletely formed larval version of a Talin. However, according to the scale grid, the softly rounded, pale white form was the same size as the two adults on the screen—about two and a half meters high.

The adults' faces were each the shape of a smoothly curving, forward sloping egg, sliced through the bottom third by a wide, lipless mouth which opened and shut, revealing an upper and lower row of small, sharp teeth. Kirk could see no nostrils as such, unless they were somehow incorporated into the asymmetrical hearing membranes on either side of the head, near where the jaw pivoted. Each adult's face was dominated by a pair of large, yellow eyes, perhaps twice the size of a human's and dotted by small black central pupils. The child's face had less slope, no teeth, and much larger eyes.

Palamas then rotated the computer composites through a full four hundred degrees. The images moved to show the mobility and gait of the Talins' long arms and legs. As he studied the images, Kirk noticed that each adult wore a biblike covering that hung from a loop of fabric around its neck, continuing down to another loop that slipped between the legs to hook over a small protuberance at the end of the spine. He guessed it was a vestigial tail.

"As you can see," Palamas explained to her attentive audience, "the Talin are saurian bipeds, though completely different in body structure from the Gornaran archosaurs. Instead, the Talin share some of the characteristics of Earth lizards and birds, notably in the loose folds of pebbly-textured skin and the thin and delicate skeletal structure. As is typical on more than ninety percent of class-M planets, there are two sexes on Talin IV and the female parent carries the live young to term. Preliminary fauna sampling runs indicate that the evolutionary predecessors of the Talin were egg-laying."

An ensign wearing a red support-services shirt raised her hand and Palamas nodded at her. "Is that what the fourth figure on the screen shows? An egg casing? It looks so large."

"No, but that's a good question. What we're looking at here is an adult hibernation cocoon. Apparently, it's an evolutionary artifact from the Talin's predecessor species. Many equatorial life-forms on the planet continue to exude a moisture-impervious substance which hardens into a protective shell. The creatures undergo this type of sealed-in hibernation during the extreme seasonal variations when water virtually disappears from the planet's equatorial deserts. The Talin themselves still retain this capability, though because of their relatively advanced technology—including extensive irrigation projects, climate-controlled housing, and efficient agriculture—a hibernation cocoon like this one is rarely seen among the Talin except in cases of extreme trauma or illness. Indeed, in most of the major nation states, there is a cultural prejudice against it—almost as if it's a reminder of their bestial past. We have noticed that in their popular entertainment, references to the hibernation cocoon and the distinctive odor of the skin secretion which forms it are usually at the level of what we would call crude humor."

"How can you tell male from female?" another crew member asked. Kirk looked again at the image on the screen and though both adult figures were virtually identical, he decided the male was probably the adult with the more pronounced cranial crest—it seemed to be composed of thick tufts of hair about ten centimeters high which ran in a stripe from the center of the head along the extended neck, getting shorter until it vanished about halfway down the creature's back. The other adult's crest was only half as high and disappeared on the neck, not the back. Of course, Kirk had seen enough different lifeforms in his career that he wouldn't be surprised if the male turned out to be the small, green, childlike figure.

"Another good question," Palamas said. "There are few obvious body structure differences and, among Talin themselves, the chief distinction seems to involve odor. The FCO suspects that pheromones are also involved, though Talin biologists have not yet formalized the concept of hormones that act outside the body, so there is no real literature or transmissions Starfleet can study." Palamas continued, looking back at the screen. "Other sex-related differences are the range of colors through which the skin can change, similar to that of the Vulcan askor or the Earth chameleon. Males can color change further into the red spectrum; females change further into the blue. Again, color changing might be far more complex than it appears to be in just the visible spectrum, but the Talin haven't investigated this so we can't know for sure, ourselves.

"Now, as you can see here, Talin children start out green and, as they mature, slowly acquire the ability to change skin color. We believe the whole phenomenon involves a mixture of conscious and autonomic control, somewhat similar to our own breathing process. The FCO doesn't claim to have a great understanding of the importance of skin-color changing—timing, setting, taboos, and so on—because it is somehow closely related to pair bonding and mating. As I've said, the Talin are very similar to humans circa 1975 to 2000 C.E., and that extends to their cultural reluctance to discuss or depict the details of their mating habits in broadcast transmissions or any publications intended for wide release. Unfortunately, those are the only data sources the FCO has been able to study in detail thus far."

"That's only because the *Enterprise* hasn't gotten there yet!" someone called out and the audience cheered and broke into applause. Kirk smiled at their enthusiasm. According to the report he had received along with his orders, one of the *Enterprise*'s functions on this mission would be to place FCO intrusive-collection specialists into important data-collection sites to extract more detailed information than was currently available.

Palamas glanced at the screenpad on her podium as the applause died down, then said, "Well, that's about all the time we have for today, so—yes, Dr. McCoy?"

McCoy stood up beside Spock. "Just one last question, Lieutenant. You say the Talin are similar to humans in the last quarter of the twentieth century?"

"That's right."

Kirk saw Spock whisper something to McCoy, but McCoy ignored him. "In other words, they're showing great promise in technology, they're on the brink of stepping out into space, they've achieved global communications, and have made a start at conquering most major diseases."

Palamas thought the doctor's words over for a moment. "Well, yes, in general, I'd say that is the case."

McCoy raised a finger and Kirk could see that he was winding up for the kill.

"And, just to clarify things, these creatures do have emotions, don't they? I mean, they don't try to hide them or anything?"

Kirk could see Palamas take a quick look at Spock. "They're not Andorians, Dr. McCoy, but the Talin do have a complex range of emotions, of which most are incorporated into their culture in an open and accepted manner."

McCoy smiled at Spock. "Thank you, Lieutenant. Great achievements. Openly emotional. I just wanted to make sure I was clear on that."

As McCoy sat back down, Spock stood up.

"Yes, Mr. Spock?" Palamas asked. Kirk could see she knew she was not going to be able to get away easily. After almost five years onboard the *Enterprise,* most of the original crew knew that when McCoy and Spock were involved in one of their "discussions," the best place to be was on another ship. Or in another sector.

"A further point of clarification, if you please, Lieutenant. Is not one of the main points of comparison between the contemporary Talin and late-twentieth-century humans the fact that Talin is currently poised on the brink of a devastating thermonuclear war between several of its most advanced nation states?"

Kirk knew he wouldn't have to ask what Spock and McCoy had been discussing during the briefing. Their questions were making it all too obvious.

"That's correct, sir," Palamas acknowledged. The fragile stability of Talin was one of the chief reasons for the urgency of the *Enterprise*'s current assignment.

"And furthermore," Spock continued, "is it not true that the root cause of the conflict between the Talin nations is based not on need but on ideological differences?"

"As far as we can ascertain, that's also correct, yes, sir."

"Ideological differences that could best be described as . . . emotional in nature?"

But McCoy wasn't going down without a fight. "You're joking, Spock. You can't honestly believe that a debate that's been going on for a century between all the different sides on Talin is an *emotional* conflict?"

Vulcans had emotions, they just didn't permit those emotions to show in public or allow them to control their actions. But Kirk suspected that the bland expression on Spock's face as he looked down at McCoy was really an unbridled display of Vulcan superiority. "Dr. McCoy, the histories of a thousand worlds offer ample proof that, at root, virtually all political conflicts are emotional in nature, no matter how well-disguised they are by ideological rhetoric."

"Good Lord, Spock, the Talin are arguing over who has the right to educate their children, who controls the water resources, at what regional level government responsibilities should be—"

"Doctor, the Talin are arguing over who is bigger and better. Everything else is beside the point."

McCoy folded his arms against his chest. "Well, at least you're the right one to be discussing *points.*"

"Doctor, I fail to see—"

Palamas leaned closer to the sound pickup on the podium so her amplified voice overpowered Spock's. "We're out of time for now, so I'd like to thank you all for your attendance today. Tomorrow, I'll continue with an overview of a few of the unique characteristics of the Talin and their planet which has made applying the Richter Scale of Culture so simple. For a change." The large viewscreen above Palamas shut down and the audience broke into appreciative applause, drowning out McCoy's reply to Spock's unheard statement.

Kirk moved against the flow of people leaving the theater so he could join Spock and McCoy. Both officers were now in a private discussion with Palamas at the podium as she gathered up her screenpad and microtapes. As Kirk approached, he heard her saying something about "the MAD deterrence."

"MAD?" Kirk asked as he stepped up behind McCoy and Spock.

"Mutual assured destruction," Palamas said. "Each of the belligerent nation states on Talin possesses enough fusion weapons and appropriate delivery systems to totally annihilate its adversary, no matter which side attacks first. The MAD theory, as it was called when it was developed on Earth, presumed that since there was no advantage to striking first, then peace would be maintained. Or at least, conflict would not escalate past the point of no return."

"A typically human theory," Spock commented.

McCoy leaned past Kirk to glower at the science officer. "It worked on Earth, Spock."

Spock raised an eyebrow. "For approximately sixty years, Doctor. Until your Colonel Green decided quite emotionally, and quite illogically, that there *would* be an advantage—"

Kirk held up his hand. "Gentlemen, I don't think we have to give the A and A officer a rundown on Earth history." He smiled at Palamas. He had forgotten how brilliantly blue-gray her eyes were.

"Thank you, Captain," the lieutenant said. "And actually, both Dr. McCoy and Mr. Spock are correct."

McCoy bowed his head. "Why, thank you, Lieutenant."

"She said we were *both* correct," Spock emphasized.

"How so?" Kirk asked.

"Historical records from the time do show that at particular times of tension, the leaders of Earth's nation states made the decision not to commit fusion weapons to a conflict because they feared the resultant escalation of hostilities would lead to a conflict in which both sides would be destroyed. Therefore, when both sides are perceived by each other to be evenly matched, then the MAD deterrence can be said to be effective."

"The key word being 'perceived,' " Kirk put in.

Spock nodded. "As soon as one side in a conflict determines that it has an advantage over the other—at the time of Colonel Green, it was Hanson Smith's surprise development of the particle curtain ten years earlier than the scientific community thought possible—then there is a benefit to be had in striking first, before the sides can be equalized again."

McCoy put his hand on Kirk's shoulder to prevent the captain from interrupting. "But Spock, even the Third World War didn't involve the use of fusion weapons. Surely that means that *something* was working."

"Doctor, the Eugenics Wars of the 1990s were not called such by historians until three decades after the fact. There was so much upheaval in your world at the time, that few, if any, of the general population were aware that the struggle between the so-called genetic supermen was actually going on behind the scenes. Only with the revelations made possible by the passage of years did Earth historians decide to reclassify key events. Because of those reclassifications, your Second World War was deemed to finally end in the early 1990s with the events immediately following arbitrarily being called the Third World War. But you are quite right in that it was not an open conflict of munitions and armies. It was a hidden and secretive conflict of science and politics. And, I need not add, of emotions."

Palamas smiled in conciliation at McCoy. "I'm afraid he has you there, Doctor. But who knows? In another hundred years, we could have new interpretations."

"History is history," McCoy grumbled.

"And it's written by the winner," Kirk said. Then, before either Spock or McCoy could continue, "But tell me, Lieutenant, is the situation on Talin actually that precarious? I know that what I saw in the FCO report was alarming, but we've seen dozens of worlds successfully pass through tense political situations. And the Talin cultures do appear to be stable."

Palamas frowned. "We have also seen dozens of worlds fail to survive situations similar to what Talin is experiencing, Captain. I think that's why the crew has become so caught up in our mission to Talin IV."

"Please, let me get those." Kirk reached out to take the screenpad and collection of microtape wafers from Palamas. He ignored the look that McCoy and Spock thought they exchanged without him seeing. If he was being obvious, then at least his actions wouldn't be misinterpreted. "And perhaps, Lieutenant, you'd like to continue this conversation over a drink in Dr. McCoy's cabin." With Scott still working overtime to get the sensor satellites adjusted to the FCO's specifications, that's where the best liquid refreshments aboard were to be found.

"Thank you, Captain, Doctor. I'd enjoy that." But she didn't relinquish any of the items she was carrying. "And I can carry my own books home from school, thanks anyway."

Kirk ignored her words and focused instead on the smile she had given him. Two more days without too much to do might be pleasant after all, provided he had someone to share them with. As he led Palamas, Spock, and McCoy from the theater, he said, "You were explaining to us why you thought the crew was so involved with our mission, Lieutenant."

"There are a number of factors, Captain. I think we're all hoping that the Talin will survive their present difficulties, the way Earth did. And since the majority of the crew is from Earth and Earth colonies, there is definitely a sense of personal involvement."

Kirk walked toward the theater doors without breaking stride and they swept open before him. "To be fair, Lieutenant, I've yet to see a mission that this crew didn't get personally involved with."

"Well, yes, sir. The crew is an extremely committed group. But . . ."

"Go on, please," Kirk said as they moved through the corridors toward the turbolift.

"I think some of the crew are hoping that this might turn into a first contact mission, sir."

Spock stopped almost as quickly as Kirk. McCoy took a few more steps before he realized he was walking by himself.

Kirk frowned. "Why would anyone think we're on a first contact mission?" The *Enterprise* had seen her share of first contacts with other civilizations, but most had been the inevitable meetings between spacefaring explorers. The Talin had barely left the orbit of their own planet and were firmly under the jurisdiction of the FCO.

Palamas shrugged. "Reading between the lines of the FCO report on the political situation on Talin, sir, there is a better than fifty percent chance that they will become involved in an all-out fusion war within the next six months."

"Sixty-four point five percent," Spock said.

"What does that have to do with anything?" Kirk asked.

Palamas looked embarrassed. "Well, sir. Membership in the Federation has been shown to have a . . . calming influence on a planet's regional disputes. Some of the crew feel, that . . . perhaps to save the Talin—"

"We'd reveal ourselves?" Kirk was astounded.

"Well, yes, sir. Something like that."

Kirk turned to Spock. "Spock, according to the FCO projections, when might the Talin be expected to be able to learn that there are several spacefaring cultures in their vicinity?"

"Apparently, Talin IV does have some unique characteristics which make a precise time difficult to calculate, Captain, but at the minimum estimation, the Talin are at least twenty to thirty standard years from achieving the required technological breakthroughs."

Kirk looked back at Palamas. "Twenty to thirty years, Lieutenant. Whoever makes first contact with the Talin, it won't be us. And I'm surprised the crew isn't more aware of General Order Number One."

"Oh, they're aware, Captain Kirk. A lot of them just can't see the point of non-interference if it means an entire race might die."

McCoy stepped closer. "You can't blame them for hoping, Jim. It's not easy for any one of us to just stand back and watch a disaster unfolding. And I'd guess that you know that as much as anyone onboard."

"Captain," Palamas said, "I know that there is no member of this crew who is planning on doing anything other than his or her duty on this mission. It's just that given the severity of the situation, they think that Starfleet and the Federation Council might make an exception to the Prime Directive."

Spock placed his hands behind his back. "As soon as an exception is made, Lieutenant, it is no longer the Prime Directive. As a historian, you should be aware of the tragedies that inevitably result when a more powerful culture attempts to set standards for those that cannot stand against it. The Federation flourishes because it is founded on the principles of informed choice and cooperation among equals. We cannot presume to have either the moral or ethical right to proclaim what other cultures should do until they have achieved a level of development sufficient enough to consider what we have to offer as equals. They must be free to turn us down, without feeling forced to capitulate in order to gain our advanced technology and knowledge. For those reasons, among many others, it is a most logical and necessary position."

Kirk could see the fire building in the lieutenant's eyes as she listened to Spock's lecture. "But as a historian, Mr. Spock, I am also aware that it was an uncrewed Vulcan robot probe that prevented a cometary fragment from wiping out half of central Europe in the early 1900s, by diverting the body to explode over an uninhabited region of Siberia. That changed the future history of the entire planet."

"That incident," said Spock, "was a preventable natural disaster, not in any way caused by the humans of the time. The Prime Directive explicitly directs us to protect emerging cultures from similar disasters, provided we do not reveal ourselves. Indeed, the *Enterprise* herself has done so many times in the past."

Palamas was not up to debating Spock. In fact, Kirk decided, there was no one onboard who was. The only reason McCoy kept trying was because he didn't know any better. Upset now, but trying not to let it show, the lieutenant conceded the argument. "I do think a case could be made for treating an unthinkable war as a natural disaster of the worst kind, but a Starfleet lieutenant is not the person to do it, Mr. Spock. It's just that I shall be very sad if we are forced to do nothing as we witness an entire race commit suicide."

"As shall I, Lieutenant," Spock said, and Kirk knew it was a rare admission for him to make to someone he did not know well.

Palamas watched Spock for a moment, as if realizing what it took for the Vulcan half of him to comment on his feelings, then nodded at Kirk. "I think I'll pass on that drink for now, Captain. I . . . have to prepare for tomorrow's briefing."

It was Kirk's turn to concede. It was apparent he would not be spending the next few hours in her company and he would not dream of trying to change her mind. "I'll look forward to hearing it," he said graciously.

Palamas said her good-byes, then headed back down the corridor, away from the lift.

McCoy watched her go, unconsciously duplicating Spock's pose by placing his hands behind his back as well. "Well, at least someone on this ship has feelings about our job."

Spock's face remained in its habitual, neutral expression. "And at least she does not allow those feelings to interfere with the proper performance of it."

Kirk saw McCoy and Spock narrow their eyes at each other, preparing to launch into yet another round. "Gentlemen, I believe we were headed to the doctor's cabin," he said to interrupt them. "Perhaps we can continue our discussion of ancient history there." He began walking toward the turbolift and heard McCoy and Spock fall into step behind him in silence. For the moment, peace had returned to his ship, even though he knew it wouldn't last. Because Lieutenant Palamas wouldn't be the only crew member who would be upset if the *Enterprise* were forced to do nothing but watch as a world destroyed itself.

But it won't come to that, Kirk told himself. *It can't come to that.*

He was a starship captain.

He would not allow it.

Two

Of all the strange and miraculous discoveries humans had made in their expansion into space, perhaps none had been as initially unexpected as the revelation that life was literally everywhere.

That knowledge had grown slowly with each step outward that humans had taken: life on Earth; fossils on Mars; spaceborne organisms blowing in the solar wind; plant analogues on Titan; and then the *Icarus*'s surprising first contact with the Centaurans and the subsequent discovery of all the other spacefaring civilizations.

At first, the realization that the *absence* of life was the exception to the rule was greeted with doubt and disbelief. There was maddeningly inconclusive evidence to suggest that perhaps some planets had been deliberately seeded by an ancient and more advanced race, unofficially known as the Preservers, and that, as a result, the natural incidence of independently arisen life could never be known. But, more often than not, detailed bioanalyses demonstrated that life was an almost inevitable by-product of planetary development throughout the galaxy. And since planets themselves had been shown to be a virtually inevitable by-product of stellar formation, contemporary scientists were more surprised *not* to find life than to find new forms around any given star.

The other startling discovery about life, which was also accepted as an inevitable by-product of universal principles throughout the galaxy, was the degree of evolutionary congruence it exhibited. If a planet had a thick enough atmosphere, then it had creatures that could fly. If it had free water, then it had creatures that could swim and extract oxygen through gill-like structures. And if a planet had existed peacefully for enough millennia without major extinctions or drastic ecological upheavals, then as surely as dilithium crystals extended into the fourth dimension, that planet would give rise to intelligent life. According to the latest Federation estimates, there were millions of such planets existing in the galaxy, and to contemplate the hundreds of millions of other galaxies wheeling beyond the great barrier surrounding the Milky Way was to experience a sense of wonder about life which could overwhelm even the orderly minds of Vulcans.

But there was more than wonder and new scientific knowledge accompanying the Federation's realization of the universality of intelligent life, there was also the burden of great responsibility. Because, for every civilization which was more advanced than those making up the Federation, there were a hundred which were less so. And every one of those less-advanced worlds would, in time, have been overwhelmed by the Federation's superior technological culture and well-intentioned aid and enlightenment—unless drastic measures were taken.

Thus, for the good of intergalactic peace, to acknowledge the uniqueness of each culture without prejudice, and in recognition that each intelligent life-form must be free to choose its own future, the Federation created its most severe, most troublesome, yet most honorable and sacred commandment: Starfleet's General Order Number One.

The principle was this: The Federation would never allow itself to act as judge and jury to a developing alien culture. Only when cultures had developed to an appropriate point where they could withstand exposure to an interstellar community would they be informed of the Federation's existence.

To set conditions of development, to monitor emerging civilizations, and, when conditions were right, to break the conspiracy of silence, the worlds of the Federation authorized Starfleet to form one of its most important branches. It was called Starfleet's First Contact Office, and the beings who ran it, above all else, were the keepers of the Prime Directive.

With more relief than Kirk thought he had ever before heard in his helmsman's voice, Sulu announced that the *Enterprise* had achieved standard orbit around the moon of Talin IV. Evidently, Kirk wasn't the only one who sensed what Sulu felt, because the entire bridge crew, with the exception of Spock, applauded.

"Well done, Mr. Sulu." Kirk spun around in his chair. "Lieutenant Uhura, when will we be able to raise the FCO?"

"Coming up on the horizon in three minutes, Captain. Subspace tightbeam standing by to send and receive."

"Very good." Kirk swung back to face the main screen, enjoying the feeling of having the ship come alive around him again. This trip had been the longest five days he had ever spent on her. "Let's have some scenery on the screen, Mr. Chekov."

"Aye-aye, Keptin." The viewscreen image changed to show the sunlit surface of Talin's moon moving eight hundred kilometers beneath the ship. It was a typical, airless planet—heavily cratered, studded with sharp, unweathered mountains and swept with dark seas of ancient lava flows. It reminded Kirk of Earth's Moon, back in the old days, before it had been spoiled by overdevelopment. At least Earth's Moon was one of the last worlds to have been treated in such a way. It might take a long time, but the success of the Federation had shown that humans were capable of learning how to change their behavior, as individuals and as groups.

Chekov abruptly turned away from his board. "Keptin, there is a space wessel approaching. Three thousand kilometers, sir. And we are closing fast."

"Spock? An FCO shuttle?"

Spock peered into his science station scope where complex data from the ship's sensor networks were holographically presented without interference from the bridge's main lighting. "Difficult to say, Captain. With the blackout conditions, we are forced to rely on passive sensor systems only. No indication of impulse propulsion." He looked up. "No indication of any kind of propulsion."

"Could it be a meteoroid?" Kirk asked.

"No, sir," Chekov answered. "Light-reflection profile indicates a regular shape. Definitely artificial."

"Then is it a Talin lunar satellite?" Kirk tapped his hand on the arm of his chair.

"It is not in lunar orbit," Spock said. He turned back to his scope. "However, the trajectory does indicate Talin IV as its likely launch point."

Kirk stepped from his chair to look over Chekov's shoulder at the deviation plotter. "We know the Talin have sent three missions to their moon. Is there any way we can determine if there's a crew on board the approaching ship, without using our sensors?"

"Not with certainty at this distance," Spock said. "However, I am running a comparison of the vessel with known schematics of Talin lunar satellites and crewed vessels."

Kirk turned to the communications station. "How are we doing with that tight-beam to the FCO, Uhura?"

"One minute to horizon, Captain. But, sir, if that *is* a Talin lunar mission, the FCO would have warned us about it with an emergency pulse."

"Assuming they knew about it, Lieutenant. Spock? How about a guess?"

"I have computer confirmation. It is definitely a Talin spacecraft, Captain."

"Is there a crew?"

"I am endeavoring to determine that. However, the ship is not a standard configuration. I am running a thermal profile and—"

"Keptin! I am detecting a radiation signature."

Kirk rapped his fist against the top of Chekov's chair. If it was an uncrewed vessel, then there was no need to be concerned. However, if there was a chance of a Talin space explorer seeing the *Enterprise,* he would have to break orbit. Unfortunately, that would mean contacting the FCO by unshielded transmissions which they had been warned might be detected, if not understood, by Talin-based receivers. Kirk still wanted to get all the details about that unlikely technological possibility. "Is it radiation from an energy generator, Chekov?"

"It is not radiating strongly enough for the amount of fissionable material on board, sir."

"Spock?"

"The spacecraft is pressurized with a sizable percentage of empty volume. Seventy percent chance that there is a Talin crew on—"

"Sulu! Take us out of orbit now. As much impulse as you can manage without using deflectors."

The helmsman's fingers flew over his board and the image on the viewscreen suddenly showed stars as Talin's moon dropped away. At the low speed at which Sulu had changed the ship's trajectory, the inertial dampers didn't even have to compensate. The ship turned without a vibration.

"No change in the Talin vessel's course, sir. Thirty-five hundred kilometers and increasing."

Kirk went back to his chair. "Uhura, how soon before we'll be in tightbeam range of the FCO outpost again?"

Uhura looked up from her controls, one hand holding her earpiece in place. "Sir, I did get a few seconds of transmission from the outpost before we broke orbit."

"And . . . ?" Kirk didn't like the look on Uhura's face.

"I'll run it through again, sir." She hit the playback control.

There was a burst of static, then a rough and angry male voice said, ". . . *Enterprise*. Pull away! Pull away! That is a crewed Talin vessel! Damn you, *Enterprise!* Why aren't you listening on the emergency channels? Get out of there! Get . . ." It ended in another rush of static.

"And that's all we managed to get, sir."

Kirk gripped the arm of his chair. "Why *haven't* we been listening on the emergency channels, Lieutenant?"

"Sir, we have been listening. But we have received absolutely no emergency broadcasts—or any other kind—for the past five days."

Kirk joined Uhura at her station. "Then how do you account for what that transmission just said?"

"I don't know, sir."

"Scan the channels now."

Uhura punched a command sequence into her main board. Nothing.

Kirk read the status displays. "All the equipment checks out."

Uhura froze. "Are you questioning my ability, Captain?"

"No, Lieutenant," Kirk said diplomatically. "But you did assign your post to less experienced officers several times in the past few days. Perhaps . . . something was missed."

Uhura was not going to accept that explanation. "I programmed this system myself, Captain Kirk. If any emergency transmission had been received, then automatic recordings would have been made and the computer would have alerted whoever had the conn, as well as me, regardless of who was at this post."

Spock came up behind Kirk. "Uhura's system was quite foolproof, Captain. She had me review the program code before assigning junior officers to the station. If the communications log does not indicate the reception of an emergency broadcast, it is because none reached us."

"It might be equipment trouble at the FCO outpost, Captain," Uhura suggested. "They wouldn't be able to use it very often, so they might not be aware of any deficiencies."

"That is a possibility," Spock concurred.

Kirk accepted their judgment. He was not inclined to argue with specialists—at least not his own. "All right. But we know their line-of-sight tightbeam transmission works." He left the communications station. "Mr. Sulu, how soon can you get us back within tightbeam range of the outpost?"

Sulu looked at Spock. "Mr. Spock, may I use full impulse once the *Enterprise* is on the farside of Talin's moon?"

"I shall have to perform the calculations to determine the length of time residual-ionization effects from the deflectors would be detectable versus the rotational period of the moon itself." Spock remained silent for three seconds. "Yes, provided you resume slow impulse within seven hundred and eighty-three kilometers of the farside cut-off and remain at least five thousand kilometers distant from the Talin lunar craft."

Sulu turned back to his board. "That's fifteen minutes to reach the farside . . . twenty seconds to cross it . . . another six minutes, then . . . we'll be in range within twenty-three minutes, Captain, taking up a polar orbit to avoid the other ship if it does come around."

Kirk looked with admiration at both Spock and Sulu. "Lay it in, Mr. Sulu. And Uhura, keep monitoring the emergency channels. In case they correct their equipment problem," he added.

Uhura smiled at the apology. "Aye-aye, Captain."

Precisely twenty-three minutes later, the subspace tightbeam broadcast from the FCO outpost came through again, and whoever was on the other side was still angry.

"*Enterprise.* Come in, *Enterprise.* This is FCO Outpost 47 on scrambled tightbeam at—"

"Outpost 47, this is Captain Kirk of the *Enterprise.* You apparently are having some equipment prob—"

But the FCO was interested in only one thing. The angry voice cut Kirk off in mid-sentence. *"Did they see you, Kirk?"*

"The Talin lunar vessel?" Kirk asked.

"Of course the Talin vessel! Put your science officer on. I want a full log download of the encounter. And so help me, if you've compromised this outpost by your incompetence, I'll see that—"

Kirk glared at the moon's surface on the main screen. No one talked to him that way. "Who is this? Identify yourself."

"There's no time for any more stalling, *Enterprise,*" the man snapped. "We need that download now so we can tell how much damage you've done. *Stator rel!"*

Kirk was surprised to hear the FCO contact swear in the Orion Trader's Tongue. He held up his hand to signal Uhura to cut his next words from the commlink. "Spock, could the Talin crew have seen us before we changed orbits?"

"Almost impossible that they achieved a naked-eye sighting. They would have to have been looking directly at us, and tracking us with optical magnifying devices. However, given the state of Talin technology, there is at least a two percent chance that some automated navigational camera recorded an image of us. If that is the case, then at worst they will not know they have photographed an alien vessel until the images are processed on their return to their homeworld. At best, we could be dismissed as a chromatic aberration."

"That's something we can handle," Kirk said. He signaled Uhura again. "Outpost 47, identify yourself."

The voice at the other end knew that the comlink had been severed on the *Enterprise*'s end and his irate tone had risen sharply. "Download your encounter log—now!"

But instead of responding in kind, Kirk sat back calmly in his chair. "Outpost 47, regulations require that you identify yourself, to enable us to know that you have not been compromised or taken over by an alien force."

"There's no—"

This time Kirk had Uhura cut the FCO off. "If you do not identify yourself, then to avoid further contamination of the alien culture, we are authorized to abandon this outpost."

Uhura opened the channel again. *"I'm going to report you, you—"*

Uhura closed the channel. "And I am going to report *you*," Kirk said. *"Enterprise* out."

When Uhura toggled the channel open again, there was only dead air. Then, the unidentified man came online again, much more subdued. "Very well, Captain Kirk of the *Enterprise.*" Kirk heard the man pause in an attempt to prevent an angry edge from building in his voice again. "For the record, Captain, I am Dr. Alonzo Richter, Special Advisor to the FCO." He paused, to let the name sink in. And it did.

Kirk turned to Spock. Spock raised both eyebrows.

Silently, Kirk mouthed the words, "Did you know?" Spock shook his head.

Richter continued. "And now, Captain Kirk, would you be so kind as to have your science officer download your *karskat* encounter log?"

"Downloading," Spock announced, ignoring Richter's use of the Andorian word for "misbegotten."

"Very good," Richter said flatly. "And I'll expect to see you here within the hour, Captain. Within the hour! Depending on the analysis of your log, we will either discuss your mission on behalf of the FCO, or why I should not report you to Command for a violation of the Prime Directive. Richter out."

Kirk sat back in his chair and put a hand to his face. This was about as good as the time when he and Gary Mitchell were both cadets and had rigged a bridge simulator at the Academy so it would respond to requests for spacedocking drills by recreating unexpected high-gee combat maneuvers. How could they have known that Rear Admiral Chan was going to tour the simulator that day? Fortunately, the rear admiral, despite being one hundred and ten, had risen through the ranks during the Romulan Wars. He had performed well on the combat maneuvers and hadn't pressed for a full computer investigation to learn who had reprogrammed the equipment. Though the tactics instructors had known there were only two plausible suspects and had started them both on a month-long, highly personalized calisthenics program.

However, Alonzo Richter's reputation was not at all like Rear Admiral Chan's. Kirk briefly considered wearing phaser armor for their meeting—though if Richter were really as bad as the stories about him said he was, Kirk knew that no amount of protection would help.

It was the most extensive communications blackout Kirk had ever operated under. The *Enterprise* was even prevented from using her transporters while on the side of the moon visible to Talin IV—and there was still no explanation why. That meant that for the next ten days at least, all travel between the ship and the lunar outpost would have to be by shuttle. Thus, in the interest of saving as much transit time as possible, Kirk brought a full landing party down to the outpost in two shuttles. That way, there would be extra room for FCO personnel to return to the ship when it was time for the mission to Talin IV to begin.

Sulu piloted the shuttle *Galileo* with Uhura, Chekov, and Carolyn Palamas. Kirk himself sat at the controls of a second shuttle, the *John Burke,* accompanied by Spock and McCoy.

As Kirk explained to McCoy what had transpired when communications had finally been established with the FCO outpost, the doctor also expressed his surprise that Richter was stationed on Talin's moon, but for a completely different reason.

"Isn't he dead, Jim?"

"Given the fact that the captain stated that he and Dr. Richter have just spoken with each other, that is a most illogical question, Doctor."

"I stand willing to be corrected, Spock."

"That has not been my experience."

"Let me rephrase that: I stand willing to be corrected by those who know better than I do."

It was going to take Kirk thirty minutes to reach the outpost by traveling in a long course that would put the shuttles' final approach within the shadows of the mountain range under which the outpost had been constructed. It would be an unbearable thirty minutes if he had to listen to Spock and McCoy trying to outdo each other the whole way.

"Dead, Bones? What made you think that?" Kirk asked to break the rhythm of his officers' conversation.

"Back in med school I took an elective course in the history of theoretical cultural dynamics. We had to study the Richter Scale of Culture and, as I recall, Richter was an old man even back then. He'd have to be well over a hundred years old by now."

"One hundred and seven," Spock said. "I continue to study Dr. Richter's work, and he has remained quite productive and formidable, despite his advanced years."

"So tell me, Spock," McCoy began, and Kirk could hear the playful challenge in the doctor's voice, "after your years of continued study, do *you* understand the Richter Scale of Culture?"

"The basic underlying structure of the Scale which identifies and quantifies similar organizational principles of disparate cultures through a systematic series of—"

"Yes or no, Spock," McCoy interrupted.

"The Richter Scale of Culture is not a 'yes or no' system, Doctor, which accounts for—"

From the corner of his eye, Kirk saw McCoy lean forward in his seat. "What he means, Jim, is that he doesn't understand it, either."

"Who does?" Kirk returned the doctor's smile. The Richter Scale of Culture was considerably more art than science, though in the absence of any other objective means of assessing the development of alien civilizations so they could be compared to each other, it was the best system the combined sciences of history, anthropology, comparative techtronistics, exopsychology, sociology, and nonhuman ethnology had yet created.

Since its original publication more than sixty years earlier, the Scale had been continually revised and refined by Dr. Richter to become the Federation's most important tool for determining at which point in a civilization's development the

Prime Directive need no longer apply. Unfortunately, over the same number of years, the Richter Scale had become so complex that only a handful of specialists could apply it to any civilization much advanced past first-level Bronze Age, or A.345-34019-1 dr.1, as the current revised Richter Scale would describe it.

For the majority of nonspecialists, it was a simple matter to interpret gross Richter Scale ratings by memorizing the basic forty-three preface-letter descriptors which ranged from AA—to indicate no tool use—to the last meaningful letter rating of Q, which was generally taken to mean no technology advanced beyond the current theories upon which Federation science was based. A forty-fourth category, the one with which the general lay public was most fascinated and Starfleet most concerned, was XX, which indicated an *apparent* culture with *apparent* technology that *apparently* was absolutely beyond any explanation based on *any* current understanding and/or theory of science.

Qualified personnel who had studied theoretical cultural dynamics for a minimum of two years could interpret more detailed Richter Scale listings which ran, in some cases, to three preface letters, combined with twenty-one explanatory qualification digits, followed by five exception letters and twelve philosophical-comparison pointers. However, to actually analyze a new technological civilization, and create a Richter Scale of Culture Rating for it, was something that perhaps only a thousand beings in the entire Federation were capable of doing with consistent results. Since most of them worked for Starfleet's FCO, given that there were almost a thousand to choose from, it was all the more surprising that someone as old as Alonzo Richter himself would have been required to make the long trip to Talin and live in a notoriously spartan FCO outpost.

"The Richter Scale of Culture is not that difficult to comprehend, Captain," Spock said.

Kirk nodded. "Agreed." A good library computer could give the textbook definitions of a complete Richter rating in perfect detail. "But I think what Bones is referring to is how difficult it is to create an original Richter rating to begin with."

"That is true, Captain," Spock agreed, though Kirk knew he would not have, if McCoy had just stated the same thing.

Kirk enjoyed the silence for a moment. But he was still concerned about the trouble he might have inadvertently caused himself. Alonzo Richter's influence within the Council and Starfleet Command was legendary. "Spock, since you've been keeping up with Dr. Richter's work, do you have any idea what he's doing at the outpost?"

"I have no obvious answer, Captain. And because I have no obvious answer, then I must conclude that Dr. Richter's presence here has been intentionally kept secret by Starfleet."

"But that makes no sense," McCoy protested. "This is hundreds of light-years away from any disputed territory with the Klingons or the Romulans. And the Talin present no new military threat to the Federation. Why keep the FCO's operation here secret?"

"Not the entire operation, Doctor. Just Dr. Richter's presence has been kept unreported."

"But why?" Kirk asked, smoothly changing the shuttle's heading. He checked Sulu's position on his board. The *Galileo* was perfectly on course exactly two kilometers astern.

"Since his presence was unreported, obviously I cannot give an exact answer. However, I can suggest possible reasons for his presence under these circumstances."

Kirk heard McCoy shift position in his seat. "Just answer the damned question, Spock."

"I can think of several possible answers." As Spock qualified his statement McCoy snorted noisily. "But I would conclude that the most likely explanation is that some questions have arisen concerning Talin IV's placement on the Richter Scale of Culture and that Richter himself has been brought in to settle the dispute."

"But differing interpretations of Richter ratings is extremely common, isn't it?" Kirk asked. "Especially the more technologically advanced a given civilization is."

"Correct, Captain. Some debates have continued for decades, all to do with minute differences in the philosophical-comparison pointers or a one-digit shift in an explanatory qualification rank. But whatever debate there is that concerns Talin IV's Richter rating, it cannot be allowed to continue over a long period of time."

"Because the threat of all-out war might mean there soon could be no more Talin civilization to rate?" McCoy asked.

"Not exactly, Doctor. Richter ratings can and have been made from studies of dead civilizations. After the number of years the FCO has observed the Talin, I have no doubt that in time a thorough rating could be evolved from existing data, even if the planet were to disappear tomorrow."

Kirk swung the shuttle into a straightline run through the shadows of the lunar mountain range and locked navigation onto automatic. He wouldn't need to return to the controls until the final landing descent began. Even then, the onboard computers could complete the flight automatically; it was just that Kirk savored the experience of bringing a craft in under his own control. But for now, he turned around to pay more attention to what Spock was saying.

"But since Dr. Richter could just as easily reevaluate someone else's rating assignation from the Richter Institute offices on Mars, it appears that there is indeed a time constraint in operation. And the most logical time constraint is the threat of hostilities on Talin IV."

"Just a minute," Kirk suddenly said. "Remember what Carolyn—Lieutenant Palamas—was saying a few days ago? About how some of the crew were hoping that this might turn into a first contact mission?"

McCoy grinned. "Yes, I remember *Carolyn* mentioning that."

"Suppose the FCO is also thinking along those lines?"

"That would be most improper, Captain. According to the Richter rating of Talin IV—"

"But that's just it, Spock! That original rating which said that the Talin are still several decades from being contacted by the Federation is apparently under review. For a civilization that is this far along, a change in its Richter rating could open the door to a Federation first contact message."

Spock shook his head, unconvinced. "I will admit that I understand why the idea of preventing a world war is appealing, but the technological-threshold boundaries that would allow the Federation to open communication channels to the Talin are stringent and the Talin have not achieved them."

"But what if they're *about* to, Spock?"

Spock eyed Kirk thoughtfully. "I take it you mean: What if the Talin are about to exceed the contact thresholds within the immediate future, perhaps over the next few months, instead of over the next few decades?"

"Exactly." Kirk's speech became more rapid as he realized he had found the explanation for Richter's presence and all the other peculiar conditions surrounding the mission to Talin. "Think of the blackout conditions. It's completely standard procedures not to use deflectors when entering an uncontacted system in which radio-astronomy technology exists. But how often have we been told to also shut down intrusive sensors and subspace communications other than tightbeam?"

Spock answered instantly. "Except under battle-ready conditions, never in my tour of duty under Captain Pike or yourself."

"And how often have we been ordered not to use transporters within line of sight of an uncontacted planet?"

Spock took a few moments to think about that. "I am not aware of any ship in Starfleet ever receiving similar orders except, again, under battle-ready conditions."

"So what does that tell us?" Kirk asked, already knowing the answer.

So did McCoy. "That along with the technology to detect ordinary radiation signals in the electromagnetic spectrum, the Talin have the ability to detect subspace signals."

"Impossible," Spock said. "There is absolutely no indication in any of the technological briefs I have read that the Talin have progressed to the point of building transtators, let alone applying the multidimensional mathematics which describe their function. And without transtator technology, the subspace spectrum of energies we use in faster-than-light communications, *and* sensing, *and* matter transmission, is unequivocally impossible."

For a few seconds, the only sound in the shuttle was the soft hum of the impulse engine running at less than two percent of its rated output. "Impossible or not, Spock, I submit that in light of the unprecedented blackout conditions and Alonzo Richter's presence, that somewhere on Talin IV right now is a device that is capable of detecting subspace frequencies. It might be the first of its kind. It might be a single crude transtator the size of this shuttle, but it's down there. It's the only logical explanation."

Spock looked uncomfortable. "It is indeed logical, Captain, but it also remains impossible."

"Is there anything worse than a stubborn Vulcan," McCoy said to the shuttle's roof.

"Several things, Doctor, including a physician who—"

But Kirk held his hand out. "Really, Spock. What other explanation could there be?"

"I cannot think of one at the moment, but my inability to suggest a second reason in no way implies that no other exists."

"But if my conclusion is correct," Kirk said, "and there is a working transtator-based receiver somewhere down on that planet, then you know what that means, don't you?"

Spock nodded his head, admitting the inevitability of Kirk's argument, if not its accuracy. "If such a device exists, then it is only a matter of days before the Talin will use it to detect stray subspace transmissions which, by their regularity and coding, will be easily identified as components of a vast interstellar communications network."

"And . . . ?" Kirk prodded.

Spock's words were a slight rephrasing of the preamble to the charter of the First Contact Office, as if he did not wish to take personal responsibility for adding more weight to Kirk's argument. "And, since the Talin will then become aware of the existence of an interstellar community of planets because of the results of their own efforts without extraplanetary interference, then according to the conditions set out in the Prime Directive, the initial first contact technological threshold will have been passed and Starfleet, through the First Contact Office, will be empowered to transmit to the Talin a message of greeting, and so begin an official, open, and nondirective dialogue between that planet and the Federation."

Kirk sat back with a look of satisfaction. "And that could all happen within the next few days."

Spock's expression did not change. "As could the Talin's self-destruction as a race."

Before Kirk could respond, the navigation computer sounded the landing-alert chime and Kirk took over the controls of the *John Burke.*

The time for talk is past, he thought, *and now it's time to test the two competing theories—Spock's and mine.* Surprisingly, he found that for all he liked the challenge of competition and the thrill of winning, Spock was the only being to whom he never minded losing.

Thus, as Kirk brought the shuttle down toward the FCO outpost, he knew that he was in a no-lose scenario, since whatever they found out next would bring victory to either Spock or himself. He smiled to himself at the controls. It was a rare and not unwelcome feeling.

As the landing-pad acquisition signal flashed, Kirk expertly guided the shuttle directly at a jagged outcropping of heavily shadowed lunar rock and, ignoring McCoy's sudden surprised protest, he flew straight into it.

Three

"I hate holograms," McCoy groused as the *John Burke* settled gently to the landing pad. "They're getting too damn real. Whatever happened to the days when you could see them flicker from the corner of your eye?"

Spock stood up in the now motionless shuttle and began to unstow the two carry cases of computer files that he had brought for the FCO's databanks. The communications blackout made extensive subspace downloading of data impossible. "Dr. McCoy, if the holographic projection of a mountain wall did exhibit a detectable flicker, then it would serve no useful purpose as a camouflage technique to hide the outpost's presence."

"I didn't say I didn't understand why it was there, Spock. I simply said I don't like them." McCoy squeezed past Spock in the narrow aisle between the shuttle's two rows of seats to gather together his medical supplies. As standard procedure, he would be making medical checks of as many outpost personnel as time allowed and, because he could not have any required supplies beamed down on demand, he had been forced to bring a broad general assortment and hope for the best.

Kirk watched through the shuttle's forward viewports as the *Galileo* under Sulu's skilled guidance silently glided through the holographic mountain wall to join the first shuttle on the pad. As soon as the craft had come to rest, Kirk saw two large pressure doors begin to slide together. The outpost's landing pad chamber was just slightly larger than the *Enterprise*'s hangar bay.

Within seconds of the towering metal doors sealing, Kirk heard the whistle of air outside as the chamber was pressurized. At the same time, now that all transmissions would be kept safely within the bounds of the lunar mountain, the communications speaker came to life. "Full atmosphere will be achieved in twenty-two seconds. Stand by." It was a woman's voice, not Alonzo Richter's.

Kirk stood up and stretched. "Not the most cordial greeting we've ever received."

McCoy shrugged. "If your guess about what's going on is right, then I wouldn't be surprised if all personnel were standing on their heads trying to—" McCoy broke off and stared at Spock. "Don't say it."

"What, Doctor?" Spock asked innocently.

Before McCoy could say anything more, the pressure equalization light came on above the shuttle's door.

"Time to go, gentlemen," Kirk said. He reached out to the shuttle's control board and slowly turned down the artificial gravity field until all he felt was the moon's point two natural field, slightly more powerful than that of the Earth's moon. McCoy moaned as Kirk felt his own stomach rise into the new, lighter field. Then he popped the shuttle's door.

As Kirk stepped out of the *John Burke,* Sulu, Chekov, Uhura, and Palamas were leaving the *Galileo.* Like Spock and McCoy, each carried one or two cases containing supplies or microtapes which they might or might not need over the next few hours. Kirk was suddenly conscious of his empty hands and even though he knew Uhura had no trouble handling them in the low gravity, he took one of her equipment diagnostics packs. It was not the time to offer to help carry Palamas's gear again, after that awkwardness in the corridor following her first A & A presentation.

As the landing party waited for an FCO official to greet them and direct them to wherever their briefings would begin, Sulu looked around the landing bay chamber appreciatively. Except for the main pressure door seals and the personnel and supply airlocks leading into the outpost itself, the chamber's walls were bare black rock. Lighting rings on an exposed current conduit provided a soft, shadowless illumination. "How did they manage to build an outpost this big without the Talin knowing about it?"

Surprisingly, Palamas beat Spock to the answer. "Talin visual astronomy is limited to ground-based optical instruments. They can't resolve any detail here much smaller than about a half kilometer."

"And unlike the Earth's moon," Spock added, "this body rotates so that during each cycle, the outpost is out of view from the planet for approximately thirteen days. Usually, most traffic to and from the outpost is scheduled during those periods."

McCoy was intrigued by Spock's statement. "Then the fact that we've been brought in during the outpost's exposed cycle could be another indication of the time pressure they're under."

Kirk nodded. Palamas looked puzzled. But before she could ask what McCoy had meant, Sulu whistled and began walking over to another section of the chamber.

"Now that's what I call 'traffic,' " the helmsman said enthusiastically.

Five *Wraith*-class atmospheric shuttles were parked against the chamber's far wall. Kirk had seen spec reports on similar vehicles, but so far the *Enterprise* had never carried one. Each was a stubby winged vehicle, smoothly rounded as if partially melted, which could carry about half the cargo and crew of the *Enterprise*'s blocky Mark 12s. The finely ribbed, spaceblack skin of the craft made them virtually undetectable to anything less than advanced mass sensing technology. But it was the unique dual propulsion systems of the Wraith which gave it its reputation of being one of the most difficult—and exhilarating—atmospheric flying machines ever built.

"Like it?" a voice asked from nowhere as the rest of the landing party joined Sulu in admiring the Wraiths.

Kirk turned to see a young, red-haired woman in a pilot's flightsuit approaching. Her eyes went to the stripes on Kirk's sleeves. "You must be Captain Kirk. I'm Carole Mallett, manager of sampling operations." Her warm smile was an unexpected surprise given the type of reception Kirk had anticipated.

Kirk automatically looked for the rank markings on Mallett's uniform before reminding himself that Starfleet ran the FCO as a completely independent operation, without ranks, answerable directly to the Admiralty and the Council. He shook her hand and introduced her to the rest of his party.

"Do you fly one of these?" Sulu asked, running his hand along the rough-finished leading edge of one of the Wraith's wings.

"I wouldn't exactly call it flying," Mallett said. "When the anti-gravity drive is engaged, it's more like choreographing a series of freefalls onto a trampoline."

"I've heard they're pretty hard to handle."

"Understatement of the millennium," Mallett said. "If it weren't for the FCO's unique requirements for covert sampling craft, I don't think there'd be any reason to build them at all."

"What's so special about them?" McCoy asked.

Mallett led the doctor to the tail of the vehicle. There were no propulsion exhaust vents, just impulse baffles. "In space, not much. We run on a small impulse unit that can give us point-oh-oh-one cee, which is good enough to get us to Talin in about half an hour. But once we hit the outer atmosphere, we switch to antigrav. The advantage is that there's no engine noise, no exhaust trail, no radiation signature, no chemical emissions. It's just the thing for exploration and sampling runs where the Prime Directive is in force and where there's a moderately high level of native technology."

"And what are the disadvantages?" McCoy asked, hearing the pilot build up to them.

"If you've ever felt momentum lag effects in your starship during violent maneuvers, then you know how painfully sluggish artificial gee fields are. When you fly one of these things, you have to think about five seconds into the future. Basically, what you're doing is gliding through a partially controlled fall, then hitting the antigrav to bounce back up before you hit the ground. And if you want to land, you have to time the antigrav reaction perfectly, otherwise you smash in at full speed or rebound like a bouncing ball. It's terrible, trust me."

"That doesn't sound terrible," Sulu said earnestly. "That sounds exciting."

Mallett smiled at Sulu and shook her head. "They all say that. Until they fly them. If you've got time, we have a Wraith simulator you can try out. If you bring your own white bags."

Sulu beamed and looked at Kirk. Kirk shrugged. For once, it wasn't up to the captain. From the moment the *Enterprise* had entered orbit, her time and crew belonged to the FCO.

"Ms. Mallett," Kirk said, "I think the first order of business will be to meet with Dr. Richter and begin finalizing your mission requirements. It is our estimate that you are operating under a severe time constraint."

Mallett nodded, abruptly appearing inexplicably upset. "They're waiting for you in the ready room off the main monitoring lab. I, uh, I'll have to let the director fill you in, past what you've already been told in the formal reports."

"And is the situation as bad as we've been led to believe?" Lieutenant Palamas asked.

"No matter what you've been told," Mallett said sadly, "it's worse. Far, far worse."

The main monitoring lab was at the heart of the FCO outpost, five levels down from the landing chamber. To Kirk, it resembled a starship's bridge enlarged ten times—a circular layout, ringed by at least fifty subsystem stations, with a central command desk instead of a conn. Five technicians, outfitted with audio inputs, sat at the command desk constantly adjusting controls while observing a master viewscreen twice as tall and four times as wide as the bridge screen on the *Enterprise*. But instead of showing a single scene, the screen presented well over a hundred identically small, rectangular displays along with ten expanded ones. Kirk couldn't make out what was being shown on most of the displays, but he did recognize adult Talin on some of the large ones. One display showed a close-up of a Talin's face and, in the background drone of noise in the monitoring lab, Kirk heard a whispery and unfamiliar alien language that appeared to be in synch with the Talin's mouth movements.

"What's all that?" Kirk asked. The overall effect was overwhelming. There was far more information than could be assimilated at once.

Beside him, Mallett smiled. "How's your knowledge of old technology? That's what they used to call television."

"Oh, of course," Kirk said. He had read about it, even seen it on Planet 892-IV. "Two-dimensional image transmission by . . . analog signals of electromagnetic energy."

"That's the technical end of it," Mallett said. "But just like late-twentieth-century Earth, there's an incredible cultural component to it as well, which is still surprising considering that there is almost no capability for interaction."

Kirk blinked. "You mean the Talin just *watch* those transmissions without the ability to alter them as they proceed?"

Mallett nodded.

Kirk wanted to ask why, but he had seen too many alien customs during his years of explorations to be truly surprised by any culture's odd habits.

Mallett continued. "We have camouflaged electromagnetic reception antennae over three two-hundred-square-kilometer areas of this moon so that one is always pointing at Talin IV. It lets us pick up about three hundred of these television public transmission channels, and more than five thousand audio-only channels— what used to be called radio, if you've heard of it"—Kirk nodded to answer her question—"as well as a few hundred thousand private communication channels every day," she concluded.

Uhura's eyes flashed with interest. "Every day? Can you process all those signals in realtime?"

Mallett could see a kindred spirit in the communications officer. "The staff here can personally handle less than one percent of all data channels, but our monitoring equipment tracks everything, checking for key words, phrases, and images, then flags transmissions we should analyze in more detail."

"Listens to everything," Uhura said, staring at the hundreds of flickering images on the main screen. "What systems are you using? What protocols? Are you on full duotronics?"

Mallett smiled. "I'll have to get you together with Mario. He runs the entire communications system here and he can give you all the technical specs."

As Mallett and Uhura continued their discussion of the outpost's signal-intercept capabilities, Kirk looked at each system station in turn, testing himself to identify each one's function from the layout of its controls and the type of data displays it had. He was surprised at the number of military monitors he saw. Then he was aware of Spock at his side.

"Captain, I believe you should look at the third large display from the right on the main screen."

Kirk turned to it, along with everyone else in the landing party, and Mallett.

"Is that a pickup from a security sensor in the outpost?" Kirk asked as he stared at the image on the screen, not wanting to believe what the alternative was.

"No," Mallett said, and all excitement had vanished from her voice. "That is what is called a news broadcast. It's like a one-way update channel."

It was then that Kirk understood the reason for the tension in his dealings with this outpost, and the reason for the unprecedented communications blackout—and they weren't the reasons he had deduced. There on the screen, from a Talin news transmission, was a blurry but all-too-recognizable image of what was unquestionably a Federation *Wraith*-class atmospheric shuttle in flight. It could only mean that the FCO itself was on the brink of compromising the Prime Directive, however inadvertently.

"I think we've done enough sightseeing for now," Kirk said. "It's time to meet Dr. Richter."

The first thing Kirk thought when he saw Alonzo Richter was: *No wonder he's so old. He looks too mean to die.*

The man was skeletally thin and his upper back and shoulders were hunched over, pugnaciously forcing his neck and head forward. He had a full head of white hair, but it was cut more severely short than a cadet's first trim, giving him a harsh, militaristic look. And the folds of ancient flesh on his face had fallen to form a deep and perpetual scowl.

In centuries past, when normal aging had changed people's appearances in this way, there was nothing that could be done. But the fact that Richter shuffled into the ready room supporting his low-gravity weight on a cane of black, gleaming wood, indicated that he was past the point where modern rejuvenation procedures would work, or that he had declined them.

Kirk and the others rose in respect for the man as the ready room doors slid shut behind him. Mallett went to help him to his chair at the head of the briefing table. But Richter pulled his arm away from her grasp and thumped his cane on the floor.

"You!" he snapped, and his voice sounded just as rough and as angry as when he had fought with Kirk over the tightbeam transmission. "You're not fooling anyone!"

All heads followed the old man's gaze to Dr. McCoy.

"Put that contraption away. All it'll tell you is that I'm dying, but they tell me I've been doing that for the past twenty years."

McCoy folded in the top of his medical tricorder. He had been trying to run it from where it hung at his side to take surreptitious readings of Richter.

"And sit down, all of you. I'm not some *patak* admiral."

Kirk saw Uhura blink at the Klingon curse, then try to hide her amusement. Richter muttered a few more barely audible Klingon epithets as he slowly made his way to his chair under his own power. He sat down with great difficulty, but with extreme satisfaction when he was finally in place. Then he sucked on his teeth, took his time looking at everyone around the table, and finally settled on Kirk.

"So you're the young troublemaker who's trying to announce his presence to the whole *kreldan* planet."

Kirk glanced at Uhura but her only reaction was one of puzzlement. Obviously, "kreldan" was an alien curse which even she had never heard.

"As I explained when we talked before," Kirk said patiently, "we were unaware of the Talin lunar mission because we had not received any emergency transmissions from this outpost."

"Of course not," Richter said. "Of course not. We were just beaming them at you nonstop for five days. Why would we expect you to pick them up?"

Kirk held his hands calmly together. "I have brought my communications officer down to run a full diagnostics on your equipment. It might have a malfunction."

Richter sneered at Uhura. "There's nothing wrong with our equipment down here. Go back to that ship of yours. Go back."

Kirk shifted forward. "Dr. Richter, I suggest that in the interest of time, we let our respective technical specialists track down the reason for the communications failure. I believe we have more important matters to discuss."

"We certainly do. We certainly do." He held up his hand to his mouth and coughed deeply. Kirk saw McCoy quickly glance down to something he held beneath the table—probably still trying to take some medical readings.

Then they all sat in silence for a few moments.

"Well," Kirk said, uncertainly, "perhaps I should begin with—"

"You'll do nothing of the sort," Richter said testily. "This is a First Contact Office outpost. A Prime Directive operation. Everything goes by the book. No exceptions. Too important."

Spock folded his hands on the tabletop before him. "We are all aware of the gravity of the situation, Dr. Richter."

Richter strained his head forward and peered at Spock as if seeing him for the first time. "Yes, *you* would be. But for these other *sal'tasnii . . ."* He shook his head and waved his hand, dismissing them all but Spock. "At least you know enough to wait for the outpost director and the communications manager to arrive."

"Of course," Spock said.

So that's what we're waiting for, Kirk thought.

"They'll be here any moment," Mallett explained. "They're preparing some datafiles for you."

A few more moments of silence passed by, broken only by the dry whistle of Richter's breathing. Then the doors slid open again and two men entered.

Mallett stood. "Captain Kirk, may I introduce you and your crew to Zalan Wilforth, the outpost's director, and Mario Cardinali, manager of communications."

Kirk stood to greet the men. Wilforth was a young pale-skinned human and, going by his name, Kirk guessed he was of combined Earth and Centauran heritage. The Centauran part was confirmed when they shook hands and Kirk felt the extra joint in the director's little finger.

Cardinali was a large human, powerfully built, probably from a high-gravity colony world. His sideburns were trimmed to an Academy point. *Just on temporary assignment,* Kirk thought. Mallett had the crispness of an Academy graduate about her, too. He was beginning to see a series of special conditions having being set at this outpost.

"So," Wilforth began without preamble, "I understand you've seen the Talin television news broadcast." He sat down to the right of Richter. Cardinali sat beside Mallett at the table's other end.

"With the television images of the Wraith," Kirk agreed. Wilforth frowned and nodded. "How much do the Talin know?"

"It's not what you think, Captain Kirk," Cardinali said.

Kirk didn't know how it could be otherwise. "As far as the Talin are concerned, they have an image of an alien spacecraft, don't they?"

"Some think so," Cardinali said. "Many Talin are forward thinking and their successes in orbital and lunar missions have awakened the . . ." Cardinali shrugged. *"Le rêve d'étoiles,"* he finished, using the Academy phrase. Without question he had come up through Starfleet, Kirk decided.

"And, as on most spacefaring, pre-contact worlds," Cardinali continued, "there is considerable public debate going on concerning the likelihood that other civilizations might exist around other stars."

Even McCoy smiled at that. Kirk knew that there would be no one at the table who wouldn't feel a special connection to a world in Talin's position. Under ordinary circumstances, and with luck, some of the Talin alive today might see the day that the dream of stars was proven to be real. But Kirk knew that he and his people were there to discuss matters of a more practical, immediate nature.

Spock joined the conversation. "I take it, then, that also as on most spacefaring, pre-contact worlds, there is considerable intellectual resistance to the idea that other civilizations might exist?"

"Most definitely," Director Wilforth said. "We have seen news transmissions indicating that sometimes there have been violent altercations between supporters of both groups. And the Talin are not a particularly violent race."

"Yet they are poised on the brink of global war," Spock observed.

"Yes," Wilforth agreed. "And frankly, that's one of the problems we're facing."

"One of the problems?" Kirk said.

Wilforth gestured to Dr. Richter. The old man's eyes were bright and alive beneath his scraggly eyebrows and wrinkled forehead. "That's why we asked Alonzo to come to this outpost. From most viewpoints, the Talin are a textbook example of a simple Richter F culture: broadly speaking—Earth circa 1975 to 2000 C.E. Eight years ago, when the initial surveys were completed, there was every indication that they would pass through Richter FF to Richter G without major incident—unlike Earth—and from there it would be just a decade or two until they hit Richter H and Starfleet would initiate communications with them. An open-and-shut first contact. There're at least twenty other worlds under FCO jurisdiction in the same predictable circumstances."

"So what's causing their problems?" McCoy asked. He still had one hand beneath the table.

"Well, if we knew," Wilforth sighed, "we wouldn't have had to ask Alonzo, or you, to help us."

"Basically," Mallett added, "the Talin are on the brink of global thermonuclear war, but there is nothing in their cultural history to suggest that they would ever be capable of reaching such a position. The FCO has never seen a culture progress so rapidly toward self-destruction."

Chekov cleared his throat. "But in the same relative time period on Earth, Russia and the United States were in a similar position."

"Yes, yes," Richter said with irritation, "but there was a long chain of historical and cultural events which made that period of confrontation inevitable as a prelude to their reconciliation and eventual cooperation to create a true unified planetary government. The Talin do not share that same historical and cultural background."

Kirk began to suspect that the FCO officials were somehow afraid to go past a certain point in describing the details of whatever problems they were facing. *But why?* Kirk thought. *What do they have to hide? They're just observers here.* And then he realized what the link was and why he detected fear in the officials. He looked across the table at Spock and silently formed the words, "the Wraith?" He saw the flash of sudden knowledge in Spock's eyes as the science officer instantly came to the same conclusion. Kirk nodded to him and Spock took control of the conversation.

"Since you maintain that the Talin themselves do not possess the cultural and historical precedents to account for their current world situation, it is logical to assume that their normal development has then, in some way, been altered."

Kirk saw Director Wilforth frown even more, but no one from the FCO said anything to interrupt Spock.

"It is therefore also logical to assume that the First Contact Office is in some way responsible for that interruption in normal development and that the disturbing Talin news image of a *Wraith*-class shuttle might be one of the ways in which that interruption has been caused."

"By God, the FCO could use a few more Vulcans like you, boy," Richter cackled. "Just saved us half a day of sitting around listening to these so-called experts overqualify their findings till Talin's a cinder. By God, more Vulcans."

"That's very close, sir," Wilforth admitted. "Very close, indeed."

"How long ago was the Wraith detected?" Kirk asked.

Mallett answered. As manager of sampling operations, she was responsible for all atmospheric and landing sorties to Talin IV. "We believe the image that has been released through the public channels was obtained during an ocean sampling run six months ago. There's a chance that the Talin have obtained other images but not released them."

"Why?" Kirk asked.

"The imaging technology used to detect the Wraith is at the leading edge of the Talin's technology. That would—"

"Of course," Kirk interrupted. "Given the state of the planet's political situation, all of its advanced technology would be coming out of the military. One side might not want to release the images, to prevent the other side from gaining information about the state of its advanced imaging technology."

"If I may," Lieutenant Palamas asked, "*are* there only two sides involved in the potential conflict? The reports we received weren't conclusive."

Cardinali answered. "Except in the case of their world's name, and a few other rare exceptions, the phonemes of the Talin language are difficult for humans to reproduce, so we call the opposing sides the Browns and the Greens. The Browns are the most powerful nation state on the primary continent, which is mostly equatorial desert. The Greens are a union of five nation states on the secondary continent—mostly temperate forest and grasslands. The two cultures have slightly different organizational and political procedures, but, from a purely objective standpoint, the main reason for the dispute between them appears to be . . . emotional."

Spock turned his head to look impassively at McCoy. McCoy rolled his eyes.

But Kirk pressed on. "What other indications do you have that the Talin have detected your observation of them?"

"That's just it," Wilforth said. "Absolutely nothing. Yet they're behaving as if they're aware of us. Both the Browns and the Greens have gone through an unprecedented upgrading of their sensor systems—mostly EM bounceback systems."

"Radar?" Chekov asked.

"Yes, that's an old name for it," Wilforth confirmed. "Plus, they've added visual tracking systems—which are what we believe caught our Wraith. But quite honestly, Captain Kirk, until they did get that image of the Wraith, we could not have possibly done anything at all to attract their attention."

"Director Wilforth," Spock began, "I do not understand why you ordered a complete communications blackout, including matter transmissions, if you are convinced the Talin's sensors are limited to the electromagnetic spectrum. Do they or do they not have transtator capability?"

Kirk suddenly felt his stomach tighten. If the Talin were still years away from developing transtators, yet they had transtator capability, there could be only one possible explanation—one hideous explanation.

"Director Wilforth," Kirk said, forcing himself to keep his voice calm and controlled, "has the FCO lost or abandoned advanced technology on Talin?"

Richter laughed at Wilforth's sudden look of discomfort. "Absolutely not, Captain Kirk. And I am most insulted that you would even think to ask that question."

"It is most logical," Spock observed.

"I don't care. As director of this outpost, I assure you that every piece of equipment is counted before, during, and after any planetary sampling run."

"Then why are you afraid the Talin will pick up subspace radiation without transtator technology?" Kirk demanded. What other explanation could there be?

Wilforth glanced at Richter, asking a question with his eyes. Richter shrugged. "If you can't trust Starfleet . . ." he said. Then he glared at McCoy again. "Just don't trust that quack. I know what you're trying to do under there with that thing."

McCoy sighed and brought both hands above the table. Kirk heard a tricorder click off.

"What information are you withholding, Director?" Spock asked.

"The Talin do not have transtator capability that we know of. However, they have what appears to be a solid foundation in the multidimensional mathematics required for the development of multiphysics—though for now they think it has no practical application. And, on the quaternary continent, which virtually all nation states had access to during the planet's age of sea exploration, there is a large, and quite anomalous deposit of . . . rubindium." Wilforth looked embarrassed.

Spock's eyebrow shot up. "Natural rubindium crystals?"

"Damn right!" Richter snorted. "How about that?"

"How extraordinary," Spock said quietly in a reserved tone which Kirk knew meant the science officer was thoroughly surprised.

But Lieutenant Palamas was not. "I don't understand the significance of rubindium crystals," she said. "Why are they important?"

"They are wery crucial to the dewelopment of subspace technology," Chekov explained. "They contain a four-dimensional molecular lattice structure on the same order as dilithium and so are able to conwert subspace radiation into transtator current—in much the same way ordinary quartz crystals conwert electromagnetic waves into piezoelectricity. You see," he added helpfully, and earnest as always, "we still use rubindium in transporter transponders just like the ones in our communicators. And they can be cut so small that we can even inject tiny crystals under our skin for—"

"I think she understands now, thank you, Chekov." Kirk turned to Wilforth. "Do the Talin know what rubindium crystals are capable of?"

"They are aware that rubindium is not normal matter. They have furthermore recognized the same temporal irregularities in approximately two to three percent of their planet's naturally occurring quartz."

Kirk was impressed. After the discovery that a second level to the periodic table of elements existed and the confirmation that dilithium was indeed a second-level crystal, subsequent investigation revealed that between two to three percent of the quartz on Earth was actually dilithium. Visually, dilithium had a dozen different three-dimensional physical configurations which could make it resemble several varieties of ordinary crystal. It was the portion of dilithium's molecular lattice that extended into the fourth dimension which made it so unique and so valuable—and that could not be determined by ordinary physical inspection or testing. In the mad dilithium rush almost two centuries earlier, Kirk remembered reading that many Earth museums became incredibly well-funded overnight simply by tearing apart their geology exhibits to find dilithium crystals which had been misidentified as quartz for generations.

"I see," Spock said. "If the Talin are at present conducting tests of rubindium or dilithium, then any strong subspace activity in their system could produce transtator current effects in the crystals being observed. And, with the theoretical mathematical foundation for multiphysics already in existence, they could conceivably come to the logical conclusion that they had detected an interstellar communications network in operation, even though they would not have developed the technology to intercept, generate, or receive messages of their own." Spock paused for a moment. "I am aware of no other culture that has ever been in a similar situation."

"Exactly, by *flaxt'a,*" Richter said fiercely, slapping his hand on the tabletop. "A whole new category for the Richter Scale. At least five more years of work to rejig the whole thing. It's wonderful. Wonderful."

"Has the FCO made a ruling on how these special circumstances might affect the application of the Prime Directive?" Kirk asked Wilforth.

"No, Captain. The Prime Directive is perhaps the most rigorously enforced regulation in the Federation, and one of the most complex. Best-guess estimates won't do. Any special ruling would have to be made solely on the basis of precise, unquestionable data."

"And you don't have that." Kirk finally saw where the conversation was going.

"No, sir, we do not."

"And that's why you asked for the *Enterprise:* to help you get it."

"That is correct."

Kirk pushed back in his chair. Normally, he would have no difficulty in performing any mission for a First Contact outpost. His general orders clearly covered total cooperation with the FCO as a sister branch within Starfleet. But the more he found out about the situation on Talin, the more he realized that it did not fall within the range of general orders.

"Director Wilforth," Kirk said at last, "what precise and unquestionable data do you have at your disposal now?"

Wilforth pushed a stack of microtapes across the table. "These are specialist datafiles and go into considerable detail, but basically, it comes down to this. First, circumstantial evidence which we have obtained through the monitoring lab facilities leads us to believe that the Talin are aware that they are under our covert observation—though we do not know precisely how that is possible. The discovery of our Wraith shuttle came only after their sensor systems were upgraded. It's an effect, not a cause.

"Second, the majority of Talin—especially those in positions of leadership—do not accept that the covert observation they are under could be the activity of non-Talin aliens. Instead, the Browns believe the Greens have advanced surveillance and transportation technology, while the Greens believe the same of the Browns."

Kirk looked over at Spock. They both understood the nightmarish situation the FCO was in. "Therefore," Kirk said, "there is a chance that FCO operations have intensified the feelings of distrust between the two sides and that the increased potential for war which now exists on Talin is the result of . . . interference."

"Exactly," Wilforth murmured. He didn't appear to have the strength to say anything more.

"How do you propose to prove or disprove your hypothesis?" Spock asked.

"That's where the *Enterprise* comes in," Mallett said. "Obviously, we need access to information that is not being released publicly."

"Information from military sources?"

"Precisely, Mr. Spock. We need to know all the details of the Wraith sighting. We have to know what phenomena spurred the Browns and the Greens to upgrade their sensor systems. And, most importantly, we have to know how far along their study of rubindium and dilithium crystals has progressed."

Kirk's mind filled with the logistics of what the FCO wanted his ship to accomplish. "The initial report said that four key installations had been identified for intrusive data collection. I take it those are military installations?"

"That is correct."

Kirk looked at the rest of his landing party. "And the results of intrusive data collection could determine if the FCO is responsible for the hostilities on Talin and, if so, determine what could be done to correct the situation?"

"Yes, sir."

"Well, Director Wilforth, you've got our work cut out for us." Kirk started to stand.

The director looked expectantly at him.

"So you'll be able to get our people to Talin immediately? We've got our collectors standing—"

"No," Kirk said plainly. "Not immediately. I'm sure you understand that in a situation like this, I have to report back to Starfleet Command for specific orders. To take the *Enterprise* into a mission that might compromise the Prime Directive is beyond my authority as a starship commander."

"But you can't report back to Starfleet," Wilforth said plaintively.

"I have to," Kirk said. "And I will."

"Captain Kirk, because of the blackout, it will take you five days to leave the Talin system. It will take you four days to hear back from Starfleet after you transmit your report—assuming they can answer immediately without the need to hold a board of inquiry—and then it will take you five more days to return."

"I'm quite aware of the time frame, Director Wilforth."

"No, Captain, you're not." The director looked down at the tabletop, afraid to meet Kirk's eyes. "You see, the situation on Talin is impossible. It cannot hold for another fourteen days. There's a very good chance it won't last even three more days. No matter what your orders say, general or specific, you don't have time to contact Starfleet."

Kirk was shocked. *Three days?* The situation was far worse than the reports had stated. Or else it had changed dramatically in the three weeks since the reports had reached the ship.

"I'm sorry to do this to you, Captain Kirk," Wilforth continued, "but I do know that when a starship commander must act within a time period which prevents communication with a higher command, that starship commander is authorized to act independently in a manner which he or she believes is in keeping with the best interests of Starfleet and the Federation."

Kirk sat back down. The director was right.

"There is no more time, Captain Kirk. And under the circumstances, as a starship commander, you are the highest authority in charge of what happens next." Wilforth looked up and finally met Kirk's eyes. "The fate of an entire civilized world and the lives of more than two billion beings rest in your hands, sir.

"What will you do?"

Four

In the deserted landing chamber, Kirk sat in the *John Burke* considering his choices. When he had been forced to operate without Command guidance in the past, the situations he had usually faced were so critical that he had had only minutes or seconds to make his decisions. But in the matter of Talin IV, Kirk had the unusual option of having hours to decide upon a reasoned course of action. The fact that he had those hours would definitely be taken into consideration by the inevitable Starfleet board of inquiry. Also definitely, in the event of error, Kirk knew the board members would not be as forgiving as they had been in the past when he had been forced to commit himself and the *Enterprise* on little more than a split-second hunch.

He heard a rapping on the shuttle's hull and turned to the open door to see McCoy. "House call," the doctor said. "Mind if I come in?"

Kirk gestured for him to enter.

"It isn't an easy one, is it?" McCoy said as he sat down across from Kirk. "But then, they never are when we're cut off from Command."

Kirk smiled at McCoy. "Though usually that's when I like this job best."

McCoy shifted sideways in his chair so he could face Kirk. "I know it's not strictly in my line of duty, Jim, but have you come up with what you're going to do about this mess?"

Kirk opened his mouth to answer just as a second rapping sounded on the hull.

"Request permission to come aboard," Spock said formally.

"The door is open, Mr. Spock," Kirk answered.

"Pardon me for interrupting, Captain, but I was curious to know if you had determined your course of action." Spock sat behind McCoy, and also turned to face the captain.

"Partially, Spock. I was just about to go over it."

"Please continue."

McCoy's eyes flashed at Spock. "Oh, yes, Captain, please do," he said facetiously.

Kirk stretched out his legs and hooked an arm over the back of the pilot's chair. "My main concern is to keep all our options open until the last possible second. The less I commit the *Enterprise* to do, the less likely the chance of inadvertently compromising the Prime Directive."

"Leaving command decisions to the last second sounds pretty risky, Jim."

"But striving to maintain the Prime Directive is most logical."

Kirk had the sudden feeling that if he ever decided on a course of action that both Spock and McCoy supported, then he would be sure to be making a mistake. "I admit that it's a compromise. But in the meantime, I'll be gathering as much new information as possible about current conditions before deciding additional actions." Kirk watched as Spock nodded and McCoy's lips tightened. *Good,* he thought, *they're still not agreeing. Maybe this plan has some merit after all.*

"The first thing that concerns me," Kirk continued, "is what that Talin lunar mission is up to. Given the state of their world's economy and the war footing the nation states are on, I don't think it's reasonable at this time to expect them to commit such considerable resources to a purely exploratory lunar mission."

"It is a troubling development," Spock said.

"So, I've sent Scotty his orders by tightbeam. He's to lock sensors on the lunar vessel the next time it passes out of line of sight from Talin. Then the first thing he's to do is to send out a quarter-second sensor pulse to see if the vessel is carrying rubindium or dilithium."

"If it is," McCoy cautioned, "then subspace resonance is going to light up those crystals like the dickens."

"But only for a quarter second, Bones. And if the sensor return indicates that crystals are on board, then the scan will not be repeated. That's well within the bounds of the Directive."

"However," Spock interjected, "if the sensor scan reveals no such crystals are present, then the Talin aboard will not be able to detect further investigation by sensor."

"Exactly," Kirk agreed. "In that case, Mr. Scott is instructed to conduct a full sensor survey of the Talin vessel. At the same time, any stray subspace signals will be blocked from ground-based stations on Talin by the moon's mass. And from those radiation signatures Chekov picked up, I'm betting that we find fusion warheads on that ship."

"Why the hell would the Talin send warheads here?" McCoy asked. "They have no bases on the moon."

"But the FCO says some Talin suspect extraplanetary surveillance. This moon is a logical place to conduct such surveillance. The early Vulcan observer missions to Earth used our moon as a base from time to time, correct, Spock?"

"That is true," Spock admitted.

"So you think the lunar mission's part of the war effort," McCoy asked, "come to wipe out the alien invaders?"

"Remember what Wilforth's data files told us, Bones: The Talin leaders don't believe in aliens. That ship's more likely to have been launched by one Talin nation state to seek out and destroy a base believed to belong to another. Which is why we have to have a complete scan of it. If the vessel *is* on a war mission, *and* it has warheads, *and* it's carrying instruments which might locate this outpost, then everyone stationed here is at risk."

McCoy looked grim. "There're more than a hundred personnel here, Jim, and their evacuation plan depends on a ship with the *Enterprise*'s capabilities. There's no way the outpost could be evacuated quickly without revealing our presence."

"Believe me, Bones, if we have to evacuate the outpost because the Talin have launched warheads at it, they'll already know we're here."

"The *Enterprise*'s sensors do have the ability to selectively disable the old style electronic components used for detonating such warheads, Captain."

"I know, Spock. I'm already having Scotty run simulations to prepare for that possibility. Though if it ever did come to us taking that action, once again they'd know we were here—and that we're technologically superior to them. And if that happens, the whole mission has failed. Ours and the FCO's."

"So much for Talin's moon," McCoy said. "What are you going to do about the Talin planet?"

Kirk frowned, showing he had still not completely made up his mind. "So far, I've told Director Wilforth that I'll take his people into orbit over the key military installations he's interested in. I'll decide then whether or not to beam down his intrusive-collection teams."

"What will determine your decision at that time?" Spock asked.

"A lot will depend on how well Scott can keep the *Enterprise* hidden from the Talin's sensors. She's not a Wraith, gentlemen. And she won't be passive. While we're in such low orbit, we'll have to use our deflectors plus full electronic and subspace countermeasures to remain invisible to the Talin sensor stations."

McCoy didn't look pleased. "How low is 'low'?"

Kirk shrugged. "Scotty's working on it. He says it's likely going to be somewhere between sixty and eighty kilometers above the planet."

"A very good estimate," Spock commented.

But McCoy scowled. "Damn it, Jim, the *Enterprise* is a starship, not a glider! What the blazes are we going to be doing literally in the planet's atmosphere?"

"Endeavoring to keep stray transporter radiation to a minimum," Spock said, "by cutting the transporter beam to the lowest gain which will still allow for the safe transmission of intelligent life-forms."

"Exactly, Spock. We'll do a preliminary test run at a higher altitude for the orbital insertions of the passive sensor satellites the FCO wants launched. If everything checks out and we've not been detected, then I'll authorize a low-orbit pass over the key installations. Then, and only if we're still undetected, I'll authorize the collection teams to beam down."

"I tell you, Jim," McCoy said, "if something starts coming at us while we're at that altitude, even I know we're not going to be able to warp out of orbit. Not that close to a gravity well."

"I understand, Bones. And so does Scotty. But the only way to eliminate all risk is to do nothing. And if I do nothing, then I have just about the same chance of breaking the Prime Directive as I would if I did the wrong thing. Right, Spock?"

McCoy turned to look at Spock, eyes wide at the Vulcan's silence. "I don't believe it. You're not going to quote the odds?"

"Doctor, I regret that in this situation I am incapable of quantifying all possible scenarios."

"Really?" Kirk asked in true surprise. "I was hoping for some input from you."

"I am still at your disposal."

McCoy shifted in his chair. "Well, what would logic dictate that the captain do, Spock?"

"Exactly what he has outlined. Uphold the Prime Directive while minimizing risk and maximizing knowledge. At this stage, there is no more that can be done."

Kirk bowed his head. "Thank you, Mr. Spock. I'm satisfied with that input."

"That's it?" McCoy asked. "That's as far as logic takes you?"

"Because of the unusual situation that exists on Talin, there are too many variables to prepare additional strategies without additional information."

McCoy leaned back against the shuttle's bulkhead and smirked.

"Bones, from the look on your face, I'd say you had some input of your own for me."

"Damn right I do," McCoy said smugly. "I bet I know why the Talin are convinced they're under extraplanetary observation even though the FCO has done nothing to alert them."

"Is that so?" Kirk asked.

"Indeed," Spock said dryly.

"Because someone else is observing them!" McCoy stated proudly.

Kirk looked at Spock.

"There is no one else in the system, Doctor. Except for ourselves, there are no alien life-forms and no alien probes. Because this is a system under FCO jurisdiction, everything that enters or leaves Talin space is monitored by the automated sensor stations in place at the edge of the system, and they have detected nothing in eight years."

"Klingons with Romulan cloaking devices," McCoy said, though less smugly. Then his smile disappeared in stages as Spock offered another explanation.

"We are so far removed from the Klingon Empire that even they, Doctor, would realize that the Organian Peace Treaty would give them no right of claim over this system. Likewise, the Romulans are too far away. Furthermore, the Talin system offers nothing of unusual value which would entice distant invaders to risk penetrating this far into Federation space. There are hundreds of uninhabited systems with natural resources of far greater value than Talin's in many disputed territories much closer to our frontiers. Not only is there no one else in this system, no others would travel to this system for what it has to offer."

"Well, Spock, at least you've got to admit it was a good suggestion. Logical even."

Spock turned back to Kirk. "If your definition of logic includes ignoring established facts, then it was indeed quite logical, Doctor."

"Thanks, anyway, Bones," Kirk said, trying to soften the blow. "It was one of the first things I thought of, too. But not even a cloaking device could fool the sensor stations surrounding the system long enough to get a ship to Talin IV."

"So that's it?" McCoy asked. "The whole plan?"

Kirk nodded.

"But it's not enough, Jim."

"Best I can do under the circumstances, and I know it's not much. To be honest, I'm not holding out too much hope that I actually will allow Wilforth's people to beam down because the last thing a war-ready nation state needs is to catch aliens materializing inside a military installation. And that means, if the Talin do have their war, that we might never recover the data we'd need to determine—even in hindsight—exactly what the best course of action should have been for me to follow."

"And we'll never know how things went so terribly wrong down there," McCoy said. He sounded stricken.

"You don't have to tell me, Bones. I can't see a way out of this one no matter what happens. I'm going to be happy just to get the *Enterprise* out of orbit in one piece and let Command and the Council work it out. The last thing I need is a run-in with a board of inquiry over the Prime Directive."

Spock nodded. "You are in a classic no-win situation, Captain."

Kirk tried to keep the look of pain from his face but without success.

McCoy turned to the science officer. "Mr. Spock, you could have talked all day and not said that."

"But he's right, Bones," Kirk said. "If things on Talin really are as bad as the FCO's updates indicate, then there are not going to be any winners in the next few days. Either here or on Talin."

McCoy stood up and put his hand on Kirk's shoulder. "I know it doesn't happen very often, Jim, but you have been known to be wrong before. And I hope this is one of those times when you're wrong again."

"So do I," Kirk said. But he knew he wasn't, and from the guarded look in Spock's eyes, his friend and science officer knew it, too.

For the first time in almost five years, Kirk was preparing to take his ship and his crew into a mission he knew he could not possibly complete with success. But to fulfill his duty to Starfleet, to defend the Articles of Federation, and to uphold the Prime Directive, he had no choice but to seek out and accept defeat.

It was the one thing he had never been taught at Starfleet Academy—and the one thing he had never learned to do on his own.

Five

No matter what Kirk thought he might face in the next forty-eight hours, he had no doubt that the best place to face it would be the bridge of the *Enterprise*. Returning there, as always, he felt renewed.

The instant the turbolift door opened onto the somehow soothing noise and activity of the bridge, Kirk saw Scotty step out of the central chair.

"It's good to have ye back, Captain," Scott said.

"Good to be back, Mr. Scott." Kirk stood by his chair, one hand on the arm, surveying his domain. Behind him, Uhura and Spock took up their stations. In front of him, Chekov and Sulu took up theirs.

"Satellite status, Mr. Scott?" Kirk asked.

"All eight ready to go when ye give the word, sir."

Kirk turned to Uhura. "Has the hangar bay reported yet?"

Uhura wheeled in her chair, one hand to her earpiece. "Three Wraiths have landed and are being stowed, Captain. All assigned FCO personnel are onboard."

"Status of Talin lunar craft, Mr. Spock?"

"Approaching farside cut-off in seven minutes, Captain."

"ETA on intercept orbit, Mr. Sulu?"

"Seven minutes, ten seconds to arrival, sir."

"Talin warhead status, Mr. Chekov?"

"No change, Keptin. Two armed, four on standby."

Kirk paused in silence. Each person on the bridge was poised, waiting for his words, his commands.

He took his chair.

"Helm, take us to Talin vessel intercept."

"Aye-aye, sir."

The *Enterprise* effortlessly slipped from her station-keeping orbit, dropping lower and faster to the moon of Talin, heading for the primitive vessel thousands of kilometers ahead. The mission had begun.

Seven minutes later, the Talin lunar vessel filled the main screen. It consisted of a main eight-meter metallic sphere ringed by six bell-shaped thruster skirts. The main sphere was connected by a ten-meter-long open grillwork tube to two six-meter spheres, one of which had folded-up landing legs. The overall structure was heavily textured with wiring conduits, three small antenna dishes, and a variety of asymmetrical bulges which could be anything from attitude thrusters to instrument bays.

"What are they throwing at us, Mr. Chekov?" Kirk asked.

"Sweeping with standard radar signals only, Keptin. Our sensors are creating perfect inwerse phase delays to show there is nothing in the immediate wicinity."

"Orbit intercept," Sulu announced. "Holding back ten kilometers, running lights out." At their angle to the Talin craft, the *Enterprise* was safely hidden within the glare from the lunar surface.

Scott stood beside the captain's chair and made soft tsk tsk noises.

Kirk smiled. "What do you make of her, Scotty?"

The chief engineer cocked his head skeptically. "They deserve an A for effort, but I don't know how they're managing to keep an atmosphere in her. My preliminary scans showed absolutely no magnatomic adhesion bonds in the whole craft."

Spock stepped up to the railing by his station. "I believe you'll find the entire pressurized crew compartment is sealed by welding and rivets."

Scott shook his head. "Och, then she might just as well be carved of wood for all the structural strength she'll be having."

Chekov turned away from the screen for a moment. "Is it supposed to be a one-way trip for them, Mr. Spock? I don't see any part of the craft which could surwive an atmospheric re-entry."

"The Talin strategy at this time is to leave their re-entry vehicle in orbit around their homeworld rather than expend the extra fuel required to send it to their moon and back," Spock explained.

"But they'll be using up far more fuel trying to slow down enough to dock with it on the return," Scott said.

"The Talin have a great deal of patience, Mr. Scott. In the past, their lunar mission profiles included a week's worth of high-orbit deceleration loops to match orbits with their reentry vessel."

Scott frowned. "Then they'll be spending extra fuel for carrying their increased life-support consumables. I don't understand their reasoning."

"Life-support consumables are minimal owing to their ability to cocoon themselves when conditions are less than optimal. There is a complete report—"

Kirk interrupted. "We are due in Talin orbit within the hour, gentlemen. Perhaps we might proceed to the next phase?"

"Aye, Captain," Scott said, going to join Spock at the science station. "The sensors are all set for ye, Mr. Spock."

But Spock stayed at the railing. "I believe you are more qualified than I at what must be done, Mr. Scott. I do not claim to have your level of engineering expertise."

Scott appeared to be surprised by Spock's compliment, and pleased by it as well. "I'd be happy to handle the procedure."

"Then please do," Spock said, offering Scott his station.

Scott peered into the hooded science scope and blue light flooded his face. "Mr. Chekov, would ye please transfer tractor beam controls to the science station."

"Transferring now, Mr. Scott."

"That's a fine lad . . . now . . . now . . . scanning for the detonators . . . easy . . . easy . . ." Scott kept a quiet conversation going with himself as he simultaneously manipulated controls for the ship's finest resolution sensor probes, as well as for the tractor beams. But Kirk tuned him out. It was just a sign that Scott was completely absorbed in what he was doing. And what he was doing demanded no less than total concentration.

Earlier, as Scott had followed Kirk's tightbeamed orders from the FCO outpost, the initial quarter-second sensor pulse had revealed that the Talin lunar craft was not carrying rubindium or dilithium. That meant its crew would be completely oblivious to further sensor scans, provided they were done on the side of the moon opposite any detectors on Talin. Subspace radiation from the ship's sensors could easily travel through the moon's solid matter. But with the sensor's focus controls tuned to line-of-sight nearspace, the radiation that emerged would be virtually undetectable by any but the most sophisticated sensing systems. And no matter how unusually advanced the Talin might be with their discovery of second-stage matter's subspace resonance effects, they were still decades away from building the transtator technology that could fully exploit that class of natural phenomena.

Scott's subsequent sensor study of the Talin vessel had confirmed Kirk's suspicions: It carried six fusion warheads mounted on missiles capable of independent launch. That information, combined with a series of methodical orbit changes that eventually would bring most of the moon's surface within scanning range of the vessel, confirmed beyond a doubt that the two Talin onboard the ship had been sent on a mission to locate and destroy what their commanders must have assumed was a hostile lunar base.

Scott's sensor study had also shown that the lunar vessel was equipped with simple mass-detector instruments sensitive enough to reveal the presence of the FCO outpost's machinery and extensive metal shielding. Judging from the way the vessel shifted orbits, those detectors would be in position to locate the outpost within two days. Kirk could no more allow the outpost to come to harm from nuclear bombardment than he could blow the Talin vessel out of space. But fortunately, in this situation at least, there had been a middle ground which even Spock admitted would not conflict with the Prime Directive. Provided Scotty's hands were steady for the next few minutes.

As Scott continued talking softly to himself, Kirk heard the lift doors slide open, followed by a familiar, shuffling walk.

"Dr. Richter," Kirk said, leaving his chair to greet the man, "welcome aboard . . ."

Accompanying the old scientist were Director Wilforth and his two managers, Mallett and Cardinali.

". . . everyone," Kirk concluded.

Richter gestured aimlessly with his cane. "Is that it?"

"The Talin vessel?" Kirk asked.

Richter sneered. "No, a *razfelsin* white whale." He stepped slowly down to the central level of the bridge, eyes fixed on the viewscreen. His almost permanent sour expression softened as did his tone of voice. "Odd that there are no markings. And how fragile it is."

"And how lethal," Spock amended.

Zalan Wilforth clasped his hands together. "Does that mean the procedure did not work?"

Kirk pointed to Scott. "My chief engineer is taking care of the warheads now. How's it going, Mr. Scott?"

Scott didn't look away from the science scope. "'Tis delicate work . . . delicate . . ." His hands moved almost imperceptibly over the station's controls.

Carole Mallett stood beside Spock. "What exactly is he doing?"

Spock watched Scott's actions carefully. "He is attempting to link our sensors with our tractor beam in order to physically alter the circuitry of the warhead detonators."

"From here?" Mallett asked in astonishment.

"It is an exceedingly sensitive operation."

Scott abruptly stood up from the scope and took a deep breath. Sweat beaded his forehead.

"Scotty . . . ?" Kirk began.

"That's the four on standby, Captain," Scott said. "They'll still be able to respond properly when they're armed, but the detonators will misfire for certain."

"And the other two that are already armed?" Kirk asked.

"Aye, I'm coming to those. But they are the trickier ones. Full of malfunction alarms and failsafe backups. Och, but the Talin are clever beasties." He bent back to the scope.

Mallett's face filled with concern. "When the Talin launch the warheads and see they don't go off, won't they know they've been interfered with?" she asked.

Spock shook his head. "Dr. Richter informs us that Talin nuclear weaponry has an accurate function rate of approximately sixty percent. The Talin who launch the warheads—if they do—should be expecting at least two to three of them to malfunction in any event. And if all six warheads are launched and fail, at least the Talin will not have any evidence of tampering remaining onboard."

Cardinali joined Mallett and Spock. "If you're rearranging electronic circuitry by tractor beam and sensors, isn't there a chance you could trigger one of the detonators?"

Scott spoke to the science scope. "Triggering them is the easy part. If it weren't for the two Talin on board, we could set the whole contraption off from half a million kilometers. But the detonators are well protected, so there's little chance of them going off on their own, even with us fiddling near them. The trick, mind you, is not to fiddle with them directly." He sighed. "There's one. Any response from the ship, Mr. Chekov?"

"Nothing showing, Mr. Scott. No alarms, no sudden computer use."

"Here goes for armed warhead number two, then," Scott said.

"I didn't think tractor beams could be so finely controlled," Cardinali said.

"Mr. Scott has made extensive modifications in virtually all systems of this ship," Spock explained. "He has—"

"Increased computer activity on the Talin wessel," Chekov announced.

"A weapons system alert?" Kirk asked.

"Can't be sure, Keptin." Chekov's hands flew over his controls. "Mechanical systems coming on line. Fuel pumps opera—"

Kirk spun. *"Scotty! Cut the tractor beam now!"*

On the screen, the Talin vessel rushed toward the *Enterprise* as four thrusters vented shimmering exhaust. Suddenly the craft could be seen to shudder violently.

"Beam off!" Scott cried, jumping back from the scope. But he was too late. An arc of transtator current crackled from the control panels as the tractor beam circuits fed back into the sensor system.

"They felt that, Keptin," Chekov announced. "The tractor beam was engaged when they changed orbit."

"How badly?" Kirk asked.

"Thrusters firing again," Chekov said, reading his board. "Their reserve fuel is adequate for orbital correction. Pressure holding."

Kirk saw that Scott was uninjured and that the fire-abatement systems had extinguished all sparks from the overloaded equipment. He turned back to the viewscreen. The Talin ship was gone.

"Where'd she go?" Kirk asked.

"Astern," Sulu said grimly. "Shot right past us. We're forty kilometers ahead of her now, leaving her orbit."

Kirk slumped back in his chair. "Did they get within visual range?"

"If they were looking through the portals, they might have seen us for a second," Sulu said.

Wilforth came forward. "Don't worry, Captain Kirk. These things happen in first contact situations."

"What things?"

"Mistakes."

Kirk's eyes flashed at the word. "Not on my ship they don't. Mr. Chekov, why weren't we prepared for their orbit change?"

"This was not one of their regular changes, Keptin. According to the pattern they were following until now, they should not have changed orbit for another two hours."

"Did they detect Mr. Scott's activity?"

"No indication of that, sir. The wessel simply changed orbit . . . at random."

"And experienced a momentum lag because of our tractor beam attachment," Kirk said in disgust. "Well, Mr. Wilforth, what's the FCO's procedure on this type of situation?"

Wilforth looked uncomfortable. "Unofficially, we hope they didn't see us."

"And if they did see us?"

"Then we hope they didn't record an image of us."

"And if they did record an image?"

Wilforth shrugged. "Between 1955 and 2018 on Earth, there were at least eighteen legitimate, two-dimensional photographs taken of Vulcan probe ships. They were, without exception, dismissed as frauds and hoaxes." Wilforth shrugged again. "The Talin are as skeptical as humans were back then, Captain. A single image of the *Enterprise,* even in the unlikely event that it is accepted as genuine, is not the same as regular observation of Wraith shuttles. It will not compromise the FCO."

"Pardon me for being skeptical as well, Mr. Wilforth," Kirk said, "but a single image of the *Enterprise* would reveal a great deal about the structural engineering required for warp balance. And that's advanced technology."

Then Kirk felt Richter's hand patting his arm. "Don't worry about it, Captain. Most technology is developed according to a strict, almost evolutionary pattern. If the Talin survive their present political situation, they'll be in contact with us long before they get around to figuring out efficient warp configurations. Most contacted races end up learning that type of thing during exchange programs at Starfleet Academy."

Kirk was uncomfortable with a mistake being dismissed so lightly, no matter how inadvertently it had been made. He was especially surprised by Richter's calm acceptance of the event. "Mr. Chekov, what's the Talin vessel's status now?"

"Settled in its new orbit, Keptin. All systems back to normal operation."

"See?" Wilforth said.

Kirk turned back to Scott, already busy replacing the science station's controls with new modules from the bridge storage compartments. "Ready to go after that last warhead, Scotty?"

"I think I might have already got it, sir. When I get the sensors back on line, I'll be able to confirm its status." Scott took his circuitplaser away from the open control panel for a moment. "Is there something wrong, Captain?"

"A few too many coincidences, Mr. Scott." Kirk swung back to Wilforth. "That Talin ship approached this moon just as we were arriving. It changed orbit just as our tractor beam was locked on to it. And it's looking for the FCO outpost after only one image of a single Wraith shuttle was recorded."

Wilforth looked around the bridge but saw that Kirk was speaking only to him. "What . . . what are you suggesting?"

"I'm not sure," Kirk said threateningly. "What *am* I suggesting, Spock?"

"That the Talin are in possession of more information than the FCO would have us believe, through means which the FCO has not revealed to us."

"Thank you, Mr. Spock," Kirk said.

"This is outrageous," Wilforth stammered.

"Isn't it," Kirk answered.

"First of all, Captain Kirk," Wilforth said, rallying, "both the *Enterprise* and the Talin vessel arrived at this moon for the same reason—because of the escalating tensions on Talin IV. Why is it so hard to accept that you both arrived at the same time while responding to the same conditions? Second, the Talin vessel is searching for a hostile base belonging to the other side—not an alien outpost. Third, since the Talin ship is on a military mission, why is it difficult to believe that it might engage in sudden maneuvers to confuse any hostile vessels that might be in pursuit? I mean, really."

Kirk pursed his lips. "Spock?"

"Each statement is logical, Captain, though for them all to be true requires a fragile chain of coincidence. Also, there is as yet no explanation for why the outpost's emergency broadcasts to the *Enterprise* were not received. Both Lieutenant Uhura and Communications Manager Cardinali were unable to find any reason for equipment malfunction either here or at the outpost."

Kirk watched the FCO director carefully. *"Could* there be another reason for the communications failure, Mr. Wilforth? Other than equipment malfunction?"

The director's face turned red with a pattern of roughly hexagonal shapes—a peculiarity of the Centauran circulation system. "Are you . . . are you daring to imply that the FCO has compromised its mission here?"

"As I said, Mr. Wilforth. There appear to be too many odd occurrences here. Should I explain them away as a 'fragile chain of coincidence,' or should I look for a single explanation?"

"Which would be . . . ?" Wilforth said, shaking with anger.

"That the Talin know that you are here and they're coming looking for your outpost—not another side in their political conflict, but for an alien base on their moon."

"Captain Kirk, really," Carole Mallett interrupted, "that would be impossible. Other than possibly observing the Wraiths, the Talin know nothing about us or our operations here."

Cardinali joined her. "And our communication intercepts have revealed no indication that the Talin leaders seriously consider the existence of alien life-forms. Captain Kirk, what we're seeing played out on this planet is a classic case of war jitters—lunar mission and all."

Kirk assessed Cardinali and Mallett carefully. They seemed sincere. But Wilforth was too hard to read. Was he really incensed at what Kirk was implying, or was he terrified that some secret was about to be exposed? Kirk decided it was time to test Richter, who had been uncharacteristically quiet for too long.

"Well, Doctor? Haven't you anything to add to the FCO's defense?"

Richter snorted. "The whole FCO's a naive bunch of *tarfel*-licking *rostonagons*. Should have done away with the whole thing years ago. The Prime Directive's an impossible piece of work so why even bother to try to uphold it?" He shook his head. "But Wilforth's telling you the truth. He's not smart enough to lie about anything like this."

The last clear spaces on Wilforth's face filled in bright red. "Alonzo! How could—"

"When you're my age, Zalan, it's easy. The last thing you feel like doing is wasting time with social niceties. Now shut up." Richter tapped his cane against the back of Chekov's chair. "So can you get that ship back up on the screen or what?"

Chekov looked to Kirk for confirmation, got it, and the Talin vessel reappeared on the screen. This time it was a view from the front.

"Are you looking for something in particular, Dr. Richter?" Kirk asked. For the moment he was satisfied that if anything improper was going on within the FCO outpost, its director, at least, was unaware of it. Richter, though, was another matter. His assessment of the Prime Directive as not being worth upholding was disturbing. Clearly, his loyalties were not firmly entrenched with Starfleet.

"Here's another mystery for you," Richter said, then coughed loudly. Sulu sat forward uncomfortably, apparently in the man's line of fire. "Take a good look at that ship, Carole. See how it's different from the others they've sent here?"

Mallett studied the screen carefully. "It's assembled from standard components, Dr. Richter. The only difference I see is that it has two lunar-landing supply spheres instead of the usual one. I presume that means the warheads are in the second sphere."

"Aye," Scott said, back at work on the repaired science controls. "That's exactly where they are."

"I don't mean the engineering," Richter snapped. "Look at it! Look at it! Where are its colors? Where are its markings?"

Cardinali shrugged. "Why does it need them? It's clearly a ship from the Brown nation. The Greens use a completely different cylindrical module design."

"Pah! If it's on a war mission, it should have the Browns' battle colors on its side," Richter insisted. "It should have a registration code on the main sphere, too. But it's blank. The whole *nyeem* thing."

"It's carrying six fusion warheads," Kirk said. "Trust me. It's on a war mission. Scotty, how's the second warhead coming?"

"It's disarmed, Captain, I got it the first time." He leaned back to stretch his back after hunching over the scope. "How d'ye manage that all day, Mr. Spock?"

"I have never done it for an entire day," Spock answered. "Dr. Richter, if the Talin lunar mission was rushed because of the so-called war jitters on the planet, it would be logical to assume that certain nonessential elements were left out of the mission's preparations, including the painting on of decorative nomenclature and colors."

Richter scratched at his cheek. "Colors are very important to these creatures, Mr. Spock. But I'll accept what you say as a theory. For the moment. Though I think you might be wrong."

"Do you have another explanation?" Kirk asked.

Richter shook his head. "Colors are so important to them that it's hard to imagine anything urgent enough to make them embark on a military mission without those colors."

"Are you suggesting that their mission is other than military?" Spock asked.

"As the captain said, Mr. Spock, they're carrying fusion warheads. That's not your typical first contact methodology in this part of the galaxy." The old scientist began to cough again.

Kirk checked the chronometer mounted between Chekov and Sulu. The *Enterprise* would be coming out of the farside protection of the moon in a few minutes. "Mr. Scott, can you guarantee that those warheads no longer threaten the FCO outpost?"

"Aye, sir. They'll hit like a ton of bricks, but only a ton of bricks. The outpost's structure could withstand all six of them impacting at once. No fear of detonation, though the fissionables will require some cleaning up. Plutonium it is, not too pure, but nothing a good environmental suit can't keep out."

"Good work, Scotty," Kirk said. "Mr. Sulu, take us to Talin IV, sensor satellite insertion orbit."

For the next few minutes, the bridge was the focus of intense activity. Scott left for the hangar bay with Cardinali and Mallett to prepare for satellite deployment. Chekov took up his position at the defense subsystems monitor to bring the

Enterprise's antidetection countermeasures on line. Ensign Fisher took over navigation. Three sensor technicians tested the repairs to Spock's science console. Spock set up Wilforth and Richter at the engineering subsystems monitor where they could follow the satellite deployment, and Uhura established a fully automatic communications scanning network to track all Talin military channels for any reference to a sighting of an unidentified space vehicle. Kirk sat quietly in the midst of the hurried preparations, the calm at the eye of the storm.

When Talin's surface filled the entire screen, Spock came to stand at Kirk's side. "All systems and personnel are ready, sir."

Kirk nodded. He knew. On the *Enterprise,* the systems and personnel were always ready. Any errors or mistakes belonged only to one person.

Spock dropped his voice, not quite to a whisper, but to something which only Kirk could hear. "If I may, you seem preoccupied."

Kirk glanced at his science officer. He hadn't spoken as a member of the crew. "Just reviewing my options."

"You expect complications?"

"Spock, we had complications dealing with a primitive spaceship that had only two crew members. And now we're facing an entire planet. Complications isn't the word for what I'm expecting."

"You have prepared for every foreseeable eventuality," Spock said.

"It's the unforeseeable ones I'm worried about."

"It is not logical to worry about that which you cannot know. Rather, you should have faith in your ability to respond to the unexpected, as you have demonstrated so ably in the past."

Kirk knew that Spock was making a touching attempt to give a pep talk to his captain, but as usual, the science officer was far too serious in his delivery of it. "Faith, Spock? Doesn't that smack of . . . emotions?"

Spock's face became completely blank, a reaction which Kirk had long since recognized as the half-human, half-Vulcan's response to minor embarrassment.

"Perhaps I have used a colloquialism where it was not necessary. I was simply trying to suggest that you have strong reason to have confidence in your skills as you have used them in the past." Spock glanced away for a moment. "I was speaking as a friend, not as a semanticist."

"Why, Mr. Spock, you're sounding more like Dr. McCoy each day."

Only someone who knew Spock well could see the subtle look of alarm that came to his face. "I most certainly hope not," he said, then returned to his post.

"We are within groundbased detection range, Keptin," Chekov announced. "Talin active sensors consist only of low-level radar. Talin passive sensors are confirmed as optical tracking networks."

"Full countermeasures, Mr. Chekov," Kirk said.

"Aye, sir. No surprises."

Kirk scanned the substations ringing the bridge, looking for alarm signals. But there were none. The *Enterprise* was undetectable to the Talin's current level of technology because her sensors could completely manipulate any electromagnetic signal sent in her direction. And with her running lights extinguished and all ports shuttered, there was virtually no chance of an optical scanning system spotting the *Enterprise* in the high orbit necessary for deploying fixed-position sensor satellites.

A paging whistle sounded from the bridge speakers. "Scott to Captain. We're ready to deploy the first satellite, sir."

"Mr. Chekov?" Kirk asked.

"All boards clear, sir."

"Lieutenant Uhura?"

"All military communication channels are being monitored. No change in readiness levels."

Kirk knew he had to make a decision. The sensor satellites were small and radar transparent. But they would orbit in altitudes accessible to the Talin and transmit data in tightbeam bursts. It didn't matter that the First Contact Office had requested their deployment and took full responsibility. *I'm the one giving the final order,* Kirk thought. He made a fist, certain that there was more to Talin than anyone yet suspected. But the bottom line was that he had no good reason for refusing to proceed. Only a hunch. And that wasn't good enough.

"Away satellite," Kirk ordered.

A few seconds passed. Kirk watched the lights on the control panel as they told the story of what was happening in the secondary hull. The hangar bay doors opened. The satellite boom deployed. The tractor beam pushed. The umbilical detached.

Scott's voice came back on the speaker. "Satellite one away, Captain."

"Shall I run a systems check?" Spock asked.

But Kirk waved the question aside. "We've got a whole planet on alert down there, Spock. Let's not do anything until all the satellites are in position. That way, if we do have to hightail it out of here, at least we'll be able to collect some data from a distance."

" 'Hightail,' Captain?"

"Strategic withdrawal, Mr. Spock."

Sulu turned around. "Coming up on second insertion point in five minutes, Captain."

Kirk nodded. "As long as the boards are clear, we proceed." But the boards only responded to active sensors like radar, and Spock had said the Talin were extremely patient. For Kirk, that meant one of the options he had to consider was that the *Enterprise* was already under optical surveillance, and that the Talin were biding their time. He didn't like that option at all.

Minutes from the deployment of the eighth and final satellite, Lieutenant Carolyn Palamas came to the bridge. She wore a communications earpiece and carried a small device, about twice the size of a screenpad stylus, which Kirk had never seen before.

Palamas took up position by Kirk's chair. The *Enterprise* was on the planet's nightside and the screen was filled with the constellations of glittering cities, tracing the rough shorelines of the primary continent.

"More than two billion of them . . ." Palamas said softly.

Kirk knew what was in her mind. There was something godlike in traveling unseen and unknown over such a planet, knowing that the power of the *Enterprise* would be enough to forever alter the planet's history and development. But in this case, the *Enterprise* was restrained by an even greater power: the words of the Prime Directive.

"For what it's worth," Kirk said, "Talin's military leaders appear to be responsible beings. They know what all-out warfare would mean and are in constant negotiations to prevent it."

"I know," Palamas said. She held up the small metal cylinder she carried. "I've been listening in."

"What is that?" Kirk took the cylinder from her. It had an FCO serial number stamped on its side and a familiar though surprisingly small computer display. "Not a universal translator?" If Starfleet engineering had begun another round of downsizing, they were going to have to start issuing new smaller fingers as well.

"Not a full translator," Palamas explained. "This is programmed just with the Talin languages. Eighteen major families and two hundred and twenty-seven dialects." She offered Kirk a second earpiece. "The crew is extremely interested in knowing what's going on on Talin. I've been preparing update digests for them."

Kirk slipped the earpiece into position and heard a computer voice re-enacting both sides of a conversation concerning a violation of airspace. One side claimed that an illegal overflight had taken place. The other side denied that any aircraft had been in the area at the time. Kirk felt his stomach tighten.

"They're not talking about us by any chance, are they?" Though he knew that Uhura would have informed him of that situation, he wanted to take no chances.

Palamas shook her head. "The incident took place about two hours ago near one of the Greens' polar airbases, long before the *Enterprise* took up orbit. Mr. Cardinali suspects a Brown highspeed surveillance aircraft was detected executing an unauthorized flyby."

Kirk pointed to the earpiece. "Who are we listening to here?"

"Regional military commanders talking over a diplomatic radio frequency. It sounds as if they're both trying to defuse the situation. It would be a lot better if the Browns simply admitted that one of their aircraft had strayed too close to the Greens' base, though."

Once again Kirk was caught by the lieutenant's clear eyes and the hope that shone so brightly in them. "Things are seldom that simple, Lieutenant. Especially in a military confrontation."

Palamas seemed not to hear. She moved closer to Kirk's chair. "I like it when you look at me that way."

Kirk smiled, but only for an instant. They had shared important time together in the past few days and he was glad of it. But the bridge of the *Enterprise* was not the proper forum for such memories. He handed back the earpiece and the translator. "You have me looking forward to the long voyage out of this system," he said softly, and it was all the acknowledgment he would make to her.

"Let me know how the situation plays itself out, Lieutenant." Kirk was referring to the airspace dispute.

"I'm anxious to know how it turns out myself," Palamas said, referring to something else. She took her translator unit over to show Uhura.

"Coming up on final satellite insertion point," Sulu announced.

Chekov followed the routine that had been established. "All boards still clear." Uhura was next. "No change in military alert levels."

Kirk gave the order to deploy the last satellite. All went smoothly.

"Shall I begin the systems check now, Captain?" Spock asked.

"Mr. Sulu, set in an automatic warp-out-of-orbit maneuver to engage at the first indication we've been detected." Kirk turned to Spock. "When Sulu's finished programming our escape hatch, you may proceed, Spock."

Wilforth stood up from his chair beside Dr. Richter at the engineering subsystems monitor. "May I go prepare the intrusive-collection team, Captain Kirk?"

Kirk had known there was a good reason for the way Richter and Wilforth had conducted themselves so conscientiously during the last orbit. They knew he still hadn't committed to allowing an FCO team to be beamed down from low orbit.

"You may *prepare* the team, Mr. Wilforth, but the final decision to send them remains with me."

"We've already agreed to that, Captain." Wilforth offered his hand to Richter to help the old man from his chair, but Richter waved his cane to force the FCO director back. Wilforth shrugged and headed for the turbolift.

"Mr. Wilforth," Kirk said suddenly, "are you intending to beam down with the team? If I give the word?"

Wilforth seemed surprised by the question. "Why, of course, Captain. It's my operation. I must take full responsibility."

Kirk shook his head. "That's not quite correct, sir. As of now, it's my operation. And I'm the one who must take full responsibility."

It took a moment for Wilforth to realize what Kirk had said. "Surely you don't intend to . . . beam down with us? Do you?"

Kirk enjoyed seeing the look of discomfort on Wilforth's face. "Come now, Director, it won't be the first intrusive-collection landing party I've been on."

"Oh, I realize that," Wilforth said, eyes wide and round. "I just hope it won't be your last."

Six

Lieutenant Kyle leaned over the transporter console and punched in a final string of setting commands. "And that's the lowest I dare go to guarantee brain function, Mr. Spock. Even then, an unexpected solar flare or energy burst could disrupt the signal so badly that . . ." He shrugged.

Spock was unperturbed. "At an altitude of sixty-three kilometers the transporter beam will be effectively shielded from solar flares by the planet's atmosphere. Energy bursts might arise from nuclear weapons detonation, but if war does break out on Talin, then we shall be under no constraints to maintain low-level power settings for the transporter. This setting should be safe."

McCoy groaned. " 'Should be safe'? Would *you* use the blasted thing at those settings to beam down there?"

Spock didn't bother to look up. "Your question is moot, Doctor. It would be foolish to expose Captain Kirk and myself to the same risk at the same time. And since Captain Kirk has invoked his command privilege to lead the landing party, I, of course, will not use these settings to beam down."

McCoy held a hand to his eyes and shook his head. "Jim, you can't be serious about this."

Kirk stepped down from the transporter platform where he had been double-checking the two tall cylinders of collection gear that would be beaming down with the landing party—*if* the landing party beamed down. "I've transported under worse conditions, Bones. And so have you."

"Don't remind me. 'Guarantee brain function'? Good Lord," he muttered.

Kirk rolled up his sleeve and held his arm out to the doctor. "Time for the transponder."

McCoy took a spray hypo from his kit and adjusted the setting on it. "You know, someday Starfleet's going to wake up and change the regulations so that the captain will be the *last* crew member to be authorized to lead a landing party."

Kirk grimaced as the centimeter-long transporter transponder was forced under the skin on his forearm. The FCO communicators that the landing party would carry, along with all their other equipment, were rigged to self-destruct in the event of capture or loss. But with the team's subcutaneous transponders in place, the *Enterprise* would always be able to lock on to each individual.

"The captain has ultimate responsibility over each mission, Bones. And ultimate authority. How can I exercise that authority or take that responsibility if I'm not on top of the situation?"

"Well, it's too damn risky."

Kirk rolled his sleeve back into position. "The system's worked so far."

McCoy frowned. "And that's the problem. The day the system doesn't work is the day you're not going to know about it because your brain will have been permanently scrambled by this damn machine."

Kirk clasped his hand to the doctor's shoulder. "As long as I know that you're waiting up here to put me back together, I won't worry."

"Oh, for—"

The doors to the corridor slipped open and the rest of the landing party entered—Wilforth, Cardinali, and two FCO technicians Kirk hadn't met. Richter and Mallett accompanied them.

"Do you require transponders?" McCoy asked.

Wilforth shook his head. "They're permanently implanted in all FCO personnel. Sudden extractions are standard operations, I'm afraid. How are things on the bridge, Captain?"

"The dispute over the polar airspace seems to be growing—though at a controlled rate. Other than that, no disturbances. And no indication that the Talin have detected us or our satellites."

"So we're approved for beaming down?"

"Not yet," Kirk said. "Sulu's going to take us down for a quick run past the main defense installation on the primary continent, just to check the effectiveness of the Talin scanners at close range. If we get by them the first time, then we'll beam down at the secondary site."

"Impossible," Richter said, leaning on his cane, and for once he didn't sound angry or provocative, just tired. "It's all so complicated—judging the development of cultures and technologies. So much room for mistakes to be made, so little chance to help."

"But that's precisely why we need the Directive," Kirk said. "Because there *is* so much opportunity for causing damage, even accidentally. It's better to let each world choose its own way."

An expression of sadness passed over Richter's face. "You only say that because those are your orders."

"Yes, they are my orders," Kirk agreed. "But I do believe in them."

"But think of all the time and effort that's wasted, because we do not help."

"Perhaps, someday, we'll know how to help other worlds without the possibility of causing harm, but for now, we do the best we can with what we know."

"Even if a world should die, Captain Kirk?"

Kirk shook his head. "This world won't die. Dr. Richter. I've been using the FCO translator to listen in on their negotiators. Talin patience is serving them well. They know what they're facing if they dare break off talking with each other." He stepped up on the transporter platform. "While we're down there, you listen in on those talks yourself. The Talin have got what it takes to survive this, and fifty years from now, maybe fewer, there's going to be another Federation starship in orbit around this world . . . and that starship won't be trying to hide."

Wilforth, Cardinali, and the two technicians joined Kirk on the platform.

"Why wait fifty years, Captain? Why not do it now?" Richter asked.

"If the Federation revealed itself to the Talin now, we don't know what would happen." Kirk felt the ship shudder around him and reached out a hand to steady himself against one of the equipment cylinders. The transporter-room communications panel whistled.

"Sulu here, Captain. We have entered the Talin thermosphere. Altitude one hundred and five kilometers. The inertial dampers are absorbing our kinetic energy in an even curve."

Richter balanced himself with his cane. "If the Federation contacts Talin fifty years from now, we still don't know what will happen."

The vibration of the ship became rhythmic. Kirk could hear the whine of the impulse generators as they absorbed more energy from the inertial dampers than they put out. "But at least fifty years from now, what happens will be the *joint* responsibility of the Talin and the Federation. We will not be in control, we will be partners."

Richter's sadness became almost overpowering. His voice was barely audible over the growing whine of the impulse system. "But fifty years from now, Captain Kirk, I shall be dead and not know anything."

It was then that Kirk finally understood Richter's impatience, but it was too late to respond. Sulu's voice spoke rapidly from the bridge.

"Altitude eighty-five kilometers, Captain. Entering the mesosphere. Thirty seconds from acquisition of primary target."

Uhura's report followed. "No military traffic, Captain."

"All boards clear," Chekov added. "We're absorbing all signals perfectly."

The vibration evened out as the atmosphere thickened and the ship's speed dropped to avoid creating an incandescent trail in the Talin sky. The energy expenditure was enormous, but the *Enterprise* could manage atmospheric flight for a brief time, though Scott would be complaining for weeks to come about the pounding the ship was taking.

"Over primary target," Sulu said. Kirk could hear the excitement in his voice.

The same excitement was in Chekov. "They do not see us, sir. We are still clear."

"Secondary-target acquisition in forty seconds," Sulu said. "Altitude seventy-five kilometers. Passing through the mesopause."

Kirk felt all eyes on him.

"This is it, Captain Kirk," Wilforth said. "Do we go or not?"

Kirk ignored McCoy shaking his head. "Mr. Kyle, lock on to secondary target. Do not energize without my signal."

Kyle set the controls to standby.

"Mr. Spock, I want a complete retrieval after one orbit."

Spock nodded in agreement.

"But that gives us less than an hour," Wilforth protested.

"If everything works out, we can return," Kirk said.

"Altitude sixty-eight kilometers," Sulu said. "Secondary-target acquisition in ten seconds."

Kirk held his hand up by his shoulder. "How are those boards, Mr. Chekov?" he called out.

"All clear, Keptin."

"Five seconds to target. Altitude sixty-four kilometers."

Kirk made his decision. He pointed at Kyle. "Energize."

The shuddering of the ship was instantly muffled by the sudden wash of the transporter effect. Kirk watched as Kyle and Richter and Spock and McCoy dissolved into the random sparkles of a quantum mist. And then the movement of the ship was gone along with the bright lights of the transporter room. Kirk felt a solid floor materialize beneath his feet, felt the sudden heat of the desert and the sensory shock of air that carried a hundred unknown scents. He was on another world. For a moment, he felt a thrill of triumph. Then the transporter effect was gone completely and he heard the others of the landing party shift around him, altering their stance in the slightly higher gravity of Talin IV.

Kirk looked around. They were in a long, high-ceilinged room, dimly lit by wall-mounted panels.

Good work, Kyle, he thought. *A perfect touchdown.*

A sudden swath of light cut through the room and Kirk heard Cardinali swear. He turned to the communications expert wondering what had gone wrong. And then he saw what Cardinali saw and knew exactly what had gone wrong.

Everything.

Two Talin stood in an open doorway, mouths open. And they screamed.

Seven

Kirk felt himself slip into a state of intensely accelerated consciousness. Even as his hand instinctively reached for his communicator to request a beam out, he knew that the *Enterprise* had already moved beyond the range of her stepped-down transporter system.

Those Talin are not supposed to be here, he thought simply. The only reason he had agreed to even consider the possibility of an intrusive-collection landing party was because Director Wilforth had assured him that each selected site would be deserted. *Or did Wilforth know? Did he bring us down here on purpose, knowing what would happen?*

Suddenly, the two Talin in the open doorway were engulfed in a shimmering blue aurora and collapsed to the roughly textured floor. The technicians whom Kirk had yet to meet rushed forward to pull the motionless bodies forward. Kirk turned to Wilforth. The FCO director held a small weapon in an unsteady hand— an egg-shaped area disruptor with a gleaming diamond emitter cone. Kirk's hand lashed out and knocked the weapon from Wilforth's grip.

"What did you hit them with?" Kirk demanded. He kept his voice to a harsh whisper. *How far did those screams carry? How many others are nearby?*

"A mild electrical charge," Wilforth rasped, frightened by the rage in Kirk's eyes. "We . . . we couldn't risk phasers because we don't know how the Talin metabolism would react to them. But a neural stun causes no long-term damage."

Kirk froze. " 'No long-term damage'? You *know* that? You've done this before?"

Wilforth couldn't speak, but he jerked his head up and down.

Then Kirk felt Cardinali's hand on his shoulder. It wasn't a fighting grip but Kirk still twisted away.

"It's all right," the communications manager said, trying to calm Kirk. "Inadvertent contact happens all the time in these conditions."

"The Prime Directive expressly forbids it!"

"But we're not *interfering* here, Captain Kirk," Wilforth said, his voice still trembling. "No harm is done. No information has been passed. Our existence is still a secret."

Kirk pointed to the unconscious Talin. The technicians attended to them with what appeared to be modified medical tricorders. "Except to them. What happens to them when they wake up? Or do you take them back with you to the moon?"

"Captain Kirk, slow down," Cardinali said. "What did they see? They opened a door, saw a few strange shapes in the shadows, then, as far as they know, they fainted. To the Talin, the effect of getting a neural shock is a bit like what happens when a human gets a violent blow to the head. There are a few seconds' worth of short-term memory that don't get laid down in the neural pathways. They'll remember nothing of us."

Kirk fought to control his anger. He had jeopardized the mission—and a planet—by trusting everything that Wilforth had told him. But as was so painfully obvious from the weapon Wilforth had carried, and the modified medical tricorders his technicians used, and even Cardinali's knowledge of Talin neurochemistry, he had not told Kirk all that he knew. And unfortunately, now was not the time to find out just how far the deception had gone.

"Who else has weapons?" Kirk asked.

Cardinali knew what the question meant. He unhooked a disruptor from his belt and handed it to Kirk. "We each have one. There's only one setting. Nonfatal. And by holding the green stud while twisting the emitter cone, you can fuse the interior circuitry so it can't be studied."

Kirk held the disruptor in his hand. "You, too," he said to the technicians who had finished with the Talin.

Wilforth nodded his head. "Do as he says," he told them. "We don't have much time."

Kirk took the technicians' disruptors and slapped them to his belt. "How long will they be out?"

"No less than twenty minutes, no more than an hour," Cardinali answered.

Kirk held out his hand. "Give me your tricorder."

The instrument was standard issue and Kirk quickly swept a half-kilometer circle for lifeform readings. "Are these signals Talin normal?" he asked as the display showed five individual readings three hundred meters distant.

Cardinali checked the readings and nodded. "But they're at rest," he said. "Or sleeping."

"That's why we expected this facility to be safe, Captain," Wilforth added. "It's late at night here. And this is just a records storage warehouse."

Kirk held the tricorder in one hand, the weapon in the other. The *Enterprise* was still more than half an hour away from returning overhead to beam them up. "How many Talin have seen a member of the FCO?" How badly had this world been disrupted?

Wilforth sighed. "As far as we know, nine." He looked at the floor. "Not counting those who might have seen one of the Wraiths on a sampling run."

"Nine," Kirk repeated. Out of two and a half billion. Perhaps the situation wasn't as bad as it might have been.

"Though according to their public broadcasts," Cardinali volunteered, "there are at least four or five thousand more who *claim* to have seen us."

"What?"

"The Talin are on the brink of leaving their planet, Captain Kirk. They *want* to believe that other life-forms exist. The same wish-fulfillment phenomena of spacecraft sighting and alien contact have occurred in the past on virtually every other spacefaring planet, including Earth."

"Earth was being observed by the Vulcans," Kirk said grimly.

"But until official contact was made, those few brief sightings and encounters did not interfere with the development of Earth," Cardinali argued. "Just as the inevitable sightings of us by the Talin will have no appreciable effect on them. The Prime Directive is safe, Captain Kirk. We have done nothing here to circumvent it."

Kirk decided not to pursue the discussion. His problem wasn't with Cardinali. It was with Wilforth, who had a convenient way of withholding information, and with Richter, who had no love for the Directive. There was nothing more he could do until they had all safely returned to the *Enterprise*.

"All right, Director Wilforth, have your people go to work. I'll watch the Talin. And the door."

Wilforth, Cardinali, and the two technicians moved quickly to the equipment cylinders which had been beamed down with them. At their touch, the storage tubes split open like metal blossoms, displaying a complex range of miniaturized sensing devices. One technician took a large, white wand which reminded Kirk of Richter's cane and began to slowly walk along a wall covered with rows of thick tubes, each the size of a human forearm.

"Those are Talin datadisks," Cardinali explained as he set up another piece of equipment on the floor. It looked like a type of primitive data terminal, almost as large as a chair. "The technician is taking micromass readings so we'll be able to reconstruct the written words and pictures stored in them."

"From only one pass?" Kirk asked.

"We're not miracle workers," Cardinali said with a faint smile. "It'll take three passes at least."

Kirk kept his eyes on the Talin. They breathed more rapidly than humans, but both breathed evenly, gently fluttering the membranes at the sides of their heads. He took that to be a good sign. "What equipment are you setting up?" he asked Cardinali.

"We've constructed a model of a Talin computer interface. The facility we're in maintains historical records for some of the nation states associated with the Greens. Much of the information is what we would call classified, so it is never transmitted outside the computer network that's in use here—which means we have never been able to tap into it." Cardinali patted the top of the device as a display screen came to life with Talin script, resembling rows of paint splatters. "Until now."

Beside him, Cardinali had several boxes of thick round objects, about five centimeters wide. "These are our own Talin-style datadisks. We made them at the outpost according to Talin specs to make downloading easier." He began slipping the disks into various slots on the side of the terminal.

Kirk did not interrupt any of the FCO personnel again and they worked swiftly and with a minimum of talking. Obviously they had rehearsed their routines many times. The readings on the five sleeping Talin three hundred meters away never varied and the stunned Talin on the warehouse floor didn't stir. Ten minutes before the *Enterprise* was due back, Kirk found himself thinking that there was a chance the landing party would be successful after all.

Then he heard a far-off explosive sound, followed by a drawn-out rumble. He went immediately to Cardinali. "Where exactly are we in this facility?"

"A basement storage area, Captain. Five meters underground. Three or four levels built above us."

"Then that was definitely a loud noise out there," Kirk said. "Thunderstorm?"

"Not here. Not in this season."

There was a second noise, louder than the first. Kirk watched as the life-form readings of the sleeping Talin began to change: temperatures rising, increased respiration, minor movement. "The ones that were sleeping heard that. They're starting to wake up."

Wilforth came over from an equipment cylinder he had been packing up. "It wasn't a weapons detonation, was it?" He sounded nervous.

Kirk flipped the tricorder from lifeforms to energy settings. "There are a couple of generating sources nearby . . . electrical . . . but everything's controlled. Nonexplosive." A sudden flurry of peak numbers rushed across the tricorder's screen. A third explosion echoed around the storeroom.

"That was something flying above us," Kirk said, fine tuning the controls. "Too small for the *Enterprise* . . . an aircraft of some sort . . ." Then he realized what they had heard. "Those were sonic booms."

Cardinali took his tricorder back from Kirk. "Zalan, pack up my terminal while I check this out."

"What is it?" Kirk asked, reading the screen upside down. He couldn't tell what Cardinali was scanning for.

"I'm trying to see if those are missiles or airplanes. Could be bombers . . . could be fighters."

"An attack?" Kirk asked, feeling shock. The negotiators he had listened to had seemed to be so reasonable, so eager for peace.

More rumbles.

"That's it," Cardinali announced tensely. "Life-forms on board. They're piloted aircraft. And with so many of them at that speed . . . they have to be military."

Kirk felt sick. The *Enterprise* was still five minutes away. But what did the landing party matter compared with a world that was going to destroy itself? "Is this facility a target?" he asked, already suspecting the answer—it held classified information.

Cardinali nodded slowly. "As far as we know, yes. An important one."

Kirk stepped over to the cylinders. "Then, let's stand ready." Wilforth, Cardinali, and the technicians moved to join him.

They waited.

They heard footsteps in the hallway outside the door. Kirk gestured rapidly to everyone to move the equipment cylinders to the edge of a bookshelf and then crouch down behind them. The *Enterprise* was less than two minutes away. *If she's still there,* Kirk thought. He knew Spock wouldn't risk coming in over a squadron of attacking warplanes.

"Give us the disruptors, Captain," Wilforth whispered urgently.

But Kirk shook his head. "If the Talin here are under attack and we stun any of them . . . they won't have a chance to go to a shelter. I won't let that happen to them."

The door to the hallway opened and bright light fell in again. Kirk peered through the crack between the two cylinders. Two Talin stood backlit in the doorway, a male and female, delicate saurians, two and a half meters tall, and impressive. Their large yellow eyes quickly scanned the storeroom as their cranial crests rippled like sea-weed. The larger Talin's gaze came to rest on the cylinders and Kirk saw the quick flicker of blue inner eyelids. The creature's wide and lipless mouth opened to reveal a serrated ridge of fine, sharp teeth. His exposed skin flushed deep red.

Then the other Talin called out with a high-pitched whistle. She had found the two Talin Wilforth had stunned.

Kirk was amazed at how quickly and gracefully the creatures moved as they knelt down to examine the unconscious pair.

The *Enterprise* was one minute away.

Be there, Kirk thought. It was an order.

Then one of the stunned Talin began to make a sound that sounded like cough-ing and the male beside him helped him sit up. Kirk watched as the awakening Talin shook his head, stared up at his benefactor, then turned to look farther into the storeroom, at the cylinders.

The creature's taloned hand shot out toward them and he began to shriek again.

"The disruptors!" Wilforth begged.

The floor shook with another cluster of sonic booms.

Kirk clutched the cylinders. *Enterprise!* he called out in his mind. *Come to me now.*

The male Talin stood. His hand went to a long pouch strapped to his bibcloth covering his chest and withdrew what could only be a chemical projectile weapon.

The ground shook again.

The Talin raised his weapon.

And the storeroom filled with the light of the ship who had come to claim her master.

Eight

The transporter room formed around Kirk and he felt the familiar transition back to the *Enterprise*'s gravity. The faces of Spock and McCoy as they waited by Kyle's console were also welcome.

Kirk jumped down from the platform. He saw Spock's eyes drop to the cluster of disruptors he had strung around him.

"Who's attacking the university? What's the situation below?" Kirk asked. He was puzzled by the way McCoy suddenly burst into a brilliant smile. "Good to see you, too, Bones."

"The university's not under attack," McCoy said.

"The situation is quite remarkable," Spock added.

Kirk looked from one to the other. Behind him, the FCO personnel broke open their equipment to retrieve the Talin datadisks. "We heard warplanes," Kirk said, still confused.

"Yes," Spock agreed. "There are hundreds in flight even now."

Kirk didn't understand. A world was at war and yet no one seemed to care.

"They are being recalled," Spock said simply.

"What happened?" Kirk asked.

McCoy's grin was blinding. "Peace, Jim. The Greens and Browns are withdrawing their forward troops. All over the planet."

"Wh-what?" Wilforth stuttered. Beside him, Cardinali and the technicians stopped their work.

As Kirk paused, wondering if he was going to have to ask more questions or whether some member of his crew might decide to fill him in, the transporter room doors slipped open and Carole Mallett ran in. Her smile was as broad as McCoy's and she went straight to Cardinali to hug him.

"They're going to make it!" she told them all. "They're really going to make it."

Before the doors closed again, Kirk had time to hear what sounded like a party in the corridor. He actually heard a noisemaker blow.

"Spock . . . ?"

"It has been a most fascinating sequence of events, Captain. The Talin had brought themselves to the brink of complete disaster."

"But that's what saved them!" McCoy's voice broke in. "They went straight to the brink—right to the edge, Jim, and they stepped back." The doctor spoke so quickly, so excitedly, that his Georgia drawl surfaced and his words ran together. "We were all listening to it on the bridge. Hell, we were all listening to it through the whole ship. Carolyn put it on the intercom.

"They *knew* they were minutes from destroying themselves, and they *chose* not to." McCoy shook his head at the wonder of it. "They chose not to."

Kirk was elated. It was the last thing he had expected to hear.

"Bones, that's wonderful. It's more than wonderful."

"It's unbelievable," Wilforth said quietly.

"But most logical on the part of the Talin," Spock concluded.

McCoy shook his head in dismissal. "Oh, spare us the logic of it, Spock. Those beings down there were scared. Cold, senseless, *emotional* fear. It was their feelings that saved the day. Not logical thinking. Emotions!"

"It was their emotions that brought them to this point in the—"

"Please, Spock, Bones, before we have to ask the Talin negotiators to come up here next." Kirk put a hand on the console to reassure himself that he was back and that all he was learning was real. "What brought them to the brink so quickly? Things weren't that bad when we beamed down, were they?"

"It was the dispute over polar airspace," Spock said. "Because of the difficulties in monitoring the area through the interference of the planet's magnetosphere, they—"

"The Greens thought the Browns were exploiting gaps in the continent's defenses," McCoy said, to cut through Spock's detailed explanation. "But the Browns kept denying it. So the Greens thought that the Browns were really up to some-thing and started to escalate their war readiness. And that made the Browns con-vinced that the Greens were making up the whole thing as an excuse to go to war, so *they* started escalating. It was like one of your bloody chess games with Spock. No one knew when to call it off."

McCoy and Spock stared at each other.

"And . . . ?" Kirk said, not wanting the story to be cut off there. "What happened?"

"The Talin negotiators intervened," Spock said. "Each side realized that there was no advantage to the other for doing what each was accused of doing."

"They blamed the whole thing on communications failure," McCoy said, "to save face. Hardly logical but it sure worked."

"And they were able to have their armies stand down so quickly?" Kirk asked.

"The Talin have an elaborate system of oaths," Spock said. "Invoking some of them carries a great deal of authority. And some of those oaths were invoked be-tween the Browns and the Greens for the first time."

Wilforth's mouth dropped open in a way which reminded Kirk of the Talin who had seen the cylinders. "The Browns and Greens invoked oaths of common kinship?"

"Yes," Spock said. "That was the term used by the translator."

Kirk thought Wilforth was going to faint.

"An hour ago," the FCO director said, "I would have sworn that would have been impossible." He looked at Kirk and frowned. "I told you we should have stunned that second pair. They didn't need to go to a shelter."

Kirk deflected Spock's question by speaking first. "We were detected by one pair of Talin and stunned them. A second pair saw us—or at least saw the cylinders beam out."

"A not uncommon occurrence during FCO operations," Spock observed.

"So I've been told," Kirk said dryly.

Cardinali came up beside him, one arm around Mallett. "Captain Kirk, this is an unprecedented moment in Talin history. Perhaps one of the greatest gifts we could give them when contact is finally established is a complete record of what transpired during this incident. I'd like permission to have the sensor satellites go to full scan under the *Enterprise*'s control for at least the next week."

Kirk began to say no. He didn't want to extend his stay in this system any longer than he had to.

But Cardinali's exhilaration was infectious. "Remember how much Earth ap-preciated the communication logs made by the Vulcans during the last decade of the twentieth century? So many questions were answered."

Kirk turned to Spock. "If we keep to tightbeam, can we stay in an orbit beyond the range of their sensors?"

"Most efficiently," Spock said.

"Very well," Kirk said to Cardinali. "Coordinate your communication require-ments with Lieutenant Uhura."

Cardinali thanked Kirk excitedly, then left with Mallett. The party sounds from the corridor sounded even louder when the doors opened a second time.

"No problem on the close orbit while I was gone?" Kirk asked Spock.

"The Talin had other matters with which to occupy themselves."

For the first time since his initial meeting with Wilforth, Kirk felt himself begin to relax. He had gone into this mission expecting the worst, yet it had unexpectedly ended with the best possible result. He knew he'd have to be careful or he'd begin to start expecting this to happen all the time. He smiled at his friends. He had won again, even though this time he hadn't known all the rules of the game.

"I guess you know that that leaves us with only one thing to do," McCoy said.

"Absolutely," Kirk agreed.

Now it was Spock's turn to be puzzled. "I do not understand. I am aware of nothing more that needs to be done at this time."

"Of course you don't understand," McCoy said as he headed for the doors. "Because *you* don't have anything left to do."

Spock looked at Kirk. Kirk smiled. "What Bones means is that since it's going to be at least fifty years before we can celebrate with the Talin, right now we have to celebrate *for* them."

Spock thought that over. "An entire planet has been saved today. A race has been preserved and someday will have a chance to spread among the stars. Yes, I believe a celebration is in order."

McCoy stared at Spock in amazement. "Well, I'll be . . . Maybe there is hope for you after all, Spock."

Kirk patted the doctor on the back. "If the Talin can make it, Bones, anyone can. Come on, Mr. Spock, we've got some logical celebrating to do."

Kirk kept reading the quartermaster's report and reached out for the coffee cup on the yeoman's tray without paying attention. The QM subprogram warned that alcohol consumption had shown an alarming increase among the crew but Kirk signed off on it. Yesterday's Talin celebration party had been the first real blowout his crew had had since the last Nobel and Z.Magnees Prize ceremonies. They were entitled. Then he became aware that he had closed his hand around empty space. He glanced up from his screenpad to see what had happened to the coffee.

The tray was out of reach. Slowly he realized that his yeoman had pulled it away from him.

"Yeoman Frietas, what are—oh."

"Hello, Captain," Carolyn Palamas said smoothly. "Did you want some coffee?" She brought the tray back within reach.

Kirk took the cup. Being fifty thousand kilometers out from Talin and monitoring the ongoing peace developments had given the bridge of the *Enterprise* a different feel. He was glad to see her there.

"Why, Lieutenant, I don't recall approving your transfer to yeoman."

Palamas moved a fraction closer. "I didn't request a transfer. It's just that someone ran off without his breakfast this morning and I thought you could use some . . . coffee."

Kirk smiled. It had been a wonderful celebration and he was happy to have someone to share it with. "What I could use," Kirk said, "is the five-day slow voyage out of this system."

"I thought you didn't like slow voyages."

"Depends on whom I'm voyaging with," Kirk said. Their eyes met and held.

"Excuse me, Captain," Spock said from his station.

Kirk turned instantly.

"Sensor satellite five does not respond to its scheduled tightbeam data upload," Spock reported.

Kirk stepped from his chair and had time to nod good-bye to Palamas as she headed for the turbolift. She nodded in return, understanding in her eyes. The mission and ship came first, always.

Kirk checked Spock's readouts. "The satellite's still in orbit. Is its power supply functional, Mr. Spock?"

"Without a tightbeam upload, the only way to be sure is with a sensor scan, Captain. But at this distance, the sensor probe would spread enough so that residual radiation would reach Talin's surface and might be detected."

"Get Scotty up here to go over the controls. He rigged the satellites. He can fix them."

"Very good, Captain. But if we are unable to regain contact with the satellite?"

Kirk looked at the image of Talin IV on the main screen—a world at peace. "Then we'll go in for a look. Nothing to worry about down there now."

The crisis abated, Kirk returned to his chair and the quartermaster's report. He looked toward the turbolift as he stepped down to the central area, but the doors were closed and Palamas was gone. *Oh, well,* he thought, *at least we've got the voyage out.*

Chief Engineer Scott appeared on the bridge within two minutes of Spock's call. "I don't understand," he said as he went to work at the engineering station, "those satellites were perfect. They'll still be working fifty years on."

"But one is not working now, Mr. Scott," Spock said.

"I can see that, Mr. Spock, but there's no reason for it. Look at these readings for yourself. It's perfectly clear. The dual-looped power units were fully coiled on the two-fifty bypasses and the L-37s were securely crosslinked to all duotronics."

Kirk leaned against the railing and listened to Spock and Scott trade technical jargon. He knew what almost everything they mentioned was but he wasn't sure how any of it should go together. It had been a long time since some of his Academy classes.

After a few minutes of increasingly incomprehensible specifications had been cited and all controls had been adjusted and readjusted, the science officer and the chief engineer appeared to have hit an impasse.

"Should we go down and take a look?" Kirk asked.

"No need," Scott said. "It's the software."

"We should," Spock said. "The hardware appears to be at fault."

Both men turned to look at Kirk. *Now this* is *a classic no-win situation,* Kirk thought. "Sorry, Scotty, but if there's the slightest chance that the satellite has been damaged somehow, we can't risk it re-entering by accident. We'll go in close enough so that we can scan for damage without flooding the Talin with sensor radiation, and once the equipment's checked out we can come back here to work on the software at leisure." Kirk hoped he had talked fast enough.

"Aye, Captain," Scott said and smiled at Spock. "And I'd be more than willin' to give you a hand with your reprogramming, Mr. Spock."

"Thank you, Mr. Scott, but I believe that will not be necessary once the satellite has been repaired."

Kirk left them to it and went to Sulu to request a change in orbit. But Sulu had overheard and the orbit was already plotted.

"Very good, Mr. Sulu, take us in."

Chekov jumped up to take his place at the defense subsystems monitor and prepare countermeasures. Ensign Leslie left his environmental station to take over

Chekov's navigation post. Kirk sat back in his chair. All operations were smooth and routine as Talin grew in the viewscreen.

Kirk turned back to his screenpad and the QM's report. The program warned that if current consumption was maintained, the ship's stores of real chocolate would be exhausted within two months. It recommended encouraging a switch to consumption of synthesized chocolate. Kirk shuddered at the thought and vetoed that suggestion with a quick flick of his stylus.

"Coming up on satellite five," Sulu announced.

Kirk glanced up. The curve of Talin filled the lower half of the screen. The satellite was too small to register though he could see its sensor echo on the astrogator screen. He signed off on the QM report and the week's medical log synopsis appeared on the pad.

"Within focused sensor range, Mr. Spock," Leslie announced.

"Scanning," Spock said.

Kirk vetoed the medical log as well. All that was in it were ten requests for Kirk, James T., to report to sickbay for a scheduled checkup or risk being put on the captain's disciplinary list.

"All equipment checks out," Spock said.

Kirk looked up. It had been subtle but there had been surprise in Spock's tone.

Scotty smiled. "You're sure I can't be giving ye some help with the software, Mr. Spock?"

Spock shook his head. "The software does not seem to be the problem either, Mr. Scott. It is no longer resident in the satellite's control circuits."

Kirk put the screenpad down on the arm of his chair.

"I beg your pardon, Mr. Spock?" Scott said.

"The control programs have been erased?" Kirk asked.

Spock nodded. "It is quite impossible, but all memory storage on the satellite is empty."

"Explanation, Mr. Scott?"

"I . . . have none at the moment, Captain. I don't know how such a thing could be possible without . . ."

"Without what, Mr. Scott?"

"Well, the password authorization . . . the encryption codes . . . the scrambling mechanisms. . . . The satellites were prepared according to FCO specifications. They're near impossible to program or extract information from by brute force."

"Mr. Spock, any theories?"

"Absolutely none. A violent subspace pulse could have burned out the transtator circuitry but we have not detected any phenomena of the required intensity. I shall have to—"

"Keptin! I have detected an energy burst on the planet's surface."

"What kind of energy?" Kirk scanned the screen. Just beyond the terminator on Talin's nightside, he saw a brilliant white flare. "Helm, magnify. Is that it, Chekov?"

Chekov looked over at the screen. "Y-yes, sir."

The viewscreen swam, then fixed on an enlarged image of the flare. Kirk could see pinpricks of red fire spring up around it. "What is it, Ensign?"

"N-nuclear, Keptin. It is a forty megaton nuclear detonation."

Kirk felt as if the ship had jumped to warp nine without warning. "Where?" he asked. On the screen, from the pattern of city lights along the coastline, the detonation appeared to be in the center of the Greens' continent—their agricultural heartland, Palamas had called it.

Chekov read off the coordinates. "The Green nation state," he said, voice choking. "Eastern administrative district. Subregion five."

Kirk stared at the glowing spark of hellfire on the screen. An entire city might already be ashes.

"Those are the coordinates of a missile silo facility," Spock said.

Kirk tensed. It was a military target. It could only mean one thing. "Why would the Browns launch a first strike now?" he asked.

"And why would they launch a first strike with only one warhead?" Spock said. He bent to his scope.

"Keptin! I have missiles launching! I have missiles launching!"

"Dear God," Kirk whispered. A regular pattern of red dots had appeared across the Green continent. Hundreds of missiles were in flight.

"Go to red alert," Kirk said. It was standard procedure, but he knew the missiles were not meant for his ship. He had Uhura kill the warning sirens on the bridge, but the red alert lights still flashed.

"Captain," Spock said. "My sensors show that detonation occurred deep underground."

"Depth, Spock? What was the depth?"

"Consistent with underground missile emplacement."

"No!" Kirk said. He turned to the screen. More red dots. A thousand missiles in flight. "It was a *mistake!*"

Uhura cut in. "Communications intercept from the planet's surface, Captain. Brown forces have detected the Green launch." There were tears in her eyes. "Captain, they're retaliating."

"Brown missiles are launching!" Chekov called out. "Brown missiles are launching!"

"It's a mistake, you fools!" Kirk shouted at the viewscreen, at the dying planet. "Spock! It has to be! The Talin warheads are faulty. Only a sixty percent accuracy rate! The Greens were dismantling their missiles and accidentally set off one of their own damn warheads!"

Spock's face was rigid. His eyes were fixed on the screen. "That would be . . . the most logical explanation."

"A mistake!" Kirk slammed his fist against the side of his chair. "No!"

"Captain?" Spock asked.

"I will not allow a mistake to destroy this planet." He burned with anger. This planet was going to survive. Any other fate for it was a personal insult.

"Captain, we can do nothing," Spock said. But his words and his tone conveyed two different meanings. "The Prime Directive forbids us from interfering."

"No!" Kirk snapped. "The Prime Directive forbids us from interfering in a planet's normal development. Look what's going on down there. Spock, that's not the planet's normal development. That's an accident. An accidental detonation has triggered off an aberrant chain of events. The Talin are not doing this to themselves on purpose."

Spock's face flickered with an expression of pain, quickly hidden. "Captain, I agree you can make a case for this being a . . . natural disaster . . . an event similar to a runaway asteroid about to impact . . . but still we cannot be seen to interfere."

"But we won't be seen, Spock." Kirk's mind raced. There had to be a way out.

There always was a way out. Change the rules, change the goals, do anything. But find that way out. "We can do it. The *Enterprise* can do it. And the Talin won't know what happened any more than they'll ever know what set off that first missile in its silo. We won't be interfering, Spock. We'll only be giving them some time. Some time to sort things out on their own. That's all."

The bridge crew froze at their stations. They would do anything their captain told them to do, but they knew their captain would tell them nothing if Spock did not agree.

Spock leaned on the railing.

Kirk held his hands out before him, imploring. "Spock . . . think it through. It works. The Prime Directive is upheld. They won't know what has happened."

Spock spoke slowly. "Yes . . . the Directive . . . is upheld." He squared his shoulders. "I shall prepare coordinates." He turned to his scope.

Kirk gave orders in an endless stream. There was no time to stop to think or consider his actions. There was time only to do, to take action, to save a world.

The *Enterprise* flooded Talin IV with sensor radiation. Within seconds, her computers established the location and trajectory of each missile arcing through the skies below.

Scott was the one who knew how the warheads worked. He took over five percent of the *Enterprise*'s computing capacity to decode and transmit self-destruct signals to the missiles in flight. They vanished from the screen by the hundreds.

Uhura knew the radio codes. Another eight percent of the *Enterprise*'s computers went to decoding and translating radio voice callback signals to bomber wings and fighters and submersible weapons platforms. Most Talin who received those messages did not turn back immediately, but they held in failsafe positions and requested verification, unsure of their commanders' commitment.

Chekov moved back to his station and took over the main phaser banks. Four hundred and twenty-seven missiles refused to respond to Scott's signals. Chekov took them from the skies with pinpoint precision.

In forty minutes, Sulu had taken the *Enterprise* around the planet twice. The Browns' missiles were gone. The Greens' missiles were gone. The bombers were returning. The submersibles were silent and still. The skies of Talin were clear.

Kirk's shirt was drenched with sweat. His voice was hoarse. The red alert signal still flashed.

Uhura cleared her throat. "Captain . . . I am on the diplomatic frequency. The negotiators are back on line. They are . . . apologizing, sir . . . they are . . . sir, they are praying to their gods together to thank them for salvation from . . . from a terrible . . . accident." Uhura wiped the tears from her eyes. "They know it was an accident, sir." Scotty went to her and put an arm around her. His hair was plastered to his forehead.

Kirk didn't turn from the screen. The nightside of the planet was scattered with thousands of small fires from the flaming debris of the destroyed missiles, but the planet was still there. A world still existed. A race still survived.

"Lieutenant Uhura," Kirk said, "download all bridge records of the past hour, unedited audio and visual, to the FCO main computer on Talin's moon. Then download duplicates of all records into two separate message buoys for Starfleet Command and launch immediately."

"Aye-aye, sir," Uhura said hoarsely.

The turbolift doors slid open and McCoy stormed onto the bridge. "What the hell is going on around here?" He stopped when he saw the small fires blazing across the face of Talin IV. "Good Lord, what're those?" He looked at Kirk, saw his exhaustion, brought out his medical scanners. "What have you done?"

It was Spock who answered, perfectly calm, perfectly controlled.

"Dr. McCoy, we have done our job."

Nine

Kirk wore his formal tunic. He knew that technically there was no need for it, but when the board of inquiry replayed the tapes of these proceedings, he wanted them to know that he took his actions and his duty as seriously as they took theirs.

Spock, Scott, and McCoy sat with Kirk on one side of the table in the conference room. Zalan Wilforth, Alonzo Richter, and Yeoman Jorge Frietas sat on the other. The yeoman operated the recording computer as if it were an extension of himself.

"Recording, Mr. Spock," Frietas said as the verification lights flickered across the computer terminal, constantly encoding all that it registered with elaborately sequenced security codes which could not be duplicated, thus ensuring that the original tapes could not be altered in any way. It was a new system designed to prevent abuses such as had occurred in the past.

Spock folded his hands on the table and began his formal recitation for the record. "The third session of the preliminary hearing into actions taken by Captain James T. Kirk at Talin IV is now in session. This hearing has been called by Captain Kirk himself because of his concern that some or all of his actions at Talin IV might be considered to have contravened the noninterference directive of Starfleet General Order One. This hearing's purpose is to gather preliminary information which may or may not support the captain's claim that all his actions were performed without such contravention. Any or all preliminary information gathered by this hearing is subject to further review and verification by Starfleet Command, if and when so desired."

Spock waited patiently for a few moments. "Director Wilforth," he said at last, "you may speak now."

Wilforth squirmed in his seat. "Oh, ah, Zalan Ko'askla Wilforth, Director, Starfleet First Contact Office, Outpost 47, Talin IV." He looked at Spock for approval.

"Please continue, Director."

"Ah, I wish to present a report prepared by the communications section of FCO Outpost 47 concerning communications intercepts carried out in the three Talin days following the accidental detonation of a native nuclear warhead on Talin IV." He held up a yellow microtape. "W-what do I do with it?"

Kirk sat calmly. This was an official procedure and, as a show of his respect for Starfleet, for once he was not impatient. Wilforth could take all day as far as he was concerned.

"Place it in the recording computer," Spock said, "and then present your summary."

Wilforth offered the microtape to Yeoman Frietas, but the young man shook his head. "You have to place it in the reader, sir. I can't touch it."

"Oh, of course," Wilforth said. He fumbled at the side of the terminal with the tape, then slipped it into place with a click. "And, ah, to summarize. Ahem." He coughed into his fist. "The hours following the accidental detonation of the warhead on Talin are being referred to as the Blue Season Miracle. Ah, Blue Season is the native calendar designation for the current . . . ah . . . calendar period on Talin. Um, anyway, the use of the term 'miracle' is important in the FCO's interpretation of events because it establishes that the Talin have clearly assigned an almost supernatural significance to what has happened on their planet. That is, they do not ascribe those events to the actions of an indigenous or extraplanetary agency.

"Briefly, the FCO intercepts show that the Talin are aware that the detonation of a missile in the Green nation state was, without question, an accident. Though, owing to the destruction it caused, the reason for that accident will likely never be determined. The Talin are also aware that the resulting launch of approximately one quarter of the Green nuclear arsenal was triggered solely by automated alert systems which were scheduled for dismantling over the next few Talin . . . ah . . . months, I suppose you'd call them.

"Likewise, the retaliatory launch of approximately one third of the Brown nuclear arsenal was also a programmed response, again not initiated by deliberate orders."

Wilforth looked around the table. His nervousness finally seemed to be under control.

"It is my expert opinion, as an FCO director, that the Talin as a race believe that an unimaginable accident nearly came to pass three days ago and that an almost equally unimaginable sequence of equipment malfunctions, programming conflicts, and even weather conditions, contributed to the failure of the warheads being exchanged.

"To support Captain Kirk's claim that what he did was not in contravention of General Order One, I should like to emphasize that because his actions preserved the Talin global communications system, the military and political leaders of the various nation states on the planet were able to enter into immediate, joint discussions which enabled them to prevent any further commitment of their remaining forces.

"It is the FCO's opinion that Captain Kirk's actions served only to give the Talin approximately fifteen to thirty minutes of extra time during which they were able to reaffirm the strong commitment to world peace that the Talin have demonstrated so often during our observation of them. The FCO believes the Talin have been saved from an unpredictable and uncontrollable disaster, not of their own making, and are now able to continue their normal and expected development as a race and a culture.

"Most importantly, according to all communication intercepts available to the FCO, Captain Kirk has accomplished this humanitarian deed without revealing in any way to the Talin that an extraplanetary agency was involved." Wilforth cleared his throat a final time. "Our conclusion is that the Prime Directive has not been contravened and Captain Kirk deserves the Federation's highest commendation for the preservation of life and peace."

Kirk didn't smile or otherwise acknowledge Wilforth's summary. As a career officer, he was used to listening to others praise him, and he knew how quickly that praise could turn to censure. He appreciated Wilforth's contribution because Kirk believed it to be true, but he also knew that the final authority to decide whether or not General Order One had been obeyed rested with Starfleet Command. However, he realized that for once he wasn't worried about second-guessing Command—he had saved an entire world, and given the politics of the Federation and the Admiralty, no one was going to go after a winner.

"Does anyone have anything more to add?" Spock asked.

No one replied.

"This hearing is adjourned."

We pulled it off, Kirk suddenly thought. *The* Enterprise *saved a world without revealing herself.* He felt a welcome rush of accomplishment. Then it was checked by one last realization. *If I didn't trust Wilforth's judgment two days ago, why should I trust him now?*

"I have this idea for a bar," Kirk said. He took a bite of his sandwich and gazed out through the herbarium's viewport. Talin was full and alive fifty thousand kilometers distant. The air around him was filled with the scent of blooming roses. The *Enterprise*'s greenhouse facility was his favorite room on the ship. Especially during ship's night.

"Funny, you don't look like the bartender type," Palamas said teasingly. On the park bench reproduction they sat on, she finished spreading out the picnic Kirk had packed.

"No, no," Kirk said, talking around a mouthful of chicken salad. "On the ship. Or a ship, anyway."

"A bar on a Starfleet vessel?" She was skeptical now.

"For times like these." Kirk turned to her and smiled. "The mission is accomplished. We're in friendly waters. It would be nice to have a place to go to enjoy these moments. Something with a bit more . . . atmosphere than the rec facilities or the mess hall. Could take the edge off waiting for shore leave, too." He took another bite of his sandwich. "Just a thought."

"Well, it sounds like a nice one. These ships can get pretty sterile sometimes." Palamas began to peel an orange, staring at it thoughtfully. "Jim . . . how do you feel about what you've done?" She sounded flustered. "Have I asked that the right way? Do you know . . . ?"

Kirk nodded. He inhaled the scent of the flowers. He remembered his mother's garden back on the farm. Just a small patch with a few rose bushes, some petunias, a rhododendron which never seemed to bloom. His father had always said flowers were nonsense on a farm. You couldn't eat them. But he was always out there with her, weeding and pruning. And smiling, Kirk remembered. They were always smiling when they were out in their nonsense garden together.

"I know what you're asking," Kirk said. "But to tell the truth, Carolyn, I don't think about it that way." He saw the confusion in her eyes. "I did what I had to do at the time I did it. And now, it's done, so . . . it's time to do something else."

But Palamas shook her head. "You saved an entire civilization, Jim. Two and a half billion beings . . . their history . . . their hopes. . . ."

Kirk put his sandwich down and took Palamas's hand in his. "I didn't save a world, Carolyn. This *crew* saved a world. This *ship* saved a world. I was just the one in the center seat, and there are lots of others who could sit there just as well."

Palamas stared into Kirk's eyes, questioning him with more than words. "You really believe that, don't you? This isn't false nodesty . . . or conceited humility . . . you honestly believe that you did nothing extraordinary on your own . . . ?"

Kirk put a hand to her face, tracing the soft contours of her cheek and her lips.

They were in friendly waters. There was room for just a few moments to themselves. "There are one or two extraordinary things I can do on my own," he whispered.

"I know." She touched his face in return.

Surrounded by the scent of flowers and life and precious memories, they kissed.

The red alert sounded two seconds later.

The paging whistle was like a knife.

Chekov's voice thundered from the intercom. *"Bridge to Keptin! Bridge to Keptin! We have missiles launched on Talin IV! We have detonations!"*

Kirk pushed his way through the turbolift doors and arrived on the bridge out of breath.

The viewscreen showed the terrible truth in full magnification. The dayside of Talin glittered with the brilliant flares of fusion fireballs. Dozens. Hundreds. More sparkling into hellish life with each second.

"Why?" Kirk said. He whirled to Uhura. "What happened?"

Uhura looked desperate. "Unknown, Captain. There has been no mention of any war preparations on any of the com channels we've been monitoring."

"Sulu! Take us in there! Full impulse."

Even as the helmsman acknowledged the order, the image of Talin swelled on the screen. The ship was in geostationary orbit in seconds, poised over the terminator.

"Chekov! Evaluation!"

The ensign's hands trembled over his controls. "It's insane, Keptin. All weapons have been launched. All weapons. There is no strategy. No plan. Just . . . they are firing *everything.*"

Kirk saw his straw and grasped at it. "Are you saying malfunction, mister? Is that it? Is that a malfunction down there?"

Chekov shook his head in confusion. "They can't want to do this. Not like that. It must be something else that caused it."

The turbolift doors burst open again. Spock rushed onto the bridge still adjusting his uniform. His mouth opened as he saw what was on the screen, but he said nothing.

"Everything's been launched, Spock," Kirk said urgently. "No plan, no strategy."

"That is senseless," Spock said.

"Exactly, Spock. Senseless. Another accident. Something to do with disarming the automated alert systems. That's the only explanation."

"Yes," Spock said. Even he was shaken by the destruction spreading on the screen. "The Talin are not capable of such . . . insanity. But without more information, we can't be sure what triggered it. We can't be certain what to do."

Kirk turned to his crew. "Bring those missiles down."

"No, Captain," Spock said. "Without data, without communication logs . . . you cannot."

"I know, Spock, I know." He thrust out his arm to point at the screen. "But look what they're doing to themselves down there." He made his decision. "Everyone: I cannot order you to do what we did before—when the situation was clearer. But I believe that something else beyond the Talin's control has caused this. And I believe we are justified in stopping it."

Kirk looked at each of his bridge crew in turn. "But I cannot order you to act against the Prime Directive."

Chekov spoke first. "Sir, I wolunteer to bring down the missiles."

"Transmitting self-destruct and call-back codes," Uhura said.

Sulu brought the ship about. "Moving in on main missile flights."

"Processing targeting data." Spock was at his station.

McCoy and Wilforth ran from the turbolift. Richter shuffled out with Cardinali and Mallett, then stopped in horror at what he saw. "My God."

McCoy was more forthright. "Those ignorant fools."

"It's not their fault, Bones," Kirk said. "It's a massive equipment malfunction. They trusted too much to their computers. Or maybe—"

"Captain Kirk, all radio frequencies are jammed, sir." Uhura jabbed at her controls in frustration. "Nothing can get through. Not even the Talin's own messages."

"Can you broadcast on subspace and phase down to radio frequencies once you're past the jamming boundary?" Kirk asked.

Uhura looked at Spock. "Mr. Spock, I'll need your help to—"

"I will begin the proper sensor alignment," Spock said.

Kirk stared at the screen, willing the miniature suns that grew silently on it to disappear. On the planet's nightside, the arc of atmosphere already glowed red from the firestorms that had erupted.

"Where are those phasers, Mr. Chekov?"

"Sir, targeting modes are not working. I can't lock on to anything."

Kirk was out of his chair. "What do you mean not working?"

"I am not getting a target-acquisition return signal. Perhaps it is the jamming. . . ." Chekov kept trying to reset his weapons systems, over and over.

"But those signals go over subspace," Kirk protested, going to Chekov's station. "Uhura said the jamming was in the electromagnetic spectrum."

Then Spock called for the captain. "Subspace frequencies are jammed as well."

"What? That's impossible! The Talin don't have the technology."

Spock looked up from his scope. "Nevertheless, subspace is jammed, sir."

"Could it be an effect of all the fusion explosions?" There were still more of them. The planet looked as if its core had exploded and was bursting through its shell.

"Perhaps, Captain, but our sensors are useless."

"What if we went in closer? Boosted power to all subspace systems and punched through the interference."

"That could work," Spock decided.

"Sulu! Take us in past the jamming layer."

Sulu hesitated for an instant. "Sir, that will take us through the ionosphere and into the atmosphere proper."

"Won't be the first time," Kirk said, fists clenched. "Take us in."

The *Enterprise* fell for the planet.

Within seconds, the rough buffeting of atmospheric flight shook the bridge.

"Chekov, try those phasers again."

The whine of the phaser capacitors echoed through the bridge.

"They're working!" Chekov cried triumphantly. "Limited range but they're working!"

"Uhura, try the self-destruct signals again."

"Yes, sir. Getting some response, sir."

Then Chekov screamed and flew from his chair as his navigation board erupted in sparks and flame. McCoy ran to him. Richter kept muttering to himself.

"Subspace feedback through phaser targeting system," Spock said.

Cardinali and Mallett broke out oxygen eaters from the emergency lockers and began spraying the sputtering console to help the automatic damage-control systems. Sulu stayed at his post, blackened with soot, breathing smoke. The ship bucked wildly.

"Shock waves from multiple explosions," he said, hands moving feverishly over the controls. "It's like flying through water, sir."

Uhura gasped and pulled her earpiece from her ear.

"Subspace feedback on all com channels," Spock said. "This is not a natural phenomenon. This is a deliberate attempt to—"

"Incoming missiles!" Sulu shouted.

"Impossible!" Kirk answered.

"We have been targeted," Spock confirmed. "Missiles are locked."

"They can't do this!" Kirk said. "They don't have the capability."

The com page sounded. Scott's voice came over the line. "Scott to bridge. If ye don't mind me asking, what the hell's going on up there?"

"Five seconds to impact," Spock announced.

"Full power to shields, Scotty! Now! Now! Sulu, get us out of—"

The viewscreen flared brilliant white until the visual compensators cut in. The ship shuddered as if it had smashed into solid rock. Uhura fell from her chair. Spock slammed over the railing. Richter cried out. And all Kirk could hear was every bridge alarm screaming at him in betrayal.

"Captain!" Sulu cried. "Impulse is gone. We're in free fall. Impact on planet's surface in one minute."

The rush of air outside the hull rose in a frantic wail.

Kirk felt his heart stop. There was only one way out. But it was madness. Madness.

"Warp us out, Sulu. Warp us out!"

Scotty shouted over the intercom. "Captain! We're within the Danylkiw Limit. Too deep in the gravity well. We won't survive the transition."

"Now, Sulu! There's no other—"

The hull metal shrieked and the ship twisted as another flight of missiles detonated against her shields. Spock pulled himself back to his feet. Green blood flooded his eyes from a gash on his forehead. Mallett sat beside Sulu, trying desperately to bring any of Chekov's nav controls back on line.

"Thirty seconds to impact!" Sulu cried. "Going to warp . . . now!"

It was like death.

The viewscreen went to black. The lights cut out. Gravity failed and there was only a long endless fall into utter darkness. Then the emergency lights flickered back on and Kirk saw everything before him blur in a highspeed vibration.

"Emergency systems on line," Spock said, voice distorted. Partial gravity returned. Color trails flickered from every object as local time slowed down.

Scott's voice was plaintive, slow, and warbling over the commlink. "Warp generators are runaway. Linked to singularity on runaway."

"Jettison nacelles!" Kirk felt trapped in thick liquid. The *Enterprise* had to cut her warp space link to Talin IV's gravity well or they would become trapped in an endless moment of time.

"Crew evacuation complete!" Spock rumbled. "Starboard nacelle away!"

Kirk felt stretched like rubber. The viewscreen flickered to show the infinite fractal nightmare of the gravitational wormhole that loomed hungrily before them. He felt a part of him wrenched away as the long white graceful form of the starboard warp nacelle flew down the maw of the beast—distorted in dizzying eddies of higher dimensional realities.

Gravity failed and they fell again. His hands gripped the sides of his chair. His feet hooked under the seat to hold him in place. Someone flew through the air beside him. Equipment consoles flared and sparked.

No! Kirk thought. *I won't let you go. I won't let you go alone.*

"Port nacelle locked in position!" Spock said. "Cannot jettison!"

Only one more chance, Kirk thought. *Worse than the last.*

He ordered Spock to eject all matter and antimatter into the wormhole. Spock didn't argue. If the singularity won, they would not even know death—only the torment of being forever trapped in the instant just before the end.

Kirk saw the twin ionized jets of matter and antimatter stream down the wormhole with agonizing slowness. Then at last they met and interacted.

The screen went blank. Time stopped.

Kirk fell into oblivion.

Ten

He awoke to the sound of a spray hypo. McCoy stared down at him. The doctor's face was haggard and bloodsmeared. "Good," he said. Then he moved on.

Kirk pushed himself from the floor of the bridge. He did it on a lean because the gravity field was out of alignment, placing the floor on a relative five-degree angle. Smoke filled the air. He heard moans. Half the station displays were out. The other half flickered with gibberish. Only a few battery lights were working, making the whole area dark and murky.

Spock staggered to Kirk's side, a greensoaked bandage covering a gash on his forehead. "It worked," he said hoarsely. "The matter-antimatter explosion pushed us past the Danylkiw Limit into normal space."

"But what else did it do?" Kirk asked. His ship was dying around him. "How long have I been out?"

"Three minutes, eighteen seconds," Spock said. He seemed weak, distracted. "Every transtator circuit in the ship appears to be fused. The subspace energy pulse directed at us was . . . incredible."

"But from where?"

"Unknown, Captain." He coughed roughly. "Unknown."

Kirk saw a shape move onto the viewscreen. It was Talin. The planet was on fire. The entire planet. It floated across the screen, then disappeared. The *Enterprise* spun slowly, adrift in space.

"We are quite powerless," Spock said before Kirk could ask.

Kirk heard a dull thudding noise and then one of the kick-in panels by the turbolift popped out of position. Scott appeared holding a hand light that sent a solid shaft of light through the smoke. He was followed by two medical technicians. Oddly, the kick-in panel on the other side of the lift was also open.

"Ah, thank heavens you're all right, Captain. I couldn't know that any of you had survived. The com system's out. The turbolift's . . ." He saw Talin pass by the viewscreen again. "Och, no . . . how did it happen? And what happened to the ship?"

"We were attacked by Talin missiles," Spock said flatly.

Kirk watched Scott's reaction to that. The fact that the Talin had attacked the *Enterprise* meant that without a doubt they had known the ship was in orbit around their planet—in direct and flagrant violation of the Prime Directive. Scott was a good officer. He'd know what he would have to do next under those circumstances.

McCoy came up beside Kirk. "Everyone here will be all right, Jim. But I can't find Mallett or Cardinali."

Wilforth limped up the rise of the deck. "But they were here," he coughed. "They were here when . . ."

"It's all right, sir," Scott said. "We passed them in the ladderways heading down to check on their equipment. But Mr. Spock, are ye sure that the Talin missiles were directed at the *Enterprise* herself?"

Kirk put his hand on Scott's shoulder. "They were, Scotty. The Talin knew we were here. They came after us."

Scott looked at the screen. He looked at Talin dying in the heat of a thousand killing suns. Already more than half the planet was enshrouded in brown and black clouds.

"Och, Captain Kirk," he said weakly. Kirk saw the knowledge in the engineer's eyes. Scott had not been on the bridge. That made him untainted, and the next in line.

"It's all right, Scotty," Kirk said gently. "You know what you have to do."

"But, Captain, I . . ."

Kirk couldn't look at his chief engineer. "Damn it, Scotty. You're a Starfleet officer. You *know* what you have to do."

Scott nodded. The funeral fires of Talin filled the bridge with their hideous glow. "Aye," he said. "That I do."

Chief Engineer Montgomery Scott faced his captain.

"James Kirk, as per Starfleet Command Regulation 7, Paragraph 4, you must now consider yourself under arrest, unless in the presence of these fellow officers you give satisfactory answer to the charge which I now bring." Scott faltered, but only for an instant. "Sir, I charge you with knowingly and willfully contravening Starfleet's Prime Directive as set forth in General Order One. Can you answer that charge, sir?"

Kirk shook his head. There was nothing more that could be done. He had destroyed his ship.

He had destroyed a world.

"James Kirk, you are relieved of your command." Scott looked toward the viewscreen.

Talin burned.

"And whatever gods there are," he whispered, "may they have mercy on your soul."

PART THREE

Talin

One

The subtle incense that lingered in the air of the embassy's waiting hall reminded Spock of his childhood. The scent had been one of his mother's favorites at the time and he was surprised at the memories that were so suddenly unlocked without effort. He realized then that he did not know when he would see Vulcan again and that the thought of never returning troubled him. He knew that reaction was not logical and decided that he would meditate on it later that evening to understand whatever had brought that feeling to him, and to control it. But in the meantime, he smelled the fragrance of kevas and trillium and in his mind he saw his mother's smile.

Beside him, Marita's baby snuffled sleepily. Spock wondered if the child, when grown, would have any recollection of his visit to the Vulcan Embassy on this day. Perhaps when the child smelled the incense again, Spock decided. The ancient structures of the Vulcan and human brain were almost identical, and scent was a key to the deepest of their memories. Spock found the linkage between scent and memory to be an interesting problem. Mentally, he began to manipulate three-dimensional images of airborne molecules to picture how they would fit within Vulcan and human olfactory nerve receptors. At the same time, he reviewed his arguments for the discussion that would follow in the next few minutes. Behind him, past the doors of the harshly lit, black granite–tiled chamber, he heard footsteps approaching, perfectly measured.

"He is coming," Spock said.

Sitting beside him on the carved rock bench, Marita looked up, puzzled. She had heard nothing but, refreshingly for a human, she did not question him. Spock had concluded it was because she was younger than most other humans he usually dealt with—only twenty-two. And despite her involvement in politics, she was still in college, still learning about her world and open to new experiences—including having a Vulcan staying with her and her partner in their small student flat.

Marita brushed a lock of long brown hair from her face and adjusted the position of her child as he snuggled into her arm. Alexander Llorente was five months old and thus far had observed proper decorum for his surroundings.

"I don't know if this is correct in the circumstances," the young woman said, "but good luck, Mr. Spock."

If she had been another person, and this had been another time, Spock might have tried to correct Marita. But he understood the cultural conventions which made her offer the superstitious wish and he accepted it as the gesture of support it was meant to be.

"Thank you. But in the affairs of Vulcan diplomacy, luck is seldom a factor."

"Then for the Talin," Marita said, not wishing to give offense.

"Yes," Spock agreed. "For the Talin."

The chamber doors swung open on perfectly balanced hinges constructed without metal. Spock rose and Marita followed. She smoothed her long skirt where her blanket-wrapped child had caused it to bunch up.

Spock held his hand up in the ritual salute. "Live long and prosper, Ambassador Sytok."

Vulcan's ambassador to Earth was magisterial in his poise and the elegant simplicity of the black robes he wore were matched in tone by Spock's own somber brown tunic and leggings. Though he did not react, Spock was disappointed that Sytok was not garbed in his ambassador's robe and jewels of office. This discussion would have had more of a chance to forward his cause if the ambassador had chosen to treat it as a formal meeting.

Sytok raised his own hand to return the salute. His face was perfectly expressionless and the short fringe of graying hair which lay across his forehead was crisply trimmed. "Live long and prosper, Spock? Have you so forgotten the ways of your home that you must speak in this alien tongue?"

Spock hadn't expected to be insulted and quickly reformulated a new and more forthright strategy for the meeting. "My associate is not experienced in the subtleties of the diplomatic dialects," Spock explained, nodding toward Marita. In truth, she barely could manage to say hello in the primary Vulcan language.

"I am pleased to meet you, your Excellency," Marita said.

Sytok glanced at her as if seeing her for the first time. He said nothing and Marita was uncomfortable with the intensity of his gaze.

The ambassador turned back to Spock without acknowledging the young woman. "What is the purpose of your request for this audience?"

"I had thought it would be apparent," Spock said innocuously, returning his own insult to Sytok.

"Your actions and motives have passed beyond the bounds of logic, Spock."

"Logic can be subtle. Patterns can be difficult to see if one's own vision is clouded," Spock countered. He watched as Sytok calculated the time remaining until his next appointment. How long was the ambassador willing to spend in the exchange of purposeless barbs? However long it was, Spock knew Sytok would not be able to wait him out. The ambassador was busy and Spock had nothing but time.

"Debates are best left to students," Sytok said. "I presume you wish aid in returning to Vulcan. Therefore, the embassy will provide—"

"No," Spock said. He hid his surprise completely. Could it be that Sytok had not deduced the reason for his visit, even with Marita at his side? But then, Sytok had not deigned to be introduced to the woman. Perhaps he hadn't recognized her.

"There was a fifty-five percent chance you would be seeking financial aid for a return ticket to Vulcan," Sytok said impassively. "There is a further thirty percent chance that you are, instead, seeking passage to a Vulcan colony world."

Spock could not resist. "What is the calculated chance that I do not wish to leave Earth at this time?"

Sytok hesitated, but only for an instant. "One point five percent."

Spock angled his head condescendingly. "I do not wish to leave Earth at this time."

Sytok was silent. Spock deduced that the ambassador or his staff had not bothered to devise a response for something that had seemed so improbable.

"I require the help of the Vulcan embassy," Spock began.

"You are still a citizen of the Federation. You require no consular help to stay on Earth."

Spock was astounded that Sytok still hadn't realized what it was he planned. The ambassador was one of Vulcan's finest.

"There is a meeting of the Federation General Council in five days," Spock continued.

Sytok remained impassive, even though Spock knew there was no doubt that he had at last surmised what Spock wanted.

"I wish to address it," Spock said.

"That is quite impossible."

"No, it is not."

Marita looked from the ambassador to Spock and back again. Neither Vulcan moved nor blinked as each stared into the other's eyes. Alexander opened his eyes as if he, too, were aware of the intense argument that raged in the subdued fashion of the Vulcans.

"This embassy will not help you," Sytok finally said.

"You do not have a choice," Spock stated. "You must."

"Spock, you have been trained as a scientist. I cannot expect you to know the intricate legal restrictions involving interstellar law and—"

"I know the law," Spock interrupted. "We had the same teacher." Spock's father, Sarek, was Vulcan's most senior ambassador and in an earlier time, before their bitter estrangement and eventual reconciliation, he had hoped his son would follow in his career path.

For the first time, Sytok allowed an expression to come to his face. He frowned, the corners of his mouth moving down a fraction of a centimeter, and spoke stiffly to Spock.

"I acknowledge that I came up through the corps with your father's guidance and instruction. I was his assistant at three Babel conferences. I both respect him and I honor him. It is because of that respect and that honor that I agreed to this unorthodox meeting."

"By law, I am a Vulcan," Spock pressed on. "By law, you are required to grant my request for an audience. Respect and honor have little to do with it."

"The waiting list for such audiences is more than seven Earth months long, Spock. It has been only three days since your request to see me."

"I thank you for your speed in complying."

Sytok frowned again. "But this is all the time I can allocate to you. I—"

"Ambassador Sytok, I wish to address the Federation General Council," Spock repeated formally. "And you have the authority and the obligation to allow me to do so."

Sytok said nothing. To Spock, it was acknowledgment that his argument was correct.

"I will also require the assistance of a junior member of your staff in order to file the proper briefs with the Council recorders," Spock added. "Of course, temporary civilian accreditation will also be necessary, for myself and my associate."

Sytok looked at the woman again, as if he had suddenly recollected the presence of the young human at Spock's side. Her baby blinked back at him.

"And which of these humans is your associate, Spock?" The ambassador's sarcasm was uncharacteristic and Spock took it to be a reflection of the deep anger that Sytok must be controlling.

"Ambassador Sytok, may I introduce Marita Llorente."

Though Sytok had not recognized her face, he did know her name. Once again, his mouth drew down almost imperceptibly.

"Spock, I cannot allow this. The organization which this woman heads has a long history of attempting to disrupt Council meetings and the legitimate work of the Federation. She cannot be admitted to a Council meeting. Even I cannot authorize that."

Marita looked calmly at the ambassador, unruffled by his rejection of her.

"But you can authorize me," Spock said. "Whom I choose to have accompany me is my own right and responsibility."

Sytok adjusted the collar of his robe and stared past Spock and the woman. Alexander burbled into the silence and Marita gently bounced him in her arms.

"What is the nature of the address you wish to make to the Council?" Sytok asked with reluctance.

"It has to do with certain legal implications of the events at Talin IV which I believe have not been satisfactorily addressed by Starfleet or the Federation."

"The events at Talin were dealt with completely within Starfleet, Spock. You of all people should know that. The Federation was never involved."

Alexander gave a small shriek, which both Vulcans ignored. Marita began rocking from foot to foot, whispering softly to the child.

"Which is precisely why I desire to address the Council, Ambassador. I wish to point out to them that there are other legal concerns at stake than simply Starfleet's jurisdictional liability for its personnel failing to uphold the Prime Directive."

Sytok shook his head decisively. "There are no other legal concerns, Spock."

"Ambassador, if you are not aware of them, then it is all the more compelling that the members of the Council who do not share your expertise in the law also are informed of those concerns."

Sytok seemed to grow impatient as Marita paced back and forth across the hard granite slabs that lined the floor of the chamber, talking to her baby. "Are you going to tell me what those mysterious, other legal concerns are?" he asked.

Spock slipped his hand into his tunic and withdrew a folded-over sheaf of printed notes. "I prefer to keep the details confidential. If I revealed the core of my argument now, then I fear I might risk insulting the Council by taking up their time in reciting information which they could already have received second hand."

"It might be faster," Sytok suggested.

"But not as accurate," Spock said. "However, these notes should enable the staff member you assign to help me in preparing the proper preliminary documents."

Sytok accepted the papers Spock held out but didn't look at them. "Why should I upset the business of this embassy by rushing through your request to speak in five days, rather than allowing it to go through normal channels?"

"If you process my request through normal channels, then I will not be able to address the Council for more than a standard year. I am aware of the usual waiting periods."

"Have you also forgotten patience, Spock? It is one of the most important lessons your father taught me."

"For myself, and my career, I have no need to rush. 'For life is long and there is much to be learned in unhurried contemplation,' " Spock quoted. "However, my concern for speed is on behalf of others."

Sytok glanced at the woman. She held her baby up and blew kisses at the child. Sytok closed his eyes and sighed. "Humans are always so agitated and in too much of a hurry."

"Indeed, the life of a human is short compared to ours," Spock observed. "But the others I refer to are those survivors who still live on Talin IV."

Sytok allowed a private, ritual expression of shared remorse to appear on his face, though none but a Vulcan could recognize the difference between it and a face of repose. "Nothing can be done for them, Spock."

"On the contrary, I believe something can be done. Please, Ambassador, read my notes."

Sytok unfolded the sheaf of papers and rifled through them in seconds. "There is nothing in here that the human woman's organization has not said before. It is merely another attempt to introduce a radical and ill-thought plan to circumvent the Prime Directive. They would force the Federation to offer aid to every known world, contacted or not, which is not as developed as the existing member worlds. Such a policy would clearly lead to tragedy and chaos."

Marita came back to the two Vulcans as Sytok spoke. Her eyes flashed with anger. "You're wrong, Ambassador. The Federation has more than enough resources to share with less developed worlds. The Prime Directive is a morally indefensible attempt to keep the wealth of a thousand worlds safely within the hands of a few powerful planetary governments."

Sytok turned frostily to Spock. "I do not have time to debate this with a child," the ambassador said. "Spock, since it appears you have more time than I, please explain to . . . your associate that the Prime Directive is the foundation upon which the Federation is built."

"Marita Llorente is correct," Spock said.

Ambassador Sytok blinked once in the Vulcan equivalent of a gasp of shock. "What?"

"A case can be made to support the proposition that the Prime Directive is morally indefensible and must be stricken from the laws of the Federation," Spock said.

Sytok blinked twice. "Spock . . . that statement goes against every principle of peace and equality the Federation is sworn to uphold . . . that statement is a complete abandonment of the ideals in which Vulcan joined with other worlds to form the Federation. It denies history. It—it is not logical, Spock."

"Nevertheless, I believe it to have merit."

Sytok looked long and hard into Spock's eyes and Spock found himself readying his mental defenses against a sudden attempt at melding. The ambassador seemed that unsettled by Spock's position.

"Do you hate Starfleet that much, Spock? Do you have such bitterness for what they've done to you that you would strike out against the Federation so senselessly?"

"I do not hate the Federation, nor do I hate Starfleet. I simply wish to improve them."

Sytok crushed the papers in his hands. "I will not allow you to dishonor the Council with such general and ill-conceived charges."

"They are not general. I intend to bring specific civil charges against Starfleet and those of its personnel who destroyed Talin by attempting to uphold the Prime Directive."

Sytok's lips actually trembled. "Is this your idea of a human joke? You intend to bring charges *against yourself?*"

Spock nodded. "Logically, I have no other choice."

"Logic?" Sytok almost sputtered. "You dare to speak of logic in connection with this absurdity? If you do this, Spock, you will be announcing to all the worlds that you have forsaken your Vulcan heritage. Don't you remember the controversy that arose at home when you decided to join Starfleet? Don't you remember how the elders said you would become less than Vulcan by being in such close proximity to humans. If you go through with this senselessness, you will prove them right." Sytok held the papers out to Spock, asking him to take them back. "As a friend of your father's, I request you reconsider. Think what will be said of you."

Spock kept his true thoughts and feelings well shielded. "I did not care what others thought when I applied to Starfleet. I do not care now." He placed his hands behind his back, refusing the papers. "Ambassador Sytok, will you or will you not prepare my credentials to address the Council as a citizen of Vulcan and the Federation, as is my right?"

Spock saw Marita smile triumphantly at Sytok. She knew so little. But her unbridled display of emotionalism helped Sytok compose himself.

"Yes, Spock," the ambassador said blandly, no trace of the hidden passion which had threatened to surface moments ago. "I shall authorize your credentials, as a citizen, to address the Council in five days' time. I must warn you though, if I place Marita Llorente's name on the forms as your associate, the Council will be likely to postpone its meeting in order to prevent her from disrupting it."

Perfect, Spock thought. The plan had worked. Sytok had become distracted by his emotions and ignored the logic of what Spock was maneuvering him to do.

"Ambassador," Spock said, "may I suggest then that you have your staff simply prepare the forms without naming Ms. Llorente directly. I believe you are able to issue a blanket credential for myself and 'others to be named later.' "

"Yes," Sytok said. "I can do that because no Vulcan has ever misused the system in the way in which you intend."

"Please believe me, Ambassador, I have no wish to misuse the system."

Sytok held the papers up in his fist. "And yet you give me this."

Spock stepped back and held up his hand to offer the salute of leaving. "Live long and prosper, Ambassador Sytok. I shall return in four days to receive my credentials."

Sytok did not offer a salute in return. "I warn you, Spock, after what happened at Talin IV, if you disrupt a Council meeting they will deport you as an undesirable."

Spock shrugged. "I will have had my say in the proper forum." He turned to go.

"And Vulcan will not take you back," Sytok said.

Spock shrugged again as if he didn't care.

And Sytok saw something in that. Spock knew it instantly. The ambassador had detected a telltale hint of deception.

Sytok glanced thoughtfully at the papers again. "This is not like you, Spock. This is not like Sarek's son at all." He looked up. "You have planned something else."

Spock knew he had to act quickly. The ambassador must be diverted again. He held out his hand to Marita, index and middle finger extended, the rest folded back.

"Marita," Spock said, "attend me."

The woman smiled seductively and matched Spock's gesture, touching her two fingers to his in the intimacy of the Vulcan ritual embrace.

Spock heard the paper rustle in Sytok's fist as he crushed it even more. The ambassador was speechless in his outrage. Spock's tactic had worked.

Still joined with Marita, Spock walked toward the chamber's exit. The carved granite doors swung open silently.

"Spock!" Sytok's voice echoed in the hall.

Spock stopped to look back at the ambassador.

"What would your father say?"

Spock raised an eyebrow. "I believe he would wish me luck."

Two

Lieutenant Kyle stuck his head out from beneath the control console in transporter room four. His blond hair and pale skin were smudged with insulation dust and blue coolant.

"I think that's got it, Mr. Scott."

Scott stood to the side of the console, using a transtator tester on the wiring circuits exposed beneath the flipped-up surface panel. He hadn't expected to hear from Kyle for at least another hour. "That's fast work, lad." He was afraid he knew why.

Kyle wiped at his face, then pulled himself out from the access opening under the console. "It was just the main node, Mr. Scott. The secondary circuits weren't touched."

Scott swung the panel down until it clicked into place. "Just like the phaser banks," he said, and he didn't like it.

"And the torpedo couplings," Kyle added. "And the main sensor sequencers."

Scott stared at the coils of power-harness cables that hung down from the openings in the room's ceiling. The starbase mechanics had done long baseline scans of the *Enterprise* and determined that every centimeter of transtator circuitry in her had been hopelessly burned out. But by actually poking and prodding their way through her, Scott and Kyle had discovered that less than twenty percent of her circuitry had actually been destroyed. Normally, that would be good news because, if the repair order were ever given, the wiring drones would only require a fifth the time to install replacement circuits throughout the *Enterprise*. But what worried Scott was that virtually all of that twenty percent of destroyed circuitry had been master control nodes. He knew that powerful subspace pulses could inflict erratic damage on a ship, but he had never heard of the damage being confined just to the most important circuits.

"I tell ye, lad," Scott said, "I don't like it. I don't like it one bit."

Kyle brushed the dust from his blue technician's jumpsuit. He looked as if he shared Scott's concern. They had had this conversation many times in the two weeks since the shipwright drones had been installed onboard to salvage damaged equipment. The drones' controllers had been surprised to find how little equipment there had actually been to salvage. But while the damage had been far less than expected, it was specific enough to render the ship useless.

"I still don't know how anything could focus a subspace pulse so precisely that it would only affect the main nodes," Kyle said. "I think it really does have to be a coincidence, sir. Or something about the way the pulse traveled through the circuitry. Maybe destructive interference built up at the main nodes because that's where the pulse signals met each other . . . maybe." His voice trailed off into uncertainty.

Scott shook his head. "Mr. Kyle, remember who you're talking to. And I'll not be swallowing any of that first-year engineering student yammer. Whatever kind of pulse hit this ship was *aimed* at us. And whoever aimed it knew exactly what it was they were doing."

Kyle looked pained. "Are you going to try to explain that to Lieutenant Styles? Again?"

"I know what I'd like to explain to that sli—" A discordant paging whistle shrieked from the companel and Scott cringed. "What the devil have they done to the power settings on that blasted—".

"Bridge Communications Center to Chief Engineer Montgomery Scott." It was Styles. It could only be Styles.

Scott leaned against the transporter console and rolled his eyes at Kyle. "Aye, Lieutenant Styles, Scott here."

"Vice Admiral Hammersmith's shuttle is arriving, Mr. Scott. Is that transporter working yet?"

"All the circuitry is back in place, Lieutenant, but we haven't had a chance to test it yet."

"Well hop to it, man. I told the vice admiral that I would have him *beamed* aboard. You've got ten minutes. Bridge Communications Center out."

The companel crackled with static, then went dead.

Kyle went over to the storage locker and broke out a box filled with various transporter test modules. They were essentially empty boxes made from metal only a few molecules thick. Any alignment or focus problems in a transporter would cause the intricately etched, reflective surfaces of the boxes to change to a dull and mottled appearance when they re-formed. They were usually the first objects to be sent through any transporter that had been subjected to repairs.

Kyle examined the test modules carefully. "You know, Mr. Scott, these look to have been banged up pretty badly. We've got some dents and bends here that could affect the diffraction patterns. Make them look perfect when they're not. I don't think they'll do."

Scott thought for a moment. There was no possible way he would authorize human transmission in a transporter that hadn't been properly tested. Then he held up his hand. "Just a minute, Mr. Kyle. I think I've got it." Scott left the room through the doors he had jammed open with an old circuitplaser. The few sliding pocket doors which had been brought back online throughout the ship were behaving about as well as the companels. Everyone on board could be seen hesitating by closed doors and rushing through open ones to avoid being sandwiched by them. Scott had taken the easy way out by simply disabling the doors to any room he happened to be working in. He found it odd that none of the starbase mechanics had figured out the same thing, and so far he had noticed three of them with eyes blackened from walking into doors. Seeing them like that was one of the few things that made getting up in the morning easier these days. Especially because of what Hammersmith had done to him.

When Scott came back to the transporter room, he carried a small mechanical scavenger drone under one arm. The device's treads whirred uselessly and its manipulator stalks waved wildly. It and two hundred and twenty-two other shipwright drones on board were controlled by a portable repair computer installed in engineering. They had spent the past two weeks crawling through the ship, beeping and bumping and getting on Scott's nerves. He was going to enjoy this.

Scott carried the drone over to the transporter platform and plopped the machine down on the center pad. It rocked back and forth for a moment, then spread its manipulators all around itself, tracing the circumference of the transmission crystal.

Scott stood back. "All right, Mr. Kyle, before its control computer figures out where it is, would ye energize the wee thing."

The small machine squealed once, then faded away in a sparkling mist.

"Holding the pattern," Kyle said as he studied the board. "Carrier storage is one hundred percent. Power consumption following normal curves." He looked up at Scott and smiled. "Seems to be perfect, Mr. Scott."

"If ye say so yourself." Scott watched the platform. "All right then, bring the little beastie back."

The transporter chime grew louder, but then was overpowered by the metallic tinkle of small machine parts raining down on the pad.

"Aww," Scott said happily.

"Um, there appears to be a realignment problem," Kyle offered.

"You think so?" Scott walked over to the companel. "Myself, I don't think it's ready for a vice admiral, but I think it should work just fine for a certain lieutenant." He toggled the paging switch. "Chief Engineer Montgomery Scott to Bridge Communications Center. I'm afraid the transporter is going to be needing a wee bit more work. You better tell the vice admiral that he should park his shuttle in the hangar bay." Scott winked at Kyle.

When Styles responded, his voice was tight with officious rage, just as Scott had expected. "Chief Engineer Scott! I told the vice admiral that we would beam him aboard and by thunder we *will* beam him aboard."

"Lieutenant Styles, sir, the only way anyone's going to be coming out of this transporter is in buckets, if you know what I mean, sir." Scott grinned at Kyle as the transporter technician put a hand to his mouth to stifle a laugh.

The companel transmission picked up a rhythmic tapping interference signal that puzzled Scott until he realized that it was that damned swagger stick hitting the side of the center chair.

"Mr. Scott," Styles said like a petulant child. "I am holding you personally responsible and I shall tell the vice admiral exactly why he was forced to experience the inconvenience of a hangar landing." Tap tap tap tap. "Bridge Communications Center out."

"Good," Scott said, "then maybe Hammersmith will come to his senses and let me go."

Kyle popped open the control console again. "Are you certain that's what you still want to do, Mr. Scott?"

Scott clenched his teeth and the muscles in his jaw tensed and relaxed, tensed and relaxed. "If Hammersmith approves detaching what's left of the port nacelle, and the ship survives the separation, she'll be someone else's worry."

Kyle concentrated on the machinery in the console. Without looking up, he said, "But the *Enterprise* needs you, sir."

"I know that, Mr. Kyle. But the *Enterprise* is more than a ship, and right now I could do a lot more for her by being away from her."

Kyle didn't move. "Do you think the Captain's all right?"

"Of course he is, lad," Scott said, wondering if he could believe it as much as he wanted Kyle to. "But if I could get off this ship, I could find out for sure."

Kyle nodded. The blue glow of his circuitplaser flared from the console as he readjusted the reassembly timing delays. This was another conversation they had had many times.

Scott decided he had better report to the hangar deck to make sure the pressure doors were working properly. He still couldn't forgive Carole Mallett and Mario Cardinali for what they had done to the doors after the *Enterprise* had been set adrift. But before Scott could leave, in walked a young female ensign in services red and a Starbase 29 insignia, waving a simple, unicorder tracker in front of her.

"Pardon me, sir," the woman said seriously. "But have you seen a scavenger drone in this area? We appear to have lost one nearby."

"Aye, certainly," Scott said cheerfully. "We did see one of the little fellas around here. Seemed to have a small malfunction or somesuch."

The woman nodded with a knowing frown. "Ah, a small malfunction. That does happen from time to time." She kept her gaze on Scott, though the engineer said nothing. "And excuse me one more time if I may, sir. But can you tell me where the . . . little fella is?"

"Why, he's right over there, lass." Scott pointed toward the transporter pad. "And I hope ye brought a broom." Scott watched the ensign stare in disbelief at the tiny mound of drone components, no doubt wondering how the chief engineer would define a *major* malfunction. Then Scott left for the hangar and his next attempt to convince Vice Admiral Hammersmith that there was no place in Starfleet for such a willfully disobedient chief engineer as Montgomery Scott.

The huge curved doors of the ship's hangar bay only opened halfway now. Their elegantly engineered folding segments had been deformed by the shuttle that had smashed through them, then further degraded by the thick sealant baffles that the starbase mechanics had roughly attached to repair the damage until the doors could be replaced.

Scott still couldn't understand what had driven the two FCO managers to do what they had done. Approximately thirty minutes after the *Enterprise* had been blasted out of the timeslowing grip of Talin IV's gravity-well wormhole, she was powerless and adrift. But even when Scott had taken command of the ship, he had not been concerned about the crew's eventual rescue. After all, the hull was secure. Local battery networks could easily keep the air circulating and the gravity functioning for weeks. And once the FCO outpost picked up the *Enterprise*'s emergency beacon, the rescue shuttles from Starbase 29 were only four days away at maximum warp. So why had Mallett and Cardinali risked their careers in Starfleet—and the safe evacuation of the *Enterprise*'s crew—by virtually destroying the hangar deck?

Scott remembered passing Mallett and Cardinali in the ladderways as he and the medical technicians climbed their way to the bridge. The FCO pilot and communications manager had told Scott that everyone on the bridge was alive with no serious injuries, and then had said that they had to salvage their equipment. In the confusion of dealing with the crippled vessel, Scott had thought nothing of their apparent panic. He certainly had not suspected that they were both determined to abandon ship. But that was exactly what the two managers had done.

The three Wraith shuttles which had been stowed on the hangar deck were specifically designed to provide as few clues as possible about advanced technology should any of them crash, so except for their heavily armored antigrav generators and a subminiature subspace radio, there wasn't a transtator in them. Whatever had rendered the *Enterprise* a drifting hulk had left the Wraiths' major components untouched.

As far as Scott had been able to determine, Cardinali and Mallett had donned environmental suits, then rigged one Wraith to fly on autopilot straight through the inoperative hangar bay doors. Without deflector shields in place, the middle segments of the doors had shattered, explosively decompressing the bay. Cardinali and Mallett had then taken a second Wraith through the gaping hole and flown back to the FCO outpost on Talin's moon. A few weeks later, after the outpost had been sealed and all personnel transferred back to Earth, Scott had heard that the two FCO managers had claimed they had been trying to get word back to the outpost to send for rescue ships as quickly as possible. That explanation just didn't seem reasonable to Scott.

In the end, after his anger had cooled, he decided that they had just been frightened. But because of the damage they had caused to the hangar bay, shuttle evacuation had been impossible and it had taken more than a day for the rescue ships to beam the *Enterprise*'s crew to safety. Fear was one thing, but endangering lives was another. Scott hoped to one day tell them just what he thought of them and their cowardice. But in the meantime, he prepared himself to tell Vice Admiral Hammersmith exactly what he thought of a certain Starfleet vice admiral who wouldn't accept resignations.

Scott watched from the hangar bay's upper observation gallery as the vice admiral's shuttle eased slowly through the partially opened doors and settled gently on a section of the deck where most of the debris had been cleared away. As the doors jerkily slid shut again, Lieutenant Styles joined him.

"What are you doing here when you should be repairing the transporter?" Styles snapped.

Scott no longer even made a pretense of being civil to Styles. He obeyed the man's orders because the vice admiral had given Styles temporary command of the ship, he did his job as best as he was able; but he would be damned if he would pretend to respect the fool.

"I'm just making sure that the vice admiral isn't sucked screaming out into space because the trained chimps ye have working the pressurization controls have confused the colors on the all-clear board."

Styles slapped his swagger stick against his open palm a few times. "Mr. Scott, I am at a loss to understand why you continue to address me in this insubordinate manner. What have I ever done to you to deserve such insolence?"

It's not what you've done to me, ye bandy-legged, spineless excuse for a starship captain, it's what you've done to my ship. "I'm afraid I don't know what it is you're referring to, Lieutenant. Perhaps we veterans of a long space voyage are just a wee bit crustier than you've come to expect after your three short months on the *Monitor.*"

"I'll have you know I've spent many years in space, Mr. Scott, and I have yet to hear highly trained Starfleet engineers refer to other highly trained Starfleet engineers as 'trained chimps.' "

"Well, it just goes to show ye, sir . . . even the likes of you can learn something new every day."

Styles slapped his stick into his hand and held it there. "Mr. Scott, I have tried to be patient with you. I understand what you must have gone through, serving on this ship for so many years, only to watch her nearly destroyed by some madman's delusions of grandeur. But I—"

"*Don't you ever—I mean ever—talk about my captain like that again.*" It was all Scott could do not to throttle Styles. "Lieutenant Styles, sir, I am a Starfleet officer and you are my commander, and I am sworn to obey you to the best of my ability. But a man has his limits, sir, and I canna stand by any longer and listen to you insult a man who is my friend. As one officer to another, sir, I ask that ye please keep your opinions to yourself so I can continue to do my job."

As soon as Scott had said the words he knew they had been a mistake. Styles wasn't a complete buffoon. Incompetents would never survive to his rank in Starfleet. He had just been remarkably insensitive. But now Scott had let him know exactly what it was that upset him so—he had revealed his weakness and Styles jumped on it instantly.

"Mr. Scott, while your misplaced admiration for a man who used to be your captain might be considered honorable by some, I want you to understand once and for all that James Kirk is a traitor to Starfleet and the Federation. And we will not honor traitors aboard *my* ship."

Scott gave up. There was no sense in continuing the fight against someone so closeminded. *Let it be his ship,* he thought. *And welcome to her. One more drone to crawl around beeping and bumping with the others.*

"I apologize for speaking out of turn, sir," Scott muttered through gritted teeth. But even he knew the words meant nothing.

"That's better, Mr. Scott." Styles flipped his stick jauntily under his arm. "Now don't you think you should be getting back to that transporter?"

"With all respect, sir, I do have business with the vice admiral."

Styles rubbed the side of his face with the large end of the stick. The ready lights glowed green and red against his skin. "What business is that, Mr. Scott?"

"He has repeatedly turned down my resignation and I would like to discuss his reasons with him."

"Resignation?" Styles said. "Why would you want to resign? You had nothing to do with what happened on Talin."

I am a Starfleet officer, Scott told himself. *I am a Starfleet officer.* "And neither did James Kirk, sir. Nor Mr. Spock, nor Uhura, nor Chekov, nor Sulu, nor Dr. McCoy."

"If you leave Starfleet, mister," Styles said, punctuating every word by tapping Scott's chest with his stick, "you'll be saying that you're no different from any of the *Enterprise* Five."

Scott felt a wave of sudden inspiration hit him. "Aye, sir," he said with a terrible smile, "that's exactly what I'm saying." And then he reached out and grabbed Styles's swagger stick and snapped it over his knee.

Styles's eyes bulged and his mouth opened and closed in shocked silence as he stared at the two pieces of his treasured memento on the deck.

But Scott felt free for the first time in months. He wondered if this was how McCoy had felt when he had swung on Hammersmith—filled with the certain knowledge that an irrevocable decision had been made. "And now if you'll excuse me, sir, I have business with the vice admiral who's been standing around on the deck for the past five minutes wondering where his welcoming committee is."

Scott smiled fiercely again as he saw the ready lights wink out on the stick, then left. He was sure he heard Styles sob behind him.

Vice Admiral Hammersmith was a powerfully built human with skin darker than Uhura's. His gold shirt was pulled tightly over bunched muscles and Scott was impressed that McCoy had actually gone so far as to hit him. But perhaps that was why the doctor had chosen Hammersmith and not some other officer. It wasn't as if McCoy could ever have hoped to actually hurt the man.

The vice admiral smiled as Scott approached him on the hangar deck. "Ah, Lieutenant Commander Montgomery Scott, I presume." His voice was deep and he held out a massive hand.

"Vice Admiral Hammersmith," Scott said, pumping hands vigorously with him. "Welcome aboard the *Enterprise.*"

Hammersmith stepped away from his shuttle as three of his staff began offloading equipment cases and supplies. He motioned for the chief engineer to follow him and glanced around the cavernous hangar bay, assessing the damage still unrepaired. "Mostly superficial," he said. "Pocket ruptures from the explosive decompression, but serviceable."

Scott was impressed. "Aye, that's true."

"See?" Hammersmith said. "I read everything you send me. Not just your resignation requests." He looked around again. "Where is Lieutenant Styles?"

"I have just broken a piece of the lieutenant's personal property," Scott said matter-of-factly. "And I believe he is too upset to make an appearance at this time."

Hammersmith shook his head. "What is it about you *Enterprise* people?" He held up his hand. "No, don't answer. Believe it or not, Engineer, I do understand why you want to submit your resignation. And I am prepared to accept it."

Scott had expected anything but that. "Why, thank you, sir."

"But not quite yet."

Naturally, Scott thought in frustration. "Then could you tell me when, sir?"

"Well, that's up to you, Engineer. How soon can you get this ship operational again?"

If Hammersmith were about to commission another feasibility study, Scott thought he would scream. He was supposed to work with machines, not paper. "Have you made your decision about her repair, then, sir?"

Scott was surprised again when Hammersmith nodded. "That's why I'm here. We're going to tow her out of system tomorrow and detach the port nacelle."

"And what if the warp reaction is still linked to the planet's gravity well?" Scott asked. "What if she slingshots?"

Hammersmith's eyes sparkled. "The experts who have been studying what they call the dimensional evaporation of the nacelle tell me that there is an eighty-five-percent chance that that is exactly what will happen. The instant the port nacelle is detached, they say that it will be drawn completely into the Cochrane subset at about warp eight point seven. At the same time, the remainder of the ship will also be accelerated to the same velocity in the opposite vector, but in normal, three-dimensional space where such velocities are against all the laws of nature." Hammersmith chuckled. "The experts tell me that the *Enterprise* will spread herself out over a spectacular starbow effect about a light-minute long, then explosively transform herself into . . . well, neutrinos or tachyons, depending on which day of the week it is and which expert's name comes first."

Scott was tired of this nonsense. "And do you believe them?"

"I believe in specialists doing the work they specialize in, Engineer. And I also believe in being prepared."

"Sir?"

"At this moment, the *Exeter* is en route from Earth at warp six. She is rigged with a cargo sling and carries the two Constitution-rated warp nacelles that were intended for the *Intrepid II*."

Despite himself, Scott felt a rush of excitement. Those nacelles could make this ship whole again. "That's quite a trip for the sake of a ship that might be a handful of neutrinos by the time the *Exeter* gets here."

"In addition to the experts' reports, Engineer, I've also read yours. I forget the technical details, but there was something about it being a cold day in Hades the day there would ever be a *partial* warp transition."

"Aye, that it would, sir."

Hammersmith's expression became intent. "I will confess that committing the *Exeter* to this run—and completely disrupting the construction schedule for the *Intrepid II*—is a gamble. Because I really don't know what's going to happen tomorrow when we blow that nacelle."

"That's all right, sir, I do. And it's not a gamble."

"That's one of the things I've been looking forward to discussing with you. Why do you have the presumption to think *you* know something that twenty of Starfleet's best scientists refuse to consider?"

Scott shrugged. "Because they're scientists, sir, and I'm an engineer. I've worked with this ship every day for almost the past five years, sir. I can tell what's going on inside her generators just by listening to them. And I was onboard the *Enterprise* when she was attacked."

"Now *that* I do know something about, Engineer. Nuclear detonations—even in an atmosphere—don't do this to a ship." Hammersmith waved his hand at the debris and exposed coils of power harness poking through ruptured wall plates.

"The *Enterprise* was attacked by more than just nuclear warheads, sir." *Why not tell him the rest?* Scott asked himself. It was probably the first and last time he'd be able to discuss his theory with an intelligent superior officer who had no vested interest in personally commanding the *Enterprise*.

Hammersmith chewed on his lower lip. "More than nuclear weapons? You haven't put that in any of your reports, have you?"

"No, sir."

"Good, because I don't recall having heard that before. What else was the *Enterprise* attacked by?"

Scott took a breath. "An extremely powerful—and precisely focused—series of subspace energy pulses that selectively burned out every major control node in the entire ship."

Hammersmith closed his eyes and rubbed at the bridge of his nose. "As I understand it, such an attack would be completely beyond the technological capabilities of the Talin. Is that correct?"

"Aye, sir, it is."

"And furthermore, such an attack would be completely beyond *our* technological capabilities. Is that also correct?"

"Aye, sir. I believe that is true."

Hammersmith walked back to his shuttle. His three staff members had finished stacking the cases they had offloaded. Now they were talking to a group of starbase mechanics who were supposed to be working on repairs to the shuttle elevator and turntable so that the undamaged shuttles in the maintenance shops below the hangar deck could be returned to active duty. But as was typical, Scott saw, the temporary workers had none of the urgency of the *Enterprise*'s real crew.

Hammersmith waved to his staff to let them know that he didn't require them at the moment, then opened a small case on the top of the stack to bring out a portable terminal. "Why wasn't this subspace 'attack' mentioned at the board of inquiry hearings?" the vice admiral asked.

"Because no one knew back then," Scott explained. "With the master nodes fused, the general scans of the ship gave the same results as if every circuit had gone. It was only when the shipwright drones came aboard and started trying to remove damaged equipment that we realized that the damage wasn't as extensive as we thought—just precisely selective."

"We?" Hammersmith asked. "Does Styles know about this?"

"No, sir. He doesn't seem to care too much about what has happened in the past. He's only interested in taking command of this ship sometime in the future."

"Nothing wrong with ambition, Mr. Scott. Now who's this 'we'?"

"Lieutenant Kyle, sir. Chief transporter technician. One of the original crew."

Hammersmith punched in something on his terminal keypad. "And he confirms your suspicions about an attack by selective subspace pulse?"

Scott wondered what the best way to describe the situation was. "To tell the truth, sir. He has seen the damage the ship has suffered, and knows it's peculiar, but he thinks it might possibly be the result of coincidence or a previously unknown destructive interference effect."

Hammersmith read whatever was displayed on his screen. He turned to Scott. "And what do *you* think it might possibly be, Engineer?"

"Deliberate, sir. The result of an unknown weapon."

Hammersmith fixed Scott with an intense gaze. "If you're right in your theory about the ship's damage, you know what that might mean, don't you?"

Scott felt the thrill of sudden hope run through him. Could it be possible? Was Hammersmith going to be someone who would finally pay attention to all that had happened at Talin? "Aye, sir, I know exactly what that might mean."

"Good," Hammersmith said. "Good. Then given your past actions and your outspoken desire to defend Kirk at any cost, you'll understand why I must remain skeptical of any new facts you present which might serve to exonerate him."

No, Scott cried to himself. *Why did it always have t' be this way? Why couldn't there be just one person in Starfleet who was willing to give the captain the benefit of the doubt for just one second?*

Hammersmith tapped at the display screen on his terminal. "And because this Lieutenant Kyle has been with the *Enterprise* since the beginning of her five-year mission, I'm afraid that I'll also have to be skeptical of any claims he might make. However, if you could get someone like Styles to back you on this . . . well, it might even be possible to reconvene the board of inquiry."

Scott felt overcome with despair. *Someone like Styles,* he thought. *Typical.* The lieutenant was probably getting ready to phaser him in his sleep at this point.

"Is there nothing else that might do it, sir?" Scott asked, wondering why the fates were punishing him so.

"I'd say that's up to you, Engineer."

"How so, sir?"

Hammersmith switched off his terminal. "If you can get this ship through the nacelle separation tomorrow, you'll have one week before the *Exeter* arrives. The deal I'll make with you is that if you give me your word that you will stick it out through the rest of the *Enterprise*'s repairs, with your full cooperation, I'll give you that week to take this ship apart and prove your theory."

Scott shook his head. "I'm afraid Lieutenant Styles would never allow it, sir. He's got too much for me to do as it is."

"Then for that week, Styles will be out of the picture. You'll report directly to me. And I will give you full run over the ship." Hammersmith held out his hand. "Is it a deal?"

Scott held back. "It's a big ship, sir."

"I'll request Kyle as well." He kept his hand extended.

"A week won't be enough time. Not for only two of us."

Hammersmith stared up at the hangar bay roof in thought, then said, "You drive a hard bargain, Engineer, but I'm going to make my final offer. I can't do anything about the one-week time limit, but whoever else you want here to help—provided we can get them here on time—I'll get them for you."

"Whoever else I want?" Scott asked.

"Starfleet personnel only," Hammersmith clarified.

Scott reached out and shook the vice admiral's hand. "Vice Admiral, sir, ye've got yourself a deal."

"Then if the *Enterprise* is still in one piece tomorrow, you've got yourself a week."

Three

Sulu stepped from the airlock and the sudden plunge into microgee was like drifting off into a warm bath, every muscle instantly relaxing. Without thinking, he moaned with relief.

"Are you all right?" Chekov asked over the helmet commlink.

Sulu touched a control on the thruster extension and made a half turn. Chekov was still in the *Queen Mary*'s open airlock, one gloved hand on either side, ready to push himself out to his friend's rescue.

"Come on in," Sulu said, "the water's fine." He waved his thickly padded arm slowly. Krulmadden might have a state-of-the-art impulse drive, but his ship's environmental suits were overstuffed antiques.

Chekow leaned out from the airlock, then floated free of it, arms extended. Sulu heard him have the same reaction to leaving the *Queen Mary*'s oppressive two-gee gravity.

"That is much better," Chekov sighed as he swung down the control arm by his side and used the controls on it to maneuver closer to Sulu, about ten meters out from the ship.

Then Krulmadden's voice boomed over the helmet speakers. "You mammals sound like you enjoy vacuum more than enjoy slavegirls. What has *f'deraxtl* training done to you?"

"Like we keep telling you, Shipmaster," Sulu said, "your normal gravity is too strong for us."

The shipmaster snorted. "You mean you are too weak. Need more *Ur'eon* exercise you do."

In the dull light of the red giant star they orbited, Sulu saw Chekov's pained expression through the unfiltered faceplate of his helmet.

"What we need is Earth-normal grawity in our quarters," Chekov said.

"Too much power. Too expensive," Krulmadden snapped at them. "Always wanting to spend my credits. You make credits, you can spend them. Leave mine alone. Now go do your work or I leave you here."

Sulu heard the click of the comlink being broken. "Let's go," he said to Chekov.

Chekov made a thumbs-up sign, and Sulu placed his own hand on his thruster control. With three quick taps, he had rotated again, then propelled himself toward the *Queen Mary*'s relative upper surface where the impulse engine was housed.

The hullmetal of the Orion pirate's ship glowed deep pink in the light of the red giant, two AUs distance. Though Krulmadden had refused to identify the star, Sulu had recognized its coordinates. It was TNC-5527 in the Minotaur Cluster, the last remnant of an ancient system which had long since lost all of its planets. The very fact that it had nothing of value to offer was why, Sulu presumed, Krulmadden felt safe in hiding out around it. Because that was exactly what he was doing now, hiding out, and with good reason.

Sulu triggered the visual sensor mounted to his helmet to begin recording images of the damage to the *Queen Mary*'s impulse engine housing. Black streaks of rippled metal showed where the border patrol's phasers had hit. Whoever the frigate's weaponry officer had been, he or she had been good. That was one smuggling route that Krulmadden would not be able to use again, and the sale of his living cargo had been indefinitely postponed.

Sulu heard Chekov's whistle, rough and full of static over the old comlink system. "Wery precise control," he said. "Another half-second of contact and we would have been blown apart."

Sulu felt a sudden chill in his suit. He had known their run-in with the border patrol had been close. He just hadn't known it had been *that* close.

"Shipmaster Krulmadden," he said, then waited for the suit's computer to reopen the comlink with the *Queen Mary*'s bridge.

"Yes, little mammal?"

"There's a five-meter secondary gash on the upper impulse housing, port forward quadrant. I know you don't want to tell us too many details about your engine configuration, but we could do a better repair job if you told us what systems are beneath the damaged area."

Sulu floated peacefully by the ship, unconcerned that Krulmadden was taking so much time to decide how much he could tell his human crewmen. For all of the shipmaster's boisterous good humor when it came to maintaining the spirits of his crew, Sulu had realized early on in his three weeks on the ship that Krulmadden didn't even trust Artinton and Lasslanlin—and they were his cousins who had worked for him for more than twenty years.

"Use sensor probe, setting three twenty," Krulmadden said finally, sounding as if he were giving the combination to the safe in his stateroom.

Sulu rotated to Chekov and watched as he slowly pulled a sensor wand from the equipment bag strapped to his leg. It took Chekov a full five minutes to align the wand and change the setting on its control handle. The suits Krulmadden had given them had to be at least a hundred years old and more unwieldy than even the ones the Academy made cadets train in.

When Chekov at last seemed to have the sensor probe properly aligned, he aimed it toward the battle damage on the engine housing. Then Sulu heard him cry out in shock.

"What is it, Chekov?" Sulu thrust himself closer.

"Ionizing radiation! All around us!" Chekov turned his head awkwardly in his helmet to catch a glimpse of Sulu. "Back away!"

Chekov suddenly spun off from the ship, cartwheeling slowly as he tried to stabilize his emergency withdrawal. Sulu took a moment longer to plan his own trajectory, then moved off after his friend. He caught up with him two hundred meters off the *Queen Mary,* where Chekov finally halted his wobbling rotations.

"We could have gone over to the other side of the ship, Chekov."

"I am not used to these thruster controls."

Suddenly, Krulmadden's voice blared at them again. "What do you do? Where do you go? What damage have you done to my jewel?"

Sulu rotated to face the ship, now small enough that he could blot it out with his hand. He swallowed as he realized how easy it would be for Krulmadden to pop into warp right now and leave him and Chekov as permanent satellites of TNC-5527. He decided he wouldn't let himself sound as angry as he felt.

"Sorry about that, Shipmaster. We were surprised by the amount of ionizing radiation venting from the hull breach." He tried to sound light-hearted. "We thought that maybe a matter-antimatter reaction might be starting."

Sulu was surprised when he heard Krulmadden laugh. "Where you think Krulmadden keeps antimatter on his jewel, stupid mammals?"

Sulu glanced at Chekov but couldn't see his friend's face through the red reflection flaring from his faceplate. However, he could hear him say, "In a magnetic bottle?"

"Ha!" Krulmadden shouted. Sulu could picture the way the green-skinned Orion's stomach would be quivering with laughter about now. "You know how much the cost of magnetic bottles? Big coils! Superconductors! Maintenance required every hundred light-years!"

Sulu was confused, and excited. Given Krulmadden's tendency to acquire illegal technology, was there a chance that he had somehow obtained a method for storing antimatter that didn't require the complexities of magnetic storage?

"Excuse me, Shipmaster, but what *do* you keep your antimatter in?"

"What antimatter?" Krulmadden thundered. "What kind of fool do you take me for?"

Sulu saw Chekov spin around beside him and motion with open palms. He didn't know what the shipmaster was talking about, either.

"Then, how do you power your warp drive?" Chekov asked.

"Time-honored methods of my parents, and my parents' parents, and my so-ons and so-forths," Krulmadden said sagely. "First-stage matter! Fissionables!"

Of course, Sulu thought, *no wonder Krulmadden was always concerned about power expenditures and the cost of fuel.* Old-fashioned nuclear generators were only a hundredth as efficient as matter-antimatter reactors. *And that probably accounts for all the extra mass and hidden areas of his ship—denselead shielding to protect his "cargo" and fuel supplies. He'd have to keep hundreds of tons of fissionables on board to give the* Queen Mary *even a minimal hundred-light-year range.*

And then it hit home—shielding.

"Shipmaster?" Sulu said, trying to remain calm. "Did you send us out to inspect the damage knowing that your fissionable fuel supply might be venting?"

"Of course," Krulmadden replied in the most reasonable voice in the galaxy. He did not sound as if he had anything to hide.

"But," Chekov added, and he wasn't trying to remain calm, "why did you not send out remotes? Why did you send us to be exposed to first-stage radiation?"

Krulmadden responded as if he had no idea why Chekov was upset. "Little mammal, if I had sent my remotes to examine the damage caused by the *stator* border patrol, my precious little drones might have been damaged by the leaking radiation. So, Krulmadden sent his newest crew! Smart thinking, yes, you must think so, too?"

As best he could, Sulu gestured to his throat with a desperate cutting motion, telling Chekov to say nothing more. Two hundred meters out from their only way back to Federation space, he did not want to make Krulmadden angry with them.

"But Shipmaster," Sulu said placatingly, "did you not know that Chekov and I could also be damaged by first-stage radiation?" Who knew? Maybe Orions were naturally stabilized.

"Of course, Krulmadden know. Krulmadden fine shipmaster!" Sulu pictured the Orion leaning closer to the comlink because his voice suddenly became louder and raspier. "But if little mammals are damaged by radiation, Krulmadden will lock them into medic booth that will make them better, no charge, no cost. If remotes get damaged by radiation, Krulmadden must go back to Rigel VIII and pay evil, very bad Andorian criminals exorbitant payments for repairs." Krulmadden wheezed with laughter. "Mammals are cheaper."

Expendable, you mean, Sulu thought, but said nothing.

"Uh, Shipmaster?" Chekov began politely, "are you certain that your medic booth works on humans?"

"If I were you, I would hope so!" Sulu could hear Artinton and Lasslanlin join in Krulmadden's merry laughter. "Please communicate again when breech is sealed. Perhaps airlock will work then, too."

The comlink clicked off again.

Sulu maneuvered so he floated directly in front of Chekov. The shadow he cast cut the glare on Chekov's faceplate and they could see each other. "What kind of exposure did we get?" Sulu asked.

Chekov shook his head in his helmet. "The sensor wand is not calibrated for humans. But whatever it was, it was off the dial. What do you suppose we should do now?"

"Fix the breech," Sulu said in resignation. "You heard what he said. If we don't, he's not going to let us back in."

Sulu saw Chekov blink as Krulmadden's voice whispered over the comlink again. "Righty right you are. And the more time you take, the longer it might take me to decide not to change my mind."

Great, Sulu thought, *even out here he can hear everything we say.* Given the pirates' paranoia—something which neither he nor Chekov had anticipated—they had not felt safe enough to risk talking about a plan to take over the ship for the past three weeks. Not that the two-gee field had left them the strength to act on any plan.

"We're returning to the breech," Sulu said. There was no other choice.

But as he glanced down to check the positioning of his fat, gloved fingers on the thruster controls, he felt Chekov tapping the side of his helmet. "What?" he mouthed through his faceplate.

Chekov smiled and nodded his head enthusiastically. Sulu saw his lips move silently to form something that looked like, "exactly." Then Chekov flipped open the protective cover on his own chest plate and switched off his suit's main power. Sulu did a quick calculation and decided that they'd have about ten minutes before they'd need the oxygen recirculators turned back on, then he shut down his own suit, feeling nervous as the status lights above his faceplate on the inside of his helmet flickered out. *It's an old, old suit,* he thought. *Sure hope it doesn't lock up when I try to restart it.*

Then Chekov grabbed Sulu by the shoulders and brought their helmets together with a bang. Sulu froze, listening intently for the sound of leaking air. But all he heard was Chekov's voice, muffled and tinny. It was one of the lowest-tech tricks they taught at the Academy, but it worked. Sound vibrations passed easily from one helmet to the other as long as they touched.

"Yes . . . I . . . can . . . hear . . . you," Sulu shouted in response to Chekov's question, making each word separate and distinct.

"Everything . . . is . . . going . . . to . . . be . . . perfect!" Chekov said excitedly.

"That's . . . what . . . you . . . said . . . last . . . time . . . Chekov! This . . . was . . . your . . . idea . . . in . . . the . . . first . . . place . . . remember?"

Chekov nodded vigorously, shaking both of them in their suits. But he kept his same bright grin in place. "And . . . now . . . I've . . . got . . . another!"

Shipmaster Krulmadden used a sonic pick to clean the remnants of his dinner from his jeweled teeth, and every time he held the madly vibrating needle to his teeth, the high-pitched grating sound of it made Chekov cringe. Unfortunately, Krulmadden had seen his reaction and apparently enjoyed it. His teeth were long since sparkling—in more ways than one—but he kept tapping the sonic pick to them in order to see Chekov jump. Except for that annoying noise, the *Queen Mary's* crew lounge was silent as everyone waited for Krulmadden's reply.

But he wasn't ready to give one. "You were not *f'deraxt'l* admiral in *statorfleet,*" Krulmadden said skeptically.

Lasslanlin and Artinton laughed at the new pun on Starfleet their cousin had made.

"So you could not have big secrets like the one you tell me." Krulmadden placed the sonic pick against his teeth until his lips blurred with vibration. "Should I kill you for liars being?"

Chekov shook his head and prepared himself to tell the story again. He couldn't understand how a being whose brain worked as slowly as Krulmadden's had ever managed to stay in control of his own vessel for so long.

"I did not make myself clear," Chekov said wearily. The combination of four hours of EVA to repair the *Queen Mary*'s hull breech, the return to double gravity, and now the added discomfort of having a medic-booth intravenous cuff strapped to his arm was rapidly becoming more than he could bear. Beside him at the brilliantly gleaming steel mess table, he saw Sulu slumped in his chair, dark circles under his eyes, struggling against anti-radiation drugs and exhaustion to stay awake. A long glistening tube trailed from his arm as well, snaking across the floor to the humming and vibrating medic booth.

"We have time, time, time," Krulmadden said expansively. "Make yourself clear, little mammal."

"First of all, what I have told you is not a secret," Chekov said.

Krulmadden spit on the floor. "A million tons of fissionables which lie around for the taking—and they have not been taken? If they have not been taken, then they must be a secret."

"No," Chekov protested. "It's just that fissionables are not considered that important. Starfleet has complete jurisdiction over the planet and it is forbidden to take anything from it."

"Besides," Sulu said weakly, "almost all Starfleet vessels are powered by matter and antimatter. Starfleet doesn't need fissionables."

Krulmadden looked over at Lasslanlin and Artinton.

"They lie," Lasslanlin said.

"So kill them," Artinton concluded happily.

Chekov tried to wave his hands in frustration but he couldn't lift them from the tabletop. "How can you say that I'm lying if you won't even go to the planet to see for yourself?"

Lasslanlin had another suggestion. "If they not lying, then can we go ourselves to the planet?"

Artinton smiled with another idea of his own. "So we can kill them now still!"

Sulu shook his head back and forth. "No, Artinton. If you kill us before you go, then you won't be able to get past the Starfleet blockade. We're the ones who know the codes and the patrol patterns, remember? You need us to get in and to get out."

"Kill them afterward?" Artinton asked hopefully. "Just one?"

Krulmadden placed his hands on the table and the metal of his rings scraped like fingernails on slate. Chekov didn't know how much more of this his ears could take.

"This is Krulmadden's problem," he said. "You wish to steal from *stator*fleet. All right, Krulmadden understands this. You wish to shame them, hurt them, all fine and good, good, good as far as Krulmadden knows. But Talin IV is Kirk's World, yes, no?"

"Talin IV is Talin IV," Sulu said grimly.

"Whatever. The planet of many names was destroyed by nuclear warheads. Updates say *all* weapons. All weapons launched when the *Enterprise* goes there and scares everyone. All weapons explode. Kill that world. Foof. No more nothing."

"That's right," Chekov said. "So what is your problem?"

"Exploding all weapons means consuming all fissionables. Krulmadden knows uniphysics. There are no fissionables on Talin IV. You lie to bring me dishonor. So I must kill you, nothing personal. Artinton, give me a dancerknife with a very slow blade."

Krulmadden held out his hand like a surgeon waiting for a protoplaser.

Artinton pulled open his vest and began looking inside. Chekov heard the clink of fine metal.

"Wait! Listen to me for once!" Chekov tried to stand but only managed to get halfway up.

Krulmadden shrugged and brought his hand back. "Okay," he agreed.

Chekov stared at the pirate's new change of mood in disbelief. How could he keep reversing himself this way? The navigator couldn't stand it any longer. He didn't care what Sulu said about trying to stay calm. He had had enough. "Listen to me, you owerstuffed, jiggling mound of flame jelly. I have told you cossacks this a thousand times and I will only tell you once more before I rip those ridiculous rocks out of your mouth with your own belt buckles!" Chekov ignored Sulu's plaintive groan. "Not all the Talin warheads exploded. They have a failure rate of forty percent. Forty percent of the entire world's arsenal is still there—refined, weapons-grade fissionables. And no one on the planet can do a thing to stop you."

Krulmadden nodded wisely. "When you say it that way, you make it sound like an appealing business dealing."

Chekov wanted to put his head on the table and go to sleep for a year. "Say it what way? I didn't say anything that I haven't said before!"

"Ah," Krulmadden said approvingly, "but this time you said it with such passion." He made a fist and tapped his knuckles on the table. "Very well, the illustrious jewel of the stars shall go to Talin IV to show our *flars* to the *stator*fleet onions!"

"I think you mean 'minions,' " Sulu said weakly.

"Whatever. We shall show them, and then we shall retrieve a cargo of fissionables that shall make Krulmadden the richest trader in all the veils of heaven's harem." He beamed at Chekov with a jeweled smile. "And if you and your *tislin* survive the medic booth's treatment, you share two percent." He held up a thick finger before Chekov could say anything. "Nonnegotiable—unless you have your own medic booth you would like to use?"

"Two percent," Chekov said, hoping that he looked convincingly beaten.

"What a good little mammal." Krulmadden reached across the table and squeezed Chekov's cheek teasingly between thumb and forefinger.

Chekov pulled away and his head thudded against the back of his chair. *But Talin has almost Earth normal gravity,* he thought. *Sulu and I can recover there.* He tried to straighten his head as he spoke. "Shall I begin to plot in the approaches necessary to awoid Starfleet's patrols around Talin?" he asked.

"No hurry," Krulmadden said.

"But we're only about five days out from Talin," Sulu said.

Krulmadden's eyes glinted. "Ah, so you do know where we are. Even without charts. Krulmadden is impressed. But Krulmadden also has other concerns for the moment. And Talin IV is going nowhere but around its lonely little sun. We will go there soon enough. A month, a year, or once upon a time."

It worked before, Chekov thought. *Might as well try it again.* "How stupid does a shipmaster have to be to decide not to pick up a fortune in refined fissionables while he has the chance?"

Krulmadden looked at Artinton. The Orion mate pulled back his vest again and began searching for a dancerknife.

"How stupid does a mammal have to be to know that there is no sense picking up one cargo until the shipmaster has unloaded his first? Or do you and your *tislin* hate the slavegirls so much you would have me offload them in empty space without profit?"

Chekov pointed weakly to the intravenous cuff on his arm. "It's the medication," he said apologetically, trying to shrug despite the cruel gravity.

"Hope that it continues to flow," Krulmadden said in what was quite clearly a threat. "And in the meantime, I am shipmaster and say where the ship goes. And right now, this ship goes to trade with Black Ire."

"What is Black Ire?" Chekov asked, trying to keep Krulmadden distracted, but dismayed that it appeared it might still be several months before they could reach Talin.

"Black Ire a who, little mammal. A trader in greenskins and, unlike your dear, sweet, understanding Shipmaster Krulmadden, Black Ire a most fearsome and dangerous *pirate*."

"I thought that's what you were supposed to be," Sulu sighed.

"Me?" Krulmadden crowed. "Fearsome and dangerous?" He leaned forward, crinkling his pudgy nose and eyebrows at Chekov and Sulu. "How much you have still to learn, little mammals. And how much I shall enjoy teaching you."

Four

"What happened to the astronauts?"

"The what?" Kirk said. He watched as Nogura stepped carefully across the environmental control board, tail lashing. Kirk had quickly learned why the most critical controls of the *Ian Shelton* were protected with clear covers.

Anne Gauvreau caught up with the cat and scooped it under her arm. "Isn't that what they used to call space explorers? Astronauts or cosmonauts or something? You know, the two Talin in the lunar orbiter. Were they still in orbit when it happened?"

When it *happened,* Kirk noted. Not "the disaster," not "the mistake," Gauvreau just referred to what he had told her had happened at Talin IV as "it."

"I don't think anyone knows for certain," Kirk said. He stretched out in the crew chair, watching the stars slip past on the viewscreen at a steady warp four. The ship was two days out from Hanover and there wasn't a lot that Gauvreau didn't know about him or Talin. Two weeks on an automated freighter *was* a long time. "I wasn't kept informed about most of what happened over the next few days. I know that the rescue shuttles from Starbase 29 went looking for the Talin ship but I don't think anything was ever found."

Gauvreau chucked Nogura under the chin as she watched a consumables breakdown scroll past on a computer display. Kirk respected her ability to be able to keep up with several different sources of information at once. Good officers had to be able to do that in a bridge environment. The human resource specialists in Starfleet called it "human multitasking."

"Do you think they crashed?" she asked. "I mean, on purpose, seeing their world destroyed like that."

Kirk watched as Komack stuck his head up above the impulse board, ears flattened. Kirk had learned how to read the creatures' minds in the past two weeks: The cat was looking for a lap.

"I don't think anyone had the resources to scan the entire moon for such a small crashed vehicle. Maybe they even landed. But there was no sign that they tried to get back to Talin." Komack stepped precisely between the impulse controls and stood across from Kirk, staring intently at him. "I suppose we can't blame them for not wanting to."

Gauvreau came over to the impulse station and pushed Komack off the board so she could lean against it. She kept her hand busy on Nogura's ears. The stars swam behind her.

"It's not your fault, you know."

"Thank you," Kirk said. Now that she had heard the whole story, he didn't question her decision to accept his innocence.

"Too bad I wasn't on the board of inquiry, hmm?" She smiled at him, trying to get him to respond in kind. Kirk knew he hadn't been doing a lot of that on board the *Shelton.* But he decided that he couldn't be blamed for not wanting to, either.

"You still haven't told me everything that went on then," Gauvreau said.

"Not much to tell. The board members had full bridge log tapes up to the point we went into warp in the atmosphere—" Kirk saw that Gauvreau still shuddered at the concept. "—so they could see exactly what had happened. They reviewed the tapes. Asked a few questions for the record to determine what the state of our minds were at various times, then made their ruling."

"One ruling or two?" she asked.

"Five actually," Kirk said. "One for each of us who had willfully—"

"No, I don't mean how many crew members they ruled against. I remember the *Enterprise* Five. I mean, did they only make a ruling to cover the second time you tried to stop the exchange of weapons, or did they rule on the first time, too? After the accidental detonation in the missile silo."

"As far as the board was concerned, they weren't separate events. The core of their decision was that if I had not interfered the first time, then the second exchange would not have occurred."

Gauvreau stopped scratching her cat's ears and let him slip out of her hands to the deck. Nogura made a soft squeaking sound as he hit, then stalked off to the ladderway. Gauvreau sat in the navigation chair across from Kirk and leaned forward, putting her elbow on her knee and resting her chin on her hand.

"Now, how did they come to that conclusion?" she asked.

For once Kirk smiled of his own accord. "For what it's worth, my science officer said their reasoning was quite logical."

"Enlighten me," Gauvreau said.

Kirk kept his eyes on the screen and the stars. He could not deny that these were painful memories Gauvreau had been coaxing from him. Yet he knew he had to face them sooner or later, so he did not resist.

"They brought in three cultural specialists from the Richter Institute. And they maintained that, from the data assembled by Starfleet's own FCO, the Talin were clearly dedicated to global peace in their world."

"Despite the fact that they were armed to the teeth?"

"Many worlds have been in similar situations and survived. The specialists said that Talin IV had had an excellent chance of being one of them."

Gauvreau sat up, plainly upset. "The accidental detonation had nothing at all to do with whatever the Talin hoped for in the long run. And it could have led them to a full exchange even earlier."

"I'm not the board of inquiry," Kirk said defensively. "I'm only telling you what they ruled. And they ruled that had the Talin experienced a small example of the effects of a full-scale war because of the accidental detonation, it would have propelled them into serious arms and peace negotiations."

"Ah," Gauvreau said, "so the board decided that you spared them that particular lesson."

"Exactly," Kirk agreed. "If I had allowed a minor exchange of weapons to take place, then the major exchange would not have followed."

Gauvreau frowned in disbelief. "Were there any Vulcans on this board?"

"Two actually. The civilian members. And no dissenting opinions."

"I don't understand how they could come to that conclusion."

Kirk closed his eyes for a moment and saw himself standing before the board. He remembered each word they had said, because each word had taken away another small part of his dream.

"The board concluded that I had denied the Talin the opportunity to learn from their own mistakes. Because they did not have to deal with the consequences of an accidental nuclear detonation, some of them were recklessly encouraged to proceed with a more dangerous action. By interfering with their normal development, I made it possible for them to engage in an activity which led to the destruction of their world. A textbook example of what happens when the Prime Directive is not upheld." Kirk opened his eyes. Gauvreau looked away from him.

"Was there no defense you could give?" she asked.

"If I had refused to resign, they would have held a court-martial for each of us who took action on the bridge. We could have presented a defense then, but if the defense weren't accepted, then each of my bridge team might have faced twenty years' imprisonment. I couldn't do that to them."

"What about what you did to yourself, Kirk?"

"That's not important."

"What is?"

"The Talin."

"But if you don't believe you contravened the Prime Directive, then why be concerned with them?"

Kirk swung around to face her. It didn't seem like her to be so cold or so callous. "Let's get this straight, Captain. At the time I made my decision to act, to the best of my knowledge and ability, I believed I was following my orders and doing my duty. In hindsight, perhaps I did not uphold the Prime Directive, despite my best intentions. But no matter what actually happened on Talin IV—whether I'm technically or legally right or wrong—I do not intend to deny that I share some responsibility for what happened." He studied her, wondering if she understood what he was saying, if she understood the concept of duty as he did. "If I caused harm to the Talin, then somehow, some way, I will attempt to right it, no matter how little I can do, and no matter how long it might take."

Gauvreau stood up and slid her hands into the pockets of her multipatched flight jacket. "You can say that despite what Starfleet did to you?"

"All Starfleet personnel involved with the Talin inquiry did their duty as they saw fit. I have no quarrel with them. The answer lies elsewhere."

Gauvreau thrust her head forward, squinting in exasperation. "Then who do you have a quarrel with? You've been tighter than a cadet's bedsheet. I keep thinking you're going to haul off and kick one of my cats. If you're not angry at Starfleet and you're not angry at yourself and you're not angry at the damned board of inquiry, then who the hell are you mad at?"

"Captain Gauvreau," Kirk said seriously, "I'll let you know when I get back to Talin. Because whoever I'm mad at, that's where I'm going to find them."

Two days later, Kirk stood in the empty cargo hold of the *Ian Shelton* and tucked his kit bag under his arm. When Gauvreau came back and paid him for his tour as supercargo, he'd be able to beam over to Hanover's spacedock, then catch a shuttle down to the colony world's freighter yards. There he could try his luck again at getting a cargo handler's job, or even pay for freighter passage to another system closer still to Talin. Eventually, he'd get back there, he knew. And even if he didn't, he knew he would never stop trying.

He heard his name echo in the vast hold of the ship and turned to see Gauvreau standing on an observation platform near the control booth. She waved to him.

About time, thought Kirk, *now we can get this over with.* Two weeks in deep space with her and he still had no idea how to read her. He couldn't make up his mind whether or not he thought Starfleet had made a mistake in letting go an officer of her wide-ranging abilities, or had been wise in refusing to promote such an eccentric, self-contained perfectionist. At least her cats liked her.

Kirk arrived at the ladder leading up to the observation platform. He was pleased when he saw that among the packages and cases Gauvreau carried was the *Shelton*'s paymaster terminal. Liquid credits were slowly being phased out throughout much of the Federation as virtually unlimited power and manufacturing technologies became automated to the point where they were self-reproducing and maintaining. When the necessities of life had no value and interplanetary resources were prodigious enough to ensure that people could have almost anything they could imagine, a simple, cashless system of barter naturally arose. But out on the frontier, Kirk knew, there would always have to be some system of portable wealth so that credits could be taken from place to place in search of scarce commodities. Then again, who knew what the future would bring?

Gauvreau stepped back and Kirk climbed the ladder to join her. He saw her three cats in the cargo control room, staring through the window at her. She would not let them out into the hold, no matter how much they cried and rubbed at the airlock.

"Sorry to take so long," Gauvreau said. "You'll be pleased to know that the whole transfer of cargo was accomplished without damage. I get a bonus for that and you're going to share in it."

"Thank you," Kirk said. Whatever else Anne Gauvreau might be, she was fair. "Did you get a chance to find out about their public transporter facilities?"

"That's what I came back on," she said. "I even got you a rate card. But . . . why not come back inside for a few minutes?" She pointed toward the airlock leading to the control room.

Kirk was in a hurry and it showed.

But Gauvreau was determined. She held up a small brown package and Kirk smelled what was in it instantly. "Real coffee," she said triumphantly. "Stasis beans from Earth. Roasted locally. You can't say no."

Kirk couldn't. He followed her back into the crew areas of her ship.

As the scent of fresh coffee filled the tiny lounge, Gauvreau unpacked another small case on the games table. "One of the reasons I was held up was because I tried to get online with the Starfleet update channels." She glanced at him. "It's completely legal. They're a public channel."

They were, technically, Kirk knew. But to intercept them, civilians usually needed a Starfleet-licensed receiver, which the *Shelton* didn't have.

"So, I still have friends in Starfleet," Gauvreau said. "And a few of them at the Starfleet office over on the spacedock let me download update files."

Kirk watched the coffee bubble up from the osmosis inverter. He was surprised at how the prospect of reading Starfleet updates didn't seem to affect him either way—he was neither interested nor disinterested, as if he no longer cared. Instead he wondered why Gauvreau was going to such lengths to let him know she had some.

"Is there something special going on out in the galaxy you think I should know about?" he asked.

"Don't give me that," Gauvreau said. "You know there is."

Kirk listened to and read the main updates whenever he got the chance. He knew that nothing had happened in the Talin system since Starfleet had blockaded it to keep out scavengers and exploiters. It had been estimated that the blockade would have to stay in place for at least five hundred years before the Talin came anywhere near their previous level of technological development. In the last two months, the only mention of Talin in the public updates had been in relation to the long-term resource allocations that the Federation was requesting for blockade maintenance. Starfleet had succeeded in doing what it had set out to do—close the datafile on the entire incident without withholding anything.

But now Gauvreau acted as if something had changed.

"Is it something you think I should know?" Kirk prompted.

" 'A good commander learns all that she can,' " Gauvreau quoted, " 'then uses all that she has.' "

"What's in the updates?" Kirk didn't want to recap Academy lectures. He wanted off this ship.

"It seems you're not the only one who wants to go back to Talin." Gauvreau slipped a microtape into a screenpad. "Recognize these names? Palamas, Carolyn. Frietas, Jorge. Let's see . . . M'Benga, Chapel, Fisher . . . about a hundred others?"

Kirk took the screenpad from her hand and scanned the list of names. There was no Starfleet imprimatur on the display but all the names were of Starfleet personnel. All the names were of *Enterprise* crewmembers.

"What is this?" Kirk said, feeling the anger build in him again as he realized something was developing of which he was unaware. "This isn't an update sheet from a public channel."

"It's a recall list, Kirk. Those officers and specialists are being reassigned to their previous posting."

Kirk felt gooseflesh crawl up his arms and neck. "The *Enterprise?*" he whispered. But his ship was dead. He had destroyed her himself.

Gauvreau nodded.

"Who authorized the recall? Where's the *Enterprise?*"

Gauvreau passed over another tape wafer for Kirk to read. "Authorization source is Vice Admiral Hammersmith, Starbase 29. And the originating source is given as Lieutenant Commander Scott, *U.S.S. Enterprise,* on station, Talin System."

Kirk read the second tape and confirmed the code designations. His hands shook. "They told me she was dead," he said. "They told me . . . she'd never be operational again." And why was Scott still on her, almost four months later, unless . . .

"Where did you get these? How recent are they?"

"No more than a few days old, Kirk. And I'm afraid I'm going to keep my source at Starfleet communications a secret. They never pass on classified or military information, but sometimes it helps to know where the big ships are going to be—especially if I've got a hold full of real coffee."

Kirk looked at the tapes Gauvreau still hadn't passed over. As a civilian, it was a violation for her to have them. But perhaps some good could come of it. "No harm done?" he asked her, indicating the tapes.

"Never," Gauvreau said. "Little more than the gossip I'd hear in a bar."

Kirk took the rest of the update wafers. Obviously, Gauvreau and her sources had gone to a great deal of trouble to pull out all recent transmissions which had contained the words *"Enterprise"* or "Talin." There were dozens of them and the story they told was staggering.

"They detached the port nacelle," Kirk read. "They told me it couldn't be done." He scrolled through the reports. "And nothing happened, per the reports submitted by Scott. Replacement warp nacelles are in transit . . . crew is being recalled . . ." For a moment, he felt as if he couldn't breathe. "My ship . . ." he said. "The *Enterprise* . . . she's . . ."

Gauvreau reached out and took Kirk's hand. "I know," she said gently. "She's going to be given to someone else."

Kirk sat back and pulled his hand away. It was one thing for him to have lost his career *and* the *Enterprise* together. Without one, what could the other be worth? But to think of someone else taking out his ship, and his crew—he was wracked with terrible jealousy.

"They told me every circuit in her was fused. They told me the nacelle was still drawing her into warp space and she could never be released."

"Here's a weapons-damage analysis report from Scott," Gauvreau said, handing the appropriate tape to Kirk. "Read it."

Kirk's eyes sped over the display. "Only twenty percent damage . . . precisely focused subspace pulse. . . ." He looked up, eyes blazing. "It was a deliberate attack. An attack beyond the Talin's capabilities." He looked back at the analysis. It wasn't signed off by Hammersmith and it was tagged as a preliminary report, but it meant there was a chance that another reason existed for what had happened to the *Enterprise.* And to Talin IV. "But how did anyone figure the damage pattern out?" Kirk asked. "To break it down like this someone would have to crawl through the whole ship on his hands and—"

And then he knew what Scott was still doing on the ship. *Bless you, Scotty,* he thought. *You never gave up.*

He scrolled through the rest of the tapes, scanning supply requisitions and personnel transfers until he had an idea of the schedule Hammersmith was on in getting the *Enterprise* back into space under her own power. He clenched his jaw. He had less than a week to get back to Talin before they'd be starting warp trials with her to bring her new nacelles into balance. A week.

"Thank you, Captain," Kirk said, standing suddenly with the screenpad in his hand. "I can't tell you what this means to me."

"I saw the look on your face when you realized someone else was going to get her, Kirk. I know exactly what it means to you."

"That's not important," Kirk said. "It's this report from Scotty. If the *Enterprise* was hit with a precisely focused subspace pulse, then there's another factor which hasn't been included in the equation." He swung his kit bag over his shoulder. "May I use the bridge to place a call to the spacedock transporter?"

Gauvreau went to the coffee osmoser and poured two cups from the flask. "Sit down, Kirk, you don't have to go anywhere, yet." She handed him a steaming mug.

"You don't understand, I have less than a week to get to the Talin system."

"The *Shelton* can make it in five days."

"I'm going to have to—what?"

"Don't look at me like that, Kirk. You heard what I said. I'm the captain and this ship's next port is Talin IV."

Kirk put the coffee mug on the table, but he no longer felt the need to rush away. Not until he found out what Gauvreau was up to. "The Talin system is blockaded," he said.

Gauvreau opened a small, soft-sided bag and pulled out two more pale yellow microtapes. "Now this one is from the public update services." She held it close to her, not letting Kirk have it yet. "You see, at the Starfleet office, I was able to request a search for everything to do with the *Enterprise* and Talin IV, because they're both within Starfleet jurisdiction. But for the rest of the *Enterprise* Five, I had to go to the public update bureaus."

Gauvreau glanced down at the tapes. Kirk didn't grab for them. He'd give her another minute to play her game. He knew what it was like to have another person hanging on every word.

"Now," Gauvreau said, "for Chekov, I found nothing. He resigned. Was last seen heading out on a pleasure cruiser to Eisner's World . . . in the company of Sulu. Same thing. No other mentions of him, either. The communications officer, Uhura, well, she was released from detention on the Moon. Was met there by . . . Leonard McCoy . . . the one who took a swing at Hammersmith . . . then they both went back to Earth, then to Mars, then to . . . Rigel II of all places . . . and then no more references, just like the others."

"That just leaves Spock," Kirk said.

"And you," Gauvreau countered. "But for what it's worth, you've been spotted on just about every seedy frontier world, doing everything *except* rockrigging and handling cargo. As for Spock, well, he's one of the reasons why the Talin system might not be blockaded for much longer." She passed over the microtapes at last.

Kirk took them calmly from her, trying not to show how eager he was for the news of his friend. But then he forgot all about keeping up appearances as he read the update story three times before he was sure he believed it.

"Spock's *suing* the Federation?"

"That's what he said at his update conference."

"And *Starfleet?*" Kirk blinked to clear his vision. "On behalf of . . . Students for Stars for the People. Who the hell are Students for Stars for the People?"

"Last paragraph," Gauvreau said. "Apparently it's a radical student organization based at Berkeley."

"Berkeley?" Kirk said in shock. "Across the bay from San Francisco, Berkeley?" Gauvreau nodded.

"But that's almost next door to Starfleet Academy. Berkeley's been one of the most conservative universities on Earth for more than a hundred years. Why would Spock get mixed up with anything so . . . ?"

"Amateur?"

"Exactly."

"From what you've told me about him, I'm sure he has his reasons."

"I'm sure he does, too," Kirk said, rereading the update for the fourth time.

"But because of the challenge he's threatening to bring over enforcement of the Prime Directive, there seems to be quite a public outcry to get emergency relief aid to Talin."

Kirk sat back at the table, feeling overcome by the sudden assimilation of this much unexpected news. He had been so singlemindedly fixed on his goal of getting to Talin IV that he had not permitted himself to remember how much he missed his crew, and how much he cared for his friends.

"Even Spock will never be able to do that," Kirk said. "No matter what they think the trigger incident might have been, as far as the board of inquiry was concerned, the destruction of Talin IV was caused by Talin weapons and Talin politics. Neither Starfleet nor the Federation could possibly allow the Prime Directive to be broken there again."

"Maybe," Gauvreau said, "and maybe not. But my credits are on your Mr. Spock. All of them." She flipped open the screen of her paymaster terminal and hit the balance button. It came up close to zero. The ship's accounts were drained.

"There should be close to one hundred thousand credits in there," Kirk said. He had seen the cargo manifest and the insurance papers from Lloyds.

"Already transferred out to pay for our new cargo," Gauvreau explained. Should be shipping up to the spacedock within the next hour.

"What did you buy?" Kirk asked.

"Emergency supplies—medical mostly. Radiation stabilizers. Water purifiers. That sort of thing. Should come in handy when Starfleet calls off their blockade."

"You're serious, aren't you?"

"According to the updates, Kirk, I'm not the only one. There are about two hundred ships already underway to Talin. And that's not counting the additional picket ships Starfleet's ordered in to manage the traffic. Something's going to give there soon. And whatever else happens, you and I will be there along with your ship and most of your crew."

She clicked the paymaster off and shut its screen down. "Now drink your coffee, so I don't have to hear you complain about the jifficoff cubes anymore."

Kirk lifted the mug and finally savored the rich scent of the brew. *Scott hadn't given up,* he thought. And Spock was doing something completely outrageous. And if McCoy and Uhura, and Chekov and Sulu had disappeared, then the chances were more than likely that they were somewhere together, also planning something. He found himself smiling at the way things had turned out. He had decided he would go back to Talin on his own because he couldn't force any of the others to share the hardships and the risks of the journey with him. Yet they had all come to the same conclusion and set out for the same goals on their own anyway. *Even when we're apart,* he thought, *we're a team.*

Kirk sniffed the coffee. Real beans, freshly roasted, steaming hot. But even without tasting it, he knew it couldn't be even half as good as what he had had on the *Enterprise*. And would have again.

Five

By standing to the side of the small window and almost against the wall, Spock could just see past the other towers of the student housing complex and catch a glimpse of clear sky over San Francisco. He looked into his human half for some connection with what he saw, but the blue of Earth's skies was still alien to him. He found it intriguing that he responded to the red skies of Vulcan in the same way— neither world held the skies of home for him.

Behind Spock, in the small and cluttered student apartment, five humans carried on two separate conversations—both about him. He followed their words easily while reflecting on the hundreds of skies he had seen in his travels, trying to recall which ones, if any, he had felt at home beneath.

After a time, one of the conversations became heated.

"Well, don't ask *me,*" Marita Llorente said in exasperation. "Ask *him.*"

"I don't think I can," Marita's companion said uncertainly. "Look at him. Isn't he meditating or something?"

"No," Spock said, and at the sound of his voice the other conversation died. "I am not meditating. What did you wish to ask me?" He turned from the window. For now, he decided that the true color of his sky was black. His home was space. He was confident he would return there soon.

Marita's companion was Penn Grossman, the young oriental human who shared these quarters with her. Spock had seldom seen a more harried or nervous creature. He had the attitude of someone who felt anything and everything which happened anywhere in the galaxy had some direct personal bearing on his life— usually negative. *At least,* Spock thought, *in regard to my presence in his life, the young man is correct.*

"Why did you have to go to the update services and tell them about the legal challenge?" Penn rocked back and forth on the worn couch where he sat beside Marita. The couch could be unfolded. It was where Spock slept. "That little grandstanding ploy could ruin everything."

Spock placed his hands behind his back, remaining impassive as he rapidly tried to recall if he had ever before heard the term "grandstanding." He guessed at its meaning from the way Penn had used it. "I assure you I was not grandstanding. It will be more beneficial to our purposes if update coverage of the General Council meeting is more intensive than normal, so that more beings will be aware of our struggle." Spock had quickly picked up the cant of Marita's organization. Typical for humans, they found romance in thinking of their political aspirations as rebellion. Many scholars on Vulcan still had trouble understanding how democracy had flourished on a planet where logic had not.

Penn's hands fluttered rapidly in front of him. "But Marita told me what happened when you saw Ambassador Sytok. He said that if the Council found out Marita would be attending the general meeting, then they'd cancel it or something so she couldn't disrupt it."

"First, I must remind you that under the terms of our agreement, the Council meeting must not be disrupted. All business which I shall present there will be conducted in accordance with the Federation's Rules of Order."

"Yeah, yeah, I know," Penn said rudely.

"Second, at no time during the update conference did I mention that Marita would be attending the Council meeting with me. All the update services reported was that I would be speaking on behalf of Students for Stars for the People to press for the repeal of the Prime Directive.

"If any of the Council members had learned of the topic of my address before it had been made public, then the meeting could have been delayed quite easily. But now that my intentions have been widely reported, the Council cannot postpone their meeting without inviting public criticism and an increased public debate on the propriety of the Directive. By holding the update conference, I have removed that choice from the Council's options and we remain in control of their agenda."

Marita clapped her hands. "Well done, Mr. Spock." She looked scornfully at Penn. "See? I told you he knew what he was doing. You should have seen the look on the ambassador's face when Mr. Spock had me do the finger-embrace thing. I tell you, this guy knows how the system works. He's just what the SSP's been needing—someone from the inside who knows firsthand how morally bankrupt the Federation is."

Penn sat back in the couch and folded his arms across his chest. "I thought that the finger embrace was something that only married Vulcans did. Or . . ."

"I assure you, Penn, that I asked Marita to attend me only to distract the ambassador from the true purpose of our visit to his embassy. Nothing else was intended by it."

One of the other three students in the cramped room chuckled. "Hey, Penn's jealous of a Vulcan!"

Penn was indignant. "I am not! It's just that . . ." He glared at Spock. "We were doing pretty good on our own. We didn't need him to come along and take over."

Spock remained expressionless though he conceded to himself that, for all of Penn's misplaced nervous energy, the young human was quite perceptive.

Marita pushed against Penn's shoulder. "Mr. Spock hasn't taken over, Penn. He's helping us. Running student rallies and uploading pamphlets is one thing . . . but Mr. Spock is the first person from the inside who believes the same things we do. The Prime Directive has got to go and Mr. Spock's the one who can make that happen." She smiled up at Spock. "Isn't that right?"

"I do not know if I can indeed convince the Council to repeal the Directive," Spock said truthfully.

"See?" Penn said, hands waving. "He admits he can't help us."

Marita stood up from the couch and gathered a stack of serving plates from a small table. "All he's saying is that he can't *guarantee* anything. He's just being truthful, Penn. You know that Vulcans can't lie." She carried the plates over to a small autokitchen set in a corner of the room. As the plates clattered in the metal-walled cleaner, Spock heard the first stirrings of the baby waking in the bedroom. No one else did.

Penn stared at Spock. "Is it true what she said? Is it true that Vulcans can't lie?"

Spock allowed a momentary half-smile to come to his lips. "Assuming that you really do not know the answer, I believe if you consider that question carefully, you will discover that no possible answer I could give would provide you with any useful information." Spock was pleased that he would not have to answer Penn's question directly. The truth was that Vulcans, as a matter of principle, strove to avoid the telling of lies at almost all cost. However, there were times when, to accomplish the greater good, it was necessary to disguise the truth. In the past, Spock had experienced no moral qualms in telling outright lies to Klingons and others who would do violence to the innocent, just as he experienced no qualms in lying to Marita and the other students involved in the SSP. Despite what they might think when they discovered his real purpose in joining them, he was not seeking personal gain. Someday, he hoped they would understand his motives, and condone them.

The student who had laughed at Penn's apparent jealousy got up from the floor where he sat. Beside him, the two other students who had been sitting crosslegged stretched out their legs. One of them knocked over a stack of music cubes. Spock noted disapprovingly that many of the cubes were not in their covers.

"So when is this other bigshot insider going to be coming?" the standing student asked. His name was Lowell and he had told Spock he intended to study law. Spock had noted the orderliness of Lowell's mind and was thankful that he was not the leader of the group. That role had fallen to Marita not because she was the best organizer among the students, but because of her unrelenting energy. The notoriety she had gained by having and caring for a child while still a student also helped attract attention to the group. It was a choice seldom made on Earth these days.

"I believe my guest is due at any moment," Spock said in answer to Lowell's question.

The young law student stood by the window beside Spock and stared out as if trying to find whatever it was that Spock had been looking at. "And he's just supposed to be another guy from Starfleet who's seen the light about the Directive and wants to make the galaxy a better place?"

Like Penn, Lowell also had his doubts about Spock's motives in becoming involved in the SSP. But unlike Penn, he seemed willing to go along with Spock, if not trust him, as long as he felt that the group might gain an advantage from their association with him—even if it wasn't the advantage they were hoping for.

"He is not 'just another guy,' " Spock said. "And he will attract even more public attention for the SSP than I."

"Hard to imagine that," Lowell said, giving up on his search out the window. "You were the first Vulcan to join Starfleet, and the first Vulcan to resign. And along the way you helped destroy a world." Lowell glanced at Spock, looking for a reaction.

But Spock gave him none. He was used to the charges and the misconceptions by now. He felt no need to correct them. There were other solutions. "I believe young Alexander is waking up," he said to Marita.

The woman turned away from her recycler and smiled at Spock. "Would you?" she asked. "You're so good with him."

Spock nodded. Since the day he had resigned from Starfleet and sought out the SSP to take his first unexpected step in his new course to correct the errors of the past, Marita and Penn had not accepted what little payment he could make for his room and board. Thus, he felt he was obliged to contribute to their lives in other ways, such as by tutoring and helping with Alexander. He excused himself to the students and went into the small bedroom.

Alexander's crib module hung against the wall near a larger bed. The walls were decorated with two-dimensional images printed on sheets of plastic and paper. Spock found it ironic that many of the images depicted pristine landscapes from other systems—not colony planets but alien worlds. He wondered if Marita could imagine what these scenes would look like if the Prime Directive did not exist. From Earth's own history, images of the fate of indigenous North Americans came to Spock. As was known now, the European colonists were not representatives of a better culture, simply a more intrusive one, and the indigenous cultures had been overwhelmed. The Federation Council was committed to ensuring that such outrages were never repeated on an interstellar scale, which is why Spock had had to be so careful and so precise in orchestrating the appearance he planned to make before them. He had no doubt that they would not be a receptive audience for what he had to say.

Alexander stopped rocking in his crib as he heard Spock enter the darkened room. He waved his stubby arms and legs as Spock appeared above him and gurgled happily as he was lifted into the air.

When Spock returned to the main room, Alexander was contentedly resting against the Vulcan's shoulder, intently tugging on a gracefully pointed ear.

Penn came over as Spock rocked the child gently, waiting for Marita to finish at the autokitchen. "I didn't think Vulcans liked to be touched by humans," he said waspishly.

Normally, when a Vulcan came into unexpected physical contact with a human, or any being with an undisciplined mind, the crude contact-telepathy transmission of uncontrolled emotion could be distressing. But children were an exception.

"The minds of babies are seldom confused," Spock observed. "And, in fact, they can be quite refreshing." However, he did have to adjust Alexander's position against him to prevent the child from deciding to chew on the ear to which he had become so attached.

A few moments later, the visitor chime sounded. It was an old building, so Marita couldn't speak to the door. She had to walk to it and open it by hand.

Lowell was the only one to recognize the man Spock had invited to join them.

"Alonzo Richter?" the student said in awe.

The old theoretical culturalist waved Marita back from the door by brandishing his black cane at her.

"What about it, you little brat?" Richter growled at Lowell. He shuffled into the room and looked around, licking his teeth and lips noisily. *"Barge g'l,* what a dump. You actually live here, Spock?" He coughed loudly.

Alexander twisted in Spock's arms to see who the new intruder in his home was. Richter stuck out his tongue at the child and Alexander began to cry.

Marita took Alexander from Spock and was jostled out of the way as the other students gathered excitedly around Richter. They all had heard his name before, even if they hadn't recognized his face.

"Dr. Richter," Lowell said, "your work is the underlying structure upon which the Prime Directive is based. Are you seriously joining us to oppose it?"

Richter frowned and made another face at the crying baby. "I'm one hundred percent behind Spock, here," he said. "And I've come a long way to be able to say that, you can be *vrelq* sure about that."

The autokitchen buzzer blared and Alexander responded with screams. Marita bounced him energetically and smiled in the face of the chaos. "The sandwich tubes are ready, Mr. Spock. Would you?"

Spock dutifully went to the autokitchen to remove the sandwich tube trays.

Richter called out to him. "And get me a bubble of ale while you're there, Mr. Spock."

Spock worked quickly and efficiently, all the time preparing for what he would say in his address to the Council, and knowing that no matter how his and Richter's plan worked out, he had to get back into space.

The buzzer sounded again. Alexander yowled. Two more requests for ale were shouted out and someone plugged a music cube into the player.

Spock had no doubt whatsoever. He had to get back into space, and quickly.

Six

Sulu jerked awake and tried to jump from his bunk as the shipmaster's voice roared from the overhead speakers. But he had forgotten the *Queen Mary*'s double-gee field. He heard something crack in his neck and fell back onto the bunk with a drawn-out groan.

"Don't complain," Chekov said from the other bunk. "At least you can still move."

"Attention, all *tislins*," Krulmadden bellowed. "This jewel of the luminous veils drops from warp in less than the time it will take you to crawl to the bridge." Krulmadden sang a few notes as if delivering a morning concert. "That is all."

Sulu rolled to his side and raised his eyebrows at Chekov, even though they felt as if they weighed a hundred kilos apiece. "And cadets think that *Starfleet* commanders are crazy."

Chekov slid his legs to the edge of his bunk and slowly rose to a sitting position. "What is this *'tislins'* he keeps calling us? Why always *'tislins'?*"

Sulu tensed his neck to keep anything from grating, and forced himself up. At least if they ever got off this ship alive, they were both going to have muscles like iron.

"Do you know this word?" Chekov asked.

Sulu nodded carefully. He did.

"Well?" Chekov said.

"I think you can figure it out, Chekov. You see, we didn't want to have anything at all to do with the slavegirls."

"So? We are gentlemen. What of it?"

"*Tislins* means that even if we *wanted* to have something to do with the slavegirls, we couldn't."

Chekov waited expectantly for more.

"Keepers of the harem, Chekov. Snip snip."

"Oh," Chekov said as the realization hit home. "Cossack," he muttered.

The vibration in the deck abruptly changed and Sulu heard the whine of the impulse engines coming to life. The *Queen Mary* was much smaller than the *Enterprise* and the sound of her machinery traveled through her more easily.

"We are out of warp," Chekov said.

Sulu sighed. "Time to meet this 'Black Ire,' I guess—whoa!"

Sulu and Chekov both flew from their bunks, then slammed onto the metal deck as if they had been snapped from a whip.

"Where did he buy his gravity generator?" Chekov complained. "Or more likely, where did he steal it? I have not felt one malfunction so badly in—"

"Hold on," Sulu said, pushing experimentally against the deck. The movement was far more effortless than it ever had been before on the ship. "That's not a malfunction. The field's been reset. It's so weak . . . it's like Mars."

Chekov jumped smoothly to his feet. He picked up one of his boots from the side of the bunk, held it over his head, then dropped it. "But look how fast that fell. This is not Mars normal. This is Earth normal. We are just . . . not used to it."

Sulu pushed off from the floor and was impressed with how painless the action was. It was better than being in Mars gravity. It was like being on the Moon.

"I wonder why he's reset it?" Sulu said.

Krulmadden's voice squawked over the ship's intercom. "Because our guests to be are from a weaker planet, little mammals. Your shipmaster is being courteous, oh yes, indeed."

"We're from a weaker planet, too," Chekov grumbled.

"But you are not guests aboard *Queen Mary*," Krulmadden crooned. "You are crew and courtesy is not required. Now to the bridge before I see what gravity setting for Jupiter does to your little hollow squishy bones."

Chekov sat on the edge of his bunk and pulled on his boots. "Let's hope 'our guests' remain onboard for a long meeting," he said.

Sulu wanted to say what he was hoping for, too, but he didn't think it was something Krulmadden would enjoy overhearing.

The bridge of the *Queen Mary* was arranged in a standard configuration—it was a circular deck ringed by elevated monitoring stations, with a main viewscreen mounted in front of a helm and navigation console, and a central commander's chair. But what wasn't standard was the way every surface in it had been finished with gleaming horizontal strips of gold and silver plating. Beneath the blazing blue Rigel-normal lighting, Chekov had to squint to keep from being blinded by the painfully harsh reflections from the bulkheads, consoles, and deck. He saw Sulu doing the same.

As Chekov and Sulu carefully entered the bridge from the ladderway entrance, Krulmadden whirled around in his chair to face them. *More like a throne,* Chekov thought. The shipmaster's bulk flowed seamlessly into a rippling gold chair that resembled a sculpture of an alien flower bud.

"Ah," Krulmadden said, "so *f'deraxt'l* mammals *can* walk upright like real bipeds after all."

Chekov peered around the bridge, trying to see if the infamous Black Ire had already beamed aboard. But all he saw was Lasslanlin at the helm. Chekov presumed that the other mate, Artinton, was somewhere else in the ship.

"If you are going to reset the grawity for Black Ire," Chekov said, "why not reset the lighting as well?"

"What weaklings you are," Krulmadden jeered. "But it is the least I can do for fearsome pirate guest to be." He rubbed a thick finger against a part of his chair where there were no apparent control surfaces and the bridge lighting dimmed to a more tolerable level. *Tolerable like high noon on Mercury,* Chekov thought. But at least his eyes had stopped hurting. He decided Krulmadden's unmarked chair control surfaces were the strongest proof of his paranoia yet. Even if someone managed to steal this ship from him, it would take days to learn how to run it. Though he guessed the two mates could be convinced to give up her secrets if the price were right.

"What's that supposed to be?" Sulu suddenly asked. "A gunnery target?" He sounded as if he were ready to laugh.

Chekov looked at the screen and saw a vessel that was even more improbable than the *Queen Mary.* The main hull appeared to be a leftover from the days of the old DY-500s when surplus submarine shells were reconfigured to transport cryogenic cargo through vacuum. And the warp pod slung on the back of the hull looked as if it were nothing more than a half-hearted attempt to disguise a twenty-year-old Mark II shuttle.

"That is supposed to be the ship of a fearsome pirate?" Chekov asked. He and Sulu looked at each other and smirked.

"It is good disguise," Krulmadden protested. "Who suspects that Black Ire hunts the spaceways in rundown cargo ship not worth fifty credits to spit for? But little *tislins* . . . see why Black Ire so clever." He palmed another unmarked surface on his chair and a tactical display sprang up in a corner of the viewscreen. "Lasslanlin! Full scan on *Heart of the Storm!*"

Chekov watched as the Orion mate engaged the *Queen Mary*'s sensors from his station. Then he waited for the results to appear on tactical. But there were no results.

"Good stuff, yes, no?" Krulmadden said approvingly. "Full sensor block. Starfleet deflectors. Very expensive. Could hide anything." He turned back to Chekov and Sulu. "The stories Krulmadden hears say *Heart of the Storm* is delusion like *Queen Mary*'s impulse pod."

"Illusion," Sulu corrected.

"Whatever. Antique outside over Starfleet prototypes inside." He widened his eyes as if they were about to burst from his head. "Warp nine Krulmadden hears, with tractor beams that reach two light-seconds, and cargo transporters that—"

A tactical alert sounded and Krulmadden popped his mouth closed and spun back to the screen. The *Queen Mary*'s shuttle came into view, sliding up close to the *Heart of the Storm.*

So that's where Artinton is, Chekov thought. *But why send a shuttle over when the pirates could be beamed aboard?*

"Warp nine?" Sulu said to Chekov. "In that crate? He's got to be kidding."

"Message arriving," Lasslanlin announced. The image on the viewscreen rolled over once and a new transmission appeared—Black Ire.

"Greetings, oh noble scourge of death and construction!" Krulmadden gushed.

"Destruction," Sulu said under his breath.

"Withdraw your shuttle at once or it will be destroyed." On the viewscreen, Black Ire looked vaguely humanoid, but through the odd twists and folds of his costume, Chekov couldn't be certain. The warbling computer distortion from the translator mask he wore—a small silver cup which covered his nose and mouth—also made it hard to tell what race he was. But the pirate was a he, Chekov decided. Thick tufts of black and white hair sprayed out from around the translator. The rest of the pirate's face and head was hidden beneath a spaceblack battle helmet and featureless radiation goggles. Klingon, Chekov decided. With a ship named *Heart of the Storm,* Black Ire had to be a Klingon.

"I send transportation to you my guest," Krulmadden said, spreading his hands in an ingratiating gesture of friendship.

"Black Ire does not travel in filthy shuttles like cargo," the pirate growled. "My mate and I must be beamed aboard your ship."

Definitely a Klingon, Chekov thought.

"But noxious one," Krulmadden said as Sulu groaned at the shipmaster's misuse of the language, "my transporter is onboard my shuttle and has, I feel such shame to say, a limited range because of the great cost of the equipment. Unless you drop all your shields completely, I cannot beam you from there to here."

Chekov finally realized what the extra equipment at the back of the *Queen Mary*'s shuttle had been. Krulmadden had obviously wanted a getaway vehicle with transporter capability but hadn't wanted to spend the credits for two transporters so he could have one in his ship as well.

"Black Ire is not fool enough to drop all shields for *Ur'eon* scum!" The pirate looked off to the sides. "Crew! Arm phasers! Lock on to that scow's bridge!"

Krulmadden cringed and held up his hands. "No, no, do not. Use your own transporters. Your own shuttle. Swim aboard if you wish."

Black Ire settled back on whatever he sat in and for a moment Chekov saw another figure in the background—a veiled female draped in a floor-length vest and tunic of shimmering red. She moved quickly out of range of the visual sensor.

"So," Black Ire said, "you invite us to beam aboard ourselves. Does that mean that Krulmadden would drop his own shields to us?"

Lasslanlin turned around in his chair and gestured to his board. Krulmadden ignored him.

"Alas," the shipmaster said, "but our screens have a slight malfunction and I regret to say we are unable to turn them off."

Chekov wondered how criminals could ever trust each other long enough to stay in business. If it was this difficult just to arrange a meeting between the two pirates, how long was it going to take to work out a way to transfer the Orion females to the *Heart of the Storm* once a deal had been struck? He wished he and Sulu had had another chance to talk privately so they could have worked out some way to free Krulmadden's captives. But at least they had the satisfaction of knowing they had enough information about the shipmaster's operations to set the Federation authorities onto him as soon as they got the chance.

"Shipmaster Krulmadden," Black Ire spat out, "you know who I am, do you not? You have heard the word about me spread through space, have you not?"

"Who has not heard of the dread Black Ire, oh dread Black Ire?" Krulmadden shook his fist at Lasslanlin who kept trying to attract his attention.

Black Ire leaned closer, filling the screen. "Therefore, you know what will happen if you betray my trust in you?"

"I cannot know, for my life would not be worth living if such a thing I ever did, oh no."

Black Ire stood and placed his black-gloved hands on his wide black belt. A black cape fell from his shoulders. *Odd,* Chekov thought, *that looks just like the one I bought in the souvenir store on Rigel VIII before I met Sulu in the bar.*

"Very well, *Ur'eon* dog. You may beam my mate and me to your shuttle and from there to your ship. But if anything should go wrong, my officers will lock tractor beams onto you and drag you into the nearest star! Now lock onto these coordinates exactly so you can beam us through the opening we shall make in our shields." He punched something in on a console out of view. A blue light lit up on Lasslanlin's board.

"We receive your coordinates, Black Ire. My shuttle pilot will beam you now."

Black Ire's image winked out and was replaced by the outer sensor view of the shuttle by the *Heart of the Storm.*

Lasslanlin almost shrieked the instant the transmission was cut. "Shipmaster! Shipmaster!"

"What is it, loathsome sore?"

"When Black Ire called for phasers armed, nothing happened," Lasslanlin said. "There should have been carrier leakage through shields so his weapons officer could lock on *Queen Mary*—but was nothing."

Krulmadden rubbed at his green fleshy face with jeweled fingers. "But why would he bluff? It costs next to nothing to power up phasers for such a simple threat."

Lasslanlin looked once at Sulu and Chekov, then dropped his voice to a whisper. "But what if he has none?"

"What?"

Lasslanlin looked to be in pain. "What if only has a sensor block? No weapons, no shields, no cargo hold full of unsynthesized metals?"

"No cargo . . . ?" Krulmadden was clearly upset by the concept. "Then how could he pay for the greenskins?"

"Perhaps not wish to pay, Shipmaster."

Krulmadden leapt from his chair and under the lighter gravity traveled a meter higher than he had intended, though he still managed to land gracefully.

"He is a pirate!" the shipmaster said. "Why should he lie to us! All of space knows of Black Ire!"

Chekov cleared his throat. "For what it's worth, Shipmaster, I have not heard of Black Ire."

"Neither have I," Sulu added. "And the *Enterprise* was always receiving updates on pirate and smuggling operations."

Krulmadden silently picked at the emerald in his teeth. He turned to Lasslanlin. "Little snail thing, have you heard all your life of the great and terrible stories of the lonesome pirate, Black Ire?"

"That's loathsome," Sulu said.

Lasslanlin shook his head, jingling his metal earrings. "Only in past few tendays, Shipmaster. Many, many subspace transmissions."

Krulmadden pulled something stringy out from between his teeth, looked at it, then sucked it back into his mouth. "Which shows what a good pirate he must be if he has hidden his crimes so well."

Chekov figured that when Krulmadden lifted off from a planet in his shuttle, he'd be lucky to know which way was up.

Then Krulmadden boasted with pride, "Good thing this fine shipmaster has hidden a few crimes of his own!"

Lasslanlin looked more confused by his cousin than usual. On the screen, the shuttle turned smoothly, then sped for the *Queen Mary.* Artinton's voice came over the commlink.

"Guests on board, Shipmaster. Coming alongside."

"Beam them to our bridge!" Krulmadden said. "We have no secrets from Black Ire and his mate! And take care to miss nothing when you energize."

"That's the first time I've ever heard anyone around here worry about taking care of anything," Sulu said.

Chekov shrugged. He had given up trying to understand Krulmadden or any of the Orions. He found himself hoping that Black Ire would start a fight when he came onboard. At least a Klingon could be reasoned with. After a fashion. Compared with Orions.

A transporter chime started and Chekov saw the swirling eddy of materialization form in front of the helm and navigation console. As Krulmadden and Lasslanlin concentrated on the slowly forming shapes of two humanoids, Chekov moved closer to Sulu.

"We should be ready to take advantage of whatever might happen," he whispered.

Before Sulu could reply, Chekov had left the elevated ramp and gone to stand near Krulmadden's chair.

As Black Ire solidified, Chekov saw that when the pirate had referred to his mate, he hadn't been talking about one of his officers. The second figure who beamed in with him was the woman in shimmering red. Though her face was still veiled, Chekov was struck by her startlingly blue eyes which shone out from her rich black skin. He was also struck by the way in which she stared at him.

Black Ire stepped forward and placed his hands on Lasslanlin's console. "So, Krulmadden, we meet—"

The distorted speech of his translator mask was interrupted by a second transporter chime. Chekov looked down at the deck as a small pile of objects appeared at Krulmadden's feet. Black Ire and the woman suddenly looked nervous and began patting themselves under their arms and on their backs as if they had just realized they had lost something.

The shipmaster turned to Chekov and gestured for him to pick the objects up. Obviously, he could not bend that low himself.

Chekov carefully lifted what had materialized. The temptation to try something was strong. He held four phaser mark ones, two stun wands, and an area disruptor. They all looked used, rebuilt, or surplus.

Krulmadden studied the weapons for a moment, then shook his head. He took them from Chekov and dumped all except a phaser one in his chair. Then he smiled at Black Ire and his mate.

"You try to bring weapons on board this jewel of peace. Krulmadden cries tears of loss and sorrow for the honor that has died today, oh yes."

Black Ire drew himself to his full height and held the back of his glove to his translator mask. *"Heart of the Storm,"* he barked, "lock phasers on this scow's engines."

Krulmadden glanced sadly at Lasslanlin. "Mate Lasslanlin, lock disruptor cannon on *Heart of the Storm.*"

The pirates glared at each other. Chekov was fascinated. Whatever happened next, things could not be worse than they were. Unless, of course, the *Heart of the Storm* opened fire on her own commander. And if they were Klingons, that was a distinct possibility.

"Shall we play this game, Black Ire, whom no one has heard of?"

"I play no game with garbage," the pirate scoffed.

Krulmadden brought his hands together and tapped his fingertips against the small phaser he held. "You are right, fearsome one. Krulmadden shall not play this game either." He shrugged and smiled.

Black Ire seemed relieved. He began to lower his glove.

"Mate Lasslanlin, destroy our guests' ship."

Before Krulmadden had even finished giving the order a glowing blue lance of disruptive energy flashed on the screen and the *Heart of the Storm* dissolved into a handful of spinning hull sections and a cloud of sparkling energy.

Black Ire and his mate wheeled to see the destruction of their ship on the screen. The woman put her hand to her mouth.

"No bodies," Lasslanlin said. "No crew."

"Mate Artinton," Krulmadden said, "stand off until I give you order to dock. Our guests have decided to stay and share hospitality with us. But might decide to be beamed back to what's left of their ship anytime I say." He made a shallow bow to Black Ire and the woman. "How kind of you to accept shipmaster's even kinder invitation."

Chekov applauded and Krulmadden jumped back as if he had expected an attack. "You are a fine shipmaster," Chekov said.

"You are pitiful liar," Krulmadden snorted. "You wanted Black Ire to be bad to your shipmaster and feed Krulmadden to recyclers so you and other mammal could sell the greenskins for yourself."

Chekov gave the shipmaster his most winning smile. "Is that not what you would have us do? You are a fine shipmaster and a fine teacher. Sulu and I have learned much from you." He made a bow as Krulmadden had done.

Krulmadden frowned theatrically. "Very well, I give you three percent of the Talin fissionables for being such toads. Now go get manacles for ex-pirate and mate."

"There is a better way to keep them captive," Chekov said slyly.

Krulmadden waited.

"The way you kept us captives!" Chekov explained. "The gravity field!" On the other side of Krulmadden, Chekov could see a look of sudden horror pass through Sulu's eyes.

Krulmadden shook a finger at Chekov. "You are a clever little mammal. The *f'deraxt'l* and *stator*fleet have not ruined you completely. Even if you do not like the company of greenskins, which puzzles me in great amounts." He went back to his chair and brushed his hand against a section of the inner arm. Chekov kept his eyes level with Krulmadden's, but concentrated on remembering exactly which part of the chair arm the shipmaster stroked to adjust the field. As the local gravity constant on the bridge began to climb, Chekov knew that at least the first part of his plan was going to work. Now the question was whether or not he could continue to function.

Krulmadden bounced from foot to foot. "Ah, feels good like home." He rumbled with laughter. "Let us make it feel *twice* as good!"

Chekov braced himself for four times Earth gravity. He felt the field climb higher. His shoulders sagged in on his chest as the weight of his arms increased. He had to struggle for each breath.

There was a thud from the front of the bridge and Chekov slowly turned his eyes to see that Black Ire had collapsed to his knees. His hands pressed against the floor and his arms trembled with the effort to support himself. Then the woman collapsed beside him.

"Ha ha! Is good is good!" Krulmadden sang.

Chekov staggered to Krulmadden's chair and leaned against it. He saw Sulu step back to hang on to the railing behind him. He felt his knees creak.

"Exercise!" Krulmadden laughed. "Good *Ur'eon* exercise for my little mammals. I go see what kind of weakling Black Ire is now." He bared his jeweled teeth at Chekov. "You do not go anywhere."

Chekov forced a smile past his sagging cheeks. He was beginning to see black sparkles in his vision as his heart could no longer keep blood flowing to his brain. *Now or never,* he thought, then leaned over the arm of Krulmadden's chair and reached for the hidden control surface.

But when he bent over he no longer had the strength to keep his back extended and he crumpled over the side of the chair, losing his breath with the sudden impact. The weapons on the chair seat pressed in on his face. He tasted blood and his heartbeat thundered in his ear.

Chekov blindly reached for the gravity control. He touched the smooth metal of the chair arm. Suddenly the bridge lights flared back to Rigel normal. Wrong control. He heard Krulmadden's grunt of surprise.

Desperately, Chekov slid his fingers over the chair arm. *It has to be here,* he thought. *I saw Krulmadden do it just like this.* He felt a slight impression in the smooth metal and stroked his finger against it. He heard a violent explosion of breath and realized it was his own. He had sent the gravity setting the wrong way and now his fingers were too heavy to lift.

The pressure of the chair arm in his stomach was overpowering. He could no longer take a breath. The bridge seemed to start spinning around him as his inner ears began to collapse. He heard Sulu calling out his name.

Then Krulmadden's black-maned head appeared above the level of his seat. The strength of the gravity field was so strong that even the powerful Orion had to crawl. But he could crawl. And from the look in his eyes he was also going to be able to kill.

"Bad little mammal," the shipmaster grunted. His thick lower lip hung down as if invisible threads pulled on it. "I crush you into spread for biscuits."

Chekov closed his eyes. He had no time nor strength for one last breath. *For Captain Kirk,* he thought, then put the last Wortham unit of energy he had into one final stab of his fingers.

He touched the metal of the arm. He felt Krulmadden's hot breath on his face. He stroked the metal away from him and—

—free fall.

Krulmadden whooped like a child on a roller whip and flew away from the chair, the phaser slipping from his hand. Chekov had known what was coming— had hoped for what was coming—and held on to the chair arms. With the pressure gone from his chest and stomach, he drew in a huge breath. His ears still rang and the bridge still spun but he could see once more.

Chekov looked over to Sulu. His friend had locked his arms around the bridge railing and was holding himself in place as if he were blowing in a gale force wind.

"Look out!" Sulu shouted. "Above you!"

Chekov twisted his head around in time to see Krulmadden swooping down from the ceiling of the bridge. Chekov ran his finger back along the gravity control and Krulmadden's trajectory changed as a triple field came back on.

"Again!" Sulu shouted.

Chekov got the hang of it. By flipping the gravity on and off, he bounced

Krulmadden across the deck until the Orion's eyes crossed and he simply flopped from one field setting to the next. Then Chekov set the field for Earth normal, grabbed one of the phasers he had kept in place beneath him, and stood up. For a moment he wavered back and forth, still feeling the bridge move beneath him, but it was only a sense memory because Krulmadden, unconscious, didn't budge from his place on the floor.

There was a moan from the center of the bridge as Lasslanlin unsteadily tried to crawl out from beneath the helm console where he had tried to escape the wild gravity fluctuations. Chekov braced himself against the center chair and checked to make sure his small phaser was set to light stun. But even as he aimed the phaser at the Orion mate, Lasslanlin's eyelids fluttered and he fell over, out cold.

Sulu walked stiffly to Chekov's side. "Good work, Chekov. I only have one question."

"What's that?"

"Did you have the slightest idea of what you were doing?"

Chekov tried his best to look indignant. "Of course, I had it planned wery carefully all along."

"Sure you did," Sulu said, but patted Chekov's shoulder in congratulations anyway. Then Krulmadden moaned and both men turned to him.

For a second, Chekov almost forgot where he was. Black Ire and his mate were standing by Krulmadden's vast body. They looked familiar somehow. But the woman was doing something completely unfamiliar with her eyes. She was picking at them. Then Chekov saw why. She held two blue lenses in her hands.

"Don't you think you should do something for him?" the woman asked Black Ire. Chekov's mouth fell open. He knew that voice.

"I don't see why," Black Ire said as he reached up to unhook his translator mask and goggles. "I'm a pirate, not a doctor."

"Dr. McCoy?" Chekov stammered.

"Uhura?" Sulu gasped.

Uhura tossed her contact lenses aside and pulled off her veil. McCoy yanked his battle helmet off and left his hair in wild disarray.

"I hope you two know how to fly this blasted thing," McCoy said. "Because this big oaf just blew up my retirement savings."

"You *paid* for that hulk?" Sulu asked in disbelief.

"Do you have any idea how much it cost to buy a used spaceship and send out hours of subspace messages to build the legend of Black Ire?"

Chekov and Uhura caught each other's eye and began to snicker as Sulu and McCoy traded complaints.

"What's so damn funny, Ensign?"

"Why, nothing, Dr. McCoy," Chekov said. "I was just thinking how wery glad I was to see you, too."

For once, the bridge of the *Queen Mary* rang with the sound of *human* laughter.

Seven

Thunderous applause reverberated in the hallway outside the Federation General Council chamber. The large, white marble–tiled hallway itself was almost deserted, making the noise that filtered out through the double-height wooden doors oddly out of place.

Sitting motionless on a padded bench beside the speakers' entrance to the chamber, Spock waited patiently. He judged that the ovation had greeted the announcement by the delegate from the Antares Corona Worlds that her system would be supporting the new agricultural trade proposals tabled by the Federation Resource Management Board. The Antares commitment had been seen as necessary to prevent a recurrence of the bottleneck transport problems that had contributed to the near-famine on Sherman's Planet. Once again the worlds of the Federation had become a bit closer knit, and once again the Federation had become stronger.

Spock reviewed the agenda he had memorized when it had been posted that morning. After the Antares declaration, the delegate from the Centaurus Concordium was scheduled to move that the Council issue its congratulations to Hudson's World on the occasion of its fiftieth year of independence. That motion would be followed by a unanimous voice vote, and then the meeting would be thrown open to civilian petitions, as authorized by their respective official representatives. Spock had been the third speaker set for the day, though he had since learned that the two speakers who were to have preceded him had now withdrawn. He estimated that four minutes and thirty seconds remained before he would be requested to enter the chamber. He trusted Dr. Richter was capable of performing the same calculation.

Penn Grossman walked over to Spock. His new shoes squeaked on the marble floor and he wore his dress tunic uncomfortably, ruining its line by jamming his hands in its pockets.

"Face it, Mr. Spock," the student said, "he's not going to show."

"Yes, he will," Marita answered before Spock could speak. She scrunched up her face and held her baby close to her. "Won't he, Alexander? Won't he?" The baby gurgled and clapped his hands. "See? Alexander knows Dr. Richter won't let us down."

Penn took a few steps away, then turned and came back. He rubbed nervously at his short dark hair as if trying to stay awake. "How can you sit there like that, Marita? Can't you see we've been tricked?"

Spock said nothing. He had tried explaining what he had done three times already. It wasn't that Penn was not intelligent, it was that he was stubborn—one human attribute with which Spock had dealt many times, thanks to the able help of Dr. McCoy.

"Mr. Spock had his reasons for doing this, Penn. I'm not mad at him."

"But you're missing out on your one chance to talk to the Federation Council! Do you know how many billion beings are going to be watching the update tapes of this meeting?" Penn wiped his sweaty hands on the back of his tunic.

"And they're going to listen to Dr. Richter a lot more carefully than they would to me," Marita said.

Spock was impressed with the young woman's powers of comprehension. When he had broached the possibility that Dr. Richter replace Marita as Spock's associate-to-be-named, she, not Penn, had immediately understood that that had been Spock's intention from the beginning.

"That's why you took me to the Vulcan Embassy, isn't it?" she had said after the first meeting with Richter. "You knew that Ambassador Sytok would warn you not to put my name on the credentials, and that was supposed to make me understand why my name shouldn't be listed. But what you really wanted to do all along was have an open accreditation form so that *Dr. Richter* could go before the

Council as your associate. And his name couldn't go on the credentials because he's under Starfleet authority, and they could have prevented him from speaking if anyone had suspected that that was what he was going to do. Damn sneaky, Spock. And very logical."

Spock had politely accepted her compliment without correcting her assumptions.

But Penn wasn't supporting Marita's acceptance of the changed situation. "Look, I don't care how buddy-buddy you want to get with this alien, but the fact is that Mr. Spock the Vulcan *lied* to you. He used the SSP as a way to gain support for this appearance. And he planned to cut us all out from the start."

"He didn't lie, Penn. He just didn't tell the whole truth."

"Big difference!"

Marita jiggled Alexander on her knee. "Mr. Spock, when you go in to address the Council, are you going to speak against the Prime Directive?"

"Yes," Spock said.

"Truthfully?" Penn asked.

"Penn, I regret to say that you have learned nothing about logic in the time you have spent with me. However, to answer your question in the spirit in which it was asked, yes, truthfully, I will speak against the Prime Directive."

The hallway echoed with the sound of the Council delivering a unanimous voice vote. Spock calculated that now only one minute, ten seconds remained.

Marita continued. "And Dr. Richter, when he goes in there, will he also speak against the Prime Directive?"

"I do not expect Dr. Richter to say much to the Council, but his presence with me will lend great support to what I have to say."

Marita looked reprovingly at Penn. "There. It shouldn't matter who does the job, as long as it gets done. Your problem, Penn Grossman, is that you're jealous."

Penn put his hand to his forehead and stared wildly around the hall as if he had just been accused of being a Romulan spy. "I am not! Why does everyone keep saying that?"

Because it is true, Spock thought, and once again he was grateful that the students' emotional turmoil had kept them from continuing their questioning of him in detail.

Spock stood up moments before the door of the speakers' entrance swung open and a Council page appeared, dressed in a traditional gray suit and white scarf. Spock handed the page the microtape of his embassy forms.

"Please note that this form is open, giving me the right to have associates accompany me."

The page slipped the tape into the reader and read through the forms, though obviously she had been briefed on what to expect. "Are these two with you?" she asked.

"Yes," Spock said. "They will not be addressing the Council with me, but by rights they are allowed to enter the meeting with me."

"How about the baby?" the page asked dubiously.

"Well, I'm certainly not leaving him out here," Marita said.

"As you wish," the page said. She flipped up the large brass wreath which was the doorpull and a hidden mechanism smoothly swung the door open again. The sound of a hundred whispered voices came out in a wall of soft noise.

"One last thing," Spock said, just before entering. "Some members of my party have been delayed. Please let them in when they arrive."

The page glanced down at her reader again and nodded. "Sure," she said. "How many?"

"Five," Spock said. He entered the chamber.

In actual voting delegates, the membership of the Federation Council numbered in the thousands. Every world, every colony dome, every LaGrange outpost, every species on shared worlds, all were entitled to representation and the Federation took heroic measures to see that as many who wanted to take part could take part. But to streamline the running of the day-to-day affairs of the Federation, the Council split itself up into hundreds of specialist committees organized along regional lines and common concerns. Full gatherings of the complete membership occurred only rarely.

In matters of more pressing importance, it was necessary for a governing body to be able to meet quickly and efficiently, and that was the purpose of the General Council. Each block of members from local regions—usually at the united system level—selected one delegate to represent them. There were fewer than two hundred and fifty of them—more than half nonhuman, but they were the power brokers of the most successful interstellar union known in the history of a thousand worlds, and it was they whom Spock prepared to address.

The meeting chamber for so impressive a body was a simple affair, two facing tiers of benches, a communications wall, a guest area in which Spock saw Ambassador Sytok standing, and a speakers' area where those who were not members of the Council—or even of the Federation—were able to make an address.

Spock waited in that last area as the Speaker of the Council read Spock's consular civilian credentials to Sukio Hirashito, this session's Council President. Marita, carrying Alexander, and Penn, hands still jammed in his pockets, waited a few meters away, closer to the speakers' door.

The Speaker, a tall Maori wearing a traditional black parliamentary robe, returned to Spock and handed him back his papers. Then he turned to face the Council members.

"The Council recognizes Spock, citizen of Vulcan, citizen of the United Federation of Planets. Bear witness, all who are in attendance." The Speaker turned back to Spock as the subtle drone of a hundred universal translators hummed alien versions of what had been said. "Come forward, Spock. The Council waits on you."

Spock went forward, knowing that each member who sat before him already knew what he was going to say, and knowing that each of them was wrong. He began his address to the Council.

"Madame President, Mr. Speaker, distinguished members of the General Council, I come before you today to inform you of a grievous wrong which has been perpetrated on the United Federation of Planets, and by the United Federation of Planets, and which demands immediate and compassionate resolution for the sake of peace."

Startled, some Council members leaned close together and spoke among themselves. This was not starting out as they had expected—with a plea to repeal the Prime Directive. By stating that he was informing them of a wrong committed against the Federation and by the Federation, Spock had spoken the formal words generally used to give warning of a real or threatened internal treaty violation. And there had not been a serious internal treaty violation within the Federation for decades.

The Speaker of the Council walked up to Spock, sensor microphones in the ceiling swiveling to capture his voice and amplify it through the chamber.

"Spock, you were to talk about the Prime Directive."

"I am aware of no topic being entered on my credentials," Spock said. "I have the floor."

The Speaker glanced back at the President, who nodded once.

"Spock, according to the words you have used, it appears that you intend to talk to the Council about matters of treaty. That is a legal matter."

"I am quite aware of that, Mr. Speaker."

"But this is a citizens' forum intended for the debate of general concerns. If you wish to use it as a legal forum, I must ask you to state your legal grounds or give up the floor."

Good, Spock thought. He would not have been able to introduce his next topic without that question being asked. But now the way was open.

"Mr. Speaker," Spock announced so all could hear, sensor pickups or not, "I invoke as my legal grounds the Fundamental Declarations of the Martian Colonies."

Not a member of the Council was silent. Two Tellarites jumped to their feet. The Speaker had to call to order twice to quiet the members. No one had any idea what would happen now, and that made the power brokers uneasy.

"Mr. Speaker," Spock said, "I believe I still have the floor."

The Speaker retreated, walking away with head bowed.

"A founding precept of this Federation is that different cultures be allowed to progress in their own time, according to their own needs and desires. Indeed, the Prime Directive is a direct extension of this principle." There was a strong murmur of satisfaction that at last Spock had mentioned what all had assumed would be his main topic.

"However, by accepting this principle of self-determination, the entrenchment of specific inequities is inevitable. That is, those cultures that achieve a certain level of technological achievement before another can claim an unfair share of natural resources." More murmurs, this time, of confusion. Was this a talk about treaties or the Prime Directive?

"This conflict was first addressed in the Fundamental Declarations of the Martian Colonies, in which the signatory bodies agreed that, in recognition of the Colonies' inability to field a full mining force, certain sections of the asteroid belt would be set aside in trust for future exploitation by Mars as their technological capability progressed and their cultural needs developed.

"This first, interplanetary recognition of the importance of resource allocation over time, has since gone on to become entrenched in all facets of Federation law. I point out to you that there is not a member of the Federation who does not have set aside by treaty, in trust, natural resources for future exploitation. In fact, such trust allocations of natural resources are automatic upon being admitted to the Federation, and are a right of every new member."

A Tellarite held two hooves to his mouth and bellowed, "Get on with it!"

"This right, originally meant to confer mining claims, has since grown to include the right of colonization. It is recognized that worlds at an early stage of space exploration cannot afford the cost of colonizing nearby systems. However, if they delay, there is the danger that other worlds might expand around them and cut off all possible colonization possibilities. Therefore, the Federation routinely allocates colony worlds within its own boundaries for the future exclusive use of those worlds not yet ready to undertake colonization."

A page handed the Speaker a note. The Speaker read it, nodded again at the President, then approached Spock once more.

"Spock, it has been brought to the Council's attention that you are expecting others to join you in your address and that those others have not yet arrived. Therefore, the Council suspects that this disjointed history lesson which you are presenting to us is nothing more than an attempt to make the Council wait for the arrival of your missing associates. I point out to you, Spock, that if that is your intention, then you can be held in contempt of this body and asked to leave."

Spock had anticipated that this interruption would have occurred two minutes earlier. Perhaps he had caught their interest.

"Mr. Speaker, each point I have raised is a necessary step in the presentation of an important matter to the Council. I ask for five more minutes of your time to prove that this is so."

The Speaker sought clues to any future disturbance in Spock's face but apparently found none. "Very well, five minutes. No more."

Spock calculated it would take three.

"In the case of the planet, Talin IV—"

The Council chamber erupted. They had been waiting for this.

"Murderer!"

"Worldkiller!"

Other insults and curses were shouted in a variety of languages. Spock tried several times to resume speaking, but the clamor of the Council members drowned him out each time. It took the Speaker most of those five promised minutes to quiet the Council to the point where Spock could continue. The response had been far stronger than Spock had anticipated. He hurriedly made cuts in the rest of what he had to say so the timing he had worked out would still hold.

"In the matter of Talin IV, a planet which is home to a species which the Federation had predicted would be ready to attempt an interstellar colonization program within the next fifty to one hundred standard years, fully forty-eight planets within a twenty-five parsec sphere have been set aside, in trust, for their future use." He paused, but his unruly audience had already been chastised by the Speaker. The members remained silent and hostile.

"Recognizing this existing, formal arrangement on behalf of the planet of Talin IV—a planet that has recently experienced a terrible disaster—I charge the Federation to provide immediate emergency relief and long-term aid in order to help this world and its people to full recovery."

After a second explosion of clamorous protest, the President of the Federation at last stood to take part. She took a small pair of antique wire-framed glasses from a case on her desk and slipped them on as she waited for the Speaker to once again bring order to the chamber.

"Mr. Spock," she began in a voice of quiet authority. "The planet, Talin IV, is under the protection of the Prime Directive. No aid can possibly be sent to it. I am surprised by your actions. The son of Sarek should know better."

Spock stepped forward into the center of the chamber. "Madame President, with respect, I submit that the Prime Directive does not apply to Talin IV."

The President adjusted her glasses. "Spock, this act of desperation does not become you, nor does it bring honor to your world. The Prime Directive holds with all worlds which are not part of the Federation."

Spock moved closer. "Madame President, with respect, I submit that Talin IV is *already* a member of the Federation."

President Hirashito lost her composure as she gaped at Spock. "On what grounds do you make this claim?" The Speaker could no longer restrain the other members. Dozens of them began to shout similar questions to Spock.

Spock raised his voice above the din. "I submit that by virtue of the planet Talin IV having assigned to it forty-eight planets held in trust for future exploitation, that it shares in the rights and privileges of being a member of the Federation and there-fore *is* a member of the Federation. *To which the Prime Directive does not apply.*"

Despite the best efforts of the Speaker and the President, the Council members did not subside until Ambassador Sytok walked out to face Spock in the center of the chamber. This time he was wearing his official garments, and the gems of his achievements gleamed in rich and colorful panels on both sides of his robe.

"Madame President, Mr. Speaker," Sytok said, raising his hand to each of them in turn. "I claim the right to speak with Spock, citizen of Vulcan, whom I charge with abusing his rights and obtaining credentials under false pretenses."

Spock ignored the Vulcan ambassador. "With respect, Madame President, the Council has not authorized my request that immediate aid be sent to Talin."

"Mr. Spock!" The Council hushed instantly at the shocking sight and sound of a Vulcan who had raised his voice in apparent anger. Sytok looked around, realizing what he had done, then composed himself. "Madame President, please allow me to address Spock's request."

"Please do," Hirashito said. She sat back down.

"Mr. Spock," Sytok began again more calmly. "I will admit that there is some logic in your request. A case can be made for claiming that Talin IV is a *de facto* member of the Federation by virtue of its property held in trust."

"Thank you," Spock said. By his admission, though he was not yet aware of it, Sytok had just guaranteed that Talin would be helped.

"However," Sytok continued sagely, "beyond that facile argument, your logic has faltered badly."

"I look forward to your correction," Spock said, adopting the words of a student to his teacher.

Sytok made his pronouncement. "You are not properly accredited to this Council to request aid for a member world, Spock." The Vulcan ambassador swung his arm around the Council chamber to include every member. "If Talin is a member and requires aid, then where are its duly appointed representatives—or its ambassadors—to make such a request of us?"

"Is that all that stands in the way of aid being sent to Talin? A formal request?"

Sytok gripped the collar of his robe in his hand. "It is enough." He turned his back to Spock and began to walk from the center of the chamber.

Spock looked back to the waiting area by the speakers' entrance door. Marita and Penn stood there with accusing looks of betrayal in their eyes. Spock had spoken against the Prime Directive as he had said he would, but only in relation to a single planet. Spock looked at Marita, knowing that if anyone in her organization would understand his intentions, she would. He motioned to her to open the door.

He saw her nod as she adjusted Alexander against her shoulder and stepped over to pull on the bronze wreath. The massive door opened slowly and Spock saw the last pieces of his presentation waiting behind it—all five of them.

"Ambassador Sytok!" Spock called out.

Sytok halted and looked over his shoulder. Then he turned slowly and fully around. The sound growing among the Council members mirrored the ambassador's most un-Vulcan look of surprise.

Spock turned to the rest of his associates. First, Dr. Richter walked into the chamber, cane clicking on the hard marble. Then came Carole Mallett and Mario Cardinali of the FCO, both gently guiding two tall figures in sweeping gray robes which swayed with the graceful rhythms of a powerful gait.

"I present to this Council," Spock proclaimed, "their excellencies—Seerl ti'La and Orr ni'Li—"

All the Council members rose, speaking in all the languages of the Federation at once.

Spock continued, knowing that at least the automatic recorders would hear what he said for future playback. "—joint representatives of the two nation states of Talin IV known as Green and Brown—"

Mallett and Cardinali stopped when they reached Spock. Powerful, pebble-skinned arms burst out from the guests' robes to flip back their hoods.

Seerl ti'La's cranial crest bristled crazily as he flushed deep scarlet and stared at the extraordinary gathering of alien creatures who surrounded him. Beside him, flushing to a deep turquoise hue, Orr ni'Li blinked her large yellow eyes. Both creatures' heads turned back and forth with quick birdlike movements. Mallett and Cardinali kept their hands on their guests' arms, constantly speaking assurances to them.

"I charge you with kidnapping these creatures!" Sytok accused. "Shame and dishonor!"

The Talin linked arms, seeking protection in each other from the threatening confusion of the Council's upheaval. Spock saw the small silver speakers of miniature translators attached to their hearing membranes. He wondered how much of what was being shouted the machine would be able to translate for them. But at least from their meetings with him, the Talin knew what he was going to say.

"—who left their planet by their *own choice* and in a space vessel of their nations' design," Spock continued, countering Sytok's charges. He raised his consular documents above his head. "To become, by the authority of these open credentials, provided by the Vulcan Embassy, the duly appointed ambassadors *to* the Federation *from* the member world of Talin. And who now respectfully ask this Council for aid to rebuild their world.

"As is their right."

Eight

The *Ian Shelton* traveled at sixty-four times the speed of light, but to James Kirk it still wasn't fast enough. He sat at the ship's navigation console as if by pushing on it he could coax a few more kilometers per second out of her. *Three more days to get there,* he thought. He was used to ships that traveled a lot faster.

Kirk heard an avalanche of small feet behind him and braced himself for the assault he knew would follow. Nogura was the first to jump up on him. Fitzpatrick and Komack took second and third place by rubbing around his legs.

"Ah," Gauvreau said as she followed her cats onto the bridge, "the captain and his loyal crew."

Kirk edged Nogura off his lap with a helpful shove and kept the other two at bay by moving in closer to the console. He had been in a similar situation before on the bridge of the *Enterprise,* but at least tribbles couldn't jump.

Gauvreau stood at his side. "So what did you want me to look at?" she asked.

Kirk pointed to a nonstandard sensor display in the upper left-hand corner of the control board. It wasn't included in the online manuals and he hadn't been able to determine which system drove it. Up to five minutes ago, he hadn't been concerned about not knowing what it was because it consistently had shown a flat reading. But now it was displaying peak numbers.

"Whatever this is set to look for," Kirk said, "it seems to have found some."

Gauvreau looked pleased. "Welcome to the mercenary world of the freighter captain. That's my salvage scanner. It's always sweeping for lost ships, old probes, that sort of thing."

Kirk thought such a scanner might make sense farther in toward the center of Federation space. But, out in this sector, there had yet to be enough traffic for there to have been many lost ships. Besides, most of the ships passing through this region followed established trade routes such as the one the *Shelton* traveled now.

"What have you found with it?" Kirk asked. "I mean, all the way out here?"

"You'd be surprised," Gauvreau said, adjusting the salvage scanner's sweep to a finer focus. "I'm always coming across some of the old impulse-powered probes from Earth, you know, the Voyagers, the Nomads, that stuff. Remember that after four or five years of full impulse at point nine nine cee, those suckers had a fifty-fifty chance of tunneling into warp space. That's why they lost so many of them, and that's why they're still turning up thousands of light-years away from Earth." She stabbed her finger at a locking button. "So far I've sold three to the Smithsonian."

Kirk watched the display home in on whatever the scanner had detected. "Is that another?" he asked. The scanner's readings were cruder and less sensitive than the sensors he was used to from the *Enterprise.* As far as he could tell, it might be picking up anything from an antique probe to a rogue planet.

"Too soon to tell," Gauvreau said. She stood back from the board with her hands on her hips. "Small and metallic, definitely. Could be another ship . . . but there aren't any power readings." She pursed her lips. "I got fifty kilocredits apiece for those probes."

Kirk checked the coordinates. He estimated that a five-hour deviation would put them close enough to positively identify the signal. He appreciated the fact that Gauvreau appeared to be leaving the final decision to him. *It's only five hours,* he thought. He just hoped Scott wasn't about to pull another one of his miracles and take the *Enterprise* out of the Talin system ahead of schedule.

"All right," Kirk said. "Let's change heading and track it down." He didn't wait for Gauvreau's reply. He simply entered in the new course and watched as the stars swung by on the viewscreen.

Four and a half hours later, Kirk knew enough about the salvage scanner to have it work with the main sensors and deliver a thirty percent increase in sensitivity.

"Not bad," Gauvreau said as she studied how Kirk had realigned both sensor systems to function together. "There's nothing like that in any of the manuals."

"Out on the frontier, you'd be surprised how quickly you learn to improvise," Kirk said, continuing his fine adjustments of the newly enhanced scanner. "When we get to Talin, we should try to have Mr. Scott take a look at your matter-antimatter intermix chambers. I'd bet he could get another half factor out of your drive for the same power consumption figures." He pressed the control that sent the sensor data to the viewscreen where the computer would reconstruct a visual image. "There, this should tell us what it is we've found."

A slowly expanding cloud of gas filled with spinning flat pieces of metal appeared.

"Debris," Gauvreau said with dismay. "It's got to be a ship."

"And it's not old," Kirk added. "Less than a day." The cloud of escaped atmosphere hadn't dispersed more than two hundred kilometers and the metal fragments were still close enough together to have returned the strong scanner signal the *Shelton* had detected. Kirk had the computer track and map the largest pieces of what he guessed were hull plates, then reassemble them in memory to try and determine what type of ship had been destroyed.

A wireframe reconstruction of the vessel slowly filled in on the screen.

"Merde," Gauvreau said as she and Kirk recognized the half-drawn graphic at the same time. "A freighter."

"An old one," Kirk confirmed. "The DY series." He had become quite expert in recognizing them.

Gauvreau reset the sensors for organics and got nothing. "Must have been a robot ship," she said with relief. "No sign of bodies."

But Kirk didn't agree. "Look at the oxygen reading from the gas cloud. No ship would carry that amount of atmosphere unless someone were breathing it."

Gauvreau reset the sensors again. "Scanning for lifepods and shuttles."

The sensor alarm chimed. "That's a positive contact," Gauvreau said. She squeezed closer to Kirk at the navigation board as they both worked the sensors together. The cats watched patiently from the chairs at the other, empty stations.

"But it's not a lifepod," Kirk said. "And not a shuttle, either." He punched in a new command line. "It's a waste trail . . . ?"

"Radioactive," Gauvreau confirmed. Her tone became flat. "First-stage matter."

Kirk felt a sudden burst of anger. Only one class of vessel left that unique signature of radioactive waste in its wake. "Orion pirates."

"Bastards," Gauvreau said bitterly.

"What weapons system does the *Shelton* have?" Kirk asked.

Gauvreau looked away from him. "You know it's illegal for a freighter to be armed, Kirk."

Kirk looked at her steadily.

"Photon torpedoes," Gauvreau conceded. "They're surplus but they're still at seventy percent power."

"How many?"

Gauvreau looked embarrassed. "Three."

"How do you launch them?"

"I, uh, sort of modified the forward waste-jettison tube."

Kirk nodded. He turned back to the board to trace the Orion's trail.

"Now wait just a minute, Kirk. The *Shelton* isn't the *Enterprise.* We're not taking on a pirate. No possible way."

Kirk didn't look up from the controls. "Don't worry, I know. But we have to get close enough to him so we can make a sensor ID that we can pass on to Starfleet when we get to Talin."

Gauvreau relaxed, but only for a moment. "Then why were you asking about weapons?"

Kirk laid in the new course that would take them after the fleeing pirate. *Good,* he thought, *he's almost on a direct heading to Talin himself. This won't cost us any more time.*

"I said: Why were you asking about weapons, Kirk?"

Kirk stood up from the board and stretched. "I estimate we'll be within optimal leading sensor range of the Orion within three hours."

"So?"

"Which means there's a good chance that we'll be inside his trailing sensor range within *two and a half hours."* He smiled at Gauvreau to try and reassure her. "Relax, it makes it easier to decide to run away when I know we've got the weapons to stand and fight."

But Gauvreau looked anything but reassured. "Tell me more about the running-away part," she said.

Two hours and forty minutes later, Kirk watched as the tracking sensors indicated that the Orion vessel was slowing and changing course.

"It's about time you started paying attention to your stern," he said, watching the sensor blip.

Gauvreau sat at the environmental station where she could control the modified waste-jettison tube, if required. "Are they coming about?"

"Not yet," Kirk answered. "We're dead in their waste trail so at this distance there's a chance we might only be a false return. They're just running a minor deviation to see if we follow or stay put. As long as we stay put, they'll think we're an echo."

"So we're staying put, right?"

"For now, we are." Kirk watched as the Orion's course changed by five degrees, held for a few minutes, then resumed its normal heading. "That's it," Kirk said. "We're an echo. That gives us at least another twenty minutes to get closer before they'll—what?"

The sensors showed that the Orion ship had suddenly dropped out of warp to relative rest. Kirk punched at the warp cut-off switch, but by the time the *Shelton* hit normal space, the Orion vessel was going to warp three at a ninety-degree deviation to its original course.

Kirk swore and Gauvreau looked with concern at him in alarm. "What happened? What did he do?"

"He's sharper than I thought," Kirk admitted. "By pulling that maneuver, he was able to get a cross fix on us. Damn. I didn't think the Orions knew about that one."

"What now?"

"He knows we're here, so we might as well keep going." Kirk entered an intercept course and the *Shelton* jumped back to warp four.

"Why?" Gauvreau demanded. "He blew up that freighter."

"Exactly," Kirk agreed. "And I'll only take us close enough to get an ID scan and then we're heading straight for Talin. We'll still be hours ahead of him." He looked up as Gauvreau headed for the ladderway. "Where are you going?"

"I'm going to put the cats in the lifepod. Let me know if the Klingon Armada shows up."

"I'm not getting anything that makes sense," Kirk said an hour later as he started his sensor scan again. "It's almost as if they've rigged their own sensor systems to relay false readings to us."

"Why do you sound so surprised?" Gauvreau said. "Even I've heard of that strategy before."

The *Shelton*'s captain was back at the environment station. This time she wore a pressure suit and orange micrometeoroid overalls. Her helmet was slung at the side of her chair. Kirk wore the same outfit. After Gauvreau had described to him the minimal power ratings of the *Shelton*'s deflector shields, it had seemed the prudent course to take. The pressure suits would give them enough time to get to the lifepod in the event of sudden decompression.

"A strategy is one thing," Kirk said, sliding the sensor controls back and forth, "but to carry this off, they'd have had to rewire their com system into their sensors. Unless they've got a couple of communications geniuses onboard, I don't see how they could have done it so quickly."

"Maybe they did it earlier?" Gauvreau suggested. "Before they knew we were here."

"Possible," Kirk said, "but not likely they'd want to limit their own com system to just short-range transmissions out in deep space. There's something very strange about that ship. Damn it!"

"What, Kirk?"

Kirk slapped his hand on the console. "They've disappeared again ... no ... there ... I don't believe it. They managed to broadcast a perfect phase delay to us so our sensors showed no return signal for a few seconds." He turned to look at Gauvreau. "Just when did Orions get so smart?"

"Why not stop underestimating them? Let's give them some of their own back."

Kirk smiled in swift response. He liked that idea. He went to work on it immediately.

Thirty minutes from intercept, the *Shelton* blazed through space, straight for the Orion vessel. Abruptly, it dropped from warp, flipped to a full reverse heading, then vented its impulse baffles at point nine nine cee. When the relativistically compressed vapor cloud cleared from around the ship, the *Shelton* rotated slowly, stern over keel, running lights out.

On the *Shelton*'s bridge, Gauvreau unstuck her hands from her chair. The inertial dampers of the freighter had not been able to keep up with sudden vector shifts. Neither had her stomach.

"Good," Kirk said. "Very good."

"What was so good about that? If the cats ever come out of their kennels they won't eat for a month." Gauvreau rubbed at her face to wipe the tears of surprise from her eyes.

Kirk couldn't blame her. It had been a wild ride and he had almost been thrown clear of his chair himself. "As far as our friends out there are going to be able to tell, the *Shelton* just lost warp drive," Kirk said. "Between the exhaust venting cloud and the system shutdown and the spinning, they're going to think we're crippled."

"This is good?" Gauvreau asked.

"Trust me," Kirk said happily. "Now broadcast an emergency beacon, but cut it off after a few repetitions."

"Terrific," Gauvreau muttered. "That way no one will ever find us."

"Don't worry. They're going to come in with their guard down. We'll get our ID scan, then pop off a torpedo, then hit warp."

"I don't know, Kirk. The way they've been behaving, I don't think their guard's ever going to go down."

Kirk scratched at his neck under the tight collar rim of the pressure suit. "Don't be so pessimistic. It's not as if we're dealing with Academy graduates here."

"Is that so?" Gauvreau pointed at the screen. "Look at that."

The visual screen painted an image of a brilliant streak passing by—the Orion vessel had not stopped.

Gauvreau read from her instruments. "We were flooded by sensor radiation, Kirk. They did a complete scan."

"Hold it. They're coming back," Kirk said, intently watching the course change indicators. "Ready with that torpedo as soon as I get them in memory."

Suddenly the Orion ship fell out of warp space directly beside the *Shelton*. Whoever was piloting her was fearless. Or an idiot.

"Steady," Kirk cautioned. "Get ready on that torpedo."

"It's not going to do a whole lot of good, Kirk. Look what they're doing." Gauvreau gestured to the screen.

It took Kirk a moment to realize what Gauvreau meant. Then he understood. These pirates were better than any he had ever dealt with before. They were even better than any he had ever *heard* of before. Standing off from the *Shelton* a half kilometer distant, the Orion ship matched the freighter's slow cartwheels, constantly keeping at right angles to the waste-jettison tube.

"I'm never going to be able to target them at this rate," Gauvreau complained.

"Doesn't matter," Kirk said. "I've got them in sensor memory now. Starfleet will be able to track them down and deal with them."

Gauvreau stared up at the viewscreen. "That doesn't help us now, Kirk. Their scanners are going to be able to see our warp engines power up. If we can't fire a torpedo for a diversion, we're not going to be able to get out of here."

The Orion vessel moved in perfect step with the freighter, waiting. But for what, Kirk couldn't be sure.

"Get ready on the torpedo," he said suddenly. "I'm going to use the attitude thrusters to speed up our rotation. As soon as the tube lines up with the pirate, fire."

"Torpedo ready," Gauvreau responded.

Kirk slid the attitude control forward and the Orion ship disappeared from the viewscreen as the *Shelton*'s rotation increased. "Now!"

The freighter shuddered as the photon torpedo was jettisoned. Kirk reached to engage warp drive. But the Orion ship went to warp first, moving toward the torpedo casing and the *Shelton*, missing both by centimeters. The *Shelton* remained in normal space. Its safety programs had not let it go to warp while another warp drive was in such close proximity. The Orion ship was now in normal space on the opposite side of the *Shelton*. The torpedo detonated harmlessly, a hundred kilometers away.

"What kind of maniac is piloting that thing?" Kirk asked.

"Kirk! They've got a disruptor cannon powering up. They've locked on us."

"Ready torpedo two," Kirk said. He'd dealt with maniacs before.

"If I try to fire, they'll blast us!"

"Just keep the tube open and I'll do the rest," Kirk said. He held his hands over the board, counting silently to himself.

"Torpedo ready."

". . . three . . . two . . . one . . . now!" Kirk hit two sets of controls at once. The *Shelton* lurched forward, directly toward the Orion ship. At the same time, Kirk used the forward cargo tractor beams to pull the torpedo from its tube and position it in front of the *Shelton*—without firing it.

The *Shelton* came to relative rest ten meters from the Orion ship. The hull creaked with the stress of the sudden deceleration.

"I don't believe it," Gauvreau gasped. "They didn't fire."

"Of course not," Kirk said. "Look what they would have hit first."

There on the screen, locked into position exactly five meters from each ship, was the sleek and gleaming case of the photon torpedo.

"Great," Gauvreau said. "So the first time either of us tries something, we'll both be blown up."

Kirk shook his head. "If they were Klingons, maybe. But whoever's running that ship is too smart to want to die. We'll work our way out of this. One way or another."

Gauvreau unslung her helmet from her chair and put it on her lap, keeping it ready.

The incoming light on the communications board suddenly blinked on.

"I'll handle the transmission," Gauvreau said, taking her helmet to the comm station. "You stay ready to get us out of here."

Kirk watched the screen as the close-up image of the Orion ship was replaced by a visual channel from the Orion's bridge.

"Who is the madman who commands your vessel?" the pirate commander snarled. He wore a black battle helmet, black radiation goggles, and a voice-distorting translator cap that covered his nose and mouth. "I am the pirate Black Ire and I demand that you drop shields and allow my crew to take over your vessel before I blast you into transporter dust! Surrender now or die a thousand deaths!"

Gauvreau didn't open a return channel. "Listen to him, Kirk. He sounds insane."

Kirk stood up, eyes fixed on the screen. "It's all right, Captain. I think I can handle this. Open up a channel back."

"If you say so." Gauvreau bit her lip. "You're on."

"What say you to my demand, spacedog?" Black Ire growled. "Or do you wish me to flay you open and take out your organs one by one?"

Then Black Ire's head jerked and he leaned forward staring at his adversary in amazement.

Kirk frowned and narrowed his eyes. "I admit I've been slow in getting around to that physical, but don't you think this is taking professional concern a bit too far, Bones?"

On the viewscreen, Black Ire clawed at his goggles and mask.

"Jim?" McCoy said, eyes wide with wonder.

Behind him, Chekov and Sulu and Uhura crowded excitedly into view.

I knew it, Kirk thought. The four of them *were* together. And heading for Talin, just as he was.

All that was missing now was Spock and the *Enterprise.* And Kirk doubted they'd remain missing for long.

Nine

Scott's footsteps echoed in the empty corridors of FCO Outpost 47. The hundred and twenty personnel who had once worked there had been recalled to Earth five days after the devastation of Talin IV and the facility had been deserted ever since. *Until last week,* Scott thought. *Everything had changed then. And maybe tomorrow things would change even more.*

"Aye," Scott muttered to the corridor, adjusting his grip on the three storage boxes he carried, "and if Lieutenant Styles had wings he'd still be a pig."

Scott continued along the corridor, remembering and savoring the look on the lieutenant's face when the *Enterprise* had survived the separation of her warp-distorted port nacelle the previous week. It had been such an odd expression of delight and regret. The delight was without question because the ship remained intact and Styles had his designs on her. But the regret Styles had felt had been because Scott was standing with him—and the twenty-being team of Starfleet experts—in the observation lounge of the *Exeter* when the separation had taken place. The chief engineer did not consider himself a mean or vindictive person, but when the *Enterprise* had remained peacefully in space before them, safely minus her damaged nacelle, he had taken great joy in turning to Styles and saying in a voice which all could hear, "I told ye so."

For Scott, the separation of the nacelle had gone just the way he had expected. For the experts, it had been a terrible disappointment, especially after all the self-important trouble they had gone to in arranging for the *Enterprise* to be towed to the edges of the Talin system.

As the time for the nacelle's removal had approached, excited groups of them watched intently through the viewports as well as on the viewscreen close-ups. After the *Enterprise* had been completely evacuated, four uncrewed workbee shuttles had been attached to the ship's port nacelle with carbon tethers. Twenty-eight additional remote-controlled workbees were attached to the ship's secondary hull. The plan was that, when the two groups of shuttles pulled in opposite directions, the port nacelle's explosive bolts would be triggered to separate it from its support pylon. The experts clenched their hands together, scarcely daring to speak to each other, expectantly awaiting the brilliant rainbow flare of destruction. Scott had just felt irritated and impatient.

With the carbon tethers pulled taut and the *Enterprise* beginning to slowly drift away in the direction of the twenty-eight pulling workbees, a bright yellow flash had sparkled from the support pylon joint on the nacelle. Then, as the experts gasped—and some braced themselves as if shock waves could travel through a vacuum—the *Enterprise* had only continued to slowly drift in one direction while the twisted port nacelle drifted in the other.

One hour later, sensors showed that the warp-compressed point of the nacelle

356 Judith & Garfield Reeves-Stevens

was still evaporating molecule by molecule. That led one of the disappointed experts to propose an alternate theory to account for the nacelle's slow disintegration. Perhaps, the expert suggested, the hull metal had been damaged by the barrage of fusion explosions to which it had been subjected and was simply undergoing a molecular outgassing effect similar to the skin leaching which occurred on primitive Earth-orbiting spacecraft centuries ago. Scott had moaned, "I told ye about that, too," but by then the scientists were digging into old historical tapes, to come up with new theories, completely ignoring the now-orphaned nacelle.

At last with the theoreticians otherwise engaged, Scott had had an easy time directing the installation of the new nacelles the *Exeter* had brought and left in orbit around Talin's moon. Once the *Enterprise* had been quickly towed back into lunar orbit to undergo her final repairs, the work had gone smoothly and now, one week later, there was little left to be done. For that Scott was grateful. But not for much else.

Scott came to the doors marked Sortie Planning Center and they reluctantly slid open before him, sticking from disuse. The people working in the vast room looked up from their tables and desks piled high with microtapes and datacubes and printouts. Despite the work—and the possibility for failure—that remained ahead, Scott felt renewed to see so many familiar faces. Vice Admiral Hammersmith had been true to his word, and then some. Already more than half the *Enterprise*'s crew had been transferred back to the Talin system to assist with the repairs, and most of the rest were in transit.

Carolyn Palamas came up to Scott to take the boxes he carried. "Thank you, Scotty. We've just got the next terminal set up."

"Careful, lass," Scott said as he passed the containers over, worrying about the delicate chiming sounds he heard as the duplicate Talin datadisks inside jostled against each other.

"I know what's riding on this," Palamas said gently, then returned to her section of the vast room.

Scott watched her go, caught up in memories. There was a time when he thought they might have been more to each other than colleagues. But the events at Pollux IV had changed that and, in a way, Scott was glad they had. Otherwise, he might never have gotten to know Mira Romaine when the *Enterprise* took her to Memory Alpha and—

"Mr. Scott, I require your assistance."

Scott felt he had been suddenly transported back in time. He had missed that voice more than he had realized. "Aye, Mr. Spock, I'm coming."

Despite the four months that they had been separated, Scott had noticed no difference in Spock when the former science officer had beamed to the *Enterprise* earlier that day—other than his civilian clothes, of course. At first, Scott had been surprised when Vice Admiral Hammersmith had escorted Spock to Scott's cabin. But given what he had heard on the update channels about the trouble Spock was causing on Earth, the chief engineer had had no doubt that his former fellow officer would be returning soon to the Talin system. Even Scott knew that logic would demand that Spock be prepared to act in case the Council debate he had ignited was finally settled and the authorization was given to begin rescue operations.

Spock had not been at all surprised by Scott's continued presence on the ship, nor had he expressed any pleasure at being reunited with him. After saying hello, he had merely asked if Scott would help him reopen Outpost 47. Hammersmith had said he was happy to loan Scott out if Scott also agreed—which he had, without hesitation.

"How're ye doing, Mr. Spock?"

Spock looked up from the large desk where he worked. The terminal screen before him displayed row after row of the multicolored paint splatters that Scott now recognized as Talin script. "How am I doing what, Mr. Scott?"

Aye, Scott thought, *I've missed the voice, if not necessarily what it says from time to time.*

"I mean, are the modified terminals working out for you?"

"Yes," Spock said. "The ambassadors have been most resourceful in helping us adapt our equipment."

Scott glanced over to Seerl and Orr. The Talin ambassadors worked with a group of young humans and Mario Cardinali, the FCO outpost's ex–manager of communications. Spread over two work benches and a corner of the floor were fifty desk computer terminals, cases open, most with circuit boards removed.

One of the two Talin—Scott still couldn't tell them apart unless Orr allowed her skin to change to a blue shade—moved quickly and surefootedly around the spread-out equipment, lifting its legs and its feet high like a strutting heron. The creature was supervising the work the young humans did to convert the standard Starfleet terminals so the machines could extract information from Talin-style datadisks. The young people were university students, Scott had been told, though he felt certain that no one in university would dare dress the way that this lot did. Scott knew that students had never dressed so outlandishly when he had been their age.

The second Talin stood to the side of the equipment work area, talking through a small translator unit to a young woman who was busily arranging rations on a set of mess trays. Scott had seen many strange things in his day, but the sight of the saurian creature gently cradling a wee baby in its arms as it talked to the baby's mother ranked among the oddest. Though at the same time, the sight of the two species united in such mundane activity made him feel secure about the Federation's future. Now if only the Council would realize what the voters had realized and authorize the aid mission which Spock had fought for.

"What can I be doing for you, then?" Scott asked Spock.

"I shall require full computer access to the main communications monitoring lab. Mr. Cardinali can provide you with details."

"Beggin' your pardon, Mr. Spock, but there's not much of any communications to be monitoring in the vicinity these days."

"True," Spock agreed, "though there are eight standard years' worth of previously captured data to analyze. The monitoring room would make the process more efficient."

"I'll get on it right away, Mr. Spock." Scott saw the clouded look that came to Spock's face. "Och, ye know what I mean."

As Scott left the work room with Cardinali, Vice Admiral Hammersmith appeared in the doorway. "Ah, Engineer, I'm glad I found you. Lieutenant Styles reports that the construction drones have finished replacing the master transtator nodes and that the warp generators in the new nacelles are locked in and ready to power up."

Scott hesitated. "So, then . . . what you're saying, sir, is that the *Enterprise* is ready to be taken out?"

"For trials first, of course," the vice admiral said. "The warp engines will have to be tuned over the next few weeks before she can be classified operational again. But Styles says she'll be ready to break orbit in six hours."

"I see, sir."

Hammersmith put his hand on Scott's shoulder. "We had an agreement, Engineer. I brought back as many of your crew as I could, and I gave you your week—and a few days more—to try and come up with more evidence for your claim that the *Enterprise* had been attacked. Now *you* owe me the services of a chief engineer."

Scott looked back in at the controlled excitement of the workroom. *Spock* must *be on to something,* he thought in despair.

"Have you found any evidence to back your claim, Engineer?"

"No, sir," Scott admitted. "But with Mr. Spock here and—"

Hammersmith shook his head. "I'm afraid Mr. Spock is here on a completely different matter. He is no longer associated with Starfleet. The only reason he was allowed through the blockade at all is because the Talin ambassadors have appointed him and these other people with him as their consular officials."

"But this outpost is Starfleet property," Scott said. He couldn't imagine Spock no longer being in Starfleet.

"Not any more," Hammersmith corrected. "This moon was held in trust for Talin IV's future exploitation and the ambassadors have invoked their right to claim it. The outpost is forfeit."

"I don't understand," Scott said.

"Mr. Scott, the repairs to the *Enterprise* went smoothly and so I had no problem assigning you to help Spock here as a gesture of goodwill from Starfleet to the Talin. However, until the Council debate over the status of Talin is concluded one way or another, there is nothing more to be done here. The Federation is more than just this one planet in this one system. Starfleet has too many ships and personnel here already. We need the *Enterprise* out doing her job and we need you on her doing yours."

"Please, Vice Admiral, I know that with just a few more days I could—"

"Lieutenant Commander Scott, I have given you all the latitude that my orders allow. Now, you, sir, are ordered to report to Lieutenant Styles, in temporary command of the *Enterprise,* in six hours, to prepare her for operational trials and return to full duty. Do you understand, Mr. Scott?"

Scott's shoulders slumped. He had come so close only to lose again. "Aye, Vice Admiral. I shall report aboard the *Enterprise* in six hours. Thank you for your patience, sir."

"Good man, Engineer." Then Hammersmith offered Scott one last piece of hope. "Of course, if you do manage to come up with something in the next six hours, I have been known to change my mind."

"Aye, sir. Thank you, sir," Scott said glumly.

Hammersmith nodded in dismissal, then entered the workroom. Scott and Cardinali left for the main monitor lab.

"What was the vice admiral saying about you trying to *prove* that the *Enterprise* had been attacked? Didn't the bridge logs show that the nuclear missiles were aimed directly at her?" Cardinali asked.

"Aye, but we weren't talking about the missiles." Scott explained to Cardinali about the unnatural pattern of damage which had been found throughout the *Enterprise*—how the most vital twenty percent of her transtator circuitry had been destroyed, but nothing else.

"And you think it's possible a focused subspace pulse was used as a weapon?" Cardinali asked when Scott was through.

"You're a communications expert. What do you think?"

Cardinali paused in the corridor and put his hand on his chin. "Theoretically, it makes sense. But I don't know anything that could generate that kind of power without setting off every energy sensor from here to the Neutral Zone. If it happened that way, then it's something that's never been reported before. And other than that, Mr. Scott, you've got me." He began to walk on.

Scott hurried to catch up with the big man's long strides. "Well, what exactly is it that you and Mr. Spock are doing for those Talin? I thought perhaps he had read my report on the subspace pulse and was coming to do some work of his own on it."

"He hasn't said anything about that." Cardinali stood in front of the monitoring lab's doors and helped them open with a strong shove. "Basically, Seerl and Orr say they were launched on their joint lunar mission because their respective governments thought something strange was going on up here on Talin's moon. I'm surprised Dr. Richter didn't suspect that it was a joint mission in the first place, I mean with their ship not carrying the colors of either nation. As far as I know right now, what we're all trying to help Spock do is find out exactly what chain of events set off that final exchange of weapons.

"Seerl and Orr want to know because they still can't believe that their governments actually went to war on their own and, I'm guessing here, Spock seems to think that if he can give the Talin the answers that they want, he can also prove that the *Enterprise* was not to blame for what happened either. But I don't know all the details."

Scott shrugged. "Well, at least we're trying to do the same thing, if not exactly in the same way." He stared around at the huge circular lab, ten times the size of the *Enterprise*'s bridge. Every one of its hundreds of screens was black.

"All right then, laddie," the chief engineer sighed, "I've got six hours to give you. Where's the 'on' switch for all this?"

One hour before Scott was to report back to the *Enterprise,* Spock entered the monitoring lab alone. Scott and Cardinali worked together at the center command console facing the master viewscreen, and did not notice his arrival until he was beside them.

Spock looked approvingly around the lab—all displays were now functional. The viewscreen flickered with a hundred focus patterns, awaiting input.

"We're ready for your datafiles anytime," Scott said.

"Please try input channel forty-five," Spock said.

Cardinali punched in the file number and ten of the smaller image areas on the master screen dissolved into one larger one. A computer graphic formed in it. To Scott, it appeared to be an illustration of the orbital mechanics of Talin IV and its moon. Also plotted on the chart were several small objects orbiting the planet, but Scott couldn't tell what they were supposed to be.

"Good work, Mr. Scott. I shall begin transferring the rest of my files here as soon as the others arrive."

"The others?" Scott asked.

"Yes," Spock said. "If my calculations are correct, they should be arriving at any moment."

"Who?"

Spock turned to the chief engineer, but before he could answer, a transporter chime filled the lab. Scott blinked as three figures took form.

Spock greeted them when the beam had faded. "Welcome, Dr. Richter, Ms. Mallett, Mr. Wilforth."

The outpost's former manager of sampling operations came forward to the command console. Behind her, the old scientist tapped his cane against the dark carpeted floor of the lab, then spit on it. "Pah. Four months later and it still stinks like *fladge* down here. Hello, Mr. Spock." He squinted at Scott. "What? You lose your *narflin* job, too, Mr. Scott?"

"Unfortunately not, Dr. Richter." Scott stood up to shake the scientist's hand but the man declined to offer it. Mallett and Cardinali hugged in greeting.

Wilforth gazed around the room with longing, then folded his hands together. "I never thought I'd see this room again."

"How are Seerl and Orr?" Mallett asked.

"Adjusting well," Spock answered. "Their guidance has helped eliminate more than forty percent of the recordings on file at this outpost from unproductive study. Apparently many of the update broadcasts which the FCO studied had a reputation on Talin for being less than truthful."

"That's something you should know about, isn't it, Mr. Spock?" a woman's voice asked.

Scott turned to see that the young woman who had been passing out rations had entered the lab. This time, she was carrying her baby herself. The Talin ambassadors walked majestically at her side, each carrying the silver tube of a translator.

"Mr. Scott," Spock said, "may I introduce Marita Llorente, organizer of Students for Stars for the People."

Marita extended her hand to Scott, balancing her baby on her hip. "And advisor at large to the Talin Embassy," she added, shaking Scott's hand with a forceful grip. "But these days, who isn't?"

"A pleasure," Scott said. Then he was aware that as Marita stepped back, the two Talin drew near. Both had extended their taloned hands in a duplication of Marita's action.

Makes sense, Scott thought. Though he had seen the Talin before, he had not been formally introduced. He reached out and took the closer Talin's hand, startled by how soft and warm the heavily textured folds of reddish skin were, and how sharp the talons were. He was more careful shaking hands with the next.

"The shorter of the two was about Scott's height and spoke into its silver translator. The Talin's voice was a melodic, whispery whistle. The translator's interpretation of it was clipped and mechanical.

"Welcome to our moon," the first Talin had said.

The second Talin spoke into its translator. "You wear a manly shirt."

Scott smiled at the compliment. He guessed red might be a favorite color.

The first Talin looked around the lab and its skin rippled, then quickly changed to a sky-blue shade. *Then that one's Orr,* Scott thought, *the female.*

"Is this the place where observation was done?" Orr's translator asked.

"Yes," Spock said. "Virtually all of your planet's communications channels were monitored from this facility."

Seerl held the translator to his wide mouth. "Yet you still have no answers."

"Soon," Spock promised.

Scott checked the time readout on the console chronometer. In forty minutes he'd be beaming back up to the *Enterprise.* "What answers, Mr. Spock?"

"The same answers you look for, Mr. Scott. Who attacked the *Enterprise.* And who attacked Talin."

"Hold on," Marita interrupted. "Talin destroyed itself. Its nuclear warheads didn't come from anywhere else. That's why the Prime Directive has got to be thrown away. So the Federation won't stand back and let something like this happen again." She looked directly at Spock. "Right, Mr. Spock?"

"Ms. Llorente, please," Wilforth said in distress. Scott had noticed the man standing at the side, trying to avoid confrontation.

Scott was bewildered by the way Marita had made her last comment. "You don't agree with that, do ye, Mr. Spock?" Had he changed over the last four months, after all?

"No, Mr. Scott. Marita and I have only agreed to disagree. I admit I used her organization's resources to further my attempts to speak to the Council about Talin IV. And I admit that I told her that I would be speaking against the Prime Directive, which is her organization's goal."

Marita shifted her baby from one arm to the other. "But what he did do was speak against the Prime Directive only as it applied to Talin. Not quite a lie. Not quite the truth. But all Vulcan."

"And you're not upset with him for that?" Scott asked.

"It's a start," Marita said. "A small step forward. The Prime Directive's grip on the Federation has become weaker because of what Spock has done in Council. Someday it will be abolished altogether."

Spock crossed his arms over his chest. "As I have said before, Marita, since the Prime Directive should not have been enforced on Talin IV in the first place, nothing that has transpired here will undermine it in any way. In the years to come, the Prime Directive can only become stronger, as a policy, and as an ideal."

Marita turned away from Spock and looked at her baby. "Well, we'll see about that, won't we, Alexander?"

As the Talin began to ask more technical questions about the communications facility, Scott motioned to Spock to join him away from the others. "I've been ordered back to the *Enterprise,* Mr. Spock, and I'm afraid that this might be the last time I get a chance to talk with you in the next few weeks."

"What do you wish to say?"

Och, someday he'll learn, Scott told himself. "I want to know if you have any proof of what you were mentioning about whatever attacked the *Enterprise* and Talin IV."

"I am working on it, Mr. Scott."

"Any chance of coming up with something in the next thirty minutes?"

"Unquestionably," Spock stated.

The answer took Scott by surprise. "What? You mean that? You'll have the answer that quickly?"

"Part of the answer at any rate, Mr. Scott." From the center of the lab, another transporter chime sounded. It was louder than before—multiple beams coming in.

"As I said earlier," Spock continued. "I have just been waiting for the others to arrive."

Scott followed Spock's gaze to the lab's center where five golden shafts of light and matter swirled into being. The sound they made was like a song.

"Captain Kirk!" Scott cried out in delight.

The last of the beams faded and Kirk looked over to Scott and raised his hand. Around the captain, Chekov, McCoy, Sulu, and Uhura did the same.

"You're back! All of you!" Scott shouted again. Without thinking he slapped Spock joyously on the back, accompanying the action with a wordless whoop of excitement.

Spock froze in position, half bent forward by the force of Scott's blow.

"Oops, sorry, Mr. Spock, sorry," Scott said, reaching out to take Spock's shoulders, then realizing that he shouldn't, then thinking that he should. "Och!" he finally said and hurried across the room to his friends—the latest additions to Talin's embassy staff, as approved by Mr. Spock earlier that day when the *SS Ian Shelton* and RRV *Queen Mary* had reached the edge of the Talin system.

Uhura's hug was the longest and most intensely felt of the greetings Scott gave and received. He was suddenly struck by the thought that of all of them, Uhura was the one he had missed most. But the loud and joyful celebration was not the time to consider those thoughts. It was a time of feeling, not thinking.

Like a statue, Spock stood motionless apart from the crush of people as the returning *Enterprise* crew reunited with Richter and Cardinali and Mallett and Wilforth, and made new acquaintances as well.

It was Kirk who approached the Talin first. "You are the lunar astronauts, are you not?"

Chekov tried to correct him. "The word is cosmonaut, Keptin."

But Kirk didn't hear as he shook hands with the saurians. He looked from Mallett to Cardinali. "They're why you smashed through the doors of my hangar bay, aren't they? You went to rescue them before they could do anything in reaction to what they saw happen on their planet."

"It was Dr. Richter's plan," Mallett acknowledged.

"Did the doctor also work out the plan for getting them to Earth for their appearance before Council?" Kirk asked.

"Partially," Mallett confessed. "Mario and I managed to get them down to the outpost and hidden before the rescue teams from Starbase 29 came into the system. Then, with all the confusion of the next few days, we were able to beam them up to the private ship from the Richter Institute which came for Dr. Richter. They stayed aboard until Dr. Richter was able to get into contact with Mr. Spock to work out the rest of the details."

Kirk nodded. "When I read the update reports of what happened in Council, I thought I detected Mr. Spock's flair for the dramatic."

"We all had a hand in what went on," Mallet said earnestly. "But no matter how it was going to turn out, when Mario and I saw what had happened on Talin IV, we knew we weren't going to let the lunar explorers die. One way or another, with or without Dr. Richter, we would have saved them."

Cardinali added, "You should have seen the looks on their faces when the Wraith matched orbit beside their ship. But it only lasted a few seconds. Almost as if they were waiting for us."

Orr stepped carefully among the humans. "We were waiting for you," her translator said. "All of our lives."

Seerl joined Orr. "But mostly since your tractor beam disturbed our mass detectors and triggered an automatic evasive orbit change."

Cardinali laughed and patted Seerl on his back. Scott was struck by how natural the gesture seemed, even between human and saurian. Perhaps that was the true legacy of space exploration, he thought. By entering a realm where *everything* was different, similarities became what was most important—cooperation, not conflict.

McCoy at last came to Spock. "Well, Mr. Spock, if I didn't know any better, I'd say you weren't happy to see me."

"I am not, Doctor." Spock's words stopped the conversations around him. "I calculated there was a seventy-five-percent probability that Cap—" He stumbled over the word, then apparently decided he meant what he said. "That Captain Kirk would arrive in the Talin system within one hundred and twenty standard days after our departure, which he has done."

Kirk acted disappointed. "Only seventy-five percent, Spock?"

"There was a twenty-five-percent chance that you would die in an accident involving manual labor or cargo handling."

"Oh," Kirk said quietly.

Scott reminded himself to ask the captain what he had been doing these last few months.

"Chekov had a fifty-percent chance of arriving here within the same timeframe," Spock continued. "Most probably in the company of Orion pirates. Sulu had a forty-eight-percent chance of doing the same."

"Why did I have less chance than Chekov?" Sulu asked indignantly.

"I estimated that there was a two-percent chance that you would, indeed, decide to become a pirate."

Chekov howled with laughter. Sulu didn't seem to want to argue the odds.

"As for Uhura," Spock said, "I regret that Dr. Richter's revelation to me that he and Mallett and Cardinali had smuggled the Talin lunar explorers back to Earth resulted in my sudden change of plans, requiring that I not contact anyone involved with the Talin incident. However, Uhura, I assumed that upon your release from Starfleet detention, you would arrive here about this time as part of the civilian relief effort."

"But what about me, Spock?" McCoy pressed. "What did you have figured out for me?"

Spock eyed McCoy warily. "Doctor, there was a five-percent chance that you would die or be seriously injured in a reckless camping accident. There was a ten-percent chance that Vice Admiral Hammersmith would change his mind about your assault on him and have you arrested."

"And what about the rest of it?" McCoy said. "There's eighty-five percent still to go. I can take it."

Spock glanced away. "And there was an eighty-five-percent chance that you would arrive here," he said quickly.

McCoy was confused. "Hold on, I *am* here. You were right. Why be unhappy to see me?"

"Doctor, there was an eighty-five-percent chance that you would arrive here *one month* from now. When I received Captain Kirk's communiqué from the *Ian Shelton* today, I admit I was quite astonished that you were included."

McCoy's smile was so wide his face seemed to expand. "Spock, you underestimated me! I'm not going to let you forget this for months! For years!"

"I know, Doctor. Which is why I am not pleased to see you."

Everyone except Spock and the Talin joined the laughter that followed. It was interrupted by the double chirp of Scott's communicator.

Scott flipped the device open. "Scott here."

"Lieutenant Styles, temporary commander of the U.S.S. Enterprise, here, Mr. Scott. I believe your time is up. Prepare to be beamed aboard."

Kirk's eyes darkened. "Styles?" he repeated in disgust. "That pompous, strutting Napoleon is in command of my ship?"

Styles's voice came back from the communicator. "Say again, Scott? I didn't quite get that."

Scott knew it was time to make his stand. "Uh, I canna beam up right now, Lieutenant."

"And why not?"

"Uh, we've had a wee bit of an emergency down here."

"Good Lord," Styles sighed. "You've got half of Starfleet orbiting over you right now. How can you have an emergency in an FCO base?"

"Communications are out," Scott said, then dropped the communicator to the floor and stepped on it.

Kirk went to Scott and put a hand on his shoulder. "Scotty, Styles is an officious nit, I know. But he is your commanding officer."

Scott was past caring. "Aye, Captain, I know. But I've spent three months taking apart the Enterprise trying to find out what happened to her and it's only now that Mr. Spock's come that we have a chance of finding out. And if we can prove that we were attacked, then the vice admiral will let me stay here until we find out who did it and why. I'm sure of it."

Kirk turned to Spock. "What do you say, Spock? Can you prove it?"

"I shall so endeavor, Captain."

"Good," Kirk said quietly. "If anyone can, you can." Scott saw a change come over Kirk then. Somehow, for just a moment, he no longer had the bearing of an officer or leader, he was just one person among many, no different from the rest.

"Thank you, Captain," Spock answered. "Now, if you take positions facing the master viewscreen, I shall present the facts as Seerl and Orr have helped me understand them."

Scott half-expected to see Styles and a security team beam in at any second. But he also knew that Styles would rather sit it out in orbit for an hour or so before admitting to Hammersmith that he had lost track of his chief engineer. As long as Spock didn't waste any time arguing with McCoy, Scott figured he'd be able to see the entire presentation, or whatever it was that Spock had been working on for the past six hours.

Spock called for the first datachannel he had prepared, and the image of a Wraith shuttle appeared in a large section of the viewscreen. Scott recalled hearing about this picture. The Talin had recorded one of the FCO's sampling runs.

"Seerl and Orr tell us that on Talin this picture was officially described as a hoax," Spock said. "The perpetrators were reported to be members of an organization that believed that extraplanetary beings were visiting Talin."

"We know about this picture, Mr. Spock," Wilforth said. "We know it didn't tell the Talin anything about us."

"Correct, Mr. Wilforth, but what is more important about this picture is what it tells us about the Talin. Specifically, the sophistication of their visual recording technology. The *Wraith*-class shuttle was designed to be virtually undetectable. However, this image proves that the Talin were able to track such craft."

Spock asked Cardinali to open the next datachannel and a flood of images—real and artistic representations—began to move across the screen. Scott thought it was one of the oddest assortments of flying vehicles he had ever seen.

"These are pictures of other, so-called extraplanetary space vehicles which were reported in the public update media on Talin."

"But the FCO has already searched through these images most carefully," Wilforth said. "There are no other Wraith photographs among them."

"Correct again," Spock agreed. "With the Talin's help, Carolyn Palamas programmed the graphic computers to sort the images and select all those showing legitimate flying vehicles not indigenous to Talin."

"We also did that," Wilforth said.

"And these are the results Lieutenant Palamas obtained." The images on the screen—some saucer shaped, some round like balloons, others angular or rounded like winged aircraft—sorted themselves into smaller and smaller groups until nothing was left.

"See?" Wilforth said. "That's exactly what we found, too. What are you trying to say here, Mr. Spock?"

Spock walked around to the front of the command console so he could address everyone, his back to the screen. "Mr. Wilforth, it is my contention that on a planet with the proven technology to capture images of fast-moving, near-invisible, covert alien spacecraft, the fact that only *one* such image exists is not logical."

"But our computers were able to scan through every image, Spock. We found nothing," Wilforth argued.

"No, Mr. Wilforth. The FCO did not scan through every image. Only every image *available* to the FCO." Spock looked at Cardinali. "Datachannel two hundred, if you please."

A new series of pictures came on screen. Twelve of them. Each a clear and detailed image of what could only be a Federation *Wraith*-class shuttle traveling through the atmosphere.

"The FCO never had a chance to analyze these images because they were obtained through military sources and judged classified," Spock said.

Richter slammed his cane against the command console to get Spock's attention. "If the FCO couldn't get these *snorled* pictures, then how the *ziq* did you?"

Spock placed a hand on the console. "The FCO did get these pictures, Dr. Richter. Unfortunately, they were obtained on the FCO's last mission to Talin—the intrusive-collection landing party sent from the *Enterprise*. Talin was devastated and the FCO outpost shut down before any of the classified and unreleased datafiles obtained during that mission could be evaluated. These pictures were finally analyzed today and as they clearly show, without a doubt, the Talin were aware of the FCO's operations on their world."

A deep voice resonated through the lab. "Well done, Mr. Spock." It was Vice Admiral Hammersmith. Scott tried to remain inconspicuous. With the vice admiral were Styles and three red-shirted security officers.

"I am not yet finished, Vice Admiral." Spock stepped around the command console to face the vice admiral directly.

Hammersmith stared appreciatively at the screen. "I tell you, Mr. Spock, when I look up on that screen and see that the Talin military had been tracking FCO missions, that tells me that you are finished. For whatever it's worth, what you've done here today is to conclusively show that whatever happened on Talin wasn't just the *Enterprise*'s fault. The blame must also be shared with the sampling personnel and director of this outpost."

"No," Carole Mallett said angrily. "I only conducted twenty sampling runs to Talin. It's inconceivable that they could have been sophisticated enough to record my operations thirteen out of twenty times!"

"The evidence is right up there on the screen," Hammersmith said. "It appears that Starfleet is going to have to re-open the board of inquiry so it can spread the blame around. Now where's Lieutenant Commander Scott hiding?"

"Vice Admiral," Spock said forcefully. "What is on the screen is only a portion of the evidence, as you call it. Mr. Cardinali, datachannel two hundred and one, please."

A second series of images came on the screen—pictures of wingless flying craft, long and streamlined with pinched-in midsections and deep grooves along their forward hulls. Scott tried to count them but there were too many. They didn't fill the entire screen so he knew there were fewer than one hundred but still there were more than five times as many as the images of the Wraiths. The only problem was, Scott couldn't tell what they were.

Neither could Hammersmith. "What are those supposed to be, Mr. Spock?"

"For want of a precise term," Spock said simply, "I chose to call them sampling shuttles."

"But the FCO doesn't use anything that looks like that," Wilforth protested.

"They are not FCO shuttles," Spock said. "Neither are they from any known world within the Federation. Or without."

Scott saw Kirk's eyes fill with excitement. "Yes, Spock," Kirk said. "That's it."

But Hammersmith didn't share that excitement. He was irritated when he spoke. "Just what are you trying to tell us, Spock?"

"According to the classified records which were analyzed today, for the past fifteen standard years, the world of Talin IV has been inundated with visits by these alien shuttles. These shuttles identified and used the same gaps in Talin's radar defenses as did the FCO. However, so great in number were the aliens' intrusions that the Talin launched a vigorous program to upgrade their detection devices. The FCO's Wraiths were not recorded because the Talin were trying to specifically find them. The Wraiths were recorded by military devices designed to detect the shuttles you are seeing on the screen now—alien shuttles."

Wilforth waved his hands at Spock. "Just a minute, Mr. Spock, this isn't making any sense. If the Talin governments officially denied the existence of these extraplanetary craft, why did they then upgrade their defenses?"

Spock asked for datachannel two hundred and ten. Scott brought it online. A geopolitical map of Talin IV appeared. Moments later, a flurry of hundreds of green dots flashed on and off across it.

"The dots represent major military outposts, airbases, space launch facilities, and nuclear power plants." Spock reached across the console and pressed a switch. The green dots were almost overwhelmed by a second flurry of flashing red triangles. "The triangles represent sightings of the alien shuttles. As you see, they are almost exclusively centered on the military installations."

Hammersmith joined Spock by the console. "Mr. Spock, there's nothing remarkable about trying to analyze military and industrial capability—no matter which Talin group was doing the analyzing."

Spock pointed at the screen. "Look at the frequency of sightings, Vice Admiral. There are far too many of them to be accounted for by any need by Talin's nations to analyze each other's military strength. I submit that these alien craft were engaged in a systematic series of provocative sorties designed for one reason only— to heighten the fear of war on Talin and to make the military and political leaders of the planet arm themselves to the point where stability would no longer be possible."

"Are you saying that *aliens* were attempting to start a war with Talin?" Hammersmith asked incredulously.

"Not *with* Talin," Spock corrected. "But *on* Talin. Preliminary tapes collected by the FCO team indicate that the incursion into polar air space, which almost brought the Talin to war while the *Enterprise* deployed satellites, was the result of provocative overflights by one or more of these shuttles."

Hammersmith shook his head. "This can't be right, Mr. Spock. It's impossible to—"

"You're wrong, Vice Admiral!" Kirk was up by Spock and Hammersmith now. "Whatever you think about the existence of any unidentified aliens, Spock is right in his conclusions. The data came from the Talin themselves. The data cannot be ignored. Someone was trying to get the Talin to destroy their own world."

"Then the Prime Directive wasn't broken!" McCoy shouted. He joined Kirk and Spock. The three of them faced Hammersmith together though the vice admiral directed his gaze solely at McCoy. Knowing what he did about the two men's last meeting, Scott wasn't surprised.

"The doctor's right, Vice Admiral," Kirk said. "The Prime Directive does not apply here. Talin IV's normal development had already been altered by the aliens' attempts to increase political and military tensions. It was right for the *Enterprise* to step in. The military exchanges on Talin were the result of extraplanetary interference. The Prime Directive compelled us to act as we did to prevent those exchanges!"

Hammersmith backed off, obviously shaken. "But to make an entire world blow itself up? Why, Kirk? What possible reason could there be to force a planet to destroy all life in a nuclear war?"

Spock reached for another switch on the console. "But not all life on Talin has been destroyed, Vice Admiral."

A new image came up on the viewscreen. It was a realtime feed of the dayside of Talin IV, transmitted from one of the *Enterprise*'s sensor satellites. Scott bristled as he saw that the insulting caption—KIRK'S WORLD—was still displayed. Behind him, he heard the Talin ambassadors make a sound of anguish that needed no translation.

The choking clouds of dust and radioactive poison which had swept the world were almost gone now. But the destruction they had brought would scar the planet for centuries, if not millennia. The land masses were still streaked black and brown. The once-white polar ice caps were gray with soot from the worldwide firestorm that had raged for weeks after the disaster. The only sign of life remaining on the planet was in the oceans now choked with the deep purple algaelike organism that had mutated and bloomed in the days after the planet's death.

"What could possibly live down there?" Hammersmith asked in sorrow and anger.

"Mr. Cardinali," Spock said, "cycle back in memory one month."

The image of the world shifted as the viewscreen presented the earlier recording. The clouds were thicker, but the ravaged land and purple-stained oceans were unchanged.

"Another month back," Spock said.

The image shifted. A brown-streaked hurricane battered the primary continent. Some patches of blue could be seen in the oceans among the purple, but more than half the planet was obscured by smoke and clouds.

"Two weeks after the incident," Spock said.

Shift. The world was wrapped in a black pall. Through small breaks in the almost solid cloud cover, fires raged.

"Two days."

The planet was hell.

"Mr. Cardinali, have the computer run through that day's recording, extracting all portions of the images that show what lies beneath the clouds to construct a composite picture of the land masses and the oceans as they appeared then."

Cardinali typed in the commands. Slowly the clouds disappeared from the image of Talin as the computer assembled the clear areas from thousands of separate shots to create a master picture of the planet's surface. Walls of fire followed the coastlines where the cities had been clustered. Forests and farmlands blazed.

Then Scott thought the computer made an error as the oceans were reconstructed. The first section cleared showed that a mutated bloom of purple algae had already appeared. More of the oceans cleared. Scott saw another bloom. And another.

He felt his flesh creep as the rest of the planet appeared as it had been that day. *The algae blooms were studded across the oceans in a regular, geometric pattern.*

"Good Lord," McCoy whispered.

"No," Hammersmith gasped.

"Exactly," Spock said without inflection. "The algaelike organism which has taken over the entire ocean ecosystem of Talin IV is not a mutation brought on by radiation. It is an artificial life-form which is not native to Talin, and which was seeded on that planet quite deliberately. Just as the nuclear holocaust was deliberately induced to ensure that the world would be made . . . fertile for it."

Scott was horrified by the atrocity that Spock had just described. He heard the Talin keen with high-pitched wails of sorrow as their translators told them what Spock had said.

McCoy's face was splotched red with anger. "Who would do such a thing, Spock?"

Spock calmly changed the display back to the pictures of the streamlined, pinch-waisted alien shuttles. "They would," he said.

Kirk's face was grim and set. "But *who* are they, Spock? *Where* are they?"

"To answer that question, we will need help from two additional sources," Spock said. He turned to Hammersmith. "The *Enterprise,* which will enable us to find the aliens . . ." He turned to face Richter. For the first time Scott noticed that the old man's face was drenched in sweat and pale with shock.

". . . and you, Dr. Richter," Spock concluded, "who have always known about them."

Ten

McCoy felt the sudden pressue of Hammersmith's hand on his arm with anxious relief. He had known that this confrontation was coming and he was glad to get it over with.

"Could you wait in my office?" Hammersmith asked Kirk and Spock, who walked just ahead with Wilforth and Richter. "The doctor and I will be along in a moment."

Kirk looked at McCoy, subtly asking if the doctor needed help, but McCoy shook his head. "I'll catch up, Jim." Then he and Hammersmith waited as the other four disappeared around a corner in the corridor.

"Don't worry, Dr. McCoy," Hammersmith said when they were alone. "I'm not going to ask you to apologize."

Fat chance of that, McCoy thought.

"Not that I'd expect you to, anyway," Hammersmith added. "I just wanted to know what the hell it is you think you're doing here?"

McCoy could feel every muscle in his body tense with anger. "I'm here to do what you wouldn't let me do in the first place—get to the bottom of this mess."

Hammersmith shook his head. "I didn't stop you from doing anything, Doctor."

McCoy spoke hotly. "You transferred Spock and me to San Francisco. You wouldn't bring formal charges against us so we couldn't get a decent hearing. And—"

Hammersmith held up a single finger and McCoy instantly stopped talking. "Doctor, you *had* a decent hearing. Starfleet chose not to bring charges when it became apparent that Kirk was going to resign. And where else would you have wanted to transfer? Another starship patrolling on the other side of the Arm? Some starbase out on the frontier? You think you would have been able to do anything about Talin out there?"

McCoy stared at the vice admiral, not following what he was saying. "So what was I supposed to be able to do in San Francisco?"

"Dr. McCoy, I sent you and Mr. Spock back to Command, to the Council, and to the headquarters of most of the intersystem update bureaus. Don't you think that was one of the best places to do something about Talin? It certainly worked out for Mr. Spock."

McCoy didn't want to believe what the vice admiral was hinting at. "Are you saying that you transferred us back to Earth *on purpose,* because we could do the most good there?"

Hammersmith's face went blank. "Of course not, Doctor. That wouldn't fall under my orders as commander of Starbase 29."

McCoy felt even more puzzled.

"Look, Doctor," Hammersmith said, lowering his voice, "I know why you slugged me back at the starbase. I know why you're feeling you'd like to do it again. And that's okay. I understand. It's because you've run out of things to say. And the only reason a person like you runs out of things to say is because you know that I'm right. And you don't like that one bit."

"Now wait just a minute," McCoy sputtered.

But Hammersmith cut him off. "No, sir, it's your turn to wait. I've already put in my years to get to this rank and I've got a few more levels to go. And the reason

I've gone as far as I have is because this is what I want to do. This is how I give something back. But like I said, Doctor, I don't know what it is you're doing here."

"I'm trying to set things right."

"I don't mean here, on this moon. I mean why were you in Starfleet at all." He held up his hand again to keep McCoy silent. "I checked your record, Doctor. You were a brilliant medical student. You could have gone anywhere and had success, wealth, whatever you wanted. But for some reason, you chose Starfleet, and then you chose a starship. And I happen to know what starship duty means for a doctor. Most of the time you don't know what to do because your only patients are probably among the fittest and healthiest humans since the dawn of time. And the rest of the time you're frantic with frustration because you're facing diseases and toxins that no one has ever seen before, or even dared imagine."

McCoy didn't interrupt. He had to admit that Hammersmith wasn't far wrong. But he was damned if he knew what the vice admiral was driving at.

"Now, I know you try to make yourself out to be some sort of rebel with a pioneering spirit and that's one of the reasons you chose starship duty. But I've watched you with your friends, and I know you envy Mr. Spock for his clear-cut reasoning—no emotions to cloud the issues. And you envy Kirk's cut-to-the-heart, full-speed-ahead ability to just make a decision and make it stick. And I wonder what might happen if you let some of Kirk's spontaneity, or Spock's logic, out in yourself?"

Struck by the vice admiral's insight, McCoy tried to make his face as unreadable as Hammersmith's. But he hadn't had the practice the vice admiral had had.

Hammersmith zeroed in as he caught something in McCoy's eyes. "Or have you already tried it? Have you already done something—out of compassion, out of logic—and realized it was the worst decision you could have made?"

"I'm not in Starfleet anymore," McCoy stated flatly. "I don't have to stand here and listen to this."

Hammersmith shrugged. "I know you don't have to hear this, Doctor, because everything I've said . . . you already know."

McCoy turned to follow the others.

Unperturbed, Hammersmith kept talking. "You know, Doctor, when we had our big argument at the starbase—with all of your objections, and your reasoning, and my counter objections and all of that—there were a couple of times there when I thought that maybe you had me and I had better work a lot harder in trying to convince you what was the best thing to do—for yourself as well as Starfleet.

"But when you finally stopped talking and hit me, that was the moment that I knew you'd lost—you'd given up."

McCoy turned back to him and spoke angrily. "You didn't win anything. I quit."

"I can see you've been spending too much time with Kirk, Doctor. I didn't say I had won. Sometimes, the point isn't to win. Sometimes the point is just not to lose. And I didn't lose. Starfleet procedures required you to be transferred, so I sent you where you could do the most good, if you were interested in doing it. But to tell the truth, I never expected to hear from you again."

"I guess you don't understand me as well as you think you do, after all." McCoy's words were clipped with sarcasm.

Hammersmith stopped beside McCoy. "I understand you better, Doctor, because Starfleet and the Federation are a lot like you. We've got humans on one side, Vulcans on the other, and we're stuck in the middle trying to make everything work. And though we might not win every fight, what I can tell you is that we are never, ever, going to lose."

Hammersmith began walking down the corridor again. McCoy decided that meant the lecture was at last over.

But the vice admiral hadn't finished with him yet. "Oh, and Dr. McCoy, one last thing. I'm a very forgiving person, but if you ever try to hit me again, two things are going to happen.

"One, I'm going to have a new set of trophies for my office wall back at Starbase 29, and two, you're going to spend six months in a regen tube growing a new pair of lungs." Hammersmith patted McCoy on the arm he had grabbed the doctor by. "I understand you, Doctor. This is just so you understand me."

Spock understood why Zalan Wilforth was so agitated. It was not just that his First Contact assignment had apparently been fatally compromised from both within and without. It was the inner conflict of his two different halves that truly troubled the man. Spock could look at Wilforth and see how his suppressed human side wanted to scream and rage at Alonzo Richter for what the scientist had done. But Wilforth's other half—his Centauran heritage—struggled to avoid the confrontation altogether. The outpost's former director was trapped between wanting the wrong resolution or none at all. Spock tried to think of something he might say to Wilforth to help ease his turmoil, but he knew from experience that help like that could only come from within. Spock wished Wilforth peace and returned to observing Vice Admiral Hammersmith. The vice admiral was someone Spock thought he could handle.

Hammersmith sat behind what had once been Wilforth's desk in the director's complex. He leaned back in Wilforth's chair, reading the data that came up on the desk display. The vice admiral's body was completely relaxed, but Spock saw how his eyes moved rapidly to scan each screen of information, absorbing everything.

The datafile came to an end and Hammersmith turned to the others in the room. McCoy sat in a chair in the corner of the office, arms folded defensively. Kirk didn't move where he stood near the office's closed door. Richter slumped in his own chair, staring past his folded hands at the floor.

Hammersmith's tone was compassionate, though it hid a trace of anger. "When did you know about them, Dr. Richter?"

The scientist exhaled with a rattling sound from deep in his chest. "I suspected them . . . I *suspected* them, when I saw the first Richter Scale rating of Talin IV. That was maybe six or seven years ago."

Hammersmith rubbed at an eyebrow. "How can a Richter Scale of Culture rating indicate the presence of alien observers?"

Richter looked up defiantly. His eyes were red rimmed, his lips moist, his skin sallow. "I *invented* the thing. I know how to read it." He tapped his cane on the floor once, but only weakly. "What you people don't understand is that life is the same no matter where it comes from. It has different colors, different forms, different chemistry, but what drives it is the same." He looked at Spock. "Even Vulcans have the same drives and needs and emotions. They just have better discipline than most."

The vice admiral tried to remain polite, despite the pressure Spock knew he was under. "What point are you trying to make, Doctor?"

"It's so predictable, life is. The development of culture, of civilization, I wrote an equation about it. It makes the Richter Scale work. And the Talin didn't *fit* the equation."

"How?"

Richter coughed. From the sound, Spock noted that the congestion in the man's lungs had increased since their trip from Earth. "If you had twenty years, I could teach you. If I had twenty years . . . Listen, the Talin culture was just like a thousand others—but for their level of understanding about the universe, for their technological achievements, they thought too much about the stars. They wanted to get to them too badly. Much more than most races do at their stage."

"I still don't understand, Dr. Richter," Hammersmith said.

"They saw something. They knew there was something more beyond their planet. It was like a transtator current through their entire culture—their literature, their art. And that desperation to leave their planet when their technology still wasn't ready—that skewed their entire Richter Rating." He tried to tap his cane again for emphasis but almost lost his grip on it instead. "This isn't just me blathering. Other people saw the problem with the rating, too. That's why Starfleet called me to consult. That's why they ended up bringing me out here. Everyone saw the problem, but I was the only one who knew why it was there."

Spock glanced at Kirk. He showed remarkable patience. Spock had no doubt that if another, younger, scientist were being questioned here, Kirk would be asking questions faster than anyone could follow.

Hammersmith persisted. "Why didn't you tell Starfleet what you suspected?"

Richter mumbled something to the floor.

"I beg your pardon, Doctor?"

"The Prime Directive," Richter snapped. "The bloody damn Prime Directive, that's why."

Hammersmith shifted in his chair, brows knitted. "Let me get this straight. *You* didn't want to interfere?"

"No! Of course I wanted to interfere. I hate the Directive. It slows everything down so much. It keeps secrets from us. Hobbles our research. Impedes . . ." He broke into a fit of coughing. McCoy was up instantly, holding a small medical scanner over the man's back. Before Richter could recover enough to push him away, McCoy had held a spray hypo to the scientist's arm.

Richter took in a deep breath. His congestion was noticeably lessened. "But what could I do about it?" he continued irritably, waving McCoy aside. "One scientist among many here. And all so dedicated to noninterference—to just standing back and doing *nothing."*

This time he managed to keep his grip on his cane as he rapped it against the floor. "But the others—the aliens—*were* interfering. I didn't know why. I wasn't sure how. But that wasn't important. The Talin saw them, talked about them, tried to hunt them down. I thought that if I kept what I suspected a secret, kept the controversy over their Richter rating going, then someday the Talin would succeed. They'd capture one of the aliens' ships. Or one of our own Wraiths."

"You wanted that to happen?" the vice admiral asked accusingly.

"Yes," Richter said. "Because then the Talin would know for certain that there were other civilizations in the galaxy. And that would mean, according to the Federation's own rules, it would be time for their 'normal' development to be at an end. The Prime Directive would cease to apply and we could finally talk to them.

Learn from them. Know so much more." Richter closed his eyes. Spock could see tears of frustration well up in them. "You people just don't understand how much there is to know. How little time there is to find it all out." He covered his face with his hands.

Kirk spoke gently but with concern. "Dr. Richter, what I don't understand is that if you were so set on circumventing the Prime Directive, why did you react so strongly when you thought there might be a chance that the *Enterprise* could be sighted by the Talin astronauts?"

Richter didn't look up. "If you, or the FCO, had done anything to break the Prime Directive, then Starfleet would have shut us down and sealed the system. But if those other aliens had been revealed, or the Talin had discovered us by their own efforts, then the whole planet would be wide open." He raised his head to look at Kirk. "Instantly. No wasted time."

Hammersmith studied the desktop for a few moments. "Dr. Richter, sir, do you understand that by not cooperating with Starfleet's First Contact Office, and by not following the provisions of the Prime Directive, that you might have contributed to the disaster that befell Talin IV?"

"I didn't want that," Richter said in a strangled voice.

"No one ever does, Doctor. That's why we have the Prime Directive. So we won't be in a hurry. So we won't rush in blindly when there are entire worlds at stake."

"Too little time," Richter whispered.

"For you and me," Hammersmith said, "perhaps. But not for the Federation, Dr. Richter. The Federation can afford to be patient. We're going to be here for a long, long time."

Spock waited with Kirk and Hammersmith outside the director's complex as McCoy treated the exhausted Richter.

"What happens now?" Kirk asked grimly.

Hammersmith was equally concerned. "I don't know, Kirk. With what Richter said in there, and Wilforth's admission that he thought Richter might be hiding something but didn't want to put pressure on the man . . . it's a mess. Starfleet's going to have to launch a brand-new inquiry. It's going to take years to sort out . . ." He shook his head. "I just don't know."

But Kirk wouldn't accept that. "What's to sort out? There were other aliens interfering with Talin IV's normal development so they could grow mutated algae—or whatever it is—in the oceans. That makes it an open-and-shut case."

Hammersmith glared at Kirk. "Don't tell me what's open and shut. I understand how you feel, Kirk. You lost your command. Maybe it was your fault, maybe it wasn't, but that's not the only consideration here."

"But it is! It all comes down to the Prime Directive. And with the presence of the other aliens—the Prime Directive does not apply."

"What other aliens, Kirk? You heard Richter in there. He *suspected* their presence. That's all. Suspected."

"What about the images from Talin?" Kirk asked.

"What about them? They're computer data from a devastated world. Those disks passed through an FCO facility where a chief scientist admits he was trying to subvert the Prime Directive. Those data could have been manipulated a thousand different ways. It will take years for Starfleet experts to authenticate them. *If* they are legitimate. There's nothing else that can be done."

Kirk was speechless.

Spock wasn't. "Excuse me, Vice Admiral, but I believe you are mistaken. There is another option open to us which might settle this situation once and for all."

"What, Mr. Spock?"

But Kirk saw it instantly. "Find the aliens who were interfering with Talin."

Hammersmith spread his arms. "Be my guest. If they're real, they've only been flying around in front of the FCO for the past eight years without anyone there noticing them. Care to guess how many years it's going to take you?"

"It will take approximately three hours," Spock said.

Hammersmith and Kirk stared at him.

Spock returned their stares with a quizzical expression. "I know where they are," he said.

In another office, Spock switched on the desk display and swung the screen around so Kirk and Hammersmith could see it. Then he called up input channel forty-five. A graphic representation of Talin IV and its moon appeared.

"A standard orbital map," Hammersmith said. "What does this prove?"

"By itself, nothing," Spock agreed. "However, I shall use it to plot additional information." He pressed a control on the desk computer. A small red triangle flashed on the picture of Talin IV.

"Is that a military base like the other ones you were showing us?" Hammersmith asked.

"No," Kirk said. "I know those coordinates. That's the site of the missile silo where the warhead exploded."

"Exactly," Spock said. He pressed another control. A small blue dot appeared in fixed orbit over Talin.

"That's a geostationary orbit," Kirk explained. "It's one of the sensor satellites we deployed."

"Correct, Captain."

Kirk put his hands on the desk to lean closer to the display. "Just a minute. Is that sensor satellite number five?"

Spock stood back. He had no need to explain anything more to Kirk.

"What's important about satellite five?" Hammersmith asked.

Kirk adjusted the controls so that the display rotated the image of Talin IV. "Satellite five malfunctioned. All its transtator circuitry was wiped clean."

"That's impossible, isn't it?" Hammersmith asked. "I mean, for an FCO sensor satellite? They're armored."

"It *was* right overhead," Kirk said excitedly.

"What is?" Hammersmith asked.

"That's got to be it!" Kirk adjusted the controls again. "Look here. The satellite was deployed almost exactly over the area of the missile silo installation. Whatever kind of signal went down to the silo passed directly through the satellite and wiped out its memory."

Hammersmith didn't follow Kirk's reasoning. "A detonation signal was transmitted from space?"

"No," Kirk said. "The warhead blew up long after the satellite was crippled.

The signal that wiped the satellite must have realigned the missile warhead's circuitry so it would go off as soon as the Talin tried to disarm it. It must have been something similar to what Scotty used on the Talin's lunar warheads." He snapped his fingers. "Spock! If a signal of that strength wasn't focused, but was allowed to spread throughout the entire system . . ."

Spock nodded. "It would effectively block virtually all subspace transmissions, which could explain the *Enterprise*'s failure to receive Outpost 47's emergency messages."

"But where did the signal come from?" Hammersmith protested.

Kirk stood back from the desk as he watched the display draw in the final details of the diagram Spock had started. "It came from the most logical place of all, correct, Mr. Spock?"

"Exactly, Captain."

On the display, the computer showed the continuation of a straightline transmission beam that reached from the missile silo, through sensor satellite five, and from there directly to the perfect base for observing Talin IV—its moon.

Eleven

The lunar dust of Talin's moon drifted up in a small eddy, disturbed by the vortex of transporter energy which swirled above it. Seconds later, the dust of that moon was marked by Kirk's footsteps.

Kirk peered through the faceplate of his environmental suit at what waited for him on the brightly lit lunar landscape. Spock's plotting had been precise, and it had taken the science officer only one hour to make his calculations instead of the three he had originally estimated.

"Kirk to *Exeter*." His voice sounded odd in the closed-in space of the helmet he wore. "The coordinates are perfect."

He heard the *Exeter*'s transporter technician reply. "Energizing."

Three more columns of sparkling light appeared. They coalesced into Spock, McCoy, and Uhura.

Kirk heard Uhura gasp in astonishment.

Spock immediately held up a vacuum-armored tricorder. "Fascinating."

McCoy checked his own scanners and grunted in disbelief. Then his voice crackled over the helmet speaker. "Forget 'fascinating,' Spock. How about downright impossible?"

On the barren rocks and soil of Talin's moon, beneath the blazing radiation of unfiltered sunlight and completely exposed to the hard vacuum of space, there was life.

Kirk moved forward with long, low-gravity strides to meet it.

What he approached was obviously a base of sorts. Parts of it were alien. Parts of it were understandable. Kirk could see about twenty of the sleek, pinch-waisted shuttles hidden in the shadows of a rocky overhang. Each shuttle was about ten meters long—though no two were exactly the same, and while some were parked neatly side by side, others were stacked on top of each other like a pile of kindling. The overhang had protected them from direct overhead observation by the Talin and the FCO, though Kirk couldn't understand why the rest of the base had not been detected by the FCO's long-range scans—especially the aliens. There were hundreds of them.

The aliens' bodies reminded Kirk of wasps, but with only two segments, mottled with black and glistening silver. Their basic shapes were also similar to the shuttles', though the creatures were only between one and two meters in length. They were supported and moved across the lunar soil by two sets of four spindly silver legs each. One set sprang from their forward segment, the other set from their hind segment, and their bodies were slung beneath their highest leg joints like a spider's.

The aliens' legs ended in wide flattened pads which kept them from sinking into the loose lunar soil. Kirk noticed that some of the creatures moved slowly around their base, while others scuttled back and forth faster than a human could run, sometimes springing ten meters in a single jump.

Cautiously, Kirk edged closer to the creatures as they swarmed around their shuttles and the large silver and black domes that were scattered nearby. So far, they had not acted as if they had detected him or the others, but he kept his vacuum phaser drawn and ready. He reminded himself that these creatures had destroyed a world.

Kirk stopped ten meters from the nearest dome—it looked as if metallic lava had bubbled out of the ground and frozen solid. The creatures crawled over it and around it, their forward legs tapping soundlessly all over its surface while their hind legs propelled them. From the corner of his faceplate, Kirk saw the rest of his landing party draw nearer to his position.

"They're not in any sort of pressure suits, are they, Spock?" Kirk asked.

"Indeed not," Spock answered. "Their exterior carapaces seem impervious to the vacuum and the radiation of space."

"Are they machines?" Uhura asked. Kirk saw her working with a large, flat computer board with enlarged controls for use by personnel in protective gear.

"That's the incredible part," McCoy answered, checking his medical scanners. "They've got organic parts inside. There are pressurized pockets in them but don't ask me how. And free water. A high metabolism rate. I wouldn't be surprised if they're living off the radiation from the sun somehow."

Kirk was fascinated by the aliens' thin legs. They seemed to be made of solid metal. "Are they some kind of artificial construct, Spock? Organics built into a mechanical shell?"

"I see no indication of anything artificial in their structure, Captain. I believe that these are living creatures, either genetically engineered or independently evolved to live in hard vacuum."

"Sir," Uhura interrupted. "I am picking up a great deal of low-level radio static. And it seems to be coming from these . . . things."

"Try to localize it, Uhura." Kirk watched as one of the creatures scurried only two meters from him without slowing. It carried a chunk of lunar rock. "Any idea what kind of sensory organs they might have, Spock?"

"None whatsoever, Captain. I am continuing with my readings."

A second alien followed the path made by the first, also carrying lunar material. Then a third carrier went by. Kirk stepped forward into the pockmarked trail left by their footpads. A fourth came along and bumped into Kirk, almost knocking him over. Kirk was shaken by the unexpected force of the creature's impact, but he stayed upright.

"Be careful, Captain. Their legs obviously have great strength," Spock warned.

Kirk remained motionless as the alien that had collided with him dropped the rock it carried and raised itself on its hind legs until its segments were at Kirk's waist level. Its forward segment angled upward and its second set of legs waved out like insect feelers until they made contact with him.

Kirk heard Spock's urgent message. "Spock to *Exeter*. Lock transporter on the captain and prepare for emergency beam-out on my signal."

"It's all right, Spock," Kirk said. He kept completely still as the creature's legs tapped lightly all over him, following the contours of his silver environmental suit and the paths of the red and blue life-support tubes. "Their forward legs are their sensory organs. It's including me in its interior map of its surroundings."

The creature finished tracing Kirk, then dropped back down to its original stance, picked up its rock, and diverted around him. Relieved, Kirk placed his phaser on its adhesion patch at the side of his suit.

"How are your pressure readings, Captain? Did the creature create any punctures?" Spock asked.

Kirk glanced down at the indicator lights built into his helmet. "All readings are green, Spock. You can cancel the transpor—"

Another creature came charging toward him. Kirk braced himself for impact. But the creature smoothly swerved just as the first one had done after its examination of Kirk.

"Fascinating," Spock said. "Apparently they can communicate through the vacuum."

Kirk's next idea was impossible, but then so were the creatures. "Uhura, is there any chance that the creatures are communicating by radio transmissions?"

"I—uh, why not? I'll try to link up with one." Uhura bounded over to where two of the creatures were stroking a small silverish bubble that appeared to have sprouted from the ground. One was exuding a dull black paste from an opening in its forward segment and then rubbing the substance against the bubble. Nearby, another creature appeared to be actually consuming rocks which had been deliberately stacked near it. Kirk wondered if he were watching the creatures process building materials.

Kirk hopped back to Spock and McCoy. "Any idea what those bubbles are?" he asked. "Or what they're made from?"

"They are composed of the same substance as the creatures' carapaces, and the coverings of the shuttles," Spock added. "Their composition is also virtually identical to that of the surrounding rocks and soils." Spock glanced down at his tricorder. "Captain, I believe that we must be looking at different versions of the same life-form. Or at the very least, different species who share the same evolutionary past."

"Are you saying the *shuttles* are alive?"

Spock pointed his tricorder in the direction of the shuttles. "They appear to be dormant in the shadow of the overhang, but their shape and coloration are suggestive of the smaller creatures."

"Jim, I'm picking up something odd from one of the bubbles," McCoy suddenly said. "That one over there."

McCoy took two long strides to land beside a bubble almost five meters in circumference. Its surface was like the creatures', mottled silver and black, shining in some areas, dull in others.

"Bones, do you think they could be egg casings?" Kirk asked. "Like a horta's?"

"That's what I thought at first, too," McCoy said. His gloved fingers worked clumsily at the scanner he held to the bubble. "I *am* getting life readings from it, but they're different from the ones I took from the creatures themselves."

"Odd," Spock confirmed, reading from his own tricorder. "There appears to be a pressurized atmosphere inside. Well insulated, and with a quantity of liquid water."

"But what *kind* of life-form's in there?" Kirk asked.

"Low-level plant analogue, Captain."

"Plant life?" Kirk repeated. "You're sure there's nothing higher?"

"Most certain," Spock confirmed.

Kirk pulled his phaser from the side of his suit, twisted the intensity setting on it, and fired at the bubble before either Spock or McCoy could say anything to change his mind.

A long stream of white vapor sprayed up from the small hole the phaser beam made. The vapor instantly changed to solid crystals and for a few moments it appeared to snow around the bubble. As the crystals sublimated in the vacuum, the area around the bubble slowly cleared again. The only difference now was that a thick sludge oozed from the hole, freezing as it fell to the ground in fist-size chunks. It glittered with a white gloss of fine frost, but the color of the sludge was apparent: purple.

"It's algae, isn't it?" Kirk said. "The same organism that's taken over the oceans of Talin IV."

Spock held his tricorder to the mass of thick, freezing material that pushed through the bubble's skin. "You are correct, Captain. But how did you decide this? It is not an obvious conclusion."

McCoy didn't agree. "Why not, Spock? The creatures are probably growing their food down there."

"Doctor McCoy, as both our readings show, these creatures do not require food. They thrive on hard radiation. The algae cannot sustain them."

Kirk saw a flurry of movement to the side. A herd of twenty creatures was leaping directly toward the leaking bubble. "Stand back, gentlemen. Looks like the repair crew has arrived."

The three men jumped away from the bubble just as the creatures swarmed around and over it. They quickly found the hole and cleaned the frozen algae away. Then Kirk saw several creatures, smaller and shinier than the others, who appeared at the edge of the repair team. The larger creatures formed a chain and passed the smaller ones over their bodies until they were deposited at the side of the bubble. The smaller creatures' footpads were twice the size of the larger creatures' pads and when they rubbed them over the hole, the pads began to glow white hot, melting the skin of the bubble to heal the opening.

"I hope you're recording that, Spock," McCoy said. "Because even seeing it myself I don't believe it."

"Captain!" It was Uhura calling. Kirk tried to find her silverclad form.

"State your location, Uhura," he said.

"Near the east side of the overhang, Captain. And you were right, sir—they *are* talking over radio frequencies!"

Uhura had found a large boulder on which to place her computer panel.

Nearby, one creature methodically ripped apart a second. The second creature did not try to escape. A small pile of other disassembled creatures was nearby.

Uhura laboriously punched in commands on the panel. "I'm patching through their main channel to our helmet speakers, sir. They seem to be able to generate low-frequency radio waves through an organ in their forward segment. They don't have much range, but the ability is definitely there."

McCoy stepped over to examine the creature, casting his shadow across it. "How can a being evolve an organ to take advantage of radio?"

Spock answered. "Life constantly adapts to use the features of the environment in which it finds itself, Doctor. Our eyes have evolved to sense electromagnetic radiation of certain frequencies. Radio waves are also electromagnetic waves at other frequencies. It is a predictable development, however unlikely."

Suddenly Kirk's helmet speaker crackled with a confused flurry of static.

"That's their language?" McCoy asked.

"That's a raw signal," Uhura explained. "I'm going to tie it through the universal translator."

"Captain," Spock began, "since this language is completely alien, it will take the translator several hours to supply equivalent cognates. I suggest we return to the *Exeter* to replenish our consumables."

"Good idea, Spock. Then we can—"

"Strange life block food." It was the clipped, mechanical voice of the universal translator circuitry. *"Strange life block food over here over here."*

McCoy smirked. "Several hours? I guess you missed reading about a few upgrades to the translator, Mr. Spock."

"No, Doctor," Uhura said. "The universal translator shouldn't have been able to even start decoding this kind of language for hours." She held the computer board at an angle to clumsily punch in more commands. "I hate these gloves," she complained.

At the same time, the translator's voice kept repeating, *"Strange life block food over here over here. Strange life—"*

"Any idea what it means, Spock?"

"I'll let you know in a moment, Captain."

Suddenly, McCoy shouted in surprise, and Kirk awkwardly turned to see four creatures grab the doctor's legs. "Kirk to *Exeter!*" he transmitted. His hand went to his phaser. The creatures dragged McCoy through the lunar dirt by his feet, sending up a cloud of billion-year-old dust.

Then they let him go.

Kirk leapt over to him. "Are you all right, Bones?"

"Just fine," McCoy grumbled. He pushed himself up from the ground. His suit was streaked with black lunar soil. "And thank you for your help, Mr. Spock. From where you were standing, you must have seen them coming."

"I did, Doctor."

"Then why didn't you do something about it?" Kirk asked.

"The creatures were simply responding to their fellow being's call for assistance. Dr. McCoy's shadow covered the creature we were observing, thus cutting off its supply of food—the sun's radiation. As you will notice, the creature's transmission has now ceased."

McCoy hopped back to join Uhura and Spock. "You might have warned me anyway."

"Yes," Spock said. "I suppose I might have. Next time, Dr. McCoy."

Kirk went to Uhura. "Good work, Uhura. How'd you get such a quick translation?"

"The creatures are speaking in a language already known to the translator, sir." Uhura turned to look questioningly at Kirk through her faceplate. "They are speaking in the primary language of Talin."

"Spock, analysis." Kirk was at a loss for an explanation. The creatures could not possibly be indigenous to Talin. Neither did the planet have the genetic engineering technology to create them.

"Sir, if my preliminary conclusions are correct, then what we see here are not intelligent life-forms. They are little more than worker insects, a group hive mentality which has worked to make Talin IV a suitable environment for growing the algaelike organism. In the absence of any language of their own, and given that they are able to transmit and receive radio messages, it seems likely that they have absorbed the Talin language by listening to the planet's radio transmissions over the years."

"Years, Spock?" McCoy asked.

"In the time that this system has been under FCO jurisdiction, no alien vessels have been sighted entering it. Therefore, the creatures have been here since before the FCO arrived."

"Sharing the same moon," Kirk mused. "And no one ever detected them."

"Since their carapaces are composed of the same material which covers this moon, it seems probable that the creatures reproduce by constructing duplicates of themselves from the raw materials at hand. The FCO's general scans would not have been able to distinguish the drones from their surroundings. I shall recommend to Starfleet that, in the future, airless planetoids should be scanned for small pockets of organic surface life contained within apparently nonliving shells."

Kirk watched as the nearby creatures finished ripping apart their victim. *No, not victim,* Kirk corrected himself. Obviously what he was watching was a part of their life cycle. No sooner were the pieces of the first creature dragged away, than another creature hurried up, also to be disassembled. One of its legs appeared to be damaged. *How efficient,* Kirk thought uneasily.

McCoy was still caught by Spock's explanation of the creatures' language. "So what you're saying, Spock, is that these things are like mindless parrots, just mimicking what they've heard?"

"Not at all, Doctor. The fact that one of them was able to complain about the shadow you cast indicates that they have also absorbed some of the language's context and meaning, just as some Earth primates have learned to use symbolic languages, though they cannot develop such languages on their own."

Kirk checked his suit's oxygen level. They would have to beam up in less than twenty minutes, and Spock and McCoy would have ample time to continue their discussion then. "Forget the details, Spock. The bottom line is that if these creatures have a language that they use, then we can use it, too."

"To do what?" McCoy asked.

"Why, Bones," Kirk said. "To talk to them."

Kirk hopped over to the creature that had complained about McCoy's shadow. It used its forward legs to grip onto a section of the creature being taken apart, then kept twisting the section around in the same direction, almost in an unscrewing motion, until it fell off. The creature being dismantled did not appear to experience any discomfort.

"Uhura," Kirk said, "can you link my helmet communicator to this one right here?"

Uhura brought her board over. "Aye, sir. Setting the frequencies now. Go ahead." Kirk moved to cast his shadow on the creature.

The translator circuits came to life instantly. *"Strange life block food over here over here. Strange life block food."*

Kirk spoke. "Would you like the food to continue?"

"Yes food eat." Uhura's link worked both ways.

Kirk stepped aside, then, after a few moments, he blocked the sun once more. The creature went into its recitation.

"Would you like the food to continue?" Kirk asked again.

"Yes food eat."

"Then tell me who you are."

The creature didn't protest or try to negotiate. *"We are the Many."*

Kirk was relieved. He had been worried that once his questions and the creature's replies had been passed back and forth through Standard, into Talin, and then into the creature's own internal system that there would be no common ground for communication. But it appeared Dr. Richter was correct. Life was almost the same everywhere, no matter what its chemistry.

"Do you know what I am?" he continued.

"You are strange life. Give back food now." As if it were running low on energy, the alien stopped disassembling the other creature.

Kirk stepped aside and let the alien have a few more seconds of light. It began to move again.

"Do you know where you are?" Kirk was carefully proceeding only one step at a time in his questioning.

"Here," the creature answered. It apparently did not need the threat of light starvation to answer questions. Though Kirk doubted with that kind of answer that he was going to be able to get much useful information from such a basic mind.

"What do you do here?"

"Work," the alien answered readily. It twisted a leg off the motionless creature before it.

"Why do you work?" Kirk asked.

The alien did not respond.

Spock did. "Captain, if you are indeed conversing with a mind that functions at little more than an instinctual level, it will not be able to understand higher concepts such as motivation. It would be like asking a paramecium why it absorbs food. It is not a conscious decision."

"But, Spock, there has to be some conscious intelligence at work here," Kirk argued. "Think of what they accomplished on Talin. They were able to manipulate the entire planetary defense system. They realigned warhead circuitry. Blocked our sensors and deflectors. Launched Talin missiles at us. How could they do all that without conscious thought?"

"Sir, everything these creatures did was achieved by altering the functions of electronic and transtator-based machinery. At the most elementary level, all that they did was to simply manipulate the data that passed through that equipment."

Kirk heard Spock take a breath. It sounded almost like a sigh. "Captain, just as birds can fly without conscious knowledge of aerodynamics, and a virus can reprogram the complex chemistry of a living host without any awareness, these creatures can apparently provoke nuclear exchanges on a planet without any conscious knowledge of the cultures they are manipulating."

McCoy was appalled by the analogy. "There's a huge gap between flapping some wings and blowing up a planet, Mr. Spock."

"Only in degree, Doctor. As we have all seen in our voyages, given enough time, virtually any characteristic can be evolved. Given enough time, virtually any behavior can be learned."

Kirk stared at the dismemberment ritual going on before him. "They've done this before, haven't they?"

"Undoubtedly, Captain. Perhaps millions of times, to achieve this level of sophistication. Their identification of the master circuit nodes in the *Enterprise* was quite precise."

Kirk's mind reeled at the destruction that these creatures might have caused throughout the galaxy to grow food they couldn't use. He wouldn't accept that it was arbitrary action. No matter how they had evolved, no matter how their behavior had been learned, somehow, somewhere, there had to be a reason for it.

He stood in the sunlight and blocked the creature's food again.

"Why do the Many work?" he demanded.

The creature still did not respond.

"Captain, it cannot answer."

"Did you *hear* me?" Kirk said. *"Why do the Many work?"* He kicked a cloud of slowly falling lunar dust at the creature but it continued its task without pause.

"Jim, let it go. Spock's right. It's like questioning a child."

Child, Kirk thought. He stared at the creature before him, silver and black mottles covering its body. He looked at the bubbles in which the algae grew—bubbles *grown* from the same mottled substance created from the lunar rock. And the shuttles, lying dormant in the shadows—the same shape, the same substance, the same . . . skin. Spock had said they were different forms of the same species, or different species with a common ancestor. That was the answer. It had to be.

"What is your work?" he asked, changing his approach.

The creature stopped moving its legs, running out of energy in Kirk's shadow.

"What is your work?" he repeated.

The translator came online. *"To sow the seeds of life."*

"Why?"

"To grow food."

But they don't eat the food, Kirk thought. *They don't need the food.*

"Why do the Many grow food? What *purpose* does the food serve?"

The creature's footpads scrabbled weakly in the loose soil as it tried to crawl out from beneath Kirk's shadow. Kirk moved with it, keeping it blocked, knowing his conversation with it was preventing it from calling for help over the same frequency.

"I said, why do the Many grow the food?"

"The Many grow the food for the One," the creature finally answered.

Kirk stopped. "The One?" he said. "What is the One?"

"The One is that which consumes the food," the creature said.

Obviously the drones were not the One because what could a hive mentality know about individuality? Kirk thought. He began to feel a cold chill of apprehension.

"When will the One consume the food?" Kirk asked.

"When the One is here."

"Where is the One now?"

A burst of static rushed from the helmet speaker.

"Uhura," Kirk asked anxiously. "What did the creature say? What language was that?"

Uhura studied the readouts on her computer board. "Sir, that wasn't a language. That was . . ." She put the board down and turned to Kirk.

"Sir, the creature transmitted coordinates."

Twelve

"Let me get this straight," Styles said. "You and the *Enterprise* aren't guilty of any wrongdoing because of a colony of vacuum-breathing, rock-eating insects, which—even though they have no intelligence—were somehow able to trick the Talin into blowing themselves up?" The lieutenant did not bother to disguise his sarcasm. "You've beamed out once too often, Kirk. I always knew it would happen."

Kirk and Styles glared at each other in the director's complex at Outpost 47. Neither had forgotten their first—and last—tour together on the *Farragut.*

But Vice Admiral Hammersmith was interested in other matters. "Stow it, Lieutenant. You, too, Kirk." He glanced down at Wilforth's desk and again read the printout sheet of the coordinates of "the One."

"How could they know our coordinate system, anyway?"

Uhura answered. "The universal translator converted the aliens' coordinate system to Talin astronomical conventions, and then to our quadrant and sector standards, sir."

Hammersmith looked at Spock. "Do you accept this as reliable data, Mr. Spock?"

"The drones had no reason to lie to us, assuming that they have the capability, sir. However, I cannot vouch for what might actually occupy those coordinates."

Hammersmith swept aside the qualification. "But you do have a theory, don't you? You must have a theory."

"Yes, sir, I do."

After a long pause, McCoy said, "For heaven's sake, tell the man, Spock."

"I believe we will find a related group of creatures who will be arriving to consume the algae which the seeder drones have planted on Talin IV."

McCoy shook his head. "Uh uh. Not related creatures. There's got to be some intelligence at work here someplace. The drones' behavior is far too complex to ever have come about by chance. The One has got to be a colony ship—an alien colony ship that sent these things ahead to prepare a world the aliens can live on. The seeder drones aren't naturally evolved creatures—they're a living terraforming machine. Only they aren't making Talin IV like Earth."

Spock closed his eyes in subtle exasperation. "Doctor, if you would study the facts as have been recorded, you would—"

"I *have* studied the facts, Spock, and that's why—"

"Mr. Kirk," Hammersmith boomed to stop the altercation. "How about you? What's your theory?"

Kirk loathed the vice admiral's use of "mister" but he wasn't going to show his anger in front of Styles. "I don't have a theory. Theories can wait until we get out there and see what it is we're dealing with firsthand."

Hammersmith nodded. "Yes, I suppose that's what has to be done."

"Good," Kirk said. "Then may I request that—"

"I'll put it into my report to Starfleet Command," Hammersmith added.

"What?" Kirk asked.

"You heard the vice admiral," Styles said. "He's going to follow the chain of command. Remember what that is, *Mr.* Kirk?"

"Styles . . ." Hammersmith warned.

"Why bother reporting it until you've gone out there and checked it for yourself?" Kirk asked.

"It's only a half light-year away," McCoy said.

"At warp six, a ship could intercept those coordinates in less than one day," Spock added.

Hammersmith held up his hands to quiet everyone. "No one's going anywhere! Is that clear?"

"Yes, sir," Styles said smartly.

"I've got more than four hundred private vessels already stationkeeping at the edge of this system," Hammersmith went on. "Starfleet's got Greenpeace and the Planetary Society breathing down its neck. Half the galaxy is geared up to send aid to Talin IV and I don't have enough personnel or ships to keep them out as it is."

"By my estimation," Spock offered, "the Council debate should have ended by now."

"Even if it *has* ended, Spock, it's still going to take two days for the subspace relay to reach us." Hammersmith almost sounded apologetic. "And I will not allow any breech of Starfleet's lawful blockade of Talin IV until the question of the Prime Directive is resolved and I am ordered to withdraw my ships."

McCoy crossed his arms angrily. "You *know* how the Council will vote, Vice Admiral! They have no choice but to rule in Talin's favor."

Hammersmith stood up behind his desk and leaned forward on his fists. "No, I don't know that, Doctor. The Council isn't ruling on wars being started by nonintelligent aliens who say they're working for 'the One,' whatever that is. They are debating the legal question which Mr. Spock raised about whether or not Talin was already a *de facto* member of the Federation when the disaster occurred. That's a mighty big loophole in the Articles of Federation and the Council's vote on that could go either way."

Spock tried to intercede as conciliator. "I agree on that point, Vice Admiral. However, you must be aware that when Starfleet receives the evidence we have uncovered here concerning alien intervention in the affairs of Talin, the question of the Prime Directive will not even have to go to Council. It does not apply."

"That's right, Spock. *When* Starfleet receives this evidence and *accepts* this evidence, then and only then will a ruling be made."

"The vice admiral is absolutely right," Styles said.

"Oh, be quiet!" Kirk ordered the lieutenant. "Look, Vice Admiral, you've got a dying planet down there. You've got hundreds of people willing to help save it. Let them do it. Take down the blockade."

Hammersmith was a man trapped in a nightmarish dilemma. "Kirk, believe me, I know what I've got on Talin IV. I wish I had a way out of this. But there are so many possible ways this thing could go, I don't have justifiable grounds for breaking orders. You lost your career over this, Kirk. Don't make me lose mine while there's still some good I can do here."

Kirk turned away in disgust. If Hammersmith wasn't going to help, then Kirk wasn't going to waste any more time with him. "Spock, Bones, we'll go out of system to the *Ian Shelton*. Her captain will take us out to the coordinates and—"

"The *Ian Shelton*," Hammersmith interrupted. "Is that Anne Gauvreau's freighter?"

"Yes," Kirk said suspiciously.

"She's not going anywhere. The *Shelton*'s a Federation registry vessel and Starfleet has commandeered her for picket duty."

"What about the *Queen Mary?*" McCoy suggested. "It doesn't smell too—"

"The Orion ship's been impounded," Hammersmith said. "And it's now serving picket duty as well. Face it, gentlemen, you aren't going anywhere. Every warp-capable ship is bouncing around the system turning back blockade runners."

The answer hit Kirk like a phaser bolt. "Every *warp-capable* ship, Vice Admiral? Is that what you said?"

Hammersmith nodded. It was his turn to be wary.

"Then you don't mean the *Enterprise?*" Kirk asked.

"What do you mean, he doesn't mean the *Enterprise?*" Styles blurted. "I've spent three months getting her warp capable again. She's got new warp nacelles and . . ."

Hammersmith looked thoughtful. "Brand new, unrated warp nacelles. Which have to be tuned into balance well away from the gravity well of a star so the ship won't risk hitting a wormhole."

"That means she's not warp capable *within* the system," Kirk concluded. "She's no use to you here."

"This is preposterous!" Styles fumed.

Kirk grinned. "You said you wished you had a way out of this, Vice Admiral. I think you've got one staring you right in your forward sensors."

Hammersmith smiled then, too. "But who do I have who can take her out?"

"Excuse me, Vice Admiral?" Styles said weakly.

Hammersmith sat back in his chair. "I mean, you three aren't part of Starfleet anymore. You're embassy officials, of all things."

"Vice Admiral Hammersmith?" Styles tried again.

"Chief Engineer Scott," Kirk said. "Just the officer you'd want to take the *Enterprise* out for operational trials."

"But Vice Admiral Hammersmith," Styles said, raising his voice. "You said the *Enterprise* would be *my* ship."

"Not too far," Kirk promised. "Maybe a half light-year or so?"

Hammersmith nodded his head in agreement, a look of peace coming to his face at last. Kirk had found his compromise. "And I'll ask Mr. Scott if he'd mind taking along some observers from the Talin embassy. Thank you, Kirk."

Styles exploded. "You can't do that! You said she was *mine!*"

Hammersmith turned slowly to Styles, eyes wide. "I beg your pardon, *Lieutenant?*"

Styles stammered.

"Did you just tell a vice admiral what he could or couldn't do?" Hammersmith began to rise from his chair.

Styles was hullmetal white. He glared at Kirk. "Someday, Kirk. Someday I'm going to catch up to you and . . ."

Kirk laughed easily. "Maybe someday, Styles. But the important thing is, that's not today."

Thirteen

The *Enterprise* coursed through the vacuum at full impulse power, racing light itself, until the orbital boundary of the system's last cold planet fell behind her.

On the bridge of the reborn ship, Lieutenant Kyle read aloud the astrogator's present coordinates. "We have left the Talin system, Mr. Scott."

Scott rose from the central chair. "Aye, and it's about bloody time." He turned to where Kirk and Spock and McCoy stood on the elevated deck by the science station. "Captain Kirk," he said proudly, holding his hand out to the empty chair. "Would you please sit down?"

Kirk stared at the conn. For almost four months he had awakened from dreams in which he was just about to take his natural place there—only to have it spin off into space without him. "I'm not a captain at the moment, Mr. Scott."

"You will be again soon enough."

Kirk shook his head. There would be time enough for that later. If there were a later.

Scott tilted his head and looked at Kirk with mock annoyance.

"Captain Kirk, you don't leave me any choice. As the duly appointed commander of this vessel, sir, I *order* you to sit in that chair."

Kirk looked at Spock. "He can't order a civilian, can he?"

Spock arched an eyebrow. "He is the commander of the vessel."

McCoy sighed. "Well, if you don't, I will. Now get down there."

Kirk stepped down to the center deck, helped by a push from McCoy. "I'll try to give her back to you in one piece, Scotty."

"I'm sure the vice admiral would be most appreciative." Scott looked around the bridge. "Och, now what happened to the other three?"

Twelve hours later, flashing through warp space, the *Enterprise* neared the co-ordinates the drone had transmitted.

"There *is* an object there," Chekov said, reading the navigation board displays. He and Sulu had also been "ordered" by Scott to take their stations, as had Uhura.

Kirk leaned forward in his chair. He had stopped thinking about how strange it seemed to see half his bridge crew dressed in civilian clothes. He only thought about what lay ahead—at the coordinates of the One.

"Sensors confirm, Captain," Spock announced from his science station.

"Well, what is it, Spock?" McCoy stood by the captain's chair, arms folded. "A spaceship, right?"

"We are still too distant to tell, Doctor. But if it is a ship, it is larger than any we have seen before."

Kirk turned in his chair. "We've seen some pretty big ships in our day, Mr. Spock."

"I believe we are about to see another."

Kirk looked back to the viewscreen. Nothing showed there yet except the computer's rendition of moving stars. "How much longer to intercept, Mr. Sulu?"

"Just over two hours at this factor, Captain."

Kirk hit the com switch on his chair arm. "Mr. Scott, how are the warp generators coming along?"

Scott answered over the bridge speakers. "You wouldn't believe the changes they've made in them since the last pair we had, sir."

"Is that good or bad, Scotty?"

"Captain, if a thing's not broke, then why fix it?"

McCoy and Kirk shared a smile. "But can you handle them, Scotty?"

There was a long pause from engineering.

"Are you still there, Mr. Scott?"

"Aye, Captain. You want to know if I can give you more power from these bairns, don't you?"

McCoy had to turn his back to avoid laughing out loud.

"That would be appreciated, Mr. Scott."

Scott sighed. "Give me a few minutes, and I'll see what I can do."

"I can tell things are finally getting back to normal," McCoy said.

Kirk settled into his chair and gestured at the brightly colored shirt McCoy wore. "Now if we could only get you some normal clothes to wear."

Before McCoy could reply, the sound of the ship changed. She had been running rougher than before, but that was part of the break-in period her new warp generators required. However, now there was a second unusual harmonic added to the sound of them.

"Captain," Sulu announced, "our speed is increasing. Mr. Scott has boosted the power output. New estimated time of arrival is fifteen minutes, sir."

Spock stared intently into his science scope. "Captain, whatever it is we are approaching, it is not a ship."

"Then what the blazes is it?" McCoy asked. Kirk could hear the disappointment in the doctor's voice as he realized his theory was incorrect. McCoy didn't mind being wrong from time to time, it was just that he hated it when Spock was right.

"Is it a collection of life-forms like the seeder drones?" Kirk asked. At full magnification, the viewscreen was just beginning to show a small gray swirl at its center.

"Life sensors are picking up readings consistent with the presence of drones, sir. But they don't begin to account for the mass of the object."

Kirk didn't like the way Spock had said that. Over the years he had become attuned to the subtle variations in his science officer's speech. Whatever he was seeing in his scope, Spock was startled.

"What *is* the mass of it, Mr. Spock?"

Spock straightened from his scope to look at the viewscreen. "According to all readings, Captain, we are approaching a planet. Slightly larger than Talin IV."

"Keptin," Chekov said, "the object . . . the planet . . . is changing course. It's . . . coming toward us, sir."

Changing course? Kirk thought. Then it *must* be a ship. "Spock, can you pick up what kind of propulsion system is being used for something that massive?"

"I can detect nothing," Spock said. "It has simply changed its trajectory."

Kirk contemplated the energies that must be involved in altering the course of something the size of a planet—a planet already traveling fast enough to cross the half light-year to the Talin system in just under sixty years.

"Lieutenant Uhura, go to red alert."

"Aye-aye, sir." The warning sirens sounded and the alert lights flashed.

"Mr. Chekov, Mr. Sulu, prepare phaser banks and photon torpedoes, all tubes."

McCoy was suddenly concerned. "Is that wise, Jim?"

"Whoever is controlling that thing has sent out an advance force that destroyed a world. And they've got a propulsion system that can move a planet-sized mass around without any indication of how they do it." Kirk frowned. "It may not be wise, Bones. But it's safe."

Kirk called down to engineering. "Scotty, we're going to need full power to the shields when we leave warp. But then I'm going to want you to stand ready to get us back up to warp speed instantly, if not sooner."

Scott sighed. "The engines aren't broken in yet, Captain. If they can't take the surge, there'll be a terrible mess to clean up in the nacelles."

Kirk stared at the screen as the object in it grew. There was still no detail apparent, only a shifting gray whorl of what might be tendrils of gas. "Don't worry, Mr. Scott. Those engines are so new they're still under warranty. If they don't work, we'll send them back to the factory."

"Aye," Scott said, "but what worries me is where they're going to send us."

"Captain, we're coming up to intercept," Sulu announced. The object filled more than half the screen now. It was spherical like a planet, and wreathed in dark fog.

"Go to impulse, Mr. Sulu. Whatever it takes to stay ahead of that thing."

The ship shuddered as she dropped from warp space with a slightly unbalanced transition. But the impulse engines ran smoothly.

"Holding at ten thousand kilometers," Sulu said.

Kirk stood to see the viewscreen more clearly. If he were outside the ship on his own, he knew he wouldn't be able to see the planet-sized object at all because of the lack of light, so far from the nearest star. But the ship's sensors were able to amplify the dim starlight from all around and make the object visible on the screen. "There it is, Bones. The One."

McCoy was not impressed. "It looks like a dirty snowball to me." He turned to Spock. "How can a planet out here have a gaseous atmosphere. I thought it was too cold."

"Those swirls of what appear to be fog are not an atmospheric phenomenon, Doctor. They are drones flying around the object. By the billions." Even Spock seemed subdued by the scale.

Kirk tried to picture what that number of drones could do to a world.

"Uhura, are they transmitting anything on radio frequencies?" Kirk asked.

"Yes, sir. Too many of them for the computers to handle. I'll try to lock into the strongest one and tie it in through the translator, but I can't promise anything."

"Do your best," Kirk said. "Spock, if those clouds are drones, then what's beneath them?"

"Maybe nothing," McCoy suggested. "It could be like a beehive. In the winter, the bees form a ball to conserve energy. They hang in the hive and slowly change position so that they each only have to spend a short time on the outside of the ball being exposed to the cold."

"An admirable speculation, Doctor, though incorrect. Sensors show that the matter beneath the drones differs from them. Though our instruments cannot yet make a clear enough reading to tell us what that matter is."

Kirk watched as Sulu made some adjustments to the impulse controls. "Is it changing course again?" he asked.

"No, sir," Sulu said. "But it is accelerating. Only by a few meters per second though. We won't have any trouble staying ahead of it . . . so far."

A rush of static burst from the bridge speakers. "I've got that signal," Uhura said. "Patching it to the translator."

The static warbled, then dropped in loudness as the translator's circuits took over. *Cold cold cold coldcoldcoldcolco—"* The speakers whined piercingly, then clicked off.

"Sorry about that," Uhura said. "Feedback on the translator. Too many similar messages coming in at the same time. I'll try to filter them down again."

Kirk watched the masses of drones writhing over the object. "What's the temperature out there, Spock?"

Spock didn't look up from his scope. "Less than thirty degrees Kelvin."

That didn't make sense to Kirk. "But the seeder drone on Talin's moon slowed right down as soon as I cast a shadow on it. How are these staying active without any sunlight?"

"Obviously, they must be receiving energy from another source," Spock said.

Uhura broke in. "Sir, I can't get anything coherent on normal radio frequencies, but there is a strong, short-range low-frequency signal coming from the object."

"Let's hear it, Uhura."

The bridge speakers hummed with a new sound, low and pulsing. "It's not like the drones' language, but I'll try routing it through that part of the universal translator."

The low pulsing noise dropped in volume. The speakers clicked. *"Hungry. Strange life. Hungry. Consume strange life. Hungry. Faster. Hungry."*

Kirk tapped at his chest. "The seeder drone said that we were strange life. And whatever that was was talking about eating strange life. . . . Mr. Sulu, is that thing still accelerating for us?"

"Yes, sir. Very slowly."

McCoy put his hand on the back of the conn. "Do you think it plans to eat us?"

"That's exactly what I think." Kirk went up to Spock's station. "Mr. Spock, is it possible that somewhere under all those drones there is another life-form?"

"It is difficult for the sensors to penetrate the mass of drone readings. They appear to be in a layer more than one thousand kilometers thick."

"A thousand kilometers," Kirk said, turning back to the screen. "Like insulation against the cold. Living insulation." He went to Uhura. "Open a channel to the subspace frequency you're putting through the translator." Uhura nodded at him to proceed.

"Who are you?" Kirk asked. He shrugged off McCoy's frown. He had to start somewhere.

"I am hungry."

"I," Kirk said. "Not 'we.' Not a hive mentality like the drones. A single individual. *The One."* He remembered the conversation he had had with the seeder drone. "What is your work?" he asked, already knowing what the answer would be.

"To consume life."

Kirk turned to Spock. *"The Many sow the seeds of life. The One consumes life.* They're symbiotes, Spock."

"Yes," Spock agreed. "That would make sense."

"What makes sense?" McCoy asked. "That thing out there doesn't make a bit of sense."

"Where are you going?" Kirk asked the One.

"To get food."

"Where?"

"There."

Kirk was certain he had solved it. "It's in communication with the seeder drones on Talin's moon. It has to be. And the way they damaged the *Enterprise,* they must have subspace capability, as well as radio."

"But how can you know they're in communication with each other?" McCoy asked.

"When I asked the seeder drone where it was, remember what it said. It said 'here.' When I asked this planet creature where it was going, it said 'there.' Simple concepts for simple, basic, rudimentary minds."

Chekov called for Kirk's attention. "Keptin, I am picking up a configuration change. The creature is . . . altering itself."

On the screen, the random gray tendrils of the massed drones were forming into a central vortex which covered half the area of the sphere's visible side. The outer edges of the gray cloud spun out ahead of the rest like clay on a potter's wheel while the inner surface became sharply concave, dipping in toward the hidden surface.

"Mr. Spock?" Kirk asked as a pale red glow began to appear in the deepest section of the growing planet-size whirlpool.

"The covering of drones is thinning, Captain. Our sensors are beginning to penetrate to whatever lies below."

The apparition on the viewscreen was no longer a solid sphere. It had opened up, the edges of it stretching outward like straining tentacles. The glow from the interior was brightening steadily, red and pulsing.

"It's trying to eat us," McCoy said, unusually restrained. "It's opening its mouth."

"Still accelerating, Captain," Sulu announced.

"Stay ahead of those tendrils," Kirk ordered. He turned to Spock. "What do the sensors show, Mr. Spock? What's inside that thing?"

Spock turned away from his scope, and to Kirk it seemed as if the science officer were abandoning it. "Captain, there is no doubt that the creature is alive." Spock sounded hesitant. The deep red tunnel which had formed within the creature, large enough now to swallow a world, flashed with odd purple bolts of energy. But the bolts arced and branched in lines which followed smooth and perfect curves, not the jagged streaks of ordinary energy discharges.

"And the lining of the creature's tendrils does have the capability of consuming and metabolizing the algae that grows on Talin IV," Spock continued.

"The lining of the tendrils?" Kirk said. On the screen, the tendrils appeared to be made of red glowing gas or shaped energy. "Are the tendrils solid matter?"

Spock stood by the railing, eyes fixed on the screen. "Not as it exists in our universe, Captain. It contains subatomic particles similar to our quarks, but the ways in which those particles interact are . . . different."

"Is the One from another dimension, Spock?"

The science officer shook his head without speaking and Kirk wondered what had so deeply affected him. Then he heard the impulse engines reset to a higher power curve as the creature accelerated again.

"All other extradimensional manifestations that we have observed have shared the same basic laws of energy and matter interaction established in the first nanoseconds of our universe's beginning," Spock said. "But this creature does not share those laws."

McCoy turned to Spock. "Are you saying that thing's from another universe, Spock?"

"An earlier universe, Doctor. One that preceded ours."

Kirk stared at the thing on the screen—now a mad, spinning maelstrom of . . . hunger. A primal hunger billions of years old. A simple, basic lifeform that had evolved over uncountable eons to acquire the ultimate survival trait—the ability to live beyond its universe.

"How?" Kirk whispered. He suddenly knew how Richter felt. So little time to understand.

"Captain, for a being to be able to maintain itself during the heat death of a universe . . . for it to be able to withstand the infinite compression of a universal collapse of energy and matter . . . and for it to then survive the creation energies of the Big Bang . . . there is nothing in our science which would even begin to suggest how such a thing might be possible."

Kirk had Uhura open the channel to the One. "What is your age?" he asked, not knowing if the creature would comprehend.

"Hunger," it answered plaintively. On the screen, it twisted as if in agony, reaching hopelessly for the constantly retreating ship it wanted to consume.

"Where do you come from?"

"Consume need consume need. Faster. Faster."

"Why?" Kirk asked.

This time, the translated voice gave no answer.

"Instinct," Kirk said with finality as he stared at the screen. "As Spock said, it's like asking a paramecium why it absorbs food. It is not a conscious decision. And this is not a conscious life-form."

Spock and McCoy watched as Kirk returned to the conn.

"Well, Doctor," he said as he sat back in his chair, "at least now you know how the One, and the Many, had enough time to develop such complex behavior. If it could survive the collapse of one universe . . . it could survive the collapse of billions."

McCoy, for once, was speechless.

"Mr. Sulu," Kirk said decisively, "take us back just beyond the distance we were when Chekov first noticed this creature change course."

The straining maw of the One receded on the screen, slowly folding closed, again encasing itself within its living cloud of insulation against the harsh environment of interstellar space. When the *Enterprise* had matched her earlier distance from it, Sulu reported that the creature resumed its original course—bearing directly for the Talin system.

"Keptin," Chekov said, "we have passed out of phaser range. Shall I arm the photon torpedoes?"

"If it can withstand the Big Bang, Mr. Chekov, I don't think there's much we'd be able to do to it," Kirk said.

"It could not have survived in that form," Spock said. "As it exists now, it *is* vulnerable to our weapons."

"Thank you, Mr. Spock, but our weapons won't be necessary. Uhura, cancel red alert."

McCoy stormed down to Kirk. "Not be necessary? Good Lord, Jim. That thing is in contact with the drones that destroyed Talin. It's probably planning to eat the entire planet by the time it gets there."

"It's not *planning* to do anything, Bones. It can't think."

"Neither can a shark," McCoy muttered.

Spock stepped down beside McCoy. "In any event, Doctor, at the slow speed with which it is traveling, Starfleet will have ample time to return and either capture or destroy the creature."

Kirk shook his head. "Starfleet's not going to capture or destroy that creature, Spock. What purpose would that serve?"

"To pay it back for all the other worlds it destroyed with the drones," McCoy said.

"To preserve the worlds which it might destroy in the future," Spock added.

Kirk turned to McCoy. "Bones, it can't be paid back. It didn't decide to destroy worlds any more than the shark knows the difference between eating a fish or a swimmer." Kirk looked at Spock. "And there are lots of planets out there, Spock. If those drones were able to mindlessly convert Talin IV into a suitable planet for their host in less than two decades, just think what the Starfleet corps of engineers could do in *six* decades to prepare one of the Talin gas giants for it." Kirk put his hands on the arms of his chair and gazed at the screen, watching the swirling gray mass shrink to a dot. "It's a big universe, gentlemen. With worlds enough, and time for everyone."

Kirk looked back at his friends. Neither one looked satisfied but that reaction pleased him. It meant he could be sure that he had made the right decision.

There were no enemies here. Only mysteries.

The *Enterprise* came about in space. Her mission, at last, continued.

PART FOUR

The New Mission

One

In standard orbit around Talin IV, the *Enterprise* resonated with the activity of her newly returned crew. Kirk moved briskly through the corridors as if drawing life from the energy they brought back to the ship. His ship. The new gold command shirt he wore made him feel as if he had returned home. He had.

In the main branch corridors leading to the cargo transporters, an earnest-looking lieutenant with a Starfleet Command insignia on his blue shirt jogged up behind Kirk, carrying a fat sheaf of printouts and a screenpad. He was balding and the last remnants of his curly brown hair were mussed and unruly, like the hair of someone who had been up all night. Kirk didn't care. He guessed that at least half of Command hadn't had any sleep for the past two days.

The lieutenant caught up to Kirk and had to walk quickly to keep the rapid pace. "Captain Kirk," he said breathlessly, the voice of a man in a hurry, "I'm Peter Bloch-Hansen, sir. Starfleet Emergency Rescue Office."

Kirk kept moving, no time to waste. All through the corridors other crew members ran or jogged, carrying equipment and supplies. There was so much to do. So much time wasted. He thought of Richter then, still in the *Exeter*'s sickbay. He knew what drove the man.

"Has the order come through yet?" Kirk asked brusquely.

"No sir, Captain," Bloch-Hansen said.

Kirk didn't bother to correct the lieutenant. Until the order did come through, he was still "mister." But no one doubted that Nogura's order was not already blistering through subspace to the Talin system. Too much had happened for even Starfleet to ignore. And when that order came, it had better include full apologies for each member of the *Enterprise* Five.

Kirk guessed it would be an easy apology for Command to make. Only Uhura's case would require Starfleet to go to the trouble and potential embarrassment of an official review board to withdraw all charges of contempt and to reinstate her. Because the rest of the Five had resigned, regulations allowed them to rejoin Starfleet service at full rank and pay anytime within six months. With a bit of bureaucratic juggling, Starfleet could even manage to keep the resignations out of the official records, as if they had never happened.

"But I do have the new figures for you, sir," Bloch-Hansen continued. He shuffled his printouts as he and Kirk weaved rapidly around the other rushing crew they passed in the corridor. "As of twenty minutes ago, there were five hundred and twelve vessels in stacked orbits around Talin IV. They'll be working in shifts to transfer their relief supplies to the *Enterprise* and the *Exeter* for mass beaming to the surface. The time/ton transfer schedules are here. . . ." He offered Kirk his screenpad.

Kirk ignored it. He kept walking. "Tell me about the Talin. Was Spock right about the survival rate?"

The lieutenant efficiently produced a printout from his bundle. He was prepared for anything. "Mr. Spock *was* right, sir. The figure is astonishing. As long as they escaped immediate blast and fire injuries, their autonomic cocooning reflex would have dropped their metabolism right down . . . uh, the life readings show just more than two billion Talin remain alive on their planet, ninety-five percent in hibernation."

Kirk stopped and looked at Bloch-Hansen with relief. That was far higher than anyone, even Spock, had hoped.

The lieutenant continued. "I estimate a complete revival program should take three years, but by that time the seeders' growth will be scavenged from the oceans."

"How's the drone contact team working out?" Kirk and Bloch-Hansen turned the corner into the final corridor. The entrance to the cargo transporter room was jammed with people, some crew, some civilians.

"The task force will arrive on Talin's moon to begin relocating the drones within a week, sir. The Talin ambassadors have given permission for them to begin seeding the gas giant, Talin VIII. It will be converted into a food source well within the next sixty years."

Kirk shouldered his way into the crowd. "Good work, Lieutenant. Let me know when the order comes in."

Bloch-Hansen stopped at the edge of the crowd. "Oh, you'll know when it comes, sir. You'll know."

As people realized who was pushing up against them, they quickly made way to let Kirk through. He passed the processing desk with a nod from the volunteer coordinators and stepped out to the open area immediately in front of the honey-combed crystal pads of the cargo transporter grid.

Nearby, Chekov and Sulu stood with Christine Chapel, checking a crate of medical tricorders. Kirk could hear the two ensigns telling the others about Lieutenant Styles's new assignment—ferrying the impounded *Queen Mary* back to Starbase 29. There was much laughter as Sulu explained how the gravity generator on the Orion ship had mysteriously been broken. It could only put out a three-gee field now, and it was tied into the warp drive so it couldn't be turned off. "I am certain the lieutenant will wery much enjoy his weighty new position," Chekov said.

Kirk looked around for Spock among the confusing stacks of boxes and knots of people. As he turned around, he bumped into McCoy. The doctor was back in his science blues.

"Have you seen Spock?" Kirk asked.

"No. He's probably hiding from me." McCoy reached out without warning and jammed a spray hypo against Kirk's arm. "There," he said when the longer-than-usual spray was done, "now you can eat plutonium for breakfast."

Kirk rubbed at the tingling spot where the radiation stabilizer had entered. "Is that going to work on the Talin?"

"It needed some modification, but M'Benga's already got the first batch processing."

"Good work, Bones. Or do you prefer 'Black Ire' now?" Kirk chuckled at McCoy's sudden look of discomfort. "How'd you ever come up with that one, anyway?"

McCoy frowned. "Someday I'll tell you about my illustrious ancestors. If I live that long." He tried to change the subject. "Has the order come in?"

Kirk looked around the huge room. It was filled with at least twenty different conversations and the hum of antigravs as boxes were received and stacked through the doors leading to the cargo hold. "Not yet," Kirk said. He suspected there would be pandemonium when it did come through. "Why do you think Spock's—"

Suddenly he felt a light touch on his shoulder. He turned to see Anne Gauvreau. Her flight jacket had a new crest proudly sewn on the front. The writing on it was in Talin splatterscript.

Kirk looked at the crates on the transporter grid. Most were marked with bold red crosses. "Is this from the *Shelton?*"

Gauvreau patted one of the crates. "Sure is. Starfleet Emergency Rescue didn't want to wait for the official word. They're buying all the medical supplies that everyone's brought in. If the supplies aren't used here, they say, then they'll still be useful somewhere else."

"These supplies *will* be used on Talin," Kirk said. There was no doubt in his voice. "So . . . until things get settled here, I suppose you freighter captains are going to be leaving this system with empty holds."

Gauvreau smiled brightly. "Not this time." She looked at McCoy and winked. "Thanks to Dr. McCoy, the T'Prar Foundation has hired me to transport twenty-six Orion females to a reorientation village on Delta Triciatu."

"Delta?" Kirk asked, raising his eyebrows.

"Seems Deltan males aren't affected by the Orion females' pheromones, so it's a good place for them to be helped to start their own lives again. And besides . . . I've always wanted to go there. . . ." Gauvreau blushed. "Look, I've got to break orbit to let another ship get into transporter range." She leaned closer and kissed Kirk on his cheek. "Thank you for making me feel I was back in Starfleet again."

"Thank you for bringing me back," Kirk said, then watched her move off into the crowd by the door. He hoped he would see her again.

Kirk turned to McCoy. "Whatever happened to those pirates?"

"In the brig on the *Exeter.* Last I heard Krulmadden was trying to buy it from her captain."

"I'm glad he's not on this ship talking to Chekov," Kirk said. He looked up with sudden interest as another crew member jostled him as she walked by with an antigrav pallet of visual sensors. It was Carolyn Palamas.

"Welcome back, Captain Kirk," she said. "The herbarium roses are in bloom again. I checked."

Kirk stumbled over a reply as she continued on without waiting for one. When he turned back to McCoy, he was greeted by a soppy smile. "Don't you start," Kirk warned.

Then McCoy looked puzzled and Kirk saw why. Spock was approaching. Like the doctor, the science officer was wearing his uniform again, tricorder hanging at his side. But he was also carrying a familiar-looking green bottle.

"Mr. Spock," Kirk said with a bemused expression, "is that whisky?"

Spock held the bottle up to read the label, as if confirming that it was true. "Yes," he admitted. "It was given to me by Mr. Scott."

"Did he say why?" Kirk asked.

"He said it was my . . . birthday present."

McCoy looked surprised. "It's not your birthday, Spock."

"Thank you, Doctor. I explained that to Mr. Scott, but he was quite emotional about it. He said, and I quote, 'Och, it dinna matter one wee bit.' And then he asked me when the party would be."

McCoy held a hand out. "Tell you what, Spock. Why don't you just give me the bottle as a token of apology and then you can stop trying to hide from me."

"Doctor, not only am I not trying to hide from you, I can think of no action on my part for which I might possibly owe you an apology."

McCoy feigned great shock. "Spock, I said there were aliens, remember? When we were talking in the shuttle at the outpost, and I said that it was obvious that the Talin were under observation by other aliens but you said, nooo, there were no other aliens. There's nothing of value in this system, you said. And meanwhile those drones *were* creating something of value—that purple sludge of theirs— right under your big pointed ears. But you didn't see it and I did. I said—"

Kirk held his hands up as if threatening to cover McCoy's mouth.

"Bones, you keep going on like that and we're all going to have to hide from you."

McCoy folded his arms and smiled smugly. "I don't care. All that matters is that I was absolutely, inarguably right and—"

"As I recall," Spock said dryly, "you suggested there were Klingons with Romulan cloaking devices lurking about."

"I said *aliens*," McCoy insisted.

"You said—"

"What *about* the aliens?" Kirk asked Spock. "Any results from the FCO's computer analysis of our sensor readings?"

Spock and McCoy didn't break eye contact. "A classic symbiotic relationship, Captain. It appears Dr. Richter was correct when he said that life everywhere was the same—even when it originates in different universes. The computers have modeled a logical relationship between the two life-forms: The seeder drones prepare planets with the purple food organism which then converts the entire biosphere into a highly radioactive algae analogue. When the One arrives in the system, it enfolds the planet and ingests the converted biosphere. In return, it carries some of the drones from system to system, providing energy to them so that they can survive the journey between the stars. Other drones it sends ahead on a smaller clump of accelerated matter, somewhat like plants spreading spores."

"How do they decide which planets to go to?" Kirk asked.

"I do not think 'decide' is the term to be used, Captain. The selection of planets for seeding is most likely an instinctual response, done without consciousness. I suspect that we may find that colonies of drones lie dormant in thousands of systems throughout the galaxy, waiting to be awakened by the first electromagnetic pulses resulting from an atomic explosion. That would indicate that fusion warheads will soon be developed on a given planet and that the planet's inhabitants could therefore be manipulated to devastate their biosphere with radiation, making it a suitable world for the growth of the algae. As the drones come to life and begin their instinctive behavior to create tension on the target planet, they send out signals to the One, informing it that a new planet is about to be seeded."

McCoy fidgeted with his tricorder and medikit. "I still don't see how anything could survive the death and birth of a universe."

"Especially if the physician present at that birth were—"

Kirk broke in again. "Perhaps, gentlemen, we should simply accept that there are still mysteries in the universe. Or the universes." He smiled at them. "Let's leave something for another ship to do, all right?"

Before either McCoy or Spock could answer, the page whistle of the ship's intercom system sounded. Instantly, every conversation in the cargo transporter room stopped. Only the background whir of the equipment could be heard until Uhura's voice came on.

"Attention all crew. Attention all crew. The *U.S.S. Enterprise,* as flagship for the Starfleet Relief Operation to Talin . . ." Kirk felt the hair on his neck bristle. He heard small gasps from the people in the room who also understood what Uhura had just said. This collection of ships had been given a name. The Starfleet Relief Operation to Talin. Uhura didn't have to read the rest. It was official.

". . . has just received this subspace communiqué from Nogura, Admiral, Starfleet Command: Effective this stardate, Earth, the findings of Starfleet's board of inquiry into the incident at Talin IV are rescinded. In addition, with remorse, Starfleet offers full and official apologies to—" The transporter room resounded with applause. Kirk felt hands slapping at his back. He struggled to hear the rest of what Uhura read. He had been waiting so long to hear it.

"Also, in accordance with Starfleet Command Regulations, General Order One, Talin IV is hereby recognized as a planet whose normal development has been subject to extraplanetary interference and thus is excused from the Prime Directive of Noninterference." The ship seemed to shake with the roar of the cheers which joined the continuing applause echoing through her. Uhura's voice was almost lost amid the tumult.

"Therefore, all Starfleet personnel are requested to take whatever action may be deemed necessary to repair the damage caused by such interference. Furthermore, in recognition of the General Council's ruling to admit Talin to the United Federation of Planets, all Federation citizens are likewise urged—"

It was no use. Her voice was completely drowned out. Kirk's ears rang. McCoy had cupped his hands to his mouth and was shouting deafening huzzahs. Kirk caught Spock's eye and saw his science officer smile, just fleetingly, and before anyone else could notice.

Then, as swiftly as it had begun, the joyous ovation quietened. It was not replaced by a return to the conversation and the activity which had preceded it. There was only silence. For a moment Kirk was puzzled. But only for a moment.

"Captain," Spock said, "the crew awaits your orders."

McCoy put his hand to Kirk's arm. "Now you really are back, Jim."

Without hesitation, Captain James T. Kirk stepped onto the transporter platform and faced his crew. He nodded to Kyle, standing ready at the transporter console, and gave his crew the order they waited for.

"Energize," he said.

Two

The shimmering veil of transporter energy fell from Kirk's eyes and he gazed onto a city of the dead.

The air of Talin was thick with the stench of rot and smoke. A sea breeze blew

400 Judith & Garfield Reeves-Stevens

up from the distant ocean where he could see foul purple waves crash against a beach of blackened wood and the skeletons of sea creatures that had washed ashore. Even the shafts of weak sunlight which cut through the overcast skies seemed gray and dull.

Kirk stepped forward onto the ash of the shattered world that had briefly borne his name. Before him was what the sensors had determined was the largest gathering of still-functioning, uncocooned survivors on the planet. Its population numbered less than four hundred.

An old Talin female was the first to see him as he took another step in the ash. She had one arm. Her bibcloth hung in tatters. Kirk could see her bones move beneath her cracked and bleeding skin.

The female cried out weakly, a harsh discordant shriek. Behind her, other Talin slowly emerged from the rubble they had made into shelters. A few hundred meters away, he saw the long shapes of soot-darkened cocoons stacked like firewood. Respectfully gathered for a better day which no Talin could believe would ever come.

But Kirk was there to make that day a reality. He looked all around him at the desolation and destruction. He saw the blasted stumps of buildings, shattered girders, fields of blackened crops.

And it was all a mistake. It had all occurred because there were still too many mysteries, still too many unknowns. But Kirk knew, at least, that *this* would not happen again. The Federation would learn. It would know what to look for next time. Other worlds would be saved by the painful lessons of Talin IV. The Federation would learn and from that knowledge, grow stronger.

A dozen Talin had gathered before him now. They pointed at him in wonder. Some covered their eyes, afraid to look at his alien form. Others reached out with trembling limbs, but were too frightened to come closer.

Kirk heard another transporter chime swell. He heard the gasp of awe from the crowd before him. More Talin were coming from the ruins. Some dropped to their knees as the golden light played upon them.

There were new footsteps behind him. Kirk glanced over his shoulder to see Spock and McCoy coming toward him, already opening their tricorders. A wall of medical supplies had also appeared, still shimmering.

He heard another cry from the Talin as the air filled with the pulsed harmonics of multiple transporter chimes. All around them the air danced with shimmering columns of luminous energy. And from each apparition came another human, or another gift of supplies.

Chekov stepped forward with Sulu and Uhura. Scott appeared with a pallet of machinery that could draw water from the air. Next, M'Benga, Chapel, Palamas. Everyone had returned to Talin.

Then, from the crowd of Talin adults, staring, pointing, shaking, not daring to believe that what they saw might be real, one female child stepped forward. Her skin was green and caked with mud, but her yellow eyes were clear and penetrating.

Alone among the Talin, she stepped up to Kirk unafraid.

Kirk twisted the dial on the small silver wand of his translator. He spoke into it for the child.

"My name is James Kirk," he said. "Captain of the *Starship Enterprise*."

He waited as the translator repeated his words in the whistles and whispers of Talin.

The child's eyes widened. She looked up to the sky, past the clouds, as if they were no longer there. She whispered one word back to Kirk. The translator spoke it to him.

"Starship."

Tears fell from the child's eyes. She turned back to her people and shouted the word to them, pointing to the skies, to the stars that waited there.

"Starship. Starship." The translator said the word as each Talin spoke it.

The child came closer to Kirk. She lifted her arms to him and he saw then in her eyes what he had seen in the eyes of a woman long ago on Earth, what he had seen in the eyes of a Tellarite child in an asteroid only weeks ago.

Kirk took the child's hands in his and lifted her up close to him, knowing that the beginnings and the endings of things were sometimes one and the same.

But this time, he knew, it would be a beginning.

"It's all right," Kirk said. "Let me help."

Epilogue

The Dream of Stars

The ship surrounds him and bears him through space, and protected by her, he sleeps.

And dreams of Iowa.

He is a young boy. He runs with his dog through fields of grain, full of the smells of things growing, and of life.

At night, he feels his father's hand, rough in his, as they walk into those fields.

The boy looks up and gasps to see the sky so black, the stars so brilliant. His father names them, magic to the boy's ears, to his eyes, to his heart, to something within him that he does not yet understand.

"Rigel," his father says. "Aldebaran, Antares."

"Yes," the boy says. He has never heard them before but he is certain that he knows them all. The names continue, the grain is forgotten. His mother waits in the house nearby, lights blazing through windows brilliant as the stars.

But the boy looks up. "I want to go there," he says, reaching out to them. His father's face is uplifted, too, feeling the heat of a thousand suns, seen and unseen, known and unknown.

The boy is five years old and he feels a pain in his chest with the weight of millennia, as if the whole species had moved forward to this one instant, to this one person, driving him on.

"I have to go there," the boy says. "I know," his father answers. He reaches down and lifts the boy high, holding him to his chest with love, holding him to look up, just that little bit closer to the stars in his father's arms. "And you will, Jimmy, you will."

The boy's heart beats faster. "I will," he whispers, clutching his father, afraid of the dark and the cold of night and the distance from the house, but hungry to see more. The challenge, the promise, the love he feels. All cast in him in that one night when first he looked up and knew where his destiny lay.

That night his house surrounds the boy and bears him through the darkness, and protected by her, he sleeps.

And dreams of stars.

Acknowledgments

For *Memory Prime*

We are gratefully indebted to the real Salman Nensi, whose enthusiastic friendship and encouragement, as well as the generous loan of his *Star Trek* collection and valuable comments and research, have made this a better book.

As writers, we thank *Star Trek* editor Dave Stern for his guidance and most importantly, patience. As readers, we also thank him for keeping the *Star Trek* universe alive in such an entertaining and faithful collection of books.

As viewers, we are also grateful to Greg and Michael Hall and everyone at Videophile for their generosity in keeping us supplied with *all* the episodes.

Mira Romaine and Memory Alpha first appeared in the original television series episode "The Lights of Zetar," written by Jeremy Tarcher and Shari Lewis. Mira Romaine was played by Jan Shutan. Some of the other *Star Trek* writers whose contributions we have specifically made reference to in this book include Gene L. Coon, Diane Duane, Brad Ferguson, D. C. Fontana, John M. Ford, David Gerrold, Vonda N. McIntyre, Peter Morwood, Marc Okrand, Theodore Sturgeon, Lawrence N. Wolfe, and, of course, Gene Roddenberry.

For *Prime Directive*

We are deeply indebted to our editors, Dave Stern and Kevin Ryan, for their support, encouragement and, most important, patience.

Once again, our "historian," Sal Nensi, has worked hard at Memory Prime to help keep our facts and references straight, and we are grateful for his fast and detailed assistance, and his friendship.

We are also grateful to Carole, Mario, and Peter, for kindly introducing us to *Star Trek* Toronto in particular and *Trek* fandom in general.

In the almost quarter century [1990] that Gene Roddenberry's *Star Trek* has been in existence, a great number of writers have contributed to its canon. We have drawn on the work of many of these writers and thank them all for the entertainment and inspiration they have provided.

The character of Lieutenant Carolyn Palamas, the ship's A&A officer, first appeared in the television episode "Who Mourns for Adonais," written by Gilbert Ralston. Palamas was played by Leslie Parrish. An older but not wiser Lieutenant

Styles first appeared as captain of the *Excelsior* in the movie *Star Trek III: The Search for Spock,* written by Harve Bennett. Styles was played by James B. Sikking.

We would also like to acknowledge the work of Vonda N. McIntyre and Shane Johnson. Allan Asherman's *Star Trek Compendium* has been an invaluable reference tool as well.

Of course, none of this would exist without Gene Roddenberry's creative vision of the future as it should be—a grand adventure.

Our thanks to all.

—Judith & Garfield Reeves-Stevens

A Look Inside

Star Trek—Memory Prime and
Star Trek—Prime Directive
with Judith & Garfield Reeves-Stevens

by Kevin Dilmore

Kevin Dilmore: I hope this isn't digging too far back for you both, but I'd like to ask about your introduction to writing for *Star Trek.* I understand that *Memory Prime,* the first story in this volume, is your first novel for the line?

Judith Reeves-Stevens: Yes, and it was the first novel we ever wrote together.

KD: No kidding? So you had been published separately at that point?

Garfield Reeves-Stevens: Yes. I had written three sort-of horror/science fiction novels.

JRS: And I was doing nonfiction and school material.

GRS: We had just come off of a science and technology textbook series for grades 1, 2, and 3.

JRS: It was a series we created as an introduction to science and technology. I put it together and then drafted Gar. The two of us wrote it, and tested everything in school with kids from fifty-five countries in grades 1 through 3, and it was pretty humbling.

GRS: We had spent three years working on that series, and that was the first time we had written together. We traveled across Canada with it—

JRS: —because it was adopted in every province. And I believe on that book tour we were sponsored in two ways: One by the text publisher, which sponsored me; and two, by Gar's fiction publisher—Gar had written a book about cloning from the Shroud of Turin. It was one of his horror books.

GRS: *Children of the Shroud.*

JRS: And so in the morning, he would be on one television or radio station talking about his horror book, and in the afternoon we would be on another station talking about children's education.

KD: Now that must have been an interesting tour. What if you had gotten mixed up in front of a class of second-graders?

GRS: (laughs) "Kids, this is how you clone at home."

KD: (laughs) So, did you decide to write together and pitch a *Star Trek* project? Or did someone approach you about *Star Trek* and then you decided to tackle it together? How did this come about?

JRS: Actually, we were so burned out from dealing with all of the separate ministries of education, and everything was so very, very serious—

GRS: Writing a textbook to curriculum requirements is almost like writing to a checklist. Requirements were set province by province, and they were all slightly different.

JRS: And they would review each of our books; there were thirty in the series. Then we would get notes from the curriculum boards, and the whole process exhausted us. Since Gar had written fiction, we thought, Wouldn't it be nice if we wrote a novel together? Gar had never written science fiction—

GRS: —Not far-future science fiction, anyway—

JRS: And we both had an interest in it, so we decided we would try writing together.

GRS: And just about that time, we were in New York visiting friends and *Star Trek IV* [: *The Voyage Home*] came out. We were looking forward to that so much because we had enjoyed the last three. We so wanted to go back into the future . . . but in *Star Trek IV,* there are only ten minutes or so that take place in the future. And we came out thinking, We don't want to wait another three years!

JRS: So, when we got back to Toronto, we called down to Simon & Schuster and asked whether they still published *Star Trek* novels.

GRS: We had gone into a bookstore and had seen a couple sitting on the shelf there.

JRS: But we didn't know what kind of a *Star Trek* book program they had. We were told they would deal only with published authors. So we sent down the books we'd written and they said, "Fine. Send us an outline." We had not met a soul in New York. We hadn't seen them and they hadn't seen us.

GRS: That was in the days of [Pocket Books editors] Dave Stern and Kevin Ryan.

JRS: So we sent them three outlines. They picked one, and that was *Memory Prime*.

KD: Of the three outlines, do you recall what the others were?

GRS: Oh, yes. One was a trilogy—

JRS: —And it involved Klingons, and took place on the homeworld of Klingon. The other was *Timetwist*. This was really interesting because they didn't want to have anything involved with time travel to the future, and we didn't get back to that until we got to a variation of it for *Federation* [the *Star Trek/Star Trek: The Next Generation* crossover novel] and *Millennium* [the *Star Trek: Deep Space Nine* trilogy].

KD: As you spoke, I was wondering whether elements didn't end up in *Millennium*.

GRS: I know they didn't want to do a story with time travel into the future because they were developing *Star Trek: The Next Generation* at the time. They didn't want us to jump that gun. In our outline, we did have a Federation starship of the future with a Klingon on it. But they said no because it was getting into *Next Generation* territory.

KD: Absolutely. Why have you written a book that could be completely contradicted in the fall of 1987 when the show premiered?

JRS: Exactly.

GRS: The Klingon trilogy was a huge idea. Kirk, McCoy, and Spock ended up being court-martialed, and, gosh, did they end up being imprisoned? I know they had to go through a Klingon trial. Hmm . . . this all sounds familiar. (laughs) It was a big three-parter, but it probably was too ambitious for our first time through, so they settled on what became *Memory Prime*. At first, I think we called it *The Followers*.

JRS: They wanted a stand-alone story.

KD: Considering the other *Star Trek* books that you have written together, *Memory Prime* seems to me the slimmest volume. So you have not shied away from ambitious projects.

JRS: And it was hard to do because we had never written fiction together. And it takes a while for two authors to develop a single voice.

KD: So how did you start developing that voice? I'm assuming that you plotted the story together.

JRS: Yes. Then, it became a microcosm of everything we have ended up doing together since. We end up passing stuff back and forth to each other so often that by the time it's finished, it's written by a stranger.

GRS: It accretes like the shell of a nautilus.

KD: (laughs) I like that, and the analogy makes sense. Gar might write one chapter and send it Judy's way, but you, Judy, might be writing another chapter farther down the story and send it back his way, and in that fashion, you make your way through the manuscript?

GRS: And whoever has the manuscript last gets her way.

JRS: (laughs)

KD: Are there specific favorite things about a story that you gravitate toward? Say, there's a Scotty scene and one of you really wants to write that. Or maybe one of you would rather deal with the parts about an alien subculture?

JRS: It's a lot of small things. Because we come at a story from different points of view, it works out wonderfully. We will leave holes for the other person to fill.

GRS: In *Memory Prime,* there was a real conscious effort on our part to give every member of the crew a "moment."

JRS: It's like ensemble writing.

GRS: But we had to cut out Uhura's moment because it came too late in the story. It sort of slowed everything down. It was one of those, as they say, pacing cuts.

KD: When plotting your first *Star Trek* story, was there anything that each of you really wanted to include?

JRS: I think the things that have always interested us about *Star Trek* are the things that have not been explained. A television show is always written on the fly. Episodes are written very quickly, so it leaves rich territory for writers to mine in other media.

GRS: I always remember that it was [former editor] Kevin Ryan's theory about why storytelling was so rich in the original series: It was on the air for only three seasons, and so much of that world and its characters remained unexplored. In *Next Generation* after seven seasons, there weren't a lot of mysteries left.

JRS: And now that we've come to *Enterprise,* it's pretty tricky finding new stories.

KD: Especially ones that do not blatantly contradict or ignore what fans know has gone before—or in this case, after. If Picard tells Riker, "You know, Number One, years ago we didn't have such things," now *Enterprise* is stuck with that.

JRS: Yes. It's much, much harder working like that. Our starting with a classic story made it much easier because we didn't have that continuity as a burden.

GRS: And in *Memory Prime,* one of the key things was that, given it was so far in the future, why aren't we seeing artificial intelligence in Starfleet?

JRS: And that always stuck with us. That's really why we wrote the book. And we loved the fact that we could develop the Pathfinders. We also love working with the big ideas of *Star Trek,* so a big question was "Where was artificial intelligence in the future?" When it came to *Prime Directive,* we loved taking on the big, iconic things about the series, and the Prime Directive certainly is one of them.

KD: In tackling the issues you wanted to address in *Memory Prime,* was there anything that didn't meet approval?

GRS: I remember we were asked to change a few things in the outline. I seem to remember we had a team of black-clad ninja Vulcans.

KD: (laughs) But I like it, though.

GRS: (laughs) Yeah, it was pretty cool. It's probably something you could do on *Enterprise* but at that time, it didn't fit in with the Vulcans as established in the television series and the movies. So we cut them out. But other than that . . .

JRS: We wanted to call the bar The Laughing Vulcan and they wouldn't let us.

GRS: No, no. We did that. Just not in English.

JRS: Well, there was something else . . .

GRS: Well, there were all the nude scenes.

KD: (laughs) There's a different venue for that kind of stuff.

GRS: (laughs) Actually, it was very painless. When the manuscript came back with notes on it from Pocket and Paramount, there were changes but just minor, technical details. At the time, the *Star Trek Encyclopedia* [by Michael Okuda and Denise Okuda] didn't exist. There was [Bjo Trimble's *Star Trek*] *Concordance.* And I know we picked up a lot of details about Zefram Cochrane and the Tellarites and the Andorians from such things as the *Spaceflight Chronology* [by Stan Goldstein and Fred Goldstein] and used those sources. There certainly wasn't a huge backdrop of reference material out there.

KD: Back then, I think that if it wasn't for Franz Joseph and Bjo, a lot of writers might have been lost.

JRS: Yes.

GRS: Yes, I remember our putting in things like the length of the nacelles and all of those fun details. But we heard, "No, no, we know what a nacelle looks like. Take out the measurements. You don't have to be that precise."

KD: Did your sitting down as fans with these characters in your hands for the first time prompt you to write things for your favorite ones?

JRS: No, we treated them as our favorite ensemble, really.

GRS: Any scene with Spock, Kirk, and McCoy, that's just gold. You could sit and write that all day. They're so well-defined, so it's always fun to put them together.

JRS: That's a favorite. You can just hear their voices in their heads. Now, what was trickier was stepping outside the characters we had seen on screen to create new races, but not spending too much time doing that or getting too caught up in the "guest stars." That's something I think a lot of first-time *Star Trek* writers have found. If you approach it like a fan, thinking there is something that would be fun to do with a character, or thinking about creating a certain kind of person you run the risk of spending too much time creating your own series within *Star Trek*. That was something we were quite aware of. We did realize how much we were relying on what we had seen, how easy it was to write the comfortable scenes because we knew that everybody knew what someone looked like or sounded like. In a way, a lot of groundwork had been done for us. Actually, this was a good thing for us to start with as a shared novel.

KD: Rather than one of you having to explain to the other any nuance of an original character that you're trying to put forward, in this case, when Judy writes, "Damn it, Jim," Gar can hear it and know what you're getting at.

JRS: Otherwise, you're having to create, as a writer does, everything from the ground up. A science-fiction writer is a world-builder, and the world of *Star Trek* is already built. We had the luxury of going out into the corners that haven't been explained; we had that nice bulwark of the series that we didn't have to explain or even create a great deal of visual imagery for.

KD: Perfect. It's like taking your first vacation together in a town you each have already been in.

JRS: (laughs) That's quite right.

KD: So once *Memory Prime* was finished, I presume you enjoyed the experience and wanted to try it again. Did you go to Pocket Books with additional outlines?

GRS: Actually, this is where it gets convoluted.

JRS: We had other writing projects going on at the same time, including *The Chronicles of Galen Sword*.

GRS: We told Pocket that we'd love to write another one. Judy said that with all this two or three hundred years of *Star Trek* history, starting with Zefram Cochrane through the original series to *The Next Generation, Star Trek* needed that James Michener–type of novel to span all that time. I think, sort of instantly, we said, *Federation.* We started working on a story that with time travel and time twists and things like that would get Kirk, Spock, and McCoy caught up in dealing with Zefram Cochrane and they would glimpse *The Next Generation.* We pitched it to Pocket, and they agreed to take a look at it. So we sent in the outline and we ended up rewriting it or amending it three times just so we weren't stepping on any toes at *The Next Generation* production. Pocket was so excited about this, Dave Stern and Kevin Ryan both basically said that they were having a lot of success with *Star Trek* hardcovers and that they were going to make *Federation* the third hardcover. They set a slot for it, we sent in the revised outline, they thought it was great. They sent it to Paramount and I think it came back within the hour saying, "Oh no, no, no. We can't combine the generations."

JRS: We had to set it aside.

GRS: So here was Pocket, who had us slotted for a hardcover, and they had us work on this story, and we had refined it and it was a really neat story, and all of a sudden there was no story to go in there. So they said, "Can you come up with something else?"

KD: (laughs) Oh, no problem.

GRS: And I remember it was a cold day because there was snow on the ground in Toronto—

JRS: And we went and took a nice, long, snowy walk.

GRS: And we thought *Federation* was such a good title—

JRS: And it was one of the prime concepts of the series, and unique to *Star Trek*—

GRS: So we started going through all of the other neat catchphrases of *Star Trek.* "Prime Directive" was the one that stood out. And there had been a science-fiction story that we had been noodling about that concerned an alien race about to have a nuclear war. We thought, Wouldn't that be a great dilemma for Kirk? That had to be the dark side of the Prime Directive: To be orbiting a planet that was basically where the Earth was during the Cuban Missile Crisis, and you're about to see an intelligent species wipe itself out with nuclear war . . . and you can't do a thing about it. Within about four or five days, we had the outline in at Pocket, and I don't think we had to rewrite it once.

JRS: But again, it was *Star Trek* dealing with big issues through science fiction.

KD: But this wasn't just a big issue story. It was one that was a crisis for the characters in the crew. All of our friends are in trouble. Everyone was split across the universe and you didn't know whether the family was going to get back together again.

GRS: Yes. And that's why the very first part of *Prime Directive* is called "Aftermath." We wanted to start with the characters in the worst possible situation. They're disgraced. They have done something horrible, or appear to have done something horrible.

JRS: And we did it so effectively that we received some of the most vehement fan mail we've ever gotten. People said, "I began this book and I couldn't get past the first two pages. How could you do that to Kirk?" Well, if they had only read on, it does get better. (laughs) We got one book sent back to us with the eyes poked out of all three individuals on the cover and a note reading "This is what you have done to my heroes."

KD: (laughs) Oh no! Was there a secret part of you that enjoyed setting this up? I mean, I thought the career of every single one of them was over.

JRS: Well, these things happen. The Prime Directive caused conflict in the original series and it came up continually. In *Next Generation,* things have moved to a different style. It's like the maturation of a large company, and it has become consolidated. In *Prime Directive,* we liked the fact that we could take everyone, throw them all around, explore how each one of them attacks a crisis, and then bring them back together.

GRS: *Memory Prime* is like an expanded episode. It is a single story and it takes place in one location; it's contained. *Prime Directive* is a story that can be told only in a novel. It takes place over months, and it really forces the characters to go through hard times. It's not the sort of thing that could have been a one-hour episode or a two-hour episode. It would be very difficult to compress even into a movie. I think this is the first time that we got into the richness of a *Star Trek* novel; instead of just being an episode we wish we had seen, this is a story that could exist only as a novel.

JRS: I think the process of going through the story outline for *Federation* got us in that mood. If you look at the stories, *Memory Prime* is self-contained; moving up to *Prime Directive,* which went over months; *Federation* then spans hundreds of years; and then *Millennium.* (laughs)

KD: One of the appeals to me of *Prime Directive* is that we got the chance to see Kirk in the private sector. Was that something you thought was fun to portray?

GRS: Absolutely. One of the most interesting events of my early teenage years was when we lived in a house that was about ten houses down from the entrance to a big freeway. One night, my father and I were home and all of a sudden these bright headlights shone through our living-room window. Somebody had pulled up to the house late at night. I looked, and there was this Jaguar parked on our front lawn. My dad went out, and there was this pilot. He was looking for the freeway, and he had had too much to drink. So my dad invited him in. Talking to him, my dad learned that this guy was a commercial air pilot and he had just had his physical that day, and he had just received a downgrading, so he could no longer be a pilot for passengers. Now he was going to fly cargo planes. And it was the most devastating thing that had happened to him. I was basically just a kid meeting this fellow who had lost his career. He had lived to fly. I remember being completely taken in talking to my dad about it afterward. Here was someone who was driven to do one thing; he had achieved that and now had lost it because he was dependent on this huge infrastructure and all these rules. He had fallen afoul of the rules, and it had destroyed him.

JRS: When we were looking at Kirk, we were thinking, What is the worst thing that could happen to him?

GRS: And it is to take the starship from him.

JRS: He wouldn't care about his reputation, but if you took the starship from him—

GRS: He would do everything in his power to get it back. The guy who ended up driving onto our front lawn, he had given up that day. But Kirk wouldn't quit.

KD: I remember really enjoying as I was reading the moments of Kirk's being charming, resourceful, and able to handle himself just fine without all of the comforts and privileges afforded to a Starfleet officer.

JRS: They were separated from where you normally saw them. That made you concentrate on them more as individual characters.

GRS: That's one of the really nice things about writing a *Star Trek* novel, and it really hit home with *Prime Directive*. It isn't a story you could tell in that length of time about brand-new characters in a brand-new setting. The strength of it is that, at that point, we have lived with those characters for more than twenty years. Virtually anybody who picked up that book would know that Kirk was the guy in the center chair of a starship, and then we could tell the story from there. There was no need to introduce the character; we all know this guy, now let's really push him.

KD: Another thing I really enjoyed was the relationship between Sulu and Chekov. How were you inspired to depict that?

JRS: Again, we're looking at areas not fully developed onscreen. We often felt as viewers that we wanted to see more of the ancillary characters beyond the "top three." We wanted to see more of them and more of their working together.

KD: And as for the others?

GRS: When the story emerged, we knew exactly what Kirk would be doing. I don't remember writing down the characters' names on a sheet of paper and listing what they would be doing.

JRS: It was more like figuring out what their first inclinations might be, who they might seek out as allies, what would be an option for them. It worked so well to separate them. You see them as an ensemble onscreen, but to separate them, especially the secondary characters, was interesting because we weren't sure what to do with them that would feel satisfying. There hadn't been much attention paid to them in the series.

GRS: But the common theme is that none of them have given up.

JRS: We love the idea that they are a team with Kirk as the leader. They are a full team. That's a mark of our writing. We like ensemble writing.

GRS: It also speaks to the strength of those characters. One of the things most enjoyable about those characters is that they are all different, they all have different opinions. They will squabble, argue, and even fight. But when they have to, when Kirk says, "OK, that's it," they are all committed; the underlying principles of what brought them into Starfleet are not different for any of them. They unite. That's what I think makes them such rounded characters and so interesting to write.

JRS: You don't realize what an achievement it was in the original series to have those characters so deftly drawn. They are like characters from literature, and it made them very satisfying to write. They are not shallow characters. We didn't know a lot about their backstories; you realize that everything was shown by how they reacted to one another. Once you actually look at them in detail, you have a very good grasp of them. I think that's why so many writers have enjoyed writing them in this shared universe.

KD: Do you think it is owed as much to performances as it is the scripts in which the characters are depicted?

JRS: Characters are a collaboration between the creators, the writers, and the performers. They all own the characters.

KD: So when you're writing Kirk, you are hearing William Shatner's voice?

GRS: Oh, yes!

JRS: The character has a voice. We can hear the rhythms and hear him. It was a very strange thing for us when we first met him [William Shatner] in person. It was very difficult to hear that voice. And I'll tell you, it was even stranger to hear it on our answering machine.

GRS: (laughs) The very first time we met William Shatner, he walked out of his office and into the waiting area where we were, and there was that shock of recognition that, "Well, Captain Kirk has just walked into the room."

JRS: In that very first meeting, you can't separate the actor from the character.

GRS: And now that we have worked with him on eight books, it's "Bill," and thinking, Oh, there's Bill on TV being Captain Kirk.

JRS: We had a similar experience with James Doohan, who did the audiobook for *Prime Directive*. We did the script, which was the only one we have ever done— the novel came in at 125,000 words, and we were down to 11,500 words when he recorded it. We were so proud of ourselves that there was still a story left. (laughs) So we went down to see him do it, and it was something. He took great care and read it a little slowly so you actually could hear the story.

KD: As fans yourselves, it's got to be a charge for you to see your works in the hands of other fans.

GRS: It is, it is. There is such affection for this world.

JRS: We feel it has been a real privilege to work in this shared universe. We never anticipated doing that. It has been something we have enjoyed from the moment it started.

KD: And it certainly shows in your work. I very much appreciate the time you spent talking about this today.

JRS: Thank you, too.